the Original Sin

the Original Sin

MARIUS GABRIEL

BANTAM BOOKS

NEW YORK • TORONTO • LONDON • SYDNEY • AUCKLAND

THE ORIGINAL SIN
A Bantam Book / May 1992

BOOK DESIGN BY GRETCHEN ACHILLES

Library of Congress Cataloging-in-Publication Data

Gabriel, Marius.
The original sin / Marius Gabriel.
p.   cm.
ISBN 0-553-07929-8
I.   Title.
PR6057.A273075   1992
823'914–dc20   91-34938
CIP

Published simultaneously in the United States and Canada

Bantam Books are published by Bantam Books, a division of
Bantam Doubleday Dell Publishing Group, Inc. Its trademark,
consisting of the words "Bantam Books" and the portrayal of a
rooster, is Registered in U.S. Patent and Trademark Office and
in other countries. Marca Registrada. Bantam Books, 666 Fifth
Avenue, New York, New York 10103.

For Linda and the Bean

*And I will restore to you the years
that the locust hath eaten.*
                    Joel 2:25

Acknowledgements

My grateful thanks go to the many people who helped me with research materials, especially to Elizabeth Murray in London, Lluis Molinas i Falgueras in Palafrugell, Bette and John Austin in Sa Riera.

My thanks also go to Vivienne Schuster and Jane Gelfman, my agents, and to Rosie Cheetham and Gene Young, my editors.

I owe a profound debt, for their encouragement and support, to my parents and above all (she knows why) to my wife, Linda.

the Original Sin

~Prologue

Costa Brava, Spain

The package arrived at eight o'clock on a beautiful summer's evening.

It came by private courier, who had brought it directly from Barcelona airport. He refused to give it to the concierge, on permanent duty at the gate house, but insisted on delivering it into the hands of the woman to whom it was addressed, Mercedes Eduard.

This meant that the four guard dogs would have to be rounded up and kennelled. Had the courier come by car, there would have been less of a problem, but on a notorious earlier occasion the Rottweilers had pulled a man off a motorcycle in the grounds and had mauled him severely. The police had been called in, and Señora Eduard had given strict instructions that the episode was not to be repeated.

The gatekeeper telephoned the main residence and was put through to Maya Duran, Señora Eduard's personal secretary.

"There's a delivery boy from Barcelona, Señorita Maya. He has a package. He won't leave it with me. He says he has instructions to give it into Señora Eduard's hands alone."

"I'll speak to her. She'll call you back in a few minutes."

Maya Duran left the poolside and went upstairs to the study, where Mercedes Eduard was surrounded by correspondence.

"There's a messenger at the gate, *querida*, with a mysterious parcel that must be delivered into your hands only."

Mercedes rang the concierge. "How big is this package?" she demanded.

"Like a big letter, Señora."

"No bigger?"

"No, Señora."

"Has the boy any identification?"

"I've got his identity card in front of me. It looks all right."

"Very well. Let him come up to the house. But see that the dogs are in their compound first."

"Yes, Señora."

She replaced the receiver.

Maya studied her with a half smile. Mercedes Eduard was fifty-five years old. Her face was handsome but not soft. Those who saw beauty in it saw the beauty of power, the magnetism of a spirit that knew discipline and purpose.

She was a woman who had exercised wealth and power; also, a woman who had known suffering. Such experiences leave their trace, and for those who knew the signs they were obvious at a glance.

Her dark eyes were ruthlessly intelligent. In her youth, the deeply carved mouth had been mobile, but she had long since learned to conceal her emotions, and these days it was usually held in a still line. She had never dyed her hair, and the black was now streaked liberally with silver.

Her body was still lithe, slim-hipped, with small breasts that had not lost their upwards tilt. To some, she was a woman of allure. Others chiefly saw something to respect, and perhaps also something to fear.

"Thank God the weekend is over," Maya said.

"Don't you find the company of our upper classes stimulating?" Mercedes asked with gentle irony.

"They're nauseating. Especially the duchess."

"Ah, yes," Mercedes said. "Her Grace." The duchess had eaten and drunk enormously over the weekend. Her youthful third or fourth husband had offered marijuana cigarettes from a gold case. They were evidently a couple who enjoyed the good things of life.

It gave Mercedes some bitter amusement to entertain such people in her house: fat cats, lapping the creamy benefit of Franco's Spain without ever having bared a claw or received a scratch in battle. She sometimes wondered whether they knew what she had been. Whether they would care, if they did.

"They imagine themselves so cultured and sophisticated," Maya said, "but all they can talk about is their money. And they eat and drink like pigs. What was the *jefe de policía* whispering to you about all weekend?"

"The policeman? He wants me to get him a kilogram of cocaine," Mercedes said, raking in her papers to file them.

Maya's eyes opened wide. "My God! Did he ask you that?"

"He specified top-quality material. For investment purposes."

Maya wasn't amused. "Mercedes, this frightens me!"

Mercedes smiled. "Don't let such things worry you. The man was trying to put the bite on me. But I've fought off bigger crocodiles than that."

"What did you say to him?"

"I told him the truth, that I had no access to that kind of commodity. I suggested he ask his immediate superior, who imports directly from Peru—in crates of little plaster Madonnas."

"And?"

"And he dropped the subject."

Maya shook her head slowly. "These people never stop astounding me. Their greed, their rudeness, their crassness—"

"I think the *jefe* may have just been indulging himself in a little thrill," Mercedes said. "He likes the idea of being a devil under the uniform."

Far away, they heard the dogs barking. Maya walked to the door. "That's the courier. I'll go and bring him up."

The courier rode up through the avenue of cypresses to the white house, the late-afternoon sun gleaming on the various black polished surfaces of his machine.

He parked the motorcycle on the gravel and stood admiring the dramatic architecture of the house, with its high glass dome and its rows of white marble columns. He often delivered items to the houses of rich people, but this house was something special. The size of the grounds, the level of security, the grandiose architecture, all breathed a wealth that was guarded, watchful.

The young woman who came out to meet him was beautiful. She was of a distinctively Sevillian type, as tall and slender as a wax taper, with large dark eyes and a full mouth. His eyes followed her buttocks appreciatively as she led him up the stairs. His black jackboots echoed among the expanses of white marble.

Mercedes Eduard was waiting for him in her study, a compact middle-aged woman who sat very still. The package was post-marked Los Angeles and bore the stamp of a commercial delivery company. She signed the receipt, and Maya led the courier out again.

With a shadow of unease, Mercedes opened the package and took out the manila folder it contained.

Inside the folder was a single photograph. It was a grainy black-and-white print, taken in poor light. It showed a girl of around twenty sitting on an upright steel chair, facing the camera. She was naked to the waist. Her upper body was lean, the ribs showing clearly. Her small breasts were brought into relief by the way her arms had been roped tightly behind her.

On one shoulder was a livid bruise. The girl's head, her face partially obscured by her snaking dark hair, was hanging down. Her eyes stared vacantly into the lens.

She wore jeans, slightly ragged at the knees. A dark stain between her thighs suggested she'd wet herself. Her ankles had been chained to the chair; a padlock dangled between her thin, dirty bare feet. The background was featureless.

Mercedes's heart was clubbing at her breastbone. She looked at the back of the print. A single sentence was printed across it in block capitals: GO TO THE POLICE AND SHE DIES.

Mercedes felt the glacial calm that had come over her at other moments of her life, the numbness of knowing that the earth had moved beneath her and nothing would ever be the same again.

She reached for the telephone. She watched her own fingers punch in her daughter's Los Angeles number. She sat listening to the faint ringing.

There was no reply. After two minutes, she replaced the receiver.

Maya Duran returned to the room. "Well?" She smiled. "What is this important package?" Her smile faded as she saw Mercedes's face. She crossed quickly to the desk and looked down at the photograph which sat there like a coiled snake.

"It's Eden," she whispered. "It's Eden. What does this mean?"

Mercedes shook her head, unable to answer. Then, overcome

by sudden nausea, she stumbled to the toilet and retched dryly over the basin.

Too stunned to help at first, the younger woman could only stare at the picture. Then she ran to the bathroom and passed Mercedes a towel.

Mercedes wiped her face with it and leaned unsteadily against the tiles. From somewhere deep inside came a memory. Another time she had rested against bathroom tiles in shock and pain, long, long ago. She made no response as Maya put her arms around her.

"I'm sorry," she said at last with stiff formality. "I made a spectacle of myself."

"How did this happen?" Maya asked. Mercedes could feel her trembling. "Have they kidnapped her? What do they want? Money?"

"I don't know." Mercedes walked over to the desk and stared down at the photograph.

The muscles of the girl's naked stomach were tensed. Together with the way her right leg was slightly lifted, indicating discomfort, they showed that she was at least alive. It was not a corpse, tied to that steel chair.

"Is there a note?" Maya asked. "A letter?"

"Just what's written on the back."

Maya turned the photograph over. Her hand flew to her mouth. "Oh, God. Have you called the ranch?"

"Yes. There's no one there." Mercedes took a shaky breath and reached for the telephone again.

Santa Barbara, California

Nobody was stirring on the grounds of Dominic van Buren's home.

It was set in almost five acres of lush estate, smoothly lawned and planted with groups of tall date palms. The distant Pacific was a sliver of aquamarine.

The house had been built in 1960, before the property boom. It was a spectacular Spanish-style villa. Many of the decorative features had been imported from Spain at the time the house was built. The handsomest artifacts had been taken from an abandoned convent, like the massive oak door, with its ornate hinges, studded with great iron nails. The smooth-worn clay tiles on the floor and the terra-cotta balustrade that surrounded the terrace had come from the same convent.

At 6:30 A.M., fountains of diamonds rose out of invisible spigots in the turf to ensure that the emerald blades stayed emerald through another roasting summer day. In the master bedroom, the distant hiss of the sprinkler was enough to edge Dominic van Buren out of the nightmare that had been making him mutter restlessly for the past few minutes.

He rolled onto his back, groaning, and swallowed the sour taste of last night. His head was splitting, and his skin was burning like fire despite the fact that he'd thrown off the sheet long ago.

An irritating buzz, like a trapped bluebottle, was scraping at his nerves. He groped in the tumbled bedclothes and located the Electrostud. Still plugged in, it was hot to the touch after having vibrated, forgotten, for hours. Excess upon excess. He switched it off and tossed it onto the floor.

His bladder was bursting. He groped out of bed and padded to the bathroom. Light stabbed at his eyes from the burnished gold taps and basins.

Relieved, he flushed the toilet and went back into the bedroom.

He surveyed the evidence of last night's party. There was an empty bottle of Armagnac on the floor, and the glass-topped table looked as though someone had been scraping patterns in talcum powder on its surface, though it wasn't talcum powder.

The girl was asleep on her stomach, head turned to one side to show a pink cheek and an open, cherubic mouth. Her back was tanned and smooth. She was considerably less than half his age, but he flattered himself by thinking she was not just here for the cocaine he had supplied her with.

He was still a handsome man, after all. The years had not been unkind to him. True, various parts of him were yielding to gravity. His hair, worn in a youthful fashion inspired by Senator Edward Kennedy, who was lately enjoying a vogue as a sex symbol, was alas now too grey to dye. But a cosmetic surgeon had just discreetly eliminated his double chin, and, all in all, van Buren felt he was a remarkably presentable package for sixty-eight.

Fortified by this thought, he turned the air conditioner up to full and crawled back into bed. He was almost asleep again when the telephone rang.

"God damn."

He clawed the receiver to his ear and grunted.

"Dominic?" The line was hollow, distant, but he recognized the voice at once.

"Mercedes, for Christ's sake. You know what time it is here?"

"This is an emergency," she said tautly. "Eden's been kidnapped."

"Kidnapped?" he repeated incredulously.

"I've just received a photograph by special courier from Los Angeles. It shows Eden, half-naked, shackled to a chair."

He rubbed his face confusedly. "Some kind of sick joke."

"It's not a joke. I've called the ranch. There's no one there."

He struggled upright. "Ah, Christ." The girl was stirring beside him. He slapped her buttock. "How much money?"

"There is no demand. Just the picture."

"Just the picture? She's really warped."

"Eden? You think *Eden* set this up herself?"

"Of course. This has her style written all over it."

"You're insane."

"Don't tell me I'm insane," he snapped. The girl, now awake, rolled out of bed and wandered, naked, to the bathroom. She didn't bother to close the bathroom door, and van Buren watched her tan naked body on the toilet seat. "She's got the idea from the Getty thing," he said.

"What Getty thing?"

"John Paul Getty the Third," he said impatiently. "The grandson. He's disappeared. Haven't you heard? They've been asking millions in ransom. Except the papers have wised up. It's all a scam."

"How can anyone possibly know that?" she asked tautly.

"Look at the situation. The family keep the kid short of money. He has his expenses—drugs, girls, booze—so he gets resentful. He stages a kidnapping with the help of some freaky friends and tries to screw a few million out of the old man. It's logical. Don't you read the papers?"

"The papers invent a lot of bullshit, Dominic. The Getty boy hasn't staged anything. And Eden is incapable of doing that. Whatever she is, she isn't that cruel. What could she possibly gain?"

"Money, of course," he said dryly. "She'll do anything for extra money these days."

"I don't believe that."

"So who's taken her?"

"Los Angeles is full of crazy people. A gang of madmen killed eight people not ten miles from the ranch."

"You mean the Manson thing? Come on. Don't let's make a hysterical melodrama out of this."

"Am I the sort of woman who is prone to hysterical melodrama?" she asked bitingly. "Is that your experience of me, Dominic?"

The girl flushed the toilet, washed her pretty face, and dried it carefully. She was not interested in the argument Dominic was having over the telephone. She wanted to start the party all over again. She had recently discovered cocaine and she adored it. She thought it made you feel like a god. There was almost nothing she would not do for the kind of uncut Colombian pure that Dominic van Buren seemed to have so much of.

"Well, what the hell do you want me to do about it?" van Buren was saying coldly into the receiver. "Call the cops?"

"No. They'll kill her. Just go to the ranch and try to find out what happened."

"What a waste of time!"

"Eden is your daughter too," Mercedes said thinly. "Be a father to her for once in your life, Dominic. God knows you owe her that."

"Well, God knows you've got room to talk," he replied bitterly.

"Dominic, you don't seem to understand. Have you forgotten how sick she is? Have you forgotten about the terrible thing she has? Please," she said. "Find out what has happened to her."

"Damn. I'll go to the ranch, if that's what you want."

"It's what I want. Don't contact the police. Call me back at midnight, your time."

Dominic van Buren heard her disconnect. "Shit," he said wearily. He slammed the receiver down and rubbed his face.

The girl had been rapturously snorting the remains of the drug on the glass-topped table. Now she came around to van Buren's bedside and stood smiling at him, bright-eyed. In the morning light, her body was flawless, except for the triangle of tawny hair where her thighs joined.

"Remember me?" she asked sweetly. "You haven't said good morning yet."

He grunted. "You shouldn't snort before breakfast. That's for addicts."

She eased her loins forward invitingly, her flat belly almost brushing his face. Her teenage voice softened into what she thought was an inviting drawl. "Let's do it again."

"Jesus. I haven't the energy."

She rolled onto the bed, graceful as a cat. Her thighs parted. "Are you sure about that?" she asked softly.

Madrid, Spain

The minister was easing on the jacket of his tuxedo. The evening stretched ahead of him uninvitingly.

Like all dinners given by the ageing dictator of Spain, the occasion would be sombre, formal, and deathly dull. Franco and his wife were the most boring hosts he had ever known. He could not remember one hour of jollity he had ever spent in their company, and he had known them for thirty-five years.

Now that Franco was eighty and increasingly frail, he was more tedious than ever. The interminable lectures in the quavering, piping voice were sometimes almost more than the minister could bear.

He sighed and studied his face in the mirror. He had once been a stunningly handsome man. But time had seen to that. He was now seventy-four, and all that remained of his looks was authority. It was a severe face. These days, the heavy features were almost always expressionless. The hair was thin and white. So was the cropped military-style moustache. Only the dark eyes, glistening in their pouches of skin, hinted at inner fires that had not died down.

He was corpulent these days, too. The starched shirt was tight on his frame and creaked when he sat. A lump of ageing lard, he thought dryly. But, by God, a powerful man yet. He clenched his right fist, as though grasping at some tangible symbol of the authority he had exercised for three decades. A diamond flashed at his cuff.

Yes. Ageing they might be, but the power was still theirs. Of course, Franco could not last forever, and when he went, they would all go. There was perhaps only a year or two left.

But they had had a good run for their money, a damned good run. For him, the exercise of power had been the ultimate gratification. It did not matter where he was now, where the journey had led. He had enjoyed the ride. Immensely.

And this twilight was far from unpleasant. The afflictions of old age were painful. Most of all, the loneliness. But power soothed all hurts: having it, using it, exploiting it.

A secretary peered around the door. "Minister? There's a call for you from Catalonia. Señora Eduard."

He nodded brusquely. He brushed some specks from the lapels of his jacket and picked up the telephone beside his bed. "Mercedes?"

"Gerard!" He was instantly aware of the anguish in her voice. "Gerard, I think Eden has been kidnapped."

"Here in Spain?" he demanded.

"No, in America. I've received a photograph of her, tied to a chair. No ransom note, just a warning not to go to the police. It came from Los Angeles."

He was silent for a moment but, apart from that, gave no sign of shock or dismay. "Does the photograph seem genuine?" he asked in his gravelly voice.

"Yes." Her voice almost broke. "Yes, it seems genuine."

"Is there a date on the package?"

He heard her take a deep, trembling breath. "The postmark says it was mailed in Los Angeles two days ago."

"How long can she survive without the drug?"

"I don't know. Perhaps a few days."

"And then?"

Mercedes did not answer.

"Have you spoken to the girl's father?"

"He doesn't believe it's genuine. He thinks Eden is trying to get money from us."

"No," he said decisively. "That's not her way."

"I know it's not. But he refuses to believe."

"The kidnappers haven't contacted him?"

"No."

"They probably won't approach him," the minister said. "He's irrelevant."

"He has much more money."

"But he would not pay. Not enough. Don't count on him for help, Mercedes."

"I won't."

The minister grunted. "I know a man here in Madrid. A South American. He specializes in this kind of thing. I don't know if he's available, or even in the country. If he is, I'll get him. His name is Joaquin de Córdoba. Don't speak to anyone in the meantime. Not the police, not anyone. Understand?"

"Yes."

"I'll call you back in a few minutes."

Tucson, Arizona

Chained to her bed in the cellar, the girl starts to scream again.

There is no sun down here, only the dim light of a naked bulb set high in the concrete ceiling. For the past few hours she has been getting too sick to do anything but lie still and cry. She is very weak, and now the only sound that comes out is a croak. Her throat is raw. Even if she had her voice, the cellar is deep, the cell has been soundproofed, and up above is empty desert. The sheets of the bed are soaked with sweat, rank and sodden. She is trembling so violently that the iron bedstead rattles and the manacles clatter like castanets.

It is coming on again, worse than before. The intensity of her agony is making her desperate. She thrashes her arms and legs feebly, feeling the iron bite into her wrists. She opens her mouth and tries to make a sound, any sound, that will give some release. The scream tears at her throat, but somehow it does not reach to the pain. How long can she bear it?

Upstairs in the house, no one is stirring. Her jailer has gone out. The door is locked, the windows are shuttered against the sun. It is going to be a beautiful day. The desert already shimmers with heat, although the sun has only been up an hour or two. The tall saguaro stand like sentinels, like a silent army, for acres around the house. No breeze stirs.

A lone coyote lopes cautiously up to the porch. Sometimes there are scraps of food here. But not today. He sniffs and pokes around the door fruitlessly. His huge ears never stop moving, hunting for the tiny sounds that can mean food or imminent death. He catches a faint whisper, a noise no human ear could detect. It comes from deep in the ground. He pauses, brown eyes alert. But his interest quickly fades. The sound is recognizably human.

He watches a pair of desert sparrows hopping in the dust, uttering their plaintive farewell: "Adiós! Adiós! Adiós!" But they are too wily to let him approach them.

He needs to find a meal before the day gets too hot, and he has to curl up, panting, in whatever scant shade he can find. He turns and trots back into the desert.

In the cellar, the girl's spine arches into a trembling bow.

Costa Brava

The two women sat in silence.

When the telephone rang, Mercedes picked it up swiftly. "Yes?"

The old man's voice was blunt, forceful. "Listen to me. I've spoken to Colonel de Córdoba. He'll be on the noon flight from Madrid tomorrow. Can you meet him at the airport?"

"Yes."

"Tell him everything," the minister commanded. "He is a man to be trusted. He is not young, but his brain is as sharp as a scalpel."

"Very well."

"Try not to worry about Eden. She will survive this."

"Will she?"

"She's a survivor. Like you. You're going to need dollars, Mercedes. I have money, both in Liechtenstein and in America."

"If I need it, I'll ask you," she said. Then, after a hesitation, she added, "Thank you, Gerard."

"You're my flesh."

Mercedes Eduard's eyes blurred. She hung up quickly, before she could betray any further emotion. "He's sending a man from Madrid," she told Maya. "A kidnap expert. We have to meet him at the airport at noon tomorrow."

"Will he be able to help?"

"I do not know." She looked up at Maya. Her face was a pale

mask with glittering black eyes. Her hands were clenched into fists, so that the well-manicured nails dug into her palms. "I want nothing of this to be known, by the servants or anyone else. You understand?"

"Yes, Mercedes."

Mercedes rose and walked to the window of her study. *If only my life had been different,* she thought. *Oh, Eden, if only I'd taken better care of you. Sin and death. Crime and punishment. Retribution following me all my life, as night follows day, as one link of a chain follows another.*

Her land stretched, parklike, towards a distant vista of the Pyrenees, their blue folds unlined with snow now that summer was here. She had built this house facing the mountains, not the sea, an orientation that was now almost obsolete among the rich people who had come here to erect their summer palaces. Unlike them, she had felt no desire to stare at the Mediterranean. Like her ancestors, it had been the mountains she'd wanted to see, every morning, when she rose.

She had sunk a fortune into this property. She had watched, four years ago, as the bulldozers had ploughed the clay earth into a landscape of her own devising for sixty thousand square metres all around. Thousands of trees had been brought in and planted at her command, rows of olives, orchards of peaches and apricots, groves of almonds and lemons and oranges.

She had watched as the lawns and rockeries and flower beds had been laid, the fountains brought to life, the pergolas and walks set out. She'd created here the green Catalán garden that she'd dreamed of in exile.

And now, it seemed to Mercedes that a cyclone had torn through it all, leaving only devastation behind.

Eden! she thought with an inner cry of agony. *Eden, my child. What have we done to you?*

Danse Macabre

San Lluc, Catalonia, Spain

Most of the nuns have been taken away already. Paco Massaguer, the local squire, has sent wagons to rescue them. Two of his men have been beaten senseless for their pains, but the terrified sisters of San Lluc have been allowed to leave.

The mob pelted them with filth as they left. With filthy words too. Some threw stones as well as dung.

Mother Josep, the Mother Superior, has refused to go. She remains behind, with four of the staunchest, huddled in the Lady Chapel.

Despite Massaguer's dire warnings of rape and murder, the rioters have not yet harmed any of them physically. Five or six men, boys really, chase poor Sister Dolors across the courtyard with a smoking firebrand. But when the old woman weeps hysterically in terror, they take pity on her.

"Come on," one of them says as he helps her to her feet, "this isn't the end of the world. It's the beginning of a new one. Go and hide yourself somewhere safe."

San Lluc is by no means a rich convent, but the mob have already taken everything that has the slightest value. They seem to be intent on plunder, sacrilege and wanton destruction, in that order. They have made a bonfire of prayer books, chests, hard mattresses and harder benches, dour furnishings of monastic life.

Mother Josep is praying that the flames will not reach the thirteenth-century roof timbers of the convent.

While she prays, she wonders whether this really might be the beginning of the terrible new world of Revelation. Or the return of the Dark Ages. Nothing worse than this has ever happened in living memory. In Barcelona, in the past week, thirty churches have already been burned to the ground.

The convent of San Lluc stands on a hill and the high walls are visible from far out to sea. It commands sweeping views of the Mediterranean in front and the Pyrenees behind. Also of the ancient tiled roofs of the village of San Lluc, which straggles a little way down the hill.

The mob must have come from these narrow streets of stone houses, or from the surrounding farms. She knows what they are—radicals, anarchists, antichrists—but as human beings she cannot find anything familiar in their faces, though she has lived here and known this area since she was a teenage novice. Rage has transformed them.

"What have we done to them?" Sister Dolors is wailing as she nurses her grazed hands. "Mary, Mother of God, what have we done to them?"

The sound of the uproar outside abruptly changes pitch. Mother Josep pauses in her prayers as she hears the sound of ragged music and wild laughter. There are also screams.

"Stay here," she hisses at the others and, gathering her habit around her ankles, hurries to the chapel door to peer out. There she stops, stupefied. "Unthinkable," she whispers, crossing herself.

They have been to the crypts where seven centuries of nuns have their last repose and have disinterred a dozen or so coffins, that they have knocked open with their spades. Now the pitiful contents are being carried into the courtyard, amid great excitement.

The village fiddler strikes up a tune; and as she watches, one of the men scoops a ragged bundle into his arms. He begins to dance to the fiddler.

Mother Josep recognizes him at once. He is Francesc Eduard,

the blacksmith. A big, strapping man of twenty-two or twenty-three, he is laughing uproariously as he dances. He loves to laugh, throwing his head back and shouting with amusement. He is handsome, strong, dark. His blue eyes flash. He is very popular with the women of the town.

The ragged bundle in his arms is the disinterred corpse of a nun.

A ring has formed around him and the rioters are clapping in time, stamping their feet, howling with laughter.

The nun too, seems to be laughing. Like all the nuns of San Lluc, she has been buried in her habit. Within the rusty black folds, her withered body is as light as a bundle of sticks and as rigid.

The tissues of her face have shrunk into a brown monkey-mask that barely veils the skull. Noseless, it peers out of the stained wimple with empty sockets and grinning yellow teeth.

"It's Pilar," she hears Sister Catalina say in an odd voice. The others have crowded around her in the doorway of the chapel and are staring at the incredible scene. "Sister María del Pilar," the nun repeats in the same scraping voice. "We buried her in 1897. She died of a cancer."

"María del Pilar," Sister Dolors whispers. "God rest her soul."

Mother Josep's eyes fill with tears. She too, can now see a caricature of Pilar's features in the monkey skull as it bobs round and round. Pilar, that sweet child. Pilar, her friend, resting with God these twelve years.

She knows why they have done this. Not just to insult. To prove that there is no God, no ultimate rest in His bosom, only this obscene declension of the flesh. . . .

"Get back inside," she commands, turning on the others with a terrible voice. "What are you gawping at? Get back inside and pray for these lost souls!"

The nuns scuttle back into the chapel, leaving the Mother Superior alone. She forces herself to watch Francesc Eduard. Her lips move in a prayer. The man is mad drunk, not just with the Communion wine they have all been swilling, but with that far more intoxicating liquor, anarchism.

Not six months ago, this splendid young man forged a new set of double iron gates for the convent. Despite his relative youth,

his work is masterful. The gates are beautifully wrought. The up-
rights and cross-bars are snakes that twine and writhe among flowers and leaves. At the centre of each gate is a cross.

Francesc Eduard made too, the great iron door knocker in
the form of a winged ox, the symbol of St. Luke. He sang, she
remembers, as he worked and his muscular arms dripped sweat.

But the young blacksmith has a fiery head on his broad shoulders. He served his apprenticeship in Barcelona and was infected
with anarchy and trade unionism there. He is said also to be lewd,
though that is often said of young persons who are only alluring
and merry. But this. . . .

Sister María del Pilar, though he does not know it, was young
and appealing when she died. Now her face, once sweet, is a horror
that he does not shrink from kissing. The women among the crowd
scream with mingled revulsion and delight.

Then Francesc swings the corpse round too roughly and with
a little dry snap, Pilar's head detaches itself, popping out of the
wimple like a sparsely-tufted football. The music falters as the
skull rolls on the cobblestones.

Francesc meets Mother Josep's eyes. He bursts into laughter
at her expression and lays down Pilar's desecrated trunk. "Come
and dance, Josep," he shouts to her, holding out his arms. "The
socialist revolution is here, don't you know that?"

But it is not the revolution, only what the newspapers will call
Semana Tragica, Tragic Week. Dozens of churches will be burned
before it is over and scores of people will be killed. But the state
will be unshaken.

Later today, soldiers will arrive to disperse the mob that is
looting the convent. Francesc is dancing his last dance. The
guardia civil's bullets will break his hips and shatter his thigh
this evening and he will never walk again without two sticks. In
these days before antibiotics and skilled surgery, he will be lucky
to live.

It will, of course, be the intervention of Mother Josep that
will save his life, not once, but twice.

First, she will insist that he remain in the convent's small
infirmary, rather than be taken to prison with the others. Her
scrupulous notions of cleanliness will save Francesc from the infections that would surely have killed him otherwise.

And second, as Francesc Eduard lies in a fever in the convent, Mother Josep will bar the police from coming in to arrest him. She will point out that he has been crippled forever, which is punishment apt and sufficient for his crime and that, after all, he has harmed no living soul. And hers is a voice that carries weight.

So he will be spared trial, but not the butchery that will be needed to save his life, nor the pain that will hammer him like iron on the anvil.

And like iron hammered when it is white hot, he will forever bear the fashion of the blows. He will hobble out the rest of his days at the forge, a crooked man, iron willed and iron faced, never again to flash his smile at a pretty young woman.

But Francesc does not know any of this and as Mother Josep turns to go back into the Lady Chapel, he retrieves Sister María del Pilar's skull and, with it under his arm, begins again to dance. . . .

november 1917

San Lluc

"It says in the paper that the Bolsheviks are killing and eating small children."

"Only after they've killed and eaten their own grandmothers." Francesc, leaning heavily on the sink with his right arm, soaped his naked chest and wondered irritably to what he owed the honour of this call. It was eight o'clock on an autumn evening, cold outside and the sun setting bloodily in the clouded west.

His visitor sat at the table. His thumbs worked incessantly on the shiny handle of the cane he held propped between his knees. He wore his hat clamped squarely on his head, his spectacles dangling on a chain from his fat waist. Marcel Barrantes, the village shopkeeper, represented the closest thing to a capitalist that San Lluc could boast.

"That man Lenin is evil. He'll only bring another kind of dictatorship, crueller than the czars."

"That would be difficult."

Barrantes watched the blacksmith covertly, gnawing at his

moustache. The man was an Apollo from the waist up, wormwood below.

His arms bulged with sinews and veins. Dark hair matted his chest. The legs, crooked like the hindquarters of a goat, gave him something of the attitude of a satyr.

"Do you think the revolution will spread?"

Francesc pulled a shirt on. "One of these fine days, Barrantes, the sewers of Barcelona will run red with the blood of those who now have their heel on our necks."

Barrantes almost crossed himself in alarm. "Men have been shot for saying such things."

A blacksmith's trade was a good one. But Francesc, with his long hair and shaggy beard, lived in near squalor. The house was slovenly. It reeked of soot and hot iron from the forge downstairs. Still, there was a great deal, Barrantes comforted himself, that a woman could do to improve things here.

He cleared his throat. "You need a woman to look after you."

"I don't see a stream of volunteers."

Barrantes looked arch. "There used to be, so I'm told."

"That was before the *guardia* improved my appearance," he said curtly.

"If the women avoid you, it's because you're so damned rude. Not because—" He was about to point at Francesc's legs, but bit his knuckle instead. "Not because of anything else."

Francesc's eyes were cold. "Is that what you've come here to tell me?"

Barrantes hesitated on the brink, then launched himself into the stream. "You know my daughter, Conchita."

"Do I?"

"A pretty girl," Barrantes coaxed. "With grey eyes and black hair. A little angel."

Francesc grunted. He started to carve at his food with a knife. "What about her?"

"Something's happened. A tragedy. A disgrace."

"You mean she's pregnant," Francesc said ironically.

"Yes," Barrantes replied heavily. "She is going to have a child. There's no question of the boy marrying her. She's ruined. You know what people are like in San Lluc. Her aunts want to send her to Andalucía, to some convent. But Conchita's only seventeen. She's my only child, Francesc. I can't bear to lose her."

"What does this have to do with me?"

"Maybe we can reach an agreement," Barrantes said.

Francesc suddenly knew why the shopkeeper was here. He was aware of an electric current running into his stomach, making the nerves flutter. Aware of a dark anger unfolding its wings. "An agreement?" he said grimly.

"You need a wife. She needs a husband. I've spoken to the girl. If you'll accept the way she is, she'll accept the way you are. It's an arrangement that—"

He broke off on a choked gasp. Francesc had lunged forward, grasping the shopkeeper's jacket with one hand, dragging him out of his chair with appalling strength.

Barrantes found himself sprawled across the table, staring bug-eyed at the knife that was quivering an inch from his face. Francesc's face was suffused with rage, his eyes bloodshot. "Because I'm a cripple, you want me to marry a *whore?*"

"She's not a whore," Barrantes panted, terrified. His fingers scrabbled frantically at the blacksmith's huge fist. "For the love of God, I didn't mean to insult you!"

"You little louse," Francesc grated. "You little bloodsucking insect."

"I love the girl," Barrantes croaked, feeling the knife at his throat, cold and sharp. "Don't hurt me, for Christ's blessed sake. I only want what's best for her."

Francesc's whole body was quivering, as though he had received some unimaginable insult. Part of him wanted to slit the shopkeeper's pudgy throat here and now.

Another part was already whispering subversion, whispering, *Why not listen? Why not? Is anything worse than this solitude, this desert?*

Slowly, his fist opened, and Barrantes slipped, gasping, back into his chair. The shopkeeper's hands were trembling violently as he straightened his jacket and repocketed his watch.

"Come on," Francesc growled. "Let's hear the rest of it."

"Don't leap to conclusions about her. She's a good girl. Her mother died when she was a baby, you know. She never had a mother's guiding hand." He wiped his mouth with a handkerchief. This interview was not proceeding the way he had imagined it would. "She's so sweet-natured, Francesc, so good. Such a pretty little fairy. So clever, always reading. She'd transform your life. Bring some light into this place."

"And two more mouths to feed."

"She won't come empty-handed. I'm not a rich man, whatever they say. But I can spare enough to give the girl a decent dowry."

Francesc grunted. "Who made the girl pregnant?"

"Paco Massaguer's elder son. Felip."

There was a silence. "Massaguer's son."

"The young shit has turned his back on her. He's away at university. In Barcelona, or Madrid, or somewhere. She's just a child. What does she know about men? Especially spoiled, rich young men like Felip Massaguer, with his poetry and his politics. I call it rape. I said so to old Massaguer himself."

"And what did he say?"

"He laughed in my face. He threw me out of his house." Barrantes's thumbs trembled as they fretted the cane. "I cannot fight the Massaguers. They would crush me."

"Of course. They own half of Catalonia. Paco Massaguer wanted to hang me in 1909, with two bullets still in my arse. And you're asking me to raise his grandchild?"

"The child might not survive. These bastards are sometimes frail."

"Oh, you're a wonderful Christian," Francesc rasped. "I can see that. You're wishing your own grandchild dead?"

"Jesus, no. But these things happen. Anyway, once the bastard is born, you can father other children, of your own. Consider it!" He was beginning to recover from his fright. He was a resilient man. "I assume there are no problems in that regard?"

Francesc snarled. "Are you asking me if I'm still a man?"

"Of course not," Barrantes said hastily, watching the knife point with wide eyes.

"I can still fuck a woman, Barrantes."

"Anyone can see that you're every inch a man," the shop-keeper soothed. Francesc opened his hand, letting the knife drop out, to Barrantes's unspeakable relief. "Will you at least come and meet her? Come and eat with us. Tomorrow night. We're having roast duck. Her aunts will be there to meet you. And perhaps," Barrantes suggested delicately, "you might think about a visit to the barber between now and then?"

"Get out," Francesc said wearily. "Leave me in peace to finish my dinner."

"You'll come?"

"No."

"What have you got to lose? Nothing. I've already lost everything. Everything!" The shopkeeper's eyes were starting to swim with tears.

"Turn off the fountain, for God's sake."

Marcel Barrantes blew his nose heavily. "Tomorrow night, then?" He knew better than to press the point any further. He rose to his feet and turned to go.

Francesc looked up. "Was this your idea, Barrantes? Or hers?"

"Don't worry," Barrantes replied obliquely. "She's a good girl. She only wants to make you a good wife."

The stairs were dark and Francesc sat listening to Barrantes's stumbling footsteps as he felt his way down. The door banged shut and he was left in silence. A pool of candlelight illuminated the remains of his meagre supper. But he had no appetite.

He grasped the wine jug and poured a generous stream into his mouth.

Though in his dreams Francesc had made love to almost every woman in San Lluc, it had never occurred to him to think of little Conchita Barrantes in that way. In his fantasies, the women who came to him were heavy-breasted, heavy-thighed, smelling of musk.

While she, the child who not so long ago used to avoid him in the street, was thin and cat-eyed, with breasts that hardly swelled the front of her dress.

Still, she was a woman. Whatever else, she was a woman.

It came to him in a rush. Jesus, Mary and Joseph, a woman, a woman in his bed again. The taste of a woman's mouth, the scent of her loins, the furnace of desire. . . .

Eight years of solitude. Of bitterness. The last woman he'd kissed had been Sister María del Pilar. He gulped at the stream of wine, spilling some down his chin.

But the bitch had already sold herself. Soiled goods. Used and cast aside by Felip Massaguer.

Paco Massaguer, the boy's father, was one of that hated class of men called *caciques*, a wielder of power. He owned factories, farms, properties in all directions, including most of the village of San Lluc. His heavy rents and rates ensured that his tenants never escaped from the crushing debts he laid on them. Sometimes a tenant's whole harvest would go to Massaguer, leaving his family lucky if they had seed corn and an animal left to pull the plough for next year.

He used his power like a weapon to bludgeon those already crushed by poverty.

It was also Massaguer, and men like him, who delivered the vote, making a mockery of whatever democracy could be said to exist in Spain in 1917. The leverage this gave them with the politicians, who in turn bribed them, ensured that their power was all-reaching.

He'd seen Massaguer's two sons many times. Felip, the elder, was a slender, pretty, delicate-looking youth of nineteen or twenty. His brother, Gerard, was a year or so younger, though it was he who seemed to be the elder of the two. He was of a different stamp, handsome and dark, with a cruel laugh. Easy to see him seducing a girl. The older boy didn't look as though he had the guts.

Francesc sat, drinking steadily and brooding.

Nipples and thighs. He groaned, shutting his eyes, feeling as though his loins would burst. A woman. A wife.

Ask the cripple, he won't say no. He hasn't had it in eight years. Clever little bitch! Knowing just how to market her stock-in-trade.

He smashed his fist onto the table once, then again and again. The sound echoed through the silent house.

Francesc decided he would not hobble into Conchita Barrantes's house on two sticks, like a beggar. He would manage with a cane, like a man of dignity.

But although he could stand for hours at the forge, leaning against the anvil, he was sweating with pain by the time he had tottered across the village to Barrantes's door.

On the threshold of the sitting room, he collapsed heavily and sprawled at the feet of Conchita and her aunts.

The women gathered around, clucking in dismay. Marcel, cursing under his breath, struggled to help the blacksmith to his feet.

"Damn, he's heavy. Lluisa, help me."

But it was Conchita herself who took Francesc's iron-muscled right arm and helped to heave him upright. Francesc looked into her face, which was as white as his own was now scarlet, and shook her away.

"A glass of wine," Marcel Barrantes said, dusting himself. "That's what we all want."

Conchita's hands trembled so that the neck of the bottle chattered against the glasses. She served Francesc first, then went back to her chair and sat with her hands in her lap.

As the pain in his legs receded, Francesc studied her bluntly. He suffered a bitter disappointment.

The girl didn't have a curve on her.

Like most men of his time, he was a devotee of round arms, fertile bosoms, buxom haunches. Conchita had none of these. She was as lean as one of the village cats, a woman barely out of girlhood, with a pale, oval face.

Only her eyes were at all interesting. They were large, dark-fringed and a clear grey. Her hair, which was black, was tied back severely. She was wearing a modest dress that came down almost to her feet.

Francesc darted an acrid look at the shopkeeper. Frankly, he'd rather bed one of the aunts, and they were nearly sixty.

"My good friend here,"—the shopkeeper was smiling, blithely unaware of Francesc's thoughts—"tells me that the Russian revolution will spread, even to Spain. But our authorities know how to deal with revolutionaries."

"With murder and terrorism," Francesc said shortly.

"Fire must be fought with fire, my friend."

"You're wrong, Barrantes." Francesc's tone was just short of rudeness. "The revolution is already here. The class struggle has been engaged and scientific materialism teaches us that there can be only one outcome."

"Karl Marx," Barrantes identified happily. "But there will never be a revolution in Spain. There may be a civil war." He smiled. "But Spain was not made for revolutions."

They began discussing Bolshevism.

Conchita sat in silence, watching the blacksmith from beneath her lashes.

Francesc Eduard had been a figure of delicious terror to her since her childhood. Yet now that she saw him with the eyes of a woman, he was not so terrifying as she had remembered. She had forgotten how handsome he was. His eyes were a striking dark blue and he possessed excellent white teeth.

There was no getting away from the fact that he hobbled. But his arms and chest were splendid. Helping him up, she'd felt muscles like living iron under her fingers.

His hands fascinated her. They were huge, knotted and scarred with his work. They were obviously immensely powerful. Yet she sensed gentleness in them.

Francesc's mood improved steadily. When the food was ready, he mellowed enough to accept Barrantes's helping arm to the table.

"You like the duck?" Lluisa, the younger aunt, leaned forward with a bright smile. She was a handsome woman with full lips and bright eyes, though she had a great mole on her cheek. She wore a large tortoiseshell comb in her hair.

"It's very good." Francesc nodded, plying his knife and fork. "Very good."

"Conchita made it especially," the aunt said with a sly glance at the girl. "Insisted on going into the kitchen to do it. She made the pudding too. You'll taste that later. It's delicious. She loves to cook."

Francesc had been placed opposite Conchita. He looked at the girl. Her cheeks were touched with pink. The colour improved her looks slightly. She didn't have the round chin, plump cheeks and rosebud lips that were his ideal of feminine beauty, but he decided that if the girl was not voluptuous, she was at least pretty. "It's very good," he said in her direction. Then, realizing that he had used the phrase twice, cleared his throat. "And what is the pudding?"

"A *crema catalana*," she said in her quiet voice, looking down at her plate.

The other aunt, María, poured more wine into Francesc's glass. "We like plain cooking here. Wholesome and plain."

Francesc had been comparing the Barrantes household uneasily with his own. Everything was bright and clean. The walls were hung with religious oleographs. The furniture gleamed with wax. Where he usually didn't even have a candle, they had oil lamps, making the dining room as bright as day.

Conchita Barrantes was used to a standard of comfort very different from the house over the forge. It would be a shock for her to come from this house to his, he thought.

"You're as quiet as a mouse tonight, Conchita." Aunt Lluisa reproved the girl. "You haven't addressed more than a word to our guest."

She raised her grey eyes to Francesc. "What will the Bolsheviks do to the czar and the czarina?"

"The women and children will probably be sent into exile." He shrugged. "Nicholas, of course, may be tried."

"For what?"

"For war crimes."

"War crimes?"

Francesc resisted the inclination to retort brusquely. "Last summer," he told her, "during the Brusilov offensive alone, one million Russian soldiers died. For nothing. The fault was the czar's. Does it really matter what will happen to him and his family?"

"Nicholas will get good Bolshevik justice," Marcel said dryly. He cocked his thumb and levelled a finger. "A bullet in the head."

"But it would be a terrible thing to kill the czar and the czarina," Conchita said, staring at the blacksmith.

"The men who started and bungled this war are the greatest criminals who ever lived," he said. "Uncounted millions have died. Why should the deaths of Nicholas and Alexandra Romanov matter more than that?"

"Because they're beautiful."

"Beautiful?" he said in astonishment. "If anything good has come out of all this senseless slaughter, it's that the corrupt old monarchies will finally be swept away."

"So Papa is right? They'll shoot him?"

"Perhaps. Who cares?"

Barrantes laughed. "Let's have some of this famous pudding, then. Lluisa, call the servant."

Francesc looked curiously at the young woman before him. The dress might have been chosen, he thought wryly, to make the girl look as unappealing as possible. It hung on her like a sack. Why hadn't they tried to smarten her up, a bit of powder, something stuffed down her flat chest?

Then she looked up and her eyes met his. Cool, grey, clear, her gaze reached into his mind with such assurance that he was momentarily stunned. He felt his stomach tighten, the blood rushing into his loins. Unable to tear his eyes away, he thought, My God, she's beautiful!

Conchita, unaware of his thoughts, saw only the intensity of his stare. The dark blue eyes were hot. He would not look away. Indeed, he seemed not to know how rude it was to stare people out of countenance. Really, it was too much. He was studying her face as brashly as though she'd been a painting!

Conchita felt the colour filling her cheeks. She tilted her head at him angrily, reproving him for that piercing stare. Then she rose to her feet quickly.

"They're taking an age in the kitchen," she announced. "I'll go and make the coffee."

"The servant will do that," her father protested.

"I'll do it better," she said and hurried out.

Francesc was tugging at his collar with his big fingers, so that Barrantes looked up.

"Too hot for you in here?"

"Perhaps it's the wine," María suggested.

"It's that stove," Francesc mumbled. "I'm cooking."

The *crema catalana* was served in plain, round clay dishes, each pale custard crusted with a brittle layer of caramelized sugar. It was smooth, delicate, voluptuously creamy.

The blacksmith avoided Barrantes for some days after the dinner. He needed time to think. Nor did the family try and contact him. It was as if both sides were waiting for the next move.

He encountered Conchita by chance one afternoon, coming down the street, carrying a basket. The wind was blowing fiercely in her face, her hair whipping backwards. He could see the outline of her slim body beneath her flattened dress. Her thighs were plainly delineated.

Her face was flushed as they met. She murmured a greeting and tried to slip by him. Francesc reached out without meaning to, or quite knowing why, and grasped her arm, pulling her back.

He stared into her face. Her skin was as fine as porcelain. He could see the veins beating at her throat and temples. There was a fine precision about the way her features were shaped, the distinctness of her mouth, the arch of her nostrils and eyebrows. Her eyelashes were extraordinarily long.

"What is it?" she asked, her mouth dry.

"You don't like to be looked at, do you?"

"It's uncouth to stare into a person's face!"

He was stung. His fingers bit into her slender arm. "Yes, very uncouth," he said roughly. "I'm an uncouth man. But then, you're a whore."

She flinched as if he had struck her. "That isn't true!"

"What are you, if you're not a whore?" he demanded.

He saw the tears start to her eyes. She wrenched her arm free and hurried away, the wind bowling her dress around her legs. He saw her bare calves for a moment, trim and white. Why had he been so harsh? Bitter regret rose in him. He had an impulse to chase after her and apologize for the way he had spoken. But he knew he would never catch her. She disappeared around an ivy-clad corner. He stumped on his way, cursing himself and her.

She came to the forge the next afternoon.

He looked up and she was standing there, those clear eyes fixed on him.

He straightened slowly.

"I want to tell you what happened," she said.

He thrust the red-hot iron into the tub. Steam billowed. "Well?" he said brusquely.

She was as taut as a bow, holding his gaze with eyes that seemed to burn grey fire.

"The baby is not Felip Massaguer's. It's his brother's."

He frowned. "What are you talking about?"

"Felip and I were never lovers. It would have been impossible, in any case. Felip is . . . incapable."

"Incapable? You mean impotent?"

"I loved Felip," she said. "But not in any—not in any carnal sense."

Francesc was impatient with her euphemisms. "Felip didn't fuck you? But the other boy did?"

He'd used the crude word deliberately and it made the colour flame into her face. "Felip is a very special person."

"Really?" Francesc said ironically.

"Yes. I know what you think of his father. But Felip is different."

"So it seems."

"He believes in freedom for the people, just like you do. He wants justice."

"Well, when he inherits his father's estates, he can give them all away to the tenants, can't he?"

She ignored the heavy irony. "What passed between me and Felip Massaguer was a thing of the spirit." Her eyes were swimming. "He—he showed me so many things. So much beauty I would never have known was in the world." She reached into her pocket and took out a bundle of papers, tied with a thin ribbon. "These are his letters to me, Francesc. I want you to read them. You'll see what kind of man he is. How he suffers for the way he is. How he feels."

Francesc took them reluctantly and laid them down. "Suffers?"

"He told me that he'd been to women many times, but something was always wrong and he could never manage—could never manage anything. He was tormented by it, but there was nothing he could do. He had another—his affections were—were elsewhere."

Francesc frowned. "You mean he had another woman?"

"He has a friend. A poet, a wonderfully gifted young man." She swallowed. "A man of his own sentiments."

"I'm damned if I know what you mean."

Her face was scarlet. "There are some men who can only manage true love with—with other men."

Francesc's mouth curled under his beard. "Ah. Is that it?" he said in disgust.

"Yes. Felip is one of those. He can't help it."

"I see," he said.

"I *want* you to see," Conchita said urgently, her hands clasping and unclasping. "That's why I've given you those letters. We were never lovers. He told me that the only person he had ever done it with was his friend. The poet." She swallowed. "You'll see that in the letters."

"So?" he prompted impatiently. "Where did the baby come from?"

"His brother Gerard raped me," she said quietly.

Francesc grew very still.

She looked down. "They hate each other. Felip will inherit almost everything. He's the elder by two years. Gerard feels that he is the better man. He's jealous of everything Felip has or takes pleasure in. I think that he must have taunted Felip about me, incessantly. In the end, Felip told him we were lovers. Perhaps to defend his manhood."

She paused for such a long time that he shifted uneasily. "Well?"

"I went to meet Felip at Fontaner's well. It was our favourite place. But when I got there, it was Gerard, not Felip, who was waiting for me. I knew he was going to do something evil, but there was no one to call for. And he had a knife." Her breaths were coming faster now and her hands were locked tight. "He held the knife to my throat. I was so afraid. He said horrible, hateful things. Until I cried. Then he raped me. There. Twice. In between, he rested. And laughed at me. And Felip."

There was a long silence as her quiet sobs slowed, then stopped. Gradually, she got her breathing under control. At last, she looked at him again. "I was a virgin until then. You understand?"

He nodded without speaking.

"I never saw Felip again. He never even wrote to me. If only I could have told him, instead of Gerard. Gerard will have told him the truth, but in such a way that Felip would never have wanted to see me again." She touched her throat with those slim fingers. "Please, may I have some water?"

He set a glass and pitcher before her. She drank slowly, her eyes closed. Through the glass, through the clear water, he saw her white teeth, the pink of her soft upper lip.

"Why didn't you tell the truth?" Francesc asked in a cold voice. "Why didn't you tell them that Felip was a degenerate and that the other boy raped you?"

"Because Felip had already told his brother that we were . . . lovers."

"And so?"

"If his brother and father knew the way he really was, it would kill Felip. His father would even disinherit him, I think. He told me that. You're the only one who knows the truth about him."

"I envy you the luxury of such finer feelings," he said angrily. "Don't you understand? If you'd said you were a virgin when the younger boy raped you, your father would have had a much better case."

"But that would have meant exposing Felip."

"Exposing *Felip*? Is that all you cared about? Were you so infatuated with Felip Massaguer that you laid down your reputation, your whole family's reputation, for his sake?"

"You mean I should have rushed home and told them all what Gerard had done to me?" She shook her head. "You don't understand. I said nothing. I *couldn't* have spoken about it, even if anyone would have believed me. It was only when I knew I was pregnant that I had to tell them."

"But your father, your aunts—don't you *care* what they think of you?"

"No," she said quietly. "Not any more." There was a long silence. She looked at his big, battered hands. "I'm sorry," she said at last. "It hasn't been easy for you to listen to me. It wasn't easy for me to tell you. But I wanted to do it, before you make up your mind about me."

"Do you expect me to think any better of you now?" he demanded brusquely.

"I just wanted you to know the truth," she retorted, her mouth trembling. "So that you knew I wasn't to blame!"

"Not to blame? You let that family of *bourgeois* pigs use you and discard you. Let them call you a whore so that Felip Massaguer could pretend to be a man!"

She choked and ran out of the forge without looking back.

He turned to the furnace and reheated the iron. There was relief in smashing the hammer down onto it, seeing the sparks fly, seeing the metal take the shape that, once cooled, it would hold forever.

By Christmas the whole village was buzzing with the unlikely courtship of Conchita by Francesc.

A round of cautious meetings between Francesc and the Barrantes family followed, culminating in a second dinner *en famille* at the shopkeeper's house, on Christmas Eve.

This dinner was a more extravagant affair than the last one. An extra servant had been procured. The table had been laid with the best white linen and the silver-plated cutlery. There was a huge bowl of fruit as a centerpiece and more oil lamps than ever.

The aunts, scenting a swift kill, had devoted much more attention to Conchita's toilette. Tonight she appeared in a cream muslin dress, with her dark hair tied back and a breath of rouge on her cheeks. As a finishing touch, they had looped a strip of brown velvet, stitched with artificial pearls, around her forehead. The effect was to make her subtle beauty positively glow.

Francesc bowed over her hand in clumsy chivalry as he arrived, the first sign of gallantry he had exhibited. He was wearing a new suit, cutting quite a dashing figure. His dark blue eyes kept drifting towards Conchita throughout the meal, something that did not escape the aunts.

Marcel became convivially tipsy. When justice had been done to the goose and the inevitable *crema catalana* that followed, he banged the table. "What about a round of cards with our coffee?"

Lluisa cleared her throat meaningfully. "Perhaps the young people would like to go into the parlour and listen to the phonograph while we play a hand or two of whist?"

"Agreed, agreed." The shopkeeper chuckled fatly.

Francesc was sitting with a fixed smile on his face. It took him a minute or two to realize that he was included in the description, "the young people." He rose awkwardly and let Conchita guide him to the front parlour.

The phonograph was a small, wind-up affair with a fluted metal horn. Barrantes was probably the only man in San Lluc to have such a thing in his house. Francesc inspected it carefully.

"When I was a boy, Father Pérez warned us about these things," he told her. "I remember him saying they were the work of the Devil."

Conchita smiled. "At least we can talk without the aunts hearing." She had never, he thought, looked so pretty as tonight. The dress and the headband were delicious. Her hair was no less black and lustrous than the phonograph records she was examining.

She put one of the glossy shellac disks onto the turntable, wound the machine up briskly and lowered the arm carefully down. A pretty waltz crackled out.

"You look very elegant tonight," he said formally.

"Thank you. You're very elegant yourself." She glanced at him shyly. "Do you want to pick some records?"

They sat side by side on the sofa and looked through the collection. He watched her slim white hands sorting through the paper sleeves. Her wrists were delicate and fine-boned. Her fingers bore few signs of work; the nails were pale pink ovals, unbroken and spotlessly clean. Beside them, his own hands were seamed machine tools.

"You're accustomed to a luxurious life here," he remarked, looking around the cozy parlour. "You have all kinds of delicacies and luxuries. Lights everywhere. Fine furniture. You saw what my home is like. Could you really be happy living at the forge?"

"I could be happy anywhere," she said simply. "As long as I was wanted."

"I don't just mean that there won't be a phonograph or servants," he said brusquely. "By now you know that I'm no gentleman. I'm ugly to look at and ugly in my manners."

Conchita met his eyes. Her mouth trembled. "You are not ugly to look at, Francesc," she said timidly.

"I'm no Romeo." He felt frustrated, unable to frame the questions he really wanted to ask her, unable to tell her the things he really wanted her to understand.

The record came to a scratchy end and she changed it for another. The magnificent voice of Caruso swelled out of the metal horn, singing a Neapolitan love song.

"Look!" she exclaimed suddenly. "It's snowing!"

She jumped up and ran to the window. It was true. The stone courtyard of the Barrantes house was blurred by a torrent of white flakes.

"Snow," she breathed, pressing her face to the pane. "I've never seen snow before."

Francesc was surprised. "Never?"

"Never in my life!" She was staring at the stuff with a joyful face. "Look how beautiful it is! Like angels' wings!" She turned to him, her eyes wide and shining. "Let's go out in it!"

"You'll get soaked," he told her.

"Who cares? I want to eat some!"

"It isn't vanilla ice cream," he rumbled, but she had already run to the back door. She beckoned to him impatiently. "Get a shawl, at least," he said, picking up his crutches and hobbling towards her. "Remember your condition."

"Shhh! Let's just go, before they hear!"

They slipped out, into the courtyard. It was not cold, even after the oily heat inside the house. Francesc turned his face upwards, winking as the icy flakes kissed his skin and settled in his beard.

Conchita was crouching, scooping a ball of snow into an appetizing sorbet. She bit into it eagerly. Francesc watched the disappointment cloud her face.

"It has no taste!"

"I told you it wasn't ice cream."

Not a soul was stirring in the village; or, if there were steps and voices, they were muted by the blanket of white. High in the spangled darkness, the lights of the convent twinkled.

"I'm sorry about what happened to you," he said.

She knew what he was talking about. "Thank you," she said, almost inaudibly.

"If there was any justice in this country, that boy would pay with his life."

She was silent for a while, her lips pressed to her snowball. "I don't think of it like that," she said at last. "I only want to think about the future."

Francesc looked down at her. Her dark hair was sequinned with snowflakes. He lifted the snowball out of her hands and tossed it aside. Her fingers were wet and icy. He took them between his own palms and chafed them gently.

He spoke quietly. "Have you considered how intimately our lives would be shared?"

She dared not raise her eyes to his. "I—I think so."

"That we would live together? Eat together?"

"Yes."

"Sleep together?"

He felt her fingers tremble. "Yes."

"Are you sure?"

"I think I am." Little clouds of vapour appeared at their mouths, hers coming faster than his.

"You're so young," he said huskily. "And so beautiful."

At last she looked up at him. He leaned forward and kissed her mouth. Her lips felt icy to him. His burned like coals. She felt the harsh curls of his beard against her chin. He was gentle at first. Then he crushed her to him, his immense strength overwhelming her.

She whimpered in her throat and he released her at once.

"I'm sorry," he said thickly.

"Don't be sorry," she whispered. "I wanted it too."

From inside the house, a voice called. He ached to kiss her again. But she turned and ran back to the house.

Francesc huddled in the mule cart. The first days of January had brought bitter winds and a piercing cold.

As he urged the horse on, he heard hoofbeats just behind him. Three riders were approaching fast. They overtook his cart and surrounded him.

He was forced to rein up, cursing.

"What's the matter?" he demanded roughly, pulling the scarf away from his face. "You're blocking my path."

All three of the riders dismounted. The leader gave his reins to one of his fellows and walked casually up to the cart.

Francesc recognized him at once as Gerard Massaguer. The other two men were Andalusian gypsies, migrants with hard-bitten faces.

The boy smiled at him. "Get down." And when Francesc didn't move, he repeated, "Get down, blacksmith, or we'll pull you down."

Slowly, subduing his initial reaction to rebel, Francesc dismounted. He lifted his sticks out of the cart and leaned on them, facing the Massaguer boy. He was a well-built, dark youth of eighteen or so, with an expression of lazy arrogance on his features. His eyes were heavy-lidded. His face was handsome, sensual.

"They say you're going to marry Conchita," he said calmly. "Is that true?"

"Perhaps."

Massaguer stood with his legs astride, jingling coins in his pocket. He smiled into Francesc's eyes. "I had her first, you know. And second."

"What do you want?" Francesc asked quietly.

The two gypsies came to stand on either side of their master. Both carried heavy clubs. "I've got some questions," the boy said. "I want some answers."

"And if I cannot give them?"

"If not, you'll be hurt. Badly." He pinched his own full lower lip, looking at Francesc speculatively from under heavy lids. "The girl bled like a stuck pig, blacksmith. Yet she claimed my brother had her first. I've been thinking about it ever since. I think my brother never touched her. He's a sodomite. And I think she knows it. That's why she's covering for him."

"I know nothing about the sexual habits of your distinguished family."

"I'm going to explain it to you, because they say you're an intelligent man. Full of crazy ideas, but a man with a brain, nonetheless. You see, if I could prove that Felip was a sodomite, my father would disinherit him, blacksmith. In favour of me."

Francesc, his eyes on Gerard Massaguer, didn't see the gypsy move until the club smashed across his face. His head exploded in hot pain. The earth was rocking. His mouth was full of blood where he had bitten his tongue through.

"We're talking about high stakes, blacksmith. A fortune. More money than five hundred blacksmiths could make in their whole lifetimes. You understand, don't you?"

This time he foresaw the blow from the other side and was able to lift his arm. A jarring impact racked into his body, making him gasp in pain. He swayed on his sticks. While he was blinded, the first man rammed his club hard into Francesc's ribs, making him double up in agony.

"After Pedro and José have broken your arms," Gerard said, "they'll break your legs, such as they are. If you live, you'll spend the rest of your life in a poorhouse bed. And what for?"

"The girl hasn't said anything to me about either of you," he gasped.

"But you're going to marry her. You're her sweetheart. Girls tell their sweethearts everything. Don't they, José?"

Grinning, the bigger of the two gypsies stepped forward, swinging his club fast at Francesc's face.

His expression changed to one of almost comical surprise, however, when the blow did not land. One of Francesc's huge hands had whipped upwards, clamping round his wrist. The club dropped. With an exclamation, he tried to pull away. Then the blacksmith's other hand closed like a vice around José's, crushing with terrible force. The man's voice rose in a rabbit-thin shriek of pain.

The other gypsy started forward with an oath, his club raised, but seemed uncertain what to do. He and Gerard Massaguer stared as José tried frenziedly to bite the blacksmith's huge fists, his teeth gnawing at the scarred knuckles.

They heard the snap of bones. The screaming grew jagged. It tailed off into a gurgle. The man slumped, his eyes rolling back. When Francesc released his hand, it flopped as limply as an empty glove.

The boy was pale. The heavy eyelids were no longer sleepy, but awake and careful. On either side of his nose, two dents had appeared, like the marks of claws. "If I don't get what I want from you, I'll get it from her. You understand me? You have no love for my brother. Why should you protect him?"

Francesc came to a decision.

"Your brother never touched her." The blacksmith spat blood. "He has other fancies."

"Who?"

"A young man called García."

Gerard stepped forward, forgetting caution in his excitement. "García?"

"Some kind of poet."

"*García Lorca?*"

"That was the name."

"I knew it." Gerard Massaguer stared at Francesc eagerly. "Federico García Lorca. She told you Felip has committed sodomy with this man?"

"She gave me some letters he wrote."

Gerard's black eyes were glittering brightly. "These letters. Where are they?"

"If you go near her again," he said, holding the boy's eyes with his own hot blue stare, "nothing will be able to protect you from me. Believe me."

"I won't go near her. Just give me the letters."

"Send your other gypsy to the forge tonight."

"Good." Gerard almost whispered. "Good. Good. You won't regret this, blacksmith." He smiled, his dark face alight, as though with a flame. "I like you. You've got balls. You'll get work from me, when the land is mine."

"Yes," Francesc said. "I'll make you a pair of good stout hinges one day and a good iron lock. To keep you in your coffin."

Gerard's smile vanished. He stared at Francesc with black eyes. There was something animal in his gaze, some dark lust. "We know how we stand, then, don't we?" he said softly.

"We know how we stand." Francesc nodded.

The two men held one another's gaze for a while. Then Gerard Massaguer laughed.

"Pedro, sling that fool over his horse."

Francesc got back into the cart, his cheek and ribs aching savagely as he gathered the reins in his hands. His face felt swollen to the size of a melon.

Gerard Massaguer wheeled his horse around. "Blacksmith," he called, "I look forward to our next meeting!" They rode off.

Francesc stared after them, wondering what he had done. Then he rapped the horse sharply with the reins. To hell with them all. Let the brothers fight it out among themselves. Everyone had suffered enough already. All he wanted was a quiet life with his woman.

It wasn't until he'd reached the forge that he realized he'd thought the words.

His woman.

spring 1918

On her wedding day, 26 January 1918, Conchita's slender frame showed unmistakable signs of the coming event. She was six months pregnant by now. The child was due in April.

Francesc stood at the altar of a God he either hated or did not believe in, he could not tell which. His iron voice echoed through the church.

Conchita carried a spray of white almond blossoms. Her white dress reached halfway down her shins, showing trim ankles in white stockings, with a pair of neat silver shoes. In the fashion of that year, she wore a simple hat that curved down over her ears and a long embroidered veil. On her hands she wore a pair of finely embroidered lace gloves that had been her mother's.

She glowed. Her advancing pregnancy had emphasized her beauty. Behind the white roses of her veil, her eyes shone. She made her responses in a quiet, clear voice and when her husband turned to kiss her at the conclusion of the ceremony, she touched his beard with one hand, her eyes sparkling up at him as though they were lovers, not almost complete strangers.

She clung to his arm so tightly as they emerged from church that the blacksmith could hardly keep himself upright.

The wind was rising and the sky was leaden. Conchita pulled the veil back over her hat so that a photograph could be taken on the church steps. The wind plucked at it and flattened the guests' clothes around their limbs. A few spots of rain had already begun to fall. Francesc, who had looked grim and tense all morning, smiled dazedly, as though not quite sure how he had come through the ordeal.

The wedding party retired for a formal lunch at a restaurant. Conchita spoke hardly at all during the meal, or for the rest of the afternoon, but that was not out of shyness. She radiated calm purpose, like a woman who no longer had doubts.

Poor thing, Barrantes found himself exclaiming. Poor little thing. Had he done right by her? It was too late to wonder. She was wedded to Francesc as surely as if the blacksmith had forged shackles around her slender wrists.

Francesc was now thirty-two years old and for nine of those years had lived crippled and alone. It was bewildering to face the realization that everything was now changed and that the radiant young woman beside him was his wife. Stranger still, that in a few months she was going to present him with the child of another man's loins.

He stared at her, at her porcelain face with its calm grey eyes, and felt an odd mixture of excitement and pain surge along his veins. She was his. Slim and lovely, she was his. Tonight she would sleep in his bed. And all the nights after tonight.

"I'm thinking of selling the shop," Barrantes was saying expansively. He had drunk a lot of champagne and his blunt-featured face was flushed, his grey moustache dripping. "One has to move with the times."

"You've had too much to drink," his sister mocked him.

"I have plans. Great plans." Marcel slipped his thumbs into the pockets of his waistcoat. "I'm going to build a cinema."

"A *what?*"

He beamed at them all. "I'm going to buy an automobile too."

"A cinema and an automobile! What are you, a millionaire?"

"I'm a man of the people," Barrantes said loudly, banging the table with his fist. "The future of Spain lies in technology. In automobiles, cinemas, radio sets. My son-in-law will tell you that. Eh, Francesc?"

Francesc lifted his glass. "I want to propose a toast. To my wife, Conchita." He hesitated as they all watched him, their glasses raised to follow his lead. "My wife," he repeated in a quieter voice. "I thought I would never in my life come to say those words." He turned to Conchita, who was sitting silently beside him. "I am no orator, Conchita. But I would give my life for you. No one will ever make you suffer again," he said, his voice descending. "No one."

She met his gaze, her eyes misty.

The afternoon proceeded with alcoholic conviviality.

By six-thirty it was already dark and had begun to rain heavily. The distant rumble of thunder from the Pyrenees hinted at worse to come. Marcel was by now maudlin drunk and weeping openly.

He clung to Conchita in the pouring rain, sobbing and calling her his little lost lamb.

"Francesc, for God's sake, treat her well," he moaned, groping towards Francesc. "Treat her well!"

Francesc impatiently endured a final embrace, then took Conchita by the arm and hurried her into the covered cart. It had been decorated with flowers that morning, but by now the rain and wind had stripped the wreaths.

Because of Barrantes's inopportune burst of emotion, they had all been drenched to the bone. Conchita huddled beside Francesc, trying vainly to shield her bouquet of almond blossoms from the wind. Francesc took the reins and set off at a fast trot up the muddy high street, leaving the others behind. It was over, the wedding, the party, the day.

The rain was turning into a storm and the cover could not shield them completely from the cold gusts that blew into their faces, nor the mud that was kicked up by the horse's hooves.

By the time they arrived at the forge, lightning was flashing brilliantly in the north and the thunder was like the ominous roar of approaching artillery. They were both icy cold and Conchita was shivering violently. "Go upstairs," he shouted. "I'll take care of the horse."

She ran into the house, clutching her bouquet and veil. He stabled the animal and emptied some hay into the manger. By the time he came in, Conchita was building a fire in the grate. He bent to help her lay on some more logs, which hissed reluctantly on the flame. He could hear her teeth chattering.

"Do you want some wine?" he asked her.

"No, thank you." She stood back in her drenched bridal gown, looking very young and very pale. The rosiness had been washed away with the rain.

Thunder pealed across the valley and the rain drummed as loud as horses' hooves on the clay tiles of the roof. Here and there a drip of water could be heard, where a tile had been cracked and not replaced.

Why hadn't he thought to make the house more welcoming? He should have had flowers waiting for her. He should have had champagne, bright lights, the sort of sweet things that would tempt a woman's taste. A woman? She was more like a lost little girl. Frills and dolls would have been more appropriate.

Francesc cleared his throat. "This isn't exactly a bridal bower. I'm sorry."

"It's our home," she said in a small voice.

"It lacks a woman's touch. I've never bothered with it much. I've just lived and slept in this place. Perhaps you'll make it more comfortable, now that you are mistress here."

"I'll try."

The moment was profoundly uneasy. Any euphoria he had felt after the ceremony was by now thoroughly dampened.

There was a sudden crash of thunder outside and she jumped.

"Oh," she said miserably. "I hate thunderstorms!"

"We're perfectly safe here. Lightning never strikes San Lluc. It's the convent, you see. It's so much higher. The lightning always strikes the steeple there. Never down here."

"Really?" She didn't seem much impressed and started again as another flare of white light heralded a rolling peal of thunder overhead. "Oh!"

"I made the lightning rod myself," he added firmly, giving her his personal guarantee against thunderbolts. "Two metres high and solid copper. You're perfectly safe."

He pulled off his dripping coat and tossed it over a chair beside the fire. He thought, what have we done? They were like two survivors of a shipwreck, souls plucked at random to share an island forever.

"Shall we go to bed?"

She nodded dumbly.

"Go on ahead," he commanded. "I'll join you in a little while."

While she undressed, Francesc hooked a kettle over the fire and made himself some coffee. He drank it slowly.

At the time he'd been shot at the age of twenty-three, he had already been an experienced lover and had learned how to please women. All kinds of women, from trembling virgins to the middle-aged widows who'd come to his forge with those odd little tasks that only he could do.

Yet it had been nine years since he'd had a woman in his bed. He had been anticipating this moment with a certain dread, wondering whether ineptitude or unfamiliarity would turn it into a humiliating disaster. Above all, he had to remember to be slow and gentle with her. And to be careful with that big belly.

When he thought he had given her enough time, he tapped at the door and came in, carrying a candle. Only her face was visible in the bed, her black hair spread across the pillow. In the dim candlelight, her eyes flickered. The poor thing was trembling like a leaf, he realized.

"We'll soon be nice and warm," he said, as though talking to a child. He blew out the candle and undressed.

Conchita heard the rustling sounds of Francesc undressing and concentrated on keeping the dark animal of her panic at bay. Stopping it from coming into sight and putting her self-control to disastrous flight.

She flinched as he slid in beside her, his skin brushing hers.

"You're like ice," he whispered. He touched her shoulder. "Don't be afraid. I won't hurt you."

She closed her eyes as she felt his big, work-roughened hand touch her stomach, warm and gentle. "Francesc," she whispered, "I'm so afraid. I can't help it."

He kissed her lips, then her brow. She felt his beard, rough and curly, brush her face.

"Just lie still," he whispered. "There's nothing to be afraid of. Making love is designed to give pleasure, not pain."

She lay rigid, feeling his hands caressing her, with the long, slow, gentle caresses of a groom. His touch was sure, calm. Conchita could smell his skin, the warm, dark scent of his body. She was unaware that she was biting her own lower lip, her teeth fastened into the flesh. No one had ever touched her like this. None of her family had been physically affectionate people and she barely remembered the feel of her mother's hands.

As soon as he had touched her skin, Francesc had become as confident, as assured, as though those years of abstinence had never passed. Perhaps it was her timidity that gave him confidence; but he thought it was something else. It was a quality she had, that of drawing him into her, so that he saw, felt, through Conchita's eyes, Conchita's skin. He could not go wrong as long as he had that secret knowledge.

He touched the curve of her breasts, his fingers brushing the silky skin, and felt himself harden with desire. But he did not move towards her until he felt her begin to relax, her breathing slowing and growing easier.

"Is that nice?" he asked.

"Yes," she murmured, her eyes opening in the darkness. "You're so gentle."

"Are you still afraid of me?"

"I'm afraid . . . but not of you. Maybe of myself." His caress was becoming hypnotic. She was aware of surfacing, of drifting to the surface of the dark pool she had been lost in. Her body jolted once or twice when muscles relaxed, as though she were going to sleep. He kissed her again and she tried to respond, pressing her closed mouth to his.

He drew back, then returned, gently. Showed her how their mouths could fit together, her lip between his, his between hers. So snug. Such a teasing snugness. So many combinations. Touching her lips with his tongue. Such tiny delicate touches for such a big, rough man. Almost like a baby, or a cat. . . .

Her head was spinning. She'd seen men and women doing this on postcards, in romantic magazines. She'd heard of this. French kissing. More wicked than ordinary kissing.

Their tongues touched. Wicked. But intimate, so intimate. And nice. A deliberate opening of the self. Like letting another soul touch yours. As though you were telling another human being about those dark inner regions where the blood surged hot, where events took place beneath the skin, in the other reality.

She felt his hand slide downward to her loins and pressed her thighs together in alarm. She was no longer quite so afraid; in fact, her heart was beating quicker and there was a flicker of curiosity, of inquisitive searching, in her blood. But she *was* embarrassed. She didn't want him to touch her there. *Not there!*

Francesc was caressing her thighs, feeling his own breath coming shallow and ragged. God, he wanted her so much. Desire was mounting in him like a fever and it was an effort to hold himself back. He lifted her nightgown. Ah, there. He was touching the soft hair, the warm, prim lips of her sex, trying to get her to part her thighs.

"Conchita," he whispered. "Let me touch you."

When was he going to put his thing into her? She parted her thighs slightly, aware that he was growing excited and tense, the way Gerard had done that day . . . no, she mustn't think of that.

His fingers were exploring her. *There.* In an agony of embarrassment, she lay rigid. The only other man who had ever put his fingers there had been the doctor who'd examined her. *I'm afraid there's no doubt about it, Señorita. You are expecting a child.* Oh, God. What was he doing?

The horde of evil memories that was being released in her mind swelled, darkened. The panic burst through. He felt her reaction and took his hand away at once, cursing himself for his impatience. It was too late. She was as taut as a bow again, whimpering, shaking her head muzzily.

"Francesc, no. No, please don't—"

"Relax!"

"Let me get up, just for a moment, *please*—"

He opened his mouth without thinking and said the one thing he knew would touch her. As it always touched women.

"I love you."

She stopped moving at once. Then he heard a little click and knew she was crying.

"Is it true?" she begged him. "Do you really love me, Francesc?"

God forgive me, he thought, taking her in his arms, the warm strength of his body enclosing her. If I don't love her now, then may it come true some day.

She was straining against him now, her hands caressing his hair, his face. "Oh, I'll try to love you." She choked, her mouth quivering. "I'll try, I'll try!"

"Please don't cry," he said, feeling her cheeks wet with tears.

There had been no thunder for some time, though the rain was still murmuring on the roof. "Oh! Do you really love me?"

"Yes, little one. Of course I do. I've married you, haven't I?"

"Yes!" she whispered. "You wouldn't have married me if you didn't love me. Would you?"

"Of course not."

Then, with a sigh, she let herself go, like the spring of a clock uncoiling and turned to him with complete naturalness.

"Take me now," she said gently. "Now."

Through the chinks of the shutter, a blue sky was shining like strips of lapis lazuli. At first she didn't know where she was. Then she stretched, feeling languid and strange.

She was Conchita Eduard. With her own husband, her own home, her own big marital bed.

She turned to Francesc, who was still half-asleep beside her, and touched his bearded cheek timidly.

He'd said he loved her.

The words hung in the air still, living in the light that was trying to flood the little bedroom.

And after all her terrors, how gentle a lover he had been. As he had promised, there had been no pain. Hardly any. Even a kind of pleasure, in the end, in feeling his body fill hers, so tight and intimate. He had been so careful of her belly. That had touched her. She'd almost wanted him to be less careful, wanted him to use her for his pleasure. There was sweetness in feeling his weight on her, the pleasing breathlessness of supporting him. In feeling his desire break on her like the sea on a smooth wet boulder, drifting back, settling into peace. . . .

"Hmmm?" He was awake now, blinking at her sleepily. He looked so much younger this morning, those furrows in his face smoothed out by sleep. "Ah. Still here?"

"This is my home. Where would I go to?"

"Back to the shop, maybe. For another husband."

"I only want this one," she said tenderly. She took his hand and kissed the rough knuckles.

"What time is it?" he asked.

"The clock struck six a little while ago. Shall I open the shutters?"

"Yes."

She slipped out of the sheets and pattered to the window. She threw open the shutters. The street outside was empty and silent. Above the lichen-covered roof tiles, a magnificent sky arched to infinity. She turned back to him, smiling with sheer joy. "Isn't it a wonderful morning?"

He had lifted himself up on one elbow, watching her with those intensely blue eyes. "Take off your nightgown," he said quietly.

Her smile faded. "What?"

"I want to see you naked."

"Francesc, no!" Despite last night, she was horrified at the idea, especially as she was now so big-bellied. "I couldn't!"

"I'm your husband," he said, "and I haven't seen you naked yet. Take it off."

"But my tummy!"

"Come over here," he commanded. She hesitated awkwardly, then went over to the bed and sat beside him, where he indicated. He reached up and unfastened the little buttons at the throat. Conchita hung her head, her cheeks scarlet. The nightgown slid down off her shoulders and settled around her hips.

Conchita's body, like her face, had a lean, fine beauty. Her spare frame seemed startled by the burgeoning belly and jutting breasts that now adorned it. But she was as delicate as a doe. Her arms and throat were slender, the peaked tips of her breasts enchanting. The nightgown hid the rest of her.

He was conscious of a feeling like relief, at finding that she intrigued him sexually. That her mystery would remain, long after a grosser woman's comforts had been exhausted.

"Shall I tell you something?" he said quietly. "I used to think you too skinny. Now I know just how lucky I am. You are beautiful." She was still gazing at the carpet. "Even with that big tummy." He smiled.

She wouldn't look up or say anything.

"Do you want to see me?" he asked. "I'm not as beautiful as you are. I'm scarred. You know that?"

Conchita nodded without speaking.

Francesc drew the eiderdown aside, revealing his naked body. Conchita turned her head tentatively to look at him.

The only naked men she had seen had been the reproductions

of Roman statues in her books. Francesc's torso was not like those cold grey shapes. He was broad and muscular, with dense black curls on the skin of his chest and stomach. The hair went all the way down to his loins, surrounding his manhood.

His thighs were wasted in contrast to his splendid torso. He had once been a beautiful man, but now that beauty was flawed, as though reflected in a mirror that had been broken. Francesc moved onto one side and showed her the jagged, livid scars that disfigured his right hip and buttocks.

She whispered his name in pity as she saw the terrible damage that had been done.

"Two bullets," he said matter-of-factly. "One went in here and came out at the front, here." He laid his finger on the star shaped scar at the side of his abdomen. "The other went in here, at the joint. They had to operate three times here and here, to get all the pieces out. It's almost useless now."

She turned forward and put out timid fingers to touch the scars. His skin was warm. He watched her face with those deep blue eyes. "It's very ugly," he said. "But I've got used to it. I hope you will too."

"I'll never get used to it," she said quietly. "It hurts me just to look at it."

"I was lucky not to die. I would have died, but for Mother Josep. And the nuns."

"But you still don't believe in God?" she asked curiously.

"I believe in humanity. God didn't save me. A woman did. A woman just like you." He smiled at her. "Look what you're doing."

Her touch had affected him. She tried not to stare.

"That means I think you're beautiful," he said, unembarrassed by his conspicuous erection. He took her hand and guided it to his loins. "It's just a man's cock," he said gently, holding her hand there. "Did I hurt you last night?"

She shook her head dumbly. His manhood filled her hand, throbbing with his heartbeat.

"But it wasn't exactly bliss either?"

"It was very nice," she said in mortification, her face hot.

"Come," he whispered, drawing her to him almost roughly. She sprawled beside him helplessly as he pulled away her night-gown. The triangle of hair between her thighs was daintily shaded, revealing the cleft of her sex, shell-pink and tender. He caressed her stomach, tracing the heavy roundness of her pregnancy. Conchita closed her eyes. He bent to kiss her breasts, making her flinch. His lips on her nipples embarrassed her. "You're as sweet as honey," he said huskily. "This morning will be better."

Their mouths met, tongues twining in that caress that had been, for her, the most satisfying part of their lovemaking last night. But now he was less gentle with her, more urgent. There was an animal quality to him that alarmed her. She felt his fingers slide between her thighs, to touch her private parts. The way she lay exposed them to his touch and she couldn't squirm away.

Was it the sight of her naked body that had inflamed him, she wondered in consternation? She'd always heard that once men saw any part of your body, even so much as the back of your knee, they became beasts.

But his ardour was also affecting her in other ways. When he reached down to touch between her legs, she was already wet, the little bud among the petals swollen and sensitive. She felt his caress touch it, bringing a sweet sensation that made her sigh. The first sound of pleasure she had so far made in their lovemaking.

She opened her eyes and found him watching her face, his eyes smoky.

"I want you," he whispered.

She put her arms around his neck, feeling a quiver of response in her own stomach. "I want you too," she said, without knowing what she meant.

His caress was slow, rhythmical. Pleasure flickered, then began to glow steadily. She was half-dazed after a few moments, as though she'd drunk too much wine. To feel him caress her in this voluptuous, surely profoundly sinful way, was a revelation. The pleasure rolled like hills. Swayed like the sea.

Conchita pressed against him, lost in the mounting ecstasy. If it became too much, she thought in distant alarm, she was going to faint. She was going to collapse, senseless. But even when it became too much, she did not faint. She just soared higher.

Francesc, watching her naked body arching beside him, saw her face flushed and blurred. He felt an intense wave of joy for this delicate, perplexing creature who was his wife. He'd feared that Gerard Massaguer might have destroyed all possibility of pleasure for her. He found himself thanking the Virgin for this woman's gift of delight.

He thought of all the women he had pleasured before her and was grateful for the skills he had not forgotten. He prolonged the pleasure as exquisitely as he knew how, wanting it to be absolutely perfect for her, wanting her always to remember this first time.

Then, when he felt the time was right, he mounted her.

"This time will be different," he whispered. He guided her legs around his hips, making her straddle him, then carefully steered himself into her wetness. She was breathing with quick, shallow breaths, her mouth open, her closed lids dewy. He sank down slowly.

She was aware of something wonderful happening. As he slid deep into her, a delicious heat seemed to melt the whole of her lower body.

Then, before he had time to move, she cried out aloud, her body convulsing. Her eyes had opened, though he could not tell whether she was really seeing him or not. Great pain, great pleasure. The expressions are the same. The same helpless soul, at the mercy of its nerve endings. The same butterfly on the rack. He felt her nails dig into his shoulders, felt the inward paroxysms of her sex. At last he let himself go and with a long thrust, came inside her.

It seemed to last an eternity, the roaring in his ears, the flood of energy from the core of his body.

Then she was holding him, sobbing as though her heart would break. He held her, tender and drained.

When she had stopped crying and nestled in his arms dreamily, he kissed her mouth. "You're not afraid any more, are you?" he whispered.

She shook her head. "I don't know what happened."

"It's what ought to happen." He smiled.

She stared at him, her eyes a rain-washed grey. "Always?"

"Normally, always."

She laid her hand on his shoulder and saw where her nails had cut his brown flesh. "I must be very immoral, to take such pleasure."

"Immoral?" He laughed.

"You've done it before," she said, her eyes clouding. "With lots of other women, before me."

"A long, long time ago," he said gently. "You are the only woman I've been with in eight years."

She considered. Eight years was a long time. "Did you care for them?" she asked.

"No, of course not." He smiled. "You're the only one I care for."

"Oh, Francesc," she said, drawing him to her, "I care for you. I do. I do."

By the second half of March, the winter storms had begun to pass. The days had warmed and lengthened. The sea, no longer grey and choppy, smiled up at the sky. In Spain, spring was well on its way.

One afternoon, in the kitchen, Conchita felt the baby kicking vigorously inside her, harder than she'd ever felt it kick before. She stood holding the smooth, drum-tight mound of her own belly, feeling that so-strange inward movement, that stirring of life within the shell.

She winced. She was due in a month and it felt as though the baby were trying to kick its way out.

None of her clothes fitted her any more. She was forced to walk with an ungainly waddle that was no faster than Francesc's limp. There was no way she could get comfortable. Some nights she did not sleep at all, but sat up beside Francesc, staring into the darkness, thinking.

There was so much love in her for the child who was to come. She yearned to feel it in her arms, to feel its mouth at her nipples, that had already begun to ooze milk.

She could hear Francesc hammering down in the forge. So far, their marriage had been unaccountably happy. Their emotional life together was proving to be rich beyond her dreams. Conchita knew that many other women found marriage a drudgery or worse. Initially, she had felt shame at her uninhibited enjoyment of their lovemaking; now she simply accepted her good fortune with the same gratitude she accepted everything else that had come with marriage.

Francesc was a remarkable person. Under his rough exterior lay wells of kindness and tenderness that continued to amaze her. Though he was certainly unpolished, he seemed to her astonishingly wise and well-informed about the world.

He had given her a new life. It seldom occurred to her that she had saved him as surely as he had saved her.

She went back to the stone slab, where she was kneading dough for the day's bread. The kitchen, like the rest of the house, had been transformed once she'd become Francesc's wife. It was now white and bone-clean. She'd had the walls plastered and limed and at her request, Francesc had made a new window to let in more light. On one wall, over the little oak table where they ate, hung a row of heavy beaten iron pans, all Francesc's work.

Over the sink was a little tiled niche, in which she had placed a small plaster Madonna. Conchita loved *La Purísima*, worshipping her with all the flushed passion of the expectant mother.

She stared at the blank, painted face as she kneaded and prayed silently. An easy birth. An unblemished child. Francesc's continued love. The face seemed to smile, as it often did.

The hammering from downstairs had ceased and she could now hear voices in the forge. She could also hear the sound of an automobile manoeuvring in the narrow street outside. At first she thought customers had come to the forge, but the voices rose in anger and became shouts.

With her heart beating faster, Conchita gathered up her voluminous skirts in floury hands and ran downstairs.

The forge seemed full of uniforms. There were four soldiers around Francesc, all armed with rifles and with bayonets strapped to their hips. Their leather belts and brass buttons gleamed in the red light of the furnace.

Francesc, a hammer in one hand, was facing them like a bull about to charge.

"Francesc!" Conchita gasped in terror. "What's happening? What do you want my husband for?"

"Attempted murder," the red-faced man said brusquely.

"Murder!"

"Some anarchist bastard shot at Don Paco Massaguer last night. He was hit in the face by some of the pellets. He might lose an eye. Get that hammer away from him!"

"I had nothing to do with it," Francesc growled. "I've never owned a weapon."

"Drop the hammer!" the red-cheeked man shouted.

Conchita forced her way through the guards to Francesc. She

took his arm and faced them, grey eyes burning in her pale face. "What will you do to him?"

"We just need to question him. Let him go, Señora."

"But he could have had nothing to do with that! He was with me all last night!"

One of the soldiers laughed. "Do you think we haven't heard that story before?"

"But why should he do such a crazy thing as try to shoot Don Paco?" she demanded of the red-faced man, who seemed to be in charge.

"Why? It's obvious *why*," the man snapped. "There's been a strike at the Massaguer mill in Palafrugell for the past six weeks. The anarchists are trying to take control, as always. Your husband's a prime suspect."

"I haven't been near the cursed place," Francesc said angrily.

"No? You've been heard to utter threats against the Massaguer family."

"That's a lie!"

"You threatened the life of young Don Gerard. You said you would put him in his coffin."

"No," Francesc replied shortly. "I offered to make him a good lock for it. There's a difference."

"Take him away!"

One of the men grasped Conchita's shoulder and tried roughly to jerk her aside. She screamed and Francesc rounded on the man with a terrible face, the hammer lifted. The guard sprang back in alarm.

"If any one of you touches her again," Francesc creaked, "I'll beat him to mincemeat."

The red-faced man rattled his carbine. "Do you want us to shoot some more holes in you and in front of your pregnant wife too?"

Francesc put the hammer down with slow deliberation and two of the *guardia* immediately stepped forward. They pushed Conchita aside and grasped the blacksmith's brawny arms, cuffing his hands behind him. The steel hoops would hardly go around his wrists.

Conchita could do nothing but stand by as they manhandled him. She started to weep. "Don't cry," he said in a low voice. "I'll be back in an hour or two."

She clung to him, almost making him fall. "But what will they do to you?"

"Some questions and it'll all be over. This has happened to me many times before. Don't worry about me."

"But what can I do to help?"

"Nothing."

"Shall I call a lawyer?"

"If he's innocent, then he has no need for lawyers, Señora. I'll take him down to the *comisaría* with Redondo. You two stay and search the house for weapons."

They refused to let Francesc take his crutches. Despairing and blinded with tears, Conchita watched him being led, stumbling, to the car that waited outside. "I'm going to get a lawyer right away," she called after him.

He twisted around to call back, "Just make sure they don't plant any evidence in the house!"

They pushed him into the black car and it accelerated away. The street was deserted, but she could make out staring faces at the windows of the houses. She ran back in, choking, then was brought up sharply by a great stabbing pain in her belly.

Gasping in agony, she had to sit on the nearest chair. The pain reached deep into her heart and up her back and she thought, *Purísima Virgen*, not now!

They dragged Francesc into the *comisaría*. With his hands cuffed behind him and without his crutches, he was nearly helpless. He was thrust up to the desk, where a few papers were stamped. Then they hustled him down a steep flight of stairs to the underground cellars of the building.

The cell they thrust him into was small and bare of furniture. A single light bulb hung high on the ceiling. Its naked light shone down on the face of the man who waited there.

"I told you I would look forward to our next meeting, blacksmith." Gerard Massaguer was smiling. "And here we are."

The cell door crashed shut, locking them in. The guards tightened their grip on Francesc's arms, holding him upright.

"I had nothing to do with it," Francesc said quietly. "Shooting isn't my way."

Gerard lit a cigar, puffing at the flame with care. "Isn't it?"

he said between clouds of smoke. "You anarchists will use any means. Bombs, guns, knives." He smiled again. "How's your little wife, by the way? I hear the baby is due any day now. Inconsiderate of you to get yourself arrested on the eve of the happy event."

"I didn't shoot your father."

"We'll find out."

"There's nothing to find out."

"That's as may be. As a matter of fact, I'm almost inclined to believe you. I don't see you taking potshots in the dark. Your approach is much cruder than that."

"If you know that, then let me go."

"Let you go? The thing is, blacksmith, you have an unruly tongue in your head. You don't know how to talk to your betters. You need to be taught some manners." His dark eyes held Francesc's. "The lesson may be painful, I'm afraid."

"Then get on with it," Francesc said through clenched teeth.

"By all means," Gerard said pleasantly. He puffed at the cigar again. Then he nodded. A club smashed into the back of Francesc's head. Axed by the blow, he sagged forward to his knees. But the others hauled him upright, dragging him to his feet in preparation for the next blow.

The two guards were hunting stolidly through the forge, knocking Francesc's tools into clattering disorder.

"There's nothing to find," she gasped at them. "We don't have any weapons!"

"We've got our orders," one of them grunted. "We have to search this place. Let's go upstairs."

Another sword blade of pain lanced through her womb and she clasped her belly, wailing out loud.

"*Ay, caramba,*" the other guard said in dismay. "It's not coming, is it?"

"I — I don't know," she panted. Beads of sweat stood out on her face and throat. "Ahhh! *Ahhh!*"

The two men looked at one another and then at the woman, who was rocking in pain and hugging her stomach.

"Come on," the senior of the two said in a low voice. "Let's get out of here before the little cow goes into labour."

"But what about the search?"

"What about it? Let's go."

"But the lieutenant said — "

"There's nothing here," the other retorted. "Come on."

They hurried past Conchita, banging the door shut behind them.

She tried to master the great pain inside her. It swelled again, robbed her breath. She wanted to lie on the floor and curl up. She fought with every ounce of strength she had. *Not yet! Not yet!*

She took a series of slow, shaky breaths, trying to calm herself. She forced herself to her feet. She felt unutterably heavy, as though the baby inside her were a lump of lead.

She walked as quickly as she dared to her father's house. She knew he would be in the shop at this hour. The little bell tinkled as she pushed her way in through the door of the shop.

"*Tresor!*" Her father's plump face creased in alarm at her appearance. "What is it, my child?"

"It's Francesc," she said unsteadily. "The *guardia civil* have arrested him."

He hurried around the counter, arms outstretched. "Merciful God. What for?"

"They say someone fired a shot at Paco Massaguer last night."

"Oh, Jesus. The mad fool!"

"But Francesc was with me the whole time!"

He peered at her, holding her shoulders. "Are you sure?"

"Papa! Of course I'm sure! You know Francesc would never do such a terrible thing!"

The shopkeeper cursed under his breath. "He's done worse. Are you covering up for him?"

"For heaven's sake, of course not!"

"What a disaster. And you in this condition! Oh, Christ, why did I ever give you to that madman?"

"We need a lawyer," she pleaded with him.

"Lawyer be damned," he said. "That would be throwing good money after bad. Why did I ever let a criminal of an anarchist take you away?"

"Papa, *please*."

"Let me get my thoughts straight, girl."

"Papa, there's no time," she said, her eyes starting to fill with tears again, "let's go to Palafrugell and get a lawyer!"

The bell tinkled behind them. It was Arnau, the wrinkled little carpenter.

"Don Josep," Conchita said, turning to him desperately, "they've just taken Francesc away!"

"I know," Arnau said gently.

"They're accusing Francesc of trying to shoot Paco Massaguer last night. I told them he was with me the whole time, but they just laughed!"

"Is there no one else who saw Francesc last night?"

"No," she said miserably. "He worked late, then we ate together and went to bed, the way we always do."

"Did they say what time the shot was fired?" the carpenter asked.

"They said around ten."

"Very well." He nodded. "I've got the horse and trap harnessed. You must come with me."

"Where to?"

"To the *comisaría* in Palafrugell. I'm going to swear that I was with Francesc last night."

She stared at him blankly. Marcel Barrantes snorted. "That's perjury, Arnau."

"Perjury or no, I'm going to do it. Men with a trade must stick together."

"Then you're as bad as he is!"

Conchita's colour had fled. "But—will they believe you?"

"They all know me," the carpenter shrugged. "I'm an honest man. They can't hold him if he has a watertight alibi."

A lump swelled in her throat. She took the carpenter's knotty hand and lifted it to her lips. Embarrassed, Arnau pulled it away and patted her shoulder. "Don't be nonsensical. We'd better hurry."

"You're crazy," the shopkeeper said in distress. "Don't get involved in this, Conchita!"

But she was already following Arnau out of the shop. The little bell tinkled briskly as the door closed.

It was late in the afternoon by the time Conchita and Josep Arnau were hurrying through the gaping brick mouth of the *guardia civil* headquarters in Palafrugell.

"Don't you say a word," he cautioned her. "Let me do the talking. All of it. Understand?"

Conchita nodded. She had experienced more fierce pains in

the jolting cart ride down from San Lluc, but had said nothing to Arnau about them. Her insides felt all out of place. She had one hand clasped anxiously at her distended womb, the other at her throat.

The *comisaría* was a bewildering confusion of uniforms, flags and dingy rooms. With quiet efficiency, the little carpenter pushed his way through the outer offices, with Conchita in tow, evading or bypassing obstacles until, down a dark and echoing corridor, they reached the presence of a *teniente* who seemed to have some authority.

"What is this all about?" the *teniente* demanded irritably as a junior guard ushered them in. He wore a formidable moustache and his hair was slicked back from a low, frowning forehead. He glared from Arnau to Conchita with hard black eyes. "Who are these persons?"

"My name is Josep Arnau, your honour," the carpenter said deferentially.

He received a piercing glare. "You look familiar. Been in here before?"

"I am the carpenter of San Lluc," Arnau explained. "This lady is Francesc Eduard's wife."

The *teniente* snorted. "We know *that* name well enough. What are you here for?"

"Your honour, Francesc Eduard is being questioned about an alleged crime which—"

"Nothing alleged about it," the officer snapped. "Last night, near San Lluc, a shot was fired at Señor Massaguer which damned near took his head off. This has anarchists written all over it, Arnau. No need to look very far to find the culprits."

"But your honour, Eduard could not have been responsible. He was in my company for several hours last night. From six until near midnight."

"You little liar!"

"It is the truth."

The officer thrust his chin forward and stared into Arnau's walnut face intently. Arnau stood in respectful silence, holding his hat in front of him with both hands. "What is this," he hissed venomously at last, "some kind of attempt to thwart justice?"

"Not in the slightest, your honour," Arnau said humbly. "I thought this information would be of help."

"This information? This bullshit, you mean. The man is a raving anarchist."

"But he was raving in his own forge when the crime was committed. I'm willing to swear a statement before a justice, your honour." Arnau glanced at Conchita, standing pale-faced beside him. He cleared his throat. "The lady is extremely anxious about her husband. Your honour can hardly fail to see the condition she is in."

The *teniente* glared at Conchita's belly. "A blind man could see the condition she is in. How long do you say you were with the blacksmith?"

"From six until a quarter before twelve," Arnau said.

"The whole time?"

"The whole time. As I say, I ask only for a judge in front of whom to swear my statement."

"Don't keep blathering about a judge, man. You're not in a court of law." He walked out of the office, leaving them standing in front of his desk.

"I'm going to be sick," Conchita gasped. The carpenter put his arm around her shoulders.

"Don't," he advised. "Wait until we're outside."

Another stabbing pain lanced between her legs, piercing her belly, and she whimpered, clasping her hands to the pit of her stomach.

"And don't do that either," he said, laying his leathery hand over her own. "A good anarchist should avoid being born in a *comisaría* of the *guardia civil*."

She gave a little laughing sob. "One thing I swear," she said tearfully, "my baby will not be an anarchist."

They waited for almost a quarter of an hour. It felt like an eternity to Conchita. The pain in her belly was acute, but it wasn't rhythmical, which she knew would be a sign of an impending birth. At last the *teniente* came back. His manner was brusque. "You'll have to sign a statement, Arnau," he said shortly. "No need for a justice."

"Willingly, your honour. And . . . Eduard?"

"Eduard is still being questioned."

"But when will he be released?" Conchita burst out desperately.

"When the interrogation is over." The officer thrust a form

at Arnau. "Fill that in. Then make your statement on the other side."

"Can we wait for him?" she asked.

He glanced up at Conchita with hard eyes. "Not in here. There are seats in the square outside."

Arnau dipped the pen in the ink bottle and with his tongue protruding slightly, began to write.

They waited in the *plaça mayor* on a hard stone bench. The old men of the square stared at them and whispered, then, one by one, drifted away. A beggar hovered nearby, plaintively whining until Arnau threw him a coin and a curse and he too left them.

They heard the bell in the church of San Martín strike nine. The doors of the *comisaría* swung open. Conchita saw Gerard Massaguer walk out, accompanied by two other men. All were laughing. She felt a terrible chill seize her heart at the sight of him. What was he doing here? She watched him climb into a car and drive away. She prayed, silently, frantically, for her husband's safety. What had they done to him?

When it was dark, the door of the *comisaría* swung open again and Conchita cried out. Francesc's broad figure stumbled out, swaying on his feet.

"Thank God," Arnau breathed as they ran to him.

She moaned in agony as she saw his face. His face was so swollen that he could hardly see out of his lids. His lower lip was burst. His nose had been torn open and his right ear was filled with clotted blood.

"Oh, Francesc," she wept, "what did they do to you?"

"Just—caresses," he said, trying to speak without moving his mouth.

"They've given you a nice new face," Arnau grunted, winding Francesc's arm around his neck. "Do you want a doctor?"

"No. I just—want to—get home." Labouriously, he was heaved into the trap. Conchita followed, not much more agile. Arnau rapped the horse with the reins and they jerked into motion and began the long uphill journey to San Lluc. A cold moon shone overhead. Francesc groped for Conchita's hand. She clung to it, trying not to cry at what they had done to him. "How's—the baby?"

She wiped her eyes. Her voice was shaking. "I felt—felt him kicking this afternoon."

Francesc turned his battered face to her. She saw him trying to force his bloated lids apart to look at her. "*Him,*" he said. "Always *him*. What if—it's a her?"

"All the better. Girls are more loving."

He squeezed her hand.

Later, lying together in bed, she spoke quietly. "Francesc, I can't go through that again. No child of ours should have to go through that either."

He stroked her face without replying.

"I want you to promise me something," she went on. "Promise me that you'll give up politics and theories. For my sake. For the sake of our children. But most of all, for your own sake."

On 14 April 1918, a Sunday, Conchita went into labour. The contractions began early in the morning and the midwife was called at 8 A.M.

Just before noon, the baby was born in the bedroom at the forge. It was nine months to the day since Gerard Massaguer had raped her at Fontaner's well.

The birth was relatively easy and once the child had been washed, Conchita held it in her arms and gave suck for the first time. Francesc sat beside her, watching. His face was mending and he managed to smile without pain.

The baby was a girl. The birth was registered later in the day by Marcel Barrantes. Francesc and Conchita had decided to name her after Francesc's mother.

They called her Mercedes. Mercedes Eduard.

2.

The Negotiator

He comes down the stairs, carrying a tray of food. The cellar is cool, roomy, well-organized.

He has built a brick cell in one corner. The brickwork is neat and regular. The structure has not intruded much into the useful space of the cellar.

The walls of the cell reach to the ceiling, completely enclosing a space just big enough to accommodate the girl's bed, with enough floor-room for her to use the toilet. The door is steel, steel-framed.

There are, of course, no windows to the outside, though there are two grilles that allow the cool air of the cellar to get in.

He stares at the brick cell he has built.

What is wrong with her?

It looks like some kind of fever to him. It could be a game. He does not think so.

What if she is dying or dead in there? He forces himself to keep calm. He thinks best when he is calm. When he gets upset, disturbing things happen. He has to keep a hold of himself.

He listens for a long while. He can hear no sound. He puts on the hood and goes in.

Her green eyes meet his dark ones with startling intensity. She is propped up against the wall, her knees drawn up tight against her chest. Her face has grown gaunt and grey. She is shivering more violently than before. Her teeth are rattling in her head. She looks very ill, even sicker than before. But she is conscious now.

"Why are you doing this?" she asks him in a low voice. "Are you going to let me die down here?"

He checks the trays. The food has still not been touched. But she has drunk the remaining jug of water, all of it.

"Is it a kidnapping? Are you asking my father for ransom money?"

The muscles of her legs and face are convulsing. They jerk as though invisible wires are yanking on them.

"Did you send him that photograph you took?"

He continues to study her.

"Don't ask for too much. It's not that he hasn't got it. He just won't pay. He'll let me die. It would be a waste."

He can smell her now. Not just the vomit. A smell of sweat. A strange, chemical sweat. Bitter. A sick smell.

"What's wrong with you?" he asks. "Are you sick?"

"No," she replies.

"Why are you shivering like that? What's wrong with you?"

"Nothing's wrong with me!" But there is a fluttering tic at one eye. He sees how tightly her hands are clasping her legs. The knuckles are white.

"Why do you scream like that?"

She does not answer.

"If you're sick, I can get you some medicine."

She stares at him, her mouth trembling. "Painkillers. Codeine."

"So you are sick," he says angrily. "Why are you lying to me? What's wrong with you?"

"I'm afraid!" she screams back at him. "I'm afraid! That's what's wrong with me!"

"You shouldn't be shivering like that," he says, more quietly. He knows something is wrong with the girl, but there is no sense in arguing about it now. "I'll bring some aspirin next time I come," he says.

"No! Codeine."

"I'll see." He picks up the tray and turns to go.

"Please—"

He turns.

"Paper. For the toilet. Please."

He nods and goes out. The steel door slams shut behind him. She hears the lock click and the bolts slide home.

It is very silent in the cell. She lowers her head onto her knees and starts to sob.

Costa Brava, Spain

"The first thing to understand," Joaquin de Córdoba said, "is that the primary consideration is money. Money first. Money last. Always money."

He put the cup carefully back in the saucer. It was exquisite Meissen, part of a service that had to be worth tens of thousands of dollars.

The room they sat in was decorated in shades of yellow that glowed in the evening sunlight. The comfortable chairs and sofas were upholstered in a Regency stripe. Heavily swagged curtains in saffron silk hung at all the windows. On the floor was an immense wool Kashan, a magnificent field of scarlet and turquoise flowers on an ochre ground.

The collection of English and German porcelain was exceptional. The paintings, too, were fine. The largest, hanging on the far wall, was a massive Victorian sunset, its rich tones binding all the colours in the room together.

De Córdoba's profession took him into the homes of many very wealthy people. He always tried to assess how conspicuous the wealth was. In this case, the answer was the usual one—too conspicuous.

What made this house different was that it had been furnished with a distinctive and vibrant taste.

He studied the two women. Both were wearing expensive suits in pastel linen, suited to the weather and the time of day. Both wore costly jewellery, the younger woman a diamond bracelet, the older an exquisite Baume & Mercier watch.

Mercedes Eduard was perhaps fifty-five. Her body was lithe and supple. Maya Duran, sitting beside her, could not be more than thirty. She had been a fashion model, de Córdoba was sure of that. Her devotion to Mercedes Eduard was clear. Adoration, he felt, would not be too strong a word.

"Kidnapping is a business. The sellers have a product for which they are determined to get a good price. You, the buyers, have the capital, which you must use in the best way possible. They'll anticipate settling for at least the going market rate—"

"And what," Mercedes Eduard interrupted dryly, "is the going rate, Colonel?"

Joaquin de Córdoba crossed his legs. He was sixty-three years old, Argentine by birth, a handsome man with silvered hair. He sat erect and spoke with a musical South American accent.

"The last few cases I was involved with closed at sums between a quarter and half a million dollars, US."

She stared at him with black eyes. "I can afford to pay much more than that."

He nodded. "But they do not know that. The important thing is not to abandon your own bargaining position, whatever happens."

"It won't be necessary to bargain," Mercedes said. "I'll pay what they ask. Within my capabilities."

"They won't begin with a price that is 'within your capabilities.' They'll start with a price they believe to be impossible. They'll expect you to bargain with them until they're sure you have reached the very limits of your finances."

"You're telling me to haggle over my daughter's life?"

"I'm not saying that," he said gently. "But we must act with forethought. They will certainly use every marketing ploy they can think of to raise the price. They will issue deadlines. They will tell you that she's sick. They will probably threaten to rape or beat her. If we mishandle the negotiations, they may even carry out their threats to some degree. This has not been unknown, though it's comparatively uncommon."

The younger woman, Maya Duran, went pale. Her eyes were huge in her beautiful face. Mercedes, however, showed no emotion whatsoever.

"If you'll excuse the metaphor," he said, "they intend to milk you to the last drop. If we make sure they feel they have got everything they can, the possibility of injury to your daughter will be greatly reduced. May I ask whether you have contacted the police?"

"Not yet."

"Neither here nor in California?"

"No."

De Córdoba nodded. "Good." He put the cup and saucer down on the table and rose to his feet. Two pairs of dark eyes followed him. He smiled faintly. "Forgive me. I need to stretch a little."

"Would you like to rest before we go further?"

"In a while. I want to explain what my services are. There are certain things I do and certain things I do not do. To begin with, my position is entirely that of an advisor. I do not make any attempts to locate hostages during kidnappings. I cannot do anything unlawful. I do not offer anything but my experience and my negotiating skills. I will deal directly with the kidnappers, on the telephone or in any other way. I have considerable experience in dealing with such people. My primary objective will be to get your daughter back unharmed."

He indicated the slim black attaché case that he had placed on the coffee table.

"I have a portfolio of credentials, together with statistics of the cases I have worked with. You are free to check them, at your leisure. I can summarize them now, by telling you that I have assisted with fifty-two cases of kidnap in South America, Europe and the United States. Of those, forty-nine had a successful outcome."

He walked back to his chair. Maya Duran was looking more composed now. He had always noted the magical effect his calm, authoritative voice could have. The older woman, however, appeared unmoved.

He lowered himself into the chair, adopting his erect, soldierly position. "My fees," he went on, "are a flat weekly rate of one thousand dollars, US. That does not include expenses or travel. Nor is it in any way linked to the outcome. I am paid solely as a consultant, for as long as my services are required, or until I decide to withdraw. No contract. No conditions."

Mercedes stared at him coolly. "You do very well out of kidnapping, Colonel de Córdoba."

He inclined his head. "It is an odd career, I agree."

"And why should I employ you?"

"Because you have never been through this before," he

said gently. "And I have been through it many, many times. My experience is your best hope of getting your daughter back alive."

Mercedes rose to her feet. "You must be tired. Maya will show you to your room. We dine at eight-thirty. If you wish to join us for drinks an hour before, you are welcome."

"That would be delightful."

They were all on their feet now. Joaquin de Córdoba looked down into Mercedes's face. Beneath that controlled, handsome mask, he thought, is a woman suffering the torments of the damned. "I assure you," he said softly, "that with the correct approach and patience, your daughter's suffering can be minimized. She may be back with you very soon."

Mercedes nodded. "I hope you're right."

He bowed over her hand with military gallantry and followed Maya out.

His room was upstairs. It opened out onto a balcony, with a superb view of the mountains. A valet had already brought up his suitcases.

"I hope you'll be comfortable," Maya said.

"I'm sure I shall be perfectly comfortable. It's a beautiful room."

"Whatever you need, please ask me, or one of the servants."

"Thank you." He smiled at her. Maya wore very little makeup, no more than a shimmer at her eyelids and lips. The lines of her face and throat were emphasized by her glossy hair. "May I ask how long you've been Señora Eduard's secretary?"

"For the past three years."

"She is facing a particularly difficult ordeal," de Córdoba said. "She will need your support. Tell me, how old is Eden?"

"She'll be twenty-one this year."

"She was born in America?"

"Yes. Mercedes went to California after the Spanish Civil War. She met her husband in Los Angeles. Eden was born there."

"Is her husband a wealthy man?"

"Yes. But Mercedes is wealthy in her own right. She invested in stocks. The wealth you see here, Colonel de Córdoba, is all of Mercedes's own creating. That is no mean achievement."

"No," he agreed. The intense pride and love in the woman's voice could not be missed. "It's an extraordinary achievement."

"I'll leave you to unpack in peace," she said.

He bowed over her hand. She smiled at him and closed the door as she left.

Santa Barbara, California

Dominic van Buren dressed, leaving the girl sleeping in his bed.

He breakfasted on the terrace, fresh orange juice, papaya and a mango. Brilliant sunshine flooded the lush garden. Peace reigned.

He thought about the telephone call from Mercedes. Eden kidnapped? With Eden's little problem, she'd be dead in three days. However, he refused to consider the possibility that it was true. The whole thing had her signature written all over it. Just the kind of shitty trick she would pull.

He had barely seen her in the past six months. Well, who needed that kind of shit? You couldn't be a parent to someone like Eden.

Chained to a chair? This was some kind of sick game. She'd be hiding out with some of her hippie friends, laughing her head off and planning what she would do with the ransom money.

A flash of anger burned in him. The bitch. He'd find her. It had been a long time since anyone had last whipped Eden into line.

He picked up the keys to the Porsche.

Midday heat and midday traffic made the freeway unbearable. By the time he was driving through the Agoura Hills, van Buren had put the Porsche's top back up and had the air conditioning going full blast. He hated coming into the smog and the tension these days, seeing all those black and brown faces, all those peeling buildings.

He'd loved this city twenty years ago, but the developers, the immigrants and the Mob were turning it into a shit pile.

He swung off onto Sepulveda Boulevard, then back along Sunset and right on Mandeville Canyon. Congestion had magically eased.

This was one of the only parts of Beverly Hills, he reflected, that remained uncorrupted. No Hispanics or Asiatics, of course. No condos, no sordid urban sprawl. Just hills and trees and canyons, beautiful stretches of California and comfortingly wealthy white people.

He turned off onto Chalon, which wound through groves of eucalyptus and conifers into the Canyon.

The wide drive of 3301 Chalon Road was not marked. You had to go thirty yards up before you met the sliding electronic gate and saw the chain-link fence behind the eucalyptus. Stopping in front of the gate, van Buren honked his horn until he saw the camera swing to study him. The gate rumbled open and he drove in.

They'd always called the place "the ranch," though it was only a large, pleasant house, facing a collection of outbuildings across a big cobbled yard. Behind it were a couple of acres of scrub and trees that backed onto Topanga State Park. The stables were the most agricultural thing on the property.

The first building, on the right as you came in, was Miguel Fuentes's house. Miguel was standing on his porch, a spruce figure all in white. Van Buren stopped next to him and lowered the window. Miguel stooped to peer into the low-slung car.

"Hello, boss. Long time no see, huh?"

"Hello, Miguel. I've come to see Eden. Is she in?"

"Uh, I don' think so."

"Well, I'll just go take a look, okay?"

"Sure."

"Do you have a key?"

Miguel produced one from a bunch in his pocket. Van Buren took it and drove on by him with a wave.

Eden's red Dodge van was parked outside opposite the group of four stables. A horse trailer was hooked up to it. Van Buren parked the Porsche next to it and got out. To his left was another house, quarters for staff during Mercedes's time, but now empty. The garden looked scruffy and neglected. Monaco, Eden's horse, had his big brown face at the door of his box.

"I see you're still here," van Buren commented. Monaco's ears flicked indifferently and he returned to his hay.

Van Buren walked across the yard to the main house.

He knocked at the front door, but there was no reply. He opened the door with his key and went cautiously inside.

·   ·   ·

Twenty minutes later, van Buren walked into Miguel's house.

Miguel didn't rise from his armchair, just grinned up at van Buren amiably. Van Buren stared at Miguel in distaste. He'd once been afraid of this man's brute, violent strength. Now that Miguel was growing older, starting to shrivel in the way old men do, he saw that Miguel had never been anything more than a crude and unclean tool that he had used to do some crude and unclean jobs.

Once, sometime in the early 1950's, soon after van Buren and Mercedes had married, but before Eden had come along, van Buren had flown down to Panama on business with Miguel Fuentes. Before going back, they decided to buy some lobster.

They'd picked up ten pounds of tails from a fisherman who had a roadside stand. It had been a rainy Sunday afternoon. They'd been pulling away from the stand when a boy of around twenty had almost rammed them in a flashy purple Buick. The boy had blared his horn at them, yelled something, then given them the finger. Miguel, his face expressionless, had got out of the car.

The boy had locked his door from the inside. But that hadn't deterred Miguel. He'd taken a pair of bolt cutters a yard long out of the trunk. Had calmly smashed the Buick's side window. Delved in with the tool while the boy cowered and deftly clipped off the kid's middle finger, the one he'd stuck at them.

Van Buren, sitting aghast in the other car, had almost fainted.

Finished, Miguel had left the boy shrieking, had replaced the bolt cutters in the trunk and had driven them back to the airport with their lobster tails. Had never said one goddamned word during the whole nauseating episode.

Miguel was now in his sixties and though his arms and shoulders were still heavily roped with muscle, the skin was starting to hang loose. His hair, once black and slick, was now a yellowish grey. His eyeballs were the same colour.

Yet there was something oddly dapper about him today, something almost dandyish. Something van Buren hadn't seen in him before. His eyes shifted away from van Buren's as van Buren studied him.

"Got a new housekeeper?" van Buren asked, cocking an eye round the room. It was spotless.

Miguel cleared his throat, lacing his thick fingers together. "Yeh. Got this girl come in every day. You know?"

"What's her name?"

"Yolanda, boss."

"Where's she from?"

"Puerto Rico."

"I see." There were cheap ornaments everywhere. From the back porch, van Buren could hear a radio playing tangos.

"You let the old housekeeper go?"

"Well, sure."

"The garden's pretty shabby. You let the gardener go too?"

"He was no good, boss. Sleeping on the job, smoking weed in the stables. He—"

"Miguel, where is Eden?"

"No idea, boss."

"Her bed's unmade. Clothes on the floor. Plates of food on the table, going rotten. The radio still playing, but nobody there."

"Normal, for Eden."

"Her car is still there, outside."

"Yeh."

"And the horse is still there."

"Yeh."

"Mercedes called me this morning. She's concerned about Eden. She thinks something may have happened to her."

"Happened?"

"Yes. Despite your unsleeping vigilance. When exactly did you last see Eden?"

"Well—uh—last Tuesday."

"That's a week ago. You're telling me Eden's been gone a week?"

"Well, that's not necessarily so. She coulda gone the day before we got back."

"Before you got back from where?"

"Uh, from Mexico."

"You and who else?"

Miguel's mouth worked. Van Buren got up suddenly and walked out onto the back porch. A dark-skinned young woman was sitting on a towel in the sun. She was wearing a pink bikini bottom, reading a comic. Shiny breasts jostled like fat brown puppies as she folded her arms protectively. A frolicsome young thing of eighteen or nineteen, with a body that was already overblown. She smiled uncertainly.

"*Buenas tardes, Señor.*"

He turned to Miguel, who'd come padding after him. "This is Yolanda?"

"Yeh, that's her."

"You're quite an old devil, aren't you," van Buren said thinly, looking at the girl.

"Come on now, boss."

"No, I mean it, Miguel. I'm impressed. So you've been on a little trip to Mexico together? When did you leave?"

"Tuesday."

"And when did you get back?"

"Yesterday, I swear it. I looked in on Eden, but she wasn't there. But I didn't think anything..."

"So, in fact, just about anything could have happened to Eden this week."

"Lissen—"

"An army of Black Panthers could march in firing bazookas and you wouldn't know a thing."

"No, Señor! Maybe she went to a show-jumping thing."

"Without Monaco?"

Miguel gestured. "Maybe demonstrations or parties. She'll be back."

Van Buren stared at him. He spoke clearly, calmly. "Has Eden cooked up some kind of a scheme with you or anybody else, Miguel? You know anything about that?"

"Scheme? What kinda scheme?"

"A scheme to get money out of Mercedes."

"I don' know wha' you talking about, boss!"

Yolanda, deciding that she looked ridiculous clutching her puppies, rolled onto her stomach and lay on them.

"Has she a man these days? A boyfriend?"

He heard Miguel swallow. "Oh, yeah. A guy by the name Craig Williams."

"Some kind of hippie?"

"No, a regular sorta guy. Real nice manners." Miguel nodded, as though he'd been impressed by that detail.

"A clever sort of boy? The sort of boy who dreams up get-rich-quick schemes? Like Rusty Fagan?"

"Uh-uh! No' like Rusty at all! A ver' nice kid. He was around yes'day, looking for Eden."

"He was looking for her?"

"Yeh."

"Go see him, Miguel. Find out what he knows. Ask him if he and Eden are trying to pull the wool over her momma's eyes. Understand? If he says he doesn't know where Eden is, maybe break his arm. Whatever. The sort of thing you do best. I have to ring Mercedes at midnight, so call me before then, okay? No doubt she'll be in touch herself soon. I'll see myself out."

The old man came to the door of the house. His mouth was working.

"Eden's okay, ain't she?" he asked van Buren. "I mean, nothing happened?"

He walked briskly down the steps, towards his car. There he turned and looked back up at Miguel. "If anything *has* happened, Miguel, you'll be the first to know. Believe me. Open the gate, will you?"

Costa Brava

"I would like you to act as my adviser," Mercedes said formally on the terrace. It was a warm evening. Cicadas shrilled in the velvety darkness. De Córdoba was too hot in his blazer and military tie. He envied the women in their sleeveless dresses, their slim arms exposed to the slight breeze.

He nodded gravely. "Then let's get to work. How did they contact you?"

She picked up the folder beside her and passed it to him. "This arrived on Monday evening."

He opened it and took out the photograph inside. He looked at the picture, his face tightening. "Just this? And you've received no telephone messages since?"

"Nothing."

He looked at the back of the picture.

GO TO THE POLICE AND SHE DIES.

Something troubled him about this cruel image, arriving unheralded and unexplained by special courier. He studied the photograph carefully, assessing the expression on the bound girl's face. He felt the distress was genuine. So was the bruise on the shoulder. Someone had hit her with a rifle butt, something like that.

"Colonel de Córdoba, there's a vital point. A point that affects this whole case very seriously."

De Córdoba nodded without speaking. He turned the photograph slowly between his fingers. "Please go on."

"My daughter is a sick woman. She suffers from a condition known as Addison's disease. Her life depends on hydrocortisone. These are prescription drugs, not available over the counter. The longer she's kept from them, the more danger she'll be in."

De Córdoba felt suddenly cold, despite the mildness of the evening. "How long can she go without these drugs?" he asked.

"It's impossible to say. If she's under a lot of stress, perhaps only a few days."

"Do you have any precise idea when she was kidnapped?"

"My ex-husband is trying to find that out. It may be difficult to say. She lives alone, and her life is not always . . . orderly."

"Any way of telling whether she has any supplies of cortisone with her?"

"Even if she has, it would soon run out."

"If the gang are professionals, they'll have studied your daughter carefully before the snatch. If they knew she had this condition, they would have obtained and laid in adequate supplies of the drugs she needs."

"How can you be sure?" Mercedes demanded.

"I can't. And even if they *are* giving Eden the drugs she needs, they may lie about it. To put pressure on you. You can expect them to play up her illness to the hilt. Abusing the emotions is what kidnapping is all about. A rape of the mind." He spoke slowly and calmly, trying to instil confidence. "Actual physical harm is uncommon. They want to keep their victim alive. She's their stock-in-trade, their only commodity."

"Until the money is paid," Mercedes said calmly.

"Yes. Until the money is paid. What I'm trying to say is that despite the Addison's disease, we must proceed as usual. For Eden's sake. You'll have to steel yourself against what you may be told or shown and follow the general guidelines I lay down."

"I can't take that chance," Mercedes said without hesitation. "I understand what you've said. But as soon as I receive a ransom demand, I intend to pay it in full. That seems to me the only hope of getting Eden back quickly."

"I must advise you most strongly to reconsider that. In my

experience, that has never produced a quick solution. *Never,"* he repeated. "It has only prolonged the agony immeasurably."

"Eden's agony may not be immeasurable." Her dark eyes stared out into the night. "This experience *must* be made as brief as possible, for my daughter's sake. I believe that if they have the money and see she's unwell, they may release her quickly."

"Please," he said gently, "consider this line of thought. If you immediately pay the initial demand, they'll assume they've underestimated your wealth and demanded far too little. They will in all probability immediately demand the same amount again. Perhaps double that. But they'll know they have reached a point of resistance. You've already paid and will be reluctant to pay more. A shock tactic will be needed to overcome your resistance."

"You mean that they will apply more pressure," Mercedes said.

"They may beat her," he said without emotion. "And send you a tape recording or a Polaroid photograph."

"She would die," Mercedes said flatly.

"Such evidence can easily be simulated. They use cosmetics to make the victim look terrible. Sometimes even sprinkle ketchup to simulate blood."

"People like that deserve the death penalty," Maya said in a tight voice. "They're animals. Filth."

"Filth, yes," de Córdoba agreed. "There are other possibilities too. If they think there's more money left in the pot, they may sell your daughter to another gang, who'll start the whole process afresh."

"*Sell* her?"

"She is a product to them. Nothing more. It's as important to your daughter as it is to the kidnappers that you pay the correct price, at the correct time."

Mercedes's face was taut. He wanted to go to her and take her in his arms. Tell her it was permissible to cry, to show emotion.

She cleared her throat. "My husband does not believe that this is a real kidnapping. He thinks Eden may have staged it in order to raise money."

"Is she likely to do such a thing?"

"I don't believe she is. He mentioned the Getty case."

"Ah, yes." He nodded. "I've been following the Getty kidnap

with some interest. The press is indulging in a lot of irresponsible speculation. It can be disastrous. I personally feel the Getty kidnapping is genuine."

"So do I."

He touched the photograph. "Was Eden short of money?"

"All young people are short of money," Mercedes replied dryly.

"Does she have any expensive habits?"

"She is capable of spending a great deal of money. Eden's life is somewhat . . . erratic. She's been through a difficult phase lately. Our contacts haven't been close in the past year."

De Córdoba shifted in his chair. "Señora Eduard, is it possible that Eden's father has also been asked for money and that he's not telling you?"

"If my ex-husband was being asked to part with his money for our daughter's sake," she said bitterly, "he would squeal like a stuck pig, I assure you."

"So they have singled you out for the ransom demand. Rather than the girl's father?"

"So it seems."

He studied her. "One other thing. Eden's illness—the Addison's disease—has she had it all her life?"

Mercedes paused. "It came on during her teenage years."

He nodded, intelligent eyes watching her. "We should begin planning our response immediately," he said. "Tomorrow we'll connect a tape recording machine to the telephone in my room. I'll answer all incoming calls from now on. In the meantime, we must prepare ourselves for the likely pattern of events. We need an operating procedure. We need to know how to respond. With your permission, I'll begin preparing you now."

Tucson

He is experiencing the first real panic of the whole operation.

Whatever is wrong with her, it is reaching its peak. She is conscious, but she can hardly speak to him for the chattering of her teeth and the jerking of her limbs. She is like a marionette whose strings are in the hands of demons.

It is a kind of shuddering agony that frightens him.

He gives her the pills and she gulps them down frantically, choking on the water.

He lays the extra blanket over her and tucks her in. There is real terror in her eyes. Not of him, but of what is happening to her. She is sobbing, silently and internally.

He sits beside her, unable to do anything. Her clothes and the sheets are soaked with sweat. Her hair is equally wet. She smells terrible.

He lays his hand on the girl's forehead. Her skin is icy cold and wet with sweat. She screams when he touches her, as though her nerve endings are raw.

"Please. I need some more painkillers."

"Where do you have the pain?"

"In my back. In my legs."

"In your back and in your legs?" He stares down at her. "Where else?"

"In my stomach. God, I feel so sick. Oh, God."

"Do you know what this is?"

"I'm so frightened. I think I'm dying."

Her trembling has affected him. He has caught it too. He feels his own body start to shiver. "You're not dying!"

"Get me out of here."

"What?"

"You could drop me near a hospital," she says unsteadily. She looks up at him, the green eyes ghostly in the hollow sockets. She was beautiful. Now she looks deathly. "Blindfold me, like you did when you first took me—"

"No."

"Do it at night. Drive me to a clinic somewhere and just drop me off a mile or two away—"

"No!"

"Please"—she sobs—"please let me go."

"You're staying here." He tries to keep his voice steady. "I'm not taking you anywhere. You either cure or die right here."

"I can't go through with it!" Her face is agonized. Her fingers are claws that have seized his forearms. "You can't let me die here! You can't! You can't!"

Her voice has risen to a scream. She terrifies him. She is like an insane person. He tries to pull away from her in horror. "Get your hands off me," he snarls.

Her nails dig into him wildly. "Please," she is saying, over and over again. Tears are streaming down her cheeks. "Please, please, please. Let me go. I need help. Can't you see what's happening to me? Don't let me die here. I can't stand it, I can't!"

He tears away from her and backs up against the brick wall he has built. He is trembling almost as much as she is.

"What is this?" he gasps. "What's wrong with you?" A dread thought occurs to him. What if she has something contagious? Some killing fever, like the killing fevers of Asia? He has touched her. Inhaled her breath.

"You've got something bad. I'm going to have to get something stronger than painkiller."

Her face is silvery with pallor and sweat. "Get me some codeine."

"No." He tries to pull himself together. "I'm going to get you some medicine. I'm going to bring you some food."

"I can't eat."

"You have to. I'll make some soup."

"I couldn't eat it."

"What could you eat, goddammit?"

"Chocolate. Bring me some chocolate." Her eyes burn into his. Her face is awful. The smell in there is starting to make him ill.

He opens the door and hurries out. Once he has locked it, he sags against the wall, trembling and exhausted. He feels as though he is in a nightmare. When he gets the antibiotics, he will start taking a course of them himself. Christ knows what she has. He walks unsteadily to the stairs.

He turns to look at the brick cell. There is a total silence. It and the girl inside it are starting to terrify him.

Costa Brava

Maya went to the kitchen and collected the breakfast tray to take up to Mercedes: orange juice, black coffee and a freshly-baked croissant. Mercedes was sitting up in bed, reading the newspaper.

The curtains had been drawn, and the morning sun made the bedroom glow.

"Good morning."

"Good morning, *querida*." Mercedes looked frail, the lines of her face drawn.

"You look tired," Maya said, pouring the coffee. "Did you have a bad night?"

"I've had better."

"What time is Dominic going to call you?"

"In about a quarter of an hour."

"Are you anticipating anything positive?"

"I'm hoping for a few answers. But anything positive, no. Not now."

"I've been thinking about Eden. When she's back, maybe you could make a fresh start with her. Really tackle her problems. Maybe I could help. I'm much nearer her age than either you or her father. I know I'm not very close to Eden. But I'm not her enemy, either. At least we've never quarrelled. Perhaps I could persuade her to get help. Go to some kind of . . ." She hesitated over the word. "Some kind of institution."

"We've tried that. Remember?"

"On a new basis. With a new attitude."

"Let's get her back first. Then we'll think about things like that."

Maya nodded and left.

Van Buren's call, as Mercedes had predicted, came through within the quarter-hour.

"Well, she's not there," van Buren said bluntly. "The house is like the *Marie Celeste*. Miguel says that's normal."

"Was there any sign of a struggle?"

"No. And there's no note, either. It's as if she just walked out. But I did find her medicine kit in her bedroom. Looked like the whole shooting match."

"She wouldn't leave that behind."

"Unless she had more someplace else."

She closed her eyes tiredly. "What does Miguel say?"

"Miguel has a Puerto Rican cutie of around nineteen to occupy his time these days. She's called Yolanda. He says she's his housekeeper. He's let all the other staff go. He and this Yolanda took themselves off to Mexico last week. He claims he saw Eden Tuesday morning, just before he left. He says he got back yesterday and went around to see her, but she was gone."

"He was away five days? And nobody else was there?"

"Yes."

"They took her while he was gone, then. As if they knew."

"The fact that Miguel's screwing this girl doesn't mean the kidnapping's genuine."

Mercedes was silent for a while, trying to digest it. Eden had been abandoned. By her father, by Miguel. By her mother. She'd been all alone, a plum ripe for picking.

For some time after the call she sat immobile. How could Miguel have done this to them?

She'd entrusted Miguel to watch over Eden. The salary she'd allotted him had been considerable, enough for him to live more than comfortably for the rest of his life. And he'd failed her.

Had the Puerto Rican girl been put up to it? Was she part of some elaborate plot? Or was it just coincidence?

Beneath her anger was the bitter knowledge that she herself was ultimately to blame. Sentimentality and carelessness. She'd been wrong to think Miguel was capable of looking after Eden.

Once, Miguel had been a rock. A man loyal as steel, who had done all Dominic's dirty work. But Miguel had softened and crumbled. He was no longer what he had been. He had gone rotten, softened by ease.

She'd thought of letting him retire last year. But then he had handled the Rusty Fagan episode so neatly, so cleanly, that she had changed her mind. She'd been over-impressed. It had been a terrible error.

Tears welled through her lids and ebbed slowly down her cheeks. She thought of what Eden was going through. She thought of Eden's unformed mind facing that monster. Her butterfly will, being strapped to that rack.

Eden was not yet twenty-one. Without strength. Without any schooling in pain, or singleness of purpose, to sustain and fortify.

For once in her life, for the first time since babyhood, Eden needed her.

And she could no longer reach her.

She reached for the telephone again.

Miguel Fuentes was still fully dressed when the telephone began to ring at 1:45 A.M.

"*Sí,*" he said into the receiver.

"Miguel, it's Mercedes. Did I wake you?"

"No. I was waiting."

"Good." Mercedes's voice was calm, uninflected. "Where is Eden, Miguel?"

"I don' know. Wednesday night she was at Palisades, jumping in a tournament. That's for sure. She came twelfth. Lots of people saw her there. She got back that night. Her boyfriend says he came to see her at the ranch, afterwards. He left around one A.M."

"Did you question him in detail?"

"I hurt him, not too bad but enough. He don' know where she is, Mercedes. He had nothin' to do with it."

"Have you questioned her other friends?"

"None of them seen her since Wednesday. It don' mean anything. Maybe she went off for a little fun."

"What kind of fun?"

"Maybe a Vietnam rally somewhere."

"The Vietnam War has been over for six months, Miguel."

"I swear I'm gonna find out, Mercé. Nothing happened to her, you'll see. She'll be okay. She'll turn up. I'll find her by tomorrow."

"Miguel, someone sent me a picture of my daughter Monday. Half-naked. Chained to a chair."

Miguel closed his eyes, listening to the calm voice. The pain in his chest was intense, robbing him of breath.

"Eden did not go off for a little fun," she said dispassionately. "Girls who have Eden's problem never go anywhere for a little fun. Do you understand what I am saying to you?"

"Yes," Miguel whispered.

"This girl, Yolanda. How did you meet her?"

"She's got nothing to do with it!"

"Was it her idea to go to Mexico?"

"I—I can't remember. No, I think we both came up with it together."

"That means it was her idea. How did you meet her, Miguel?"

He closed his eyes. "I got this friend, Álvaro. Yolanda's his cousin. He brought her round to me because she had no place to go and no papers and she was going, you know . . . on the streets. I took care of her awhile. And she ended up staying. I love her, Mercé. She has nothing to do with this. I swear."

"Is that why you betrayed Eden? For a Puerto Rican hooker?"

"I didn't betray you, for Christ's sake! Maybe I wasn't thinking straight, maybe I was foolish, but—"

"You left my child unprotected to go on holiday with a *whore*." Mercedes's voice had risen to a savage rasp, all the more terrifying because of the quietness that had preceded it.

"Oh, Jesus, Mercé. I didn't know it was going to happen. The poor little thing. I'm so sorry, I could cut my right arm off."

"Find out if the Puerto Rican girl is involved in this."

"I swear she isn't!"

"You won't know until you have applied sufficient pressure."

Miguel felt the pain spreading upwards into his shoulders, into his throat and jaw. He started massaging his breastbone with a trembling hand. "You mean hurt her? Jesus, Mercé, what are you asking me? I couldn't do it!"

"You must do it. When you have finished with her, do the same with your friend Álvaro. Find out what they know. Whether someone paid them to do this. Above all, I need to know where Eden is, fast, because she may be dying."

"Mercé, for the love of God!"

"I will wait to hear from you, Miguel."

"*Mercé!*"

She disconnected.

Miguel Fuentes put the receiver down and rested his head in his hands. The pain was terrible, restricting his breath like a vice around his chest. He rose and stumbled to the bedroom.

He needed Yolanda, needed her warmth, her comfort. At least until tomorrow, he desperately needed to forget Mercedes Eduard's quiet, commanding voice.

Tucson

She is curled up on the bed with her back to him. He stares at her. She has not eaten any of the food he brought her last time. The beans have congealed on the plate. She has drunk a little water and that's all. Her ribs are sticking out. Her hip bones are sticking out.

"If you don't eat, you're going to get sick."

She seems not to know that he is here. He picks up her left wrist. It is shackled to the other with a long steel chain that loops through the iron bed frame. She whimpers a little, but her eyes do not open. He checks her pulse against his wristwatch. It is very fast and it seems to flutter irregularly. The skin burns feverishly. He is uneasily aware of how frail she is. He does not like touching her.

When he releases her wrist, it flops back onto the bed lifelessly.

He touches her forehead. The skin is damp and heated. The trembling is like a frightened dog's, long rippling spasms that subside and grow.

"Time for another photograph," he says to her.

There is no response. He repeats the words, more loudly. "Come on, wake up." He shakes her shoulder, hard. "Don't screw around. Sit up."

He hooks his arms under her body and tries to haul her upright. At last, there is some sign of consciousness. She begins to whimper again, hands weakly beating at him.

"No," he hears her moan. "No, no, no!"

"Come on." The chain is tangled around her. He pulls the links free. He notices that her wrists have been chafed bloody by the manacles.

She has been jerking on them until she bled.

Christ, she must be crazy.

He props her against the wall. For a moment she stays there, though her eyes remain tightly closed. But her head lolls forward, long black snakes of hair trailing over her face. He catches her with a curse and tries to sit her up again. Her eyes open slightly, but the eyeballs are rolled back. Her mouth is open and he sees a strand of saliva crawl down her chin. Her hands flop sideways.

Now he is sweating.

"Jesus," he mutters. "Come on, Eden. Snap out of it. You were okay when I brought you here."

She has started the whimpering sound, wordless and persistent.

"I know you're screwing around," he tells the girl. He props her up again and this time holds her in place with one hand. With the other, he picks the plastic jug off the tray and tries to make her drink. The water runs down her chin, soaking her soiled T-shirt.

"Drink," he commands. "You'll get dehydrated."

He coaxes a little water into her mouth. She chokes violently. He feels her lean muscles tense as she coughs, eyes rolling back in her head.

"Drink. Or drown."

He forces her head back and pours water into her mouth. Again, she chokes and starts to flap at him with her manacled hands. Not much water has gone down.

He is enraged. He hurls the plastic jug against the wall. It does not break, of course. He has carefully selected everything to be unbreakable. A gout of water splashes the supine girl.

She slides back down onto her side. He rises to his feet and looks down at her. He cannot take a picture of her like this. She looks dead.

He does not want her to look dead in the photograph.

He has an idea. He takes the jackknife out of his pocket and pulls out the sharp blade.

His hands start to tremble.

He rolls the girl onto her back. Her ghostly face twitches in her coma, or whatever it is.

His hands are shaking badly. His breathing is unsteady. He has to force himself to concentrate. This place stinks. The smell reminds him of other places, evil places, where pain and death had their empire.

He grasps a lock of her hair in his fingers, saws jerkily. The blade is sharp and it cuts cleanly. But the shaking makes him clumsy. The point of the knife grazes her cheek and before he knows it a bright ribbon of blood streaks across the sweaty skin.

"Shit."

He stares at the blood, swallowing. His mouth is dry. In his hands is a thick strand of black hair. He reaches out, unthinkingly, and smears the hair with the blood.

He studies the lock of black hair, with its smear of blood. It will do better than a photograph.

Costa Brava

Maya went downstairs to the indoor swimming pool. There she slid into the cool blue water.

When the house was being planned, they'd decided to include

the pool as an integral part of the structure. It had been placed in the crux of the house, between the sleeping quarters and the living areas. It was in reality a vast conservatory, covered with a high glass dome.

To Maya it was, quite simply, a little piece of heaven. There was always a luxuriant summer in here. The pool was set in a thicket of plants, a humid indoor jungle that Maya had created and continued to tend. It contained tall tropical trees, some of which flowered or made bright fruit in their season. The plants towered upwards, embracing, twining, their glistening leaves unfolding in riotous growth. It was a Douanier Rousseau jungle, with pool by David Hockney.

She'd wanted lianas, monkeys and exotic birds too, but Mercedes had laughed her out of that. As it was, she spent hours each week in here, tending to what Mercedes called her rain forest.

She paused for breath at one end and saw Joaquin de Córdoba's tall figure standing at the poolside, watching her. He was wearing a bathrobe and holding a towel, evidently wondering whether to join her. She smiled at him.

"Hello," she called. "Join me for a swim?"

"I don't want to disturb you."

"You won't."

He smiled. "Very well."

The Argentine radiated an authority that calmed Maya and filled her with confidence. She had liked and trusted him instinctively.

He swam companionably at her side for a few lengths. Though he was clearly a fit man, he only stayed in the water for a few minutes before hauling himself out.

He was already seated and wrapped back in his robe by the time she decided to emerge.

Maya smiled at him as she walked over to where he sat. The wet swimsuit delineated the athletic perfection of her figure, swelling over her breasts, showing off the muscled plane of her midriff, the flare of her hips. Her legs were long and slender, but equally well-muscled.

De Córdoba passed her a towel. His brown eyes followed the pure, unself-conscious movements of her body as she dried herself.

In some women, he was thinking, beauty is an open thing, as

candid and simple as the face of a daisy. Maya Duran's beauty was a thing of dark subtlety. A jungle flower.

"This is a most wonderful place," he told her. "Like something from the jungles of Peru."

"It's an eccentricity"—she smiled—"for which I have to take partial blame. I'm the gardener in this domain."

"You have a wonderful gift with plants!"

She sat down beside him. "And you are very gallant."

"If you mean that it was an empty piece of flattery, you're wrong. I think that this is one of the most beautiful gardens I've ever seen."

She looked pleased. "Well . . ."

"Tell me something: Where does Señora Eduard's husband live?"

"He lives in Santa Barbara, California."

"I know it well. It's a lovely place. When did they divorce?"

"In 1966." Maya hesitated. "He has nothing to do with this matter, colonel."

He found the statement an odd one, but he did not pursue it. "I see."

"She married him in California. That's where Eden was born. But the marriage was never a very happy one. It ended very acrimoniously. Dominic was not a good father. He has no deep feelings for Eden any more. Mercedes has almost no contact with him now and she doesn't even like to hear his name spoken. She certainly doesn't trust him."

"Yet she left Eden with him?"

"Mercedes wanted Eden to stay in America for a number of reasons. Mainly, she felt there was more opportunity for her there. And Eden is very much an American girl. She thought it was the right decision at the time. Now, of course, she blames herself very bitterly for what has happened. . . ."

"You say Dominic van Buren wasn't a good father to Eden?"

"He thinks only of his own pleasure. That's his overriding problem. Eden was at a boarding school when the divorce was finalized. The arrangement was that Dominic was to look after her in Santa Barbara on the weekends and she was to come to Spain for her holidays. But Dominic neglected her. He was too busy enjoying himself. She stopped going to Santa Barbara on weekends.

She would tell her father she was staying with friends, but God knows what she was really doing. Sometimes he wouldn't see her for weeks on end. She just ran wild. By the time Mercedes found out what was really going on, it was too late."

"Too late?" de Córdoba asked sharply. "What do you mean, too late?"

Maya coloured slightly. "Too late in the sense that she had become something of a rebel. And she'd lost all her interest in academic work. She managed to graduate from school somehow, but her grades weren't good enough for an Ivy League college. She went to UCLA, but it was a disaster. She dropped out last year."

"To do what?"

"To bum around. She still rides. And she's had some odd jobs: working in a boutique, making cheap jewellery, that sort of thing."

"Where did she live once she left school?"

"At the ranch, in Beverly Hills. Mercedes bought it for Eden. It's a country house with some big fields and some wild land. It was perfect for Eden's horses."

"Was she all alone?"

"Oh, no. She had Miguel to look after her. Miguel is an ex-employee of Mercedes's husband, a security guard. When she left America, she appointed him watchdog over Eden."

Not a very good watchdog, de Córdoba thought, but didn't articulate the words. He had learned more from this girl in two brief conversations, he reflected, than he ever would have done from Mercedes Eduard herself. He glanced at her and found her eyes on him.

Maya smiled slightly, guessing his thoughts. "Mercé hasn't forbidden me to answer any of your questions, colonel. When you speak to her today, I think you'll find her a little more open to you than she was last night."

He nodded slightly. "I can only repeat that trust is the most important thing you can give me."

"I'm afraid Mercé is not very good at trusting people," she said with a touch of wryness. "Her life has not always been easy."

"But it has been remarkably successful," de Córdoba observed. "Your employer is an exceptional woman. And she's very fortunate in having you. What sort of businesses did her husband run in America?"

"Import-export. He shipped consumer goods to South America and brought back fruit and curios."

"And they split it all at the time of the divorce?"

Maya's perfect mouth turned down in distaste. "He kept everything that was his. As I told you, Mercedes made herself rich in her own right."

"So Dominic van Buren is at least as wealthy as his ex-wife?"

"Oh, yes, colonel. At least."

He nodded. And yet they had approached the mother, not the father. Why?

"I have not called myself 'colonel' since 1955." He smiled. "It makes me feel extremely ancient. Perhaps you could call me Joaquin."

"Thank you. And I prefer Maya."

"Agreed." He nodded.

She rose and he stood up with her. "Please, Joaquin," she said gently, "remember what I've said about Mercedes. She finds it difficult to give her trust."

He nodded. "I understand perfectly."

He watched her walk away, the smooth curves of her buttocks alluring as peaches under the black swimsuit. She glanced over her shoulder at the door and left him with a fleeting smile.

Mercedes Eduard was sitting at her desk. Before her on the desk was a folder she had taken from the steel Chubb safe. In it was a single sheet of drawings dating from the last years of the fifteenth century. They were by Hieronymus Bosch, a page of pen-and-ink studies of cripples and beggars.

She had paid a great deal of money for the work at a New York art auction some years ago. She'd wanted it because she considered it a unique work of art, but she had seldom looked at it since. Now she stared at the tiny details absently.

Every kind of deformity was here, perfectly drawn. Amputated and twisted limbs. Patches. Rags. Faces that suffered or leered. Jaunty hats. Crutches, sticks, ingenious props fashioned to dangle ingenious aberrations. All the pain and the bitter humour of the world, captured by a great, twisted genius.

If she had to start selling her possessions to raise money for Eden's ransom, this was where she would start. There was a dealer in Amsterdam who had once offered a fortune for these wretched little people.

The door opened and she heard Maya come into the study.

"You look exhausted, Mercé."

"Yes," she replied. "I am tired."

Maya's eyes rested on the drawing. "What are you looking at those for?"

"I was trying to brace myself to sell them, if I have to." Mercedes tapped the Bosch sheet. "Which one of these drawings affects you the most?"

"They're all gruesome." Maya peered at the paper in distaste. She pointed to a drawing low down on the page. "That one," she said. "I hate it."

It showed a man both crippled and blind. Under each armpit was a crutch to support his deformed legs. In his mouth he held a stick, protruding forward, with which to feel the way in a dark world. At his heels, their teeth fastened in his coat, were two angry hounds.

Mercedes smiled grimly. "That's the one I like best. It contains the greatest truth."

Maya grimaced. "I'll go and get the mail."

Joaquin de Córdoba was standing on the balcony of his grey-and-buff room, smoking a cigar. The weather had cooled perceptibly overnight, becoming clouded and damp. His back ached, a sign of worse weather to come. The sky was grey and heavy with rain. The Pyrenees in the distance looked as though they were white with snow, though it was only faraway sunlight. A sombre shadow had fallen over the magnificent grounds of the estate, over the orchards and the woods and the gardens.

He heard the knock at his bedroom door and tightened the cord of his dressing gown before turning.

"Yes?"

The door opened and Maya Duran came in. She was wearing a bright yellow dress, her short hair tied back with a matching ribbon, the colours of summer. But as he tossed his cigar away and came towards her, he saw that her face was white as paper.

"Another package arrived this morning," she began without

preamble. "There was a lock of Eden's hair in it. And some—"
She swallowed. "Some blood."

He stood very still. "Any message?"

She nodded. "Just the amount. Ten million dollars."

"Ten million?" De Córdoba was staggered. He had never
come across a demand for that much money in his whole career.
"I'll get dressed right away," he said.

"There's something I want to show you, before you come
down. Something you ought to know." He paused. She was holding out a black plastic binder. "Something Mercedes has been trying
to hide."

He didn't take the binder. "What is this?"

"Mercedes had Eden followed by a private investigator in Los
Angeles last year. This is his report."

"In that case, it's a confidential document," he said quietly.

Maya's brown eyes held his. "You have to understand the
truth about Eden. Please read it."

He took the binder from her. He put on his glasses and walked
out onto the balcony to read the contents.

The report was dated from the end of the previous year. It
ran to ten pages, with an appendix and a sheaf of photographs.

The first two pages were taken up with superficial—at least
to de Córdoba—details of the girl's private life and he skimmed
impatiently through accounts of protest marches and demonstrations, lectures missed and courses cut. The nucleus of information
was contained on the third page:

[22]   Over the three-week period of surveillance, the subject
       employed controlled drugs to a conspicuous extent. The
       drug involved was heroin.

[23]   A total of eleven purchases of this drug were made over
       the period that she was observed. Purchases were made
       by her current companion, who then took the drugs to
       the subject and, as shown in accompanying photo-
       graphs, sometimes assisted the subject to administer the
       drug to herself.

[24]   Purchases were made from known dealers.

[25]   The existence and degree of drug dependency cannot

be determined without access to a doctor's report or other medical records. However, the subject was observed injecting heroin on various occasions, a method associated with addicts, rather than casual users. It should also be noted that the subject is spending an estimated $400–$800 per week to support this habit.

[26]   The subject's association with her current companion, Terence O'Neill Fagan (a.k.a. "Rusty"), is highly relevant. Fagan is an occasional cocaine user, but almost certainly not an intravenous heroin user. Has typical "minor drug offender" record (see appendix), although no arrests since 1970. He has been identified as a tout or procurer of drugs for other youthful, wealthy "clients." Evidence to support this view was obtained during a previous investigation by this agency (see Appendix B).

[27]   This agency estimates that Fagan resells purchased drugs for a profit of up to 500 percent to his "clients," who in exchange secure anonymity and safety.

De Córdoba turned to the photographs. The first one he selected showed a striking, dark girl of around twenty, emerging from the doorway of a nightclub. He recognized her as Eden van Buren. Beside her, his arm around her waist, was a tall, rangily-built young man of about eight years more. His face was open, pleasant. He looked like the male lead of a successful daytime soap.

The next was a grainy black-and-white print, taken with a telephoto lens through a window. It showed Eden sitting on the edge of a bathtub. She was naked to the waist, her upper body lean and small-breasted, like her mother's. The open-faced man was in the bathroom with her. He appeared to be filling a syringe.

The next photograph had evidently been taken shortly after the first. The location was the same. The man was now watching. The girl's head, her face partially obscured by her snaking, dark hair, was hanging down as she focussed her attention on the needle she was in the process of thrusting into the crook of her left elbow. She held one end of a tourniquet between her teeth. The other was wrapped tightly around her thin upper arm.

She was so angular. So pathetic.

De Córdoba closed the binder and looked up at Maya Duran. She was watching him tensely.

"Thank you for showing me this," he said.

"It makes a difference, doesn't it?"

"Yes. It might make a difference." He handed her back the binder. "This man Fagan. Is he still associating with Eden?"

"No," Maya said quietly. "He took his own life at the beginning of the year."

De Córdoba met her eyes. The calm expression on her own face had not changed. "I see," he said heavily. "And the Addison's disease?"

"Mercedes wanted to hide the truth. She thought it would put you off. Eden has never had Addison's or any other disease," she told him. "Eden is a heroin addict."

3.

The Forge

San Lluc

It is a time of new things, of wonders.

Like Grandfather's new Ford, which is the very essence of excitement. No one else in San Lluc has an automobile. When Grandfather drives them all to the beach, with her in the front seat, on Papa's lap, bursting with pride, the dust swirling around them, people stare in awe!

Grandfather's cinema house, the Tivoli, is a dim palace of dreams.

And Papa's forge, the heart of their home, is the back door to Hell itself! His muscles gleam with sweat as he beats glowing iron into the shapes it will forever hold. The blows send sparks shooting. When he opens the mouth of the furnace, scarlet and roaring, she flees in terror.

And then it is announced that Mercedes is going to school.

Aunt Lluisa is deputed to lead Mercedes to her first day of school. Mercedes is not very fond of her. But when she is abandoned among a throng of other children in the classroom, all with strange faces, she watches her aunt's broad back depart with tears in her eyes.

The school is a square, drab building with a bell tower, surmounted by a rusty iron cross. It has a sandy playground, in which lime trees provide surfaces for the engraving of countless initials.

It is a church school, run by a number of grim-faced nuns from the convent and a male headmaster. The teaching methods place a heavy emphasis on discipline, especially on beating. The older nuns are particularly partial to the cane.

One day Sister Eufemia sets about Mercedes in a fury, slapping her face with hard hands until the child cowers under the desk, shrieking. She is bewildered by shock and pain. No one has ever hit her in her life.

Sister Eufemia hauls her back onto her seat.

"I see you take after your father," she hisses. She thrusts her meaty face against Mercedes's. "A rebellious spirit and a proud heart. That is blasphemy and vice. Learn to quell the evil in your blood if you do not want to burn, child."

Mercedes cries all day. She learns to avoid provoking Sister Eufemia. But her intelligence cannot be hidden. She leaps ahead, not only at reading and writing, but at arithmetic and geography too.

And most important of all, at her catechism. She is moved to the very front of the class.

Her first year at school flies past.

One day, some weeks before her first Communion, Sister Catalina takes her aside. Mercedes loves her best of all the nuns.

"I shall not be here to teach you next year," she says gently. Mercedes's dismay shows in her face. "Will you miss me?"

"Yes, Sister."

"I am old, Mercedes. It is time for me to retire and devote my days to prayers and to thoughts of what will come next. But you may come to see me, sometimes, at the convent, if you like."

Mercedes nods.

"God has given you intelligence, Mercedes. One day you might become a sister of Christ, like Eufemia." She is telling her rosary as she speaks. "Like me. You might come to teach other children, here in this very school. You would like that, wouldn't you?"

Mercedes nods.

"But though you are a child now, you will one day be a woman. In a woman, many things matter far more than brains. Purity. Obedience. Your soul is white, Mercedes. Unstained. It is like a snowy piece of paper on which you will write the story of your life. Do you understand me?"

"Yes, Sister Catalina."

"Lucifer was once proud and bright. He too had great gifts. But through pride he fell. He fell into the bottomless pit of error and he grew black and hideous to look upon. A long time ago, before you were born, your father committed a terrible sin. A sin that fell like a great black stain on his soul."

"What did he do?" she asks in fright.

"A foul thing," the nun says with sudden passion. "A thing that must not be spoken of."

"What?" she persists

Sister Catalina lays a hand on the child's shoulder. "He was punished for it," she says. "God struck him and lamed him for all to see. And until he repents, the sin will always be there. Inside him. Always."

Mercedes stares at her in silence. Her heart is thudding painfully.

"Beware, Mercedes," she says, shaking the girl's shoulder to and fro. "Beware. Remember that whatever you write on that white soul of yours will stay there forever until the great day of Judgement. And then the Recording Angel will tell God what you have written there and God will decide whether you are to go up through the gate of doves, or down into the fiery pit below."

Mercedes asks in dread, "Will Papa go into the fiery pit?"

Sister Catalina takes her hand off Mercedes's shoulder. "If he repents and comes back to the church, he will be saved. If not, no force in the Universe can take that stain away, Mercedes. It is there forever, black and odious."

Mercedes thinks of the gaping mouth of the furnace, scarlet and roaring. She knows Papa will never repent and come back to the church. Fear crawls at the back of her mind.

She takes her first Communion in December. All in white.

april 1925

San Lluc

They came to San Lluc a few days after her seventh birthday: three *guardia civil*, with their carbines slung over their shoulders. They were looking for Bertrán Cantarell, a factory worker who lived in the village.

Perhaps there would be shooting.

Mercedes, her heart pounding, ran behind them to see.

Bertrán had barred his door. They shouted at him to come out, but he would not. So the *guardia* smashed the door down. People began to gather in the street. The *guardia* unslung their carbines and went in.

A little while later, they led the man out. They had reslung their carbines and there had been no shooting. But Bertrán's nose and mouth were bleeding and had gone a funny shape. His hands were cuffed behind him. Bertrán's wife, Sofía, and his son clung to him, screaming. A *guardia* pushed them roughly away and kept them back with his pointed rifle.

There was a pain in Mercedes's stomach by now, a sick pain that made her want to run. But she couldn't. She was clinging to a woman's skirt, unable to look away.

A fourth man had arrived. He went into Bertrán's house and began throwing things out of the door into the street. Mercedes and the others watched in silence. The three *guardia civil* smoked a cigarette between themselves, talking about bullfighting. Bertrán looked at his wife and child over the heap of their belongings, without speaking.

Sofía's face held naked terror and grief.

Chairs, clothes, a table, a few tin plates. There was not much to throw. Soon it was all in the street.

Then Bertrán was marched away down the road between the soldiers. Their distinctive hats towered over his bare head. A woman put her arms around Sofía and the boy and drew them away. Someone else tried to gather their possessions.

What was Bertrán's crime? She asked Grandfather, who was standing in the square with some of the older men.

"Never you mind about that. Go play with your rabbits."

"They threw all his things into the street."

"It's a damned good job we've got a strong government," Grandfather said to the others. "These people have even tried to assassinate the king."

"*Bertrán?*"

"Not Bertrán." Grandfather smiled. "But people who think like him. And this is all they can expect in return." He tapped

Mercedes's shoulder significantly with a plump forefinger. "You tell your father that, Mercé."

Mercedes ran home to the forge. Mama was there, talking to Papa as he worked. She looked pale and worried.

"Was Bertrán a bad man?" Mercedes asked Papa.

"No. Only a poor one. As you grow older, Mercé, you'll find that very poor men are seldom bad. And that very bad men are seldom poor." Papa lifted Mercedes onto his knee with his huge hands. His dark blue eyes glowed. "San Lluc is a sleepy backwater. But there are thousands of San Llucs. And there are cities too, thronged with millions of men and women. A great movement is afoot in those villages and cities, like a mighty sea that is rising. One day that sea will break and sweep through Spain. And it will wash away all the injustice, all the misery that defiles our land."

"Francesc, that's enough," Mama said urgently, reaching for the girl. Papa laughed as he let Mercedes slip off his knee. Mama hoisted her up in her slim arms. "My goodness," she gasped. "You're getting to be a very heavy little lady. I wonder if I can still carry you upstairs?"

It seemed she could. But she would not discuss Bertrán Cantarell and what he had done. Mercedes was left with an undercurrent of foreboding. It had never occurred to her that doors could be smashed down. She'd always felt so safe once the door was shut and bolted. Could someone smash their own door down?

Mercedes Eduard was an elfin child. She was very pretty, with signs that she might attain real beauty in womanhood. Her eyes were large and dark and sparkled with intelligence. Her hair was long, thick and very black. It twisted, rather than curled, into long, heavy ropes that Papa called her Medusa's serpents.

She was unaware of the angry currents that flowed and counter-flowed through Catalonia and through the whole of Spain. How could she be? At seven, Mercedes had hardly ever been out of San Lluc.

She knew the village with the intimacy of a village child. She knew each dark stairway, each door, each of the winding streets. She could tell who lived in each house, who was behind each shuttered window.

She never felt that she loved San Lluc, or that it was beautiful;

but she did and it was, though she only realized that when it was too late to matter. For now, her mind was wrapped up in the present, eager for the future.

Lleonart Cornadó, who was one of the biggest boys in the class and almost eleven, said in the playground that Bertrán was dead.

"They've put a lead weight around his neck and chucked him in the sea," he said. Lleonart was showing them his muscles as he talked. He sat in the low branch of a tree at the far end of the playground, the throne from which he usually held court.

"See that?" He rolled up his sleeve and braced his biceps. The muscle swelled, white and impressive.

"Why would they do that?" Mercedes asked.

"You'd like to know, wouldn't you?" Lleonart grinned. He was a freckled boy with a sly smile and hazel eyes. He showed them his other biceps, touching his clenched fist to his nose in a stylized Adonis pose. Three of the other girls came to watch. Girls were fascinated by Lleonart Cornadó. Even Mercedes, in a vague way. They always drifted towards him, especially when he was giving an exhibition.

"But why?" Mercedes persisted.

"'Cause he's a dirty little Lenin, that's why. Like someone else we know." One of the girls snickered and nudged her companion. "That's what they do to anarchists," he said. "Tie a lead weight round their neck and chuck them in the sea. They sink right down to the bottom, choking and drowning. Then the fish eat their eyeballs out. That's what anarchists deserve." He held a braced biceps out to the girls. "Feel that. Like iron."

The girls squeezed the hard white muscle with little gasps and shudders. One or two of the boys followed suit.

Lleonart winked. "Want to feel something else that's like iron?"

"Don't be disgusting, Lleonart," a boy said. They all knew what was coming. The girls crowded closer, wide-eyed.

"Go on," one of them said.

Lleonart unbuttoned his fly, digging inside with his fingers. "Get an eyeful of . . . *that!*"

The girls shrieked in unison.

"Put it away, you pig," the same boy exclaimed. But they were all staring as Lleonart proudly manipulated himself.

"It's *revolting*!" Fina, the oldest of the girls, said disdainfully. She was ten.

"No, it isn't." Lleonart Cornadó leered. "It's a delicious sausage. Want a bite, anyone?" He offered himself to Fina. "Go on, Fina. You know you like the taste."

"Go on, Fina," one of her girlfriends hissed, nudging her hard. The girls' faces were avid.

"I wouldn't *dream* of it." Fina lifted her snub nose and tossed her pigtails. "It would *poison* me."

"No, it won't," Lleonart said eagerly. His eyes were bright. "Go on!"

The others started a chorus of encouragement. Fina grinned and leaned forward.

Mercedes turned away and wandered across the dusty playground. She'd seen it all before. Lleonart didn't care who sucked his sausage, boy or girl, and Mercedes knew what happened in any case. It held no interest for her.

What was really on her mind was the idea of someone sinking into the sea with a weight around their neck. Choking and drowning. Then the fish would eat out his eyeballs.

Lleonart was a liar. Lleonart had just said that to try and frighten her. It couldn't happen.

But Mercedes had seen a man's door broken down and his home violated. She'd seen a man bleed after being struck by other men. *It couldn't happen* didn't reassure her any more.

Then, one night, Bertrán returned. At first Mercedes thought he was drunk. He walked into the village square very slowly, holding himself as though he were a bundle of old clothes that would fall apart. Then the light from a window fell on his face. It was bloated and discoloured, like a carnival mask. One eye was clotted shut with dried blood.

She ran back to the forge, barely able to tell them what she had seen. Papa, grim and silent, went out to find Bertrán. Mama put her to bed. Mercedes begged her to leave the candle on, because she saw Bertrán's monstrous face in every shadow.

Bertrán and his family left San Lluc in the morning and did not return.

According to Tia Josefina, who worked in the bakery, it was to do with the long-drawn strike taking place at the factory where

Bertrán worked. Bertrán, she said, had tried to sabotage a valuable machine. The Massaguer family, who owned the factory, had been greatly angered.

"They put their mark on him, all right," Mercedes heard her tell a customer. "They've given him a hernia. And he's pissing blood. And where will they get the money for a doctor?"

Mama made a *zarzuela* that night, a succulent stew of shrimps, clams and chicken. But Mercedes had no appetite for it. She felt ill. So Mama sent her to bed with a hot water bottle. She hugged herself tight.

Mercedes was proud of Papa, whatever they said.

Mercedes could recognize Papa's work on houses everywhere, from the heavy iron rings on the doors to the whimsical weathervanes that swung on the rooftops.

It all had his touch. Ornate locks and bolts, burglar-guards and balconies, iron pots and griddles, a thousand things that had come from his anvil and gone into people's lives. But noblest of all were the gates he'd forged for the convent.

The ironwork was marvelous, strong and delicate. The writhing snakes seemed almost alive, the petals of the flowers looked almost soft. She loved those gates. They made her so proud.

Mercedes went up there to see Sister Catalina from time to time. They would meet in the shady gardens and she would give Mercedes a glass of milk and a piece of biscuit.

Lately, Sister Catalina talked less and less. She was thinner and more transparent than ever and she fell into long silences nowadays, seeming hardly even to breathe. Mercedes knew she didn't hear anything during those silences. It didn't matter. She just liked being there. She liked to see those gates and touch their black, serpentine curves with awe. She liked the tranquillity of the stone-flagged courtyards, across which the black figures of nuns drifted like shadows. She liked the sense of height, the closeness of the blue sky above.

Sometimes she thought she might like to be a nun. From up here you could see far out to sea and far inland to the mountains. You could lean over the walls and look down onto the houses of San Lluc, beggar children clustering round a rich woman's skirt. It was easy to believe in God, up here.

April became May. Among the fields, countless poppies had

started to bloom, as though a million cats had caught a million birds and sprinkled a billion tiny spots of blood.

may 1927

San Lluc

This morning a crowd of children was standing around an automobile parked outside the schoolhouse.

Mercedes saw at once that it was a very different vehicle from Grandfather's Ford. It was long, sleek, gleaming red, with dazzling chrome work. Each huge wheel was a glittering basketwork of wires.

"It's a Studebaker Sedan," Juan Capdevila said with awe. Juan Capdevila was Mercedes's best friend and was an authority on cars. He had stick-out ears that he could wiggle. He looked like a very skinny bat.

The bell began to clatter. Reluctantly, the children dragged themselves into the assembly hall.

This morning, the teachers on the dais at the end of the hall wore especially stern expressions and there were one or two strangers among them. When prayers were over Señor Sánchez, the headmaster, cleared his throat solemnly.

"Most of you children know that Spain is fighting a war in Morocco," he began. "A heroic war against a savage and barbarous enemy. In wars, men are sometimes called upon to make the sacrifice of their lives. Today I want to talk about someone who has made that greatest sacrifice of all. A brave soldier who died in the field in Africa."

He crossed himself and everyone else followed suit.

"His name was Lieutenant Felip Massaguer and he was the eldest son of a family who have been generous benefactors to the church and to this very school. He died like a hero, leading a bayonet charge with the greatest possible courage. His last words were, 'Long live Spain.' The school is commissioning a plaque to commemorate his brave death. We will observe a moment of prayer."

Before dismissing them to their classes, the headmaster had a last announcement.

"I wish to see Mercedes Eduard in my study after assembly."

Mercedes tucked her tingling hands in her armpits. It could only mean a punishment If anything, girls got it worse than boys, on the palms, with a thick length of cane.

Lleonart Cornadó kicked her slyly on the ankle, then wrung his hands in mimed agony. Juan gave her a sympathetic pat on the shoulder. She dragged her feet to the headmaster's office.

Señor Sánchez was behind his desk. But he was not alone. Another man was sitting across the desk from the headmaster. Mercedes recognized him as one of the strangers who had been at assembly that morning.

"This is the Eduard girl," Señor Sánchez said.

"Is it, indeed," the stranger said in a husky voice.

The eyes that stared at her were black and very intense, with heavy lids and long dark eyelashes. There was something in them — anticipation? curiosity?—a fleeting impression that was instantly veiled.

The headmaster toyed with his spectacles. "You heard me speak about the heroic death of Lieutenant Felip Massaguer this morning?"

Mercedes nodded.

"This is that man's brother, Señor Gerard Massaguer."

Gerard Massaguer. Mercedes felt a moment of stark terror. Was it going to be worse than a beating? Something to do with Papa? She remembered Bertrán Cantarell shuffling into San Lluc with bloated face and broken body. She began to tremble.

"Señor Massaguer has just returned from Africa, where he visited the grave of his brother. He came to bring us the sad details. I summoned you because he asked to see our star pupil."

"So," Gerard Massaguer said. He crossed his legs lazily. "You're Mercedes Eduard, eh?"

"Yes, Señor," she whispered

"Your fame spreads far and wide. I hear that you excel at all your subjects. Is that true?" Mercedes said nothing. "Well?" he demanded sharply. "Cat got your tongue?"

"N-no, Señor."

"Do you excel?"

"Yes, Señor."

"Even at arithmetic?"

Mercedes looked at the headmaster blindly. "I—I think so, Señor."

Gerard laughed. He was beautifully dressed. On the lapel of his suit, a little square of black material had been daintily pinned. He looked like a film star to her. His hair was slicked back in two gleaming waves. On the little finger of his right hand was a big diamond ring.

"No false modesty, Mercedes Eduard. That's a poor sort of virtue. I like to meet people who know their worth." The black eyes considered her from under hooded lids. "Come here."

Mercedes obeyed, her heart pounding. She could smell the man, a scent of cologne, new clothes, male skin. He studied her intently. "Yes," he said at last. "She has an intelligent face. Wouldn't you say, headmaster?"

"An intelligent face, indeed, Señor Massaguer."

"Good blood must have gone into her somewhere." The full lips curved. "She may turn out to be a beauty someday soon. Those are very fine eyes. Who is the girl's father?"

"The blacksmith at San Lluc. Francesc Eduard."

"Ah. That troublesome fellow."

"Indeed, Señor Massaguer, an anarchist. And worse."

"How old are you, Mercedes?"

Mercedes's throat was dry. "Nine."

She felt the man's hand take her chin in strong fingers, lifting her face. She met the black eyes of the stranger, unable to look away for the biting grip. "You're trembling, Mercedes. Are you afraid of me?"

Mercedes didn't answer. She felt the fingers tighten, crushing her cheeks against her teeth until she winced.

"Don't be afraid of me. I'm very interested in you, Mercedes."

The headmaster, waving his spectacles gently, was looking on with an indulgent smile.

"Very interested," Gerard repeated. "I shall be watching your progress with great attention. I expect great things of you."

He released her at last. Her cheeks felt numb, squashed out of shape. She longed to rub her bruised face, but didn't dare.

"Now. Let me hear you say your nine times table."

Mercedes began to recite.

"*Faster*," Gerard cut in brusquely. "Don't take all day over it."

Mercedes launched out again, as quick as she could. The dark man listened to her, frowning. At the end, he turned to Sánchez. "Does this child get beaten often?"

"Hardly at all." The headmaster smiled.

"Bad," Gerard said silkily. "She needs beating. All girls do. If she shows any sign of slacking in her studies, headmaster, any sign that she is not doing as well as she should, I expect you to beat her severely. *Most* severely. Until she screams for mercy. Agreed?"

Sánchez nodded gravely. "It shall be as you say, Señor Massaguer."

Was it meant as a joke? Mercedes was shivering now. Gerard leaned back in his chair, considering the child. "Tell me, what does a little girl like Mercedes Eduard dream about?"

"I—I don't know, Señor."

"There must be something you really want. Something you would give your right arm for. Well?"

"I'm saving up," she whispered. "For a—a bicycle."

"A bicycle. Well, put this in your piggy bank."

She saw the coin gleaming between the man's outstretched fingers.

She gasped as she took it, her eyes wide and dazed. It was a *duro*. Five whole pesetas, a huge silver thing that covered her palm. On it, the head of the boy king, Alfonso XIII.

The headmaster sat up. "Really, a most princely gift. What do you say, girl?"

"Thank you," Mercedes whispered, clutching the coin in her palm.

"Thank you *very much*," Sánchez corrected her.

"Thank you very much."

"If you've done well, next time I see you there may be another. If not—tears."

Mercedes nodded dumbly.

"Well, Sánchez." Gerard Massaguer rose to his feet, consulting a slim gold fob watch. "Time runs on."

"Of course, of course." Sánchez shooed Mercedes out. "Get back to your lessons. And don't lose that money, or I'll break your fingers!"

Mercedes flew out into the playground, the money clutched in her hand. She could hardly believe it. Not a beating at all. Gerard Massaguer, the most powerful man she knew of, had given her a silver *duro*!

The red Studebaker gleamed in the sun. A young woman was leaning negligently against the polished bonnet. She was very slim and her golden hair was almost as short as a boy's, but she was very pretty. She was smoking a cigarette in a long holder.

She wore a white print dress that had been gathered into a bow at one hip, an arrangement that lifted the hem enough to show slender ankles and high-heeled doeskin shoes.

Mercedes's heart contracted. How *beautiful*. An angel. She imagined herself standing like that, negligently, against the car, an angel with blond hair.

She hid behind the thick trunk of one of the lime trees as Sánchez and Gerard emerged from the study.

"Sorry to keep you, my love," Gerard said to the girl. He tapped the headmaster's chest familiarly. "I meant to ask you whether that girl's father interferes in any way. Does he put ideas into the girl's head?"

"It seems not," Sánchez replied. "Eduard seems to have calmed down considerably since he married the Barrantes woman."

"Don't you believe it," Gerard said with contempt. "I know that kind. They don't change their spots. Until the next time, Sánchez."

He opened the door for his fiancée. Mercedes watched the Studebaker roar off.

She looked at the coin in her hand. It was as though she'd peeped into a new world.

She ran to her classroom, where the history lesson was already halfway through, and muttered an apology to the teacher as she let herself in. She went to her chair next to Juan. Her fists were tightly clenched.

"Let's see," Juan whispered, turning his skinny bat's face sympathetically to his friend.

Mercedes held out her fist under the desk, then slowly opened her fingers. Instead of the red weals Juan was expecting to see on Mercedes's palm, the huge silver coin gleamed.

Juan's eyes opened so wide his ears went into spasm.

Mama wasn't back from work when Mercedes got home, but Papa was in the forge, making hinges for Josep Arnau, who was standing talking to him.

Breathless with having run all the way from school, Mercedes spilled out the enthralling news of the day. She had to shout against the roaring of the furnace.

Josep Arnau listened with a grin. But Papa's face grew rocky.

"Look," Mercedes finished on a panting, triumphant note. She held out her hand. "Just *look* what Señor Massaguer gave me! And he says he's going to give me another when he comes to the school again, if I've done well!"

Francesc took the coin and tossed it into the mouth of the furnace.

Mercedes gasped. *"Papa!"*

"No daughter of mine will take money from the Massaguers," her father said in a stony voice. "No daughter of mine."

"But it was mine! Give it back!"

Francesc picked up the hammer. "Go to your room and do your homework," he said harshly.

"You're a thief," Mercedes wept. "A *thief!* Give it back to me!"

Arnau clicked disapprovingly, pulling at his grey hair. "Don't talk to your Papa like that, Mercedes."

"He stole my money!" Tears were streaming down her face. "He's a thief!"

Her father's dark blue eyes were hard with fury. "Take your money, then." With the pincers, he raked the coin from the furnace and dropped it into her palm.

Mercedes clutched it without thinking. The metal seared into her palm. She tried to throw the coin down, but it had stuck to the flesh and would not come free. She screamed as the pain blossomed intolerably. She flailed her hand wildly.

The coin fell to the ground at last. It had scorched a perfect red disk in her palm. She crouched, sobbing over her pain.

"Don't call me a thief, Mercedes. Not ever again." He dragged

Mercedes to the trough and plunged her hand into the water, as though she was a piece of iron he had just shaped. "You will never take anything from Gerard Massaguer, as long as you live. Nor from any of the Massaguers. Do you understand me?"

Mercedes pulled away from Francesc. Her black eyes seemed to blaze out of her white face. "*I hate you*," she hissed. She ran blindly out into the street.

Francesc started forward, his face livid. The carpenter laid an anxious hand on his shoulder, stopping him.

"Children are funny animals." Arnau, father of four and grandfather of six, patted the blacksmith's broad back sympathetically. "They aren't bits of iron you can beat into shape, or bits of wood you can carve. Especially girls. Girls are more difficult."

Francesc shrugged him off and grasped the jug of wine that stood near the door, in the coolest spot of the shop. He drank deeply, trying to loosen the knot of pain and anger in his chest.

He'd seen Gerard Massaguer's black eyes staring out of Mercedes's face.

She was not his child. She never would be. He stared unseeingly at the motes of dust that danced brightly in the forge doorway and wondered what Conchita would say when she found out.

Barcelona

The *burr* of the trap was followed by the twin flat cracks of the shotgun. After each report, one of the flying clay disks vanished into a cloud of fragments. There was a sprinkling of applause from the spectators.

The shot, a young marquis, broke the shotgun open and ejected the spent shells. He was doing well this afternoon. He stretched his back, then shouldered the gun again.

"Pull."

Burrr.

Crack. Crack.

In the pavilion, Gerard Massaguer crossed his grey-flannelled legs, his hands laced behind his neck. Marisa was practicing with the other women competitors. She had already won the first two rounds and was due to shoot again in a short while.

The marriage would be a good one, he knew that. Marisa was

Italian. Her family had excellent connections. Her uncle was an Italian duke and a close friend of Mussolini. Various cousins enjoyed high-status positions in the Fascist hierarchy. He and Marisa would be honeymooning in Rome and Florence after the wedding and he would be presented to Il Duce. He was looking forward to that honour. People might laugh at his histrionics, but Mussolini was a very great man. Fascism, as a force in international politics, was here to stay.

The future was theirs. The Communists were being slowly but surely beaten back all over Europe. In Portugal, Italy and Germany, the street battles had already been fought and won. Fascism offered stability, prosperity. It was the philosophy twentieth-century Europe needed. It built ramparts against anarchy.

Someday soon Spain would be Fascist too. It was the only solution. Communism had to be stopped. And by God, it would be stopped. Someday soon.

The Marquis came sauntering up the alley, his shotgun over one arm. He was replaced by Félix Martínez, current idol of the bullring. He drew a round of applause, especially from the women, as he strutted, tight-buttocked, to his place. The shiny queue bobbed at the back of his head.

Women loved a winner. A killer.

Marisa was never so excited, or so exciting, as when he conquered her by force. Like last night. Gerard drained the glass, enjoying the heady taste of the gin. He closed his eyes, thinking of how he'd impaled her on the silk sheets, his cock thrusting deep into her body like a weapon. Hearing her whisper his name as his seed gouted into her.

Then she'd reversed their positions. Straddling his face so that he could satisfy her again with his tongue. Fingers parting the petals of her sex to expose the place she wanted him to minister to.

And twenty minutes later, she'd been discussing Puccini with his cousins over the dinner table, chin on hand, her violet eyes wide and innocent. If she'd leaned any closer, they'd have been able to smell his come on her breath.

Magnificent! She would have been utterly wasted on anyone else.

Gerard was revelling in a deep sense of contentment. Of achievement, even. He felt as one favoured by the gods.

Felip was lying in a sandy grave in Morocco, no longer able

to come between him and his inheritance. He'd never rested easy about Felip. There had always been the chance, a remote one, that Felip would pull some heroic deed out of the hat and win back his place in Father's heart.

It had been a serious disappointment to him in 1918, when he'd given that nauseating correspondence to Father, that Father hadn't actually disinherited the little sodomite. There had been a thunderous row, of course. But packing Felip off to the army in the hope that it would "make a man of him" had been very far from a proper solution.

"Pull!"

Crack. Crack.

"Good shooting!" He applauded the bullfighter politely, then adjusted the square of black material at his lapel.

Eight or nine young women were sitting in a circle around a table a little way away from him, all in wide-brimmed hats. Ostensibly, they were watching the shots, but he'd caught the long-lashed glances that came his way and had sensed the murmured remarks.

"Of course, he inherits everything now . . . father's as rich as Croesus . . . engaged to Marisa de Bono . . . lovely, isn't she . . . and he's *so* good-looking . . ." Giving the group a more careful glance, he noted that he'd bedded at least three of them on various occasions in the past. Three down, six to go.

Felip getting himself killed was a magnificent solution, actually shedding glory on the family. Why, even he, Gerard, was bathed in the romantic glow of having a heroically martyred brother. That thought gave him keen amusement.

Leading a bayonet charge with the greatest possible courage . . .

He grinned to himself. Wonderful stuff. It would all go on the monument. Even Father believed it, at least partially.

The truth, as he'd had it from that cynical young officer, after the fifth cognac in a stifling army club in Morocco, was somewhat less glorious. Felip had been captured by a handful of fuzzy-wuzzies in some godforsaken gully half a mile from camp. They had cut open his belly and tried to haul out his bowels. Felip had been unfortunate enough to be rescued at this point. To everyone's profound relief, however, he had succumbed in hospital a day later, screaming for his mother.

Gerard signalled to the waiter for another drink and gazed around the pavilion with his heavy-lidded eyes. Society photographers mingled with the spectators, scribbling and clicking. The latest fashions were on show.

Crack. Crack.

His drink arrived and he swirled the ice cubes thoughtfully.

Meeting Mercedes Eduard this morning had been an extraordinary event. He had gone to see the girl out of pure curiosity, but he had come away dazzled by her. She was a masterpiece. They would never make a yokel out of her. His blood ran in her veins. Her breeding made her soar above the others.

It had been a profoundly stirring experience. He'd never felt anything like it before. He hadn't been able to stop thinking about her all day. The child was beautiful. Her eyes were intoxicating: Massaguer eyes. He'd wanted to kiss that trembling mouth, touch that snaking black hair. He'd wanted to crush her in his arms. If they'd been alone, he'd have done so. Would have crushed his mouth to hers . . .

My daughter.

He pondered telling Marisa that Mercedes was his child. He decided against it. Women were jealous creatures. She would want to present him with *bambini* of her own and would not appreciate Mercedes's prior arrival.

But he vowed to make something of the child someday. When she had grown. Yes, he would make something of her. And woe betide that brutish blacksmith if he got in the way. The child was *his*.

He thought of Francesc's great paws, the way he'd crushed José's hand. A dangerous oaf. Well, it was easy to deal with such men. He remembered the beating they had given him. The glowering brute wouldn't be so insolent a second time.

He let his hand drop casually onto his lap, feeling his penis swollen and hard against the flannel. He watched the group of demure young Señoritas from under lowered lashes, unobtrusively stroking his erection.

In his mind's eye, he saw a child's face. The future was his. *Crack. Crack.*

San Lluc

Marcel Barrantes had put on a lot of weight since he'd sold the shop and bought the Tivoli and now carried an imposing paunch before him. He was crying with pity and anger in his kitchen.

"Poor little thing," he moaned. "That *bastard*. How could he do such a vile thing?"

He dabbed iodine on the child's palm and she squirmed with the excruciating pain.

"Why was Papa so angry?" she gasped.

"Don't call him that." Marcel's piggy eyes were pouched and watery. "That man is not your father."

She stared at him through her tears.

"He's *not* your father," Marcel repeated. "Not your *real* father. How could that ugly beast have produced you, my chick?" He put the iodine away with trembling hands and blew his nose. "No. You come from finer stock than that, Mercedes. I thought Eduard would be a good father to you once. But I made a terrible mistake. I should never—"

He bit off his words and stamped out of the kitchen, into the pantry. He poured himself a glass of wine and gulped it down, trying to control his emotions.

When he turned, Mercedes was standing in the doorway, watching him. Her face was as white as linen. "Who is my real father?" she asked in a still voice.

It was starting to dawn on Marcel what he had done. He flushed, blinking tears from his swollen eyes. No words came.

"Is Gerard Massaguer my father?" she asked.

Marcel nodded. The child had to know sometime.

Mercedes no longer felt the pain in her palm. She felt changed. Altered. As though she was not Mercedes any more, but someone or something else. As though she would never be Mercedes again.

They had lied to her. They had lied to her all her life.

She turned and ran.

"Wait!" Marcel hurried after her. "You can't go back! Stay here! Lluisa and María are cooking a goose. With dumplings!"

But Mercedes ran out into the sunshine, her hair streaming as though a knot of black snakes were writhing around her head.

"Oh, Francesc," Conchita said that night, "why did you do it?"

His voice was rusty. "It kills me to think of the girl turning away from us, to *them*."

"She'll never turn away from us, my love. Mercedes loves you. She's your daughter."

"Gerard Massaguer is wealthy. He has land, fine clothes and possessions. What if one day he says to Mercedes, *I am your father*? And what if Mercedes looks at Francesc Eduard on that day and sees only the village blacksmith, a black, rough man who can hardly read? A bumpkin who's lied to her, calling himself her father with no true claim to that title?"

"She doesn't have to find out."

"What if she does? Am I to stand by while Gerard Massaguer steps in at the end and says, *This is my daughter*?"

"No, Francesc, no," she said miserably, stroking the stubborn locks of his greying hair.

"I'll have to find another way. I've been sitting here, thinking that. I'll have to teach the girl, Conchita."

"Teach her what?"

"Teach her right from wrong."

"You mean your politics," she said sorrowfully. "Francesc, you promised me you would never force your anarchism down the girl's throat. For pity's sake, let her just be a child."

"She needs more. I don't want them to be able to tempt her with baubles, Conchita. When she finds out, she can make a choice based on logic, not on blind emotion. A choice based on political awareness, on a sense of justice, on a knowledge of good and evil."

"At her age?"

"It's time to start treating the girl like an adult. She's more mature than any boy of her age. I'll start tomorrow."

"Oh, Francesc..."

She rose and went into Mercedes's bedroom. The child was sleeping fitfully. Her face was pale, her black hair tumbled on the pillow. The gaping blister on the palm of her right hand made Conchita wince. She understood what feelings lay in Francesc's heart, or at least she thought she did. But would he have done that to his own flesh and blood? She despised the question, but it was there nevertheless.

As she slept, Mercedes's downturned mouth and brooding eyelids gave her a look of Gerard that disturbed Conchita deeply.

Mercedes began sobbing in her sleep. Conchita stroked

her hair helplessly. Who knew what was going on in a child's head?

june 1928

San Lluc

"Hey, *you*."

Lleonart Cornadó dug Mercedes in the back.

She and Juan Capdevila had sought out the far corner of the playground, trying to find a peaceful place among the screams and whirling bodies of the lunch break, but Lleonart Cornadó had found them.

"Leave us alone. Get away."

"This is *my* place," Lleonart retorted. "*You* get away."

"I was here first."

"*I wath here firtht!*" Grinning, Lleonart yanked at Mercedes's long black hair.

Mercedes turned a furious face on him. "Leave me *alone!*"

"Get lost, Lleonart." Juan Capdevila was at Mercedes's side. He thrust his ugly bat's face up into Lleonart's belligerently. "Just leave her alone."

"Or what?" Lleonart challenged.

"Or I'll make you!"

Lleonart stared, then laughed contemptuously. He was easily the strongest boy in school. "You? You ugly little runt. I could—"

He broke off, staggering backwards as Juan pushed him hard in the chest.

"Just leave her alone," Juan repeated menacingly.

Lleonart's freckled face flushed red with anger. "You'll pay for that, Capdevila. What do you hang around with this little bitch for, anyway? Her father digs up nuns' corpses and her mother's a whore."

Mercedes flew at him, a feral animal, all teeth and claws. Lleonart was quick enough to catch Mercedes's wrists before the nails could rake out his eyes. But the girl's wild strength was almost too much for him. "She's trying to kill me! Get her off!"

Without hesitation, Miguel and Ferran, his two courtiers, launched themselves onto Mercedes.

Juan moved as quickly, flinging himself onto Ferran's back, wrapping his arms around the bigger boy's neck.

A knee exploded violently into Mercedes's stomach. Gasping for breath, she tottered back. Something very hard slammed into her nose. Exquisite pain spread claws deep into her skull. The world had suddenly gone red and roaring, like the mouth of the furnace in the forge.

She reeled away, sightless and helpless. She could not match them in this kind of fighting. She cannoned into a body and heard Lleonart Cornadó's voice say, "Get them on the ground and we'll teach them a lesson."

She clawed at the voice. Her nails raked a face and a voice squawked in pain. She tried to kick, but it was all over in seconds. Strong arms hurled her to the ground. Her face was forced into the ground so that she could taste the earth in her mouth. A foot descended on her shoulder, pinning her down.

"Try to kill me, would you?" Lleonart panted. "Little anarchist bitch. I'm going to teach you a lesson."

Then something hot and wet began to rain onto her cheek. The bitter ammonia taste of urine ran into her mouth.

Lleonart Cornadó was pissing on her.

Enraged, she tried to roll away, but Lleonart's foot jammed her back down onto the ground. The piss streamed over her face, her hands, her back. The other two were whooping with laughter.

Unbearable. She tried to endure. Her time would come. Lleonart's bladder voided itself slowly. The rank stream ended with a few drops. Then he released Mercedes and rolled her over with his foot. The freckled face grinned down at her, sly eyes bright.

"Look at you, Mercedes. Cleverest girl in school. And I've just pissed in your face! I'll piss in your anarchist father's face and your whore mother's face too."

Mercedes lay still, the emotion in her too big for words or gestures. She just watched Lleonart with burning black eyes, knowing that she was going to kill him. Soon.

But Lleonart was unaware of that. He laughed raucously, turning away. The other two released Juan and also rose. The three of them linked arms as they walked away, gloating over their easy victory.

Mercedes tried to pick herself up. Her legs and arms were like rubber things. She felt Juan's hands support her. The ugly bat's face, now sporting a rapidly-swelling scratch down one cheekbone, peered at her sadly.

"I'm sorry they did that," Juan said. "I might have been able to fight them off. Except you scratched me in the face and knocked me over."

Mercedes swayed on her feet. "Sorry," she muttered thickly.

Juan surveyed his friend in dismay. Mercedes was filthy and torn. Her long black hair was streaked with mud and piss. "We'd better get you washed before the next lesson, or Sánchez will go mad."

He led Mercedes to the lavatory and shut the door. Using his handkerchief and a liberal supply of soap and water, he started working on Mercedes's appearance. Mercedes submitted, thinking about how she would kill Lleonart. *With a rock*, a voice hissed. *Hit him on the head as he comes out of school. Smash his brains out.*

The hatred in her seemed to reach from somewhere deep inside her, extending into her fingertips, filling her with a vibrating force. She was very white and there were little dents on either side of her nose, like claw marks. She leaned against the wall, the tiles cold on her naked shoulders. She pressed the wet handkerchief to her nose as Juan washed her shirt in the basin, trying to give her comfort.

"I'm going to get him," Mercedes said through gritted teeth. She wasn't crying any more. She examined the handkerchief. The bleeding was stopping gradually. "I'm going to kill him," she said quietly.

"He deserves it." Juan wrung the shirt out and gave it back to Mercedes. "It's wet, but at least it's clean."

Impulsively, she reached for Juan Capdevila and hugged him tight. "I'm going to kill him," she whispered into her friend's ear. It wasn't his fault they'd overpowered him. He had fought valiantly for her. She kissed his bony cheek, hard. Her fingernails bit into Juan's shoulders. "Really kill him."

•　　•　　•

She was careful to have her satchel packed before the final bell went. When it rang, she was ready to go. She hurried out as soon as Sister Eufemia had dismissed the class, well ahead of the others, even Juan. She did not turn to the right, towards San Lluc, however, but ran down the road towards Pals, the way Lleonart would walk.

She had been planning this all day. She knew exactly how she would do it.

She knew where to strike. At the ochre mine.

The ochre mine lay twenty yards or so off the winding footpath that led to Pals, buried among a thicket of cork oaks and wild rosemary. It had been abandoned for years.

Most adults had long forgotten the place, forgotten even to forbid their children to play there. The braver children sometimes explored the pitch-dark galleries as far as they dared. But nobody knew how far into the earth they went. You could hide something in those unexplored depths for years. Forever.

Panting, she crashed through the undergrowth, oblivious to the thorns that scratched her knees. Reaching the spot she'd chosen, she hunted for a suitable rock. At last she found what she wanted, a jagged piece of shale as heavy as an ax head, but not too heavy to wield with force. The shape was like a falcon, poised to strike.

Her heart was racing and there was a taste of blood in her mouth, like rusty iron. Her body was shivering and her dark eyes were as wild as an animal's as she peered through the aromatic screen of rosemary, wild sage and grey thyme. Cicadas shrilled without ceasing in the afternoon heat. She could see the footpath clearly from here.

She settled down to wait, sweating.

Conchita filled a pail of water at the well and heaved it upstairs to start cooking the evening meal, something she did every day as soon as she got home from the cork factory.

Over the sink, she began to rinse soil out of the onions they would eat tonight.

She longed to move out of the village. With the trade Francesc had now built up, they could open a proper workshop in Palafrugell or La Bisbal, some place where there was activity and life and not just dust and dead dreams. A town where a man like

Francesc, with his past and his politics, would not stick out so dangerously. Somewhere Gerard Massaguer's grasp could not reach them so easily. Somewhere Mercedes could be happy.

She loved her daughter with a blind passion that did not bear explanation or study. But she loved her husband for reasons that she could easily enumerate. For his kindness to her. For his innate goodness. For his strength. For the way he had loved Mercedes, from the start.

In 1918 he'd promised Conchita that for her sake, for the child's sake, there would be no more meetings in Barcelona, no more talk of revolution, no more speeches. He'd stayed true to that promise so far. But she knew that his views had strengthened, rather than subsided, in the past decade.

She sighed heavily. Mercedes was an only child. That was not good for her. Or for them. Why had no other children come? She was now twenty-eight, at the height of her beauty, in the full bloom of her womanhood. She'd expected at least two children of Francesc's by now.

He made love to her almost every night, with pleasure and affection. And every month her terms came.

Perhaps the fault lay with him? Had something been damaged when he was shot?

Mercedes was probably, unless something miraculous happened, his only chance. That was why he had reacted so fiercely to Gerard Massaguer sniffing around Mercedes. That was why he burned to transmit his political views on to the girl. To make Mercedes's mind an image of his own.

Because Mercedes's flesh belonged to another man.

She put a rabbit into a clay casserole with onions and herbs and a half litre of red wine and put it into the oven. She unfastened her apron and looked out of the window. Saw the stone walls of San Lluc. A stone village. Dusty earth streets and faded wooden doors. And above the clay-tiled rooftops, a pure blue sky.

She checked the clock on the wall. Mercedes was due back from school in a short while.

Mercedes watched the groups of children file along the track. Her fingers gripped the rock convulsively. Her teeth were clenched tight. Sweat dripped into her eyes and she blinked it away painfully. She'd seen Juan go past, and Fina, swinging her pigtails.

Then her heart gave a great swallow dive inside her. Lleonart was walking down the track, his bag slung over his shoulder, his eyes on the ground. And he was alone. Mercedes felt the shivering energy flood into her fingertips from that deep place inside. There was no hesitation in her. She rose in a half crouch and called out.

"Lleonart!"

At first she thought Lleonart hadn't heard. Then the boy stopped and looked uncertainly into the thicket.

"Lleonart!" she cried again, fingers working tensely around her rock.

"Who's that?" Lleonart called back.

"Come here! I've got something for you!"

She could see the sly hazel eyes hunting among the greenery. "Who is it?" Lleonart asked. "Mercedes Eduard? Is that you?"

"Come here!" Mercedes called again.

"What do you want? Another beating?"

"I've got something for you."

"What?" Lleonart asked suspiciously. He still couldn't see Mercedes.

"Something special!"

"Well, bring it here."

"I can't."

A group of children came by and Mercedes sat in silence.

"Well?" Lleonart shouted, when the others had passed on. "What have you got for me, Mercedes Eduard?"

"I'll suck your sausage," she called.

Lleonart's freckled face changed. These days he couldn't get the girls to do it any more. Not since hair had grown down there and stuff came out smelling, so they said, like a dead fish. He hesitated, licking his lips.

"I'll suck it as long as you like!"

Lleonart scratched his leg, considering. He couldn't resist. "You're on," he said, wading into the undergrowth. "But you'd better do it nicely, or I'll kill you. Where are you? Mercedes?"

"Over here."

Mercedes sat very still, watching Lleonart make his way into the thicket. She was utterly sure of what she was going to do. The boy cursed as prickles scratched his legs and caught in his socks. "Ouch. Where the hell are you?"

"Here. By the big tree."

"Couldn't you have chosen an easier place?" He was already fumbling with his fly, his almond eyes hunting Mercedes. He passed within two yards of her without seeing her, fondling himself.

Then the world went white and silent.

She rose to her feet and stepped after Lleonart.

The rock was already raised high above her head. Swinging in her hand. Curving like a falcon towards Lleonart Cornadó's temple. Striking.

A thud. A jar that went up Mercedes's arm, back into that deep lair inside her. Jolting her.

Lleonart's legs crumpled like ears of corn. He went down without a murmur. Blood spouted from his head. Shuddering oddly, he flopped onto his back.

Then he lay still.

There was a knock at the door and Conchita heard her father's voice calling from downstairs.

"I'm in the kitchen, Papa," she called. He came puffing up the stairs, his cane thudding on the treads. She kissed his florid cheek. He smelled of wine, as he so often did nowadays.

"All alone?"

She nodded. "I don't know where Mercedes is. She's very late. She was due home from school hours ago. I suppose she'll be dreaming on the road somewhere."

"Hmmm." Her father gestured with his cane at the jug of wine on the kitchen bench. "May I?"

She smiled. "If you must drink at this hour."

"What's the hour got to do with it?" He tucked the cane under his arm, lifted the jug and drank deeply. His moustache was almost all white now and the wine stained it red.

"Aren't you going to sit down?" she invited.

"I'm not staying long." He took another long gulp and put the jug down. Leaning heavily on the cane, he began to fret at the smooth-worn handle with his thumbs. "Look here," he said abruptly, "I came to talk to you."

Conchita smiled. "What about?"

"About that girl."

"You mean Mercedes?" She cocked her head. Under the lard

that covered his features and made them expressionless, she could detect emotion. "What is it, Papa?" she asked gently.

"I want you to take her away."

"Take her away where?"

"I want both of you to come and live with me. And her great-aunts. Away from Eduard."

She laughed in sheer surprise. "Papa, don't be silly. Francesc is my husband. He's Mercedes's father."

"Francesc is not her father," Marcel retorted.

"Of course Francesc is her father."

"No, he's not. And don't think I don't know what Francesc is doing to the girl. He's filling the child's head with dangerous rubbish, Conchita. Poisoning her. Turning the child into a little anarchist. Teaching her to think that throwing bombs and burning down factories is the right way to behave." He glared at her. "How can you permit it? Do you want her to grow up like *that*, full of bullet holes and hatred?"

Her mouth tightened. "She could do a lot worse than grow up like her father."

"That man is *not* her father," Marcel snapped. "And what's more, the girl knows."

"She knows what?"

Marcel belched, covering his mouth with his hand. He looked at the floor suddenly. "She *knows*."

Conchita froze, staring at her father with eyes that were suddenly cold. "What are you talking about, Papa?"

"Look at the way the girl is doing at school! She used to be top of the class. Now she's the dolt. She used to be such a good little girl. Now she's a fury—"

"You said Mercé knows," Conchita cut in quietly. "What did you mean by that?"

"She had to know." The old man began jabbing at the ground with his cane, like a petulant child. "She had to know sometime, didn't she?"

"You told her," she whispered, feeling hollow. "You told her that Francesc is not her father!"

"Is that such a crime?"

"I can't believe it," Conchita said, sitting down. "When did you tell her?"

"When Francesc did that terrible thing to her. With the red-hot coin."

"All those months ago?" Conchita was white and trembling. "You mean the girl has known for all these months, almost a *year*?"

Her eyes welled with tears of grief. Suddenly she knew what had changed Mercedes. Understood it all. "How could you? How could you do such a thing, Papa?"

"It's the truth, isn't it?" her father blustered. "She had to know."

"And you thought you would be the one to tell her?" Fury flashed in her. The child had been dealing with this horror. With no one to comfort her. With no one to explain to her. "You thought you would take that decision?"

"It had to be taken," he said defensively. "You know how I love that girl. When she came rushing into my house, screaming with pain, with that horrible thing on her palm—" He shrugged. "You'll say I was wrong. But I could have killed Eduard at that moment. If he'd been standing there in front of me, I could have shot him with a pistol."

"It was a vile thing to do!"

"It was a vile thing he did to Mercé. What right had he to do such a thing?" Marcel Barrantes asked, his voice rising to a shout. "Just because her *real* father chose to make her a present! It's not as if *he* showers the girl with largesse! Why, he barely gives her a centavo to buy a sweet with. The girl might as well be the daughter of a tinker!"

Her fury had lasted long enough to dry her tears. Now it was gone. She rose. "Papa, go home," she said quietly. "Don't come here again."

"Is that it?" he said loudly, putting one fist on his hip. "My own daughter is throwing me out of her house, like a dog?"

"Just go," she repeated.

"After all I've done for you! After all I've put up with from you and that fanatical boor—"

"When Francesc finds out what you've done," she said softly, "he'll probably kill you. So just go home, Papa. And stay away from us."

Marcel Barrantes opened his mouth to shout back at her. But there was something in her eyes that silenced him.

He shook his cane impotently, then turned on his heel and stumped clumsily down the stairs.

She bit her knuckles to fight back more tears. The full horror was only beginning to sink in. They'd thought there was nothing more to the change in Mercedes than Francesc's harshness.

God, how much damage had been done to the child? What had she been going through all these months? Never saying. Just staring at them with those betrayed, hating eyes. Jesus.

Where was Francesc? Where was Mercedes?

Suddenly she felt her heart turn over inside her. *Where was Mercedes?* She knew in her blood that something terrible had happened.

Lleonart's eyes were open, gazing up at the blue sky. So was his mouth. His blood dribbled into the soil from the hole in his temple.

Mercedes stared down at him, the rock clutched in her hand. She wasn't sure if Lleonart was dead or not. But she knew she had to finish it now. Crush Lleonart's head with the rock, then drag his body into the ochre mine, down the darkest and deepest tunnel. Then go home as if nothing had happened.

She straddled Lleonart's chest and raised the rock high above her head, ready to smash down into the freckled face.

Lleonart was still alive. He heaved suddenly and made a strange gurgling sound. "No—"

Mercedes lowered the rock, then raised it again, aiming at Lleonart's forehead.

"No! Do—on't!" The hazel eyes weren't sly any more. They were pleading. They bulged with naked desperation. Imploring. His face was so white that the freckles were as dark as the blood that now also spattered his skin. "Don't," he managed to gargle. "Ple—ase, ah, please—no—"

Mercedes wanted to do it. Wanted to carry it through. But she found she couldn't.

The shivering electricity had gone out of her. The shouting rage had stopped echoing inside her mind. She felt empty. Calm, almost tranquil.

She felt as though someone was pushing her upraised arm gently downward. Slowly, she lowered the rock.

Lleonart's eyes rolled whitely backwards, then fluttered closed.

Mercedes lifted her head and looked around. Yellow ochre, blue sky, green trees. Heat and the chirping of insects. A lizard scuttled across a rock.

She felt Lleonart's chest heaving between her thighs and wondered why she hadn't killed him, after all.

"I'm so—rry," Lleonart gasped. "Sorry . . ."

"Shut up," someone said calmly.

Lleonart's eyes flickered.

To have been prepared to kill him, she decided, to have been able to kill him, was just as good as having done it. Just as good.

Yes. Just as good, any day. Really, it was so easy. Now that she had learned how.

She got off him and squatted over his face. She pulled her pants aside. Lleonart lay still as she voided her bladder on him. He was too dazed even to turn his face aside. Doing it gave her no pleasure. It was simply justice.

She stood up when she had finished.

"Now you know what it's like," Mercedes heard her own voice say, matter-of-factly. "I should have killed you. You were lucky."

Lleonart started to cry as she walked away.

4.

~Spoiled

summer 1953

Prescott, Arizona

He thinks of his father's voice as a scythe. It sweeps through the church, and the unrighteous fall like corn before the blade.

Joel is nine years old. He sits in the front pew, beside his mother.

The Reverend Eldred Lennox is a brimstone preacher of the militant variety. A hundred years ago, he would have worn a Colt over his cassock. He rants his sermon and his aim is deadly. The guilty quake in their Sunday shoes.

But after a while, exhaustion sits heavy on Joel's lids.

His chin nods onto his chest. His spine relaxes and he begins to slide imperceptibly off the hard, polished seat.

When the child crashes onto the floor, there are giggles throughout the congregation, hastily stifled by handkerchiefs and prayer books.

The Reverend Lennox pauses in his sermon as his son picks himself up and creeps back to his place.

The enormity of what he has done appalls Joel. His mother does not even deign to look at him. But there are dark patches on her bony cheeks, and her mouth is as tight as a scar.

The anticipation of punishment fills him with despair.

· · ·

When the front door has closed on them, his mother whirls on him with blazing eyes. "You made your father a laughingstock in front of those clodhoppers and their fat wives. A priest of God!"

She thrusts him into the corner and presses his face against the wall. The flat smell of the paint is familiar, comforting in his misery. He feels the full weight of his worthlessness, his powerlessness.

Father is counting the collection money. "Four dollars and thirty-five cents," he says bitterly. "The godly are generous with the servant of the Lord."

"Four dollars? God damn them," Mother cries. "May God smite their pious faces and tight wallets. What do they think we live on? Manna from heaven?"

"The afternoon service will bring in less."

Mother turns on the child violently. "Why should I feed him, on four dollars and thirty-five cents, so that he can sleep on the Sabbath day?"

"He is our son, Miriam."

Mother laughs sharply. "Well. An empty belly might keep him awake during the afternoon service."

Joel hears Mother preparing the meal in the kitchen. The food is brought in and put on the table behind him.

Father prays. Joel stands unmoving, listening to them eat. The smell of the food fills his mouth with saliva and he has to swallow. He closes his eyes. His stomach hurts.

After the meal, Mother pulls him away from the wall.

"Well?" she demands.

He does not look up. "I'm sorry, Mother," he whispers.

She thrusts a plate into his hands. On it is a piece of bread and a slice of meat.

"In the cellar," she says curtly.

"Mama, no!"

"Take him, Eldred."

Father grasps his hand and pulls him down the stairs, into the dark.

At the cellar door Joel tries to pull away. The food falls off the plate. The blackness smells of mould and the grave. Within, among the shadows, are the shapes of monsters.

Terror chokes him. His eyes fill with tears. "Dada, no!"

Father thrusts him into the cellar. "I want you to understand the meaning of darkness, Joel. So that you can understand what it means to offend God and have his back turned on you."

"Dada, please! Please!"

The door slams. The bolt rattles.

Black, black. The hell he has heard about since babyhood. Shapes throng around him. Claws grab, jaws gape. He cannot see them, but they are coming for him.

Whimpering, he stumbles to the door. It does not yield. He hurls his body against the wood.

Again and again.

september 1956

Los Angeles

Things were rustling in Eden's room.

"Over there. . . ."

"What about this one?"

"Shhh. . . ."

"Here. . . ."

She snuggled into the pillow. She was not ready to wake yet.

"Look at her, Mercedes." (Daddy's voice.)

"She's exquisite." (Mama's voice.)

"Look how long her eyelashes are. She's all pink cheeks and black hair and white satin."

She felt Mama's hand touch her face. "She's ours."

"Eden . . . wake up, darling. It's your birthday!"

"Open those beautiful big green eyes."

She yawned and peered up at them. It was morning. Mama drew the curtains. Her room turned bright and hazy. Sunlight splashed on the toy cupboard, on the satin canopy over her bed, on the pink-striped wallpaper.

Daddy grinned.

"Hi there, Daddy's treasure. Forgotten your birthday?"

Her eyes widened. "Oh!"

Her room was transformed. Boxes. Cylinders. Packages. Tissue paper in green, red, gold. Ribbons and lace and bows. Presents of every shape and size and colour. For her.

"Which one shall we unwrap first?" Mama asked. "This big green one? Or the little gold one? What about this one, all in pink ribbons?"

"That one!"

She ran to it. It stood in the corner, the biggest parcel of all, way bigger than she was.

"It's a very special present from Mama and Daddy. Shall we help you open it?"

"She'll manage," Mama said. "Pull the ribbon, Eden."

She fumbled, enthralled, with the wrapping. At last the paper rustled aside.

Eden was lost. The rocking horse had brilliant eyes and a snow-white mane. His harness was red leather with brass stirrups. His hoofs gleamed black.

"His name's Dapple."

Eden buried her face in the shimmering white mane.

"I think she's just fallen in love."

Daddy lifted Eden into the saddle. She took the reins in her hands. She urged with her hips and the wooden horse dipped and reared with slow majesty.

Daddy stuck his pipe in his mouth. He put his arm around Mama. "Well, she soon got the hang of that."

They watched her rock. Eden had forgotten all the other presents. She was entranced, hypnotized by the motion.

Mama smiled oddly. "You know, I never had toys. Not toys like this. I played with my mother's rabbits. Bits of wood."

"Eden's never going to want for anything," Daddy said.

Prescott

"Your Daddy's sech a fine man, Joel."

"Yes, ma'am."

She glances at the sharp white steeple that rises over yonder, against the deep cobalt of an Arizona autumn sky. "Sech a true Christian. A man of the highest moral fibre."

"Yes, ma'am."

"You jest take it easy, now."

Mrs. Schultz goes back into the house.

Today is Saturday, the day he gardens for Mr. and Mrs.

Schultz. He gets twenty cents for the afternoon, which, of course, he must put in the collection box. He has been clearing stones from the dusty yard. The sun is like a hammer. Now he sits in the sparse shade of a mesquite tree, resting.

He takes the wax out of his pocket and begins molding it in his hands. Old Mr. Schultz, who keeps bees up in the hills, has given it to him, a scrap at a time, over the past year. Now he has a lump the size of a tennis ball, grey from endless kneading.

His lean fingers work unceasingly. He stares in fascination at the wax as it metamorphoses. It is a little thin coyote. In seconds it becomes a face. It lengthens into a snake, contracts into a frog, humps into a tortoise.

The endless succession of transformations fascinates him. It is as if his fingers are things apart from him and he merely a watcher.

He is a thin child, already showing signs of growing tall and rangy. His face is taut, pale. The nose is slightly hooked. The eyes are dark, almost black. They are striking. They hold a watchful glitter.

Joel's fingers move and suddenly his father's face is there in the wax. Aquiline, thin-lipped, it has materialized as if by magic.

He holds it close to his eyes and stares at it. The likeness is uncanny. It glares at him angrily.

He digs his thumbs quickly into the eye sockets. The skull balloons, explodes. He mashes the face into a Gila monster, squat and ugly.

Immediately, guilt sears him.

"My, my," Mrs. Schultz says, making him gasp. "You're real clever with that stuff."

Joel stuffs the wax into his pocket and stumbles to his feet. "Mr. Schultz gave it to me!"

"Why, of course he did. I know that. You can jest about make it do what you want, hey?"

"I'll get back to work, now."

"No need to hide it. You got a talent, son." She gives him a glass of lemonade and watches him indulgently, thinking what a strange, old-fashioned child he is, so full of fits and starts.

Many people say the Reverend Lennox's son is a simpleton. Mrs. Schultz knows he is only a little odd. Different from the others in some way she cannot quite pin down.

He is watching her in that odd, peering way he has, like a little old man. His mouth is working.

"Ma'am?"

"Yes, Joel."

"Ma'am? Please don't tell my father."

"'Bout what, son?"

"'Bout the wax, ma'am."

She stares at him. She is sixty-three years old and though she has never had a child of her own, she flatters herself that she knows something about children. But this boy baffles her. You never know what he is going to do or say next. Perhaps that is part of his charm.

"Now don't tell me," she says jocularly, "that your Daddy don't allow you to have an old itty bit of wax!"

"*Please*, ma'am."

She sees suddenly that his dark eyes are swimming with tears. Instinctively, she reaches out and touches his shoulder. The small thin body is quivering like a greyhound's.

"Well, of course I won't, if you don't want me to. It'll just be our secret. That satisfy you?"

"Yes, ma'am," he says.

She can tell by his face that he does not believe her.

"I promise, Joel," she says gently.

He nods uncertainly. Nothing adults have ever done to him has led him to trust what they say or do. He hurries away from the woman and begins gathering the stones in the dust.

Though he works so hard at school, his grades are poor. He is put at the back of the class and can barely make out the blackboard; the teacher's chalk marks dance in a dim scribble that makes no sense to him. His eyes ache and his brain buzzes like a trapped fly.

Even the Good Book is a torture. He has to memorize a passage each day. From the book of Joel: *And I will restore to you the years that the locust hath eaten.* But although he has a quick and retentive memory, the words will not stand still to be caught; they dance on the page and make his eyeballs throb. His evening recitations for Mother and Father end in tears.

He sleeps badly, with nightmares and sweats. Confused dreams press his bladder, making him shame himself by wetting the bed. During the day his exhausted mind fades and he falls into fresh errors.

The cellar terrifies him. Each time is worse than the time before. The suffocating horror of that hole is more than he can bear.

The monsters are only pieces of old furniture. The grasping talons are only an old iron bedstead. But the terror does not leave him. The terror is rooted deep in his mind and will never go away.

He knows he feels terror because he is wicked. The righteous are strong in the Lord. But he is not of the righteous.

Not of the righteous.

spring 1957

Los Angeles

Mama took her to Dan Cormack's Riding Academy. Mr. Cormack had a face like seamed leather and his hands were rough, but he had kind eyes. He said Eden was just old enough to start on one of the Shetland ponies.

"Get the little gal kitted out," he drawled. "We'll see what we can do with her."

So Mama and Françoise took her to the riding shop on Rodeo Drive.

They bought jodhpurs, pink and fawn and white. They got a velvet riding hat and a little whip. They bought boots, English leather, because English leather was the best.

Eden looked at herself in the shop mirror, wearing her hat, her jodhpurs and her boots.

"You look beautiful, *chérie*," Françoise said.

Everything was wrapped in boxes with ribbons and put in the trunk of the Cadillac. The next week, she started riding lessons with Dan Cormack.

Mr. Cormack's Academy was in Laurel Canyon. There was a stable yard with doors all the way round. A horse's head poked out of each door. Eden always brought a bag of carrots so she could give each one a little treat.

The horse she rode was a Shetland pony called Mister. He

wasn't much bigger than Dapple the rocking horse, but he was a lot harder to ride.

It made you ache all over. But she tried very hard, because Mama and Daddy said if she did well, they would buy her a pony of her own soon. And by and by she could jiggle around the ring without falling off once, though her hat would tip down over her eyes until she could hardly see.

"That's not too bad," Mr. Cormack said approvingly. "Ain't gonna keep you on a Shetland forever, neither. Pretty soon, gonna have to graduate you to something with a longer stride."

After her lesson, she loved to lean on the fence and watch the jumping.

There was a tall, dark boy who jumped a snow-white horse called Mahler. Mahler soared over the jumps like a cloud, his mane and tail streaming out behind him. The beauty of it made Eden's heart lurch inside her.

"I'm going to do that," she told Mr. Cormack. "I'm going to jump like the boy on that white horse."

"It's called a grey," Mr. Cormack said.

"Just like him," Eden said.

spring 1958

Prescott

"It's not that you don't have the ability," Miss Greaves says, giving him the report card and folding her hands. "You're a clever boy. I won't say you're the most forthcoming child I ever taught. You've never been sociable. Have you?"

Joel stares at Miss Greaves's shoes, which are brown and masculine. He does not know what to answer.

"Well, you may be a hermit crab, but you're intelligent enough. We know that. You've just stopped caring. Your exercise books are a disgrace. Your writing is an insult to your teachers. I do my best to help you, Joel. I give you more time than the rest. But you've just stopped caring."

He glances up at her with that strange, peering look of his. "No, I haven't," he whispers.

"You sure about that?"

"Yes, ma'am."

She stares at the bowed head and wonders what is happening to the child. She does not like the Reverend Eldred Lennox or his hatchet-faced wife. She is herself a Presbyterian and does not care for rigid hellfire creeds like the Reverend Lennox's.

She feels a little sorry for the family's straitened circumstances. But then, if the Reverend Lennox had a little more charity in his doctrine, she believes the world would show a little more charity to him. Hellfire is not a prosperous creed.

She pities the boy. It cannot be easy, growing up in that biting atmosphere of lye soap and sanctity. God alone knows what sort of mother that woman must make, with her vicious temper disguised as righteousness and her meanness of spirit masquerading as piety.

But that is none of her business. Her business is the child's academic performance and she applies herself to this with all the staunch dedication of a small-town schoolteacher.

"Well, if you're sure you haven't stopped trying, there must be something else the matter," she says decisively. "I'm going to call the school doctor next week and get him to check you over. Your eyes, especially. Okay?"

"Yes, ma'am," he whispers.

He walks out into the afternoon sunlight. The smell of creosote bush is faint on the air. It has not rained for months in the mile-high city and everything has become tinged with dust.

He sets off home. He has a mile to walk. He wishes it were fifty.

Mother hardly bothers to disguise her hate for him any more. It is there in her eyes, in her voice. She begrudges him every morsel of food, every inch of space that he takes up. He must be silent and motionless in the house to escape her wrath. Father ignores him. Father is wrapped up in the Lord. But Mother has made him her scapegoat.

He knows what a scapegoat is. A creature upon whom the sins of others are laid.

"But the goat, on which the lot fell to be the scapegoat shall be presented alive before the LORD, to make an atonement with him and to let him go for a scapegoat into the wilderness" (Leviticus, 16:10).

If only he could go out into the wilderness like the scapegoat and never come back. The desert is a wilderness. But that would mean death. The desert kills.

He stops and opens the report card. He holds it close to his eyes and squints at the comments. They are chilling.

Arithmetic: Poor.
History: Extremely poor.
Geography: Very poor.
Art: Shows imagination, but neatness very poor.
Natural Science: Weak.
English: Must try harder.
Religion: Adequate.
General Comment: Joel's progress gives great concern to all of us. If he does not learn to apply himself harder, he will fail this year.

But how can he apply himself harder? There is nothing in his life but work and punishment. He has no toys except his ball of wax. He has no friends. He swallows the lump in his throat. He cannot apply himself any harder than he does. It is impossible.

He dares not take this document home.

He sits for a long time under the shade of a picket fence. Then, out of his desperation, comes a kind of weary courage. He gathers himself together and drags himself home to face his mother and father.

Who will restore to him the years that the locust hath eaten?

Joel cowers in the corner as the storm rages. Father sits rigid, his Bible in his lap. Mother and Miss Greaves claw at one another.

"I am astonished at the presumption," Mother rasps. "Coming into our house with such filthy accusations!"

"I have the doctor's report right here, Mrs. Lennox." The paper shakes slightly in Miss Greaves's hand as she holds it out. "Read it for yourself."

Mother thrusts the paper aside. "You had no right to bring that quack to our child without our permission."

"The State of Arizona gives me the right to call in the school doctor if I feel that a child in my care needs medical treatment—"

"As if to say we abuse our own son."

"The plain and simple fact is that Joel is not well. Quite apart from the fact that he needs glasses to read with, his body is covered with marks and bruises."

"Joel is incurably clumsy," Father says. "He bumps into things."

"That cannot account for so many bruises!"

"Do not raise your voice to my husband under our own roof!"

Father leans forward. "We have sacrificed ourselves for that boy."

"For that defiant and delinquent child!"

"I have never found Joel to be defiant or delinquent." Miss Greaves is struggling to keep her voice level.

"We have your own reports to confirm his shiftlessness," Mother says.

"Perhaps," Father cuts in, "the schoolmistress is trying to create a smokescreen to cover defects in her own teaching methods."

Miss Greaves flushes and sits up. "There may well be defects in my teaching methods," she says tightly. "But I have always taken a special interest in the boy."

"Please," Mother says with a bitter smile, "spare us your frustrated spinsterhood, Miss Greaves."

"I beg your pardon?"

"Joel is not your child, no matter how much you might wish it."

The schoolteacher's face changes from red to white. "No," she replies with difficulty, "he is not my child. It might be better for him if he were."

"So," Mother jeers. "Now we get to the bottom of this charade!"

"I know a troubled child when I see one," Miss Greaves quavers. She points to Joel, who is cringing in his chair, his hands clasped over his ears. "Look at him. Look at the marks on his chest and back! Are you proud of the way he is?"

"Get out of this house," Mother hisses.

"Let her spit on us," Father says bleakly. "Let her smite us."

"What do you do to him?" Miss Greaves demands, looking from the woman to the man. "Just what is it you do to him to make him so afraid?"

"How dare you?" Mother says, her eyes gleaming with fury. "How dare you?"

"He's terrified of his own shadow. He's as thin as a rake. He has the marks of beatings and he falls asleep in my classroom. How do you account for that?"

"We do not have to account to you! You are an impertinent, malicious, meddlesome old maid!"

Miss Greaves is breathing through her nose. "I am not the subject here. Joel is."

"You wish to exact a humiliation from me," Father says. "Very well. Neither my wife nor I have ever raised a hand to that boy. Are you satisfied now, Miss Greaves?"

"No," she says quietly. "I am not satisfied."

"He is the spawn of Satan," Mother bursts out. Joel begins to cry silently.

"That poor, quivering boy, the spawn of Satan?" Miss Greaves is now even whiter. "He is your son!"

Mother sneers. "There are things about your precious pupil that you cannot even guess at, schoolmistress."

"What do you mean?"

"'A good tree bringeth not forth corrupt fruit,'" Father recites ponderously; "'neither doth a corrupt tree bring forth good fruit. For every tree is known by his own fruit. For of thorns men do not gather figs, nor of a bramble bush gather they grapes.'"

Miss Greaves stares. "Are you saying that he is not your—" She bites off the words. They stare at her in silence. Finally she rises to her feet. "Nothing matters but the boy's health," she says. "I am more determined than ever that Joel shall receive the help he needs. I am speaking as his schoolteacher. Not in my private capacity. Do you understand me? If Joel does not have glasses to read with by the end of next week, I will take him to the optician myself. And if I ever see the signs of violence on his body again, I shall take the matter to the police."

Without looking at Joel, Miss Greaves walks out.

Mother slams the door behind her and locks it. She turns to Joel. Her face is terrible.

Santa Barbara

She loved going to the airfield.

Mama and Daddy usually took her on weekends. There were six planes altogether, white and red, with the words along the side:

VAN BUREN AIR FREIGHT. Of course, the planes were almost never all there together. Usually there were just a couple, parked by the hangars. The others would be flying.

She herself had been up heaps of times already, of course, and was quite blasé about the whole thing.

The planes went as far as South America. The pilots often brought her presents: masks, carvings, toys. Every time she went to the airfield, there was sure to be something waiting for her, something exotic and beautiful.

Once, someone had brought her a little black monkey from Colombia, but Mama wouldn't let her keep it. And once Miguel Fuentes even brought a real shrunken head, with its wrinkly mouth stitched shut.

"Musta talked too much," Miguel guffawed. Of course, she wasn't allowed to keep the head either.

Miguel Fuentes took care of things for Daddy. He was squat and ugly and everybody was frightened of him, but when he hoisted her up and grinned at her, his eyes twinkled like a laughing dog's.

But this weekend, Mama and Daddy didn't take her to the airfield as usual. They all drove up to Santa Barbara in the new car.

The car was a Cadillac Eldorado Brougham, white and tan, and Daddy put the top down. The breeze was warm and smelled of pine trees. Mama put on a scarf and dark glasses. Eden sat in the back with Françoise, the French *au pair*.

There were mountainous clouds in the sky, white and gold against the blue. When they reached Santa Barbara, they stopped for ice cream. The sea was vast and green and boys were surfing on the swells.

Then they went to see the Plot. It was just earth and trees and the sea down beyond the pines.

Eden licked ice cream off her sticky fingers. "When will there be a house?" she asked.

"Soon, darling. They'll be laying the foundations in a few months."

"Can I have a pony?" Eden asked.

"Of course you can have a pony. When you're a little older."

"How much older?"

Daddy came to study the drawings. "Know what I was thinking for the bathrooms? Green onyx and gold taps."

Mama shook her head. "Gold taps are vulgar," she said. "And

green onyx is positively obscene. We'll have white marble, the way we planned."

"How about white marble and gold taps?" Daddy said.

"Marginally better. But still ostentatious."

Daddy laughed. "Honey, this is California, not Europe. The year is 1958. It's okay to be ostentatious."

He waltzed Mama across the grass. Mama started laughing. She had a laugh that was low and soft and made you want to laugh too.

"What's vulgar?" Eden asked.

"Money's vulgar." Daddy grinned around his pipe. "But money can achieve anything. Anything at all. You remember that, honey."

Prescott

He is frantic in the darkness.

He can hear something moving around him. Scuttling and scratching. A rat. Or worse.

He has been down here for so long. So long!

It is usually two hours. Sometimes three. This time it has been a day and a night. He is exhausted and starving.

The light in his mind has been fading. Like a torch left on too long, it dims and flickers.

The creature scuttles. Joel shudders, eyes staring wide, though he can see absolutely nothing. His fingers work together. He has hidden the wax in the yard. He knows better than to bring it into the house. She finds everything. So he has been molding shapes in his mind. But the inner light is going out and he cannot work in the dark.

They have forgotten him. He is going to die in this darkness.

The air has grown foul. He can no longer fill his lungs and breathes in short gasps. The light in his mind dims to a red point. He can hear rodent teeth scrape at wood or cardboard. What if it noses his own warm flesh? What if it fastens its teeth into his thigh, his face?

Panic rises in him. The red point in his mind goes out. The darkness rushes in. He has been abandoned to the forces of evil.

The rat scuttles across his feet.

He kicks out wildly. His shin tears on something hard and sharp.

Something grabs him from behind. He fights away. Hooks grasp his clothing, scour his arms. He fights, struggles. He is enmeshed.

Scaly things writhe around his feet. Fangs are bared at his throat. He feels leathery wings fold around his face. The terror rushes up from his stomach to his brain.

The monsters are pressing in from all sides. He flails with his arms. His hands smash into things he cannot see. There are noises, pain.

His breath comes in great whoops, but the oxygen-poor air gives him no energy. His heart hammers against his breastbone as though it wants to burst out of his body.

He succumbs to the deepest instinct of all. To run.

The cellar is only a few yards wide and crowded with lumber. He runs into a pile of chairs. Something rams into his stomach, winding him. Something else hits his mouth, mashing his lips against his teeth.

This is how he gets the bruises on his body.

The choking air makes his lungs heave. He writhes over the monsters, feeling their bony carapaces and knuckles beneath him. He is sinking into their clutches. The horror is driving him mad. He claws out with hooked fingers.

Then, his heart bursting, he lies still.

A streak of gold. His nails have clawed a streak of light in the darkness.

It does not fade. It glows in front of him. He stares at it for a while; then he reaches out with trembling fingers and scratches again.

More streaks appear.

Wild with sudden hope, he scrabbles at the flecks of brightness with both sets of nails. They multiply and grow. Soon, he is dazzled by the brilliant scribble he has made in the darkness.

He is clawing at a small window that has been painted out. He presses his face to the glass and squints. Through the scratched paint he can see red earth. Earth and flowers at eye level. The world.

The back yard.

The little window under the back porch. Beside the water barrel. The little window that has always been painted white.

He has found a way out.

He pounds on the window, but it has been nailed shut. There is no catch to open it.

He screams.

There is no one to hear him.

He is desperate to escape. He grasps around him for a tool. His fingers close on something. It is the arm of a chair, loose and squeaky. He wrenches the arm back and forth until it splinters and comes away. He batters the window with it.

A pane smashes, showering him with glass. Then another. The hot air of the outside world breathes into the cellar. He keeps battering at the window until all four panes are broken. He can hardly see for the bright dazzle of sunlight.

He hammers at the jagged wooden cross that remains until it too gives way.

Then he claws his way through the little hole. He is oblivious of the cuts and gashes he is making in his knees and hands.

He crawls into the sunlight and feels its heat sweep down on him. He is crying, partly with pain, partly with sheer relief. He staggers to his feet, blinded and exhausted. The desert air is clean and dry.

"Oh, my good God Almighty! Oh, land sakes. Joel? Is that you?"

He squints blearily. Mrs. Pascoe, the next-door neighbour, has heard the noise of breaking glass. She is staring over the fence at him. Her jaw hangs open.

She is looking at a trembling boy, masked with filth and broken glass. Blood trickles down his legs. Blood seeps from his mouth and nose. His fingernails are broken.

She cups her own cheeks in her hands.

"Oh, land sakes." Her voice quavers into a scream. "Reverend! Reverend Lennox! Reverend Lennox! Reverend Lennox!"

Father comes around the corner.

He stops short when he sees Joel. His bony face turns white.

"He came crawlin' outa there!" Mrs. Pascoe points a shaky finger at the broken window. "I heard the glass breaking, and when I looked he was crawlin' outa there, like a—like a rat!"

Joel meets his father's colourless eyes. He sees the stupefaction there and knows the enormity of what he has done. But he is too weary to care.

"I 'most died of the shock, Reverend. That boy's like a wild animal! What in Hades were you doing down in the cellar, Joel?"

It is Father who answers. His voice is rusty. "He has obviously been exploring where he should not have done. He"—father's voice catches—"he has locked himself in the cellar somehow. Your mother has been looking for you, Joel."

Joel stares at his father.

"That is the truth," Father says, more harshly. "Is it not, Joel? You went exploring in the cellar and locked yourself in. That is what happened. Is it not?"

Joel shakes his head slightly.

Mrs. Pascoe sighs. "That boy ain't normal, Reverend."

"He is afflicted." Father reaches out his hand. "Come, Joel. You are filthy. You must be washed."

Joel does not move. His father has lied. He has heard his father lie to Mrs. Pascoe. It is a revelation so vast that nothing else seems to matter any more. His father has told a lie.

The Reverend Eldred Lennox takes his son's hand and leads him into the house. Mrs. Pascoe watches them go, clucking her tongue.

Inside the house, Mother is waiting. She has been watching through the window.

Like Father, she is white-faced.

"He is an abomination," she whispers. "He was conceived in evil. He is only capable of evil."

"He climbed on the chairs," Father says. Joel can hear his voice tremble. "He reached the window and smashed it."

"What did that woman see?"

"She saw him emerging."

"What did you tell her?"

"I told her the boy had locked himself in the cellar."

Mother stares at Joel with loathing, almost with fear. "He is evil, Eldred. Look at him. He should never have come into this house. He cannot stay here. We cannot control him."

"We will control him," Father says. "We shall control him."

"How?"

Father thrusts him forward. "Wash him, Miriam. I am going to board up the window he has broken."

Mother gets a bowl of water and a cloth. She does not speak as she sponges Joel's face, arms and legs. The sponge is cruel on his cuts, but he does not cry out.

Father lied to Mrs. Pascoe. Father hid the truth.

He has not thought it until now. But he has known it, somewhere inside, for a long time. That Father and Mother are not like other parents. That what they do to him is shameful. Inhuman.

It dawns on him for the first time in his life that it is they who are wicked. Not he.

He looks into his mother's face. It is gaunt, pinched. It has the beaked nose and hooded eyes of a bird of prey. Her mouth is thin. Her hair is grey, colourless. Her eyes are grey, colourless. Yet she has a colour. Her colour is cruelty.

Under the piety, under the godliness, they commit sins worse than any of his.

"Don't look at me!" she hisses. But he cannot tear his eyes away from her, until she slaps his face aside. He feels the sting of the blow almost with relief.

"Stand there."

Mother takes the bowl to the kitchen. The water now looks like raspberry juice.

He hears Father's hammer echoing in the cellar. He stares at the room. It is plain and bare. The furniture is ugly. There are no ornaments, no paintings on the walls. Nothing to suggest that the people who live here love their dwelling, or take pride in it. The things that have been chosen are as hard, as angular, as comfortless as possible.

He sees, as if for the first time, how wretched his home has been, how much unhappiness he has endured. They have outraged him. If they had simply beaten him, as some children are beaten, it would have been better, cleaner, than what they have done.

Who will restore to him the years that the locust hath eaten?

His emotions churn in him, all the fiercer since he is not a child who possesses the means of expressing his passions. He feels dizzy. He hears Mother and Father talking in whispers. He hears things moving in the cellar.

Then he hears his father's slow tread coming up the stairs.

He hears a rattle of metal and looks up. Father is standing in the doorway.

"You have behaved like a wild animal," Father says. "Like a wild animal, you shall be chained."

Joel sees the shackles in his father's hands.

He turns to flee, but Mother grasps his hair. He fights for his life. He is in the grip of an emotion he has never felt before. He bursts with rage. His wiry body has the strength of desperation, but they drag him down the stairs to the cellar, kicking and clawing.

"I hate you!" he screams. "I hate you! I hate you!"

He tries to kick them, tries to bite, like a dog. He gets Mother's hand in his mouth and closes his jaws on the bony knuckles. Her scream of pain fills him with a fierce, sweet joy.

Mother hits him with all her force across his face. The blow sends him reeling.

"Miriam!" Father yells.

"God forgive me," Mother gasps. She is clutching her hand. "He bit me!"

"Do not strike him," Father says. "That woman—"

"He drove me to it. He is evil!"

"He is our son, Miriam."

"*He is not our son*," Mother bursts out. "Look at his eyes. Those are Satan's eyes. Black, black and evil!"

Father thrusts Joel onto the old bedstead.

Joel no longer resists. His hatred swells in his chest like a flood.

Father puts the manacles around Joel's wrists. They click shut around the slender bones. He loops the chain through the struts of the bedstead and padlocks the chain to the manacles.

Like an animal, he has been fettered.

The man and woman stand looking at him. Joel raises his eyes to them. As he looks at them, he feels a moment of such intense passion that he is almost afraid of himself.

Father takes a breath as though he is going to speak. But something in the boy's eyes stops the words.

He takes Mother's arm and leads her out.

The door slams shut. The darkness envelops him.

april 1960

Santa Barbara

The Fairchilds had a garden party to introduce Mama and Daddy to all their friends in Santa Barbara.

There were around fifty people on the shore of the small artificial lake. In the lake, there were white water lilies and flamingoes.

The birds moved like dainty, elegant women. They were pastel pink, a very fashionable colour that year, and could twist their long necks into knots. Everyone said they were exquisite.

Mr. Fairchild (Uncle Max) had a plastics company and he said that plastics were the thing of the future. Mrs. Fairchild (Aunt Monica) was blond and pretty and English.

The Fairchilds also had a gazebo, all overgrown with scented jasmine and a summerhouse, and a croquet lawn and a tennis court, where Margaret Fairchild had been teaching Eden to play. Margaret was eleven, two years older than Eden.

Despite the flamingoes, the Fairchilds were conservative and occasionally dull. Mama said they were a pair of boring wasps. But Daddy said if he could loosen them up, the Fairchilds were going to be their best friends here in Santa Barbara.

It wouldn't be long, now, before they came up here to live.

The builders had worked steadily since last autumn. The house looked almost like a house, instead of just walls and empty squares. You could make sense of it at last. Daddy had already joined the Santa Barbara Yacht Club and had a boat in the harbour.

"So you're going to Europe next month, Eden," Aunt Monica said, passing a piece of cake to Eden.

Eden nodded, filling her mouth. Mama and Daddy and Aunt Monica and Uncle Max were all standing together in a group, with lots of other people around them.

"You must be so excited. What's your itinerary?"

Daddy answered for her, because she didn't know what an itinerary was. "Paris, Venice, Rome, Barcelona, London."

"How lovely. A grand tour! What fun you're going to have."

"Is she old enough to appreciate it?" Uncle Max asked.

"Eden's always ready for a good time," Daddy said. "While we're in Spain, we're going to look around for some stuff for the house. Antiques. Paintings. Ceramics. See what we can pick up. Prices ought to be pretty good."

"I'll bet your Mama's family are going to spoil you to bits," Uncle Max said to Eden.

An older man named Howell Carlisle, who was a professor of something somewhere, asked Mama, "When did you leave Spain?"

"In 1943."

"So you were there during the Civil War?"

"Yes."

Howell Carlisle accepted some pipe tobacco from Daddy's leather pouch. He puffed to get his pipe going. "Were you in a combat zone?"

"It wasn't like Dominic flying fighters in the Pacific. But there was a lot of fighting."

Howell Carlisle's wife, who had a rouged, wattled face like a turkey, leaned forward. Her eyes were wide. "You saw actual *fighting?*"

Mama looked into her champagne. "I saw people die, if that's what you mean."

"Did you lose relatives?" Aunt Monica asked.

"I don't think there was a single Spanish family who didn't lose relatives."

"Oh, dear," Aunt Monica said contritely, as though she had dropped something that had broken. "I didn't know. I'm sorry."

"I suppose they were massacred by the Reds?" Uncle Max asked.

Mama smiled in an odd way. "No," she answered. "As it happens, they were killed by Franco."

There was a silence. Then Uncle Max said, rather stiffly, "I see. I didn't realize your family were on the other side. I assumed . . ."

Mama sipped her champagne. "I have relations on both sides. Most people did. But my immediate family were Republicans."

"Republicans?" someone asked.

"She means Communists," Howell Carlisle said.

"Technically speaking, they were anarchists."

"Max, you're introducing all your friends to a ferocious red-hot Red." Daddy grinned. "What are they going to say at the country club, eh?"

Uncle Max laughed shortly. He was staring at Mama.

"Well," Aunt Monica said firmly, "*I* never liked Franco. He's a strutting little Fascist. Don't glower at me, Max. Franco's no better than Hitler or Mussolini."

"Whatever he is," Uncle Max said, frowning at Aunt Monica, "he held out against Bolshevism at the right time."

"Gee, Max, that dates you." Daddy laughed. "I haven't heard anybody say *Bolshevism* for years."

"We don't want to talk politics today, Howell," Aunt Monica said briskly. She turned back to Mama. "It must have been a terrible time for you, Mercedes."

"War is war," Mama said. "You can't do anything about it. It just happens to you."

Aunt Monica said, "Surely it's going to be very painful to go back, Mercedes."

"It was all a long time ago."

"Mightn't it be dangerous for you?" Uncle Max asked.

Mama smiled. "Oh, I think General Franco has forgotten about me by now. And I'll be going back on an American passport. Don't worry, Max, I'm not a ferocious red-hot Red. I wouldn't be here if I was, would I?"

"You might be playing Mata Hari." Howell smiled. "Plotting fiendishly to bring Santa Barbara society crashing to the ground."

Everyone laughed. Daddy patted Eden's head. "You're learning things about your Mama today, aren't you?"

Eden was bored with the conversation. "Can we go look at the flamingoes?" she asked.

Margaret took her hand and they walked down to the edge of the lake, which shimmered and dazzled in the midday sunlight.

"We're going to have flamingoes too," Eden said.

A week later, they all went out on Daddy's boat. The yacht harbour was a forest of slender masts that rose out of the water. Behind, the Santa Ynez Mountains were golden and rugged in the early morning light. The palm trees along the quay were rimmed with the same golden light. Only the faintest breeze touched their shaggy heads.

The other way, the open sea was blue and oily-smooth. Their destination was a mauve smudge in the morning haze—the islands of Anacapa, Santa Cruz and Santa Rosa.

The sea was very calm. The boat sliced through the water towards the islands. They grew into humps, then into places and then you could see the trees and hills on them.

When they reached the little bay at Anacapa, they moored the boat and everyone had a swim in the glassy water. There was no one else for miles. They had lunch on deck, cold salads and things.

After lunch it got very hot and very quiet. The grown-ups sat drinking gin, and she and Margaret played games in the shade of the awning, their cheeks and noses masked in white suntan cream.

Then they got sleepy and dozed.

She woke up sometime later, hearing Daddy say, "Come on, Monica. Try it."

"If Mercedes won't, I won't."

"Mercedes has tried it already."

"Then why won't she now?"

"She's just a stick-in-the-mud. Come on."

Eden rolled sleepily to the window and peered down into the cabin. The four of them were sitting around the table. They were all in their swimsuits. Mama wore a black one-piece swimsuit. Aunt Monica wore a powder-blue bikini with white polka dots. There was a bottle of gin and some lemons on the table between them.

Daddy had a big grin on his face.

"Are you sure it isn't addictive, Dominic?"

"I guarantee it isn't," Daddy said. "Sigmund Freud used it. He thought it was wonderful. Wrote a whole book about it."

"Where do you get it from?"

"Oh, one of my pilots brings me a little from Colombia now and then."

Aunt Monica asked Mama, "Is it really worth trying?"

Mama shrugged. "It's an experience."

"I'll go first," Daddy said. He leaned forward, over the table. He sniffed loudly, several times. Then he leaned back and closed his eyes.

There was a silence. "Wow," Daddy said after a while. "Pharmaceutical quality. The best. The very best. Do yourself a favour, Max." He pushed something over to Uncle Max.

Uncle Max hesitated. Then he said, "Okay. If you say so. Here goes."

He held something under his nose and sniffed. They all looked at him.

"Do you feel any different?" Aunt Monica asked.

"Do I feel any different? I don't know. My nose has just vanished. What else am I supposed to feel?" He looked disappointed.

"I'm going to try it," Aunt Monica said.

She also leaned forward. Daddy held something out and said, "Inhale it right into your nose. It won't hurt. Good. Just like that. Now the other one."

Aunt Monica sniffed mightily.

"Mmm," she said, wiping her nose. "Mmm."

"What do you feel?" Uncle Max asked, staring at her.

"My nose has gone numb. And my mouth has turned to ice. Feels so cold. Oh. Oh. Oh, my goodness."

Daddy chuckled. "You like it?"

"Oh, my *goodness*." Aunt Monica's voice rose excitedly. "Oh! That's rather marvelous, isn't it? Oh, my *heart*. I feel wonderful. Quite wonderful."

"Give me another sniff," Uncle Max said. Eden saw Daddy pass him a little tin. He scooped something out with a tiny spoon and snorted it vigorously up his nose.

"Oh, my God." Aunt Monica stood up, her hands on her head. "Oh, my God. This is better than French champagne. This is wonderful. Smashing." She sat down again and started to laugh, peals of gay, silvery laughter. Daddy joined in, throwing his head back. And then, after a while, Uncle Max started chuckling too.

"I guess that *is* pretty good," he said.

Only Mama sat quietly, watching them all, saying nothing.

"I feel so *cool*," Aunt Monica said. "So *delicious*."

"You look pretty delicious too," Daddy said, and they all laughed uproariously.

"This beats anything," Uncle Max said. His beaky face was flushed and his eyes shone. "Beats anything. I feel I could fly. Look, I feel just terrific. Just terrific. Say, Dominic. How long does this last?"

"Oh, about a hundred years," Daddy said, and they all laughed some more.

"What happens if we take some more?" Aunt Monica asked.

"Try it and see," Daddy said.

They started another round of blissful snorting and sniffing out of the tin.

Mama got up and came up the ladder. She stopped short when she saw Eden sitting by the window.

"Eden! I thought you were sleeping."

"I woke up. Mama, what are they doing?" Eden demanded.

"Just fooling around. Let's go for another swim," Mama said. She took Eden's hand. They woke Margaret and went into the sea. The water was cool and translucent. You could see your toes among the pebbles. Little fishes nibbled Eden's tummy, making her giggle.

"Is Spain like this?" Eden asked.

"Yes. Some parts."

The boat was dazzling white on the still sea. Gulls wheeled over the island, squawking lazily. The distant coast shimmered in the afternoon haze.

They paddled in the water. Mama kept her straw hat on, and her face was speckled with light and shade.

Shouts and hilarity came from the boat. Aunt Monica's voice rose above the rest, shrieking with laughter like a schoolgirl. She sounded almost wild.

"Boy," Margaret said. "They're sure having a good time."

All three of them paddled to shore. The laughter from the boat followed them across the water.

"Here's a real beauty." Mama picked up a shell and put her arm around Margaret's shoulders. "Look at the rainbow colours inside."

Eden wandered behind them along the beach, her attention alternating between the shells and the distant boat.

By and by, Daddy came swimming out to them. Eden ran to the edge to meet him.

"Hi, girls." He grinned, dripping and bright-eyed.

"Where are Max and Monica?" Mama asked.

"At a guess, making the beast with two backs. It's gone to their heads. Among other places." Daddy sniggered. "Did you see the way they blossomed? Talk about Dr. Jekyll and Mr. Hyde!"

"I assume you think that was very clever," Mama said in a

quiet, icy voice. She looked furious and her eyes flashed black and dangerous. For a moment, Eden was afraid.

Daddy put his arm around Mama's waist and kissed her neck. "They'll be begging us for more," he said. "Begging us. We'll be their best friends ever. We'll be *the* people to know in Santa Barbara."

Mama pulled away. "I see. This is your idea of winning friends and influencing people."

"Exactly," Daddy said. "This is my idea of winning friends and influencing people."

Mama shook her head. "You fool."

"Those two had to loosen up sometime," Daddy said. "They'll mellow down in a while." He grinned at Eden, bright-eyed. "Come on, honey. Show me your shells."

may 1960

Paris

They descended from a vast, metallic blue dome and found Paris sweltering in summer heat.

Paris smelled unique, of diesel fumes and acrid cigarettes and strange foods. French was a language that growled and spat, like an ill-tempered poodle. In order to speak their tongue, the French had developed lean faces with protruding lips and sunken cheeks, which Eden found slightly alarming. Even Françoise, dealing with porters and taxi drivers, cultivated the same sort of face and looked quite different.

After the quiet luxury of their Super Constellation, it was terrifying to be hurled into the maelstrom of Parisian traffic. This was not the orderly procession of large cars Eden was used to. The cars here were small, shabby and eccentric. They looked and behaved like hungry sharks, snapping at each other's heels, diving at each other's throats.

Eden stared out of the back window of the taxi and wondered where on earth they had come to. The buildings were grand but old. The streets were crowded. The predominant impression of greyness was relieved by stalls of flowers and fruit on the sidewalks. It all looked *old*.

Once they entered the splendour of the Ritz, however, everything changed. A luxurious hush descended. The growling and spitting became a husky purr. Bald heads gleamed as they bowed. It was hard not to be awed by the accomplished fawning of the staff.

Françoise was bright-eyed. "I never thought I would *ever* be staying in the Ritz," she whispered in Eden's ear.

They were conducted to their suite on the fifth floor, their feet sinking soundlessly into plush carpeting.

The chambermaid, a neat little creature in black and white, threw open the doors to their balcony. Eden ran out and looked out over the Place Vendôme. The noise of traffic floated up to her. A sudden feeling of excitement kindled in her. She was in Paris. Far from home. Abroad in the wide world.

Room service brought a bottle of champagne in a silver bucket. They sat on the balcony while their luggage was unpacked and drank it. The murmur of traffic was endless. The whole of Paris seemed to hum, like a giant engine. The very air throbbed faintly with excitement.

"Call your mother and say you've arrived," Mama told Françoise. Françoise hurried to the telephone.

Daddy reached out and took Mama's hand. "How's it feel to be back in Europe?"

Mama didn't answer.

"Why are you sad?" Eden demanded, seeing the shimmer in Mama's eyes.

"I'm not sad," Mama said. "I just feel happy. Strange and happy."

After the champagne, though they were all tired, Mama and Daddy took her for a walk among the marble statues and clipped hedges of the Tuileries.

Eden floated on a sea of roses. The smell of Paris was starting to intoxicate her. An old man was selling *brioches* from a little handcart. Mama bought one for her. It was fragrant and light. It had a taste that lingered on her palate with a long, sweet note, like new music. The grand tour had begun.

•   •   •

Paris was a kaleidoscope that never ceased changing. Certain arrangements of lights and colours would stay with her for the rest of her life.

Roses struggling sweetly to escape from their intricate formal beds.

The neon rainbow of the city by night.

A street circus, performing impromptu in a cobbled boulevard: a clown in yellow and purple with orange hair and a scarlet nose, who danced in green shoes a yard long; a giant in a leopard skin who lifted huge weights in his teeth; a man who blew great plumes of flame out of his mouth; a dwarf who collected pennies.

The olive face of the Mona Lisa, smirking at her from the depths of centuries.

Pigeons rising in a cloud around the Arc de Triomphe when the hourly cannon went off.

The taste of bread and chocolate, an impossible combination that worked so marvellously.

The ride up the Eiffel Tower. And when they'd reached the top, with all Paris spread out at her feet, Papa went to the souvenir stand and bought her a little perfume bottle—eggshell-thin glass, painted with swirls of purple and gold, with a gilt stopper. For years, that little bottle was to sum up French chic for her.

Magic was always waiting. Even the Seine, on first acquaintance a dull-brown river, could catch fire. Years later, Eden would remember standing on a bridge at twilight and watching the hulk of Notre Dame reflected in a sheet of flame, a moment of enchantment.

It was in the kaleidoscope of Paris that she first began to become aware of herself as Eden, a person apart from all others, different from all others; and in Paris too, that she began to see Mama and Daddy in the same way, as people with their own distinct lives and characters.

The first realization came to her sitting at a café on the Champs-Élysées, watching the endless stream of traffic, the endless parade of people. The flow of humanity never stopped. Like a drop of water falling into a pool, the thought fell into her mind that she was apart from them all. No matter how many others there were, she was Eden. And Eden was Eden.

The second came to her in a famous modiste's shop in the Faubourg St.-Honoré.

They had given her a little gilt chair to sit on while Mama tried on clothes. She found herself thinking that Mama fitted in here. Back home in California, she was always somehow different. Watching the other customers, it occurred to Eden that Mama was one of *them*, dark and compact, quiet-spoken, with that sudden beautiful smile. She spoke French nearly as well as Françoise and it was hard to tell that she was not a Parisian, like the other dark, compact, beautiful women in the shop.

Now, instead, it was Daddy who was different. His height, his boyish grin, the way he walked and gestured, all stood out. She studied him as he stood talking to one of the assistants who fluttered around Mama. His pipe, his floppy hat, his dark glasses, all were unlike anything men wore here. His very *shoes* were American. Back home, he was orthodox. Here, he was a foreigner.

She wondered suddenly about herself. Was she a foreigner, like Daddy? Or did she fit in here, like Mama?

She slipped off her chair and went to the mirror to check.

She stared at her reflection. A little girl stared back with serious green eyes set in a pretty, oval face. She had a short, straight nose and a full mouth. The chin was round and determined. Her hair was black and long. If it had not been held back with a red alice-band, it would have fallen in thick coils around her face. She wore a red dress and white socks.

And that was Eden.

She lived inside that little girl. In there was her soul, the thing that made her different. Just as Mama and Daddy had souls. And the other customers. And the assistants. And everyone in Paris. And everyone in all the world. Millions of them, all separate, all different. It was dizzying when you thought of it like that, and yet it didn't matter, because no matter how many others there were, you were still you, and you were Eden.

Barcelona

Françoise was there to meet them on the docks as their ferry steamed into Barcelona. They saw her among the crowds, waving a straw hat.

"Françoise!" Eden called. "Françoise!" She was bursting to

tell Françoise all about Italy and to show her the beautiful presents she had bought her in Venice and Rome.

Spain was blisteringly hot, even hotter than Rome. The sky overhead was unflawed. The light had a hard, white quality that hurt the eyes.

Outside, Françoise scooped Eden up in her arms. She was wearing a plain white dress and her skin was damp with the heat.

"*Chérie!* How is it with you?"

"I got you a glass dolphin in Venice! And a silk scarf in Rome!"

Françoise laughed and hugged her. "My little traveller!"

"Great to see you, honey," Daddy said, looking at Françoise's tanned arms and legs. "You look as though you've been on the beach."

"I have! I wore my bikini, but a policeman sent me home. He said it was immodest. Imagine, immodest! He said you're only allowed to wear a one-piece in Spain."

"You should have taken one of your pieces off, then." Daddy grinned.

Françoise giggled. "The taxi's waiting in the street."

They got into the taxi. Françoise said, "There was a little confusion about the hotel. We're booked into the Palace instead of the Ritz."

"Oh, no," Mama said in an odd voice.

They looked at her. She was pale. "It was a mix-up, madame," Françoise said apologetically. "The Ritz was full. The Palace is a beautiful hotel, madame. It's old, but wait till you see the furniture, and the ceilings and the bathrooms—"

"I know the Palace Hotel," Mama said quietly. She put her dark glasses on. "Wasn't there anywhere else in Barcelona?"

"All the good hotels are full. It's the height of the season."

Daddy put his arm around Mama. "What's wrong, honey? You look sick."

Mama shook her head. "I'm sorry. I suppose I'm just a little jumpy, being back after all this time. It's nothing."

"Has the Palace Hotel got bad memories for you? We can go to a smaller place."

Mama was silent for a while. Then she said, "Everywhere has memories for me. I'm sorry. We'll stay at the Palace. It doesn't matter."

The Palace Hotel was as impressive as Françoise had promised. It was a white neoclassical structure embellished with columns, like a wedding cake and had gay yellow awnings on all the balconies.

Their suite was huge and airy. Fans revolved slowly on the ceiling, wafting a cool current of air around them. Running the whole length of the suite was a balcony that looked out over the Plaza de Cataluña, an expansive square with trees and fountains and ornamental lawns. As in Paris, the roar of traffic was incessant.

Mama was suddenly ill. She rushed into the bathroom and slammed the door behind her. Daddy shrugged irritably at Eden's questions.

"Your mama's being a mystery woman. This place obviously upsets her."

"But why?"

"The war, I guess."

"What happened to her in the war?"

"You ask her," Daddy said dryly. "She won't tell me."

Later, Mama emerged, her face pale and drawn, apologizing.

"You need some fresh air," Daddy said. "Let's all go for a walk."

They went out and walked down the Ramblas.

Mama's sickness started to fade. "I'm glad to see there's some gaiety left in Barcelona," she said. "This used to be such a happy city."

"It seems gay enough to me," Daddy said.

"Before the war it was . . . different."

"You were younger." Daddy grinned. "That was the difference, honey."

Françoise laughed. Eden wondered again what had happened to Mama in the Palace Hotel.

San Lluc

It was baking, shadeless midday by the time they reached the village in their rented car. No cloud marred the deep blue sky, but a faint mauve haze softened the horizon.

Orchards of gnarled, silvery olive trees lined the road as they approached San Lluc. Men in hats were scything hay. The heat had made the vineyards wilt, but the grapes were darkening. There was almost no traffic apart from horses or donkeys and carts.

San Lluc was a little outcrop of stone houses in an ocean of golden fields. On the hill above it, a ruined building stood open to the sky.

They entered the village and parked in the main square, next to a cart, between whose traces a donkey stood flicking his long ears. Nothing was stirring. Eden felt that she had plunged into an ocean of silence and peace.

San Lluc was enchanting. It was a place from another time, with earth streets and plants growing out of all sorts of unexpected niches in the walls and roofs. Lots of the houses were abandoned, with fallen-in roofs and crumbling walls and no glass in their windows. The house where Mama had been born was one of these.

It stood in a little square, overgrown with bougainvillaea. The doors swung listlessly in the big arched doorway; inside, two donkeys munched hay steadily among a tangle of rusty farm implements. At the far end was the blackened mouth of a furnace, now choked with cobwebs.

"That was my room up there." She pointed to a little window high up under the eaves. "My parents' room was next door. That was the kitchen window. We kept rabbits down in the yard. I used to play with them for hours. They were all the toys I had."

Eden thought of her cupboard full of playthings at home. "Doesn't anybody live here any more?"

"Not any more."

"Where are your mama and daddy now?"

"In heaven," Mama replied.

Daddy was taking photographs. "It's so picturesque," he said. "I had no idea it would be so beautiful. I wish we could take the whole place apart, stone by stone, and crate it all up and take it back to California with us."

Mama looked around. "It was even lovelier before the war. There weren't all these abandoned houses. There weren't all these ruins."

Mama was strange this afternoon. But then, she had been strange ever since they'd come to Spain. Eden had expected she would be pleased to be in the place where she had been born, but her moods were unpredictable. She was very quiet, but she seemed happier than she had been in Barcelona.

They wandered up the street, meeting no one, admiring the pots of geraniums, peering into the old well, staring up at the façade of the *ajuntament*, photographing odd corners.

"I'm starving," Eden said at last.

"Is there anywhere we can eat in the village?" Daddy asked.

"Only the *fonda* in the square. It's not exactly *cordon bleu*."

"That's okay. Let's go."

There were a few tables outside, but it was far too hot to stay in the sun any longer. They went into the cool interior. The people who were eating quietly at a few tables looked up with nods but did not speak to them.

"These people—do they know who you are?" Daddy asked.

"Yes," Mama said. "They know who I am."

"Why don't they talk to you?"

"They're afraid to. Someone might be listening. They know my family were Reds."

"But that was twenty years ago!"

"Remember who's in charge. Franco hasn't forgiven his enemies."

"You're being absurd."

"Dominic, there are still tens of thousands of people who've been in prisons and labour camps since 1939. Hundreds of thousands more in exile, who can never come home. Their only crime was being on the wrong side. Why do you think there are so many abandoned houses?"

"Jesus." Daddy looked over his shoulder. "Are *we* in any danger?"

"No," Mama said.

"Well, I know you have an American passport. But aren't you an enemy of the state?"

"There were some charges against me once, but they were dropped. I have a distant cousin in the government. He took care of it. There's no problem, Dominic."

Daddy still looked uncomfortable. "If I'd known how bad it was, I'd probably never have come up here."

"You're quite safe." Mama smiled dryly. Eden was staring at them. Mama touched her face. "Don't frighten her."

"You're the one who's frightening *me*," Daddy said. "After lunch we'll go take a look at that old convent up there."

"There was a fire," Mama said.

Eden stared up at the blackened stone walls. "Why haven't they ever fixed it? Where are they all?"

"I don't know."

"Are they in heaven too?"

"Some of them."

Mama took her hand and they walked around the hulk of the convent. The ground was strewn with little white daisies. It was very quiet and peaceful up here. You could look down and see the tiled roofs of the village below, and then the plain and then the blue sea beyond.

Daddy was staring at the huge iron gates that hung askew on their hinges. "Look how beautiful these things are," he said.

Mama nodded. "My father made those."

"Are you serious?" Daddy asked.

"Oh, yes. Before I was born."

The bars were writhing snakes, entwined around roses. Eden reached out and touched the iron. It was hot from the sun, as though it had come fresh out of the furnace.

"He was a magnificent craftsman," Daddy said. He was looking excited. "Mercedes, these gates are works of art. They're just going to rust away up here. And there are other things lying around, beautiful things. Those tiles on the floor—they've got to be three hundred years old. It could all be salvaged!"

"Who's going to salvage it?"

"We are! We'll speak to the local bishop, or whoever's in charge of ecclesiastical buildings and offer to buy all this stuff. We could have it shipped back to the States."

"Oh, Dominic . . ."

"Think of it," Daddy said eagerly. "This oak door could be our front door. We could easily get the builders to fit it in."

Mama looked ill. "These things hold memories for me. I don't want to be reminded of them every time I open my front door. . . ."

"Don't be silly," Daddy said, taking her in his arms. "These gates are practically a family heirloom. Your own father's work, Mercedes. Think of it. And those tiles—they're all hand-made.

Unique. There's enough to do the whole house. They'll make it something special, something exceptional. They'll add something you just can't buy any more in California. Jesus! It'll make the Fairchilds' house look like a shack!"

Mama pulled out of his embrace. "This is sanctified ground."

"No, it's not. Only the chapel and the graveyard."

"Why should the church want to sell these things to you?"

"Come on." Daddy grinned. "Money can achieve anything, honey. If we offer the right price, they'll jump at it. This place is going to rack and ruin. If we salvage what's left, at least it'll be preserved, won't it?"

"Maybe it's better left to rot peacefully up here," Mama answered in a distant voice. "I don't think any of it will bring us luck."

"Don't be so doom-ridden." Daddy laughed. "Look, if we tell them who you are, that your father did this work—"

"No," Mama said shortly. "My father's memory is not exactly venerated by the church. Leave him out of it. And leave me out of it too."

"Okay, I'll say we want to put it in a museum in Santa Barbara."

"But that's a transparent lie."

"Sweetie," Daddy said patiently, "if I walk into the monsignor's office with a wad of hundred-dollar bills in my hand, do you think he'll care what story I spin?"

"Could we *really* take them back to California with us?" Eden asked, looking at the gates.

"Of course we could," Daddy said. "You'd like that, wouldn't you?"

"Yes!"

"It's a great idea, isn't it?"

Eden nodded, thinking of possessing those writhing black snakes.

"I'll find out who to talk to," Daddy said. "This stuff will be ours in a week. You'll see!"

They stayed in a tiny hotel in a fishing village right on the sea, a short way from San Lluc. Every dawn the fishermen went out in their brightly-painted boats and every afternoon the beach was strewn with their nets, laid out to dry. They swam and sunbathed and feasted on seafood, just as Daddy had predicted. It was the happiest time Eden would remember.

One afternoon, she and Mama went for a ride in a fisherman's boat. Daddy and Françoise didn't come, because Françoise got sick on boats and Daddy had a headache and had gone to bed for the afternoon.

They sailed around the cliffs to a tiny little cove, where the water was as clear as Venetian glass. But when Mama stepped out of the boat onto the rocks, she slipped and cried out and suddenly there was bright red blood welling out of her heel. Mama laughed and said it was nothing. But the heel wouldn't stop bleeding and they needed a bandage, so the fisherman rowed them back.

Mama sat in the boat, holding her heel, while Eden ran up the beach to the little hotel to get bandages and Mercurochrome, so that Mama wouldn't get sand in the gash.

But when she opened the door of Mama and Daddy's room, something terrible was happening.

Daddy and Françoise were on the bed together. They had no clothes on and Daddy was doing something to Françoise that was making her gasp and gasp and gasp.

Eden was unable to move. She couldn't speak a word. They didn't notice her. The bed was rattling and Françoise was making that desperate noise, and Daddy's naked buttocks were pumping at her. Then Daddy was growling at Françoise in a strange, hoarse voice, and Françoise clawed at him as if in agony, and their bodies started convulsing violently.

Daddy was killing Françoise.

Eden found her voice at last. "*Daddy!*" she screamed in terror. "*Daddy! Don't!*"

They turned blind, sweating faces to her.

Françoise said, "*Oh, mon Dieu,*" and pushed Daddy off her. She ran to the bathroom with her hands covering her face. Eden saw her white breasts swinging, caught a glimpse of the dark triangle between her thighs.

Daddy sat up. There was a thing sticking out of his groin, like Uncle Max's, but erect, angry. He looked as though he were very drunk. "Get out of here," he said thickly.

"Mama cut her foot," Eden whispered.

"Get out of here!" Daddy roared at her. "Get out, you little fuck!"

Eden turned and ran as though the hounds of hell were after her.

By the next day she had a fever.

Mama said, "I think she's caught too much sun. She's not well at all." She held Eden in her arms and stroked her face. "She's so hot. Do you think I should call a doctor?"

"For a bit of sunburn?" Daddy said. "Don't be silly."

So Mama tucked her up in bed with an aspirin and Françoise came and gave her a kiss on the brow and looked at her with imploring eyes.

But it was not a sickness that aspirins would help. Like Mama's gashed heel, something had been torn and blood was leaking out. Her fever rose steadily. She tossed and sweated in her bed. She didn't want to think of Daddy and Françoise naked together, but the fever filled her head with terrible dreams, from which she awoke, screaming.

The doctor came and said it might be Malta fever, from drinking unpasteurized milk. He prescribed sulpha drugs but said they probably wouldn't do much good. The hotel staff came with soups and puddings and sympathy, but Eden just lay shivering and wretched, her skin pale under the summer tan.

Daddy hardly spoke to her. When he came to her bed and looked at her, it was with a cold, wary expression in his eyes that chilled her.

It was the same face as before. The same look. Like a stranger's. Somehow blind. As if he wanted her to die.

She knew Daddy hated her now, because of what she had seen. He had called her an ugly name. She did not know what a little fuck was, but his tone had been pitiless.

Daddy frightened her. When he came in the room, the fever would burn like a furnace. She would scream if he touched her. He appeared in her febrile dreams. He would kill Françoise. Then he would come to kill her.

In her lucid moments, Eden knew that Daddy had betrayed them all in some terrible way. But *she* was the guilty one. *She* was the one who was going to die, because of what she had seen.

The fever raged for days. She entered a limbo world where nothing was quite a dream and nothing was quite real. Shadows of familiar people came and went. Voices spoke and music echoed. She saw strange visions. Often she heard cavalry thundering through her head and saw the penumbra of a vast army on the move. She vomited whatever she ate. Her joints ached, and her skin burned and her head was a swollen balloon.

She heard her mother crying at her bedside.

Then, as suddenly as it had come, the fever went. She lay on the drenched sheets, exhausted but cool, and could eat again. She slept profoundly, but normally, for twenty-four hours. Within a couple of days, she was well enough for Françoise to take her down to the sea.

Françoise sat on the rocks beside her and cried until her face went red and begged her not to say anything about what she had seen.

But Eden didn't have to be told. Whatever it was Daddy had been doing to Françoise (and Eden knew better than to ask what it was), it was something that Mama must never know about. Like Françoise trying on Mama's clothes, only much, much more secret and shameful.

"It wasn't my fault, *chérie*," Françoise sobbed. "Your father made me do it. I'll never do it again, I swear. I swear!"

Eden stared at the horizon and heard the distant thunder of that dark cavalry.

Daddy smiled at her again. But the cold look in his eyes was still there. All her pleasure in the holiday had died. She wanted to go home.

Then, one afternoon, Daddy came back to the little hotel in high good spirits.

"I've arranged everything," he said triumphantly. His pipe stuck up at a jaunty angle, and his eyes sparkled. "I've bought the convent."

"You've *what*?" Mama demanded incredulously.

"I've bought the whole building." He tossed his hat across the room. "Bought it for a song!"

"Are you saying the convent belongs to us?" Mama said, with a strange expression on her face.

"Well, the demolition rights do, anyway." He grinned at Eden and for the first time in days she smiled back, hesitantly. "They want it pulled down. I've subcontracted with a local builder to do the work. We get the gates and everything we want. He gets the rest. The way it works out, all we'll have to pay is the shipping costs and a couple of hundred dollars and we get the doors, the iron gates, the balustrade and the floor tiles!"

Mama shook her head in disbelief. "I don't believe it!"

"All we need now is a shipping agent." He looked so jolly that Eden went up to him timidly and crept onto his knee. He put his arm around her and hugged her. It was almost as though everything was going to be all right, after all.

But she knew that nothing would ever be the same again.

5.

~The Party

San Lluc

An unbelievable turn of events: Spain is a republic!

Yes. It's true. There have been nationwide elections. The results have been pouring in. A Republican landslide! On 14 April 1931, which is Mercedes Eduard's birthday, the republic is proclaimed.

The monarchy has fallen. Alfonso XIII is king no more.

Seven years earlier, anarchists tried to assassinate him in Paris. He survived, to reign under the aegis of Primo de Rivera, the dictator he called his Mussolini. Last year he was shorn of this prop when Primo fell.

Informed by the Guardia Civil *that they will no longer protect him against the Reds who thirst for his blood, this jaunty, pleasure-loving sportsman departs hastily for Cartagena, where a ship awaits to take him into exile—so hastily that his children and Victoria Eugenia, his English-born wife, are left in the royal palace in Madrid, with two dozen rococo halberdiers to protect them from a vast mob that has gathered outside.*

Many of the crowd have dressed themselves after the fashion of the French Revolution. Perhaps there will be a massacre! But the crowd are in too joyous a mood to want Victoria Eugenia's blood. They retreat chivalrously when requested to do so. Victoria Eugenia leaves, surrounded by weeping ladies-in-waiting.

Neither she nor Alfonso will ever see Spain again. Alfonso will die in Rome, in 1941. Nor will their son, Don Juan de

Borbón, ever call himself King of Spain. Thirty-eight years later, however, the dictator Franco will name their grandson, Juan Carlos I, his heir as head of the Spanish state.

That is all to come. At this moment it is inconceivable that a king will ever sit on a Spanish throne again. Democracy has arrived.

Spain explodes with joy.

Most of Spain, that is. The day is full of portents and ironies.

In Zaragoza, thirty-nine-year-old Francisco Franco has been standing on his balcony in a state of considerable agitation. Normally a phlegmatic man, this dedicated careerist is the youngest general ever to have been appointed in the Spanish Army. During the turmoil of these past years, Franco has widely been tipped as the future leader of a military government— once the Red menace has been swept away, of course. At this moment, he sees that bright hope slipping away in a welter of barbarism and anarchy.

Suddenly he blurts out, "Things can't go on like this!"

He resolves to take troops into Madrid to restore . . .

To restore what? For the moment, there is nothing to restore. Baffled, he sits down instead and writes a letter of allegiance to the republic.

His younger brother Ramón, on the other hand, is overjoyed. Nine months ago, he flew over the royal palace in his airplane, intending to bomb it, but at the last minute dropped pamphlets instead. He is a young man of (at the moment) passionate democratic persuasions. He is also a national hero who undertook the first South Atlantic air crossing to Buenos Aires. He fills his glass and drinks to the new republic.

In the streets of Madrid, Barcelona, Valencia, Seville, huge crowds gather to rejoice with tears or laughter, to sing revolutionary songs, to wave the purple, red and yellow flag of the republic. They hug one another, climb lampposts and monuments, drink and dance. Spain has seen light at the end of the tunnel.

Even grim Francesc Eduard, in the village of San Lluc, is pleased. He will be a hard-line anarchist until the day he dies, but at least, as he says, "There will now be a state to dismantle."

The rest of Spain is drunk with the prospect of democracy. But has the victory been too easy? Can anything as wonderful as this last?

The prospects for the new republic are not, of course, very favorable. The Great Depression of 1929 lingers on. A world-

wide recession still has Spain and every other European nation in its fist. Fascism is emerging as the preferred ideology of the Right. Army generals are already wondering when and how to strike. Democracy has never been a Spanish forte.

When the long-awaited general election takes place, it will produce a parliamentary monster: 116 Socialists, 90 Radicals, 60 Radical Socialists, 33 Catalán nationalists, 30 Left Republicans, 27 Right Republicans, 22 Progressives, 17 Federalists and 16 Galician nationalists. Ranged against them, some 50 bewildered deputies of the Right, wondering how a stable government is to be formed from so many conflicting shades of Red.

Paco Massaguer, rattling with emphysema in his huge four-poster bed, shakes his head.

"This cannot be," he wheezes.

Marcel Barrantes, dying of heart failure and loneliness in his own house in San Lluc, is equally gloomy. "There will be a civil war," he predicts, as he has predicted many times before.

Of course there will, and soon. Look what awaits Spain over the next five years: This government of the Left will swiftly encounter armed insurrection from the Right. The government of the Right which follows will topple to armed insurrection on the Left. Finally, another government of the Left will be tumbled by armed insurrection on the Right.

And then there will be no more republics.

This, too, is all to come and awaits en los años venideros, in the well of time that has yet to be drawn. For the time being, it is fiesta *in republican Spain.*

San Lluc

Two days later, life had almost returned to normal in San Lluc. The whine of Josep Arnau's buzz saw and the smell of freshly-sawn logs filled the village. In the forge, Francesc was busy. Nowadays the searing blue light of the welding torch was replacing the red roar of the furnace, but the work was still hard and demanding.

Republican flags still flew bravely all over the village. There had been a *fiesta* in the square on the fourteenth, with the village band blowing till their cheeks almost burst and every soul who could walk had joined hands to dance in the stately circles of the *sardana*, the Catalán national dance.

Some veteran royalists, of course, had been sorrowful to see even so unworthy a monarch as Alfonso XIII tipped off his throne. A few on the extreme left, like Francesc Eduard, wanted something far more radical than a republic. But for the most part, San Lluc had celebrated with uninhibited delight. There was a real sense of freedom in the spring air. Anticipations of reform and prosperity fluttered like starlings over the bright green fields. And Mercedes had been enthralled to find the celebration coinciding with her own thirteenth birthday.

She was suddenly a princess. Many of the older men and women had kissed her on the fourteenth, calling her *la niña bonita*, the pretty girl. One old lady had given her a silver religious medal. An old man had given her a glass of sweet almond liqueur to drink which had made her head spin. She'd thought it all a simple tribute to her birthday until her mother explained.

"*La niña bonita* is the name people used to give to the republic in the old days," Conchita told her. "They used to dream about the day the pretty girl would be born. So they're happy for you, but they're also celebrating that their dream has come true."

Mercedes nodded, a little disappointed. It had been a good day, anyway. And there was no school this week. Of course, the republic wasn't the end of the struggle, not by any means. As Papa always said, the end of the struggle was complete freedom for the workers and complete equality for all. Anything less was a compromise. But the republic was a start. Now at last some wrongs would be set right.

She squatted in the yard, playing with the rabbits. Though Conchita kept the animals for food, the girl treated them as pets and loved them for their long ears and silky pelts. She cradled one in her arms. It was delicious to press her face against the warm, silky fur. It lay passively, its nose quivering.

"Pretty thing," she whispered, stroking it. "Pretty, pretty thing."

From the kitchen window, Conchita looked down on her. She had grown so fast. Nothing fitted her any more. Her long black hair irritated her so much that Conchita had braided it into two long plaits that hung down her back. She was always out of doors and she was as brown as a gypsy.

Her breasts were swelling. Womanhood was already coming over her. Almost every month she had a period and she treated them calmly and efficiently. Soon, boys would be buzzing around her like bees around a bowl of honey.

"Pretty, pretty," she heard Mercedes say. She watched as the child put one rabbit down and picked up the other, tenderly kissing its unresponsive face.

She had such capacity for love. If only they could give her a brother or a sister . . . but that hope grew increasingly forlorn with each year that passed.

Please God, she was sailing in open waters.

Conchita thanked God for Mercedes's health and happiness. Few traces remained of that terrible time of three years ago. Lurking somewhere in her was the murderous temper that could transfigure her. But it hardly ever showed nowadays. She would never forget that time. Lleonart Cornadó, now a grinning butcher boy in his father's shop, would bear that scar on his temple to his grave. Francesc refused to see it, but Conchita knew in her heart that Mercedes had, in the moment she wielded that stone, possessed the will to kill. Only physical strength had been lacking. Only that.

Sometimes, when she thought of that, she looked at her daughter with doubting eyes and remembered the man who had begotten her. . . .

She and Francesc had fought so hard to win back Mercedes's trust. Gaining ground had been slow and painful, but she felt, this spring of 1931, that they had succeeded. Once again, that soft look of love could be seen in the dark eyes.

And the girl was still doing well at school. She spent much time devouring books. She had joined three libraries and brought home a bewildering assortment of literature. Conchita, who loved books and had always encouraged Mercedes to read, was glad. She had a retentive memory and could recite poems, chapters of history, screeds of the anarchist theory her father taught her.

That was the only dark stain on Conchita's happiness: Francesc's continuing insistence that it was his solemn duty to "educate" the child in his own way.

Perhaps Mercedes accepted this education to show that she had forgiven her father.

She talked about *collectivization* and *anarcho-syndicalism* as though the words meant something to her. She could quote wholesale from Bakunin, hair-raising stuff about revolutions and terror. The girl had been with her father to rallies and trade union meetings. She had dozed or (for all Conchita knew) listened attentively to the ranting speeches of Russian agitators, anarchist assassins, half-educated Asturian miners with dynamite in their pockets, and God alone knew who else.

Francesc had even taken her to the front lines of strikes, among the placards and the flying rocks. Once she had come home sobbing hysterically, having seen a man shot ten feet away from her.

It appalled Conchita to think of the dangers Mercedes had been exposed to. It appalled her even more to think of the political opinions she was imbibing. But there was nothing she could do. All you can do, she thought, is trust in your innate strength. And in the kindness of fate.

Her daughter was already out of her hands. She was already on the anvil of life, awaiting the hammer.

Mercedes looked up at her mother and smiled. Conchita felt her heart squeezed by the sweetness of that smile.

"I'm going down to the olive grove, Mama."

"Who's going with you?"

"Nobody," Mercedes said simply.

Conchita nodded. She would read alone among the trees for hours, as likely some nonsense about the Wild West as a weighty tome about the history of Germany. "Take care on the road."

It was early afternoon. Mercedes walked slowly down the road to the field of olive trees. The book she was reading at the moment had seized her imagination powerfully. It was called *The Scarlet Letter*, and it was a translation of an American book, written by someone with an unpronounceable name. She was fascinated by the solitary courage of the heroine and by the strangeness of her child.

It was so like her and Mama. After all, Mama was an Adulteress too, wasn't she? If Mama hadn't married Francesc, she thought, that was how they might have lived. The two of them, alone in the woods. Fending for themselves. The idea appealed to her fantasy. Just her and Mama, in a house of their own, free as the birds. It wasn't that she didn't want Papa there any more; it was just nice to think of the two of them, all alone.

Of course, Francesc was the most interesting man in the world.

And she admired him so much. They were friends. But she couldn't say she really loved him. Perhaps she had until she'd found out, but not after. Not if she was being honest. And it was Papa himself who was teaching her to be honest, never to lie about her feelings. Never to lie about anything.

She didn't think he really loved her, either, not deep down inside. He cared. He wanted her to understand so many things. He was more like a dedicated teacher than a father. But he didn't love her. Love was a warm, hungry thing. Papa didn't feel that for her. She didn't mind. As long as they didn't deceive one another, she didn't mind.

She opened the book as she walked and found her place, starting to read at once, her eyes intent.

The sound of an automobile approached, driving up the road behind her, and Mercedes stepped onto the grassy verge to get out of the way. Looking over her shoulder, she saw it coming up in a haze of dust. It was a big, open-topped limousine with two men in it. As she waited, it slowed down, until one of its gleaming black haunches came to a halt beside her.

Mercedes looked up. The man at the wheel was a chauffeur in a peaked cap. The other, sitting behind him in a dark suit, was Gerard Massaguer.

She met his black eyes and the impact of recognition was icy cold.

They stared at one another for a long moment. Then he leaned over and opened the door of the car for her. "Get in," he commanded.

She hugged the book to her breasts, not moving.

"Come on, Mercedes," he said with sudden command in his voice, "get *in*."

It was like a hand pushing hard against the small of her back. She stepped into the automobile and sat on the seat opposite him. He leaned across her to shut the door and again she caught that smell, that mix of cologne, expensive material, man's skin. Her heart was pounding against her ribs.

Dust hung in the air. The chauffeur sat stolidly, waiting for instructions, the engine running quietly. Gerard Massaguer's eyes assessed her face, dropped to her breasts, then to her bare brown legs. She sat motionless, thinking, *You're my father.*

"It's some time since we met, isn't it?" he said at last.

She nodded silently.

"So much to do," he said, as if in explanation. "So little time."

It was in fact almost four years since their meeting in the headmaster's office. Since then, she had caught only occasional glimpses of him, passing in his car, or walking into a bank or a shop in Palafrugell. She had seen his wife too, more ravishingly elegant than ever. And two years ago they'd had a child. A son. Her half-brother.

She didn't think that Gerard Massaguer had ever consciously thought of her in all that time, though she was wrong.

"And it was your birthday two days ago, if I'm not mistaken?"

She nodded again. "I'm thirteen."

"Well. We have to celebrate. Drive on," he commanded the chauffeur. "Go to Las Yucas."

The car slid smoothly forward. "Where are you taking me?" she demanded.

"For a birthday celebration," he replied.

"I have to go home," she said, frowning. What if someone saw her and told Papa!

"Why?" He smiled. She remembered that smile so well. He sat watching her, fingers laced across his flat stomach. The car was picking up speed.

Mercedes sank back against the seat, feeling her stomach turn over. "My mother's expecting me!"

"Not for an hour or two," he said. "Enjoy the ride." He reached out and plucked the book out of her arms. He looked at the cover and gave a snort. "They tell me you've become a bookworm. Eh? Bookworms don't come to anything. They lose themselves in fantasies, and life passes them by."

The interior of the car was the most luxurious place she had ever been. The seats were upholstered in cream leather that smelled intoxicatingly good. Everything else was panelled in gleaming walnut or carpeted in crimson wool. There were little fold-down walnut tables, upon one of which Gerard had been reading the newspaper, and even an open cabinet in which Mercedes could see cut-crystal tumblers and a decanter of some liquor. A silver stork mascot was poised on the long, gleaming hood.

He sat in the car like an oriental prince. Were they alike? He had a face as handsome as any film star's, though there was a slightly frightening darkness to his looks. Everything about him was black. Black hair, black eyes, thick black eyelashes and eyebrows. His mouth was sensual and cut deep into his face. He returned her gaze steadily, always with that dark glitter of amusement.

Well, Mercedes supposed, their eyes were the same colour. So was their hair. But whether they looked like one another could only be told by someone else. Or maybe by staring into a mirror together.

Las Yucas was a small restaurant overlooking the sea. It had been named after the tangle of yuccas that grew outside, a huge bouquet of green bayonets. From here, you could watch the fishing boats sail into the harbour every evening.

The chauffeur parked outside and started polishing the car while Gerard took Mercedes inside. The low room, which contained some two dozen tables, was cool and empty. Gerard Massaguer shouted for the landlord and pulled out chairs for them by a window.

The proprietor hurried out of a back room with a tablecloth at the ready. "What can I offer the *señores?*" he asked.

"French champagne," Gerard ordered. "The best you have. Good and cold. And something to eat. It's this lady's birthday."

"*Si, señor!*" He spread the cloth in front of them and hastened out again.

Mercedes clenched her fists in determination. "I know who you are," she said forcefully.

Gerard leaned back in his chair, considering Mercedes with his heavy lids lowered over his eyes. "So," he said. "Who am I?"

She took a breath. "You're my father."

"What damnable insolence." He leaned forward, black eyes like the muzzles of a shotgun. "You could be put in jail for repeating such a filthy lie. Your father is that anarchist blacksmith, who will soon be hanged."

"He isn't my father!"

"Isn't he?" Gerard's face was flinty, terrifying. "Then your mother's a whore."

"She's not!"

"You're the bastard brat of some village Romeo. A fleck of scum on the surface of life, worth nothing, counting for nothing. You dare to claim I'm your father? I'll see you whipped until you scream for mercy!"

Mercedes had gone white and was trembling violently. "You can whip me if you like. It's true."

"Oh! I see." He showed his teeth in a cruel smile. "You think you'll get more money out of me with a bit of blackmail. How crude."

"I don't want any of your money," she quavered.

"Who put you up to this little game? Your mother? Your father?"

"No one put me up to it," she said in a tight voice. She was fighting back tears, her throat a giant ache. "You're—my—father." Her fingers were biting into the seat of her chair. "You *are!*"

The landlord came bustling in with a dewy bottle of champagne and several bowls of *tapas*. Mercedes turned her head away, her eyes blurred with tears. Through the open door, the sea was a flickering sheet of ultramarine. She felt so utterly, completely alone. Pain had swelled inside her like a vast blood blister.

The champagne cork popped and the proprietor chuckled fatly as he filled their glasses. *"Salud,"* he wished them and then slyly added, *"Y viva la república!"*

"A charming sentiment," Gerard said silkily. The man retired and Gerard held out a glass to Mercedes. "Come on," he ordered. "Drink."

She shook her head. The movement threatened to make her brimming lids spill over. "I don't want any."

"It's your birthday," he pointed out calmly.

"I don't care. I hate you. You're a *liar*," she added with passion. "I know all about your crimes."

"My crimes?" he asked, still holding out the champagne.

"You sent *pistoleros* to break up a strike in La Bisbal! I saw them shoot a man in front of the factory!"

"You were there?" He studied her thoughtfully. "Your father is certainly seeing that you get a broad education."

"You're an enemy of the people. You own factories and land. You exploit the workers. You crush their rights!"

He put the glass down in front of her. "I pay them damned good salaries for doing next to nothing, I know that."

She met his gaze with hot, wet eyes. "You're finished, anyway. There's a republic, now. They'll probably execute you for your crimes."

The deeply-chiselled mouth turned down slightly. "What a bloodthirsty little Red you are."

"Well, at least put you in jail for *years*."

He smiled. "Tell me something, Mercedes. If I'm such a terrible criminal, why are you so keen to call me your father?"

"Because it's true." She watched him pick up an olive and put it in his mouth. "I don't care what you say to me, it *is*."

He spat an olive stone carelessly onto the floor. His eyes had grown cold. "You're a very intelligent child, so they tell me," he said softly. "If you were a little more intelligent, you would realize that there are certain things that are not spoken of in front of servants, or in public places, where there are other ears to hear."

The cool words cut her more than the rough insults had done earlier. Yet, as she shrank back in her chair, she also felt a warm trickle of pleasure somewhere inside her. He'd as good as admitted it!

Mercedes examined the earthenware bowls that had been placed in front of her. It was a feast. There were cold fried prawns and sardines crisp with batter, pickled mussels and other shellfish, rounds of rich country sausage, olives, almonds and slices of cured ham, a whole array of salty delicacies. She began to pick at the food. It was delicious. He watched her eat. When she grew thirsty, she picked up the champagne glass in greasy fingers.

Gerard lifted his own glass. "*Salud*," he said with some irony. "*Y viva la república*."

She pulled a face at him before drinking. She didn't really like champagne, though the crisp bubbles were refreshing. "Aren't you afraid?" she asked, hunting through the bowls for more of her favourite things.

"Of what?"

"Of the republic, of course."

He laughed contemptuously. "Your precious republic won't last six weeks."

"Why not?"

"Because the army will take over. Do you think they'll sit by idly while Spain turns into a Soviet state?"

"Russia is a worker's paradise," she said, spearing a mussel. She had started to eat voraciously.

"My dear girl, the way the Russians treat their workers makes me look like an angel, I assure you."

"A devil, you mean."

"You have a little of that strain in yourself, come to that." Gerard studied an olive. "I hear you almost knocked a boy's brains out a while ago."

She was silent for a moment, a strange expression crossing her face. "He's all right now," she said quietly.

"No thanks to your ministrations. I've seen the scar. Why did you do that, Mercedes?"

She shrugged. Her eyes were open, yet they were closed to scrutiny.

"He must have made you very angry."

She made no answer to that. When she spoke, her voice was clear. "If the army tries to take over the republic, there'll be a war. We'll fight them," she told him briskly. "Everyone says so."

"And whoever fights the army will get shot," he returned equably.

"I don't care. *I'd* fight against them."

"And I'd fight *for* them," he retorted. "And if I met *you* coming the other way, I'd put a bullet right through you."

"I might put a bullet through you first."

"Yes," he said pensively, "you might. You're a dangerous person to tangle with."

She looked at his tie pin. It held a bright diamond, flanked by two rubies. The tie was silk and shimmered like the sea. "Would you really?" she asked. "Shoot me?"

"No question," he replied. "If you were coming to take away what was mine."

"But it isn't yours. You stole it from the people. Or your family did."

"That's an argument of very doubtful validity," he replied laconically. "However, if the people are really of that view, they're welcome to try and take it back. If they can."

"They will!"

"I wouldn't count on it." He leaned forward. His face was heavier than she remembered, blunter. In later years, he would grow jowly. "Let me give you a little piece of advice, Mercedes. Always choose your side well in advance. And always choose carefully. We have the army, the navy and the air force on our side. In Africa, we have tens of thousands of Moroccan troops, the best and fiercest in the world. We hold all the guns, all the tanks, all the airplanes. We have ships and submarines. Best of all, we have all the money. And nothing wins a war like money. Abroad, too, we have powerful friends who will help us if we need it. Are you too young to grasp all this?"

She was staring at him. "No."

"Good. Then think what you have on *your* side. An undisciplined rabble of peasants with flails. Spineless factory workers. Unemployed gypsies. Starry-eyed teenagers and decadent intellectuals. The only foreigners who will help you are the Russians, the most treacherous and untrustworthy nation on earth. No guns, no money, no organization. Are you so sure your side is going to win?"

Mercedes gulped at the fizzy champagne and belched slightly. "Yes! Because we're the people!"

Gerard smiled. "Remember what I've said, Mercedes."

"You could always save yourself, you know," she told him. "You could collectivize your farms and factories. Then the workers would love you instead of hating you."

"Oh, I can live without their love. In fact, I believe I prefer their hatred. Though I admit it's marginal. Fundamentally, I don't give a damn."

"I know." Mercedes nodded. That was exactly the way the owning classes spoke and thought. She swung her legs. "I've seen your wife. Lots of times. She's Italian."

"Yes." He nodded. He was barely touching the food. His eyes seldom left her, though the way he veiled them with his lids made it hard to tell how close his scrutiny was.

"She's beautiful."

"You think so?"

"When I grow up, I want to look just like her."

"I assure you," he said, "that you will never look remotely like Marisa."

She was hurt. "I could dye my hair blond."

"You're going to be beautiful enough in your own way," Gerard said gently. "You're beautiful already."

Better pleased with that, she watched him fill her glass. Her head was starting to spin, whether from the champagne or the excitement she couldn't tell. "Well, I want to wear clothes just like her," she said. "And have jewels and a long cigarette holder just like hers."

"Then I advise you once again to consider changing sides," he said. "No self-respecting Red would spend a thousandth of what Marisa spends on clothes. As for what she spends on jewels . . . "

"How much?"

"More than you could imagine." Mercedes considered the question with her forehead wrinkled and he smiled. "I see that your education—or should I call it indoctrination?—is not a hundred percent complete yet."

"Why do you say that?"

"Surely you've seen what Communist women look like?" he said mockingly. "They wear baggy trousers and workmen's boots. They put tractor oil on their hair."

"They don't!"

"They'd rather be shot with shit than wear pretty jewels or a smart dress."

"Shot with *shit*?" The phrase was new to her. She giggled into her champagne. "You've got a son. Alfonso."

Gerard sat back. "Named after our late-lamented king, of course," he said dryly. "My father said it was unwise to name a child after a living Spanish monarch, but Marisa insisted. Alfonso Xavier. He's almost two years old now."

She tried to look sober. "Is he a pretty baby?" she asked, searching for another shrimp.

"Marisa thinks so."

"Does he look like me?"

"Not in the slightest."

She raised her eyes to Gerard's for a moment. "Your wife, Marisa, does she know about me? I mean, who I am?"

"No," Gerard said calmly. "But then, who are you? A blacksmith's daughter from San Lluc. Why should she bother herself with you?"

"You know why," she said in a low voice. "Why don't you tell her about me?"

Gerard considered her. "I don't really know," he said lazily.

"Is it because you're ashamed of me?"

"I wasn't very pleased with you when you tried to brain the butcher's son."

"You don't know anything about that," she said, unsmiling.

"Someone told me he pissed in your face."

Mercedes's cheeks whitened for a moment. He watched the two dents appear on either side of her nose and recognized the symptoms with something like exultation. He could almost feel the anger surging in her with a stallion's bared fangs and flailing hooves. She's my blood, he thought. Mine. My virtues, my vices!

"If that's the case," he said casually, "then I think you did the right thing. Some actions are intolerable. Tell me. Did you mean to kill him?"

He saw her eyes glitter, imagined he heard the thunder of those sharp hooves. Then it was gone. The child had been teaching herself! She had a stronger hand on the reins than he himself did.

He refilled her glass and Mercedes drank greedily, the colour coming back to her face. Gerard took out a gold cigarette case and extracted a cigarette. He put it between his lips and lit it with a gold lighter. Mercedes watched as he tilted his head back and blew a long plume of smoke upwards.

"Is that nice?" she asked him.

"Smoking?" He shrugged, eyes narrowed against the smoke. "It's a vice. Therefore it's enjoyable."

"Can I have one?"

Gerard smiled slightly. He lit another cigarette, then passed it to her. She took it gingerly and put her inexpert lips to the butt. A cautious puff. Another puff. Then, predictably, some coughing.

Why had he paid so little attention to her over these last years? So much to do. So much to occupy his time. Trips to Italy with Marisa. Meeting Mussolini. Meeting the German air minister, Göring. Developing his relationships, his business contacts, his lines of influence.

He studied her through his lashes. He had missed her. Sitting here, he was again aware of that extraordinary excitement in his belly. A feeling he had with no other human being, not even with his son. He loved the boy, of course, but this . . . this was different.

"Are you bored?" she asked suddenly.

He laughed. "A true woman's question. No, not so far. In fact, I'm being well entertained. I would certainly have been infinitely more bored if I'd gone where I was going before I saw you."

"Where were you going?"

"To see a lady."

"A lady? Not your wife?"

"A lady, not my wife." He nodded. His smile mocked her.

She puffed on the cigarette, trying to imitate him. She picked up the glass in her other hand. Then she gasped with sudden insight. "Are you having—an *affair*?"

"Certainly not," he said composedly. "Affairs are extremely tedious. I just fuck her now and then." Mercedes gaped at him, almost spilling her champagne. "I suppose you don't know what that means."

"Of course I do," she retorted. She had to squint to keep him in focus, now. "A man and a woman making a baby."

"Not unless they can help it," he said, blowing out another cloud of blue smoke. "Fucking and babies are usually best kept separate."

"How do you do that?"

"There are ways and means. It's the woman's obligation to know how."

"But *how*?"

"Bits of sponge and things," he said vaguely. "Ask your mother."

She examined the cigarette with distaste. She looked a little green around the gills. "Can I put it out now? It's making me feel sick."

"Then I think you'd better."

Mercedes stubbed the coal out clumsily. She was going to be achingly beautiful, Gerard thought. Ripeness would come suddenly. Look at those breasts, sharp enough to tear her shirt. She'd be ready for her first sexual experiences soon. Some hayseed Romeo would bundle her into a hedge and hoist her skirts, grunting . . .

Gerard felt a fierce pang of jealousy twist inside him. I'd like to be the one to show you, he thought.

But she's your daughter.

So what?

"What's your house like?" she asked, cradling the glass. She had drunk nearly half of the bottle herself. She'd be falling out of her chair soon.

"It's the usual thing," he said laconically. "The furniture is upholstered with the skins of workers I've shot. We dip peasants in tar and set them alight, so we can see to count our gold."

Mercedes giggled again. He was really a very amusing man.

But she had eaten a great many shrimps and mussels and mushs-rooms and pieces of salami and her head was reeling in a rather alarming way. She took another gulp of champagne to steady it. "No, r-really. Tell me what it's like."

"Nothing ostentatious."

"What's 'ostentatious'? Oh, I know. *Pretentious display.*"

"Exactly. No pretentious display. Just the best of every-thing."

She rested her chin lopsidedly in her hand. "Why didn't you marry my mother? I know why. Because she was poor and simple and you were too ashamed to have her as your wife!"

He was sitting with one leg crossed over the other and one arm stretched out along the chair back. "You sound like a penny novelette."

"You abandoned her," Mercedes said. "You abandoned both of us." Her head was spinning dizzily. She felt very drunk and rather tearful. "Oh, I feel so sick!"

Gerard tossed some bills onto the table. Her legs were quite numb and she wondered with distant alarm how she was going to be able to walk out of here without falling over.

Gerard's hand closed around her arm and she clung to him gratefully as they walked out. Her balance had completely gone and the way the world teetered around her made her feel dreadfully sick. The cigarette. The champagne. The way the world *swooped.*

"Oh, oh," she whispered, "I feel so ill!"

"It'll pass." The air outside made her feel a little better. He helped her into the car. "Take us back to San Lluc," he ordered the chauffeur. Mercedes tried to lie down on the seat, which smelled so deliciously of expensive leather. He hauled her upright. "Sit up, or you'll make yourself sick," he advised.

"I'm going to be sick anyway."

"Not in here, you're not."

"Hold me," she whimpered.

She felt his arm around her shoulder, drawing her close. Then she was snuggled against him, her face pressed into his shoulder. That smell. Cologne, cloth, skin. Her nausea receded. She clung to her father. His body was warm and hard. All thought left her and she lay passive, blissful.

His hands caressed her and she drifted into a doze. Much

later, the limousine came to a stop and she raised her head languidly. "Are we here?"

"Yes," he said, looking down into her drowned face.

"Thank you so much—so much for the party," she said, articulating with care.

She felt his mouth close on hers and with a spasm of emotion, she flung her arms around his neck and hugged him tight, as tight as she could.

His hand cupped the youthful cone of her breast, his thumb rubbing against the nipple.

The sensation was electrifying. Mercedes squirmed. Gerard's tongue thrust into her mouth, probing roughly. His arms were like iron, preventing her escape. She was too weak to struggle. She felt his hand slide between her legs, his fingers probing. There was roaring in her ears.

He touched her, in that secret place. It was a violation. It was evil, yet she felt a kind of wild thrill. It was all swimming in her head, pleasure, pain, disgust, excitement. She arched in his arms, hating him, loving him. She did not know whether she was fighting against him or pressing herself to him. She was panicking for want of breath, wanting to scream. The sensation between her legs blossomed like a sinful orchid, purple and black and gold. It was agony, it was sweet beyond belief...

Gasping, she drew away from him, her face white and stretched. For a moment she stared into the devouring black eyes. Then she grasped frantically for the door handle and stumbled out into the road.

Gerard's heart was pounding in his chest. He felt as though some feral drug had been poured into his veins, robbing him of his humanity. He was close to orgasm. His throbbing penis was wet. He felt that if he touched himself, he would explode.

The child was watching him in a state of shock. God, she was so beautiful. He wanted to get out of the car and take her, right there in the road. His body trembled with a desire he had never experienced before. He had to get away.

"Until next time," he said in a shaking voice that sounded strange to him. He tapped the driver's shoulder.

The big black car eased forward and receded down the road. He did not look back.

Mercedes gasped for breath, holding her throat, which seemed about to close, robbing her of oxygen. His taste was in her mouth, strong and acrid. Between her thighs, her body was stickily wet. She turned away, fighting for air. She had to get home.

Then a giant fist closed on her stomach. She leaned forward and vomited agonizingly into the road.

6.

~The Burglar

spring 1968

Prescott

"Of course, I'll leave it entirely up to you. The verse. The design and so forth."

Joel nods.

"I'm real sorry about this, Joel. Your father—"

Mr. Maxwell reaches out, as though to touch Joel's shoulder. But he sees the young man stiffen and he drops his arm. He walks away, embarrassed.

Joel has already selected the stone. He lifts it onto the workbench with a grunt, his muscles tightening against the weight.

He has grown tall and strong. The thin child with the peering, timid manner has become a six-footer with wide shoulders and a muscled throat. The lean face has filled out, becoming aquiline, with rocky cheekbones that fall away sharply into gaunt cheeks and a steel-trap jawline. His dark hair curls around his ears. He wears a full moustache that disguises his mouth.

He is very handsome. But there is something frightening about him. Perhaps it is the dark, almost black eyes. They stare, sombre and intense, from under craggy brows. They are like fissures that lead to danger faults, deep within the rock. In their depths lies an intimation of the earthquakes to come.

The girls of the town have started to pursue him, all the more eagerly for the taut air of potential calamity that hangs around him.

The vibrancy of inner torment lures them on. Joel Lennox carries with him, like James Dean, the intoxicating breath of self-destruction. And that fascinates them.

The hands that restlessly moulded wax into a million shapes have grown powerful and competent. They work with assurance as he traces out the letters on the stone. The stones come from the supplier in Phoenix. Some have raised surfaces upon which the mason can carve something: a kneeling angel, a pair of doves.

Joel is capable of cutting anything you want into the marble, with a skill that amazes everyone. Though he is only twenty-four, his work is being sought after by art collectors as far afield as Los Angeles. He is an artist, not merely a craftsman. For now, he must work for Mr. Maxwell. Soon, though, his sculpture will fetch prices high enough to let him set up his own studio.

But despite his skill, he will not adorn this stone. It does not take him long to cut the single verse:

> *For every tree is known by his own fruit.*
> *For of thorns men do not gather figs*
> *nor of a bramble bush*
> *gather they grapes.*

Then, lower on the stone, in larger letters, he carves three more lines:

ELDRED CALVIN LENNOX

PASTOR

4 OCTOBER 1904–14 APRIL 1968

Outside the church, people shake his hand and murmur platitudes. He nods without speaking. Despite his youth, they are intimidated by his manner, his height, his eyes. They soon drop away.

He walks into the church, where the coffin has been placed on trestles. The casket is open. There are no flowers, no wreaths.

Joel looks down at his father.

His mother has allowed no hand but her own to touch the dead man. She has laid him out in his black vestments with his white collar. The bony fingers with their mauve nails are clasped stiffly around a Bible. The closed eyes have sunk. Despite whatever it is his mother has done to try and keep the face human, the thin lips have parted, showing a row of teeth, and the face is already skull-like.

Joel stoops over the corpse briefly, but does not touch it with his lips.

Finally he looks at the woman who is seated beside the coffin, shrouded in charcoal cloth from head to foot. She too, is grasping a Bible. She has been watching her son. Her eyes gleam behind her black veil.

"Have you finished the stone?" she asks in a dry voice.

"Yes."

"You left space for my name beneath his?"

"Yes, Mother."

"It will not be long before you have the pleasure of carving it," she says with a bitter smile. "Then you will be free of us, Joel. I imagine you can hardly wait."

He takes a chair and places it on the other side of the coffin. He sits, folding his arms, staring straight ahead. They do not exchange any further words.

He thinks of the years that the locust has eaten.

A small crowd has followed the coffin to the cemetery.

The mourners sniff loudly. The service is short and plain. Joel reads the Ninetieth Psalm, his quiet voice betraying no emotion.

The coffin is lowered into the stony trough that has been dug for it. Shovelfuls of earth thud onto the wood.

It is over and the crowd files away, tipping hats to the widow, shaking hands with the son. Soon the two of them are left alone at the graveside.

"Is that the best you could do for your father?" she says in a bitter voice, gesturing at the plain gravestone.

"It seems adequate to me."

"Adequate?" Miriam Lennox lifts the veil from her face. Her hair is white these days, her face chiselled by time. Anger has tightened the thin mouth and brightened the colourless eyes. "After all he gave you?"

"Tell me, Mother, what more do I owe him?" Joel retorts coldly.

"Rich people pay money for the stones you carve. Could you not spare a grain of your gift to honour your father?"

He meets her eyes. "In all his life, Father never uttered one word of praise for my gift. He despised it. It would have been hypocritical of me to carve anything on his tombstone."

She sneers. "It is fitting that his monument should be this meagre thing. He suffered humiliation every day of his life. His poverty. The ignorance of his parishioners. The hatred of his own son."

"He inflicted humiliations on me that were far worse than anything he ever suffered."

"You broke his heart," she rasps, "with your whoring, your rioting, your evil ways."

"He died of a stroke!"

"You killed him."

"He tried to crush everything I ever did. You both did." He takes an unsteady breath. "I have had to fight for my life since I was a little child, Mother."

"You fought because of the evil in you." Her eyes glitter. "Because of the hatred the Devil sowed in your heart."

His anger breaks. "You're the ones who hated *me!* Jesus Christ, you must have hated me so much. The things you did to me. Degrading! Inhuman! You crippled me." He is trembling violently. "You made my life such a goddamned wretched misery—" He stops and wipes spittle from his mouth.

She sees the veins standing out on his fists and laughs, a cracked sound. "Strike me, if that is what you want. The Devil is raging in you, my son. He possesses you utterly."

"There is no devil in me!"

"He controls you, as a puppet master jerks a puppet. He fills your mouth with obscenity. He inflames your loins. He drives you to filth and degradation."

"Mother, for God's sake!"

"Oh, don't be a hypocrite," she hisses, her teeth bared. "I know what you do to those painted little whores! I know why they follow you! You brought their slime into our house, their cheap perfume. You flaunted your iniquity in your father's face. That was what killed him!"

"You're the one who's evil," he says in a shaking voice. "You make me want to—"

"What, Joel? What is Satan telling you to do now? Does he want you to kill me too?" A terrible eagerness comes into her eyes. "Or is it something worse?"

"Stop, for God's sake!"

"Does he want you to violate me, on your father's coffin? Is that it?"

He raises his fist, speechless.

Hectic colour blazes in her cheeks. "Do it, Joel! Do it and let Satan have his triumph!"

He turns away with a tormented sound and stumbles back to the old Chevrolet, leaving her by the grave. He gets in and rests his forehead on the wheel, trembling and nauseous. The blood is pounding in his temples.

He takes from his pocket the piece of paper the government has sent him. He stares at it blindly. It summons him to a distant country to fight a distant war. It gives times and dates and places for his departure.

She does not know about this yet. He has not told her.

He knows he need not go. He could easily get a student deferment. But he will not. He will not ask for this cup to be taken from him. He has to get away from Prescott.

And this piece of paper will take him a long, long way.

Barcelona

Mercedes Eduard lay face down on the black marble slab. It was heated from beneath and the smooth stone was agreeably warm against her naked body.

The masseuse's hands were strong but gentle. Mercedes lay inert, hovering on the edge of sleep, feeling only the sure, gentle hands.

Today is my fiftieth birthday. I have lived half a century, she thought.

The masseuse ran her oiled palms across the firm muscles of calves and thighs. Mercedes could feel her own flesh springing under the probing fingers.

My body is still supple, she reflected. I can say I have kept my looks better than many. But nothing else is left me of the things by which women measure the success of their lives. I have no husband, no lover, no home, no family. I left all that behind me.

All my life I have left behind me the things I loved most.

The masseuse touched her shoulder. "All done, Señora Eduard. A brisk swim will do you good now."

She sat up. The masseuse wrapped a towel deftly around her.

The other masseuse had also just finished, and a second woman was sitting up on the slab beside her. Mercedes glimpsed a slim, naked body before the white towel closed around it.

Her eyes met the other woman's. She was in her mid-twenties, dark-haired, with velvety brown eyes. Mercedes realized, almost with a start, that the young woman was truly beautiful, her face and throat shaped by superb, subtle lines. The face was vaguely familiar.

She smiled into Mercedes's eyes. Mercedes nodded formally.

She showered the oil off her skin, changed into her swimsuit and went to the pool. A faint haze of steam hung over the surface of the water. There was no shock to her system as she plunged in. Everything in this club, she thought wryly, was carefully designed not to give anybody's system a shock of any kind.

But the aura of quiet luxury was infinitely soothing. America taught me how to enjoy being pampered, she thought. Wealth, the panacea for all pains...

She swam a few lengths, then drifted a little, keeping away from the other women in the water.

The girl who had been beside her in the massage room came to the poolside. She was wearing a black one-piece swimsuit. Her figure was tall and lithe, with long, well-muscled legs. She moved with the musical grace of a professional dancer or model. She dived into the water cleanly and swam over to Mercedes. "A massage makes you feel wonderful," she said cheerfully.

"Yes," Mercedes nodded.

"I've only seen you here once or twice before. You don't come very often, do you?"

"Not very often."

"I try and come every day." She sleeked the black hair away from her temples, smiling at Mercedes. "Membership is so expensive. I feel I have to get my money's worth. I force myself to use every piece of equipment in the place, even the torture instruments in the gym."

"You look very fit."

"My name is Maya Duran." She held out a dripping hand.

Mercedes usually discouraged attempts to be friendly. She

valued her privacy. But this young woman had a calm assurance that set her apart from the brash *beaux mondaines* of this city. Her beauty had an exotic darkness. Mercedes touched the cool fingers briefly. "Mine is Mercedes Eduard," she said. "There's something familiar about your face."

Maya Duran laughed. "I'm a model. If you buy fashion magazines, you've probably seen my picture."

"Yes, I've seen your picture."

The other woman checked the clock on the wall. "I'm going to have an early lunch in the restaurant here before I go to the studio. Would you care to join me?"

Mercedes was faintly surprised to hear herself answer, "Yes, thank you. I think I will."

The restaurant was half-empty. The diners were all women, elegantly coutured and coiffed, heads together in confidentialities. Most were nibbling on salads, mindful of costly wardrobes at home.

Mercedes and Maya sat by the window. The younger woman was open without being a babbler. She told Mercedes about her eight-year career in modelling, unaffectedly mentioning the prestigious magazines she had worked with, the covers she had been on. She was also openly curious about the older woman.

"You're not married?" she asked Mercedes, glancing at her bare ring finger.

"I'm divorced."

"Any children?"

"A girl of fifteen. She's at boarding school in California."

"I would have hated that, at fifteen."

"Oh, I think Eden's quite happy there. She has friends. She goes to her father in Santa Barbara for two weekends a month and she comes to me for her school holidays. We travel together a lot. Last summer we went to Italy. In the autumn we chartered a yacht and cruised for three weeks off the Greek islands."

"It sounds very glamorous and exciting," Maya said. But Mercedes caught the undertone in her voice.

"A family shouldn't live like that," she said with a little shrug. "Glamour and excitement don't make up for stability. But divorce sets its own rules. Are you married?"

"No. Actually, I don't think I'm the marrying kind."

"Surely you're too young to say that."

"I'm twenty-seven."

"You look younger."

"Thank you." Maya smiled. "The torture instruments must be paying off." She certainly gleamed with health. She was wearing a pale blue Chanel suit with beautiful gold buttons. She wore no jewellery. It occurred to Mercedes that she had seldom known a woman who wore not a single trinket of any sort.

"Today is my fiftieth birthday," Mercedes said, then wondered why she had uttered the words.

Maya Duran put down her knife and fork. "Oh! But that's wonderful!"

"Is it?" Mercedes asked dryly.

"Let's have a bottle of champagne," Maya said eagerly.

"I'd rather not."

"But you must celebrate," Maya said, waving to the waiter. "It's positively obligatory."

"I don't want champagne," Mercedes said.

"I'll be glad to pay for it. Waiter!"

Mercedes laid down her fork. "If I wished to celebrate my birthday," she said distinctly, "I would be quite capable of deciding how, and when and with whom." Her icy tone wiped the pleasure from Maya's face.

The younger woman opened her mouth, then closed it again and looked down at her plate without expression.

They sat in silence for a moment. The waiter arrived and hovered at their table, waiting for the order.

"I was presumptuous," Maya said quietly to her plate.

"No," Mercedes said with an effort. "You were trying to be kind. Waiter, a bottle of your best champagne, please."

When the waiter left, Maya lifted her eyes to Mercedes's. "You didn't invite intimacy. I apologize for trespassing."

"I should be the one to apologize," Mercedes said. "I was very rude. It's very gracious of you to bother with a dull, middle-aged stranger."

"You're lovely," Maya said. "And I'm not being gracious. I've always wanted to talk to you. From the first time I saw you, I felt something. An affinity. A warmth. Something. I don't know the word. But I know the feeling. We're going to be friends."

.   .   .

Lunch ended on an upbeat, lifted by the champagne. They were both laughing as they walked out into the spring sunlight.

Maya turned to Mercedes and gave her a card. "Let's do this again soon. I've had the most delightful lunch."

Mercedes smiled. "So have I."

She watched the elegant figure walk across the carpark and get into a sporty red Lancia. With a throaty growl of engines and a quick wave, Maya was gone.

Mercedes looked down at the card in her hand. It read simply, MAYA DURAN, followed by a Barcelona number.

By most standards, she thought suddenly, my life is two-thirds over. What am I going to do with the third that remains to me?

Los Angeles

Eden dreamed she'd been bound in chains. She was helpless, crushed by the manacles.

Mama and Daddy were in the same room. But they didn't see her. They didn't know she was there.

She could see Mama's face, white and strained, and she knew it was a bad fight. Daddy was shouting. Horrible things. Horrible things about Mama.

Eden wanted to block her ears, shut out the ugly words, but she couldn't move.

Then Daddy saw her at last. But he didn't come to unchain her. He started shouting at her. He got to his feet, and his mouth was moving and the words that came out were terrible. There were cracks in the walls and the ceiling was coming down. The house was crumbling. The weight of all that stone was going to fall on them and obliterate them all. And Daddy didn't care.

And she couldn't move. She knew if she could stop Daddy's words, the walls would stop falling, and they would all be safe. So she screamed to drown him out.

She screamed so loudly it tore her chest and deafened her.

She woke suddenly, soaked in sweat. She was sitting bolt upright. Her heart was hammering against her ribs. She became aware that the Dormouse, who slept in the bed next to hers, was also sitting up.

"Did I scream?" Eden gasped.

"Shhh, no. You just sat up."

"I wanted to scream. I was having a nightmare. About my father." She felt unbearably shaky, her stomach churning. "God, I feel sick."

"Hush," the Dormouse whispered. "You'll wake the whole dorm."

"Screw the whole dorm."

"Go back to sleep." The Dormouse lay back down and rolled over.

Eden sat staring into the darkness.

Chu Lai, South Vietnam

The helicopter tilts and rises slowly into the air.

The two dozen conscripts on the ground stare upwards at the machine as it rises away from them.

The whirling downdraught buffets them, whipping caps off, flattening their ponchos against their bodies. The grass swirls and streaks around them. They huddle to the ground until the thunder of the helicopter's rotors fades away.

A black NCO strides among them, screaming at them to pick up their gear and form up. They obey in a daze. They are blinded, their possessions scattered, their faces streaked.

These boys have come to join A Company, 3rd Brigade, 25th Infantry Division of the U.S. Army in Vietnam. They are part of one of the mightiest military forces ever to stand in Asia, but they do not look very fierce as they shuffle into a dishevelled line and follow Jeffries into the base camp.

Like the others, Joel Lennox's hair has been cropped close to his head. He looks very young. They all do. They look like boys, bewildered and weary.

The country is alien and unwelcoming. Joel stares around him at the olive drab and the red mud and the blue swirl of smoke. A misty green plain of flooded rice paddies stretches out around the camp. In the distance, dim mountains loom threateningly. The air is wet and heavy. There is a rich stink of decay, excrement, a steam of foreign vegetation.

The jungle is a rotting hell where the enemy thrives, invisible to American eyes. The enemy is a creeping animal who, they have been told, can live in the trees, in water, under the ground. He seems impervious to bullets, high explosives, needle bombs, defoliants, the concentrated might of American technical ingenuity.

They march into base. The camp is chaos and order in one. Roads are ankle-deep courses of mud. Tanks and trucks loom in the grey drizzle. Personnel and vehicles churn to and fro in a welter of noise. Over it all, rock music blares from loudspeakers. There is a gory carnival atmosphere, summer camp with howitzers.

The unit of construction seems to be the sandbag. Fat and heavy with rain, untold myriads of them cloak every hut, every structure, every dugout.

A soldier, sitting half-naked on the hood of a jeep, oblivious to the rain, grins at them and shouts out, "Happy birthday, happy Easter, merry fuckin' Christmas!"

"What's he mean?" Joel asks the man next to him.

"Means we gonna have a birthday here, gonna have Easter here, gonna have Christmas here. Gonna be here a fuckin' year, man."

Sergeant Jeffries leads them to a hut. He tells them to form a line and goes in to see the captain. They start muttering among themselves.

"Hear those guns."

"Only one thing on my mind. Gettin' outa this shithole alive in one piece."

"Think there's any pussy around here?"

"Smell the air. Like the whole fuckin' place is rotten."

"Wonder how far away the fuckin' gooks are?"

"Wonder if this fuckin' rain ever gonna stop?"

"Wonder . . ."

The black NCO emerges from the hut, snarling. "Shut your mouths, dammit. You with A Company now. You better start acting like soldiers. And shape up, for fuck sake. You look like the slums of Saigon." He goes back in.

They glance at one another and shut their mouths. They make an effort to keep in line.

There is a distant rumble. It steadily becomes an overwhelming roar, mobile thunder. Six olive-green helicopters are approaching across the plain. Their snub noses are slick with rain. They move fast, with urgency. Vehicles, among them ambulances, stream onto the landing field to meet them.

As the choppers land, their rotors create a storm that lashes the camp, drowning out all other noise, even the rock music. Muddy water whips off the puddles and flails the new arrivals. They break their line and run to the chain-link fence that surrounds the landing field.

They have an excellent view of the scene through the fence. It is one they have seen many times before, on their television screens at home. It all has a familiar look. The soldiers who spill out of the choppers are filthy with mud. They carry all sorts of weapons. Some wear ammunition belts slung around their bodies. They are clearly fresh from combat.

Some are wounded and have bloodstained field dressings on heads or limbs.

Some are limp forms that have to be carried.

The new arrivals hang on the fence, watching in silence as medics hustle the wounded to ambulances. Four men are man-handling one of the limp forms out of a chopper. They are clumsy and the man's equipment slides out of his lap to the ground.

But it is not equipment. It is something wet that unravels from inside him, purple and yellow and slippery. One of the medics grasps at the stuff and tries to cram it back into the man.

Sergeant Jeffries comes out of the captain's hut. He opens his mouth to scream at the new arrivals for breaking ranks but sees that most of them are doubled over, losing their lunch. He looks past them. Then he shuts his mouth and stands with his hands on his hips, shaking his head slowly.

spring 1969

Los Angeles

A few seconds before the police opened fire, Eden turned and ran. She had seen the rifles aiming at the marchers from behind the phalanx of plastic shields, the squat canisters fixed on their muzzles.

"Come on," she yelled. "We gotta get out of here!"

She was already fighting her way through the chanting crowd when the canisters began to rain down, spewing tear gas.

The stone throwing stopped. The marchers, welded a second earlier into one vast, angry beast, now exploded into ten thousand panicking individuals. Faced with the billowing white clouds, they streamed chaotically sideways and back.

But a host of helmeted, black-clad figures had appeared at the corner of Westwood Boulevard, blocking off the retreat. The protestors were trapped between the wall of tear gas and the batons of the National Guard.

She crammed a handkerchief to her face and followed a group of young people who were scrambling over a hedge into someone's garden. The owners of the garden, a prosperous-looking middle-aged couple, watched in stupefaction from the porch of their Tudor-style house as the National Guard followed with swinging batons.

The protestors tried to scramble over a fence into the next property. The fence collapsed, bringing twenty of them down. At once, the guardsmen were upon them, clubbing, kicking.

The white cloud of gas had drifted across the garden and Eden suddenly caught a lungful. She tried to gasp for air, but only sucked more of the searing gas into her throat. She choked and gagged, writhing among the other bodies.

Something struck her a stunning blow on the shoulder. Her arm went numb. She was hauled roughly to her feet. Through streaming eyes, she saw her captor towering over her, black and menacing.

A voice yelled, "Let her go!"

She was brought up with a jerk. The owner of the house was blocking their way. "Let her go," he repeated. "I saw you hit that girl. She didn't do a thing."

The black pig's muzzle turned on Eden. Dark eyes surveyed her through goggles.

"I'll take care of her," the voice said. "You go and chase the big ones."

The guardsman hesitated. Then he thrust Eden into the householder's arms and ran back to chase the others.

Her savior put an arm around her shoulders and hustled her onto the porch and into the house. He slammed and bolted the door. His wife was shutting windows against the creeping gas.

"Water," Eden whispered desperately, clawing at her throat.

"Vile stuff," the woman said. "They needn't have used it."

Eden gulped at the water, her whole body shuddering. "Thanks for rescuing me."

"We have a daughter," the man replied. "She's grown up, now, but . . . those guardsmen didn't have to be so brutal. You're not a student, are you?"

"No. But I soon will be."

"What's your name?" the man asked.

"Eden."

The woman looked down at Eden. "Do you really care about the Vietnam War that much?" she asked with a half smile.

Eden nodded. "I think it's the worst thing that ever happened in the history of the whole *world*."

The couple stared at her. She was beautiful, with the oval face and slender body of a Botticelli angel. Her hair, which seemed black enough to absorb light, coiled in thick snakes around her shoulders.

Despite her streaming eyes and filthy clothes, she was arresting. Her breasts and hips were not fully ripe beneath the jeans and T-shirt. But her face was, at least superficially, adult, with a firm chin and full cheekbones. The generous mouth and intense green eyes had a reckless, slightly wild radiance. Expressions moved across her mobile features, like clouds across a summer sky.

"Don't worry about me," she told them. "I do this kind of thing a lot."

"You need to wash that filthy stuff off yourself," the woman said. "Come along."

The woman washed Eden's T-shirt while Eden stood under the shower, the stream of water driving the stinging needles of the tear gas off her skin.

When she had finished, she opened the shower door and stepped out, her naked body streaming water. The older woman handed her a towel.

"Do your parents know where you are?" she asked.

"My father has no idea. He hardly knows the Vietnam War is on, really. But, like, the *shame* would get to him. His daughter with a lot of long-hairs in some riot."

"Don't you have a mother?"

"She's in Spain. They're divorced. I'm at boarding school."

"Oh. I'm sorry."

"Don't be," Eden said coolly. Her green eyes were unsmiling. "Boarding school is better than living at home the way it was. I hate my father." She dropped the towel and sat on the edge of the bath, indifferent to her own nakedness. The woman glanced at the slim, pretty body. The bruise on the arm was purpling rapidly. She looked so vulnerable, so unequipped for life. Yet there was something daunting about this child-woman's poise.

"Hate is a very strong word."

"Oh, I guess I don't really hate him." Eden shrugged. "I just hate what he's become. He used to be okay. When I was a kid, I mean. Then he changed. It's like he's not even there any more."

"How's that?"

"Well, what with his parties, his little girls and all the coke he does, he doesn't have much time to be a human being any more." Her mouth twisted. "He's too busy having fun, fun, fun."

"Your father takes cocaine?" the woman asked, wide-eyed.

"As much as he can get."

"And when you say little girls, you mean . . ."

"I mean underage hookers," Eden said bitterly. "Kids my age that screw old men for money. In fact, he likes them younger and younger every year. Maybe he'll end up screwing babies." She laughed, but the woman didn't join in.

"Oh, dear." The older woman stood with the dripping T-shirt in her hands.

"It's his problem," Eden said. But her eyes had grown hot, as though she was holding back the tears.

"I suppose it is," the woman said wryly. "I'll go and find you some of my daughter's clothes."

By the time Eden was dressed in a clean dress that was a little too big for her, the street outside was deserted and the wind had swept the tear gas away. The man was standing on his porch, sorrowfully surveying his wrecked garden.

"I guess the coast is clear," Eden said. "Listen. Thank you for rescuing me. I'll send the dress back to you."

"Keep it. Or throw it away."

Eden kissed the woman, took the bundle of her soiled clothing and walked out of the house. She didn't look back as she hurried through the garden into the street.

The couple stood amidst the wreckage of their garden, staring after her.

Barcelona

"I'm going up to the Ampurdán for a fortnight," Mercedes told Maya over a lunch of champagne and oysters.

"How lovely. Where will you stay?"

"Near a little village called San Lluc."

"Oh, I know San Lluc. It's an enchanting place. You'll be able to unwind completely."

They made a point of lunching together at the club these days. Their talk was always easy and amusing. Mercedes had begun to look forward to the meetings with a glow of pleasure. Maya's dark beauty had brought a warmth into her life in Barcelona on which she was starting to depend. Her visits to the club had risen from one or two a month to one or two a week.

"As a matter of fact," Mercedes admitted, "I'm looking for a property to buy in the area."

"You couldn't make a better investment," Maya said, sipping champagne. "Prices there are going to rocket. San Lluc is becoming very fashionable."

"So I noticed," Mercedes said ironically. "San Lluc is my home."

"Your home?"

"I was born there. My father was the village blacksmith. My mother was the shopkeeper's daughter. I was born in the forge. Why are you shaking your head?"

"To look at you in your Yves St Laurent suit," Maya said, "with those beautiful diamonds, nobody would guess you were born in a blacksmith's forge. You're so poised. So sophisticated."

"San Lluc certainly wasn't sophisticated when I was born," Mercedes agreed dryly. "Anything but. It was always a beautiful place, though of course I didn't realize it as a child. "

"Things must have changed a great deal, Mercedes."

"They have." Mercedes studied the pearly rainbow of an oyster shell. "There are restaurants and bars, and a nightclub, and even a discotheque. Rich people from Barcelona are buying the ruins and turning them into chic weekend cottages. The house I was born in has been turned into maisonettes. There was a Porsche parked where my father's anvil used to stand."

"The whole world is changing, Mercedes."

"Yes, it is. The world grows old. I have changed too. I used to have dreams and illusions. Now I find I've become the sort of person I used to despise."

"That happens to everybody," Maya said gently.

"It shouldn't. People should have some illusions left, even after fifty years. I've lost so many, Maya."

"The only way not to lose illusions is never to grow up. And you shouldn't despise yourself just because you can afford oysters and champagne."

"There's more to it than that. What's modelling like?"

"Modelling is like . . . like being in a silent movie. No one cares what you think. If you try and say something, it's a curiosity, like a dog walking on its hind legs. They don't really listen. They're just surprised you can do it at all."

Mercedes smiled. "I understand."

Maya checked her watch. "Damn. Talking of work, I have to rush. Good luck with your house hunting, Mercé. Call me when you get back."

She kissed Mercedes's cheek and was gone.

Mercedes returned to Barcelona two weeks later. She had not stayed in San Lluc itself, but in the five-star hotel that had sprung up on a spur of land overlooking one of the enchanting, rocky bays. For two weeks she had explored the surrounding countryside in the company of a local land agent.

The day before coming back to Barcelona, she had gone with the agent to the notary in Palafrugell and signed for the purchase of six hectares of land, around fifteen acres.

The plot was magnificent. It was not far from the village, near the sea, but with fine views of the Pyrenees. It was exactly what she had been looking for. She had already chosen the site for the house she was going to build, though the architecture of the place was as yet unformed in her mind.

She called Maya before unpacking.

"Mercedes!" Maya's voice lifted. "How was your visit to San Lluc?"

"It went well. I was wondering whether you'd care to have dinner with me sometime this weekend."

"Of course I would. Where and when?"

"Would Saturday night at La Catalana suit you?"

"Perfect!" There was unaffected happiness in the other woman's voice.

"I'll pick you up in my car."

"I'll be waiting," Maya said.

Mercedes hung up. This would be the first time she and Maya had met outside the confines of the health club. She had missed the girl.

Why do I think of her as a girl? she wondered. She is a grown woman. Perhaps it was Maya Duran's openness, her lack of guile, that made her seem so youthful.

For a painful moment, Mercedes was reminded of another guileless young woman she had known, over thirty years ago, in San Lluc. She winced at the memory and went to take a bath.

Maya was waiting in the foyer of her apartment building on Saturday night. She greeted Mercedes with a wonderful smile. But she paused as she saw the Daimler limousine purring at the kerb.

"Is *this* your car?" she asked Mercedes.

"It's my going-out car."

The chauffeur stepped out and opened the door for them. The two women settled themselves beside one another in the leather-upholstered interior. Maya stroked the burr walnut inlays of the Daimler. "It's absolutely magnificent. You must be seriously rich."

Mercedes shrugged. "I'm comfortable."

Both women were wearing striking evening dresses, Mercedes's in midnight blue, Maya's in maroon silk.

"That dress is new, isn't it?" Maya said. "Did you buy it especially for tonight?"

Mercedes laughed softly. "Did I forget to cut off a label somewhere? Yes, I bought it especially."

"It's beautiful. It suits you. Classic styles will always suit you."

"I wish I had your flair for clothes." Mercedes looked at Maya's dress, which was sculpted above the breasts to show ivory-smooth shoulders and a perfect throat. As at the club, she wore no jewelry, but she looked heart-stoppingly lovely. "You look exquisite," Mercedes said.

"Thank you. The dress is five years old. But it's Balenciaga and it never goes out of style. So—we're definitely celebrating tonight! Did you buy something?"

"Yes. I've bought six hectares of land."

"But how exciting! I'm dying to hear all about it." She smiled at Mercedes, genuinely pleased.

La Catalana was famous for its seafood cuisine, its sumptuous decor, and the celebrities who went there. It was already crowded and noisy when they arrived and would be crowded, Barcelona-style, until three or four in the morning, as diners continued to come and go from cabarets and nightclubs.

Heads turned to stare openly at the two glamourously dressed women as the maître d'hôtel led them to their corner table. Waiters fussed around them with various flattering attentions, easing them solicitously into their places. Two glasses of champagne materialized in front of them.

The chef was already bustling out to their table, beaming. He kissed Mercedes's hand.

"Luis, I want you to meet my dear friend Maya Duran. Maya, this is Luis Marqués, the famous chef."

"*Encantado.*" He kissed Maya's hand too. "The lobsters are good tonight."

"Then we put ourselves entirely in your expert hands," Mercedes said. "Perhaps you wouldn't mind choosing the wine for us too?"

"Leave it to me, Señora Eduard. Delighted to meet you, Señorita Duran." He bustled back into the kitchen.

"Am I really your 'dear friend'?" Maya asked, her head on one side.

"Of course you are."

A waiter arrived with a plate of oysters on the half shell. They were pearly fresh, elusively luscious. They started to eat.

"What will you do with the land you've bought?" Maya asked.

"I'm going to build a house."

"Just one? On six hectares?"

"Just one. Just for me. I'm going to live in it. I've been staying in an apartment in Barcelona for eighteen months, and I'm sick of the sound of traffic."

"Well, San Lluc will be a good antidote to that. You'll end up running around with one shoe on, and a long white veil flowing around your hair."

"I might." Mercedes smiled. "But solitary, eccentric splendour rather appeals to me. What other options are open to me in my old age?"

"A beautiful young man who can make love twenty times a night," Maya suggested solemnly.

Mercedes laughed. "No, thank you. No complications of that sort. I'm going back home, Maya."

The lobsters were brought in. There were a dozen of them, split and grilled, the succulent white flesh still sizzling. Fragrant beds of saffron rice were laid on their plates, and Luis himself bustled out to position the shellfish just right, and dribble hot butter sauce on them. He waited, glowering, until they tasted the dish and pronounced it superb. Then he left with a beaming face.

"Part of the reason I want to build a house is Eden," Mercedes went on. "So she can have somewhere to stay when she comes to me, somewhere to keep a horse. Somewhere to call home. It's better than nothing. As a matter of fact, Eden's coming out this summer. We're going to Paris."

Maya looked up. "Does she like fashion shows? I can get tickets to the summer couture collections. Chanel, Cardin, Yves St Laurent, whatever she's interested in."

"She only seems to wear Levi's and T-shirts these days," Mercedes said wryly. "But that's a lovely idea. It would be an education for her."

Maya smiled. "I'll find out who's got the boldest collection this year and get you some good seats."

"Thank you, Maya."

They ate in silence for a while.

"What does your ex-husband do for a living?" Maya asked at last.

Mercedes patted her mouth with the napkin. "Dominic's retiring this year. He's in air freight. He exports glossy consumer goods to various South American countries."

"What is he like as a person?"

"Very charming. Dominic was a fighter pilot in the Pacific during the war. When I met him, he was so handsome, so dashing. I thought he was wonderful. But he changed."

"In what way?"

Mercedes's face had closed. "I married him because I thought he loved life. But I was wrong. He just loved pleasure. He took pleasure more and more seriously as he grew older. Until pleasure mattered to him more than anything else.''

"You mean he had affairs with other women?''

"Also with other things. With drugs. With money. With the good life. With anything that gave him gratification. In the end, he was like a handsome tree that's been eaten away from the inside by termites. It looks tall and proud, but it's hollow and ready to fall, and the birds no longer nest in its branches.''

"Oh, Mercedes.'' Maya's fingers reached out and closed around Mercedes's hand. "Don't look so bitter. Please.''

"It's all right. It's all over now. Dominic takes care of Eden during his two weekends. He's just responsible enough to be a father for four days a month.''

Maya rested her chin on her hands and stared at Mercedes with her brown, luminous eyes. "Why did you come back to Spain?''

"To find myself,'' Mercedes said. "No, that sounds juvenile. I know what I am. I came back to find what I used to be. Not to recapture, you understand. Just to remember. Even if I wanted to be that person again, I couldn't any more. I have changed too much.'' She smiled. "Maya, you remind me rather painfully of someone I used to know, long ago.''

"Who was she?''

"Her name was Matilde. She was the best friend I ever had. She used to ask me questions just the way you do. Quiet, searching, endless questions.''

"What happened to her?'' Maya asked.

"She went away.''

"Oh. I'm glad I remind you of your best friend. If you let me, maybe I can become what she was.''

Mercedes felt her face change. She was aware of warmth choking her throat. She was almost angry with this beautiful young woman for penetrating her defences so easily and so disturbingly. "You don't know what she was. You can never know.'' Mercedes took a breath to steady herself. She closed the subject determinedly. "If Luis will let us choose our own dessert, I'm going to have some fruit. But I can recommend the black cherry *bavarois*—if you like sweet things.''

•   •   •

Two days later, she called Maya again.

"I've had an idea. Why don't you come with us to Paris?"

There was a silence. "Surely Eden won't want me intruding on your holiday?"

"Oh, it would be such fun! Eden would be able to learn so much from you. She's so gauche and you're so . . ." She didn't finish the sentence. "I've got a suite booked at the Ritz already. It's very comfortable and there's plenty of room, so it wouldn't cost you anything at all. We'll go to the fashion shows—you, me and Eden. We'll stuff ourselves on French cooking, spend a fortune on clothes, kick our heels up. What do you say?"

An excited laugh came down the line. "It sounds rather a wonderful idea."

"Are you busy then?"

"No."

"Then will you come?"

She hesitated for a second. "Yes. I will."

"Good." Mercedes smiled. "That's settled."

summer *1969*

Paris

Eden van Buren sits between her mother and Maya Duran, in the front row, with the fashion editors, the buyers, and the very special guests, who all loyally wear one of last year's models.

Eden is the only person in the room wearing jeans.

She pretends to be bored by the models who prance down the long catwalk, bombarded by flashes from the dozens of cameramen. But in reality the collection is riveting.

It is a free-form mélange of classic Parisian elegance with psychedelic patterns and colours. The materials are exotic. There are shimmering silks and patterned voiles, diaphanous chiffons through which navels and nipples tease the cameras.

Excitement is washing around the room. Flashbulbs explode like summer lightning. Reporters scribble furiously. The buyers are bright-eyed.

The collection is brilliant. Tomorrow, next week, everyone will want these designs. Whatever is being shown elsewhere in Paris this week, this is where it's happening.

The great couturier, said by so many to be burned out, has resurged, phoenix-like, from his own ashes. He has produced, in this final year of a turbulent decade, what is undoubtedly the wittiest and most elegant summing-up of the past ten years' trends.

It is all here: flower power, LSD, free love; the Beatles, Carnaby Street, Haight-Ashbury; John Lennon, Angela Davis, Twiggy; yé-yé and go-go; hippies, yippies and spacemen.

Sensation!

This celebrated hotel in the Faubourg Saint-Honoré, with its tall Corinthian columns and its rococo gilding, has never seen anything like it. The heavy rock music seems to shake the chandeliers, making them emit a faint whimpering tinkle.

Even Eden van Buren, blasé, world-weary, sixteen-year-old Eden, is in the grip of the excitement. She has slid to the edge of her seat, green eyes bright.

Maya Duran glances at her with a smile. Her friend's daughter is ravishing. Where Mercedes's face is calm and composed, her daughter's beauty is restless. Eden's mouth is full and passionate. As she rapturously follows the show, her lips are slightly parted, as though awaiting a kiss. Her colouring is the same as her mother's, though there is little facial resemblance. Her eyes sometimes have the hard green glitter of emeralds, sometimes the dumb pain of a hurt child.

She treats her mother with coolness. Only now and then, as though wrenched from somewhere inside her, are there moments of love, abrupt kisses, rough embraces. For the rest, she remains aloof.

Mercedes has confided to Maya that Eden is even worse with her father. There is no favouritism. She blames them both equally bitterly for the break-up of the family. She is deliberately showing them her independence, the hard carapace she has had to develop.

Maya hopes that Eden will learn to adjust soon, before the pouts and tantrums become entrenched and her sweet nature curdles permanently.

At the end of a long four hours, the famous couturier himself emerges to accept the accolades of his public. They rise to their feet, clapping feverishly.

On the general wave of euphoria, Maya, Mercedes and Eden are borne out of the room. Eden is bubbling, more like a teenager than Maya has yet seen her. She walks between the older women, clinging to an arm of each, talking excitedly about the collection.

Mercedes waves at a taxi. They have to hurry. They have a reservation at Maxim's before the next show.

Two hundred and thirty-eight thousand miles from Paris, an ex-fighter pilot named Neil Armstrong clings to the ladder of his landing craft and scuffs gingerly at the ground below with his boot.

"The surface is fine and powdery," he reports to a listening world. "I can kick it up loosely with my toe. Like powdered charcoal."

Then he takes a little jump off the ladder. "That's one small step for a man," he intones, "one giant leap for mankind."

Soon he and his fellow astronaut Buzz Aldrin are gambolling on the surface of the moon like children. The people of the Earth watch the galactic revelry on countless millions of televisions. The fuzzy images leap and bound, their great golden helmets reflecting the distant blue ball in the black sky above them. Their voices crackle across the vast distance.

"Beautiful," says Aldrin. "Beautiful. Isn't that something? Magnificent desolation . . ."

The lunar landscape is bleak and cratered. Here nothing grows, no creature makes a sound, no breeze stirs the Stars and Stripes the two men have planted. No terrestrial desert was ever so silent, no mountaintop so remote, no island so empty of life.

The loneliness of the two men is absolute. The concerted endeavours of the mightiest nation on earth have put them here, farther beyond the reach of their fellow humans than any men have ever been before.

They caper in space, weightless, alone.

Chu Lai

Joel Lennox, too, stands among desolation. He too has been sent abroad by his country, at the spearhead of a mighty technological undertaking. Here too the ground is charcoal and bears no sign of life.

He stands holding his M–16 cradled in his arms, fumbling to reload the weapon. He is trying not to listen to the screams that come from the place where the Rangers are conducting their interrogation. Tears have made tracks through the filth on his face. His eyes have been inflamed by smoke. His throat is raw.

Though not one hut of the village is now standing, and though Vietnamese dead litter the earth, the loss has not eased. Five of their comrades are dead. Four more are badly wounded. The ambush they walked into this morning was perfectly planned, and the hail of fire that hit their patrol was devastatingly accurate.

The Americans have wreaked terrible retribution on the village. They have raked the huts with concentrated fire, slaughtering humans and their animals alike. Then they have set fire to the village.

But the destruction is ultimately meaningless, and they all know it. The Vietcong have melted back into the forest they came from, leaving no trace behind them.

And now the Rangers have arrived to ask their questions.

Joel walks through the smoke to the clearing. He moves with the animal wariness of the combat soldier, his head swivelling this way and that, high-strung senses alert. His face is gaunter than ever. The cheekbones look as though they will cut through the skin. A tic pulls at the corner of his mouth. The dark eyes are terrible. The fissures in the rock have opened wide and the agony within is plainly visible.

By now he has almost forgotten that there is a world other than this jungle, this war. He has almost forgotten that there are other ways of talking, other ways of behaving. He has become so completely immersed in the war that he is almost no longer a living man. He is a tenant of the realms of death.

He sees what the Rangers are doing.

The wives and children of the two farmers are being forced to watch. Their screaming is added to that of the peasants themselves, a symphony of agony.

Other Rangers smoke cigarettes in silence as they watch. A few American soldiers have also gathered to see, though most have retreated from the scene, nauseated. They are not saints. In the bloody course of the afternoon, women have been raped. Children are dead. Old people are dead. Water buffaloes have been butchered with machine-gun fire.

But that was in the rage of loss. This is beyond most of them. They are muttering among themselves, pale-faced. It is moments like this that bring home to them into what an alien war they have blundered into, what an alien world.

Joel watches the faces of the two suffering men. They are distorted into the masks that all human faces assume in extremes of pain. He has seen the faces of his own men like this. Boys from Colorado and Washington, Oklahoma and New Jersey. Faces that torment his dreams.

He sees Nguyen Van Khoi draw his heavy-bladed knife and stoop to inflict worse outrage on the writhing body.

He lifts the M–16 and tucks the butt into his shoulder. He sights carefully past Nguyen. One of the Rangers, quick-eyed, screams a warning. But it is too late. Joel's first burst rips the peasant's chest open like an old mattress. His next kills the other man equally cleanly. The screaming abruptly stops. Then the soft weeping begins.

Nguyen whirls on him, furious. A dozen Rangers are pointing weapons at Joel, fingers white on their triggers.

Joel crouches. He holds his M–16 pointed directly at Nguyen. They may chop him to pieces, but he will have time to kill the little Ranger captain. He waits, mindless, prepared for death.

Nguyen sees the expression on the American's face. The big man with the terrible eyes is ready to kill and be killed. He is impervious to fear or logic. He has gone beyond, into the dark dominions where nationality and uniform no longer matter. The dominions where men do anything that strikes them as reasonable.

Nguyen waves his hand very slowly, signalling his men to lower their weapons. They obey. Joel backs away from the Rangers, keeping his muzzle trained on Nguyen's belly.

"We're moving out," he tells his men. "Let's get back to the APCs."

Then he straightens, turns his back on the Rangers and walks away.

"You fool," Nguyen shrieks after him. "Your superiors will be informed of this!"

"Go fuck yourself," he says quietly.

They round up the rest of the patrol and move back to the armoured personnel carriers. Luke Jeffries, the big black sergeant, slaps Joel's back resoundingly.

"Mah friend," he says in a soft Alabama drawl, "you seem a little confused about which side you're on. Ah thought those slant-eyes was gonna take you out there and then, you sentimental motherfuckah."

But the words are kindly and Joel nods brief thanks. He longs for base camp and a hot shower. The smell of death is on his skin. He knows that soap will not remove it.

Woodstock, New York

Eden danced barefoot in the mud, her face lifted to the sky. Her eyes were closed. Her face was exhausted, vacant. Her black hair was tied back with a headband. Her wet jeans and smock clung to her body. Her nipples were taut through the transparent cloth.

A few others were dancing too. But in the torrential downpour that marked the second day of the largest rock festival in history, the remainder of the almost half-million-strong audience sat quietly sheltering in tents or huddling under blankets, waiting for the sun to shine again.

It was like a scene from some biblical epic, a vast multitude spread out on the bare ground, awaiting a prophet.

Nearby, the group of hippies in whose minibus she had hitched the long, long ride from Los Angeles sat under their tent, sharing a joint. They watched Eden dance with dreamy eyes.

They had driven nonstop for three days, across the Rockies to Salt Lake City, then through the prairies of Wyoming and Nebraska to Illinois, then from Chicago, in driving summer rain, through Cleveland, Pittsburgh, Philadelphia, into New York State.

As they'd travelled upstate, they'd joined the vast army of young people converging on Max Yasgur's dairy farm, fifty miles from the little town of Woodstock. They had arrived just in time to catch the opening band, the newly-formed folk rock band, Crosby, Stills, Nash & Young.

The hippies had come with cooking pots and bags of macrobiotic beans, being vegetarians. But today in the open field, with pouring rain, they had been forced to go hungry.

They had supplied themselves, however, with plenty of drugs.

To while away the tedium of the journey, they had given Eden a microdot of LSD. She had swallowed it on Interstate 80, near Iowa City, and the effects had not worn off yet.

She floated in a rippling world of shapes and lights, her inner being welded to the music, the rain, the rainbow sky that shimmered above her.

She felt that she was experiencing a mystical union with all things. The galaxies had become as soft and tender as kitten's fur. It was a wondrous and healing experience, which was soothing the pain she carried within her.

She lifted her arms to the sky and saw the rainbow reach down to her fingertips, flowing into her. The rain was golden. It enveloped her in radiance. The mud that squelched between her toes was the primordial ooze of life, the common sap of all things.

A short circuit finally cut the band short and the music fizzled out into silence. The huge crowd began clapping ironically. Eden, unaware, kept dancing through the mud, hands raised to the sky like a priestess.

Later, she opened her eyes and saw a Christ-like face above her. Golden hair hung in a wave around his pale brow. His beard was golden too, curling around a sweet, pale mouth. His blue eyes were windows to the sky. She could swim through them into the heavens beyond, lose herself in their vastness.

She felt his body moving in hers. Her jeans were around her ankles. She felt him sliding into the vacuum tube of her newly-unlocked loins.

So this was why he had come. This was the great ceremony he had come to celebrate. The rainbow closed around them. She smiled up at him, her eyes filling with tears of joy.

He was inside her, moving around within her hips, among her organs. Gold and blue clouds exploded through her mind. She clung to him, praying in a language she herself did not understand.

On the third day, she awoke in the tent, down from her acid trip, starving and exhausted. Her clothes were filthy, and everything smelled terrible.

She was also furious with the blond-haired boy.

"How could you do that to me while I was stoned?" she demanded bitterly. "I didn't even know what was happening."

"It was beautiful," he said dreamily.

"For you, maybe." She stared at him in disgust. Off acid, he was not Christ-like at all. He was just a thin, ratty-looking boy with dirty hair and a beard, smoking a pot pipe. "You creep," she said angrily. "It was my first time!"

"Be cool. Won't be your last."

Jimi Hendrix was playing *The Star-Spangled Banner* on his guitar. The titanic screams towered up to the sky, a dinosaur sound.

It was now five days since she'd skipped out of Mount Pleasant, not telling anybody where she was going. There would be hell to pay when she got back. But she didn't want to stay here any longer.

She had missed most of the festival through being stoned. She had lost her virginity to a stranger. And now all she saw was squalor and chaos.

She trudged through the mud to the information stand, and stood in line for an hour to use one of the telephones that had been set up.

"Dad? It's me."

She listened wearily to the explosion at the other end of the line.

"I'm at Woodstock," she said. "Woodstock, New York. At the rock festival. Yeah, I'm okay. I'm sorry. I'm *sorry*. Listen, if I get to La Guardia, can you have a ticket to LA waiting for me?"

Chu Lai

He hears the sound of ripping calico. A flame streaks through the air and into one of the amtracs. The vehicle and the men in it erupt in a blinding flash. The explosion flattens several of the soldiers nearby, including Joel Lennox. Limbs and debris rain down.

The unmistakable, shattering roar of enemy fire opens up on them.

The Americans scramble wildly for what cover they can find, attempting to answer the fire. Joel Lennox tries to scream at his men, telling them to get behind the armoured vehicles. But there is no breath in his lungs, and he cannot rise. There is a strange numbness. He looks down at himself and sees that his side has been torn open. Blood is spouting through the rents in his uniform.

He has been wounded before. This time he knows it is serious.

He clamps a hand over the wound unthinkingly. The blood continues to jet out between his fingers. There is no pain, just the dreadful numbness. And his right leg will not respond. He rolls along the ground towards the nearest APC. The air is being torn by bullets. There are screams. His men are being cut down, massacred.

He is desperate to do something, but the wound robs him of strength. Then the pain comes. It crushes the breath from his lungs, tears at his soul.

And I looked, and, behold, a whirlwind came out of the north, a great cloud, and a fire infolding itself, and a brightness was about it, and out of the midst thereof as the colour of amber, out of the midst of the fire.

And then blackness.

spring *1970*

Prescott

They show him into the room where his mother lies. He still moves with painful slowness, his arm pressed to his ribs. He is very thin. The tan he got in Vietnam has faded and his gaunt face is white.

"Mrs. Lennox," the nurse says. "Your son."

The old woman on the bed opens her eyes slowly. Now, at last, her eyes have colour. Pain and the imminence of death have darkened them.

"I told you," she says with an effort, "that it would not be long, Joel."

"How do you feel, Mother?"

"I feel like death," she says. Her eyes close again.

The nurse pulls up a chair for Joel and leaves them, closing the door. The white room is bathed in stripes of light through the venetian blinds. Joel stares at the tubes that lead from machines into his mother's withered body. In the corner of the room, a screen registers each beat of the failing heart with a glowing green dot.

She does not move for so long that he thinks she has fallen

asleep. But she has been gathering her strength. The dark eyes open again and fix on Joel's. There is a glitter in their depths.

"So," she whispers. "They have brought you from your hospital to see me in mine."

"Yes, Mother."

"Do you have pain?"

"Sometimes."

"Show me."

He hesitates, then unfastens the khaki shirt the VA hospital gave him to travel in. He pulls it aside so she can see the wound. It curves around his lean flank, over the hipbone. The marks of the stitches are still angry and red.

Her mouth twists. "Is this how they sent you back? Like a gutted herring?"

"This is how they sent me back."

She is silent. Then she closes her eyes again. "You will heal. I will not."

He fastens his shirt and sits awkwardly in the chair beside her. "And you?" he asks. "Do you have pain?"

"There was one great pain at first. Not now. They have given me drugs. I did not want them. But they give me them, nevertheless."

Her bedside table is clear except for the black Bible that lies beside her. Her face is like the skull of a bird of prey. The eyelids are so thin that he can see the bulge of the iris through them. Her hands lie on the sheet like claws. Her chest barely moves. He wonders how long she will live.

"Not long," she says. He is startled that she has read his thoughts so easily. Her mouth stretches and her chest quivers a little. She is laughing. "Not long, Joel. If you stay long enough, you will see the ghost leave my body. You will have the pleasure of carving my name on that plain little stone. Of throwing earth on my coffin. I am thirsty, Joel. Water."

He pours her a glass from the carafe and holds it to her mouth. She drinks a tiny amount, just enough to moisten her lips. She meets his eyes again. He can see the dark gleam of laughter still lurking in their depths.

"Well?" she says. "Have you any questions to ask me before I go to join him?"

He puts the glass down. His fingers are trembling slightly. "You promised that one day you would tell me. Everything."

Her hand twitches. "Is that what you came for, Joel? For yourself? Not for me? Still, always, yourself?"

"I came for the truth."

She laughs her silent laugh. "The truth. The truth will set you free. Do you believe that?"

He grits his teeth. "Yes."

She closes her eyes again. Her face is a mask of malicious amusement. "Very well, my dear son. I will tell you what you want to know. My dying gift to you. I will tell you every-thing."

summer 1970

Santa Barbara

At 6:30 A.M., as always in the summer, the sprinkler system turned itself on. The air became a mist of diamonds. The one-acre lawn began to sparkle like a carpet of tiny emeralds.

Nobody was moving yet, but there were obvious signs of the party that had taken place in the night.

A champagne bottle floated, neck up, in the shimmering water of the swimming pool. There were dozens of other bottles strewn around the edge of the pool. The barbecue area was chaotic. Swarms of flies were already droning over the congealed platefuls of last night's ribs, lobster tails and steak, and drowning themselves in half-empty glasses of champagne or brandy. It would be nine-thirty before the servants materialized to start clearing up the mess.

The flies were in for a bonanza. By nine-thirty, they would have had time to feast, mate, and lay their eggs, a complete cycle of life.

So many parties had taken place here over the last decade. But this had been one of the most magnificent of all. This had been Dominic van Buren's retirement party.

And it was not over yet, though all the guests had gone home. In the master bedroom, Dominic van Buren, his eyes bright but unfocussed, was squatting between the splayed thighs of a teenage girl, a straight-edge razor in his hand. Both were naked.

"Take it easy," she said, anxiety surfacing through her thickened voice. She was not quite as stoned as van Buren, and was experiencing some qualms about this game. "Don't you cut me, now."

Van Buren was still soaring on the wings of the long night's debauch. Consoled by Quaaludes, zonked on marijuana, sustained by cocaine, he was not in a world that could bleed.

He had everything he needed spread out on a towel beside him. He swayed slightly, crooning, as he lathered the girl.

The girl was very young, very pretty, and a natural blond. She had been a party gift last night of some special friends from LA, people who understood his varied tastes. The best kind of friends.

Though he was retired, shut down, sold out, Dominic van Buren had secreted enough uncut cocaine to ensure that he would be supplied with friends and playmates until he couldn't get it up any more.

Though she was not quite a child, she'd been perfectly presented, with an oval face free of makeup and long, shiny golden hair. Her name was Tammy. The night had been full of delights. He had saved her till last.

When he had finished shaving her, he surveyed his handiwork.

"Pretty little pink smile," he said dreamily. "I love that pretty ... pink ... smile."

"What you want me to do?" she asked.

"Pink candy. So nice to lick. So good to taste."

She reached down and parted herself with her fingers. "You wanna eat me?"

"Leave yourself alone."

She lifted her head and peered at him. "Wanna spank me, Daddy? Wanna spank Tammy's naughty little botty? Make Tammy cry? Huh?"

"Bathroom." His bleared eyes had a mean look in them now. "We'll go to the bathroom and get dirty."

"You want me to wet on you? Things like that?"

He smiled at her lopsidedly. "Yeah. Things like that."

"Okay," she said. "I'm bursting, anyway. Got a full load."

Surreptitiously, she palmed the tube of KY jelly. They made their unsteady way to the bathroom. The drugs made Tammy stagger a little in the ankle-deep pile carpet, but she managed to keep smiling.

The bathroom was all crystal and gold, with huge mirrors that reflected their naked bodies. In a saucer on the basin were gold cuff links and a diamond Rolex worth twenty or thirty grand at least. She eyed these appraisingly. The house was crammed with priceless stuff, antiques and art. The payoff was going to be good. She'd been right to let him shave her, though she hadn't wanted to let him near her with a razor, not in his condition.

She caught sight of herself in the mirror and giggled. "Far out. I look like Barbie." She stiffened her slim body and stared ahead with her blue eyes wide, in imitation of the doll. "Barbie wants Ken. Ken? Ken?"

Van Buren frowned. "Come on, stop dicking around."

"Okay," she agreed. "Where you want it?"

"In the shower."

There was a marble seat in the shower. He sat on it and pulled the girl onto his lap. He held a little glass vial under his nose, broke it and inhaled heavily. She could see the mist whirl up his nostrils. His capacity was impressive. He had taken enough drugs to waste a rhinoceros.

"Whoo," Dominic van Buren said, rolling his eyes upward.

A deep flush spread across his upper body. His face seemed to congest and distend. So did his penis. He pushed his erection under her and squinted into her face.

"Do it."

"Better be careful." She giggled. "I'm a dirty little girl, you know. Barely house trained."

"Do it."

She linked her arms around his neck. "Ooh. Tammy dying to go pee pee. If Daddy not careful—"

"*Do it*," he said roughly.

She concentrated for a moment, then smiled.

Van Buren felt the hot stream flood over his engorged penis. He growled, his heart racing.

"Ooh," she said in mock dismay, wide-eyed. "Ooh! Tammy can't hold it in any longer!" She wriggled, spreading the flow over him. "Ooh! Ooh!"

A blast of lust exploded into his brain. Van Buren felt himself become a blade, a flame. He grasped her slight body, thrust at her with brutal urgency.

"I haven't finished yet," she exclaimed, struggling. "Hold on—"

He was grunting inarticulately, his eyes blind. They struggled to the marble-tiled floor. Tammy's bladder was still voiding helplessly, wetting them both. She struggled, but his strength was far greater than hers.

"Wait," she gasped. "Wait, I need my jelly—"

Van Buren rammed himself into her body, seeing the pain twist her face. He was far too big for her, but he took a savage pleasure in the violation. He gritted his teeth, forcing himself in.

"Oh, Daddy, take it easy, take it easy," the child whimpered, clinging to him.

He crushed her to the floor, thrusting into her small body. He barely heard her screams as he began to ram at her.

Later that evening, from his hiding place in the garden, Joel Lennox watched van Buren leave the house with the child. They got into the Porsche convertible and drove down the palm-lined drive towards the gate.

He waited until the Mexican maid left the house, locking up behind her. She walked to the staff cottage. Her husband, one of the gardeners, met her at the door. The door closed. Music started up. He was certain the main house was now empty.

Apart from the Mexicans, he had seen no sign of security guards on the grounds. There was an air of complacency about this house, as there was over the whole of Santa Barbara, a feeling that big-city crime hadn't reached these lush pastures.

It was a beautiful house, large and immaculately maintained. It was worthy of the estate it stood in, unmistakably Mediterranean in concept, yet fitting gorgeously into this prime slice of California.

He circled the house at a distance, moving in the shadows. All the windows were protected by ornate iron guards. He had no doubt that they were connected to the alarm system. There was no chance of getting through them.

But at the back, he found a portion of the roof that was accessible via a pergola.

He tightened the knapsack around his shoulders and swung

himself up onto the pergola. The vine was covered in fragrant flowers, but was luckily thornless. Standing on the beams, he could easily reach the scrolled ironwork of the window above. He grasped it in both hands and with a grunt, hauled himself upwards, his feet pushing against the wall.

He dragged himself over the gutter and onto the roof. He lay with one hand pressed to his side, gasping. The exertion had strained the wound, which was only partially healed, and pain shot through him like red-hot pincers.

When he had recovered, he examined the roof tiles. They were of the Italian type, each set on the next with a dab of cement. However, plenty of lime had been used in the mixture and it was relatively brittle. He took a small, high-tensile-steel crowbar from his knapsack and prized at one of the tiles. After some effort, the baked clay snapped. A piece slid off the roof and fell into a flower bed below.

He paused, listening for danger signals. There were none.

Making as little noise as he could, he began working more tiles loose, using the palm of his hand as a hammer against the curve of the crowbar. The more he removed, the easier it became, until he had a stack of twelve or fourteen beside him and a gap in the roof about two feet square.

Beneath the roof tiles was a layer of thin, flat bricks. These too yielded to the crowbar, the first with effort, the rest more easily.

The last layer he encountered was the asbestos insulating board. He sawed through it with the razor-edged commando knife.

Blackness yawned. He peered down into the loft, listening. There was no sound. As he'd expected, the roof was not wired.

He was in the house two minutes later.

It was well-lit, no doubt to give the illusion that it was not empty. But he ignored his surroundings. He moved quickly down the stairs, concentrating on avoiding rugs, checking each doorway carefully for photocells.

In the grandiose hallway, he found what he wanted, the unobtrusive little panel that concealed the alarm system controls. Several lights were glowing in the fascia. There was a key switch, but no key in it.

He took a screwdriver out of his knapsack and warily removed the fascia. Beneath was a tangle of coloured wires and circuits. He explored circumspectly, then set to work on the switch mechanism.

Ten minutes later, he managed to turn the switch. There was a click. The lights in the fascia stopped glowing. He stood motionless, listening.

"Hello," he said aloud, his voice rustling in the silence.

He pushed open the double doors of the main reception room. There he stopped dead, as though he had walked into a solid wall.

He had never seen such a beautiful room in his life.

The focus of the room was a massive eighteenth-century stone fireplace. There was more sculpture, pottery, magnificent Spanish baroque furniture. On the walls hung a collection of superb oil paintings. A glorious Persian carpet, to his eyes as wide as a football field, covered the floor.

Joel felt something shrivel in his soul. For a moment he was once again the peering child, surrounded by a world he did not understand.

He closed his eyes. "Jesus," he said.

He walked through to the dining room.

Here, too, was the same crushing assurance of taste and style. A vase of irises stood on the ebony table, darkly reflected in the polished wood. On the wall was a Japanese triptych, three large painted panels depicting a pond with blossoming lily pads and white cranes stalking frogs. Through the sliding glass doors was the central patio, where sago palms and rubber plants flourished around a real pool with real lily pads.

In another room he found a gleaming grand piano. Upon its black surface stood a group of silver-framed photographs. Most showed a teenage girl on various horses. The girl had black hair, pulled back to show a clean throat and profile. Her face was pretty, intent on what she was doing. Only in one picture, standing beside a lofty horse and holding a trophy, was she smiling. She showed regular white teeth, though the green eyes were solemn.

He was fascinated by the images. He studied each one intently. Finally, he took them from the silver frames and put them in his knapsack.

Upstairs there were eight or more bedrooms and as many bathrooms. But it was easy to tell which was the master bedroom, for it was as big as a whole city apartment, with six great arched windows looking down onto the patio and the lily pond.

The bed was circular and covered with a fur spread. On the ceiling above, recessed lights were arranged in a matching circle. At each bedside was a large vase of white lilies. Above the bed hung a big oil painting, a female nude with tanned skin and sultry black eyes.

He knew the mistress of the house was no longer here. But he looked for some sign of her presence, nevertheless. He opened cupboards, pulled out drawers, searched the twin dressing rooms and the twin, marble-clad bathrooms. His feet made no sound on the ankle-deep pile carpeting.

But there was no sustained female presence here, only evidence of transients who had left a bottle of lotion, a shower cap, a hairbrush, a pair of slippers. There were a few women's toiletries in the bathroom. But not hers. He knew. Her shoes, her minks, her bottles of French perfume were all gone.

He found Eden's room at the end of the corridor. Her name was on the door, on a painted china plaque: EDEN.

The room was in darkness, but he risked using his flashlight, since the windows faced over the pool, away from the staff cottage. It was a large room, furnished for a little girl, but a very special little girl. An empress, whose wishes were sacred law.

He played the light around. His beam lit on the rocking horse. It was superbly carved and painted, with real leather trappings and a real mane and tail. He reached out and touched it. It rocked slightly, rolling coquettish wooden eyes at him.

A big dresser held a couple of dozen silver cups. A vast, fluffy-white polar bear stood in one corner. Propped against a wall was a scarlet-hulled yacht with masts five feet high and real sails and rigging, flying a little French flag.

At the foot of the bed was a dollhouse, on the same large scale. Each tiny room was exquisitely furnished. The whole thing must have cost thousands of dollars. All the toys together must have cost tens of thousands.

He jerked open the cupboards. They were filled with a girl's clothes, shoes and trinkets, all neatly pressed and laid out. There were rows of boots and riding hats, everything spotlessly clean and orderly.

"You little bitch," he said savagely. "You spoiled little *bitch*."

He shone the flashlight into the display cabinet. The dozens of glass horses glittered in the moving light. They were charming, feminine things, all the colours of the rainbow. They pranced on slim, translucent legs and tossed elegant, translucent heads.

The pressure of his rage crushed him. He wrenched the cabinet from the wall and hurled it to the ground.

It burst open, panes shattering, glass ornaments spewing across the carpet.

He swung on the dollhouse and kicked it, splintering the wood. He rained blows onto it. Dolls and exquisite pieces of furniture rolled out. He crushed them under his feet, stamping, kicking blindly. He turned his rage on the room like a flame-thrower.

At last he stopped, gasping for air.

The rage had not gone. It was like a coiled spring, unbearably tense. He stood as though on the edge of an abyss. There was a terrible scream in him, wanting to burst out of his throat with each rasping breath.

He had not heard a sound during the explosion of violence. But he knew there must have been a lot of noise.

He pulled the commando knife from his belt and crouched in the darkness, waiting for the staff to come running.

Had someone come into the room then, he would have let the scream erupt, and would have leaped forward with the blade outstretched, slashing, stabbing, gouging.

But the silence continued unbroken. The servants had heard nothing.

Almost imperceptibly, the rasping breaths became sobs. Then he fell to his knees among the broken glass horses, the sobs tearing at him. They shook his whole body, as a dog shakes a rat. The knife fell from his fingers, and he covered his face with his hands, crying as though his heart had broken inside him.

Beverly Hills

They rode down through the canyon in the evening sunlight. The smell of eucalyptus was sweet on the warm air. The Dormouse followed behind Eden, she and her horse casting a rounder, shorter shadow on the grass.

The Dormouse (nobody ever used her jaw-breaking real name, Antigone Pringle-Williams) was a tubby blond, already developing a conspicuous bust. She was the daughter of an English actor who had successfully transferred to Hollywood and whose second wife wanted her out of the way.

Despite her dumpy shape, she was the only other girl at Mount Pleasant who took riding as seriously as Eden did. She jumped nearly as well. Riding and a common sense of having been rejected by their families drew the two girls together.

A school minibus took the girls to Dan Cormack's Academy in Laurel Canyon four times a week for their riding lessons. It was the only way Eden could get out of the school's high-security ambit. They figured even she couldn't get up to too much mischief at Dan's.

They were wrong.

It was here that she and the Dormouse had their regular appointment with Pedro González, the little Mexican gardener who supplied them with the drugs that they shared out back at school. She did not meet Pedro near the big white ranch itself, of course, but in the narrow canyon that was part of the estate, where they took the horses to relax after the workout.

"There's Pedro." She paused. "Hey. It isn't Pedro."

Alarmed, the Dormouse reined up. She squinted at the figure that waited on the path. The man was tall, definitely not the little Mexican gardener. "Who is it?"

"I don't know."

Something about the waiting figure suddenly made the Dormouse's flesh creep. "It could be the cops," she squeaked.

"Don't be silly."

"Come on, let's get out of here!" The Dormouse wheeled her horse around and trotted briskly back towards the ranch. "Come *on*," she shouted over her shoulder to Eden.

But Eden kept her ground, watching the stranger. Apprehension wrestled with curiosity inside her. Then her customary recklessness won the day and she rode slowly forward to meet him.

The man was young, in his twenties. He wore denims and a black T-shirt. He was tall. His arms, folded across his chest, were powerful and veined.

His face was bony, hawk-nosed, with angular cheekbones. It was a strikingly handsome face, but it had a tense, almost cruel cast. His dark hair had been cropped close to his head. He wore a full moustache.

It was his eyes that caught Eden's attention and held it. They were very dark, almost black. They stared at her with a hard glitter that disturbed her. They were, she decided, definitely weird. The expression in them was almost frightening. For a moment she felt a qualm before that dark stare. The Dormouse had been wrong. This man was not a cop. But he might be something worse.

She stopped the mare and looked down at him. "Where's Pedro?"

"Who's Pedro?" he asked in a harsh voice. A twitch tugged at the corner of his mouth.

She gathered the reins in her hands and looked around. The little canyon was blind at the far end. To get in here, he must have climbed down the rock face from one of the properties up along the ridge. It was overgrown and deserted here. But at the slightest sign of danger, she reasoned, she could use the mare's speed and power to get away. "You don't work for Dan," she said. "What are you doing here?"

"You're Eden van Buren," he said, jerking the words out. "Aren't you?"

"Maybe I am."

"There's no maybe about it." He held something up for her to see. She leaned forward. It was a photograph of herself, taken at a showjumping event the year before. "That's you," he said.

"Where did you get that picture?" she asked indignantly. She reached out for it, but he put it back in his pocket. "Who are you? What do you want from me?"

"I want nothing from you." The frightening black eyes were wide, intense. "I just want to see you. Look at you. Hear you talk."

"How do you know my name? Who gave you that photograph?"

His eyes devoured her. "You're beautiful," he said. "Like your mother."

"You know my mother?" she asked.

He reached out and took the loop of the reins in one hand. Suddenly, her getaway looked a lot less easy.

"Let her go," Eden said sharply. She jerked at the reins, but could not get them free of his grip. "Look," she said tensely. "I don't like this. Tell me what you want, or get out of my way. Or I'll call the cops."

He gave her a strange smile. "How are you going to call the cops, Eden?"

"My friend will call them. In fact, she went back to call them, just there." She was still hauling on the reins, but he was very strong. The mare shifted nervously under her. "Let *go*, damn it."

"Don't shout at me," he said quietly.

"Who the hell do you think you are?" she said, her voice rising. "Let go the horse. You're scaring me."

"I told you not to shout at me." The tic at his mouth was fiercer now. "Just keep calm."

She dragged on the reins. "Let her go, I said."

The mare tried to rear, but he put his weight on his arm, keeping the animal's head down. "Keep still!"

She'd left the goddamned whip at the ranch, or she would have cut him across the face. "Help!" she shouted, as loud as she could. "Somebody, help!"

He moved with animal swiftness. With his free hand, he grasped Eden's forearm and jerked her off the horse. She tumbled forward with a scream. He dragged her to her feet, standing between the horse and the girl, immobilizing each with a hand. His black eyes blazed into hers. "Keep still," he snarled at her. "All I want is to *talk*."

The mare was trembling, her eyes rolling. "Easy, girl," Eden said, her mouth dry. "Easy, now. Nothing's happening. Everybody's calm."

She was talking to the man as much as to the horse. His strength, the explosive violence, had terrified her. His grip was like iron, his thumb digging into her forearm.

A fear-pain was swelling in her stomach. Her mind conjured up the bloodstained horror of the Sharon Tate killings last year, just a few miles from this canyon. Charles Manson's eyes had been like this man's, wild and glittering. This man might even be a deranged survivor of that terrible Family.

She prayed that the Dormouse *would* have the sense to summon help at the ranch.

"Okay, take it easy," she said shakily. "You don't have to

hurt me. I don't have any money. Nothing. You can take my watch if you want. It isn't worth very much."

He did not seem to be listening to her. The devouring eyes were fixed on her, drinking her in. "You're sixteen," he said, almost talking to himself. "You look like a grown woman already."

She tried to pry his fingers loose. "You're hurting my arm. Please."

He didn't let go. "What sort of life do you have?" he said, the dark eyes never leaving hers.

"Uh—what?"

"Tell me about your life."

He must be deranged. What crazy words would chime with his crazy thoughts? "I have an ordinary life," she stammered. "I never hurt anyone!"

"How do you know who you hurt?" he said with an abrupt flare of rage. His grip on her arm tightened painfully. "You've been pampered since the day you were born. Spoiled. Indulged. Cocooned. You don't even know there's a real world out there."

"I know about the real world."

"The world beyond private schools and yachts and thoroughbred horses? Come on!"

He had authority. It was there in the prematurely lined eyes, in the way he spoke, despite the crazy words he used. He watched her as though he wanted to eat her with his eyes. "Whatever you think you know about me," she said cautiously, "you don't know everything. I care about injustice."

"Injustice? Your parents are millionaires. All your life you've wallowed in privilege and luxury."

"What do you want from me?" she demanded. "An apology for the fact that my parents are rich?"

"No," he said in a still voice. "It's too late for apologies."

He released her at last and walked without a backwards glance into the eucalyptus trees.

Drained, Eden sank to her haunches and watched his tall figure disappear into the dusty vegetation. She heard the sound of twigs snapping under his feet. A little while later, she caught the more distant sound of rocks tumbling as he scrambled up the side of the canyon, but she could not see him for the trees.

"You okay?"

She looked up. Pedro, the gardener, had appeared at her side.
"Yeah," she said, wiping tears off her cheeks. "I'm okay."

"I was waiting by the tree, like always," Pedro said. "I see him coming down the side of the canyon. Creeping, like a wolf. So I hid."

"Great," said the Dormouse acidly. She had watched from afar and ridden back when the coast was clear. "Thanks for warning us."

"I figured he was a cop." Pedro shrugged. "I woulda been the one to be bust, not you. I still got the hash. You don't."

"Pedro, he was probably a rapist," the Dormouse exclaimed. "Would you just have sat and watched while he cut our throats?"

"He was much bigger than me," Pedro said obliquely.

"He wasn't a rapist," Eden said quietly, stroking her mare's neck.

"He was a soldier boy," the Mexican said.

Eden looked up. "Why do you say that?"

"The way he move. He knew what he was doin'. Like he'd been trained."

"He knew who I was," Eden said quietly. "He came especially to meet me. He asked all kinds of crazy questions."

"Scary. Should we tell the cops about this?"

"What's there to tell?"

"Well, it was weird."

"If I ever see him again, I'll call a cop."

"Next time you see him might be too late," the Dormouse said significantly.

All this talk of the police was making Pedro shuffle nervously. "So you want the stuff or no?" he said. "I gotta get back to work."

"Not if it's the same crap as last time," the Dormouse said in a businesslike tone. "I nearly choked on it. What was it—horse shit?"

"That was a bad consignment," Pedro said. "Got something real special this time. Acapulco gold."

"No shit?" the Dormouse said with heavy irony. "Okay, give us your Acapulco gold, Pedro. And get us some blues for next time. Okay?"

"Yeah, okay." The little gardener turned his back on the girls and dug into the crotch of his underpants with one hand.

The Dormouse rolled her eyes at Eden. "You reckon it gets a little extra something from being stashed under Pedro's balls?" she muttered.

Pedro passed them the limp package and Eden gave him the six dollars. "The blues, now they gonna cost a little more," he said, pocketing the money. "Ten dollars."

"Shit," the Dormouse said. "Ten dollars for this kiddy-toy stuff?"

His face became sly. "Hey. If you got the *cojones*, I can get you something a lot heavier."

"Like what?"

"I can get you H."

Eden stared at him. "Heroin? That's heavy, all right."

"For smoking, not shooting. You sprinkle some on tinfoil, put a flame underneath and breathe."

"I don't know about that, Pedro."

"You never tried stuff like this," the little gardener whispered. "The sweetest, best feeling in the world. I promise. Gets you so far up you'll never want to come down. Man, you'll think you up there on the moon with Neil Armstrong."

"How much?"

He spread his hands. "Show you I'm not greedy. The first sample's on me."

"Okay." The Dormouse nodded. "And you show us how to do it."

He smiled at her.

"This whole drug trip is getting expensive," the Dormouse complained as they rode slowly back to the ranch. "Hey," she asked, brightening, "do you know where your father keeps his stash?"

"Yeah. In his safe. And I don't have the combination."

"My stepmother uses coke," the Dormouse said wistfully. "I've never tried."

"It doesn't do shit. Cocaine's for people who want to spend a lot of money and feel shit-hot and not get stoned. Forget it."

"It's a real upper, isn't it?"

"Who wants to be up?" Eden growled. She was preoccupied

with thoughts of the strange man who'd pulled her off her horse. "Coke doesn't change a thing. You're still you."

"I don't take drugs to stop being me," the Dormouse said.

"I do," Eden retorted briefly.

She returned to her thoughts. The episode in the canyon had been the biggest adventure of the year. When she told them all back at school, their eyes would pop.

He had been sexy, in a frightening way. The way he had looked at her. As though he wanted to eat her alive.

She wished she'd known he was a soldier. She could have told him about the big protest in Washington. If he was cool, he'd have realized she did care about things. If he wasn't, she'd have enjoyed watching him freak out.

But by the time they were dismounting at the ranch, she had decided to say nothing to the other girls. Or to the police.

The episode had not been an adventure, at all. It had carried overtones that had disturbed her in odd ways she couldn't explain.

She could not share what had happened. There had been something between herself and that tormented man. Something special. Some kind of common feeling.

A bond.

7.

~Matilde

july 1936

San Lluc

The Spanish Civil War is at hand.

There have been weeks of tension. Everyone anticipates that the army must soon stage a coup d'état against the divided and tottering republic.

Summer begins to sear Spain. The fields bleach to white, rocks crack with the heat. Passions are at breaking-point. The tension becomes unbearable.

On 12 July, José Calvo Sotelo, ex-Minister of Finance and one of the most respected conservatives in Parliament, is murdered.

It is the necessary spark. The army begins its coup at last.

Seville falls to the insurgents in two days. Then Cádiz, Granada, Córdoba.

In four days, the insurgents have captured one third of Spain. They are looking eagerly towards Madrid and Barcelona. Franco has already sent urgent requests for war matériel to Italy and Germany. Hitler sends transport planes so Franco can get his Moors from Morocco to Gibraltar. Mussolini sends bombers.

Here it is. Everyone knows it: the Civil War is here.

The generals form a junta in Burgos. Thousands of men join the Fascists.

Anarchists demand arms from the Generalitat, but the

government is reluctant to put rifles into the hands of these wild-eyed men, no matter whether Franco is coming or not.

Weapons are stolen. Militias are formed.

Real fighting begins. In Barcelona, five hundred die in pitched battles between rebel soldiers and partially-armed mobs of civilians.

On the night of 19 July, fifty churches burn in Madrid.

The next day, 2,500 officers, men and Fascist volunteers barricade themselves in the barracks. Communist miners from Asturias blow the gates down with dynamite. There is a wholesale butchery of officers that leaves the parade ground strewn as if with khaki leaves.

And among these greater tragedies, on 25 July, the convent of San Lluc burns.

Once again, as in 1909, a mob has made its way up to the convent with pitchforks and clubs and a handful of guns.

And this time the mob means business.

Montserrat Martínez, the Mother Superior, remonstrates with a gang of men.

They grow angry. They are mostly very young, some not out of their teens. They are a type that will become dreadfully familiar in the months to come, on both sides of the conflict. These are the young killers of Spain, the ones who do it for pleasure.

These are the uncontrollables.

They take her into the courtyard and pick an impromptu firing party of seven. She prays. No one is quite sure whether they will go through with it or not.

They thrust her against a wall and form up a few yards away. Suddenly, it breaks on Montserrat what a terrible sin they are about to commit. She raises her hand to bless them.

There is a ragged volley, surprising everyone except Montserrat Martínez, who hugs the scarlet lilies that have opened upon her breast. She slides to the cobbles, eyelids fluttering.

Eagerly, they hunt more offenders. A priest who is found at the altar is also dragged into this same courtyard. He is shown the body of Montserrat, and he begs them to allow him a confessor before they kill him.

"Confess to us," a boy of nineteen jeers. "Confess that you're a Fascist and a traitor to the republic!"

He is still on his knees when they shoot him. He rolls a few feet and comes to rest almost touching the body of Montserrat.

The church is, of course, the least defended and most exasperating appendage of the state. But no one can really explain where this anger comes from. It is simply here, red and alive. Over twelve hundred priests, monks and nuns are to die in the province of Barcelona alone. Seven thousand such in all Spain. Tens of thousands more innocents will die in the same way.

The mob swells and gathers strength.

It becomes a madness.

Nuns are kicked and beaten, even the elderly and frail. Two youths try to cut off the hands of a nun whom they cannot stop from praying.

The youngest of the sisters, a novice of seventeen, is raped by several men on a table in the kitchens and afterwards shot.

Sister Rita Fábregas is thrown into the well, where her screams echo hollowly for a quarter of an hour before she drowns. Two others are shut into a cell filled with blazing mattresses.

The afternoon runs red.

At around seven the roof beams of the great building catch alight. Soon, a sheet of flame hundreds of feet high competes with the setting sun. It soars into the sky, keeping away the night for many hours. Then it starts to flag and flutter and droops wearily. Darkness closes in. Timbers collapse into red coals, and thousands of roof tiles pour downwards, opening the convent to the night sky.

Specks of soot drift down on the village, which has straggled like a beggar child around the convent's skirt for centuries. The fire ebbs.

Elsewhere, Spain is still burning.

"We can say she's a housemaid," Conchita told him.

"A housemaid," Francesc repeated.

"Yes," Conchita said firmly. "A housemaid. Come to work for us."

"And who would believe that?" he asked dryly.

"There's no reason for anyone to disbelieve it."

Mercedes stared at the girl's shorn head, which proclaimed her to all the world for what she was, a young nun who had fled from the convent yesterday afternoon. Conchita had found her wandering in the fields, and had hustled her home. They had taken off her habit, washed her and dressed her in one of Conchita's smocks. She was shivering uncontrollably though she was wrapped in a blanket and the night air was hot and still heavy with the stink of yesterday's burning.

"I've spent the past week trying to beg machine guns from the Generalitat so that the workers can defend themselves against the army," Francesc reminded her with some bitterness. "How do you think people will react when I tell them we have taken a *housemaid*?"

"It's not a question of your reputation," she retorted. "It's a question of this child's life."

The girl shrank involuntarily as Francesc peered at her. "Did they hurt you?" he asked roughly.

"They threw a stone," Conchita replied for the nun. "She has a cut on her shoulder, nothing worse. Mercedes dressed it." She touched the nun's hand. "You wouldn't mind that?" Conchita asked the girl gently. "Posing as a maid until we can get you back to your home?"

The nun shook her head, then began to cry in an odd little wailing voice.

"Her name's Matilde Nicolau," Conchita said, putting her arm around the girl's shoulder.

"Well, Matilde Nicolau," Francesc said shortly, "you're not in any danger, girl."

Mercedes, sitting in silence at the table, stared at the nun. Matilde was a sizable, rather plain girl, with blue eyes that were rimmed pink with crying.

"Of course she's in danger," Conchita snapped at Francesc. "If they caught her, your precious anarchists would cut her throat."

"She'll have to spend the night here, at any rate," Mercedes said. "She's exhausted. She can sleep with me."

"Take her, then," Conchita said.

Mercedes rose, as dark and compact as the nun was pale and awkward, and took her arm. As Mercedes led her up the stairs to her bedroom, the nun stopped crying and wiped her eyes wearily. She stumbled at the top stair, and Mercedes supported her.

"Get in the bed," Mercedes told her. "I'll wash. I won't be long."

She had been up to inspect the convent today, with some others from the village, and her hair smelled of smoke and soot, but that would have to wait until tomorrow. The bed creaked as Matilde crept between the sheets. It was narrow, Mercedes thought, but not too narrow for the two of them. She heard sniffs and choking sounds from the nun.

"Where do you come from?" Mercedes asked, drying herself.

There was a long silence. Then: "Sitges."

"You'll have to try and get back there."

"Yes."

"How old are you?"

"Twenty-four," Matilde said in a small voice. "And you?"

"Eighteen." Mercedes pulled on her nightdress, shaking her dark hair loose. "How long have you been a nun?"

"I'm only a postulant."

"What's that? Like a novice?"

A pale face peered back at Mercedes over the sheet. "I haven't taken all my vows yet."

"Are you still going to? Now that the convent's gone?"

"Yes."

"D'you really still want to become a nun?"

"Yes."

Mercedes sat on the bed, tying back her hair.

The young nun thought she was ravishing. She had the sort of lithe body she herself had never possessed, and the sort of face that was seldom seen inside convent walls.

"We're anarchists," Mercedes said. "In fact," she added, with what looked like a gleam of irony in her dark eyes, "my father is the leader of the anarchists in this area. You saw how he limps? The *guardia civil* did that to him in 1909."

Matilde fidgeted with the sheet at her chin. Mercedes saw that her hands were raw and red from work.

"Don't look like that. We won't eat you." Mercedes studied her. "So you ran away yesterday afternoon."

"I wanted to stay. To protect the older sisters. But the men started throwing stones, and Sister Inmaculada—she's my spiritual counselor—pushed me into the garden. She told me to run, and I panicked."

Matilde's eyes were too painful to touch. She dug her fingers into her temples, sobbing through her open mouth like a child. Mercedes watched her grief intently, but without trying to comfort her.

"Why?" Matilde said blearily. "Why do they do such things to helpless priests and nuns?"

"Because you've gorged yourselves at the tables of the rich and powerful for too long. Because you never came to starve at the tables of the poor."

"I never ate at a rich man's table in my life!"

"Whose side has the church always been on? Always on the side of the oppressor. But paid out of the pockets of the poor." Her clear voice held a throb that was like stirring music. "Every worker's death or birth or marriage meant money in your pockets, payment for your bit of mumbo-jumbo, or it wasn't legal. Yet you, who don't marry, wouldn't let us divorce."

"So now they murder and rape nuns!"

"I didn't say I approved of that."

"But you approve of them wanting to destroy the church!"

"The church destroyed itself," Mercedes said calmly, "a long time ago. The church is an empty house. It's time to shut the door and lock the bolt."

"You're very glib," Matilde said with bitterness.

"You asked me a question. I tried to answer."

"But you're only eighteen," the older woman said. "Those are your father's words, aren't they? Tell me, Mercedes, do you really believe in them?"

"Tell me, Matilde, do you really believe in your Creed?" she replied in a mocking echo.

"I'm going to pray."

Matilde slid out of the bed and kneeled at the side of it. She rested her forehead on her clasped, reddened hands and began to pray in a rapid whisper.

Mercedes watched her. She had been sorry to see the old building burn. It had been as though a part of herself had gone this afternoon. Not a living part, but something dead and nerveless. Like having your hair cut. You felt an abstract regret as it fell from the scissors, but afterwards it was a relief. A burden gone...

She heard the voices of her mother and father rise in argument downstairs. The words were indistinguishable, but the tone was angry, bitter. Matilde rose to her feet. Mercedes pulled the sheets aside for her to get in. Matilde's soft flesh smelled of the Maja soap that Conchita had given her to wash with.

"Shall I put the light out?" Mercedes asked her.

Matilde closed her swollen lids. "Yes."

She reached up to the switch on the wall over the bed. In the darkness, they lay silent, each occupied with her own thoughts. The murmur of Francesc and Conchita's voices swelled and ebbed and finally drifted into stillness.

Mercedes's mind returned to the subject that had been dominating it to the exclusion of all others for two weeks. The war. It was here at last.

The immensity of the idea sent a shiver down her spine, made ice crystals form in her blood and sparkle dangerously along her veins. War. War against fascism. Not just in Spain, but in all of Europe. In all the world!

She imagined victory as the iron gates of a dungeon opening. She saw the first ragged, blinded prisoners stumble out. Watched the trickle become a flow, a flood of millions, surging towards freedom, reaching up to the light, the tumult of their voices beating against heaven.

It was a vision of such majesty that she was awed by it. It drew her with a mystical force, summoning her with a call she could not refuse. An invocation.

What if she were to meet Gerard in the smoking ranks of battle? Would she kill him? She saw herself holding a pistol to his heart, looking into those heavy-lidded eyes. *Gerard Massaguer, you have sinned against the people.*

Her face became rapt. She did not hear Matilde sobbing beside her.

Sleep stole slowly over the house.

Refugees from Andalucía began to arrive over the next few weeks. They brought with them horrific tales of Fascist cruelty. Tales of rape and slaughter *en masse*. Of looting, arson, bestiality. Of testicles crushed, eyes torn out.

In a surge of fury, dozens of local *bourgeois* families were hunted out and taken away by militias the next day.

"You mustn't go out of the house," Conchita told Matilde Nicolau urgently. "Don't even go to the window. You understand?"

She gave the postulant a scarf to cover her cropped hair, and a pinafore like a servant's.

"If anyone speaks to you, pretend to be simple. You're my cousin from Sitges. Your name is Carmen Barrantes, and you've come to work for us. You're not quite right in the head. Do you understand?"

Matilde nodded, fear making her wide-eyed.

Peeling potatoes together at the kitchen sink one evening, Mercedes tilted her head critically at Matilde. "If a man had wanted you in Sitges, would you have ended up in the convent?"

"That's a cruel question!" Matilde burst out.

Mercedes widened her eyes slightly. "Is it? Why?"

"Because my faith is more than that! And you have no right to assume that no man wanted me in Sitges, or anywhere else!"

Mercedes's expression changed subtly. "I didn't mean to offend you."

Matilde dug at the eye of a potato with her knife. "Well, you did."

"Did you leave someone in Sitges, then?"

"I'm not pretty and graceful like you," Matilde said in a toneless voice.

"But you are pretty. You have lovely eyes."

"Have you got someone here? A boy? A—a—man?"

"I hate all men." Mercedes slashed at the potato she was peeling. "I hate them."

"Have you ever . . . been . . . with a man?"

Mercedes smiled. "Have you, Sister Matilde?"

Matilde had not confided in a lay person since she'd left Sitges. It had been almost four years since she'd even talked with someone of her own age. "There *was* someone in Sitges," she said. She gnawed at her fist for a moment. "A widower, and ever so ugly. They wanted me to marry him because he was the only one who would have me. He had some money. Once when he got me alone, he started kissing me . . . squeezing me . . ."

"Did he do it to you?" Mercedes asked.

"He wanted to. He made me touch . . . his *thing*."

"Dirty old goat," Mercedes said sympathetically.

"He was one of the reasons I came to San Lluc. It was too awful. Spending the rest of my life with him. He stank."

"Then you're better off."

"I know what you're thinking."

"What am I thinking?"

"That I only became a nun to run away from a smelly old man."

"What else could you do?" Mercedes said gently.

"There were other men. Ones I liked better. But I would have still joined a convent, if that was God's will. You didn't answer my question. *Have* you been with a man?"

"No," Mercedes said, after a slight pause.

"You're a virgin?"

Again, that slight pause. "Yes."

"They say it's wonderful," Matilde ventured.

"I wouldn't know. I never think about it."

"Never?"

"It's a subject that doesn't interest me. It's frivolous."

"I don't think it's frivolous. It's a very serious thing."

"All that grunting and fumbling?" Mercedes said in disdain. "Oh, you can trip over them doing it any summer's night, in the lanes. Anyway, I have something infinitely more important."

"What's that?"

"A cause."

"Which cause?"

"The war, of course. I'm going soon. Joining up."

Matilde gaped. Her voice was incredulous. "You don't mean it!"

"But I do," Mercedes replied. "I'm going to join the militia."

The postulant forgot to peel. "There's no place for women in the war, Mercedes."

"I can shoot a rifle like any man. Drive a truck. Nurse the wounded. Anything they want me to do. Anything."

"Mother of God. What do your parents say?"

"I haven't told them, not yet. But they won't be able to stop me. I'm eighteen. I'm a woman now."

Matilde stared at Conchita's little statue of the Madonna, her mind flooded with images. She mused for a while. "Nurse the wounded," she said in a slow voice. "I could do that."

"Me too. If they want me to. But I'd rather fight. I want to make a positive contribution."

Matilde whispered, "Could you ... actually ... you know, kill someone?"

"Of course," Mercedes said calmly. "Anyone could."

"I could never hurt another human being." She was astounded at the serene way Mercedes spoke, awed by her certainty. "Not *ever.*"

"Couldn't you? Couldn't you kill those men who raped and shot your friends?"

The other was silent for a while. "No," she said at last. "I pity them. I hate them. I have to try and forgive them. But I couldn't kill ... not ever."

"You and I are different," Mercedes said lightly. "I see the necessity for killing. You don't. The word *forgive* kept the workers of Spain slaves for a thousand years. Now we understand another reality. To kill those who oppress us. All I have to do is pick up a rifle and it's done."

They busied themselves with other preparations for the evening meal. Matilde had been made painfully restless by Mercedes's words. "When will you go?" she asked.

"Soon. In a month, maybe."

"A month!"

Conchita came into the kitchen, smiling. "What are you two talking about so earnestly? Not the dinner, I see. Let's get a move on, or we won't be eating until midnight."

The floodgates of confidence had been opened.

That night, they lay together in bed and talked for hours, until exhaustion lay heavy on their lids and a village cock began to crow faintly outside.

It was ideas and dreams that kept sleep away from Mercedes Eduard. But it was Mercedes herself who disturbed Matilde, disturbed her with a painful, sweet trembling. This girl-woman was a tiger to her lamb. Those hypnotic black eyes, that sweet Joan of Arc face, that throb in the voice, all intoxicated her.

Quite suddenly, her own faith seemed an ephemeral thing. A thing of convenience. She had believed in her calling for four long years, but in this house, with the convent burned, the last wraiths seemed to have seeped into the air like ether from a badly stoppered bottle.

The cock crowed louder, more confidently. The eerie night was almost over, and neither had slept. In the darkness, great armies were trudging towards battle. Matilde Nicolau, without a home and perhaps without a faith, lay in her enemies' bed and faced an uncertain future.

"We ought to sleep," she said dully.

"Yes," Mercedes agreed. "You go ahead. You need rest, poor thing."

That "poor thing" almost started Matilde off crying. In a thickened voice, she asked, "Aren't you going to sleep?"

"I don't seem to be able to. Ever since the war started. I just lie awake at night, thinking. Making plans..."

"Would you like me to hold you?" Matilde hesitated, her face flushing. "Sometimes, in the convent, when we couldn't sleep, we held each other... like sisters..."

Mercedes didn't answer, wondering whether she liked the idea. The postulant, perhaps taking her silence as assent, reached for her gently and drew her close.

She allowed herself to be cradled, her body not stiff, but not yet yielding. Her head was pillowed on Matilde's soft bosom, Matilde's soft arm around her shoulders. "You'll sleep now," the older woman whispered, her mouth against Mercedes's hair. It gave Matilde a throaty, intensely sweet feeling to have the girl's slender limbs in her embrace. Tenderness unfolded in her. With her other hand, she stroked Mercedes's arm lightly, surprisingly gentle and deft for such an ungainly woman.

Mercedes relaxed slowly, closing her eyes. Almost immediately, the velvety petals of sleep opened. Just before she slipped into darkness, she felt Matilde's lips touch her face.

Seville

For the duration of the war, Gerard and Marisa Massaguer's home is to be here in Seville. They are unable to return to Catalonia, where the Massaguer estates have recently been turned over to the government.

They are installed in the exquisite house of a prominent Republican intellectual, currently facing a death sentence.

While the war lasts, any Spaniard who exerts influence on

the Italian government is worth his weight in gold. Gerard Massaguer's contacts with the Italian High Command have made him into an important figure in the nationalist cause.

As Gerard once told Mercedes Eduard, nothing wins a war like money.

But Franco still does not have enough. Tens of thousands of elite, highly trained Italian and German "volunteers" are pouring in to swell his ranks. Military equipment, too, is pouring in. It all has to be paid for. An ingenious solution is found.

An Italo-Spanish investment company, SAFNI, is set up to pay for all this foreign aid. It is a delicate trade. The machinery relies on certain key individuals. Such as Gerard Massaguer, who is given one of the biggest offices, one of the plushest limousines.

He also has his finger in HISMA, the Nazi version of SAFNI.

The total trade will eventually run to well over $200 million. Even a few points of that will amount, by the end of the war, to a very large fortune. Gerard has expectations of serious wealth.

He remains a beguiling man, for all the signs of good living. Though he would detest the notion that he is a dandy, his regular trips to Rome and Berlin have enabled him to build up an extensive wardrobe of the kind of fine clothing that is unobtainable in Spain. And his meetings with Hitler and Mussolini have given him a presence, a prestige, that counts for a great deal, both socially and in business.

Fashionable, successful and increasingly powerful, Gerard is enjoying his war thoroughly.

San Lluc

Two days later, at lunchtime, Mercedes exploded her bombshell.

"I'm going to volunteer," she told Francesc and Conchita. "I'm going to join the militia."

"Mercé, darling, no!" Matilde saw Conchita's face whiten and crease with pain. "You can't!"

"I *have* to go," she told them. "I can't stand by while Spain hangs in the balance!"

"You can't help Spain," Conchita said passionately, reaching for her daughter's hand. "What will you do in the militia? Help to arrest and shoot innocent fathers of families?"

"I must, Mama. Hundreds of young people have already gone from Palafrugell alone. The republic has to be defended—"

"Not by girls of eighteen!"

"I'm a grown woman," Mercedes said gently, squeezing her mother's hand. "I have to go where my sense of duty sends me."

"Francesc!" Conchita pleaded, "Speak to her, for God's sake."

Francesc looked up from his plate. The cobalt eyes had lost little of their intensity, though the lined face was weary and the hair and beard were greying. "You're a grown woman, yes," he said in his harsh voice. "No one can stop you from going. But you're also very young. And you're needed here. You could delay for six months, Mercedes."

"But why should I delay?" she exclaimed, her cheeks flushing under the dusky skin.

"Because that might help the war effort more than a precipitate departure." The blacksmith massaged his bad leg as he spoke. These days, it was almost totally useless and he relied heavily on his sticks. "We must all make some effort. Of course. I have to decide for myself what my own contribution is going to be." He paused. "The Russians are going to send us tanks and armoured cars. They'll need people who understand machinery. I've been asked to join the militia. To help establish a motorized regiment. I've been offered officer's rank, if I want it."

"Papa! How wonderful! We'll fight side by side!" She turned, radiant, to her mother. "Did you know this, Mama?"

Conchita nodded silently.

"I don't know whether I can accept," Francesc said heavily. "My age. My impediment."

"But they need you!"

"They are grasping at straws," he said flatly. "A fifty-year-old cripple might just be a burden on the people in their time of need, no matter how strong his commitment." His piercing eyes turned on Mercedes. "Just as you, Mercé, have to decide whether an eighteen-year-old girl can really help the militia. Or whether you will just present added problems and added dangers for the men who have to do the fighting."

Mercedes shook her head briskly. "It isn't that complicated, Papa. They need us, whatever we can offer. If Spain calls, we have to go."

"You did this," Conchita said bitterly to her husband. "Filling her head with ideology all these years. Now look! Look at what you've achieved! Oh, Mercé!" Conchita's eyes glistened with unshed tears. "Mercé. I can't lose both of you."

"Put off your decision, Mercé," Francesc said. When he tried to speak gently, his rough voice became a croak. "At least until I know what I'm going to do. If I have to go, you must stay with your mother, if only for a while longer. She can't be left alone, not in these times."

Mercedes's face flushed deeper, then paled. Her long lashes dropped over her eyes.

"But if I decide to stay," Francesc went on, "you can go whenever you choose."

That night, as they lay together in the darkness, Mercedes demanded of Matilde, "Don't *you* think I should go? You're on the other side, of course, but don't you think I should?"

"I'm not on any side," Matilde said. "And I think—I think you're so noble. But your mother . . . it breaks my heart to see her face when you talk of going."

"Do you think it doesn't break mine?" Mercedes said angrily. "I can't help it. I hear drums in my head, pounding. I *have* to go. I can't ignore the call." Her voice throbbed. "Do you remember 1931, how the masses spontaneously took arms to defend the republic? That was glorious. They're doing the same now, Matilde. They're streaming to battle in their tens of thousands, with only one purpose. To win."

Matilde reached out timidly and touched Mercedes's hair. Sometimes she felt so much older than this girl of eighteen who talked of war and killing. Yet Mercedes thrilled her, awed her. She was a phenomenon Matilde had never dreamed of, neither in the salt sea air of Sitges, nor in the quiet of the convent. Over these past days, she had prayed for Mercedes with a burning intensity. She had prayed for Conchita too, who had taken her in, and even for grim Francesc; but mostly for Mercedes. "They need you too. Think of what your father said."

"Shall I tell you a secret?" Mercedes asked, staring at Matilde through the dark. Matilde nodded. "He isn't my father."

Matilde's cropped hair crackled on the pillow as she turned her head. "He isn't?"

"I've never told a living soul," Mercedes said, her voice dropping to a whisper. "He raised me. He gave me his name. But my real father is—"

"Who?" Matilde asked breathlessly.

Mercedes laughed softly. "You won't believe me."

"I will! And I'll never tell anyone, not on pain of death!"

"It's . . . Gerard Massaguer."

"*Gerard Massaguer?*" Matilde was stunned into speaking aloud.

"Shhh. You'll wake the house. He and my mother must have had an affair. But he abandoned her because she was poor and of humble stock. She was already pregnant with me when she married Francesc."

"He's so handsome," Matilde murmured, swept away by the glamorous images. "I've seen him often. He's beautiful, like a panther."

"Yes," Mercedes said tightly. "He is handsome. He is also an enemy of the people."

"You look like him. Of course you do! Oh, I see it so plainly now! You have the same eyes, the same mouth! That's where you get your beauty!"

"Don't shout," Mercedes commanded. Matilde's voice had risen to a squeak.

"But it's like a fairy tale!"

"He has another child. Alfonso. He's seven years old. My half-brother. He'll probably never know he has a half-sister. Isn't that ironic?"

"It's more than ironic. It's symbolic. Have you seen that painting by Goya? The two men in the river, both doomed, fighting each other with clubs? That's Spain. That's you and your father!"

"I've often thought about what would happen if we met on the battleground."

Matilde was enraptured, a child listening to a play. "What would you do?" she breathed.

"It would depend who had the upper hand," Mercedes replied. "If it was Massaguer, he would shoot me."

"No!" Matilde crossed herself.

"Oh, yes. And if I had the upper hand, I would shoot him."

"Shoot your own father!"

"I would try."

"Mother of God! Oh, Mercé! Oh, thank you for sharing it with me." She took Mercedes's hand in both of hers and drew it to her lips, kissing it timidly. The confidence had overwhelmed her with gratitude. And she was the only one Mercedes had ever told! She did not see in that the loneliness of Mercedes's life. She saw only the gift of trust. It was a soul treasure, a distinction, something unspeakably wonderful. "I'll never forget it. And I'll *never* tell."

"None of that is important. What is important," Mercedes said, "is that now is a time for action. Not for thinking and agonizing. Why can't my father see that?" Her fingers clamped tight around Matilde's, making her gasp. "Should I listen to them?" she demanded. "Should I let them sway me? Shouldn't I just go, maybe even tonight and leave a note for them to find in the morning?"

"No," Matilde said in a quavering voice, "don't go. Not tonight. Stay here."

"I feel that if I don't go soon, I'll catch fire. I'll burn up in spontaneous combustion."

"You've got a fever." Matilde felt Mercedes's forehead. It was cool and dry, not flushed at all. She could see Mercedes's eyes gleaming in the dark, and she felt that dark gaze meeting her own. In a surge of emotion that she hardly understood, she began to babble advice. "You have to think, like your father says, what's best, I mean, what's best for your cause. For Spain. You could go, yes, but would that be the right thing, my goodness, who can tell? What if you were captured? What would those Moors do to you? The thought is unbearable!"

"Nonsense," Mercedes retorted. "I'd willingly die tomorrow if it helped the republic an inch."

"But would it?" Matilde's fingers were working around Mercedes's hand, still captive between her own. "If they hurt you, or if they killed you, I'd—I'd—" She laughed oddly, then sobbed. "I'd die."

"It's not me who has the fever. It's you! You mustn't get so upset, Matilde."

"I can't help it. I can't. You're so magnificent. I adore you."

Mercedes couldn't help laughing. "*Hostia.* Are we making an anarchist out of you?"

"I adore you," Matilde whispered. Suddenly, she had taken

Mercedes in her arms and was covering her face with kisses, her heart threatening to burst out of her chest.

Mercedes stiffened, knowing that if she fought away, she would wound Matilde mortally. She let the other woman kiss her cheeks, kiss her eyelids and temples. Then, gradually, she tried to draw back.

"Don't push me away!"

"It's just that, well—"

"Yes, yes," Matilde said in a tiny moan. "I'm plain and lumpish and the sight of me disgusts you."

"You don't disgust me," Mercedes said gently.

"I do! My eyes are like a pig's! And my hair is all cut off!"

"You're overwrought," Mercedes said, touching her face in the dark. "We've talked too long. We should go to sleep now."

"Let me kiss you good night. Please."

Mercedes let the other woman take her in her arms again and felt the warm lips that sought hers. Matilde's touch was gentle, tremblingly light.

"Oh, my dear . . ."

Their lips pressed. Mercedes felt warmth unfold in her, a tenderness that was sweet yet uneasy. Matilde was no longer lumpish and ungainly. The moist mouth was like a flower, trembling on the point of opening. The arms that held her were sure, comforting. She longed suddenly to melt into that softness, to let Matilde envelop her.

She turned her face aside, her heart fluttering uncomfortably.

"Just lie in my arms," Matilde whispered. "Go to sleep."

Mercedes drifted, as if on a warm ocean. Then the deep claimed her.

Matilde was awake long before Mercedes the next morning. She propped herself up on one elbow, watching her. In sleep, Mercedes's face lost those small signs of tension at eyes and mouth that made it so commanding when she was awake. Now she was as serene as a child, her face an angel's. Her mouth was deeply carved, the shape of her eyelids and nostrils so consummately delineated that her face seemed to Matilde's adoring eyes like the face of an angel.

"You're so beautiful," she whispered. She kissed Mercedes

on the mouth, as lightly as a feather landing. "So beautiful. So precious."

An imperious expression crossed Mercedes's face and she began to waken. Her lids opened. Their eyes met. For a moment, neither spoke.

Then Matilde said, "I love you."

Mercedes smiled, a lopsided smile that Matilde had never seen before, and reached out to touch Matilde's face.

"Do you really?" she asked.

"Yes," Matilde whispered.

"You're the first person who ever said that to me. I'll remember. Always."

For two weeks, the summer reigned unchallenged over San Lluc.

Francesc Eduard was summoned to Gerona by the militia and was asked to join the staff of an armoured car division, to take charge of supplies and provisions that it was hoped would come from Moscow. He was offered the rank of major. Because of his disability, he would probably never see action, but he would be able to play an important part. He agreed.

Two days later, he left his family to go up to the barracks in Gerona. From now on, they would only see him at weekends. Conchita made no effort to dissuade him. But after his departure, she became silent and grim.

Matilde set up a little shrine in their bedroom. She hung a wooden cross on the wall, over a small table, on which she put a Bible and a rosary. She would kneel here and pray, as she had done at the convent, for them all.

Occasionally, Mercedes would mock her religiosity, but for the most part, she tolerated it, watching Matilde at prayer with ironic eyes.

The war had begun in earnest. In the south, Franco's army moved out of Seville and began its slow, bitter progress towards Madrid. Mérida, then Badajoz, fell. So began the long march along the course of the Tagus River, through fields and villages, towards the capital.

Skirmishes, compared to what would come in Europe after 1939, the impact of these victories was intensified by the rumours of slaughter that accompanied them. The insurgents' crack troops, twenty thousand Moors and Foreign Legionnaires, deliberately

spread terror as they came. After each battle there was a massacre
of the enemy wounded and captured. Each village that was taken
became an arena for looting and reprisals. Had a landlord been
killed here? Had a priest been murdered? Vengeance followed
swiftly. Officers ripped the right shoulders from the shirts of all
the male villagers they found. If the flesh bore the bruises of rifle
recoils, it was a death warrant, old man or young boy.

The three women in San Lluc read in Republican newspapers
how the bodies were sometimes burned with gasoline, just as Francesc had said, or more often left by the roadsides, where the summer sun soon made them hideous.

Killings multiplied like flies. Mass executions of men of fighting age were accompanied by the individual murders of anyone
deemed to be an intellectual or a leftist by the Rebels. School-
teachers, doctors, artists, local government officials, all were
gunned down in "purges." Neither grey hairs, nor eminence, nor
innocence, were any plea.

Mercedes, forced to accept the check to her own plans, remained with her mother in San Lluc, fretting. She practised her
driving on the anarchists' cars and trucks in Palafrugell, running
errands for them whenever she could.

She knew that her friendship with Matilde was deepening into
something more than friendship. Yet she did nothing to either halt
or accelerate it. At nights they embraced in the narrow bed, their
bodies pressed together. Sometimes Mercedes allowed Matilde to
kiss her and stroke her, awakening feelings that stirred her sweetly.
Less often, she returned the caresses. Sometimes they lay talking
in whispers until the dawn.

Mercedes's yearning to join the conflict was like a flame inside,
consuming her. Matilde, halfway between her friend and her lover,
watched her burn, and prayed that the madness, for that was what
she thought it was, would pass.

She offered Mercedes what comfort she could. She, too, had
found herself trapped in the forge house, not only because of her
passionate devotion to Mercedes, but because Sitges, her beautiful
seaside home town, had become a stronghold of anarchism, indeed,
the killing-ground for many thousands of men and women being
"purged" in Barcelona.

Her family there gave out that she had died in the fire at the
convent, in order to protect themselves, and when she sent a letter

to them there, they did not answer it. Perhaps they preferred to think of her as dead.

Though Mercedes refused to believe it, Conchita insisted that the postulant's life was far from safe. Matilde ached to venture outside, but Conchita would not hear of it. She remained in the forge house, day and night.

Occasionally, a fit of claustrophobic panic would overwhelm her.

"I get so afraid sometimes," she told Mercedes one night. "I could cry with terror."

"But you're safe here."

She turned to Mercedes with a desperate look. "I can't go back to Sitges. I can't go anywhere! What's going to become of me? What will happen to me in the end?"

"We'll look after you," Mercedes said, touching her arm. "We'll find somewhere safe for you to go."

Matilde clung to her. Mercedes could feel her tremble. "Where?"

"Some place where there isn't any fighting. Don't cry, darling."

"There's nowhere where there isn't fighting," Matilde wailed. "Everywhere is blood and violence. Oh, Mercé, I'm so afraid!"

"You could come with me."

"Where?"

"To the war. You'd be on the wrong side, of course, but you could be a nurse. It wouldn't be exactly safe, not with bullets whistling around our heads. But we'd be together."

Matilde stared at her, open-mouthed. "Would you take me?"

"Of course I would."

Matilde swallowed her tears, digesting the idea.

It was that point of high summer when the sun was beginning to put the finishing brush strokes to his masterpiece. The hay was already being gathered in. Crops were ripe, roads were dusty, the sea held not a ripple or a wave. Intense heat and light flooded the landscape. It was almost impossible to stay indoors in such weather. Matilde suffered tortures of claustrophobia, and Mercedes's heart went out to her.

"If she doesn't get a breath of fresh air," she told her mother, "she'll go stark mad in this house."

The two young women planned an outing on the weekend, a walk in the countryside that lay around the village. They put on big straw hats and took wicker baskets as a kind of disguise. Mercedes went bare-armed, while Matilde had to wear a blouse to cover her white skin.

"What if you meet someone?" Conchita asked worriedly. "You know how people gossip."

"No one will see us," Mercedes promised. "And if they do, I'll say she's our cousin. Who's going to care, anyway? I'll look after Matilde, Mama."

They slipped out of the village in the dead hour, after lunch, when the baking streets were deserted, and took a country lane that wound between farms and oak woodland towards the next village.

The lane was lined with brambles and wild fig trees. The fruits of both were ripe. It was an apparently endless abundance, a prodigal cornucopia of sweetness. Matilde, in particular, was a glutton for fruit and gathered with delight.

"You can feast on blackberries and figs until you're sick," she said happily.

"Or shit in your pants, whichever comes first," Mercedes replied.

Their baskets grew heavy as they walked. They met no one. It was the first time Matilde had been outside since the burning of the convent. Her hair had at last begun to grow, though it was still very short, and she had not shed what Conchita called "that convent look." She was in ecstasies at the air and the sunshine. Mercedes saw tears of joy trembling on her lids.

It was very hot. Across the fields, farmers were scything hay, piling the cut grass into tall golden stacks. Here and there a horse or a donkey stood harnessed to a cart, patiently flicking its ears. The distant bang of a hunter failed to silence the shrill cicadas.

The lane took them through the yard of a small farm. A stone well stood under a tree. Heat and sugary figs had made them both fiercely thirsty. They hauled the bucket up and dipped their cupped hands in the cold water to drink. It was delicious and they said so.

"Good water, eh?" an old woman called from a window. "Better than silver."

"Better than silver," Mercedes agreed, gasping at the coldness.

A mile farther along the path, they started growing tired. They left the road and walked into the oak woods. When they found a shady bank, they sprawled onto the ground.

By now it was almost too late in the summer for flowers, but Matilde had managed to gather a handful of cornflowers, gentians and pink valerians. She arranged her flowers in her lap and began weaving them into a fragile garland, with a few stray ears of ripe wheat and some rose hips for variation.

Mercedes lay on her back, watching sleepily. "What are you doing?"

"Making you a crown."

"Have you got the energy for games? God, it's hot." She closed her eyes and dozed until Matilde leaned over and tried to crown her with her creation. The wreath fell apart almost at once, scattering the younger girl's black hair with flowers and wheat.

"Idiot." Mercedes sighed irritably, raking the petals out of her hair. "I was almost asleep!"

Matilde smiled down at her, her eyes warm with love. "My little bad-tempered queen. I'll go with you to the end of the world."

"You may have to." She looked up at Matilde seriously. "Maybe the world is coming to an end."

"My world is you."

Heat and exertion had flushed Mercedes's skin. A vein pulsed in her throat. Matilde leaned down and kissed the red, deeply carved mouth. She laid her hand gently on the other woman's breast.

"It's too hot for that," Mercedes complained peevishly, turning her face away. She clasped her hands behind her head.

Matilde brushed the soft hair of Mercedes's underarm with her lips. The animal fragrance was enthralling. She nuzzled, tasting the bittersweet of Mercedes's sweat.

"Don't," Mercedes said languidly, squirming. "I stink."

"You smell like a rose."

"Like a sweaty horse."

"It's precious." Matilde's mouth was quivering. She slid her tongue against the musky skin. "It's a narcotic. Opium. Deadly nightshade."

Like a drunken bee in an orchard, her mind was blinded with the intensely vivid colour of Mercedes's scent and taste, and her head swam giddily.

"I'm in love with you," she whispered hotly. "I'm mad about you."

She kissed Mercedes's throat, then began to unfasten the buttons of her blouse.

Mercedes's eyes were smoky. "What are you doing?"

"Loving you, my darling." She opened the blouse with trembling fingers, baring the soft swell of Mercedes's breasts.

Mercedes felt a flutter of panic. "Not here!"

"There's no one to see."

"Are you going to devour me, like a fig?"

"Exactly like a fig," Matilde whispered.

She felt Matilde's mouth at her breasts, felt the warm tongue caress her nipples. She cradled Matilde's head in her arms. It was heady to be devoured like this, to be loved like this. Matilde's ardour was like summer wine.

Mercedes was more innocent than Matilde perhaps realized. She received Matilde's love with an embarrassment that burned for a short while, making her cover her face with her hands. Then pleasure came, not as a surprise, but as a long-forgotten friend.

Melting, wordless, she allowed Matilde to possess her body completely. It was as though what was happening could not be stopped. There was no wrong, no right. Though later there would be decline and dissolution, the fruit had ripened, had opened its scarlet, seeded interior to the sun. She felt the other woman's mouth seeking between her thighs, tasting the secret flesh that no other had ever touched.

She closed her eyes and surrendered to the hot delight. It grew, blossomed and swelled. It filled with sweetness and warmth until it opened like a flower and Mercedes's body arched in moaning pleasure.

Until the sun swelled and burst and Mercedes gasped out her ecstasy under the trees, among the rustling oak leaves of last year's summer.

Seville

Gerard Massaguer returns from a trip to Rome with the promise of further Italian aid for Franco. He reports directly to the Generalísimo in Burgos, with Marisa and Alfonso at his side.

"One thing you can say for Mussolini," he remarks to his

wife after the audience, "is that he has presence. Franco reminds me of some po-faced plaster saint."

"You should try conversing with his wife," Marisa says wryly, touching the medal that Franco has hung on her husband's chest.

They go out to the opera.

Now thirty-seven, Gerard Massaguer is achieving his peak. His heavy-lidded eyes stare with considerable power from a face that is startlingly handsome. His dinner jacket is exquisitely cut and he wears a diamond pin that glitters brightly in the soft light. He is becoming both wealthy and powerful. The scent of it is on him. Women, in particular, can smell it. And with women, as in business, his success is already legendary.

Gerard enjoys his cigar at the intermission. There is no more potent pleasure than having and exerting power. His word has taken on weight. It means life or death. He has entered a cabal, the select few who will hold the reins once all the mess has been cleared away. It is a good feeling. Alfonso, his son, will inherit not only wealth and prestige. He will inherit Spain.

He thinks of his daughter, that exquisite child. He aches to see how she is maturing. Just the thought of her fills him with a strange longing, a longing neither his wife, nor any of his many lovers, can excite in him.

Has she, as she once promised, taken up arms for the republic? How does she look now? Has she grown even more beautiful, even more alluring?

He is terrified by the thought that she might die by some Moor's bullet. What can he do to protect her? Nothing. She is out of his reach. He remembers the perfect shape of her immature breasts, the feel of her tongue sliding against his.

He will see her again. He will. When Catalonia falls, she will be his, this time forever. So he tells himself. But he is afraid for her. The burning of the convent of San Lluc, and the atrocities that occurred on that day, have made headline news on the nationalist side. Doña Carmen herself, Franco's ultra-Catholic wife, was shocked, and attended a special *Missa Solemnis* for the souls of the dead Catalán sisters in Burgos.

Of course, atrocities occur daily, on both sides, each one fuel for the propaganda machines of the other party. It is the winning side, however, who will finally get to write the score.

Gerard knows which side that will be. And Gerard knows that a heavy reckoning has been laid up against the village of San Lluc.

San Lluc

Night world.

A secret world. A world within a world that Matilde had never fully admitted, not even to herself. The convent nights had been short and dark, and what passed in them was always buried by the first prayers at break of day. No one ever spoke of the things that happened in the absence of light. Of the comfort that was given when the storms of the soul raged.

This love, if it was love, was never confessed to any priest, or spoken of at any counselling. These meetings were not between nuns, but between women. Between bodies. They were not to be acknowledged. They were not to be forgiven.

But Matilde's love for Mercedes neither began in the dark nor ended with daylight. The night world had become a day world, and she had been forced to see herself, and acknowledge what she was. Mercedes's body was slim and lithe, her skin like silk. Her bones were fine, the muscles on them taut and elastic. She was a miracle. She smelled as fragrant to Matilde as the days when the nuns distilled lavender oil or attar of roses. She tasted of youth, a youth that had already fled Matilde Nicolau. Of happiness, too, that had gone. Of salt and soap. Of teenage skin. Above all, of innocence. It was her innocence that conquered.

She knew that Mercedes was still burning for the war. She knew that her own love was not strong enough to hold her in San Lluc, and that one day soon, Mercedes would go and she would be left alone. She formulated a prayer.

Please let her not suffer. Let her not be killed. If her life is in the scales, let mine be taken instead. If pain awaits her, let it come to me first. She used the same formula each time she prayed.

They made love again and again over the succeeding weeks, without exhaustion or weariness. As yet, there were no words. Afterward, barely speaking, Mercedes would slide into sleep with the finality of a burial at sea.

"You'll have so many men in your life," Matilde said to her one luminous dawn. "So many men will love you. This will mean nothing to you, in the end."

"It will always mean something to me," Mercedes replied with unexpected passion. "You're the first person who ever loved me. I don't want men. I hate them. I *hate* them. I only want you."

Matilde's hands and mouth were hungry, plundering, gathering. Desire replied in Mercedes, quick and eager.

They planned another excursion, this time to the ruins of the convent.

The convent was a sad spectacle, and Matilde started to cry as they saw the damage that had been done. The inside was completely gutted. Most of the floors, and the whole roof, had completely gone. So had the spire on the little Lady Chapel where Mother Josep had taken refuge in 1909. Every window had been smashed, and the grounds were strewn with the charred remains of furniture and books. The great iron gates that Francesc had made thirty years earlier had survived almost unscathed. Seeing those gates affected Mercedes oddly.

"My father made these," she said quietly.

Matilde stared at the fine workmanship with reddened eyes. "An anarchist did that work for the church?"

"And he did it for nothing too. Why not? The church always gets the best of everything. During *Semana Tragica*, he tried to burn this place down. The *guardia* shot him, and he ended up in the Infirmary, right here. Mother Josep, who was the Mother Superior then, saved his life. Now you're sheltering in his house." She reached out and traced the sinuous iron ribbons of the metalwork. "It's like these snakes. Welded together whether they like it or not. Twisting and twining. Biting and making love. Sometimes I think there isn't any logic in it at all."

They wandered around the walls, which had been daubed with anarchist and anti-church slogans. Someone had painted political slogans in huge letters which could be seen right across the valley.

"That was my room, up there," Matilde told Mercedes, pointing to a small window on the very top floor. "I used to watch the dawn, nearly every morning, after Matins."

"Do you want to go inside?" Mercedes asked. Matilde shook her head in silence, afraid of what she might see and feel. Mercedes looked through a gaping window into a blackened inner room. "I had a friend here, once. A nun who taught me at school. Her name was Catalina. I expect she's buried here, if they haven't dug her up."

Matilde shuddered. "God, it's awful."

"Is it upsetting you?"

"To do this to a convent—" She gestured helplessly. "It isn't politics. It's barbarism."

"Well, it'll never open again," Mercedes said decisively. "Not if the people win this war. It might be turned into a barn, or maybe into a museum of superstition, like they have in Russia. But there won't be any more Matins or Vespers here."

"It's like the Dark Ages coming back. It terrifies me."

"The other side burn churches too, though they claim to be such good Catholics. And Hitler burns synagogues. Mussolini has the Pope in his pocket. If the Dark Ages are back, the Fascists brought them, not the Reds."

Matilde's mouth was quivering again. She looked up at the blackened windows. "I wonder where they've all gone. All my friends. All those sisters."

"Would you go back?" Mercedes asked curiously. "Supposing Franco won tomorrow and rebuilt the convent, would you take your orders?"

Matilde stared with unseeing, pale blue eyes. "No, I suppose not," she said after a while. "Not after everything . . . that's happened. But I'll always love the church. As much as you hate it."

"I don't hate it," Mercedes laughed. The evening breeze whipped dark snakes of hair across her mouth. She pulled them free with slender brown fingers. "But it doesn't fool me. What are those vows you take? Poverty, obedience, chastity? The first two ought to be wealth and arrogance. As for chastity . . ."

"Most nuns and priests keep their vows holy," Matilde said stiffly, "all their lives." Mercedes just watched her with a slightly malicious gleam in her dark eyes until Matilde flushed. "I know what you're thinking. But it wasn't like that! You know it wasn't."

"I don't know anything," Mercedes smiled.

"Then why are you looking at me like that?"

"Well, *you* can't have been very chaste, Sister Matilde," she said dryly. "You obviously learned some naughty things in this place."

"Don't be hateful," Matilde exclaimed hotly. "You and I are quite different from . . ."

"From what?"

"From anything that happened to me in the convent."

"Well, you certainly know your stuff," Mercedes said. "You must have had good teachers."

"No!"

"No?"

"Yes, things sometimes happened. Yes. We were only women, after all, trying to live a holy life. It isn't easy, you know. But if things happened, it was only on very rare occasions. And not the way you think! Not like—not like you and me!"

"Well, well." Mercedes still had that look in her eyes. "I was merely commenting on how skillful you are."

Bitterly wounded by the callous mood that had overtaken Mercedes, Matilde turned away. "I love you. And if you don't know that by now, then you're blind."

"I'm just wondering whether you're turning me into a *tortillera*."

The slang word for a lesbian cut Matilde to the quick. "That's ugly, Mercé! I'm not a *tortillera*. Nor are you."

"I thought that's what a *tortillera* was," Mercedes said innocently. "A woman who wants to make love to other women. Who likes touching their breasts and kissing them between the legs. The way you like to kiss me."

Matilde's round cheeks flushed scarlet. She turned back to Mercedes. "You seem to like it too!"

"I never said I didn't." Mercedes's eyes were smoky. "But isn't it all just a tiny bit degenerate?"

"You're the one who said you hated men!"

"That doesn't mean I want a love affair with a woman."

"You don't have to touch me again if that's how you feel," Matilde said with a quavering attempt at coldness. "I'll go and sleep in the attic."

"What, with the beetles you hate so much?"

"I'll go away. You don't ever have to see me again."

"But where would you find such a pretty little lover?" Mercedes asked mischievously. "With such beautiful breasts and thighs, as you were telling me last night?"

"Why are you doing this?" Matilde demanded. "It's cruel to taunt me with my own love. I can't help it. If it comes to that, you've corrupted *me*, not the other way around!"

Mercedes widened her eyes in a parody of surprise. "How do you work that out?"

"I never had a love affair in here," Matilde burst out. "I never slept with anyone every night, the way I do with you. I never loved anyone!"

"And do you love me?" Mercedes asked, her head on one side.

"You know I worship you!"

Mercedes looked at her for a long moment. Then her expression relaxed. She held out her arms to Matilde, who rushed into them with a sob.

"There," she murmured. "I was only teasing you."

"You're so cruel sometimes," Matilde said, her voice muffled against Mercedes's shoulder. "We're not lesbians!"

"We're a pretty good imitation," Mercedes said, with a lopsided smile that was lost on Matilde. "Would you rather have a man's cock, if you could?"

"No!"

"Nor me."

"You'll fall in love," Matilde sniffed. "You don't really love me. One day you'll meet the right man. And then you'll forget me forever."

"Will he know all the naughty things you do?"

"You can teach him," Matilde said. "Say a nun showed you how."

Mercedes stroked Matilde's cheek. "I didn't mean to upset you. I'm just so frustrated. I want so much to *do* something for Spain . . ."

"I know."

"And perhaps I was a little jealous."

Matilde lifted her snub-nosed face. "Of what?"

"Of this great lump of shit," Mercedes said, nodding at the ruined convent.

Matilde stared, then laughed. "You say some funny things."

The sun was low over the distant sea. Long purple shadows stretched around them. In the golden light, Matilde thought

Mercedes had never looked so beautiful. "I love you," she whispered. "Maybe I'm a *tortillera*, but you aren't. You're...just Mercedes."

"Oh, I quite like being a *tortillera*." She slid her hand into Matilde's blouse and cupped Matilde's soft breast. They looked into each other's eyes, Mercedes deliberately caressing Matilde's nipple between her finger and thumb until it hardened and Matilde shuddered with pleasure. "Let's go back home," she whispered, kissing Matilde's lips. "And see how well I've learned my lessons."

Mercedes came home from the post office at lunchtime on Thursday, as always, and knew at once that Matilde was gone.

Conchita was sitting on a chair in the kitchen, her face bitter, though she was no longer crying. "They took her away," she told Mercedes flatly.

"Oh, God, no. Who?"

"Militiamen. Thugs. I don't know who."

"What did they look like?"

"I don't know their badges and their piebald uniforms the way you do."

"Did they have anarchist badges?"

"Some of them did. But I'd never seen any of them before. They said they were looking for reactionaries. Someone must have denounced Matilde. I don't know who. Some busybody."

Mercedes's skin was like ice. "Where have they taken her?"

"They wouldn't say. They took about ten others. Even old Luis Quadreny, your grandfather's friend."

Mercedes felt so sickened that she had to sit down. She stared at her mother as if at a stranger. "Tell me what happened."

"It's because of something that happened in some wretched village in Alicante. Now they have to have their own massacre to set the balance right." Conchita's face was lined, hard, as though her beauty and her tenderness had been ironed out that morning. "They came into the village in a lorry. So young, just youths. Young men with killer's faces. One of them had a list of names. They started rounding people up. Five came into the house with their guns. They knew who they were looking for. They found that little shrine she'd made upstairs. They brought her down here and started questioning her. She didn't have any papers or anything to incriminate her. But her hair...and you know that look she had, that nun's skin..."

"Yes," Mercedes said in a dry voice.

"I tried to tell them she was my cousin. They wanted to listen, some of them. But the others asked her outright if she was a nun." Conchita Barrantes's grey eyes were dry, but she seemed to be crying within. "She wouldn't deny it, Mercé. She wouldn't. If she'd just said, No, I'm not a nun, they would have left her in peace. But she just sort of...smiled. I always thought her a lump of a girl, God forgive me, but I never saw anything braver in my life. She smiled at them and wouldn't deny her religion."

"She was only a postulant," Mercedes said.

"Yes, she was only a postulant. A few weeks ago, you asked her if she was proud of what the Fascists are doing in the south. Let me ask you now, are you proud of what *your* side have done today?"

"It's an error," Mercedes said flatly. She felt unreal, emotionless. "They won't harm her. I'm going to find her."

"You'll never see her again," Conchita retorted in a hard voice.

"The anarchists in Palafrugell will know where she's been taken. I'll go down now. We'll get her out."

"Out of their clutches?" Her mother laughed abruptly. "Do you really know them that little? They would have taken me, too, if I hadn't been Francesc Eduard's wife. Do you know what one of them said to me? *A woman like you should be ashamed of harbouring an enemy of the State.* If she was an enemy of the State, Mercé, then it isn't a State I want anything to do with. You can have it, you and your father."

"The State isn't at fault," Mercedes said, staring at her hands. "Every individual action of the State cannot be just. It's impossible."

"Oh, Jesus. Spare me the ideology." Conchita's voice rose tightly. Something seemed to have snapped inside her. "I carried you in my belly, Mercedes, when you were only a curse to me. I bore you, screaming. I watched you grow into what you are. When you started drinking in that anarchist cant of your father's, I was appalled. As horrified as if I'd found you lapping raw blood. But I let myself be convinced that it was best for you. I never interfered with your education. And now I wonder what you've become. I wonder what all of you have become, all you children of Spain. Pitiless. Mindless. Drinkers of blood. Creatures with a doctrine where their souls should be."

"It's *war!*" Mercedes was shouting suddenly, her eyes glaring. "Don't sit there lecturing me about pity! Don't you listen to the radio, Mama? Don't you read the papers? Don't you know what we're facing? Don't you know what is ranged against us?"

"I know that Spain is being swallowed up by evil," Conchita said wearily. "And I know that you are part of it."

Mercedes stared at her mother for a moment, then rose to her feet. "I'm going to Palafrugell to find Matilde," she said shortly, and ran out of the house.

She sat tautly in the bus to Palafrugell, fighting back the urge to pray. It was an error, a dreadful error. They'd see that as soon as Matilde opened her silly mouth and showed them she couldn't possibly be an enemy to anyone.

But the anarchist leader in Palafrugell was unable to answer her question. Carles Romagosa, an old friend of her father's, spread his hands.

"It wasn't the anarchists who carried out those arrests. They may have worn anarchist insignia, but they were more likely Trotskyites or Marxists. They've been doing a lot of killing under our name, so the blame falls on us."

Mercedes felt a horrible flutter of panic in her heart. "Killing?"

"I wouldn't hold out much hope, Mercé," he said heavily. "Especially if she was a nun. The people who do this work are young butchers. Ex-criminals, Christ knows who. Uncontrollables. They kill for pleasure. They've even killed good anarchists before now."

"Where would they have taken her?"

Romagosa scratched his beard. "To a field somewhere. A beach. Some remote place. What time was she taken?"

"At nine this morning."

Romagosa checked his watch. "By now she'll be dead."

Mercedes's stomach turned over. "Oh, God. They wouldn't harm her without a trial first. Without a judge, a tribunal!"

He gave her an odd look. "Don't you know what happens, Mercé? How they do these things?"

"Carles, give me a car," she pleaded urgently.

"And how will you find your nun, between here and Gerona?" he asked dryly. "By second sight? I'll make some telephone calls. Wait here."

He left her fretting in the office and went out to make his calls. Her imagination tortured her. Matilde. She pictured some young exterminator tearing off her skirt, jeering as he forced her white thighs apart ... *Matilde.*

Romagosa was back in ten minutes. "Trouble with this *mierda* of a war is there are too many fucking sides," he said bitterly. "And no one knows who's killing who from one hour to the next."

"Did you find anything out?" she begged.

"Maybe. A PSUC lorry is said to have gone out in the direction of Mas Bolet this afternoon. That's apparently where they've had some of their 'trials' lately." He rose with her. "But I'm coming with you. I don't want you turning up there on your own."

He equipped himself with a submachine gun and brought along a wizened anarchist militiaman named Perón, who carried a Mauser rifle. They took an ancient, olive-green Citroën from the garage, because it had the fullest tank, and rode out of Palafrugell, the anarchist pennant flickering from the aerial.

"Still eager to go off to war?" Romagosa asked her as he drove. "Bide your time. You can't leave your mother alone in San Lluc. Your father's doing ten men's work for the republic already. Be content with that."

"Maybe they're still waiting for orders," Mercedes said. "Maybe they're questioning them first."

"Maybe," Romagosa grunted. "You were taking a chance, hiding this nun. Those maniacs might have taken the whole lot of you, if they'd felt like it."

They didn't speak after that, but Mercedes could tell from Carles Romagosa's expression that he held no hope for finding Matilde alive. A terrible foreboding had settled in her stomach and would not go away.

The sun was high. It was a magnificent afternoon. A slight haze hung over the countryside and it was bakingly hot. The road to Mas Bolet lay through some of the richest land in the Ampurdán, golden acres of wheat and silver valleys of olives. The hay had all been harvested and stood in tawny stacks in the fields. The leaves of vines had begun to droop in the heat, but beneath, the clusters of grapes were growing heavy and musky. It all passed by Mercedes as in a dream.

When he spoke of "Mas Bolet," Romagosa had been referring not to the tiny village of that name, but to the abandoned eighteenth-century farmhouse after which the village had been called.

It lay some two kilometres outside the village, along an overgrown track that climbed a rocky hill. It was still a fine-looking structure, though it had not had a roof for seventy years. Its massive walls had been built of the local dark brown stone and it possessed a proud circular defence tower that rose stolidly against the sky and could be seen from as far afield as Begur.

They reached it along the track, Romagosa driving cautiously with one hand, the other cradling his submachine gun in his lap. But all appeared abandoned, the overgrown yard empty of persons or vehicles. Mercedes's heart sank in despair as they stopped and climbed out. The silence was massive. Perón walked across the yard with his rifle, his head down, then pointed at the earth. They followed him to see. The grass had been torn up, recently, by the tyres of a heavy vehicle. It had driven around the farmhouse.

Without speaking, they walked slowly around the building, the two men carrying their weapons at the ready. At the back of the farmhouse, the stink of death hit them.

"This is where they do it," Perón said impassively. He nodded towards three mounds that lay in a blackened clearing. "Pile them up and burn them. Shovel some dirt on top afterwards. Come the winter, rain'll wash that away and you'll see skeletons underneath."

Romagosa was walking in the other direction, down a slight incline, away from the building. He stopped and after a while called, "Here."

Mercedes was aware of her legs carrying her, but her mind had gone blank. It wasn't real. It was happening to someone else.

Some ancient spades lying around. A trough in the reddish earth, maybe a metre wide, three metres long. Partially filled, not to the top. Where the earth had settled, outlines of limbs. The back of a head. A man's hand protruding from the soil, stubby fingers spread.

"Made them dig their own grave," Romagosa said laconically. "Then shot them in it. Couldn't even be bothered to bury them properly. You want to look any farther?"

Mercedes lowered herself into the shallow pit without speaking. She was suddenly aware of standing on half-interred limbs and she stumbled to her knees, wanting to vomit, her hands buried in the earth. Slowly, her head hanging, she started to scrape the soil away from a face.

"Jesus. Give her a hand, Perón."

The soldier groaned. But he climbed in beside her with a spade and started to dig. After a few strokes, he swore in disgust. He threw the spade back out and continued digging with his hands.

They dug in silence. Romagosa smoked a cigarette above them, whistling a few snatches of a popular song from time to time. Scrabbling in the soil, Mercedes found a man's stubbly face under her fingers, eyes shut, mouth full of earth. She stared at it blankly, then covered it and moved on. The next face was that of an older man, balding and bearded. His eyes were half-open.

"This one's a female," Perón said.

Mercedes turned. Romagosa tossed aside his butt and peered in.

Matilde was lying on her side, her face turned upwards. Her hips and legs were trapped under another corpse. The back of the dress she wore, one of Conchita's old ones, was clotted with dark blood. Perón swept the soil off her face gingerly. "Been shot at least four times. Revolver, probably. This her?"

Mercedes nodded. In death, Matilde's eyes were wide and staring. Her mouth gaped. Her expression was somehow gross, as though her features were suffused with anger. Mercedes had never seen that expression on her face in life. Her limbs felt as stiff and heavy as bronze.

"That's the *rigor mortis*," Perón said, as Mercedes tried to pull Matilde clear of the man who half-lay on her. "They'll all be stiff as boards until tomorrow. Best leave her. You can't do her any good now, anyway, can you?"

"No," Mercedes said. She felt a great wrenching sob begin at the pit of her stomach. "Can't do her—any—good—now."

"Hey, don't start that." Perón took her shoulders and pulled her to her feet. Mercedes could not move. The sobs were tearing her open, taking her over. Her mouth had locked open and it was as though her very heart were being jerked out of her.

They couldn't make her respond, so Perón and Romagosa pulled her out of the grave, cursing. She was blinded and paralyzed with grief.

"I didn't know this was a friend of hers," the officer said, panting. "She said it was just some nun they were sheltering."

"Been a bit of a shock, I suppose."

They held her between them, trying to support her against the great tearing sobs that wouldn't stop. In between, ragged gasps of air. All that she had locked inside. All that she had denied. All pouring out in violent contractions like those of birth.

"Come on," Romagosa said at last. "Let's get her in the car and take her home."

Halfway back to San Lluc, she stopped crying, quite suddenly, and lay against the seat, staring out of the window with glazed eyes. The two men exchanged glances and shrugs.

Matilde laughing. Matilde crying in her arms. Matilde loving her in the darkness. Matilde so afraid, not knowing where she would go next. It was as though she'd only realized how much she'd loved Matilde after her death.

And only now could she see how selfishly she had behaved, how callously, how carelessly.

She'd never said, *I love you*. Not even to her corpse, in that terrible grave.

It was all over. She felt a sense of termination so complete that it was as if her own life had ended at Mas Bolet, as if she were lying in that red earth, and someone else was here in her place.

She found tears again, later, and wept brokenly for many hours.

She and her mother sat in the kitchen while darkness fell, not talking. Later, she looked up to find her mother's eyes on her.

"I'm going," she said in a dead voice.

"I know," Conchita nodded.

"Whether it's evil or not, I can't help myself. You were right. I'm part of it. I have to go."

"I know," Conchita said again.

8.

~Claws

spring 1971

Tucson

The morning dawns mild and dry in southwestern Arizona. By mid-morning, the sun towers in a vast, cloudless heaven. The temperature is up in the 70's.

Joel Lennox's house is cool. It is set above the Golden Gate pass, high in the hills west of Tucson, a low, compact adobe with beamed ceilings and tile floors. The house is not large, but it is very beautiful. He has built it with his own hands.

Crudely carved in mesquite, pine and walnut, the furniture has been painstakingly hunted out and assembled. The pieces glow with having endured much use. There are Navaho and Zapotec rugs on the floor. Some older, finer examples adorn the walls—there are no paintings. Among the collections of Hopi baskets and pottery are some rare and valuable examples. There is a fine Spanish colonial chest next to the fireplace.

A large, handsome sandstone carving has been set into the wall above the fireplace.

There are other sculptures, free-standing and relief, lying almost casually around the house. Some are in sandstone, some in smooth green soapstone. One, a beautiful portrait head, is in marble. It is work like this that paid for the land and the materials of the house.

Joel Lennox sits with his face in his hands. He has passed a dreadful night. He has lain in his own sweat, tormented by grief and anger, by nightmares and visions. His own pain, the pain of others, has haunted him in terrible shapes. The things they have done to him and made him do, will not let him be. He cannot shed them. It feels as though he has not slept for years.

And he can bear it no longer. The decision has been forming for weeks. Now it is here.

He walks to the cupboard and takes out the M–16 rifle he keeps there. The weapon fits into his hands with the intimacy of long familiarity.

From a drawer he takes an ammunition clip and methodically fills it with glinting bullets. The actions have the flavour of a ritual. His mouth is dry and he keeps swallowing. He walks out onto the porch and down into the garden.

His garden is the Sonoran desert, majestic and vast. It is here he has built his house. His land is seventeen acres of creosote bush, prickly pear and cactus, cholla, agave and ocotillo, mesquite and smoke tree. Gaunt arms, thorns, pastel colours. Drought. And silence. All around, the dim violet mountains. Land that had no value to others, but was priceless to him.

The saguaro is the fleshiest living thing here. It is the plant he loves the most. Beckoning giants, the cacti rise up to forty feet. Their ribbed and spiny bodies sometimes sprout thick, upraised arms. Others are solitary monoliths. Most bear holes made by nesting woodpeckers. In this season they are swelling out, losing the shrunken look of summer. They are filling with sap.

They are beautiful creatures, regarded by the Indians as human like themselves. To Joel Lennox, they are more. They are his people. His flesh.

He stares at the desert. He came here for shelter. He came out into this wilderness, a scapegoat, to be at peace. But peace has eluded him. He has been unable to escape the torment of his own emotions.

He sits on the step. He rests the rifle on the ground, butt first. He flicks off the safety catch and takes the muzzle in his mouth. This way there can be no mistake. No note, no regrets, just a painless exit.

The cold steel digs into the roof of his mouth. A bitter mineral taste of oil. Clean, sharp sensations. He can just reach the trigger with his thumb. He is calm and still as he pushes against the spring, feeling the trigger yield a millimetre. Two millimetres.

He thinks about silence. About peace.

There is a hawk, high in the sky. It seems not to move, but it is soaring, soaring, free.

"You gonna do it?"

He hears the voice as clear as a bell, although there is nobody standing by.

"You call this justice? Go on, then. Do it, motherfuckah."

Now he knows the voice. An Alabama drawl, soft and slow. It belongs to Luke Jeffries.

He lets the trigger slacken, his eyes opening.

"Listen," says Jeffries's voice, "ain't you learn' nothin' out there? Better kill than be killed. Better fight than give in. You remember?"

He begins to tremble violently, so much so that the steel sight rattles against his teeth. Bathed in sweat, close to vomiting, he is forced to take the muzzle out of his mouth. He grits his teeth, taking deep, hissing breaths through his nose. The blood is pounding in his ears.

He stares around blindly, as though Jeffries might actually be there, even though he knows Jeffries died in Southeast Asia three years ago and came home in a coffin labelled, "members missing."

There is no one there. Sweat is splashing into his eyes. The muzzle of the M–16 wavers in erratic circles. It is always this way, when death is near. The trembling, the rage.

He shuts his eyes and sees the images burned onto the retinas. After a while, the trembling subsides enough for him to get to his feet. He lifts the M–16 and aims at the nearest saguaro, a thirty-foot titan bearing a candelabrum of uplifted limbs. The plastic stock cuddles tightly against his cheek.

This time he does not make the mistake of hesitating. He sights on the saguaro and pulls the trigger at once.

The bullet rips through the cactus, leaving a long, ragged hole. The report rolls away across the desert. Birds take to the air in alarm. His shoulder is numbed. A deeper silence seems to have fallen over the desert.

He sights again and fires again. Another numbing blow. Another long rip in the flesh. His flesh. The cactus he loves sways with the impact.

Sweat keeps pouring into his eyes. Rage is swelling in him, erupting. He pushes the selector button to full automatic fire and braces himself. His teeth are bared and he can hardly see. The saguaro is a dark, blurred silhouette in a red world.

He squeezes the trigger and holds it down.

Bullets churn into and around the saguaro. Astringent green gobbets spatter and fly. The noise is shattering, an assault on the ears, on the thorax and brain. Long before the clip is empty, the cactus is already falling, cut through.

It hits the earth with the heavy thump of tons, just as the clip empties. With its limbs outstretched, it lies prone, arms outflung among a swirl of dust.

Lennox lowers the rifle and sits heavily on the steps of his porch. His breathing is torn. His anger fills him, bitter and emetic. He almost killed himself. Almost. Made a victim from the day of his birth. And almost blew his head off on his own porch.

He tries to form a word, his tortured diaphragm fragmenting it. Then he gets it out.

"Somebody," he gasps. "Somebody has got to pay."

"Yeah?" says Jeffries, close beside him and laughs softly. "Who gonna pay you, man? Who?"

"She will. She'll pay." He rests his forehead against the rifle. His face is tight around his skull. "I'll make her pay."

Beverly Hills

She was having the dream again.

Mama and Daddy were fighting. Eden could see that Mama's face was white and strained, and she knew it was a bad fight, one of the worst. Daddy was shouting horrible things at Mama.

Eden couldn't bear to listen. She tried to block her ears, but she couldn't move.

Then Daddy saw her at last. His face was congested and dark. He got to his feet, shouting at her.

His mouth was moving, and the words that came out were terrible. She saw the walls crack, the ceiling crumble. The house was coming down. It was all a jumble, a roar. The walls were falling on her. On them all. They were all going to be destroyed.

She knew Daddy's words were making the house collapse. So

she started screaming to try and drown him out. She screamed and screamed. She screamed so loud it tore her chest, deafened her.

She was awake, abruptly, sweat soaking into her hair. She was sitting upright in bed, her heart pounding in her chest like a hammer. The nausea and the shaky feeling were unbearable.

"Did I scream?" she gasped.

But there was no one there to answer.

She groped with trembling fingers for the strip of tinfoil. She coaxed the greyish powder into a thin trail on the foil. Then she put the plastic tube in her mouth, and clicked the lighter on. She trailed the flame under the tinfoil. The heroin melted, began to sublimate. She sucked rapturously at the greasy smoke, following the line as it burned away.

Then she lay back on the pillows, holding it deep in her lungs, her eyes shut. It felt like the whole night was inside her. Her chest swelled with stars and moons and planets. A marvelous alchemy was taking place in there. Tiny alveoli feeding her blood with the junk. Her blood humming through her veins to her brain, golden, rich. Her brain receiving the gift, exalting her mind. All pain and fear vanishing. Everything vanishing but the magnificent feeling of being high. High, high, high.

Rusty Fagan arrived at Spooky's apartment around two in the afternoon, which was extremely early for Spooky. Spooky's customers didn't start appearing until three or four, which was when he usually got up.

Nevertheless, Spooky dragged himself out of bed and blearily opened the door to let Rusty in. Since there were a dozen assorted bolts and latches, this took some time.

At last the fortified door swung open. Rusty's nose wrinkled at the smell inside the apartment.

"Jesus," he said, as Spooky laboriously re-locked the door behind them, "this place smells like a Saigon whore house."

Rusty had been in Nam in '69. He liked to do the heroic veteran routine. As a matter of fact, Spooky had spoken to some brothers who'd known Rusty Fagan out there, and they'd told him Rusty spent his entire tour in Cam Ranh Bay, slinging hash in a rest and recreation centre.

The most action Rusty had seen was jumping on Vietnamese women who could be bought for a steak or a piece of fish. The brothers said he jumped them anyway, whether they wanted the steak or not. They said he'd once raped a thirteen-year-old kid on a pool table.

Not that Spooky was going to reveal any of this knowledge to Rusty, who was a foot taller and seventy pounds heavier, and who could be a nasty son of a bitch when he felt like it.

Rusty Fagan, for his part, felt nothing but contempt for Spooky, the same contempt he felt for all addicts. Spooky was a dealer, but that didn't earn him any respect. He dealt to support his habit. He was turning over a thousand bucks a week, and he never had a dime, and he lived like a pig. One day the cops would bust him and he would scream out his mind in a police cell.

Originally, Spooky's full nickname had been "Spooky Tooth." While he'd smoked the drug, as Eden did now, his front teeth had blackened. After he started on the needle three or four years ago, the nickname dwindled to just "Spooky."

It suited him, even though he was black. He moved around like a ghost, a scuttling, twitching little ghost. Rusty perched on the table and considered Spooky with disdain.

"You got my stuff?"

"Sure."

"Gimme, then."

They weighed the heroin and haggled over a price. Spooky really did not like Rusty Fagan. Rusty was a bad dude.

Rusty liked to deal a little scag on the side. On a very intimate basis. Only one very special customer at a time. Right now, he was busy making Eden van Buren his very special customer. He had met Eden at UCLA, earlier this year. Her career as a student looked to be a short-lived one.

What Rusty did was, he bought the stuff from the dealers, fairly cheap, because he bought large quantities. Then he sold it to Eden, a shot at a time, for about two thousand percent profit. He fixed it so that when Eden tried to go behind his back, she always found the dealers had just run out, or were just waiting to score themselves, so she couldn't get any.

Eden was kind of innocent. It didn't occur to her that Rusty had told all the other dealers she knew that if they sold to her direct he would cut their balls off. Contrary to popular belief, most junk dealers were not muscular thugs with pistols in their vests, but helpless fucked-up addicts, only a grade less pathetic than their customers. None of them wanted trouble. So they did what Rusty said.

And Eden believed Rusty when he told her only he could reliably get the stuff for her.

That, too, was a good business. Eden was a very rich kid. Rusty knew there were thousands of dollars to be made.

But Rusty wasn't in it just for the money: Spooky knew, with an addict's sharpened perceptions of such things, that what Rusty really enjoyed was fucking with people's heads.

Eden was gorgeous. Not just physically desirable. She had something else, a mystery, an allure, a something that kept you staring at her, fascinated.

Rusty wasn't just making money, or getting laid. He was plundering that mystery. Possessing the secret.

Spooky pocketed the money Rusty gave him. "Never felt the urge yourself, huh?" he asked.

"No."

"Scared of the dragon. Right?"

Rusty was counting dollar bills. "It's just not my scene."

"I can dig that. It's a devil, right? A dragon. It fucks you up. A hundred and five percent. Man, it's a good thing Eden's got you to take care of her."

"Yeah," Rusty grunted. "A very good thing."

Rusty Fagan drove back to his apartment, feeling good. He had certainly never tried heroin. He was knowledgeable about it, as he was about a lot of drugs. He took the trouble to read all the drug literature.

Heroin fucked you up, as Spooky said. Really. And personally, he would have said you got a far better buzz out of cocaine, especially if you know where to get good stuff, which Rusty certainly did. Cocaine was wonderful. It was very fashionable. *The* up and coming kick. It wasn't even addictive, if you didn't start ladling it up with a soup spoon. (Rusty's reading of the drug literature was somewhat selective.)

Rusty Fagan preferred to deal with those in a weaker position than himself. It wasn't that he was a bully. It was just that he couldn't bear not to be the stronger party.

Leverage.

Leverage was what it was all about.

When someone was at a disadvantage and you held the whip-hand, you knew just where you stood. There were no nasty surprises in store for you. You could call the shots and the shots were neat and tidy and very profitable as a general rule.

You could use leverage to get anything from them. You got to look into their eyes, see right into their minds. You could watch them squirm, and that made you feel good. So good. Better than coke.

The only trouble with addicts was, it got messy. Users were a drag when they were up, a worse drag when they were down. You couldn't depend on them.

Not that he couldn't handle it. In fact, handling it was part of the pleasure.

Eden van Buren was certainly a heroin addict by now, though she probably did not know it yet. She was still floating in a cozy dream-world. He would wake her. By and by. When the time was ripe.

The real trick would be to get her on the needle.

She hadn't asked yet, but she soon would. And then he would need someone to show her the way. He thought he knew just the person.

San Lluc

Maya watched Mercedes talking to the site foreman.

They came up every weekend now, to check progress. The house was taking shape, fast. The pool, set into the foundations of the structure, had been completed. Now the high glass dome above it was being installed. The great house was going to have a heart of glass, cool and clear, with blue water at its centre.

The whole business of building a house on this scale and of such splendour, had seized Maya's imagination. Quite apart from any other consideration of their relationship, she felt deeply privileged that Mercedes had consulted her about the design of the house and had included her in so much of the planning.

It would soon be Mercedes's birthday. Her fifty-third, and the third that Maya would have celebrated with her.

Over the past three years, their relationship had steadily deepened and matured. They had become friends of a particularly close kind. Maya had sensed, especially at first, a profound reserve in the older woman. An unwillingness to be drawn into intimacy. Almost as though Mercedes were afraid of the relationship that might develop. Mercedes never spoke of her friend, Matilde, the woman who "went away." But Maya knew that Mercedes's reserve had much to do with that experience.

Friendship had grown, a gentle, unhurried thing. Maya had come to love Mercedes Eduard over the past three years, and their relationship had steadily excluded others.

Mercedes walked over to her. "He says they'll finish by mid-August," she told Maya.

"That's wonderful."

"Yes." Mercedes took her arm. "We'll be living here by the autumn."

"We?" Maya said in surprise.

Mercedes slipped her arm through Maya's and led her towards the car. "Come on. Let's go down to the boat."

An hour later, they were lying together on the sunbaked after-deck of the Feadship, moored in one of the beautiful, solitary coves that dotted the coastline. They were completely private. The crew of three who ran the motor yacht for Mercedes were all forward, out of sight.

Mercedes said, without preamble, "I want you to stop working."

"What?"

"I want you to leave your job. I want you to come and work for me. As my personal secretary, for want of a better word. Most of all, I want you to come and live with me in that house."

Maya picked herself up on one elbow and pulled off her sunglasses. "Are you serious?"

"I've never been more serious," Mercedes said quietly. She smiled up into Maya's eyes. "Your work doesn't fulfil you. You don't particularly like living in Barcelona. What we have together is more important than any of that. Isn't it?"

"Yes," Maya said. "It is."

"Then this is the most logical thing. To have you in Barcelona and me up here, would be unbearable. We would miss each other too awfully. You must have been thinking along the same lines."

"I never anticipated that you would offer me a job," Maya

said with a slight smile. "I don't want to be paid for being your friend, Mercé." She held out her slim wrist, where a diamond bracelet glittered icily in the sunlight. "You've already covered me in jewels. I don't want money."

"I wouldn't consider it on any other terms. Besides, there would be things for you to do. You could do just as much as you wanted to, or as you thought the salary warranted. That is the offer. Think about it. You don't have to answer until the house is ready."

"But we both know what the answer will be," Maya said gently.

summer 1971

Beverly Hills

This is what she has been waiting for.

This is what she has been longing for, this draught that will quench her thirst forever; yet now she is afraid.

Donna examines Eden's arm intently. She digs her thumb into the crook of Eden's elbow. She exclaims in mock-envy at the eager vein that pops.

Eden tries to smile. "Is that good?"

"I don't have a vein like that in my whole body. You're a regular Charles Atlas. What I wouldn't give for a line like that." Donna wears tight denim jeans and a denim jacket, with a pink scarf around her head. Her skin is the colour of white clay. She wears a perpetual down-turned smile. When Donna is stoned, her pale blue eyes are like Orphan Annie's, pupil-less disks that stare lifelessly. When she is not stoned, her smile becomes savage, and invisible fingers tweak at the clay in odd places.

But Donna is an expert with the needle, a genius. She will hit Eden up without pain or accidents, blast her straight to the moon. That is why she has chosen Donna.

Eden reminds herself of that and tells herself she is excited to the point of euphoria. But when Donna starts tying the tourniquet around her arm, showing her how to slip it, she tenses and draws back.

"Whatsamatter?"

"Nothing. I don't know. Am I going to get hepatitis or something?"

"Come on. You got it like a doctor's office in here. Alcohol, distilled water, new needles. You think I bother with all this shit?"

"No, but I do."

Donna shows Eden the needle, still in its cellophane wrapping. "Look. Just what the doctor ordered. Okay?"

Eden looks at the rest of the stuff, the syringe, the spoon, the water, lying on her coffee table.

"You gonna chicken out?"

"No," Eden says in a low voice.

Donna is not in a patient mood. She is waiting for her own fix. "Well, come on, then."

"I'm just going to wait a moment," Eden says, still staring at the syringe. "I need to settle down."

"Yeah, well, while you're making your decision, I'll just go ahead on my own. Maybe that'll give you the idea."

How did things ever get this far? What has happened to her? She feels as if she has swallowed a cannon ball, hard and cold inside her. But there is no time for second thoughts. Donna is already tapping the heroin into a spoon, deftly mixing it with water. She reaches for the lighter. The fix is about to go up Donna's tracked arm.

"Wait," Eden says. She does not want to be sitting here while a stoned Donna excavates in her arm with the needle. Her doubts have gone. She grasps the end of the tourniquet in her other hand and pulls it tight. "Do it."

Donna has to make an effort to put the stuff down. She kneels at Eden's feet and begins slapping and stroking the vein she has chosen. She is muttering softly to herself.

"Say goodbye, babe," Eden hears her say.

"To what?"

Donna grins at her. She doesn't know shit. Rich kid, looking down at her with those cool green eyes. "To everything."

Eden watches Donna fill the syringe.

"Everything you hate," Donna says dreamily.

The heroin is dirty-looking, yellowish.

"Everything you love."

She wants to ask Donna what it's been cut with, but bites her lip. Anyway, she doesn't want to know. She is not going to turn back now.

Donna raises the vein farther, rubbing at Eden's arm with her fingers.

"Alcohol," Eden commands tightly. She does not want septicaemia, whatever the occasion.

Shaking her head, Donna swabs the site with the alcohol. She has shot up with water taken from toilet bowls, using needles shared among a dozen strangers, so blunt they had to be sharpened on a matchbox. Eden will be a lot less picky in a month or two. "You all ready now?"

Eden nods. Her body is prepared. There is menace in the air. But her anxiety has gone. She decides that she loves this ominous awareness. Fear has turned into a deep, dark thrill. Like watching for the nuclear flash in the night.

She has been ready for this, more than ready, for a long time. Chasing was good, but never good enough. Heating it on foil, drawing the rich sublimate into her lungs, feeling her brain blossom, feeling her body become weightless and pure, everything fading away except the intense light of her high.

But that was a flirtation, delicious foreplay that had only one end. This.

Today she will catch the dragon.

Donna flicks the syringe with her nail. "See? Gotta make sure there's no air in the works. Bad for the heart."

"Yes."

Donna slides the needle into the vein without ceremony. Eden barely winces. There is no pain.

"Untie," Donna commands in a thick voice. Eden fumbles with the knot of the tourniquet. It falls to the ground. She has been holding her breath till her chest hurts, and she lets it out slowly, unsteadily. Now there is no barrier between her and the junk.

First Donna draws the plunger out, not in. A scarlet tongue of Eden's blood licks into the heroin, mingling in the glass tube. Then Donna shoots it all back in, fast. Eden watches as she draws out one more syringeful of blood to flush the last traces of the drug. That too, is shot quickly back in. She slips out the needle and presses a cotton-wool ball to the puncture.

"Bend your arm," she commands.

Eden obeys.

She is a thousand miles from land, a thousand miles from anywhere. She is waiting. It is in her blood, making for her brain, fast. There is a complete silence within her body.

A monumental, majestic stillness.

From a long way away, she is aware of Donna washing out the needle, ready for her own hit.

Where is it? When will it come? She waits. Donna looks at her.

"How're you doing?"

"Okay."

It is in her blood. It is coming on. She feels it begin at the edges of the room, flowing towards her. Faster now. It will be a flood. The cotton-wool ball drops as she grasps the arms of her chair to avoid being swept away. It rushes into her body with the force of a dam bursting, surging up, towards her brain.

It is thundering towards the top of her skull, filling the universe with noise and heat and light. It is too much. She won't be able to bear it. Life has been tapped within her and is exploding like a geyser. This is what she has been looking for. Nothing matters beside this. No pain. No joy. Ecstasy is so intense in these seconds before impact that she tries to scream out loud, but no sound emerges.

It smashes into her brain, exploding her cranium.

Her cerebrum erupts. She feels each one of those billions of cells flying outward, disassociate from all others, each one singing its own thin song. Her brain cells fill the room in a sparkling cloud. She is dissipated, as ethereal as cirrus clouds stretched across the sunset.

She is no longer Eden. She understands ecstasy.

Silence.

The blood slowly surges back down, through the golden tracery of her veins. It fills her body with love, more intense, more sweet, than any love has ever been. Mother, father, lover. It spins a golden web around her, cherishing her in joy.

"You feel it?" Donna is ready to hit herself up with the rest of the heroin. Eden raises her head slowly to look at her.

"Lethe. Wonderful."

"What's Lethe?"

"The river of . . . forgetfulness."

Stoned talk. Donna peers into her face. "Jesus, yeah. I remember that."

"God. God." Eden takes a deep breath. "I didn't know. I mean, I knew, but I didn't know. God. This is . . ."

Donna has lost interest already.

"This is . . . all I ever want."

Donna ignores her. She shoots herself up, staring at the wall. After a while, she puts her head back, shuts her eyes and says softly, "Oh, yeah." She nods once or twice.

Later, she studies her own arms. They offer few more sites. She has wrecked a lot of veins injecting crushed-up Demerol tablets, amphetamine, shit like that. She will move onto her thighs next. And in the end, there is always the femoral vein in the groin. There is always somewhere.

She glances at Eden as Eden gets unsteadily out of the chair and moves to the sofa like a sleepwalker. She lies back against the cushions, on the nod.

Where she is now. Wonderful. More wonderful than flight. Greater than sex. Different from the rush, but just as good. A golden twilight in which she floats, high as an angel.

Donna looks up and sees that Rusty Fagan is standing there. He is staring at Eden.

"Yeah," Donna nods. "Makes you envious, doesn't it? I'd give my left tit to have my first hit again."

"Whatever turns you on," Rusty says. "Any problems?"

"Nah. She took it like a lamb."

"Good. Here."

He takes some bills from his pocket and gives them to Donna. Donna takes the money and counts it.

"You can split now," Rusty says.

But Donna is in no great hurry to leave. This house is a super-comfortable pad to gouch out in. Beverly Hills, yet. Countryside out there, not smog and traffic. It also contains a thousand and one pretty things that could be picked up by a girl with a habit to support. Things with a ready resale. After all, Donna is already thinking about the next hit and the next.

She wanders around the house, eyes hunting for the right object. She finds it on a table and picks it up when Rusty's back is turned. She studies it eagerly. A paperweight. A beautiful thing.

She holds it to the light. Within the crystal globe, a glass butterfly is imprisoned forever.

She grins slyly. Baccarat or something like that, it has to be worth big bucks. Enough to keep her well for a week. Maybe enough to cut her in dealing to other junkies for a while. She slips it into her pocket.

"I said you could split now."

Rusty's eyes are hard. Donna knows that look. If she does not go now, he will hurt her. Anyway, she has the paperweight in her pocket.

"Okay." She goes over to Eden. The drug has made her lovely, vacant. Her hair is spread out, black snakes that coil around her pale face. Her mouth is dark red. Each of her cheeks holds a hectic disk of colour. Eden has an oval face, perfect skin. Her eyelashes and eyebrows are black and lush. She looks very foreign. A Spanish gypsy. Donna has never seen her so stilled before.

Donna resists the temptation to touch her.

This is sacred. Eden has taken herself a new lover, a lover no man will be able to compete with. This is the closest anyone will ever come to possessing Eden. No one, as far as Donna knows, has ever managed to cross the barrier she has inside, that gate she has erected. She won't let anyone. Will not let people in.

Strange girl, with her money and her politics and her horses. Her protest marches and her long words. Strange, fiery doll.

"Sweet dreams," Donna says quietly to her.

She nods to Rusty and leaves.

autumn 1972

Pacific Palisades, California

The curtains were being held open. She rode out through them, under the sign that read PALISADES SHOW JUMPING '72, into the warm evening air, blind and numb.

A groom reached up to take the horse's head and she slid off. She stooped to check Monaco's legs for cuts. She could see none. Aware at the edge of her vision that Dan Cormack was approaching, she pulled her hat off and unfastened her jacket.

"You're getting worse."

She ignored the gritty voice and started tugging at Monaco's girths.

"Much worse." She felt a hand descend heavily onto her shoulder. "What the hell is wrong, Eden?"

She had no option but to turn. Dan Cormack's face was cordovan leather. A face like an old saddle, polished and creased and seamed. As a child, she'd thought that if you prised the creases of his face open, you would see the saddler's stitching within.

She met his faded blue eyes and fought away the pain in her head. "I guess my heart wasn't in it," she said briefly.

"Damned right your heart wasn't in it. Leave that stuff." He drew her away from the panting, sweating horse, one hand still grasping her shoulder. "Every time you get a chance to win, your mind slips outa gear. I see you slump over in the saddle like your backbone turned into asparagus. You get a glazed look. You high on dope or something, Eden?"

The metallic voice of the loudspeaker, boomed around the ring, announcing her final marks. They were terrible.

The back of her neck was sweltering under the heavy knot of black hair. The nerves at the base of her skull were tight and quivering. The claws had started to dig in.

"I thought you were gonna really make progress this year. You told me you were gonna tackle this concentration problem."

"Dan—"

"You told me you were gonna win some prizes, Eden."

The next rider rode past them, through the curtains and into the ring. Applause greeted him, then an expectant silence.

"I think I'll go take a shower," she said.

"I have a recommendation." Cormack blocked her way as she tried to walk by him. "Come back to me for more ring work. Three days a week, two hours a time. Proper training."

"I don't have time for all that ring work, Dan."

"You already dropped outa college. What else you got to do?"

"I can't live, eat and sleep horses."

"That's what you wanted to do, once." The leathery face creased into what might have been a smile. "I'll make the time if you will. Evenings, too, if that's what you want."

"Thanks, Dan," she said flatly. "I really don't have the time."

"Then what do you come here for, wasting everybody's efforts and energy?"

Her voice sharpened. "I beat half the kids here tonight. That's enough."

"Hell, no, it ain't enough." His voice roughened. "You should be at the top. Like you once told me you wanted to be. Remember? You have the capacity to excel, Eden. I see you progressively throwing that away, and it makes me angry. Your riding's just disintegrating. Today you came in the middle. Next time, maybe you'll come at the bottom. The time after that, you might not even bother to participate."

From inside the ring came the clatter of a jump being knocked over, and the half-dismayed, half-gratified gasp of the audience.

"Ain't no excuse for that, Eden." He tried to speak gently. "Throwing it all away. It's an insult to God."

They faced one another among the ordered chaos of the saddling-up area. The groom led Monaco past, a rug over his flanks.

"That horse deserves better too," Cormack said. "You keep knocking his legs against those bars, he's gonna lose his confidence. If he doesn't hurt hisself first."

She slung her jacket over her arm. "I'll go take that shower now, Dan."

"And there's another thing. You look right sickly to me. Like you might be anaemic, or something." He took her arm. "Ever thought you might have something? A deficiency, maybe a dietary thing?"

"For Christ's sake, Dan."

"Jennifer was commenting on how much weight you've lost. You're downright skinny. And getting white as a ghost. She was saying maybe you should consider vitamins . . ."

She shook his hand off. "I don't need any vitamins," she said angrily. "And I'm at my perfect weight."

"Now, I'm not saying extra pounds are any friend to a jumper. But ain't no use shedding that muscle tissue. That's what makes you strong, gives you your power. Jennifer was saying—"

"I'm not interested in what Jennifer was saying. I don't like being discussed behind my back by busybodies."

Cormack's faded eyes widened. "*Busy*bodies? Girl, Jennifer's known you since you were knee-high to a horse turd."

"Know what I hate most about the showjumping scene?" she said bitterly. "The gossip. The tattletales. Everybody poking their noses into everybody else's business. There's no privacy. No barriers. Nowhere a person can just be alone."

Dan's craggy brows came down. "The only people who need barriers are people who got something to hide, Eden. What is it you need to hide?"

Eden stared at him. "Fuck off, Dan," she said coldly. She pushed past him and walked to the changing rooms. Dan Cormack stared after her.

Jennifer Cormack came to stand beside her husband. She had overheard the last few sentences and her face was hard.

"Snotty little rich bitch," she said shortly.

"Something's wrong with that girl, Jennifer."

"What's wrong with her is that her parents ruined her from day one. She was already spoiled rotten when she first came to you for lessons, when she was five years old. Forget her."

"Uh-uh. It's more than that. More than that. And I reckon I know what it is." He shook his head slowly. "I think I'm gonna invest in a long-distance call to her momma."

The women's room was full of riders in various stages of undress. She sat down and cried a little. She was slipping out of control. She felt exhausted. Her nerves were quivering in her flesh, spidery branches in a cruel wind.

No one paid her much attention. A sweaty rider crying in the women's room on a competition night was not an unusual occurrence.

She pulled off her shirt and bra and unfastened the heavy knot of hair at her nape. It tumbled down her back in thick coils. There was some relief from the claws, but not much.

She pushed through the steamy crowd of female bodies to the showers.

The spray felt like needles piercing her sensitized skin. She stood it as long as she could. She was shivering when she came out, though the water had been hot. Her nerves were tightening all the time, claws digging in along her spine. Not much longer, now. She couldn't stand it much longer.

They never told you about this part. They never said it would be so bad. It was as bad down as it was good up.

Rusty. Why did he do this to her? He knew she was competing tonight. He knew what happened to her when he left it too long. Why did he enjoy tormenting her?

She regretted jumping so wretchedly.

She regretted swearing at Dan Cormack. How many more friends did she have left to hurt and alienate? How many of the women out there already hated her, jeered at her behind her back?

Sometimes she felt they must all know. All of them, even Dan.

Could she apologize to Dan? He would probably cut her dead. Maybe later.

The need surged in her, white-hot filaments in her flesh. She sank down on the teak slats, onto her knees and wept silently.

Tucson

Joel Lennox gets back to the house after dark. He is tense and tired and he gets out of the van to stretch his shoulders before he starts unloading.

The autumn air is like champagne, especially after dark. It is cooling, but through the soles of his boots, he can feel warmth radiating from the ground.

He glances around. The desert at night is silent. The stands of saguaro are moonlit sentinels. He catches the shape of an owl, gliding down towards some quivering rodent.

The van is filled with bricks and bags of cement. He has gone upstate to buy them, at a yard near Phoenix, and has only returned to Tucson after sundown. He has few neighbors, certainly none in his sightline, but there is no need to advertise the fact that he is doing a little building work at the house.

He begins unloading, carrying the materials straight down to the cellar. It is hard work and he starts sweating. As he works, he tries to think about the job ahead of him, wanting it to be cool and clear in his mind. Without emotion, the way it has to be. He still has a lot to plan.

But there is too much distraction in his head, and his quarry trembles elusively in his thoughts, a rabbit seen through a heat haze. His eyes feel parched and his skin seems to crackle as the sweat breaks through it. He loses his concentration and stumbles. Bricks cascade to the ground.

He focuses his thoughts on the work, muscles working stolidly.

The van slowly empties. The neat piles in the cellar grow.

When the work is done, he goes downstairs and examines the site. He has already acquired the iron-framed bedstead. It is just the right age. Just the right design. A heavy, dark thing. It stands waiting in the corner, like a bed of torture, rather than one of sleep. There are struts through which to loop the chains.

He had to weld flanges onto the feet of the bedstead, so that he could bolt it to the concrete floor. It is completely immovable now until he takes out the bolts.

The structure itself will be built around the bedstead. He has already marked the floor.

Tomorrow he will start building the cell.

Los Angeles

"She was here last night," Spooky told Rusty.

"Uh huh," Rusty said.

"Around four o'clock in the morning. Begging for a shot. Pleading. Crying and shivering."

"I hope you didn't do anything silly," Rusty said blandly.

"No. I didn't do anything silly. I got my orders, don't I?"

"Yeah, you have your orders." Rusty snapped his fingers. "Gimme."

Spooky shuffled to the back of the apartment, closing and locking the door behind him. Rusty had never found out where he kept the stuff. Spooky was as secretive as a pack rat. One day, he thought with amusement, he would kick the door down, burst in there with a yell and catch Spooky at his little hidey-hole. Scare the shit out of him.

Spooky gave him the parcel. "It made me feel like a piece of shit, man. Having to turn down a friend who's cold turkeying on the doorstep."

"Yeah?" Rusty went into the kitchen and weighed the parcel on the plastic scales that stood among the grimy cups and plates.

"It ain't even good for business." Spooky watched Rusty with bleary, reddened eyes. "Word gets around I'm not good for a score, my customers'll start drifting away."

"Spooky, old boy, your kind of customers are never going to drift away. I make that twenty-five grams, right?"

"Right. Top grade material." Spooky glanced at Rusty, not directly, but sideways. "How do you square it with your conscience, man?"

"Square what?" Rusty said with quiet menace. "You used to sell to her, didn't you?"

"Yeah, but I never did what you do to her. Ripping her off. Keeping her hooked."

"Keeping her hooked? Me? Does she look like she needs encouraging?"

"No, she don't need encouraging. She don't need to be turned into a slave either."

Rusty folded the money into a little tube and pointed it like a gun at Spooky. "Don't fuck with me, you little shit."

"Okay, okay."

"Eden was born to be a junkie. Nothing you or I can do about it. She needs looking after. I'm protecting her. Looking after her interests. I'm just ensuring there are no fuck-ups. You understand me?"

"I'd call her wandering around desperate at four in the morning a pretty good fuck-up."

"I had things to do."

"I'm sure you did." Spooky was still looking at Rusty with that sideways look. He really did not like Rusty.

When Spooky saw Eden these days, he felt that a bright light was going out. He felt that he was being used in a very ugly game. And he felt, even though drug dealers and addicts are not prone to pity, a lingering qualm of compassion for the girl who was now waiting for her shot in Beverly Hills.

"Where do you get your stuff?" Rusty asked casually, examining the heroin.

Spooky shrugged. "That's my business. If you need some more, call me."

"You're not going to tell me, huh?"

"No."

Rusty still had the money. He considered Spooky through

narrowed eyes. "I could hurt you. I could tie you up and put your balls in that blender."

"What for? Think you can cut yourself a better deal with the big boys?"

"Maybe. If I knew who they were."

"Wouldn't do you any good, even if you did know. They coloured folk, Rusty. Wouldn't deal with you. You try to approach them direct, they'd put a knife in your guts."

"You smokes always carry a knife, huh?" He smiled and tossed the money to Spooky, who fumbled it into his pocket. "We'll talk about it again, sometime. Well, I appreciate your help, Spooky."

"Sure."

Rusty laid a hand on Spooky's frail shoulder as they walked to the door, digging his thumb into the thin muscle. "If I find you've given Eden so much as a headache pill, I really will put your balls in the blender. If you have any balls left, that is." He dug his thumb in, hard and Spooky screeched, trying to squirm away. Rusty held him like a gaffed fish. "Don't forget. You give her nothing. Nothing. You understand?"

Spooky could only screech again, but that was a pretty good answer, so Rusty let him go.

Rusty drove his Alfa Romeo towards Beverly Hills, weaving smoothly in and out of the afternoon traffic. He was nodding in time to the cool beat of Ahmed Jamahl.

He drove through the ranch gates, waved hi to Miguel Fuentes, and drove on up to the house. He was anticipating a storm.

All addicts were at their worst when they'd been waiting a day or so. Eden had been waiting since five yesterday evening, which was when he'd gone out to score for her. And hadn't come back. It was now almost four. She would be screaming for it.

But that was also exciting. That was when she was at her most naked. He was already deciding what he would make her do before he gave it to her.

Since buying the packet, he had cut the twenty-five grams into fifty little bags. He had four of them in his pocket. He wondered, as he got out of the car, whether it wasn't time to put the price up. The stakes could get higher. A lot higher.

The sky was blue. It was a beautiful day. Even the smog

seemed to have lifted a little. Eden's horse peered out of the stable at him, and he clicked at it. He felt good.

He walked up to the porch. He'd hardly reached the door before it flew open.

"Where have you been?" she hissed furiously, a bottle of wine half-empty in her left hand. Some greeting. She was glazed with booze, but still venomous, her slight body quivering with bitter energy. "How could you do this to me, Rusty?"

"Hey, I'm sorry. I had problems."

"All night?" She slammed the door hard behind him. "All morning? You've had problems all night and all morning?"

"Well, the car broke down."

"You *knew* I was waiting."

"Some transmission thing," he was saying. "I was stuck in this all-night garage for hours. Gonna cost me a mint. Then as soon as I got to the agency this morning, a whole lot of other shit turned up. Like one of the girls smashed a whole dinner service. Our insurance don't cover that much. The client is going to sue. A whole dinner service, can you imagine? Some clumsy wetback with a hangover."

"Why didn't you *call*? How could you just *leave* me like that?"

"Aren't you listening? I've been in the agency until a half-hour ago."

She was like some small, feral animal, white teeth bared. "Liar! You wanted me to freak out. I've been calling there all morning. You didn't show!"

"And just how much wine have you gotten through since I left?" Rusty demanded. "You smell like a brewery."

"I had to go out *myself*. I went to that place on Manchester, but there was no one there. I saw Spooky, but he said he didn't have any. I've had to buy *booze*."

"Now. I've told you not to try and score for yourself, haven't I? Haven't I told you it's dangerous? You'll get yourself mugged, or get sold some real bad shit that'll kill you."

"For Christ's sake." She glared at him from under her ragged bangs. "Just give it to me, will you?"

"Pretty please?"

"*Please.*"

"Okay, I'll give it to you," he grinned, and took out one of the bags. "See?"

"Give it to me!"

He waved it out of her reach. "When you talk to me nicely."

"You bastard!"

"That wasn't what I had in mind." He looked at her speculatively. "Maybe we should get it off before you shoot. What do you say?"

She whispered, "God," clenching her teeth and closing her eyes.

"Unless you have a better idea." He unzipped his fly. The way he was standing, the expression in his eyes, said it all.

She took a breath, then kneeled on the bare wooden floor in front of him.

"That's a pretty good idea," he murmured. He felt her soft tongue pleasing him. He had taught her well.

After a while, he began moaning with pleasure. He spread his legs and held her head in his hands, swaying his hips, easing himself luxuriously in and out of her mouth.

"Bite me," he commanded roughly. "Harder. Aah. Harder, Eden."

She could hear him groaning and grinding his teeth, and she braced herself for what was coming. He rammed himself into her, hard against her gullet. She started to choke. Then with a harsh grunt, he came.

He held her there, his fingers knotted in her hair, not letting her escape as her gorge flooded.

After a while, he sighed luxuriously and let her go. Her mouth was full, but she knew better than to spit or gag. So she snatched the bag out of his hand in silence and ran upstairs to the bathroom, trying not to vomit.

Rusty watched her go, feeling weak and wonderful. That, at least, was one thing she could do well. She looked terrible today. Skinny little bitch. He'd once thought her the prettiest thing he'd ever set eyes on.

Upstairs, Eden slid the needle into a vein, flushed, re-injected. Then she fumbled the tourniquet off. She was shaking violently. She leaned back against the tiles, closing her eyes. Her teeth were clenched. She waited for the flash that would loosen those terrible claws.

She was silhouetted against the bathroom window. The photographer in the garden shot another six frames through the huge 2000mm lens. He made a careful note in his log book.

Beverly Hills

Eden opened the door. Her eyes widened as though she'd been expecting someone else. Then they narrowed.

"What do you want, Father?"

"Hello, Eden," Dominic van Buren said without much warmth. "Aren't you going to let me in?"

Eden's response was to brace her free arm against the jamb, conspicuously blocking the doorway. "What are you here for?" she demanded.

"Does a father need a reason to come and see his daughter?" van Buren asked.

"It's been months since you even called me," Eden retorted. Her eyes were bitter as she surveyed her father up and down. "There's gotta be some reason for you to tear yourself away from all those wunnerful, wunnerful parties in sunny Santa Barbara. What is it?"

"Don't be more gauche than you have to, Eden."

"Tell me the reason, Father. Or I'll shut the door right now."

"Okay," van Buren said with elaborate patience. "The reason is that I'm your father, and I'm concerned about you."

"Concerned?" Eden laughed with such a harsh note that van Buren winced.

"You could call *me*, you know," he said, trying not to sound defensive. "The lines go both ways. What happened to your mouth?" Eden had a lovely mouth, leaf-shaped and sensitive. Right now, the lower lip was puffed up and there was a scab of dried blood where the soft skin had been broken. "Who did this to you?"

"Father, do me a favour. Just go home."

Anger snapped in his eyes. "You're not too old to spank, Eden."

"Why didn't you call before you came?" Eden demanded. "It was stupid to just *arrive*."

Van Buren stared at his daughter. Such a sight in her tawdry clothes and lank hair, cut into God knew what style by God knew who. She could be so ravishingly pretty, and she had a fabulous figure, but most of the time, these days, she just looked like shit. "I didn't realize I had to make an appointment to see my own daughter," he said with ponderous sarcasm. "Who've you got in there?"

"Nobody."

"Then I'm coming in." Van Buren pushed past Eden into the house.

Eden rounded on him with blazing eyes. "How *dare* you just barge in here? This is *my* house. Mom gave it to *me*. You have your own place! You have no right to come in here!"

"I want to know how you got that cut lip," van Buren said, ignoring her.

"Oh, shit. I did it my*self*, Father. Now please leave!"

"How, did it yourself?" van Buren asked. "Are you telling me you hit your own self in the mouth?"

"*Jesus*." The girl turned away from her father and plumped herself furiously down in the sofa. "I dropped something on the bathroom floor. When I bent down to pick it up, I hit my face on the basin. That's all. Okay?"

"A likely story." Van Buren stared at his daughter intently. She had all the elegant graciousness of a pig. He hadn't seen her for months, but there seemed little change in her. She was very thin and pale, that was true, and her clothes were unusually scruffy. And the house was in a mess. But then, Eden had never been much of a conformist.

"What're you looking at?" Eden demanded irritably.

"I'm not sure. God knows you're no beauty." He sat down opposite Eden, hitching up his trousers at the knee so they wouldn't lose their crease. "I've been hearing all kinds of things about you," he said meaningfully.

There was no flicker of guilt on the thin face opposite him. "Oh, yeah?"

"You look like hell."

"Thanks."

"What's that all over your blouse? Blood?"

"Coffee, Father. For Christ's sake, don't make a drama over

everything." She met van Buren's eyes contemptuously. "Okay, you're in. Now what do you want?"

"I want to talk to you."

"About what?"

He leaned forward and quickly jerked up the sleeve of Eden's blouse. Eden was too surprised to pull away. Van Buren examined the skin carefully, then checked the other arm.

"What the hell are you looking for?"

"Needle marks," he said succinctly.

"Let me guess," Eden said with a hard smile. "You saw some heavyweight sociologist on Channel 28 last night, saying every kid in LA is either a prostitute or mainlining dope these days." She drew the zip of her jeans down with a rasp. "Do you want to check my panties as well?"

"There's no need to be gross. I don't know *what* you're doing to yourself these days. Just tell me, are you on drugs?"

"No more than you are," Eden replied disdainfully, zipping herself up again.

Van Buren bristled. "What do you mean by that?"

"Oh, Father. Do you think nobody knows how much cocaine you snort?" Eden propped her feet up on the glass-topped table and met her father's frosty glare. Despite her sordid appearance, she had a presence that was daunting. Ever since she was thirteen, van Buren had been wary of his daughter's cutting tongue and contemptuous eyes. "You probably take more drugs than I do. Librium, Valium, coke, not to mention all the bourbon, coffee and cigarettes you get through." She laughed at van Buren's expression. "Listen, Daddy. If you're asking me whether I ever take drugs, that's a silly question. But if someone's given you the idea that I've started mainlining—no *way*, José. I'm not crazy."

"You swear it?"

"Father." She quirked her bruised mouth wearily. "Haven't I just told you? I wouldn't go near that shit."

"I hear different."

Eden shrugged lean shoulders. Her face was sulky, baleful, drawn. But not guilty. "I don't care what you've heard. It isn't true. I've never used hard drugs. Who's been telling you all this crazy rubbish about me?"

"People." Eden was being so aggressive about this. That puzzled him. He'd expected furtiveness. Guilt. He was wondering exactly what the signs of addiction *were*. Pinpoint pupils? Those truculent green eyes looked fairly normal. Bad skin? She was pale, but not covered in loathsome sores or anything. Well, at least the girl wasn't drooling in a corner with needles sticking out of her arms.

Maybe Mercedes had got it wrong? Maybe the private investigators had been mistaken?

"What are you supposed to be doing with your life these days?" he asked, glancing around the house. "Not keeping this place clean, that's for sure. It's a pigsty."

"It suits me fine."

"When does your help come?"

"I don't have servants anymore."

"You don't? That must make a change for you," he said dryly.

"Maybe. I've just decided I'm not a complete bourgeois."

Van Buren pulled his lower lip. "Okay. Make me a cup of coffee and I'll go."

"Why not just go?"

"Make the coffee, will you?"

With an exasperated sigh, Eden got up and stalked to the open-plan kitchen. She switched on the espresso machine and hunted for the coffee jar.

Who had been talking to him? Miguel? It was possible, though she didn't think Miguel knew. Maybe someone else, one of her so-called friends from UCLA.

She surveyed the grimy kitchen. There weren't even two clean coffee cups to use. Not surprising. Most of her cutlery and crockery was wallowing in two sinks full of grey water. Irritably, she groped for what she wanted and rinsed the utensils off.

She was feeling far from steady. She was dizzy and dreamy, the way she always was with a brain full of scag. It gave her the strength of purpose to act convincingly in sudden situations like this, but it also seemed to fade away so soon. They weren't highs any more, they were mediocres. And when the mediocres wore off. . .

These days she shot up just to feel normal. Just to feel like her own damned self, instead of a screaming animal. Actually being high only seemed to last a matter of a minute. And the animal need came sooner, and more urgently, after every shot. Already, she was thinking about the next one and praying that Rusty wasn't going to play any more games with her. She'd grown to depend on him. Utterly. There was only enough in the packet for another shot. What if he stayed away again? Panic fluttered in her at the thought.

Van Buren walked into the kitchen and Eden turned to him.

"Father, who's been telling you—"

Her father's palm cracked across her face hard. "What's this?" van Buren snapped.

Stunned, Eden stared at the packet of syringes and needles in van Buren's hand. *Christ.* He'd been into her bedroom. He'd even found the little envelope of dope. Fury surged in her. She snatched the syringes away from her father, her eyes blazing.

"Get out of here," she screamed. "You snoop! You interfering old bastard. Get *out* of here!"

"You've got a filthy mouth." Van Buren slapped her again, so hard this time that the half-closed cut on her lip opened, welling blood. Eden saw stars. The syringes fell to the ground and she groped after them, starting to sob.

Van Buren, his pale eyes cold, grabbed his daughter by the hair and dragged her, whimpering with pain, into the sitting area. There he thrust her into the sofa, where Eden curled up in foetal misery, her lip running scarlet with blood.

When van Buren spoke, his voice was deadly quiet.

"You disgusting little worm. You nobody. You *nothing*. So you don't go near hard drugs?"

"Get *out!*"

"I'm not going anywhere till I've got the truth out of you," van Buren said. "Sit up."

Eden just curled up tighter, paralyzed with impotent fury. "Leave me alone. I hate you!"

"How do you take it?" van Buren demanded grimly. "How, Eden? It isn't your arms. Where do you inject the stuff?"

"Get out!"

He grasped Eden's blouse by the collar and pulled hard. The flimsy material ripped down the back, exposing Eden's thin ribs. Eden screamed, twisting away. *Rusty.* Why didn't he come back and save her from this nightmare?

"Take your jeans off."

"*No!*"

"Take—them—off," van Buren gritted.

He was filled with a sick anger, his stomach hard and tight with it. He dragged the ruined blouse off Eden. The girl's torso was painfully thin, her breasts diminutive, with rigid nipples. "Take them off or I'll tear them off!" he shouted.

Sobbing convulsively, Eden unfastened her jeans, her fingers fumbling. Van Buren reached out and dragged them down to Eden's knees, panting with the effort. A pair of peach-coloured briefs came into view and then Eden's lean legs.

It all went out of van Buren, the rage, the passion, everything.

Both of Eden's thighs were tracked with needle perforations. They followed the course of the veins, many of the marks raised and pigmented from infections. Dozens of them. Hundreds of them. Like an infestation of evil brown insects in the white flesh.

He staggered back, the red fading out of his cheeks.

His voice was appalled. "Eden. Oh, my God. What have you done?"

Santa Monica, California

Eden lay curled up on the bed, staring at the wall. Her hair was clean and neatly tied back, evidently the work of some kindly nurse. She was wearing a white blouse and plum-red velvet cord pants, and she could have passed for twelve, though she was soon going to be twenty. Her hands lay, half-open, on the pillow.

Sitting on a chair beside her bed, Dominic van Buren felt a pang of emptiness pass inside him. It was so hard to accept that this was Eden, ferociously rebellious Eden. Still so hard to accept that she could ever end up like this, a helpless addict, a patient in a place one step from a lunatic asylum.

She hated the clinic. She wouldn't go near the other patients, many of whom admittedly looked in worse shape than she did. She kept to her room, lying here like a dead thing.

Accusing.

She accepted what they did to her with a passivity that was in itself an accusation.

A spiritual change had come over her. It had started that day at the ranch, even before her admission to the clinic. As if her will had somehow collapsed. Persuading her to accept treatment had been surprisingly easy. There had been little struggle. Surprisingly little. Perhaps, deep down, she had been seeking help, without knowing it. Most addicts, the doctors here had told him, lived with real and terrible fears.

There was a darkness about her these days that seemed to suck your energy in. Though she spoke in monosyllables, would hardly meet your eyes, she exhausted you. You left the clinic feeling as though she'd drained your strength.

The methadone had flattened her, naturally. It took away the anguish of withdrawal, but it seemed a joyless medication. As though it cut out the high notes and the low notes and left only a grey monotone. That was what affected him so intensely, that inaudible grey monotone.

Van Buren's mother had been a psychiatric patient for many years of his childhood. He could recall seeing her after the electroshock treatments they gave her for her bouts of hysteria, sitting vacant and dead-eyed on the lawn in front of the hospital. Just like Eden, now. That was when he had first heard the grey drone of a dead brain. They had burned his mother's psyche out with ECT.

She had been in need of love and attention, but his father had put her in a mental hospital instead, where they had given her electroshock.

Even now, his worst nightmares were of being imprisoned in a yellow deck chair on a green lawn, white-coated attendants drifting to and fro in the background. With that dead sound in his own head.

Or walking down endless corridors, past countless rooms, in each room a bed, on each bed a woman lying staring at the ceiling with lifeless eyes and lolling hands.

He looked out the window. Bright wintry sunlight outside, and a sea-breeze stirring the palm fronds.

"Don't you want to go and sit in the garden awhile?" he suggested. "It isn't too cold. You could put on a cardigan."

She did not answer.

He grew irritable. "Come on, Eden. I'm doing my best, for Christ's sake. I want to help you. Don't sulk with me."

"Is that why you put me in here?" she said to the wall. "Because you want to help me?"

"We didn't *put* you in here. You're here on a voluntary basis."

"When can I leave, then?"

"You can't leave until they've got this terrible thing out of your system."

"So it's not voluntary, after all?"

"We're not going to sit back and watch you kill yourself," he snapped. "Don't be Jesuitical. It doesn't suit you. Eden, please look at me. It's a damned long drive from Santa Barbara just to look at your backside."

After a while, she sat up and faced him. Her face was a pale oval. Her green eyes were dead. Whether she was deliberately putting on the dead eyes and the dead voice, or whether the methadone was doing that to her, it depressed him unutterably.

"Are you okay?" he asked uneasily. She reminded him so much of his mother. "Are you doing this on purpose? Is this your way of punishing me?"

"I don't want to punish you," she said calmly.

"You punish everyone who tries to help you."

"You're not helping me," she said quietly. "You think you've done me good, walking in and smashing everything? You haven't. You're destroying me."

"You were destroying yourself."

"My life is my own. It's mine and I want to live it the way I want."

"Oh, God. If you knew how banal and childish that sounds."

"Yeah."

"Eden? *Eden?*"

Eden did not answer. She was wrapped in silence again.

He rose heavily to his feet. "Okay. Interview over. Your mother's waiting to see you. I'll say goodbye."

"I don't want to see her."

"She's come all the way from Spain, Eden."

"That's her problem."

Van Buren walked out of her room. Mercedes was waiting outside. She wore a plain but beautifully-cut grey suit. Her expression was sombre.

"How is she?" Mercedes asked in a low voice.

"Go and see for yourself," he said, walking past her. "I'll wait for you outside."

Mercedes hesitated at Eden's door, then went in.

• • •

"You spied on me," Eden said in a low voice. "You paid strangers to spy on me. It was a sick thing to do."

"Yes," Mercedes said calmly. "It wasn't very nice. But you don't communicate with us any more, my child. Why didn't you tell us you'd dropped out of college?" Eden did not answer. "Why didn't you tell us you were becoming addicted? Why didn't you tell us *any* of it? Didn't you think we could help you?"

"Where is Rusty?" Eden stared at her mother. "Are you keeping him away from me?"

"Is he all you care about? Even now?"

"Yes," she said quietly. "He's the only one who cares about me."

"He's the only one who cares about you," Mercedes repeated, with irony. "That showed, didn't it?"

"Have you told them not to let him see me?"

"No."

"You have, haven't you? You've told them not to let him see me. Not to put his calls through."

"Knowing what we do about him," Mercedes said heavily, "would you blame us?" Mercedes reached for Eden's hand. "Eden, listen to me. Fagan had arranged it so that other dealers wouldn't sell to you. So that he had total power over you. He made you pay five, ten times what the drug cost him on the streets. He was exploiting you. Ruthlessly. In every sense."

Her hand lay cold and dead in Mercedes's. "I don't want you to go near Rusty," Eden said. "Stay away from him."

"You're afraid that he'll stop bringing you the stuff. Can't you see?" Mercedes said, squeezing the cold fingers. "You're getting free of him. Free of heroin. When you get out of here, you'll never need to think about drugs or Rusty Fagan again. They'll both be out of your life."

There was a flicker in Eden's eyes. "What do you mean, out of my life?"

"Just that. Gone."

"*No!*" Eden suddenly jerked her hand away, eyes blazing at her mother. "If you hurt Rusty, I'll never speak to you again. I'll kill myself!"

"Don't be hysterical."

"You're planning something. I *know*. I know you are. I know your evil mind. Whatever he is, I love him. If you do anything to him, you'll destroy me."

Mercedes was almost afraid of the passion in the eyes she'd thought extinguished. "Nobody's planning anything, Eden. But this boy was *abusing* you."

"Yes," Eden said. "He abused me." There was bitterness in her face. "He liked to humiliate me. He enjoyed making me grovel. He liked to make me go cold turkey. Before he'd give me my shot, he'd make me do things like scrub the floor. Sometimes I had to get on my knees and suck his cock. Like a whore. Other times he'd screw me, at his leisure, knowing I was screaming inside. All sorts of things. Whatever came into his head. He was very inventive."

"For God's sake," Mercedes said, disgusted.

"As a matter of fact, I've learned how to enjoy being abused," Eden went on, in the same taut voice. "Some kinds of abuse can be fun, in a sick way. The good thing about being an adult is that you can choose the kinds of abuse you want to submit to."

"What are you talking about?"

"Rusty gave meaning to my life."

"You call that meaning? That's disgusting."

"Not as disgusting as your life," Eden said, with such coldness that Mercedes's temper snapped.

"Okay," she exploded, "you sucked his cock. You grovelled on the floor. Wallow in your degradation, if that's what role you've chosen. But he was killing you. He was killing you! Can't you understand that?"

"Something has got to kill me. It might as well be something I love."

"*What?*"

Mercedes stared at Eden. The fire was dying slowly out of her eyes. Mercedes could almost see the emotion sag out of her veins.

"I'm so tired," she said, matter-of-factly.

"Why do you want to die, Eden?"

"Everybody wants to die. Don't they?" She lay back on the bed and turned her eyes back up at the ceiling. "It's the common complaint."

She's insane, Mercedes thought, shaken. Her mind has gone.

"You won't miss me," Eden went on, in the same calm voice.

"You have Maya, now. She's your new daughter. You love her better than you ever loved me."

Mercedes rose to leave.

"If you touch Rusty, I'll never forgive you," Eden said. "Not ever again."

Dominic was waiting for her in the parking lot, next to his powder-blue Porsche convertible.

"Well?" he challenged.

"She's a skeleton with dead green eyes," Mercedes said. "She must weigh less than she did when she was fourteen."

"Yes," he said heavily. "She's like a lost soul. I'm starting to hate going in there. Maybe some kind of alternative therapy would be better."

"Acupuncture, homeopathy, herbalism? That hardly meets the case, Dominic."

"Not necessarily."

"I don't trust gurus in designer robes. She's better where she is."

"Today they said they wanted to start some kind of encounter sessions. You, me and Eden together with the head shrink there. I ruled that out. It wouldn't help. The girl hates us both."

"She's consumed with Fagan."

"Yes. She's still obsessed with that bastard. She more or less told me that as soon as she gets out of Hebron she's going straight back to him."

"She said that? That she would go back to him?"

"She sees him as some kind of saviour. Or some kind of possessing demon, I can't tell which. He's still trying to contact her. He comes to the clinic, but they turn him away. And he calls her every day. They say they don't put his calls through. Who knows? Maybe they're lying. But one thing's for sure. As soon as she comes out of this place, he'll be back on the scene."

"Perhaps not."

He stared at his ex-wife. She looked good. Her skin was tanned and youthful and her face had not changed much in twenty years. "What are you going to do?" he asked.

"I have to go back to Spain," she said. "I'm in the middle of some crucial business I just can't leave. I'll try and get out again in a few weeks."

"What about Fagan? Should I get an injunction?"

Mercedes shook her head. "That won't be necessary. He'll lose interest in her."

"You really think so?"

"Soon." Mercedes's voice was flat. "He'll lose interest in her very soon."

january 1973

Tucson

Joel Lennox has made himself a meal but the simple food lies untouched before him on the table. He has been watching television. For the past hour, he has been watching with the sound turned off.

It is over.

Nineteen years have passed since Dien Bien Phu. Eleven years since the first few thousand troops went in. Five years since Hanoi's request for talks. Four years since Nixon's "six months." A matter of weeks since the heaviest bombing action of the war. And at last, America's involvement in the Vietnam War is over.

Today, 27 January 1973, the treaty is being signed in Paris. The cameras film the Stars and Stripes hanging limp and sodden in the French rain. After the sacrifice of 58,000 dead and 300,000 wounded, after the expenditure of $150 billion, after the loss of her international prestige and her internal unity, the United States has called it quits.

A festering ulcer has been ripped out of the national flesh. There is joy at home, according to the television, but it seems joy of a rather numbed kind.

Everyone knows that Hanoi will go back to war with Saigon within weeks, and will win within months. Vietnamese politics will turn out just as they would have done a decade ago, five decades ago, except that they will do so in a land now churned into mud by high explosives, charred by napalm and shrivelled by defoliants, poisoned by the hatred of a million dead or crippled.

Having desolated Indochina, the Americans are giving it back to the Viet Cong.

And now viewers can begin to forget the flickering images, begin to forget the blazing huts and the mutilated children, the lines of corpses, the tortures and the massacres. Forget napalm and Agent Orange. Forget My Lai. Forget Kent State. Forget protest marches led by men in wheelchairs.

On the screen are silent images of these things, a valedictory montage. Icons of a war irretrievably lost.

Men in combat fatigues spew from helicopters; a machine-gun disgorges its fury into an impassive sea of reeds.

The faces of politicians and generals mouth inaudible sentences; inert black bags are lugged into ambulances.

A child flees screaming and naked from an exploding village.

Seen from the high eye of a B–52, bombs drift down into the jungle; the shockwaves ripple through the dense foliage, dissipate and die. Again and again.

For the last time, the camera's eye turns to these scenes. Soon it will forget everything.

Think about the next story.

Joel Lennox rises and switches off the television. Richard Nixon's portentous face shrinks to a dot of light. He is watching an image from his own war, one of the thousand scenes he can recall without thinking.

And all for nothing. He sees an unimaginably vast army in his mind, an army of shadows, trudging through history, trudging to nowhere. From darkness into darkness.

But he has a goal. The cell is finished downstairs. The bed is waiting.

It is all ready.

San Gabriel Reservoir, California

"You know," Miguel said, "I always thought you were kind of a nice kid. Always so polite. No' like these kids you seem to meet nowadays, fulla shit. I guess that was all just a act, uh?"

He started whistling.

Rusty was still moaning. His wrists were trapped between his ankles. He would never have believed the old man could move so fast, or have so much strength.

When he'd pulled the gun on Rusty, a big, old-fashioned Colt revolver, Rusty had instinctively made a grab for the weapon. He'd figured, in the split-second of making the grab, that the odds were easily on his side. Miguel was over sixty and Rusty was a fit young man.

Miguel had stepped back and kicked him squarely in the balls, caving him in like a house of cards. Then, while the agony had still been racking him, Miguel had thrown him into his own Alfa as easily as though he'd been a sack of wheat.

Miguel had the gun in his pocket as he drove. He was wearing pigskin gloves. Rusty's hands were cuffed to the steel frame of the seat, next to his feet. He had to crouch like an ape. His head didn't even show through the window. He barely knew where they were. He could only guess that Miguel was taking him east, out of the city. He'd known they were on a freeway for a long while. Then he'd prayed that a trucker might look down as they passed, might notice him crouching in this contorted position and perhaps call the cops. But it was late at night and they had passed no trucks.

Miguel stopped whistling. "Yep. Just a act," he repeated. He fiddled with the radio, trying to find a station he liked. Eventually he got a Spanish-language station that was playing lively tangos and pasodobles. He smiled contentedly. "Know where we heading, Rusty?"

Rusty shook his bowed head.

"We heading to San Gabriel reservoir. Tha's a pretty place. When we get there, I gonna blow your brains out."

Rusty felt vomit rise in his throat. When he painfully tried to lift his head, Miguel hacked him in the back of the neck with a hand like an axe. The pain dazed him.

He heard Miguel go on, calmly, "Keep your head down, muchacho. Yeh, I gonna blow your brains out. But we got to make it look like suicide. You unnerstan'? I need your cooperation. I need you to write me a good suicide note. We gonna be there in maybe ten minutes. Okay? So meantime, you be putting together a good suicide note in your head."

He glanced down at the hunched boy beside him, Eden's boyfriend Rusty, the handsome young man with the intelligent, knowing eyes.

He'd told Miguel they'd called him Rusty because he'd had coppery hair as a kid. Yet even now that his hair was darker, the name still suited him, with its homely, guileless feel, its boyish ring.

"I got a pen," he said, "and some paper outa your office. If you wan' some ideas, I can sugges' a few." He heard a sound from the bowed figure. "You okay down there?" he asked.

A little later, he pulled the car off the road, onto a dirt track. It was a bumpy ride, and Rusty felt bile surging up in his throat. A faint smell of dust entered the Alfa through the ducts.

"We here," Miguel announced cheerfully, after ten minutes. "End of the road. Hey, wha's so special about these Italian imports, uh? Mos' uncomfortable fuckin' car I ever drive. I gonna be glad to get back in the Caddy, lemme tell you."

The engine cut out.

"Listen," Rusty said, fighting back bile. "I'm not the one you want to kill." His voice shook. His eyes were squeezed shut. "All I was doing, I was trying to protect Eden. I swear it."

Miguel smiled without humour. "Bullshit. You really been screwing Eden good. How much you make out of her? Five thousand bucks? Ten thousand? You fucked her life up. Now somebody gonna fuck your life up."

"That's what I'm trying to tell you," Rusty choked. "I wasn't the one turned her on to scag. I swear I wasn't! But I can tell you who was. I can give you the evil little bitch's name."

"Okay," Miguel said easily, "gimme the name."

"In exchange for my life," Rusty said.

"You don' got no life to exchange," Miguel replied. He reached out and took Rusty's right ear in his thick fingers. He twisted it hard enough to make Rusty scream. Rusty would never have believed someone could hurt you so badly just by twisting your ear. "You wan' me to tear it right off your head?" Miguel asked.

"No!" Rusty gasped.

"Gimme the name."

"Donna Andretti," he blurted out. "She's a junkie, a tall hippie chick—"

"Yeah, I know Donna." Miguel twisted Rusty's ear harder. "Weird chick, uh? But you paid her to do it, di'n' you? Di'n' you?"

Rusty shrieked.

"Was that a 'yes'? Yeah. You're the one. Ay, you see that poster? NIXON'S THE ONE?" He chuckled heartily, releasing Rusty's ear.

Rusty heard Miguel lift his bag off the backseat. "Be with you in a moment," Miguel said. He got out of the car and closed the door.

For a long while Rusty crouched alone in the car, his mind frozen, immobile on the brink of the void.

He was trembling violently. He felt desolate and cold. Unreal. He was going to die, and he wasn't ready. He prayed there would be no pain. No horrors.

He heard the silence. Heard night insects chirping.

Then the door opened and Miguel got back in the car. Rusty felt the cold muzzle of the revolver grind into his ear. With his other hand, Miguel reached down and unlocked the handcuffs. He freed him from the seat, but left his wrists chained together.

"Open your eyes," Miguel coaxed. "Straighten up, muchacho."

Rusty opened his eyes. Miguel had put the roof light on. He was sitting alongside Rusty, the revolver just touching Rusty's belly.

He was completely naked except for a pair of bright yellow rubber gloves. It was a surreal image. Deep shadows fell in the wrinkles of his face and his belly. He was a muscular old man with a deep chest. His pubic hair was white, his balls heavy under a stubby penis.

Outside the car was pitch darkness. Miguel had chosen a moonless night. Nearby, Rusty could just discern a shimmer of water.

"Tha's the San Gabriel reservoir," Miguel informed him. "Appropriate, uh? You gonna be meeting San Gabriel in a minute or two."

He put the sheet of notepaper on the dashboard and put a pen into Rusty's cold hand.

"Okay. Write."

"I can't," Rusty whispered.

"Sure you can," Miguel assured him. "I help you. Start like this, okay? *I am taking the only way out.*"

Rusty started crying. Miguel dug the muzzle of the revolver into his groin, with enough force to make him gasp.

"*I am taking the only way out,*" he repeated firmly.

Rusty clutched the pen and wrote the words wildly.

Miguel nodded approval. "Don' worry about the writing going everywhere. You suppose' to be upset, uh? Okay. *My life has no meaning.*"

Rusty wrote that too.

"Okay. *I am glad to be leaving this world.*"

Rusty started crying again as he wrote the words. "Jesus," he sobbed, "that's so fucking corny. Nobody is going to fall for that!"

"It's in your writing," Miguel said calmly. "Tha's wha' counts." He studied the note critically. "Not too bad. About says it all, don' it? No need to sign it." He smiled. "I gonna make this quick, Rusty. You very lucky. Say thank you, Miguel."

"Thank you, Miguel," Rusty whispered.

Miguel reached up and flipped the light off. In the darkness, he popped rubber plugs into his ears. He said, "Open your mouth, Rusty."

The muzzle of the revolver pushed its way in through Rusty's spitless lips and into his mouth. Miguel's expression had been mild and friendly up till now. Rusty would not have seen it change, even if the light had been on, because his eyes were tightly closed.

Miguel forced the barrel into Rusty's gullet and jerked it brutally into the right position. Rusty gagged helplessly, writhing. He could smell the bitter rubber of Miguel's gloves.

Miguel pulled the hammer back with a loud click. He waited until he heard Rusty's bowels void loudly into his pants.

His voice had thickened. "This comes to you courtesy of Eden's Mama, Rusty."

Then he pulled the trigger. The muzzle flash glowed through Rusty's billowing cheeks.

When Rusty's limbs had stopped jerking, Miguel unlocked the handcuffs. He put the revolver into Rusty's flaccid hands and pressed his prints all over it, not forgetting the thumb on the hammer and the index finger on the trigger. Rusty's ruined head lolled acquiescently.

He dropped the Colt onto the floor and got out of the car. He was lavishly spattered with blood and tissue, but he was humming quietly. He examined the hole in the roof of the Alfa and hoped the police would be able to locate the bullet, somewhere out there in the bushes.

He walked down to the water and waded in. It was a cold night and the water was far from warm, but he enjoyed the sensation keenly. He swam around slowly, plunging his head in and rinsing his hair. When he felt quite clean, he got out, dried himself on the towel he had brought, and got back into his clothes.

He had left the other car a mile and a half away, but he was in the mood for a walk. He put the ear plugs, the rubber gloves and the cuffs into the bag with the towel and set off briskly.

He was proud of the way he had done the job, and he was looking forward to telling Mercedes that Rusty had just lost all interest in Eden.

Los Angeles

The staff at the Hebron clinic telephoned an urgent message to her father, but by the time he arrived at the clinic, Eden had hitch-hiked down the freeway to Venice.

At around midnight, she knocked on Spooky's door. Spooky had been gouching out in front of the television set, watching the peace treaty being signed. The Vietnam War was over.

When he saw Eden on his doorstep, his eyes widened.

"I thought you were in Hebron."

"Not anymore," she said in a tight voice.

He let her in without comment. She looked terrible. Like a corpse, white and ghastly.

"Are you okay?" he asked in alarm. She just stared at him. "You heard about Rusty," he said heavily. "Is that why you here?"

"I need to score, Spooky."

"I can't give it to you."

"Yes, you can."

"You been on detox, Eden. What they put you on at Hebron? Methadone?"

Eden was fumbling out five-dollar bills. "I need ten grams."

"Ten *grams*? What are you going to do, OD yourself because of Rusty, that piece of shit? Best thing he ever done in his life was blow his brains out."

She stared at him with empty eyes. "You think Rusty killed himself, Spooky? I didn't think you were so naive."

He frowned. "What the hell you talking about?"

"I have people who look after me, Spooky. People who take care of me. Didn't you know that?"

She looked terrible to him. "Listen, I'll give you a ride back to the clinic right now."

She held the money out to him. "Come on, Spooky."

"No."

"Ten grams, Spooky."

He dug his hands into his pockets and tried to look determined. "Listen, Eden—"

"No, *you* listen." She was trembling. Her voice throbbed in her chest, as though it hurt her to talk. "Don't try to play God with me, Spooky. I've had too much of that lately. I've had enough. If you don't give it to me, someone else will."

She stood there, her eyes meeting his, as green and hard as stones. He looked away, gnawing his lip. Then he took the money.

9.

~Sector 14

january 1937

Granados, Aragón, Spain

A truck picked them up at the station and they clambered aboard it, heaving their kit. They were in high spirits, despite the bitter cold. They had sung revolutionary songs all the way from Barcelona, passing a goatskin of wine around.

There was still some wine left, and they finished it on the way to Granados, swaying in the back of the truck. They were arriving at the front.

Granados was a small hilltop town, surrounded by sparse groves of almonds and olives. It had been the site of bitter hand-to-hand fighting the summer before. The anarchists now occupied it, and had made their headquarters here.

At Granados they stopped singing.

The truck drove down through the main street. It had to weave its way between craters and heaps of rubble. The town wore a shocked, deserted look. It had been raped by violence.

Only the shells remained of many houses. Roofs gaped, windows were blank, woodwork had been charred by fire. The possessions of ordinary lives lay shattered among the fallen masonry— beds, sideboards, washbasins. Mercedes stared in silence at the parade of destruction that passed by. She was shivering, despite the wine. There was a foul smell in the air, partly excrement, partly decay, partly the reek of explosives. Almost no one was to be seen in the streets.

The truck stopped in the square while the driver went to headquarters for instructions. It had once been a fine marketplace with a stone cross in the middle, but the cross had been knocked down, and most of the buildings around the square had been gutted.

They stared around them without much to say. Ochre earth and grey stone, blackened by fire in places, matched a yellow and grey sky above. It was overcast. A keen wind was blowing from the north. The winter of 1936–1937 was growing harsh. Though it was January, they were still in their summer uniforms.

"What a mess," someone said at last.

"It's not so bad." A young street sweeper named Ignacio Pérez, who had excelled with the bayonet in training, offered cigarettes around and lit up. "What the fuck. A bit of cement will patch things up." He blew smoke at the ruined church. "Anyway, this place was a rat's nest of Fascists. They've learned better now."

The rest of them began to talk, quietly at first. Some of the villagers were apparently still living here. Two crones in black crossed the square. One of the girls called out to them, offering to buy food or wine. But they had nothing to sell, and hurried past. By the expressions in their eyes, these old women did not regard the Republican army as their liberators, nor, presumably, the nationalists as their enemies.

Mercedes huddled around her kit bag, hating the ugliness. This desolate village was her first instruction in the reality of war.

"What's the matter, Mercé?" José-María Calvet laid his lean hand on her shoulder. "Are you upset?"

"I feel sorry for these people," she told José-María in a low voice.

"The villagers?"

"Yes. They didn't ask for this."

"It's war," José-María said. "And Ignacio is right. They harboured a column of Fascists."

"Now they're harbouring us. Did they have any choice?"

"Everybody has a choice."

"See there?" Ignacio Pérez was speaking with increasing excitement as his confidence recovered. "You knock a hole in the

wall with a pick and throw hand grenades inside. Boom! Shake
the bastards up a little. Then in through the windows, shooting as
you go. No quarter. That's the way to clear a house!"

Mercedes shivered again. José-María put his arm around her
shoulders. He came from a family of brilliant Barcelona intellectuals. The Fascists had murdered his father two years ago. José-
María himself had been a law student at the time he'd signed up.
He was good-looking, with soft brown eyes like chocolate. But
he was delicate, almost fragile. The others laughed at him for his
fastidious habits and long words, and because he was scrupulously
clean, like a cat.

He was devoted to Mercedes, however. He had appointed
himself her guardian and mentor, though he was only a year or
two older.

"This is ugly," he told her, "but it represents a victory."

The word jarred on her. "Will the whole of Spain look like
this when we've finished?" she asked him dryly. "We'll be standing
victoriously on a stinking mountain of ruins."

"Remember what Buenaventura Durruti said, Mercé. We're
not afraid of ruins. We can live in ruins for a while, if we have to.
We'll build it all back again. We're the workers. Our hands built
every city in Europe." His hands did not look capable of laying
a brick. Or of pulling a trigger. But he was solemn with conviction.
"We're going to build the world anew when this is all over. The
Fascists can destroy it as they leave, but we carry a new world in
our hearts."

She nodded. She had heard the phrases before, though never
in this setting. Still, she allowed their ringing promise to lift her
heart again. "Yes," she nodded. "We'll build it all again."

"I wonder when we'll get our rifles," Ignacio Pérez sighed.

The driver returned. "Sector 14," he told them. He got into
the cab and set off out of the village with a jolt. Mercedes was glad
to leave the desolation behind.

The countryside was barren and rocky. They had reached the
mesa, the arid central plateau of Spain. The fields were abandoned.
They lay half-ploughed and strewn with boulders, as though war
had interrupted the work and it had never been resumed. Mercedes
wondered when the ploughing would ever be finished.

Most of the vegetation was dusty and exhausted. But along

the edges of the fields were dozens of wild pomegranate trees. The fruit was now ripe, hard-skinned scarlet and magenta globes beginning to split open and show their myriad-seeded contents.

The heavy clouds broke. Overhead, the sky was an infinite eggshell blue, the coldest sky she had ever seen.

The front, which had loomed in their imaginations so luridly, was no more than a dry river bed. The enemy were camped on the opposite bank, a long way off. A few puffs of smoke hung in the air from rifle fire, but there were none of the cannonades and barrages they had anticipated.

The driver pulled up by a grove of carobs. "Here you are," he called from his cab window. "Sector 14."

A few militiamen were sitting around a fire. They looked dirty and battle-hardened. The recruits clambered off the truck, self-conscious under the watching eyes. A young *teniente* was waiting for them with a grubby list of their names. He was a thickset man with a boxer's broken nose and heavy brows.

He called a roll, studying each recruit critically in turn. There were seven women in the group and his face grew sourer with each one that answered.

"Right," he concluded. "I am *teniente* Manuel Ribera. I'm in charge of Sector 14. From now on, you take orders from me. Follow me."

"Hey, *teniente*," Ignacio Pérez called as they hurried after the officer, "when do we get our rifles?"

"What do you want rifles for?"

"To fight with, of course."

Manuel Ribera turned. "Ever fired one?"

"Well—no—"

"What fucking use is a rifle to you, then?" the *teniente* asked.

"We learned how to take a Mauser apart at the barracks," José-María said. "And how to put it back together again."

Ribera spat. "Just make sure the enemy don't take *you* apart, four-eyes. These are your quarters."

Their "quarters" were a long heap of leaking sandbags, behind which a trench had been dug. They peered at the structure in disbelief. It was like something badgers had made and befouled.

Mercedes walked slowly around it. Far from the snug fortification she had envisaged, her home from now on was to be this. A filthy ditch containing a foot of mud, with a few sheets of corrugated iron for a roof. It was a vision from the Dark Ages.

The whole area stank terribly of excrement.

"Jesus," Ignacio Pérez remarked glumly. "No chance of getting lost. Just follow the smell of shit and you're home."

Mercedes met José-María's eyes. He seemed to have crumpled. She wondered how he was going to stand up to the winter ahead.

A sudden explosion ripped the air. As one, they flung themselves into the mud, covering their heads. Shrapnel whined and clattered.

The *teniente*, who had not moved, watched their reactions dryly. "Mortar shell," he said, as they cautiously raised their heads.

They clambered rather shamefacedly to their feet, trying to wipe mud away.

"This isn't the Ritz," he said shortly. "There are rats and lice. And there aren't enough blankets to go around. But at least it's sheltered from the enemy's machine-guns. You're going to have to make yourselves as comfortable as you can. Stay out of the firing line for the time being and don't get in anybody's way. That applies especially to the females." He glanced at the women with undisguised scorn. "Okay?"

He walked away.

Mercedes and the other women huddled together against the wind. They were all stunned. Whatever their expectations had been, the reality was a shock. There was not only no comfort here. There was no privacy. They would be living in the utmost squalor. There were no provisions for modesty here. Even the toughest of the men looked discouraged at the prospect of this winter.

After a while, they pulled themselves together and set about making their redoubt more habitable.

"Can't we clear all this shit up?" Mercedes demanded, appalled by the smell. But no one would join her in the Herculean task.

They set aside a women's section, under the least rusty sheet of iron, and tried to make a fire. Unpleasant discoveries continued. They were out of the firing line here, a concession to their inexperience, but there was no water nearby and no shelter from the terrible wind.

There was almost no firewood available either. It had all been gathered long ago. They managed to accumulate a few heaps of twigs, and huddled around their glow for warmth, sharing cigarettes.

They also learned that the food they had, which, apart from what they could pillage, consisted mostly of tinned Argentine beef, was eaten cold. There were no facilities for cooking.

And Manuel Ribera had been right about both the rats and the lice.

As they worked, bullets whined spasmodically to and fro. Occasionally one would hit a rock and ricochet into the air with a whimper. Though everyone ducked when this happened, there seemed to be little danger at this range.

Now and then, too, a mortar shell exploded overhead and shrapnel would whirr into the trees. There were field guns some miles away, firing with a distant thump. Once a shell fluttered overhead towards Granados and exploded with a *crump* outside the town.

Manuel returned after a couple of hours and inspected their arrangements. Mercedes saw the contempt in his eyes. It occurred to her for the first time that he would see them not as conquering heroes, but as a useless encumbrance. A liability. He went away again without comment.

Up till now, the enemy had seemed irrelevant compared to their immediate discomforts. But once they had unpacked their gear, a group of them climbed up to the forward parapet, where the wind was keenest, and strained their eyes in the dull light. They were rewarded with a glimpse of the nationalists, little grey figures moving against the scrubby hillsides opposite.

"What are they doing?" Mercedes asked.

José-María had his field glasses to his eyes. "Looking for firewood," he said.

"They don't look very dangerous," Mercedes commented.

"There's a column of Moroccans among them," one of the veterans said. "Hard buggers. We fought them in the summer, not far from here. Best not to be captured by them, especially not if you're a woman."

The Moroccans had a terrible reputation for rape and throat-cutting. Mercedes strained her eyes to see the enemy better, but the wind made her eyes sting.

It was now blowing from the enemy, revealing that the nationalist lines stank just as badly as their own did. No doubt they, too, had their lice and rats. The sordid realities of war were dawning on Mercedes.

There were other stenches too, of rotting food and the dead horses in the river bed. The worst smell of all was the smell of unwashed humanity. She realized with a wave of depression they would all soon smell exactly the same.

The first weeks passed in increasing wretchedness and boredom. They began to get acclimatized to their misery. Sporadically, there was firing, and once an aircraft dropped a bomb farther up the line, which injured no one. Otherwise, the days were spent in frozen sentry duty, or in the endless hunt for food and firewood. Unarmed and inexperienced as they were, there was nothing constructive they could do.

The appearance of the mail after the first fortnight was a cause for wild excitement. There was a letter from Conchita, full of love and concern. She had been appalled that Mercedes had elected to go to the front, and Mercedes was moved to tears.

Hunger grew keener. They gathered baskets of hibernating snails when they found them. Roasted on a sheet of corrugated iron over a fire, they were a feast. Sometimes people stumbled on forgotten potato patches, where a few winter tubers could be dug up. But soon there were not even snails or shrivelled potatoes to be found.

The veterans did not seem to take the slightest effort to make the trenches either more comfortable or more sanitary. The brutishness of life was infinitely depressing.

Mercedes's beauty drew male eyes. The veterans would saunter over and chat to her, their eyes flicking hungrily to the swell of her bosom. Occasionally, they would suggest a quiet walk among the pomegranates, but she grew adept at turning aside these propositions.

José-María gazed at her with adoration. Like little Juan Capdevila at school, he had become her faithful squire. He was always at her side, eager to protect and serve her. She gave him little encouragement, but he seemed content just to be near her.

·   ·   ·

By February, they were all thinner, dirtier and hungrier and starting to wonder what they were doing here.

Mercedes began to be aware of the rampancy of sex. The high-minded, almost puritanical spirit of anarchism had weakened and vanished here at the front. Boredom and loneliness turned everyone's thoughts to the opposite sex.

Some of the "militiawomen," Mercedes realized, were simply prostitutes. Others, sexually experienced, unashamedly took as many men as they could get.

One afternoon, hunting for firewood, Mercedes was startled by a violent moan. It came from an old shepherd's hut a few yards away. Expecting to find someone wounded, she ran to the door.

What she saw, as she peered into the hut, was a muscular pair of naked male buttocks in violent motion between splayed female thighs. She didn't recognize the man, but the woman was a buxom blonde named Federica Ossorio. Bewildered, she took a moment to realize that they were coupling on the naked earth.

Their movements were savage, as though their aim was to hurt, rather than give pleasure. Federica moaned encouragement, heavy breasts wobbling with the force of the man's rutting.

Mercedes turned and walked away from the hut. Her heart was pounding sickly. The image had burned itself into her mind so intensely that for several days afterwards she could recall it at will, just by shutting her lids. She was unable to meet Federica's eyes for a week, though Federica was one of the women who had showed the warmest friendliness towards her.

Mercedes was deeply troubled by the question of her own sexual identity. Was she now a lesbian? Would she ever be able to love a man? Matilde had died and had taken the answer with her.

Ever since Los Yucas, she had told herself that she hated all men. Gerard's kiss had excited and disgusted her. It had done something to her. It had left a bruise inside, a place still so tender that she shuddered from touching it.

She watched the varied sexual exploits of women like Federica with incomprehension. It was easy to pretend moral disgust; that was a good cover for her own inability to understand. It troubled her that she felt no spark of attraction towards the men around her, not even the handsome ones whom the others desired.

She certainly felt no desire to lie with any man here, not even

José-María. Despite his intelligence and undoubted good looks, he did not excite her.

When she thought of Federica's splayed thighs, she felt a twisting in her stomach, but could not tell whether it was revulsion or excitement. What appetites could lead to such an act? She did not know.

And then the rifles arrived.

They crowded eagerly around Manuel as he passed out the weapons, with their formidably long bayonets. They tried to guess the make, which was unfamiliar to them.

Mercedes studied hers carefully. It was a Lee Enfield, but on inspection it was so old and corroded that she could hardly believe they were serious. The barrel and bayonet were pitted with rust. It dated, she decided, from the late nineteenth century. The others were equally dismayed.

"There's nothing wrong with them," Manuel snapped. "They just need to be cleaned."

"They need to be put in a museum," José-María said gloomily, wiping the rust off his fingers.

Manuel Ribera showed them how to clean the rifles, pulling a rag through the bore and oiling the action. Then he took them for some shooting practice in a nearby field. He pinned a target to an olive tree and instructed them in the workings of the sights. Mercedes sprawled in the dry grass with the others, the stock cuddled to her cheek. For the first time since leaving Barcelona, she felt that she was doing something positive for the war. There was considerable excitement.

Mercedes sighted on the target, as she had been told. It looked very small and far away. She pulled the trigger. There was a loud bang. The recoil was unexpectedly painful and the shot had apparently gone wide.

Manuel had been watching her. "For Christ's sake," he said patiently, "keep your eyes *open* while you pull the trigger." Like José-María, he had developed a protective attitude towards her and had started making a pet of her in his rough way.

She operated the bolt, aimed, and keeping her eyes as wide as she could, pulled the trigger again.

There was a blinding flash of light and something smashed brutally into her face.

She found herself lying on her back, stunned. She could see nothing. Her right arm was numb from the shoulder down.

Numbly, she realized that the ancient rifle had exploded in her face. Her eyes began to burn agonizingly. She writhed on the grass, terrified that she had been disfigured and blinded.

She felt Manuel's strong arms grasp her wrists and through the ringing in her ears, heard him cursing. Then she was lifted onto a stretcher and consciousness left her.

After hours of drifting in a roaring darkness, she awoke croaking for water. Her face had been bandaged and one hand throbbed painfully. Someone brought her a glass of water. She grasped that she was in the field hospital at Granados.

"Am I blind?" she asked in dread.

"You were lucky," a voice told her laconically. "We've had people in here with the same thing who've lost their jaws or hands. One bloke got the bolt imbedded in his skull."

"Clean the fucking thing properly next time," another voice advised. "If you're going to go around blowing up all our fucking rifles, we'll lose the fucking war by summer."

"*Am I blind?* Tell me!" she begged

The bandage was unfastened. Callous fingers pried her swollen lids apart. Through blurred and weeping eyes she dimly saw a pair of white-clad male nurses peering into her face. "Happy now?" one asked.

"Oh, yes," she sobbed in relief. "Am I going to be scarred?"

"You might have a few small scars later on. Here, and maybe here. But nothing serious. You'll be all right. You're a lovely girl. You shouldn't be out here. You should be back home in Barcelona in your boyfriend's bed."

"Yeah, cleaning *his* fucking weapon," the first added. "They shouldn't send women out here. You're worse than fucking useless."

"Your thumb's broken," the kinder *sanitario* advised her. "We strapped it up for you. You'll be discharged in a few days." He wrapped her face up in the bandages again.

Tormented by a splitting headache and by a clanging in her ears that would not go away, she was glad to sink into a stupor.

They discharged her as soon as she could see properly again. As the *sanitarios* predicted, the swelling went down and she was left with only a few light scars on her cheekbones, which in time would fade.

But it was a week before her ears stopped ringing, and ten days before she got another rifle, just as ancient as the first. She cleaned this one for several hours before attempting to fire it and reamed out a heap of black rust.

It was not explosive, but the rifling inside the barrel was completely gone, so it was wildly inaccurate. The rounds she fired moaned weirdly as the bullets tumbled. Much of the time the ammunition, part of a lot of 28 million out-of-date cartridges bought from the Mexican government, did not go off at all.

Manuel also gave her a heavy calibre pistol, an awesome and far more practical weapon, and three hand grenades. The grenades, which had three-second fuses, terrified her. She stashed them in her sleeping bag for an emergency.

When she got back to the lines, she found that the others had taken to climbing up to the forward parapet to fire pot shots at the enemy. The veterans watched these displays of fighting spirit indulgently.

Manuel Ribera encouraged her to join them. She obeyed. After having been blown up by her own rifle, she was not squeamish about firing at the enemy. She lay down among the sandbags and took sight on one of the distant grey figures. She fired carefully, but the little grey creature scampered safely back to its trench, and Manuel laughed.

It occurred to her suddenly that she had fired her first shot in the defence of Spain.

It also occurred to her that she had held, for a moment, a human life in her hands. She thought of the day at the ochre mine, smashing her rock onto Lleonart Cornadó's head. How easy it was to kill!

She had started trembling. She leaned her forehead against the cold sandbag and closed her eyes, feeling sick.

"Good, good." Manuel patted her shoulder. "We'll turn you into a marksman yet."

Her fit of faintness did not last long. The enemy were well out of effective range, and her only real chance of killing someone with this venerable weapon would be to stick it in his ear before pulling the trigger.

From then on, she had no such qualms about firing her moaning rounds at the enemy.

This was a war of rat's bites. The real fighting was now taking place elsewhere, to the south and the west. Here, the armies had bedded down for the winter. There would not be any action until the spring. What they were doing here was almost play acting.

Manuel cheerfully remarked, "This is a picnic compared to last summer. Nothing will happen here until the winter's over. At least we're stopping them from advancing."

If the enemy only knew, Mercedes thought, just how ill-equipped and inexperienced they were . . .

But death was not far away. Ignacio Pérez was the first of their lot to be hit. A mortar shell, exploding unluckily close to him, tore open his thigh. They found him screaming, trying to stop the spouting arterial blood with his fingers. He was rushed to the field hospital, but they later heard that he had bled to death.

It seemed unreal. Nobody could quite believe it.

Now it had begun to rain by day and freeze by night, and the daily search for food and firewood had become of overwhelming importance, so Ignacio Pérez passed unremarked, "to sweep streets in heaven," as José-María sighed, "or wield a bayonet in hell."

For two days they came under fire from a sniper who had made a nest in a thicket in the river bed. Though they all crawled on their stomachs, keeping their heads well down, his fire was deadly. He succeeded in killing three of theirs.

Neither the sight of blood nor of corpses upset her any more. Not now. Since she'd looked into Matilde's face in that awful trench, she knew that bodies were only meat. Dying was the important thing, not death. The actual moment of death mattered intensely, like the moment she'd first fired on the enemy. But after that, nobody cared.

Manuel finally shook the sniper out of his perch with a grenade and shot him, and life in Sector 14 turned back to the eternal search for food and warmth.

One morning as the women were washing in a group, Federica Ossorio nudged her. "Manuel Ribera has eyes for you, you know."

"Does he?"

"Sure. He's a real man too. Not like that moon-calf, José-María."

Mercedes shrugged. These communal washing sessions were always an opportunity for ribald talk and reminiscences. "José-María is very sweet."

"Sweet?"

"He's got a brilliant mind."

"A brilliant fiddlestick." Federica leaned closer. "Don't you ever think about sex? With your looks, you could have all the best-looking men here."

Vanna Coll, a plain-faced and dedicated anarchist with heavy glasses, who disapproved violently of sexual licence, spoke sharply. "Leave her alone, Ossorio. We're here to fight a war, not get VD."

"Go fuck yourself," Federica replied rudely. "Who's got VD, you four-eyed old bitch?"

Vanna's face froze.

Federica turned back to Mercedes. "Manuel fucks like a bull. Believe me, I've had him."

Mercedes smiled tightly.

"She's too cold and hungry to think about fucking," someone said.

"She's a little virgin," another giggled.

"I'll fuck anybody. I'd fuck Francisco Franco for a plate of hot potatoes," someone else put in.

Federica grinned. "Franco doesn't like women, everyone knows that. He can only do it between the pages of a Bible." She pulled up her shirt and washed her heavy breasts. "Eh, Mercé?"

"That's a dirty lie put about by the Reds," Mercedes said. "God has provided for the Generalissimo's sex-life."

"How?"

"Haven't you heard that he keeps the hand of Santa Teresa by his bedside? Every Sunday morning, it rises miraculously off the table and gives him a hand job."

Federica doubled over with laughter. So did the others, even Vanna Coll.

The humour covered her uncertainty. She could not stop watching herself. Sometimes Federica's breasts, large and coarse-nippled, reminded her painfully of what she and Matilde had been.

At other times, she felt revulsion. Was she frigid? Perhaps that was better than being a *tortillera*.

She had no answer. It did not arouse her when the others discussed sex, though she could tell by their eyes that some women found talking about it as exciting as the act itself.

Manuel Ribera certainly did not attract her. She recognized his powerful masculinity, and did not dislike the way he protected her, but she felt no desire towards him. His mind did not mesh with hers, so his flesh did not rouse her.

Matilde's love had been gauzy, as exquisite as the touch of butterflies' wings. It had grown out of tender feelings. The sex she saw here was gross and rough. It was the rutting of animals, something to be guffawed over later. No man, she felt, could ever understand her the way Matilde had done.

The only one who was different was José-María. He was the only person with whom she felt any affinity here. He was sensitive. His gentleness touched her. In that he was like Matilde.

But the others laughed at him. There was a fragility about him that said he would not survive long. He had no strength. And that, paradoxically, repelled her.

Manuel might fuck like a bull, but he had no soul. Whereas José-María was all soul and no masculinity.

Or so, at least, she felt.

She was so hungry one afternoon in early spring that she walked among the wild pomegranate trees and picked one of the fruit. She settled down in the dry, crackling undergrowth to peel it.

The dozens of glazed red seeds inside were beautiful. She could have strung them like glass beads. The tart flesh did nothing to satisfy her hunger. She ate more for the sake of eating than for anything else. And to be private for a while.

She had already discovered that her San Lluc dreams of the glory of war were quietly dying. To be starving, to be freezing cold, and to have your most intimate parts infested with crawling lice could not be called even remotely glorious. To be dismembered by a mortar bomb, or bayonetted in the mud, was not a noble death.

Though she would never have admitted it, she had already begun to suspect that the republic was never going to win this war.

She had suppressed this feeling, of course, as they all did. But increasingly she felt a sense of disintegration, that everything was going sour around her.

She thought of her romantic dream of meeting Gerard Massaguer in the smoke of battle. She knew now that a man like Gerard would not be caught within miles of a place like this. He had not entered her thoughts for months. She had stopped thinking about Gerard Massaguer from the moment they'd entered Aragón. She had shut him away.

Now, spitting out pomegranate seeds, she remembered the taste of the champagne. She remembered the feel of the cigarette smoke in her lungs, making her head swim.

Always choose your side well in advance. And always choose carefully. Are you so sure that your side is going to win?

She heard a sudden rustling in the undergrowth and snatched at her rifle, pulling the bolt.

"Who's there?"

"Only me." It was José-María, peering through the trees at her. "Do you want to be alone?"

"Yes." But she relented at the sight of his expression. "It doesn't matter. My thoughts weren't very good company. Come and sit with me, if you want to."

He stooped to study her face. His fingers brushed her cheek. "Those scars are healing. There probably won't even be a mark, later on."

"I was lucky not to lose my sight. My looks come second."

He was looking at her with a strange expression. "You're very beautiful," he said quietly. "You could be a Greek. Your eyes are so black, so lustrous, so dark. Your face is a perfect oval. Did you know that?"

"No," she said quietly.

He touched her lips. "Your mouth is so soft. Don't go down into the underworld, Persephone. I would go into mourning forever if you did." As though embarrassed by what he had said, he sat back awkwardly on the bank. His frail body seemed lost under the leather straps and ammunition pouches he wore.

"You sound depressed," she commented.

"Aren't you?"

"No more than usual."

He sighed. "I feel depressed all the time. But I'm so peaceful when I'm with you. You're the only person here I can talk to. You're not like the rest of them. Apart from you and me, nobody here seems to have read a book in their lives."

"They've done other things."

"Yes. They've done all sorts of things I haven't. And some things I could never do." His face twisted. "Filthy. Copulating in the ditches like animals. Eating with their fingers out of tins."

"Well, they're the proletarians you talk so much about," she reminded him gently. "There are worse things than copulating in ditches. They only need to be educated. That's the job of people like you, clever people who understand things."

"I can't teach them anything," he said glumly. "They think I'm a joke. I'm not on their level."

"Maybe you don't belong here, José-María."

"Do you?" he asked. "They should never have brought the women out here. It was a mistake. Your father was right."

"I don't mind eating out of a tin."

"But you don't copulate in ditches." His face was pleading for a moment. "Do you?"

"I don't copulate anywhere," she said in a rare moment of candour.

His expression changed subtly. "You're a virgin?"

"Yes," she said, after a pause.

"So am I," he replied quietly. He reached for her hand. She took it and felt his thin, cold fingers close around her own. "They all desire you. All the men."

"I haven't noticed," she smiled.

"I have. I notice everything you do or say. You're special." He lifted her hand abruptly to his mouth. Though his hand was like ice, his lips were warm. She looked at him compassionately, almost pityingly.

"You're special too, José-María."

"Do you mean that?" he asked eagerly.

"Yes."

"May I kiss you?" he asked. His voice trembled slightly. "I mean on your mouth?"

She hesitated, then nodded. He took his glasses off with unsteady fingers and leaned forward. His mouth was as soft as a child's. He put his arms around her, clumsily and drew her to him. His ammunition pouches got in the way, but she did not flinch. She felt neither yearning nor revulsion, only a distant tenderness. She wondered whether they were going to make love here, under the pomegranate tree, two virgins in time of war. She knew she had no desire for the act.

She reached up and stroked his cheek tenderly. He laid his hand on the swell of her breasts under the blouse.

"I love you," he whispered huskily. "I love you, Mercé."

She thought of Matilde and felt a wave of sadness pass through her. Her eyes closed and she parted her lips.

His tongue probed the warm, wet inside of her mouth uncertainly. He was an inexpert kisser, too shy and too clumsy. She couldn't respond. To show any expertise would be to hurt him cruelly. If they were to make love, she realized, she would have to show him everything. The blind leading the blind.

She unfastened her blouse and guided his hand inside. She heard him gasp as his fingers encountered the naked skin. His fingers trembled as they explored. He found her nipples, rigid with the cold, and began to caress them eagerly. She kept still. She had retreated to somewhere high above, looking down on herself, carefully monitoring her feelings. Was there pleasure? Was there excitement?

"Let's lie down," he whispered. "Please."

She obeyed, lying on her back, with the lattice work of the pomegranate tree above her, criss-crossing the pale sky.

José-María kissed her breasts. She cradled his head in her arms, feeling his mouth hungry at her nipples. He was not trying to give pleasure. This was the desperate suckling of a child, taking without giving. He didn't know anything.

She stroked him, feeling the lean body tense and shivering with desire. His hunger throbbed in him like a powerful motor in a frail housing. And she felt nothing. Just her own heart beating slowly, steadily, in her breast. She felt as though the ghost of Matilde were watching her with an ironic smile. Perhaps there had only been excitement with Matilde because it had been wrong. Dirty. The thrill of sinning. Perhaps she was a pervert, after all.

She laid her palm gently against his loins and felt his erection under her fingers, the oddly guileless arrangement of the opposite sex, straining against the coarse material of his trousers. He moaned helplessly as she stroked him there. His face, which had been flushed with passion, now went white. Mercedes watched his eyes glaze.

Instinctively, she knew she was in complete control. She could make him spend, now, and avoid the whole issue. And keep her virginity for other times, other doubts.

She made her decision with a pang of sorrow. She did not want him. She pressed into him hard, and kissed his lips. Three or four slow rubs of her hand were enough. He gasped out her name and she felt his loins convulse under her palm, a long dying shudder. The rough material grew hot and moist.

She kept her hand pressed to him until he grew slack and his body relaxed.

He looked up at her. His face was scarlet again, but this time with humiliation. "Oh, Mercedes," he stammered, "I—I'm so sorry!"

"Don't be."

"But I'm so ashamed!"

"Why? It was beautiful."

"But I—"

She hushed him. The poor boy had no idea she had done it deliberately. She rocked him in her arms, despising herself for the way she had manipulated him, but aware of relief that it was over.

The sound of an airplane was in the air. There were often planes overhead, high against the pale winter sky, but this one had a different engine note. Somebody was shouting from the trenches. They both rose to their feet, looking for the aircraft.

It was passing overhead. As Mercedes squinted upwards, she was aware of a shrill, swelling whistle.

José-María grasped her arm. "It's a bomb," he screamed.

Then there was a huge concussion that flung them both backward. A rain of dirt and broken branches beat down on them as they sprawled, deafened and half-unconscious. Her first instinct was to get up and run wildly, but José-María dragged her down. "Stay down!"

There was a second explosion. The blast thrashed through the trees. Mercedes burrowed into the soil like a terrified animal.

A third bomb, farther away. Through the ringing of her ears, she could hear wild screams from the trench. José-María pulled her to her feet. His glasses had been smashed into the ground and his face looked naked without them.

"Come on," he gasped, "before it comes back again."

They stumbled towards the vast column of smoke that towered up from the redoubt where Mercedes had been sitting half an hour earlier. Equipment and corpses lay scattered like a confusion of driftwood after a storm. The first body she came across lay in a heap across the sandbags. The man was dead, a bloodstained scarecrow whose stuffing had been ripped out. A woman was crawling blindly towards shelter, her hands scarlet with blood.

In the dugout was a tangle of bodies, the wounded, the dead and the living. She saw blood spraying brightly from a half-severed limb. A man was screaming like a castrated pig, though there was no apparent wound on him. Sobbing for breath, she began helping to drag the wounded out of the dugout. Hands grasped at her for assistance, mouths open in entreaty. Several people had been buried under debris.

The stretcher bearers were already careering across the fields in their battered ambulances. The slaughter had been all the worse because most people had been caught completely by surprise. It was as though they had been playing a game up till now, and the rules had suddenly, viciously changed. She had to fight against shock to make herself move.

More ambulances arrived, from other parts of the line. The dead were laid in rows, to be disposed of later. They made a terrible monument. The blast had torn off arms and legs, crushed chests and skulls. Those at the centre of the detonation were truncated things without limbs or heads.

There were a dozen or more dead. Another two dozen at least had been wounded and some of these were obviously going to die.

One of the last bodies they found was Federica Ossorio's. She lay at the bottom of the barricade, her eyes open, staring curiously up at the pale sky as if at some strange new vision.

The long silence of the winter had ended, it seemed, forever. In the wake of the air attack, heavy machine-gun fire began from the enemy lines. Their artillery, apparently reinforced, had begun a constant sullen thudding. The shells passed overhead with a sound like ripping calico and began landing on Granados. Soon they could see smoke rising from the direction of the town.

Toward evening trench mortars started lobbing shells at them from across the riverbed, at first aimlessly, then with increasing accuracy. The mortars made a horrible whistling noise as they came down, exploding with a blast that rocked the brain and filled the air with mud and whining shrapnel. The fact that their redoubts were so widely scattered made it hard for the enemy to be accurate. But they were forced to crawl to and fro in the mud, belly-flopping whenever they heard that shrill whistle overhead, and occasionally there were screams. Stretcher bearers hurried backwards and forwards.

Through some piece of mismanagement, they themselves had dozens of mortar shells in unopened boxes, but no trench mortar to put them in. They did not even have a machine gun with which to answer the attack.

It was Mercedes's first experience of being under steady fire in all her months of war. She was aware, suddenly, of being a bag of soft organs, every inch puncturable, none of it defended. She tried not to imagine the savage pain of steel ripping into her, but it seemed her skin had an imagination of its own, because it crawled and prickled. The sharp ammonia stink of explosive permeated everything, even the wretched meal they made, silent and afraid.

The pounding continued through the night. It tailed off during the next morning, which brought renewed fears of another air-attack. Exhausted, they did their best to reorganize themselves, scanning the sky anxiously for enemy aircraft.

Mercedes's nerves were ragged and trembling. Her hands seemed unable to grasp anything. Things fell from her nerveless fingers. The others were equally demoralized. The change from boredom to sudden terror had eviscerated them. To these untried, unhardened volunteers, the carnage had been stupefying.

The strafing and shelling had broken their nerve. Many were vomiting, others were crying helplessly. Most had fallen into a state of apathy, oblivious to the curses and kicks of their officers. The blood of the dead seemed to be everywhere, on the clothes of the living, on their equipment, on their hands and faces.

The field hospital in Granados, they heard, was filled to over-flowing with terrible injuries. They also heard rumours that the anarchist headquarters had been hastily moved out of the town. This caused dismay until a messenger on a motorcycle came to tell them that HQ had been relocated at a nearby country house.

The rest of his message was ominous. "There'll almost certainly be an enemy attack tonight. Probably in the early hours of the morning."

"Well, we'll be ready for the bastards if they come," Manuel promised grimly and stamped off to organize their defences.

The mortar fire began again in the afternoon, building up into a pulsing barrage that continued into the black and windy evening. Mercedes's ears were aching from the noise and her brain throbbed. In the darkness, the mortar bombs glared red. They crouched in the mud, knowing that when the barrage eased off, the enemy would begin moving across the river bed towards them. The expectation was horrible.

"I want the women to stay down below the barricade if any shooting starts in the night," Manuel warned fiercely. He had been badly upset by Federica's death. "I don't want any more casualties. Understand, Mercedes?"

She nodded. There was no argument from the other women either. But she retrieved her weighty pistol and the grenades from her sleeping bag.

The rest of them sharpened their bayonets and greased their useless Mexican ammunition. José-María hunched beside Mercedes in the trench.

"I'll protect you," he kept assuring her. He was trembling even more than she was. Selfishly, she wished he were elsewhere. If the enemy got into their trench, she knew he would be more of a hindrance than a protection. But in the end she fell asleep in José-María's arms, jerking spasmodically each time the mortars cracked.

The attack came just before sunrise. The enemy must have cut their way through the wire without being detected by the sentries.

It began with a roar of grenades that awoke her in terror, her heart leaping into her mouth. She clutched at José-María, not knowing where the attack was coming from. For a few minutes there was a chaos of screaming and firing.

"There they are!" someone shrieked. Against the sullen dawn sky, dark shadows moved towards them. Fear became a wild pain in the heart that she could no longer resist. Against Manuel's orders, she clawed her way up the sandbags. With numbed and trembling fingers she pulled the pins out of her hand grenades. She hurled them, one after another, over the barricade towards the shadowy, scurrying figures.

José-María dragged her back down by her legs, cursing. "Take cover, for God's sake!"

The grenades erupted in quick succession. Earth showered them and her deafened ears seemed to pick up screams. Sprawling behind the sandbags, she wondered dizzily whether she had killed anyone.

More grenades blasted the night. The darkness was lurid with green and red flashes. At any moment she expected the enemy to come charging over the parapet, bayonets thrusting. She clutched her pistol tightly, praying the ammunition wasn't dud.

Then Manuel came loping past. He grabbed José-María by the arm and dragged him to his feet. "Come on, get out of the mud. Come on, all of you. They're outnumbered. We've got to counterattack. Come *on*, damn you."

The men scrambled over the barricade. Hoarse, inarticulate shouts receded beyond the sandbags. The firing intensified.

Now there were only women left in the trench. She could hear one of them weeping beside her. If she was to be killed, she herself prayed, then let it be quickly. Not mutilation. Not the screaming, animal death she had seen yesterday.

The firing grew sporadic after ten minutes, then started to die down. There were isolated shots for a while, as a few men continued to fire into the darkness, but no more grenades were thrown. There was a confusion of footsteps running to and fro, and a call for the stretcher bearers.

"What's happened?" a woman's voice implored.

Someone came scrambling over the barricade and slithered down among them, panting. There were shrieks from the women, but it was Manuel.

He was jubilant. "We've beaten the bastards off. Not bad, for our first effort this year!"

A ragged cheer went up.

"Where's José-María?" she demanded, clutching at Manuel.

His voice changed. "Over there."

She felt a knot pass through her heart. "Has he been hit?"

"Yes."

"Badly?" she asked.

"Can't tell."

"I want to see him!"

He looked unhappy. "Come on, then."

She rose and followed Manuel. "He's the only casualty," Manuel told her. "It would be him, poor bastard."

The sun was rising over the mountains by now, cold horizontal rays throwing long shadows along the ground. José-María was several yards beyond the barricade, lying on his side in the mud, whimpering. His hands were clasped at his mouth, as if in prayer. She knelt beside him helplessly. "Where are you hurt?" she asked.

He only shook his head, unable to speak. His legs seemed immobile. Manuel rolled him over and examined his stomach. Mercedes saw that his uniform there was dark and oozing wetly. There was a smell of excrement from the wound. Manuel pulled a disgusted face at Mercedes.

"Oh, God," she moaned. "You'll be all right, my love. You'll be all right!"

She tried to unbuckle the useless leather belts that held the ammunition clips. Manuel stopped her. She took José-María's head in her arms and kissed him. His face was cold and clammy. She tried not to cry, but nothing seemed to be able to stop the tears from welling out of her eyes.

He didn't speak. The rising sun bathed him in a golden light. Within a few more minutes the stretcher bearers arrived. As they loaded José-María, he began screaming weakly, his head thrashing from side to side. She begged them to be gentle. They hurried off with him into the sunrise.

Manuel put his arm around her. She clung to him, feeling as though her heart would break. He stroked her hair as she sobbed, his big hands striving for gentleness.

"He'll be all right," he promised her. "They'll patch him up. Don't you worry about him."

Then someone pointed and said, "Look," in a panicky voice.

They turned and stared across the river bed. During the night the enemy had advanced five hundred metres. A new line stretched across the valley, much closer than before. Machine gun posts had been set up and they caught the glint of a periscope in the early morning sun. The attack had been no more than a distraction for the advance. Suddenly, the whole character of their position had changed.

"From that range," Manuel said quietly, "they'll be able to

drop mortar bombs right into our laps. If we don't get reinforcements soon, we'll have to retreat."

The word hung heavily in the air.

"Over here! Over here! One of them's still alive!"

They hastened over to where the others were congregating. There were three dead enemy soldiers lying on the ground, heaps of mud with teeth bared in mirthless grins. For all she knew, she herself had taken one of these strangers' lives.

A fourth nationalist soldier lay huddled against a tree, moaning. He had been wounded in the side. His uniform was soaked with blood and his white face stared with dread at the group that was forming around him.

"What are we going to do with him?" a man asked Manuel. "Shall we get the stretcher bearers for him?"

"No," Manuel said in a rough voice. "No stretcher bearers for this scum." He drew his revolver and walked over to the wounded man. He cocked the pistol and pointed it at his head.

A woman screamed. Mercedes turned her face away unable to look. In the silence, the wounded man started praying in a gasping voice.

Mercedes's body jerked as she heard the hammer click emptily on a spent bullet. Manuel pulled the trigger again. Again the flat click. He cursed violently. He had emptied his revolver during the attack.

The wounded man rolled onto all fours and tried to crawl away from Manuel. Manuel began hunting in his pouches for more bullets. "For Christ's sake," he snarled at the silent bystanders, "shoot the bastard, one of you!"

Nobody moved. Their faces were grey, appalled. To blaze away in the dark at a charging enemy was one thing. This was different.

Manuel could find no more bullets for the revolver. He ran after the crawling man and kicked him with immense force in his wounded side. The man did not scream, but flopped to the ground and writhed there. Manuel's face was a mask of hate. He drew back his boot and kicked the squirming thing in the same place again, jerking it off the ground.

Then again. At last it made a sound, a kind of dry croak. Blood leaked from its opened mouth.

There was a babble of voices, protesting, pleading with Manuel. Mercedes found her own pistol in her hand. She walked forward. Her mind was blank. Her world had gone white and silent.

She knew she would miss unless she went up close. She pressed the trembling muzzle to the man's temple. The pistol kicked in her hand with a crash and the man's head jerked sideways. The cordite burned her nostrils. The soldier's body was quivering, but she did not look at what the bullet had done to his head. She was emptied of emotion. Her brain seemed to have stopped working. Blood seeped into the wet earth.

The others were staring at her, as though frozen by what she had done.

"Good girl," Manuel said, patting her shoulder. He took the pistol from her hand, pushed the safety on and replaced it in her holster. With his arm around her shoulders, he led her back to the redoubt. Her feet dragged with exhaustion. The others began to follow in silence.

She wondered numbly whether she had shot the man out of mercy, or in revenge for José-María. She wondered whether it mattered. Perhaps it did, in a distant way. What mattered more was the numbness she felt inside.

She felt that she, too, had died a kind of death.

She felt that nothing in her life would ever be the same again.

That afternoon, a truck arrived with a visitor for them, a forty-year-old woman dressed all in black.

The visitor was Dolores Ibarruri, *La Pasionaria* herself.

She looked older than her photographs, her hair pulled back into a tight bun. There were dark shadows under her eyes. Her face was grave and sombre. But when she stood on the tailgate of the truck to address them, her voice was deep and sonorous and a spark burned in her eyes.

"I have come, as a woman, with a special message to the women here at the front. You have done magnificent work. You will never be forgotten. When we have won this war, and peace once again reigns in our land, your names will be written in gold in our history books. But I am here to tell you that the time has come for you to go home."

There was a stunned murmur. Mercedes felt her stomach twist inside her. She looked up at the cold blue sky, barely hearing the rest of the speech. The unreal feeling persisted. All of this was happening to someone else. The war, the deaths, it was all alien to her.

There had been no news about José-María. The field hospital had too many casualties to deal with. But she felt he was alive. He couldn't be dead. It was impossible.

La Pasionaria was giving them news of a great battle at Guadalajara, which she said had changed the course of the war. A Republican victory was now inevitable. The people were on the brink of triumph over the forces of fascism and revanchism. Now, she told them, Republican policy on women in the militias had changed, and the women were being withdrawn from the fighting.

"From now on, your place is at the rear. You can do more good at home than out here," she said, her voice reaching over the cold wind. "Go back to Barcelona. Go back to Tarragona and Zaragoza. Go back to the workshops, the factories and the hospitals. Go home. Get yourselves ready. The lorries will be coming tomorrow morning to take you away."

She got down off the truck. Many of the women were openly crying with relief at the prospect of leaving the front.

Mercedes stood silent, holding her rifle. Was this where it had all been leading, all the suffering, all the hope? To this dismissal? She thought of Federica, lying dead in the mud. She thought of José-María, and of the man whose life she herself had extinguished that morning. She had killed a man in the name of the republic. A helpless, wounded man who had tried to pray.

At the very last minute they had made her into a killer. And now they were sending her home.

La Pasionaria was given a tour of the line. The enemy, perhaps aware of who was present, were firing more or less constantly, and the tour was hurried along to the tune of ricochets. After she had left, the women started gathering their few possessions, watched glumly by the men. Some were protesting bitterly, especially those who had formed attachments with the women.

"Shut your faces," Manuel said. "This is the best thing that's happened all year. We can't fight a war with women and children hanging around our necks. We can't watch them being shot and blown up. Once they've all gone back home, we'll be able to *fight*."

Mercedes borrowed a bicycle and rode along the rutted roads to Granados, to see José-María.

After the past few days' fighting, the hospital was chaotic, full of terrible sights and sounds. Shells kept landing in the town and a thick pall of smoke was over everything.

The courtyard milled with ambulances and stretcher bearers. Parked discreetly farther back were several hearses, the old-fashioned horse-drawn kind. Wounded men lay everywhere, on mattresses on the floor, or even outside, in the cold air, awaiting evacuation to Barcelona. There were far more doctors and nurses too, than when she'd been admitted before.

Mercedes asked several tight-faced nurses where José-María was, and was ignored until she found a young auxiliary with eyes red from crying.

She described José-María. "He's young, dark-haired. He was wounded in the stomach last night."

"Shot?"

"I think so."

"If that's the case he'll be in no fit state to receive visitors."

"I have to go back to Barcelona tomorrow morning," Mercedes pleaded. "I just want a glimpse of him before I go. He's my friend."

The auxiliary shrugged dully. "We'll ask matron. Stomach wounds are at the end. I'll take you."

She followed the nurse through the abattoir. Bodies lay so thick along the floor she had to pick her way through them. Dulled or feverish eyes followed her. Some men were screaming, their anguish apparently ignored. Here and there, scarlet stains seeped through the bandages on faces, hands, chests. Haste and dirt were evident everywhere. There was a smell of putrefaction that caught in her throat and made her gag.

This is what hell is like, she thought.

The ward at the end was comparatively the quietest. Here the shutters were drawn over the windows. Mercedes waited at the door while the auxiliary went in and spoke in hushed tones to the matron there. After a while, she came back and nodded for Mercedes to go in. There were six beds in the room, which had once been a handsome salon. All the beds were occupied by silent figures.

José-María was in the first bed. His thin body didn't make much of a heap under the orderly bedclothes. His face lay on the pillow like a mask of yellow clay. His eyes were not quite shut, but only a rim of white showed between the puffy lids. Beside the bed, a bottle of blood was suspended, a line going into the vein of one thin arm.

"They operated this morning," the matron told Mercedes. "Took out half his bowel. He's lost a lot of blood. He's on morphia, but he might just be conscious. Husband?"

"A friend." Mercedes felt a swelling in her throat. She had to force herself not to look away from him. "Will they send him back to Barcelona?"

"In a few days. If it's worth it."

"Isn't he going to live?" she asked numbly.

"He'll be lucky if he does," the matron replied. "They usually die of shock or peritonitis. Only five minutes, please."

She walked away and left Mercedes there. There was no chair. Mercedes stooped and kissed José-María's forehead. He was cold, but still sweating. He made no sign that he knew she was there. Her almost lover. He lay like the dead.

"José-María, can you hear me?" She touched his face gently. "I have to go back. We all do. I've come to say goodbye. I have to leave you here. I don't want to, but I must. Please forgive me. José-María? Can you hear me?"

She thought she saw his eyelids flicker. But she couldn't be sure. She was determined not to cry any more, though her throat ached. She kissed him again, on the mouth. His lips were soft, like a sleeping child's. She couldn't bear to stay any longer. She had to go.

"I'll see you in Barcelona. Don't die," she whispered. "Please don't die! I'll see you again."

She turned and walked out of the room.

"How will I know what happens to him?" she asked the matron.

The matron wrote a number on a piece of paper. "You could try calling this number. Every now and then a call gets through."

She nodded and rode her bicycle back to the lines in darkness. How many more times in her life was she to leave someone who loved her dying or dead in her wake? First Matilde. Now José-María. Perhaps it was her curse to prove fatal to those who cared for her.

In her nightmares that night, José-María and the man she had shot merged into one ghastly, crawling thing that moaned and bled and followed her. Its hands clutched at her, beseeching, imploring.

She awoke the next morning to that familiar, awful smell. She stared around her at the filth and the disorganisation of Sector 14. It was as if she had suddenly perceived the uselessness of it all. Dolores Ibarruri was right. They had no contribution to make out here.

They should never have come.

The lorries were waiting. She had few possessions to gather. She gave away her blankets to her friends and passed her pistol and her crotchety rifle on to a teenage recruit from Zaragoza.

In all, she had spent three months at the front. Saying her farewells to the men, Mercedes knew she would never see them again. She knew that the war had already changed from fiasco to tragedy, and that they would all die.

Manuel hugged her tight. "Goodbye, little virgin," he grinned. "See you in Barcelona. Don't cry, for God's sake."

She climbed aboard the truck with the others, the whores and the martyrs, the crying and the laughing. She was exhausted to the bone.

Barcelona

Two days later, on a Friday, another truck let them out in front of the anarchist barracks in Barcelona. They gave her a bed in a crowded dormitory. A new batch of recruits was about to be sent off to the front, and they stared at her with wondering eyes.

She telephoned the hospital at Granados several times, but could not get through to the matron.

She wandered the streets, trying to marshal her scattered thoughts. The city whirled around her, impossibly noisy and huge after the front.

Barcelona had undergone a change.

The gaiety had faded. The flags looked ragged. Hunger and despondency had set in. Wretched refugees from other provinces were to be seen in the streets, begging for food.

A counter-revolution had begun. The hard-line Communists were trying to take control of the city. Brutal killings were being carried out by NKVD-trained thugs, intended to remove the most committed anarchists and to "purify" the revolution.

Anarchists and Communists were shooting at each other from

balconies and across rooftops. Interrogations, sometimes with torture, were said to take place in cellars. There were denunciations, counter-accusations, murders, bombings. The battle had turned inward. The world had gone mad.

People no longer looked you in the eye. It was as though the whole city had received some intimation of the end. As though the city knew what the reality of this war was going to be.

The realization of what was happening disgusted Mercedes profoundly. The ideas she had learned from her father had been powerful and romantic, while they'd lasted. They'd exercised a strong grip on her teenage imagination. But the raw violence of the struggle had filled her with disgust. She hated what it had done to her.

She hated the memories she would always have. She could no longer listen to the harsh, declamatory rhetoric of revolution without a feeling of nausea.

She felt that she at last understood the muted, pessimistic humanity of her mother. It was not a philosophy. It was not something that could be articulated. It was something more female, an understanding of suffering, something instinctive her mother had always had. Maybe it was no more than a feeling of outrage at the hideous things men did to one another. But it was something she could understand.

She regretted only that she had not come to that understanding before the war had scarred her and turned her into a butcher of her own kind.

She would take no more part in killing. She would find work in a hospital. Better to try and save the lives of her comrades than to take those of her enemy. But first, she was going home for Easter.

She went to the railway station and bought a return ticket to San Lluc.

She rang the hospital at Granados again. When at last she was connected, they told her that José-María Calvet had died a few minutes after she'd left the ward.

10.

Withdrawal

august 1973

Tucson

She awoke crying, lathered in sweat. She knew where she was before she opened her eyes. The knowledge didn't leave her, not ever. Even when she slept, her nightmares were about this place. She moved from sleeping nightmare to waking nightmare.

As soon as she was properly awake, she began retching. She leaned over the toilet, and painfully brought up a thin watery gruel. It looked bloodstained, as it had several times before. Her abused stomach must be bleeding again. Her head felt as though it had been split open with an ax. She peered at the tray, hoping there would be some aspirins left, but there were not. She'd taken them all hours ago.

She lay back on the pillow, disgusted by her own smell. Her skin had a clayey look, moist and dead. She thought she even smelled dead, like something in which the processes of life had stopped and the processes of decay had started.

The dim light bulb overhead flickered. She watched the glowing filament until her eyes were blinded by a host of incandescent worms. Then she closed them and watched the afterburn fade.

It felt like morning. It felt like early, early in the morning. She wondered if the sun was rising up above, in the world she had left. She preferred the idea of dawn to, say, late afternoon. Or worse, late in the night. It was absurd to feel that such things mattered. But they did.

She had no watch. And she had lost count of the meals, because she'd been unable to eat so many of them. Without darkness or daylight, she'd very soon become disoriented. And so many hours had been swallowed in the dark pit of her sickness. The sickness had erased wide patches of her consciousness, or so it seemed.

It had waxed and waned, like a storm that came and went, tearing at her for hours at a time, then drifting away. She was a tree who had lost every leaf. She felt a terrible sadness for herself, for her loss, for what had been done to her.

She'd expected to die, but she hadn't. She'd expected to go mad, but she hadn't done that either. Not yet. She'd endured. Lessened, pared down to the green bones, she endured this morning too.

She felt slightly better after she'd vomited. For the moment the storm was rumbling in the distance, not near enough to hurt.

She opened her eyes and lifted her thin arms to study them. Under the manacles, the skin was puffy and scarred. She could see the muscles of her forearms clearly under the grey skin. She must have lost a lot of weight in this hole.

She was a long, long way from Los Angeles. The journey had lasted at least twelve hours. Maybe eighteen. Maybe twenty.

When he'd come into the kitchen with the M–16 pointed straight at her chest, she'd thought at first she was hallucinating. Then her heart had begun to lurch.

She'd gasped the first inane words that came to her mind: "Hey. How'd you get in here?"

But, of course, that had been easy to answer. He'd had no problem at all getting in.

Miguel was gone. The old man's presence always made her feel safe, even these days, even now that he was white-haired. But he was in Mexico with that tacky girl.

The staff quarters opposite the main house were also empty. Miguel had let the gardener and his wife go, and the replacements hadn't arrived yet.

In fact, the whole ranch had an air of abandonment. The garden was overgrown these days. Most of the property was in darkness. Even the electronic gates had been switched off, since

Miguel wasn't there to monitor the closed-circuit TV. And she'd been there alone, waiting for her last shot of the night, the extra big one that let her sleep through till morning.

The kidnapper had just walked in.

He was unrecognizable. He had a ragged half-beard and ragged, uncombed hair. In between, his face was a streaked mask of green and black camouflage paint. The eyes glittered as black and feral as an animal's. He was taut as a bow. For a moment of blank terror she'd thought he was going to fire, tear her body apart with bullets.

She'd risen to her feet, holding her arms out, as if to stop the bullets.

The butt of the weapon had slammed into her shoulder. She'd stumbled and sprawled onto the floor. He'd stood over her, pointing the muzzle of the gun at her face. She'd seen his black eyes half close in that bizarre mask of a face, and had felt the void open inside her, the empty anticipation of imminent death.

She remembered the smell of the wax on the pine floorboards.

Had seen his finger curled around the trigger. Saw the rifling inside the barrel that gaped at her hungrily.

She'd lain frozen, waiting. *Rape, murder, pain* had flashed through her mind. *Miguel,* she'd thought in anguish.

Then he'd hauled her to her feet. She'd screamed at the wrench to her shoulder, and he'd pushed the muzzle of the rifle into her throat. "Shut up. Not a sound. You understand me?"

She was choking, her eyes staring blind with terror. She'd managed to nod.

He'd stared at her, eyes black as midnight. "Come on, Eden," he'd commanded. "You're coming with me."

Shackled to struts in the back of the van, her hands and feet had gone numb. By the time they'd got here, wherever here was, agony had become stupor. She had wet herself twice. She'd been numb and shocked, and starting to jitter for her fix. He'd had to carry her out of the van. He hadn't spoken.

The air had been warm. She'd heard outside noises. Birds, wind. A sort of dry, sweet smell. Then he'd pushed her into a building of some kind, and down a set of wooden stairs into what she'd guessed must be a cellar or a store room. She'd felt his strength, heard his unsteady breathing.

When he'd started undressing her, she'd thought he was going to rape her and had tried to fight. But he'd only pulled off her shirt. She hadn't been wearing a bra. He'd shackled her to the chair.

Her blindfold had come off. She'd started screaming, then. She didn't want to see his face, because she knew if she saw his face he would have to kill her, so she couldn't identify him afterwards. If she saw his face, there would be no afterwards.

He'd cursed her angrily and had pulled on her hair, hard. But she hadn't opened her eyes until he'd promised that he was wearing the hood. Even then, she'd raised her face with dread, slowly.

The flashlight had exploded in her eyes, blinding her more effectively than the blindfold had done.

Then he'd unshackled her from the chair and had shackled her to the bed. He'd taken the chair out. The black hood stared at her through neatly cut eyeholes. Nothing more had been said until the steel door clanged shut and the lock had clattered, and she'd looked around her and started screaming again. Screaming her head off. There had been no answer.

Why had he pulled her shirt off to take that picture? To increase the impact of the photograph, of course. By now her father would have received it. She wondered how Daddy had taken it.

She wondered whether the police were hunting for her, whether it was in the papers, on television. Or whether it was being kept quiet, and no more than a handful of people knew she was missing. She wondered how much he had asked for. Fifty thousand? That was too little. Hardly worth the risks. Double that. Maybe as much as a quarter-million.

That would have given Daddy a jolt. For once in his life, he would be really hurting on her account.

She wondered dreamily how you quantified the value of a human life. Was she worth a million bucks? What was the value of a Vietnamese child in some burning village? An American President? A murderer on death row? Did they all have different values, or maybe the same value, or no value at all?

Withdrawal was not something she had experienced often.

Deprivation had seldom gone beyond minor discomfort before. She'd always had enough money to buy as much heroin as she wanted. An addict's paradise. Because of that, her habit had grown without limits, a monstrous plant whose huge, rank blossoms had required huge feeding.

She had learned that tolerance to the drug was almost without limits too. The more she shot up, the more she had needed. It was almost impossible to overdose, once her tolerance had grown sufficiently.

Of course, everything else had lost its importance.

Her exterior life had steadily crumbled as heroin became her god, took her soul. It had all gone, even the riding. Until the night she had walked out naked into the darkness and had fallen into the abyss.

Blindfolded and terrified in the van, she hadn't thought about the prospect of withdrawal at all. Not until much later. None of that had occurred to her. But after twenty-four hours, the sickness had begun in earnest.

It started, as always, with a pain in the back of her neck. The claws digging in. But soon it had enveloped her whole body. The real agony consisted not of the pain, though that was terrifying, so much as of the torture holes that she sank into, with no one to pull her out. The torture holes were funnels of desperation. Like someone holding her head under water until the need for air was gigantic, making her whole body kick and flail.

She fell into the holes three or four times a day. The need would begin to gather in a knot at the base of her skull, an unbearable tightening of the consciousness. Like the onset of madness, like the desperation of a breakdown. A craving for release that had no limits and no bottom. She would be able to smell it, taste it. She could feel it tingling in her blood, but it would never reach her brain.

She would remember huge scores she had made in the past, remember towering highs she had been on. The needle-tracks would start to itch and burn. She would remember the feel of the needle, popping into the skin. Then it would start scraping at her stretched nerves until they shrieked, scraping them right down to the bones.

The walls of the cell would crowd in on her, compressing her space even smaller, even smaller. She would become convinced the walls were actually moving, that the cell was a terrible machine that would eventually close on her and crush her.

She would watch the concrete ceiling slowly descend. Her life would start running out, second by second. Her heart would start to race, her mind screamed in overdrive, like a motor slipping its clutch. Her skin would crop out in the huge goosebumps that gave the whole withdrawal process its ugly name. Her fingers would turn into claws. Her spine would arch as though it wanted to break. She would watch the walls and the ceiling close in and begin to scream.

And minutes would turn into hours.

At its worst, the walls closed in on her completely and the light went out. Then the external world would cease to exist. She would be imprisoned in the tunnels of her own mind. She would creep agonizingly forward. When the walls tightened their grip, her breath would almost stop. She would be entombed, paralyzed. Until slowly the walls moved and let her inch her way forward, twisting and writhing along the shafts. And the darkness and claustrophobia began to ease and she would fall into an exhausted, feverish sleep.

Being chained added a refinement to the torture. Often, she would come out with her wrists bruised and aching.

Next to all that, the coughing and the vomiting, the pains in her back and legs, the fever and the sweating, had been no worse than her childhood bout of scarlet fever.

She'd almost told him, more than once. At the start she'd reasoned that if he was part of a professional gang, maybe he could get her the stuff. Or something else, maybe morphine. But she didn't think like that any more. Now she knew he was part of no gang. He was alone.

And he was an amateur. A crazy amateur. He talked to himself. Argued with invisible presences in the room. He was unbalanced. Dangerous.

So she hid her addiction. Hiding it was a way of life and possible even in the stark confines of this cell.

She'd let him think she had some kind of fever.

He brought her antibiotics. That had been almost funny, in a gruesome kind of way. He was still forcing her to take them, though the damned things only made her feel worse. The painkillers helped, but he never brought her enough. She'd begged him for codeine, but he only brought aspirins.

Lately, she'd been crouched around one bleak thought: that he was working on his own. And that was very bad. Bad for her.

Working on his own, it would be far easier for him to just kill her, rather than to work out any complicated routines for keeping her alive and letting her go.

Joel Lennox walked out onto the porch.

At ten o'clock in the morning it was already fiercely hot. It would reach 105 degrees down on the valley floor today, maybe 130 degrees in the sun.

He was used to it, of course.

No, not used to it. He loved it. He loved the heat and the solitude, the purity and the cleanness of the desert. He loved the height of his aerie, towering above Tucson. It was his home, his garden, his refuge. His immense and glorious fortress.

He thought of the girl down there in the cool dark. If he brought her up here, she would shrivel, with that frail skin and those huge night eyes. She was a creature of the dark.

She'd been sleeping when he'd taken down the last tray. But she had seemed a little better, breathing easily. A normal sleep. No shivering or whimpering.

He leaned against the wooden railing. When he'd seized the girl, he'd felt emotions that had been dead in him for years. Feelings of excitement. Of vindication. A feeling that he was fighting back. He'd lost a lot of that since she'd got so sick.

Now he had to regain his balance.

He had been monitoring the California press carefully. There was no hint that Mercedes or Dominic van Buren had contacted the police. He was pleased by that, though he felt he had little to fear from the police. It was impossible that the girl could be traced to this isolated house in the desert, hundreds of miles from Los Angeles. Almost nothing could link him to the crime. But the publicity, a massive police enquiry, would have cramped him a little and he hoped they would continue to keep silent.

That a local missing-person enquiry had begun in LA was, of course, possible. But there was no way that could affect him. Eden van Buren would be no more than one of dozens of missing girls in Los Angeles this summer.

He walked around the back of the house, to the shed he had built. The sun smote his shoulders like a familiar old friend. He squinted at the cobalt sky. No clouds were in sight. A shimmer hung over the ground, making the saguaro seem to wobble.

In the cool of the shed, he let his eyes adjust to the shade. Sheets and blocks of stone were stacked neatly at the back, beside the big masonry saw he had bought second-hand in Phoenix. His tools, electric and manual, lay in neat rows on the benches. Pieces of work lay around, some half-finished.

The new carving he had been working on lay on its trestle. He lifted the sheet of canvas off it. It was very big, a wide, flat slab of pale stone on which he was carving a Navaho woman and a flock of sheep. She held a lamb in her arms, against a backdrop of craggy hills. The subject was well-worn, the sort of western kitsch he tried to avoid; but he had breathed something special into it, an authenticity, a tenderness.

She was looking up into the sky, as though maybe the lamb was going to be a sacrifice. Her attitude expressed some dynamic emotion, hope, or perhaps fear.

He had made the drawings from life. He would have preferred the model, a young girl who worked in a store in Tucson, to have posed for him while he cut the stone, but he couldn't take the chance of bringing anyone up here who might notice something odd. He was known to like solitude, and not to like visitors. A solitary artistic temperament. He knew some people tapped their foreheads behind his back. They had always done that, ever since his childhood. Fuck them. It suited him fine.

He picked up the hammer and the slender, sharp chisel and sat in front of the work. The stone was a commission. It was going to be set into the wall of a house being built in the foothills by Keith Hattersley, a rich man who saw himself as a patron of the arts. He had little empathy with Hattersley, the owner of a fast-food chain, but he knew the carving would be standing there in pride of place long after patron, artist and model were all dust.

He began to work. As he chipped, his thoughts fell into place, tranquil and ordered.

He worked on the drapery for a while, then turned to the woman's face again, pecking at the stone, flaking away the dross, bringing out the smooth lines of youth.

After an hour and a half, he rose to his feet, took the hose and washed the stone down, rinsing away the chips and the dust. The carving came up clean and crisp, darkening as it soaked up the water. He played the jet over it awhile, then turned the hose off.

He watched the water evaporate. In this heat, it took only a minute before the stone paled and dried again. It was coming along fine. His eyes drifted over the flowing lines he had sculpted.

He had touched the stone and was bringing out the spirit in it. There was sorcery in his fingers.

He reached out and caressed the work and felt good.

Santa Barbara

Dominic van Buren contemplated the day ahead as he showered. He'd just had his morning toot and he was feeling cool, alert, happy.

Plenty to do this morning. Friends to see, shopping to do, a lunch appointment with Leonora. A busy schedule. And then, this afternoon, he was going to the polo match.

He was pleased at the prospect and was whistling as he towelled himself dry.

The internal telephone buzzed discreetly and he scooped it up.

"Yup?"

"Mr. van Buren, Señor Fuentes is here."

"Miguel? Okay, I'll be out in a few minutes."

He chose fawn cotton slacks with a matching shirt and slipped on a lightweight cashmere cardigan against the cool of the air conditioning. He was still whistling.

He shoehorned a pair of lizard-skin pumps onto his feet and walked out of the bedroom.

Miguel was waiting in front of the carved stone fireplace in the salon. He stood holding a panama hat in both hands. His shoulders seemed to have sagged since van Buren had last seen him. He looked shrunken somehow.

"Good morning, Miguel," van Buren said briskly. "Found Eden yet?"

"No, Mr. Dominic."

"No news at all?"

The old man's eyes were swollen and red, as though he'd been crying. The lines in his face were deeper-cut. "I did what Mercedes asked," he said in a low voice. "I questioned Yolanda."

"And?"

"She ha' nothin' to do with it, Mr. Dominic."

"You're sure?"

Miguel looked up. For a moment, a hot bitterness washed over the filmy eyes. "Yeh. I sure."

Dominic smiled faintly. "You gave her the third degree, did you? Pulled out a few fingernails?"

Miguel looked out of the window without speaking.

"Well, that's the sort of thing you do best," Dominic said lightly. "If you couldn't get anything out of her, there was nothing to be got. I hope you weren't excessive, Miguel. She's not disfigured, or anything?"

Miguel mumbled something.

"What's that?"

"She gone. Back to Puerto Rico. Back to her family."

"Ah, well. And what about your friend Álvaro?"

"He ha' nothin' to do with it either."

"You questioned him too?"

"Yeh."

Dominic considered the old man's wretched face. "Okay, Miguel. I'll tell Mercedes you've done well. In the meantime, keep looking for Eden. She won't have gone far."

Miguel nodded and walked slowly out. Dominic went onto the terrace for breakfast.

He shook the newspaper open. There were two main news stories. One was about heavy fighting between North and South Vietnamese troops, only 25 miles north of Saigon. The other was about Richard Nixon's recovery from a bout of viral pneumonia. Nixon would soon, a spokesman said, be returning to the Watergate-embattled White House.

Beneath the lead stories was an item about the disappearance of Paul Getty III. Van Buren read it attentively.

"Italian police," the report concluded, "continue to classify John Paul Getty III as a 'missing person,' rather than as a kidnap victim. They point out that young Paul, heir to the world's greatest fortune, had openly speculated about 'staging his own kidnapping' in order to get money out of his grandfather. Ransom demands fluctuating between $1 million and $10 million have been received but police say that there is no proof Paul is 'in the hands of anybody.'

"Another possibility, that Paul has run away with a 'bewitching' green-eyed beauty, the daughter of a Belgian diplomat in Rome, is also being investigated. 'We are not ruling out the likelihood,' one police official said, 'that this is a crudely-planned attempt by some of Paul's friends to get cash.' "

Van Buren snorted and flipped the page. Damned right it was. How peaceful life was without Eden! The longer she stayed out of sight, the more peaceful it would get. Really, it was the answer to a prayer.

Mercedes was a fool to fall for Eden's games. After all they'd been through with Eden. Mercedes must be losing her touch . . .

Mind you, the world was certainly full of crazy people. It *was* just possible that Eden had gotten herself into bad trouble. Black Panthers or SLA, or something. God knew that was the sort of thing she was prone to. The best thing about the Vietnam War ending, as far as van Buren was concerned, was knowing he didn't have to bail Eden out of police stations after riots any more.

Or there was the other possibility. Another Godawful Manson episode, like 1969. Blood on the walls. An end to all their problems, including Eden's.

Well, he thought philosophically, squeezing lemon onto his papaya, she would turn up again, one way or another. She was the original bad penny.

In the meantime, the thing to do was just enjoy the serenity of her absence.

He checked his watch. He would leave in a few minutes. He would snort a little coke first, make sure he was extra-primed for the morning's activities.

Costa Brava

"I've assembled three million dollars in cash," Mercedes said. "It's available in Switzerland. It can be transferred to America in a matter of twelve hours. I've also been offered a further million dollars, if I should need it, by a friend in Madrid. That makes four million dollars."

De Córdoba nodded. He was in her study, facing her across the desk. The curtains had not yet been drawn against the evening that was closing in. In the light of the desk lamp, Mercedes Eduard's hands were clasped, immobile. They were still youthful hands, strong and smooth. But they gripped one another so tightly that the oval nails were bloodless.

Her voice tightened. "Maya is going to Amsterdam tomorrow, to dispose of some... assets. I hope these will bring in a further two million. The remaining money is going to be much harder to raise."

"You already have far more," he said gently, "than you are likely to need."

"I have other assets. The cars. The boat. This house and its contents."

"I would strongly advise against your disposing of any more *assets* for the time being. With four or five million dollars at your disposal, you are in an excellent position to..."

"To barter? To haggle for Eden's life?"

"To manipulate them, rather than let them manipulate you. Letting them know you have so much money available would be a terrible mistake. To have the money in reserve is good. But as I said before, we should be aiming at a settlement figure of far less. Well under a million, if we can. At most, around the half-million mark."

"If they agree to negotiate."

"They will. Besides," he added gently, "if you can't raise the money, you'll be forced to compromise, anyway. Would your ex-husband help?"

"Dominic stopped caring about Eden a long time ago."

"Because of her..." He hesitated.

Mercedes met his eyes. "Maya has told you the real nature of Eden's sickness," she said.

He nodded. He was glad that the subject had been brought up. "Yes," he replied. "She told me about the heroin."

Mercedes's face was in darkness, but he thought he saw colour touch her smooth cheekbones. "I lied to you. I was stupid."

"Not stupid," he said gently. "It's a hard thing to admit, even to yourself."

"Do you think the kidnappers will find out?"

"That she's an addict? I don't know how she could hide it," he said gently. "They'll have seen her go through the withdrawal syndrome."

"What will they do to her... when they know?"

"If they're professionals, they'll do nothing."

"They wouldn't try to obtain the drug for her?"

"I very much doubt they would bother. Why should they risk giving her needles and dangerous drugs? Her addiction makes little difference either way. If she truly had an illness, something which would have given them added leverage, then it could have been very serious. But she hasn't. In fact, the longer she stays off the drug, the better for her."

When Mercedes's mouth relaxed, it became vulnerable, soft. The skin of her face was delicate, porcelain-fine. "I shall try and have more hope. But the distance is terrible. She's so far away. I keep thinking of her going through withdrawal, all alone. With no one who loves her nearby. Maybe in some cramped place. Maybe without air, without light—"

He was distressed at the tears that glistened on her dark lashes. "Please, please. Don't torment yourself."

Her eyes were blurred. "So much of it is my fault. I blame myself for what has happened to Eden. For the addiction. For everything. If I'd been a better mother, she'd never have turned to drugs. The blame, ultimately, is mine."

He wasn't sure how to comfort her. Sometimes kidnap relatives were corroded by an irrational guilt. A sense of having failed to protect their loved ones.

"We live in strange times," he said. "Our children are angry with us. Perhaps with reason. We have been materialists. We allowed things to go wrong. The war in Asia, the problems of poverty and drugs... What Eden is going through may change her way of living. For the better. May bring her back to you in the end. That, too, is possible. Life is full of strange ironies, don't you think?"

"Yes," she said, "life is full of strange ironies. Do you have children?"

"I had a son. He died a young man."

She turned her dark gaze on him. For a long while they looked at one another. Then she reached out and laid her hand gently on his chest. "Thank you for your patience, Joaquin," she said.

For a moment he felt the full power of the woman's allure. It rocked him, stirring his heart and his loins. He wondered whether his reaction had shown. "I'm glad to help," he said huskily. "I want her back, just as you do." He tried to sound professional, calm. She nodded.

She took her hand away. But he thought he could feel the warmth of it burning into his flesh through his clothes.

Tucson

It was happening again. Her whole body had started to tremble, her skin was breaking out in an icy sweat. She rolled onto her back. Her legs were shaking badly, drumming against the bed. She stared up at the ceiling with darkened eyes.

She felt naked, as though her very substance was draining away from around the bones, leaving her skeletal, raw. She needed the drug. She needed it so badly. It was the only thing that could enrich her blood, give her back life.

She took a long, shaky breath. The walls had started to press in on her, the way they always did. But today there was a difference. A lessening of intensity. At first she would not recognize it. She cringed. Yet the attack was less venomous. All the sensations were a little less cruel.

She pushed against the walls with her will, timidly, driving them back. She thought they obeyed. A tiny victory. The feeling of panic subsided in her throat a little.

Eden rolled onto her side and stared at the tray. He had brought her some cereal in a bowl, milk in a plastic jug, toasted sourdough bread spread with butter and some kind of jelly. A mug of black coffee.

Breakfast. It was morning again. Another day had passed.

She squeezed her eyes shut and fought against the need in her.

I don't want to think about you. Go away. Leave me alone.

"Go away," she said aloud, then repeated the words, more strongly.

It seemed to work. The walls were not pressing in so ominously. The trembling was still there, but it wasn't dominating her whole body, as before. Maybe he had been right. Maybe she was getting better. She tried not to think about cooking up a shot, about the feel of the needle popping into the vein...

She reached out and picked up a slice of toast. She touched the spread with the tip of her tongue. It was strawberry jelly. The taste was hauntingly sweet. It made a colour flood her mind, a pale transparent pink, like the inside of a strawberry. She could actually taste the fragrance of the fruit under the sugar and the preservative and God knew what else.

It was the first thing she had been able to taste since she'd been brought here and now taste was like a new sense to her.

It endured on her tongue, that tiny scrap of confectionery, with a long, honeyed note. It made her think of bracken, and cool woods and leaves.

Slowly, a scrap at a time, she licked the jelly off both slices of bread until it was all gone. She heard her own stomach gurgle in astonishment. The bread itself was damp and unappealing by the time she'd finished.

She turned to the cereal. Some kind of flakes, coated with sugar. She let one dissolve on her tongue.

Another kind of long, sweet note. She chewed the flake when it was moist, and it tasted golden-brown, wheaty. She ate half the bowl, without milk. Then she poured in some milk and ate some more.

The coffee was acrid. She couldn't drink it. But she drank a little water and lay back on the bed with a sigh. She felt full. She was aware of energy seeping into her veins.

How wonderful. She had eaten. The wonder of it persisted, only slightly dimmed by the fact that after ten minutes she was sick again.

When he came down with her evening meal, after dark, he saw that she had eaten some of her lunch too, the egg and bacon. She was sitting on the bed, turned towards the door. She looked ill, but alive. Not dying any more. He had the odd feeling she had been waiting for him.

As he changed the tray, she lifted her manacled hands.

"Please," she said.

It was the first time she had spoken in days. He glanced at her warily. "What?"

"Take these off."

"No."

"Why not?" she asked quietly. "Look at what they're doing to my wrists. They're rubbing the skin raw." She showed him the chafed places. "It's inhuman to keep me like this."

"They stay on," he said shortly.

"Why?" she demanded.

He didn't answer. She was staring at him, something she had never done before. And her eyes, he noticed, were brighter and clearer than he had seen them before.

It made him uneasy. He was going to have to stop coming into the cell. He was going to have to go back to the system he had originally planned, that of pushing food in through the flap. He'd only started coming into the cell because she was so sick. Now she was improving, he didn't want to see her any more.

"You don't need the handcuffs," she said. "You've got me locked up in here. I'm not going anywhere. Are you afraid I'll be waiting behind the door to strangle you with shit paper and make a dash for freedom?"

She was pleading, but her voice was stronger. Almost angry.

He put the tray of food down on the floor without a word and picked up the old tray.

"How can you keep me down here, chained like an animal?" She was glaring at him, her slight body trembling. "Do you think I'm not human? Is that it?"

He had another distrustful moment, wondering whether she could see the shape of his face under the hood, maybe tell enough about him to give a description, or recognize him later. "It'll work best this way," he said in a toneless voice. "There's the least danger for both of us."

She gritted her teeth. "What am I going to do to you, break your arm? I must weigh ninety pounds. You probably weigh twice that. What're you, six-three, six-four?"

Anger licked at him. She already knew his voice. Now she had picked up his height and weight. He had been a fool. He had to get out of here, now. He turned to go.

"You lousy son of a bitch." Her eyes were blurred with tears. Her mouth trembled. "You lousy, heartless son of a *bitch*."

He unlocked the door, went out and slammed it shut behind him. She sat staring at the blank sheet of steel with blurred eyes.

She wondered whether her father was going to negotiate, and felt a spasm of fury at the thought.

Don't argue, Daddy, you bastard. Don't haggle. Just pay him what he wants and get me out of here.

"I'm so sorry," Maya whispered.

"Don't be," Mercedes said gently.

"I tried so hard..."

"You did your best."

"I failed you!"

"Hush." They were sitting on the bed in the blue light of early evening. Maya's suitcase lay still waiting to be unpacked on the floor.

That the diamonds and the drawings had brought in only a paltry half-million dollars had been a bitter disappointment. But she had not been profoundly surprised. She had long ago learned the truth of the maxim that there was one price when you were buying, another when you were selling.

At least the money was now available, deposited by Maya in a Swiss bank account before reentering Spain. "I'm the one who should be sorry, for having sent you on such an errand." She brushed the hair away from Maya's face. Maya's velvety brown eyes were swimming with tears. "Don't cry any more," Mercedes said. "Let's not think about it. The money is nothing. I'll find it somewhere else."

"How much more do you need?"

"Even if I accept the million Gerard has offered me, more than five million."

"My God. It's so much. So *much*. Where will you find it?"

"The house. The estate. I've contacted an agent. I'm putting it all up for sale. The house and land. The paintings. The carpets. The furniture. But it will take time. And it will be underpriced," she added bitterly. "We've already seen what happened with the diamonds and the drawings and they were the most readily disposable assets."

"There's nothing else?"

Mercedes shook her head. "Nothing."

"That leaves Dominic," Maya said slowly.

"Yes."

"He hasn't even called since they sent the hair."

"No."

Maya looked into her face. It was a mask. The narrow, straight nose and calm mouth were almost severe. Only the eyes, dark and enigmatic, held pain in their depths. It seemed to Maya that the streaks of silver in Mercedes's hair had intensified over the past weeks.

"You'll have to ask him," Maya said. "Won't you?"   ·

De Córdoba had never been a heavy sleeper. The ringing of the telephone at his bedside penetrated his sleep at once. He switched on the light, started the recording machine and groped for the handset.

"*¿Digame?*"

There was a pause, filled with the echoing noise of a long-distance line. Then he heard a harsh American voice say, in English, "Give me Mercedes Eduard."

De Córdoba's heart was suddenly pounding against his ribs. He heard a slight click as Mercedes lifted the receiver in her bedroom. He leaned forward to make sure the tape was turning in the machine. "Señora Eduard is unavailable," he said. "Who is this?"

"She's available to me," the voice said. "I'm the one who has the girl. Put her on."

De Córdoba waited to see whether Mercedes would speak.

"Put her *on*." The voice had risen sharply.

He gave Mercedes another moment to reply. When she did not, he began speaking again. "My name is Joaquin de Córdoba," he said carefully. His voice sounded odd in his own ears, strained. "I am the family's representative. Señora Eduard has given me full powers to negotiate on her behalf—"

"Fuck you!" The voice cut in savagely. "Fuck you and your *negotiate*. I don't want to talk to anyone but her. Put the bitch on. *Now*."

Still Mercedes said nothing. "Please," de Córdoba said gently. "Keep calm. Before anything else, we need some kind of assurance from you that you have Eden and that she is safe and well—"

"She's not safe! I'll cut her to fucking ribbons!" The voice was shaking. De Córdoba bit his lip in silence. "I'm going to call back in fifteen minutes. If anyone answers the phone but Mercedes Eduard, you'll never hear from me or the girl again."

The line clicked dead. De Córdoba sat immobile for a while, then slowly reached out and stopped the tape recorder. He checked his bedside clock. It was 3:15 A.M. Early evening over most of America. "What do you want to do?" he said into the telephone.

"I'll come to your room," Mercedes replied and hung up.

He rose and wrapped a dressing gown around his lean frame. As he combed his hair in front of the bathroom mirror, his own face looked sallow and weary. But he felt the adrenaline circulating through his system. So it had begun. They had made contact at last. He took a bottle of whisky from his cupboard and poured three glasses.

Within minutes, Mercedes arrived with Maya. Mercedes was in a silk robe, the younger woman had pulled on a tracksuit.

"The waiting is over," he told Mercedes and kissed her on both cheeks. Her skin was warm and fragrant. He passed the drinks around. He lifted his own glass slightly. "To a rapid and successful conclusion."

He played them the tape he had just made and they listened in silence. Maya's face tautened at the crude threat, but Mercedes seemed icily calm, unruffled by the abrupt awakening and the savage voice on the tape machine. Without makeup, her face was oddly youthful, the skin smooth and soft. There was no trembling of the mouth or fingers.

She went to sit on de Córdoba's bed, beside the telephone.

"Do you want to go through the drill again?" de Córdoba asked her.

"No. I remember what to say."

"Good. The important thing is to stick to the lines we've agreed. Don't let them frighten you with threats. Don't be distracted by what they say they'll do. That's all part of the technique. You understand?"

"Yes."

"They will try and exert control over you from the start. They'll try and give all the orders, make all the arrangements. You must show them you won't be browbeaten."

"I know what I have to do, Joaquin." Unexpectedly, Mercedes reached out and touched his arm, as though it were he, and not she, who needed comforting. "Don't worry. I'm capable of dealing with it."

"I know you are," he said with a brief smile.

Maya spoke for the first time. "He sounds so . . . unstable. So emotional." She hadn't tasted her drink, but stood clutching the glass so hard it looked as though it might break in her fingers. "What if he's some kind of madman?"

"He's just tightly strung. At this stage, they're as tense as we are," de Córdoba said. "There's bound to be aggression. It's fairly standard. Abuse and hostility at first. They may use filthy language. Their aim is to intimidate you, get you off-balance. Later, they'll probably grow familiar with you. At the end, they'll be impatient and frightened. Try and ignore their threats."

"I will," she nodded.

"Later, we'll listen to the tape over and over and see if we can pick anything up about their mood. For now, we have to concentrate on what we agreed to say. Don't be distracted by ugly words, Mercedes."

"I won't." She drained the whisky and set the recording machine to simultaneous playback, so they would all be able to listen in on the conversation. She checked her watch. "Five more minutes, if he's punctual." They sat in silence.

The great house was as still as a tomb. Not even the night noises of the garden penetrated the double-glazed windows. De Córdoba watched Mercedes Eduard. Her calves were bare beneath the gown, smooth and firmly-muscled. She had slid one foot out of its slipper. It was a small foot, with slender toes. The toenails had been painted the same pale pink as her fingernails, and were flawlessly manicured.

Her face was expressionless, the eyes unfocussed. He wondered whether he should have written her a script to follow. He hoped she was going to be able to deal with whatever they threw at her, and wished it were he, and not she, who was going to field the call. They would want to terrorize her at first. That was why they had insisted on speaking to her. They would want to show her how vicious they were.

Perhaps it would be better if she broke down. Showed them how willing she was to cooperate. That would simplify things, in one sense. They might feel she was not holding back.

When the telephone began ringing again, Maya's body jolted violently. Mercedes started the tape machine and picked up the receiver.

"This is Mercedes Eduard," she said in her fluent, accented English. There was no reply. They all heard the echoing silence on the other end. "I am listening," she said.

The voice that came out of the echoes was harsh, tight. "I've got your daughter, Mercedes."

"Have you?" Her voice was cool. "I would like to speak to her, please."

"You'd like to speak to her?" There was a crackle down the line, that might have been a laugh. "That will cost you. Have you got the money?"

"I want you to understand one thing," she said unemotionally. "I am not going to negotiate with you, whoever you are, until I have proof that my daughter is alive and well."

"I can always let you hear her scream." They heard the rasp in the voice. "Is that the kind of proof you want?"

"No," Mercedes said quietly and coldly. "I want something more specific than that. I need evidence that you have Eden and that she is alive. I gave my daughter her first horse when she was five years old. Ask her his name. Ask her what breed he was. Second, I need a name for you. So I can be sure I'm not dealing with hoaxers. From now on, you must identify yourself as Paul."

"Are you crazy?" The voice was rising. "Who do you think is in charge here?"

"Nobody is in charge. Contact me again when you have the answers to the two questions. And don't forget. Paul."

"You cunt! I can do what I like with her. Anything! You hear me?" His ragged breathing was audible down the line. "I can starve her. Beat her. Rape her."

De Córdoba saw Mercedes's naked toes dig into the soft pile of the carpet.

"I can kill her if I want to. I can cut her open—"

Mercedes slammed the receiver down, silencing the venomous voice. This time, her hand was shaking slightly.

"Jesus," Maya whispered. She had risen involuntarily. "Mercé, what are you *doing*?"

"You took a chance," de Córdoba said dryly. "You should have let him calm down."

"No," Mercedes said. "He didn't want to calm down. You heard his voice."

"I warned you to ignore threats and obscenities," he said patiently.

"You've taken a terrible risk, Mercedes." Maya was still white. "You've provoked him."

"I've shown him he can't frighten me as easily as he thinks he can." She looked at the other two wearily. "At the moment, that seems to be what he wants, rather than the money." She looked at de Córdoba. "He didn't mention anything about her addiction. You noticed?"

"Yes."

"Perhaps they haven't found out yet," Maya suggested.

"Perhaps." There was a silence. Mercedes rose to her feet. "I'm going back to bed."

"He might call again," de Córdoba said.

"I don't think so. He'll wait. He'll want to punish me. But he'll do as I say in the end."

"Don't you want to re-play the tape?" de Córdoba asked.

"You play it if you want to. I've heard what he had to say."

De Córdoba was awed by her composure. He opened the door for her. "You did well," he said. "Very well."

She smiled at him. "Eden is my daughter."

The Argentine closed his bedroom door. The two women had left a warm scent of perfume in his room. He walked over to the recording machine. He ran the tape back and listened intently to the crackling voice.

The intonation did not seem particularly provincial to him, though he was no expert on North American accents. The voice was strong, youthful. Not a crude voice. A confident, authoritative voice. But there was something that vibrated in it, making the hairs stand up on the nape of his neck.

I can kill her if I want to. I can cut her open—

He listened to the tape again, then again. On the relistenings, he was struck by the glacial calm that Mercedes had maintained. By contrast, his own voice in the first conversation was quavery and nervous.

But there was no question about the other voice. The emotion that vibrated in it was recognizable now.

It was hate.

Feeling slightly sick, de Córdoba reached for the whisky bottle.

The dark holes of the hood turned on her grimly. She could sense the anger that had come into the cell with him, could feel danger vibrating in the air.

"Your first horse. What was it called?"

"My first horse?" she repeated blankly.

"What was it called?" With the hood on, he was like a medieval executioner. His fists were clenched, the veins prominent. "What breed was it? Come on, don't screw me around!"

She stared at him for a moment. Then her heart lurched so violently with excitement that it seemed to lodge in her throat. "They want proof I'm alive! Am I going to get out of here?"

"Just answer the question."

"His name was Alfie. Alfie. He was a Shetland. He was brown and white, piebald—" The words were tumbling out of her. "Did they tell you to ask that? Are they going to pay? Just tell me if—"

"Your mother's playing cute," he said. His voice was tight. He took a small tape recorder out of his pocket and sat on the bed. He put the machine down in front of her. "She thinks this is a hoax. So you're going to send her a little message."

"My mother?"

"You're going to tell her not to be smart. You're going to tell her just how bad you feel. I think you know what I mean."

Complete shock made her face blank. "You're tapping my *mother*? Not my father?" She was stupefied. "Why her? Why not him? He has much more money." Her green eyes were wide. "How much are you asking for?"

He paused for a moment. "Ten million dollars," he said.

She was stunned. "Ten *million*? You're crazy! She'll never be able to find that much money!"

He stared at her. "You better pray she does," he said. "Now shut your mouth and concentrate on what I'm telling you. You've got ten seconds to speak to your mother. Ten seconds. Understand? Tell her how much you want to be out of here. Tell her not to be clever with me. Just remember, the more you cooperate, the quicker you'll be home."

"No!"

He switched on the tape recorder and held the microphone to her mouth. "Ten seconds. Starting now."

Eden stared at the microphone. It had never occurred to her that he would ask her mother for the money. She'd always assumed Daddy was the target. For the first time in days, she felt the impotent rage rise in her. She shook her head. "I won't do it," she said in a low voice.

"You want me to get rough with you?"

"I don't care. I'm not doing that to her."

He lowered the microphone slowly. "We can do this the easy way," he said with deadly quietness, "or we can do it the hard way. But we're going to do it. If I have to hurt you, I will. Now, talk."

"No."

He thrust the microphone at her. "*Talk.*"

She shrank back against the wall, shaking her head. "I won't do it," she whispered.

He grasped for her and she screamed involuntarily. She tried to roll off the bed, past him.

"Talk to her!" He caught her arm, making her scream. She had forgotten his frightening strength. "Tell her how much you love her!"

"No," she gasped. "Fuck you! I won't!"

"You have to do everything the hard way," he said bitterly. "Don't you?"

"You're despicable," she said, cowering away from him.

He grasped her wrist and twisted her elbow up behind her back. The excruciating pain in her shoulder made her scream.

With his free hand, he held the microphone up to her mouth. "Tell your mother to get you out of here." His breath panted hot against her ear. "Tell her to make this stop."

"No," she whispered.

He jerked her trapped arm. Red-hot claws tore at her sinews. She whimpered in agony. "Ask her," he rasped. "She loves you so fucking much, doesn't she? Beg her."

Eden shook her head, her teeth clenched. He twisted harder until the pain grew immense. She could feel the joint opening, the ligaments straining. Blackness swelled up in her vision. Then something broke in her. "Mama," she sobbed. "Mama, please. Get me out of here! Please! Please!"

He released her and she curled up into a foetal ball, her arm limp at her side. The pain spread slowly through her body, leaving her shoulder hot and numb. She was crying silently.

He was shaking and the tape machine rattled in his fingers. He ran the spool back a short way, then played it. Eden heard her own voice, wailing tinnily from the machine.

He rose and stood over her. She could hear his rasping breaths.

"I didn't want to hurt you," he said.

He slammed the door shut as he went out.

She cradled her dead left arm and stared at the steel slab that shut her in. He must be negotiating with her mother, right now, or he wouldn't have wanted the tape.

The silence flooded around her. Had it really happened? Or had it been a dream, a hallucination brought on by her solitude? Already, the reality was fading. How long had she been here? As long as a month? No, surely far less than that. But her past, the outside reality, was starting to fade. It was growing hard to remember a time when she hadn't been in this cell, chained to this bed. Her life had shrunk.

Ten million dollars. The sum was too vast to comprehend. It would destroy Mama to have to pay that. Guilt loomed over her, a giant crow. She had never been anything to Mama but trouble. How much pain had she caused her? Their relationship had been so fucked-up for so long.

A sudden cramping pain in her stomach made her hunch forward. She clutched herself in anguish. The pain held a long note, then intensified. She gasped, curling up until her knees touched her forehead. Perhaps it had been the fight. Or perhaps it was the sickness coming back.

Without warning, the need surged, overwhelmingly intense. It had been hours, days since she'd thought about it. Now every nerve had become an open mouth that screamed out for junk. Her body stretched taut, the physical pains sublimated in the general agony that had overtaken her.

God, how badly she wanted a hit right now. She wanted it with a violent longing that choked her.

She was a tiny, flickering light in an ocean of empty blackness. The overwhelming emptiness of the universe was crushing. It echoed around her, an infinity of loneliness and guilt. Her own meaning had vanished. She was naked. Defenceless.

She wanted the shelter of her opiate. She wanted to pull that warm, loving embrace around her, to protect her, to isolate her from pain, from solitude, from the fear of death. She wanted to be back in the pleasure dome, back in the bright white heat.

Like an exile at the gates of paradise, she covered her face with her hands and wept as though her heart would break.

After a while she looked down at the tray. The water jug was full. Suddenly, she couldn't stand her own filth any longer. She forced herself to sit upright, fumbled off her jeans and panties, and pulled her T-shirt down over her arms.

The manacles on her wrists were linked by a long chain that was looped around the iron frame of the bedstead, so she couldn't get the T-shirt right off. She left it bunched up on the chain, and now naked, sat on the edge of the bed. She picked up the jug and scooped up a handful of water.

She washed her face first, then her loins. God, for even a sliver of soap. The water raised her flesh in goosebumps. Under the chicken-skin, fragile bones. It was like washing someone else's body, impersonal and unfamiliar. She smeared water across her ribs and breasts, under her arms, around her neck. It felt cool and clean.

Afterward, she dried herself with the sheet, which was grimy and wrinkled, and washed her pants in the last of the water. It wasn't much of a toilet, but she felt marginally better.

She uncrumpled the sheet and draped it over the edge of the bed to dry. She put the wet pants and T-shirt back on. She didn't want him coming in and finding her naked. She left the jeans to dry a little.

The air of the cell, which always felt tepid, was now cool on her naked skin. Her contortions had tired her. She lay back and let her body relax slowly. All the time she'd been on junk, she'd almost never dreamed. The only time she saw things in her mind's eye had been when gouching out after a shot. Actual sleep had been dead and black as the grave. But here, she had dreamed with an intensity and a reality that sometimes terrified her.

All kinds of dreams came: monstrous things that chased her; dim memories from her childhood, that lingered sweetly long after she had awoken; sometimes things that made no sense at all, and subsided back into the swamp of her unconscious as soon as she wakened.

She dreamed now, as sleep came. The first dream was strange, because she knew the woman in it wasn't her mother but her grandmother. She had no memories of her grandmother. She had never seen even a photograph of her. What she saw was an image she'd composed from things her mother had told her, long ago. She saw the grey eyes and dark hair, and heard a gentle voice speaking Spanish.

Then she dreamed of the horse her mother had bought for her, Cypsele. She dreamed she was riding around the ring, in hot Mediterranean sunlight. She was taking every jump perfectly, soaring through the air. She dreamed she was free of junk. She slid off the horse into her mother's waiting arms. Her mother's eyes were dark and warm. She was the only one her mother's eyes warmed for. She nestled up against her mother, becoming very young, losing herself in the love she had long ago rejected.

Then the dream changed.

She was at home. But something was terribly wrong.

She was bound in chains, heavy and cold, immobilizing her.

Mama and Daddy were nearby. But they didn't seem to see her. They didn't hear when she called.

They were arguing. Mama's face was white and strained, and Eden knew it was one of the worst fights ever. The things Daddy was shouting at Mama were horrible, frightening. Things about Mama.

Eden wanted to cover her ears, but the chains held her arms fast.

Daddy saw her at last. He came to her. She saw the thing sticking out of his groin, erect and threatening.

But it wasn't his thing that made her scream. It was what he was saying. His mouth was moving, and the words that came out were terrible. It was all a jumble, a roar. The walls were coming down. And the ceiling was falling. And she couldn't get away. And Daddy's words were bringing the house down.

She screamed to try and shut out his words, and stop the house from falling in and crushing them all. She knew if she could drown out his words, they would be safe. She screamed so loud that it tore her chest, deafened her.

She was awake, soaked in sweat. She was sitting bolt upright. Her heart was hammering against her breastbone as though it wanted to burst out of her body.

"Did I scream?" she gasped.

The chains were real. But the grey walls held. Impaled on an unbearable emotion, she writhed onto her side and buried her face in the pillow.

Santa Barbara

Dominic van Buren was alone by the poolside. His housekeeper brought the telephone out to him.

He accepted the instrument. "Hello?"

"Dominic, it's Mercedes."

"Mercedes?" He lifted his legs onto the chair in front of him and waggled his white loafers. "Hello. How are things? Any news from Eden?"

"Do you care?" He could hear the bitterness in her voice and smiled slightly. "You haven't even bothered to call in a week."

"You seemed to have everything so well in hand. What's new? Another hank of bloodstained hair in the mail?"

"Eden's kidnappers have contacted me by telephone."

"Ah. To what purpose?"

"To threaten. I've demanded that they give me some proof that Eden's still alive before I go any further."

"Alive? Don't be so Latin. Of course Eden's alive. She's the one who's planned the whole escapade."

"This is *not* an escapade."

"Well, you're entitled to your opinion. Just as I'm entitled to mine."

"Dominic, I spoke to the man who has her in his power." Mercedes's voice was constricted. "Eden is in deadly danger. If she isn't rescued, we will never see her again."

"Bullshit. It's a spoof. She got the idea from the Getty kid, and now she's trying it on with us."

"Can't you understand that Eden is *incapable* of doing something like that to us?"

"Eden is capable of anything." He laughed. "I never thought you, of all people, would fall for something so transparent. You must be losing your grip. If you're so sure it's for real, go to the police."

"*No.* No police."

"Just pay up? You're really getting set to send ten million bucks to some unknown who claims to have kidnapped Eden?"

"I see no other way out. Unlike you, I do not believe that this is a hoax or a gimmick. I believe she has been kidnapped. They threatened to torture her, Dominic. I believe that if the money isn't paid, or if we go to the police, they'll carry out their threat."

"You think so? Then pay the ten million bucks, sweetie, and set your mind at rest."

"Paying ten million dollars is not so easy, Dominic." The strain in her voice was clear.

"I'll bet it isn't. She'll probably settle for ten thousand. That'll keep her in junk for a couple of months, at least."

"You know what I am asking you."

"Oh, yes," he said. "You're asking me to squander millions of dollars. That's what you're asking me to do."

"I'm asking you to lend me the money." Again, he felt that her teeth were clenched around the words. "I undertake to pay it back."

"How?" he asked succinctly.

"Dominic. Please."

"Don't you think it rather odd," he said sharply, "that they're asking *you* for the money, and not me? It's almost as if they expected me not to fall for the ploy. Or as if they had singled you out for . . . punishment. Hmmm?"

"Nothing can be ruled out," she said quietly.

"True. Except that, if you fall for this, you'll be financially ruined. And Eden will have won her little game."

"Dominic," she said, "you cannot hide behind the pretence that none of this is real. Eden has never been a perfect child. But then, neither of us have ever been perfect parents. She had very little chance of finding stability—"

"No, Mercedes. No. I'm tired of heaping ashes on my head

over Eden. The truth that you won't face is that she's rotten. Born rotten."

"That's an atrocious thing to say!"

"Is it?"

The silence stretched out. "You can believe what you choose to believe about the reasons for Eden's problems," Mercedes said at last, her voice weary. "The fact remains that if the kidnapping is real, and I don't come up with the money, they'll start mutilating her. They'll kill her in the end. Can you face that?"

"Put it this way, Mercedes. I am fond of my house and my lifestyle. I am no longer fond of Eden. I am not prepared to risk my financial security on what is almost certainly a vicious prank on her part."

"Your financial security? Is that what you care about?"

"Oh, yes. Very deeply. But while we're on the subject of relative values, let me say this." Anger was churning in him now, worms in his gut. "In the unlikely event that Eden *has* got herself into deeper waters than even she can navigate, then let her sink or swim, Mercedes. Let her rescue herself for once, without our footing the bill."

"How can she rescue herself?"

"That's her problem. You, of course, may pay whatever you want to pay. Just don't ask me to part with a penny. Not one red cent. I want nothing to do with it. That's my last word."

He slammed down the receiver.

He rubbed his stomach. That call had stirred up his ulcer. The worms in his stomach were slithering around, making their way up his gullet. He felt quite ill with anger. Damn Mercedes. Damn Eden. They had pretty near ruined his life between the two of them.

He hurried into the house, into his study and opened the safe.

He chopped the cocaine into lines on his desk and snorted it all up expertly. Soon, his spirit was soaring again. He enjoyed the sense of elation, lying back in the chair.

What the hell did it matter, anyhow, any of it?

He looked out the window. A little gust of wind made the palms sway and dabbled cats' paws on the flawless surface of the pool. The afternoon was cooling. The sun was sinking into the sea. He picked up the telephone and dialled Leonora's number.

Costa Brava

The second call came late on Tuesday night. Joaquin de Córdoba in his bed, and Mercedes in her study, lifted their receivers simultaneously. As before, de Córdoba spoke first.

"This is Joaquin de Córdoba. Who is calling?"

"Get me the woman."

The voice was unmistakable.

This time she came on the line directly. "This is Mercedes Eduard. Who is calling?"

"Paul. The horse's name was Alfie. He was a Shetland pony."

"Yes," she said, and relief made her voice catch slightly. "Yes, that's right."

"Just to convince you," the voice went on bleakly, "here's a little message from Eden herself."

A scream of pain came down the line. Then they heard Eden's voice sob, "Mama, Mama, please. Get me out of here! Please! Please!"

The voice was abruptly cut off.

"*Eden!*" Suddenly, the weeks of self-control, of emotional abstinence, came to an end. De Córdoba, sitting on his bed, heard her voice break as she cried out. "Don't hurt her! Please! You don't have to hurt her!"

The Argentine, in his room, stared at the carpet as he listened to her weeping. There was no other sound on the line. Her tears were bitter, harsh. They took a long time to subside. "Please—" Mercedes whispered at last. "She has never done you any wrong. Don't harm her."

"I'll do as I want with her. She is mine." The voice was exultant. "She is in my power."

"Yes. Yes."

"I hurt her because you got clever with me."

"I had to know—"

"I can make your daughter's life just as easy or just as painful as I want. You understand that fully now, don't you?"

"Yes," Mercedes said. "I understand that."

"You have only one way to ensure that she stays in one piece. Do as I say. Exactly, to the letter."

"Yes. Yes, I will."

"Cooperate, and she stays well. Get clever, and she bleeds. Understand?"

"I understand."

"If I have to hurt her again, it will be your fault. Again."

"I want to cooperate. I want Eden back. Believe me." Whether faked or not, de Córdoba thought, the broken tone of Mercedes's voice was masterful. There was none of the arrogant coldness of last time. Her obvious submission was making the kidnapper relax.

"Are the police listening in on this?"

"No, I swear it. The police know nothing, not here, not in California."

"It doesn't matter, anyhow. Have you got the money?"

"I'm trying. I'm trying so hard. But it's difficult. Almost impossible."

The voice was a snarl again. "You want me to cut off one of your daughter's fingers?"

"I can't raise so much capital so soon!"

"Don't lie to me. You have the money."

"You're wrong. Why do you think I am a rich woman? I'm not. You're asking for so much. I don't know where I will get it from."

"Sell your house!"

"I've been selling everything I can—" Her voice trembled, grew even more urgent. "Please. For Eden's sake, listen to me. I can pay you what I have, now. It's a great deal of money. It's all I have. Accept it. Let my daughter go. You could wait for a long time and get very little more."

"The sum is ten million. Nothing less."

"I can never raise that kind of money. It would take me years."

"Jesus!" The explosion of distorted sound made them both jump. The man was literally screaming into the telephone. *"You're dangling your daughter's life on a string, you know that?* What kind of woman *are* you? You're haggling over your own flesh and blood. This is not some fruit stand." The voice descended slowly from its furious peak. "I know how rich you are. I know how you made the money. I know more about you than you can possibly imagine. You think you can fool me? I *know* you. Don't plead poverty with me, you bitch."

The last words had come out in a savage hiss. Mercedes was silent. De Córdoba's mouth compressed. Argue with him, he urged her silently. Don't let him browbeat you.

Then, astonishingly, a laugh came down the line, slow, malicious. "I can wait until you see sense," he said. He sounded almost relaxed after the outburst. "Your daughter isn't expensive to maintain. She doesn't eat much. I just hope she's alive—and sane—by the time you decide to stop being clever."

"Sane?" Mercedes said abruptly. "What do you mean by that?"

He ignored her. "When you have the money—*all* the money—put a private ad in the *New York Times* classifieds. The ad will say, 'Wanted, castle in Spain. Any price paid.' Then put your telephone number. Understand?"

"Please! Tell me how she is. How her health is—"

"Nothing. Nothing until I see that ad."

The line went dead.

"Joaquin?" Mercedes's voice was tight. "Are you in bed?"

"Yes. I'll come to you."

"No. Stay there. I'll come to you."

Her face was white and tense against the dark blouse and slacks she wore. Her eyes were bruised-looking. She was alone.

"You did very well," he said. "Wonderfully well."

Her eyes pleaded with him. "You think so?"

"You let him get to you with that recording. But otherwise you were almost perfect."

"But he is not prepared to negotiate, Joaquin. He wants it all."

"He wants a lot, yes. But he will negotiate," he said, with rather more confidence than he felt.

"How can we negotiate with him? He is insane. And he said he wouldn't contact us again!"

"We'll contact him. We'll wait a week. Then—"

"A *week*," Mercedes gasped.

"Yes," he nodded. "A week. Long enough to let him cool down. Then we'll take out the advertisement. The wording will go something like this: 'Castle in Spain. Cannot raise full price but will pay what I can. Please get in touch.'"

She was crushing her fingers together. "What if he doesn't buy it?"

"He will. He'll get in touch with more abuse, more threats. That will be the time to mention a concrete figure. Say one million. From there, it should be much easier. We can plan to settle at around one-point-five million. Which," he added dryly, "will make one of the highest kidnap premiums ever paid."

She was looking at him with dark, haunted eyes. "He sounded so . . . adamant."

De Córdoba felt how much she was depending on him, trusting him. "The question is how much they expect," he said gently. "The going rate, as it were, is between a quarter and half a million dollars. They will have known that before they started. The ten-million figure is an opening bid. I told you that when we first began. Didn't I?"

"Yes."

"It's important—for Eden's sake—that you sound plausible. They have to believe there is no more money."

She nodded. "He still hasn't mentioned her addiction. What does it mean?"

"Perhaps she has been through the withdrawal syndrome without his noticing."

"Could he be so blind?"

"She might have been able to hide it from him."

He saw Mercedes's eyes swim suddenly. She raised a shaky hand to cover them, but was too late to prevent his seeing the tears spill out and slide down her cheeks.

"Please. Mercedes . . ." He touched her arm. Then, when she did not resist, he drew her gently to him. He did not pat her shoulder or stroke her hair. He just held her lightly, feeling his own heart leap and quiver at the closeness of her, the warmth of her body. She wept silently, her forehead touching his chest. He could hear the little choking sounds in her throat. "Her voice was recorded," he said quietly. "In all probability faked."

"It was Eden's voice. The pain was real."

He had felt the same thing, but he shook his head. "It will have been engineered somehow." Again, he tried to inject confidence into his voice. It was not difficult. Holding her like this, with the dark, scented cloud of her hair touching his cheek, he felt tenderness swimming in his veins, as though he were a schoolboy. *A sixty-three-year-old schoolboy*, he jeered at himself. *You old fool, are you falling in love?* But his self-mockery was not bitter.

"You must try not to let it upset you. You must try and get back your self-command."

"It's my fault," he heard her whisper. "My fault."

"Of course it isn't."

"But it is. It is."

He released her and gave her his handkerchief. "That isn't logical, Mercedes. You're not to blame for Eden's kidnapping, any more than for her addiction."

"You don't know me," she said in a voice that throbbed. She dried her eyes. Her face was strained. She looked suddenly old. "You don't know what my life has been."

He was nonplussed. "Of course, we all have our dark side . . ."

"Not all of us are evil."

Despite her emotion, he was tempted to smile. "I cannot believe that you have been evil, Mercedes."

"Believe it," she said quietly. She crushed the handkerchief in her fingers. "I have been many things. Perhaps now I am being asked to pay for what I have been. I will pay. I will pay. I am just terrified that Eden will have to pay the final price, rather than I."

He felt a shadow cross his mind. "Are you saying this man knows you personally? That he's connected with you in some way?"

"I don't know. I can't think. But anything is possible."

"He said he knew how you had made the money. He implied . . . something. What did he mean by that?"

For a moment he thought she was going to answer him. Then she shook her head. "Not now," she said.

"I hold many secrets, Mercedes. If there is something I don't know, something that affects Eden, you should tell me now."

"It doesn't affect Eden," she said. "I will tell you, but not tonight. Later. I've had enough tonight. I'm going to bed, Joaquin."

De Córdoba nodded reluctantly. Her face, lined with weariness and stained with tears, seemed to him more seductive than he had ever seen it. He did not focus on the signs of age and grief. Instead, he felt the immense privilege of having been permitted to hold her, to see her tears. He felt as though he had been admitted to a magic and secret presence, allowed to touch the unicorn.

"Sleep well," he said, stooping. He had intended to kiss her cheek, but she must have moved her face, because their mouths met. He felt her lips, soft and warm, against his. Something swelled in his heart, something at once painful and sweet. Then she turned and walked quickly from his room.

Had it been accidental? Deliberate? The memory of her mouth was alive on his.

He went mechanically back to the bed, not allowing himself to think about her. There was nothing to think about in any case, only his own unruly flesh. Her scent remained on him. It seemed to be spinning a web around him, trapping him in something silky and stuporous.

He played the tape again, listening carefully to the voices.

"What kind of woman *are* you?

"I know more about you than you can possibly imagine.

"Don't plead poverty with me, you bitch."

As before, the hatred in the voice was conspicuous. And as before, he noted the plethora of I's and me's. De Córdoba had a recurrence of that sick feeling at the pit of his stomach. If this was a private vendetta, something arranged to harvest pain, rather than money, then all his experience and knowledge would be useless.

In fact, the more he interfered, the worse he would make things. He could only do harm.

He poured himself a small whisky and drank it reflectively. Mercedes was hiding much from him. He felt that, increasingly. Perhaps it was time for him to confront her. Demand that she share her private suspicions, her private knowledge with him. And then, if he felt he was in over his head, he should withdraw discreetly and hand over to someone else.

He swirled the drink. He thought of how her body had felt in his arms. The warm pressure of that soft mouth against his. Sixty-three, he thought suddenly, is not so old, after all. She is only a few years younger than I.

The direction of his thoughts brought a wry smile to his mouth. How absurd he was. How foolish to let fantasy creep into this comfortable, masculine room. Yet he knew he could not leave her, not when she needed him so much.

He turned in. Later, back in his shallow sleep, he heard her voice again. *Not all of us are evil.*

Tucson

Half a mile away, a cloud of dust hung in the desert air. He went out onto the porch, lifting his hand to shade his eyes. A car was moving along the dirt road towards the house.

He watched the cloud of dust drawing closer.

He was naked to the waist, wearing only faded denims and trainers. He thought about getting the gun, then dismissed the idea. He just had to stay calm.

He caught sight of the car at last, a cream Cadillac Eldorado. He felt anger lurch into his throat. It was Hattersley, the fast food man. He awaited his arrival with clenched fists.

The big limousine pulled up in front of the house, and Keith Hattersley got out, greying, tall and paunchy. He was dressed in cords, hand-tooled boots and a denim shirt with pearl buttons. A blond woman got out on the other side. She was much younger than Hattersley, who was in his fifties. A pneumatic bosom pushed against her open-necked shirt. Her haunches filled her jeans tightly. She, too, wore expensive boots.

Hattersley took a Stetson off the backseat, put it on and grinned engagingly. "Well, hi there, Joel boy. Ain't it a scorcher?"

"It's hot," he acknowledged briefly.

"See ya dressed for the weather. Showing off your physique, hey?" Hattersley led the young woman up the porch, one hand placed familiarly on her buttocks. "This is my friend Lilah. Lilah, meet Joel Lennox, one of the finest young artists we've produced."

He probably meant it to flatter. It sounded as though he was exhibiting Lennox as his own invention. The blond gave him a wide-eyed smile. She had pert features with a big, soft mouth. Her name was picked out in gold letters on a chain around her neck. He briefly took the small soft hand she put out, saying nothing to her.

"Thought we'd stop by and take a look at the work in progress," Hattersley said jovially.

He chose the words carefully. "I only show my work when it's finished. Not before. You know that."

Hattersley shrugged. "Well, sure. To the *public*, sure. But I'm the patron here. I guess that gives me a special privilege."

The man had come up here with his mistress to show off a little, play the generous Mycænas. Joel did not look at either of them. "It's not ready to be seen yet."

Hattersley glanced at the blond, then at Lennox. "Come on, Joel boy," he said, still smiling. "Are you telling me I don't even get a peek at it before payday?"

"I showed you the drawings, Mr. Hattersley."

"Yeah, but the drawings ain't the real thing, Joel. I'd like to cast my eyes over the actual carving. Where is it, out back in the shed?"

Lennox didn't move. The blond spoke in a little-girl drawl. "Keith, honey, maybe we should come back when Mr. Lennox is ready to show the piece."

"The builders are gonna be ready for that stone in a couple of weeks. I want to take a look at it."

"I don't think it's a good idea."

"For who? For me or for you? I'm paying five thousand bucks for that piece of stone," Hattersley said in a hectoring tone. "I already gave you two thousand down, boy. I think that gives me the right to take a look at it. Yes, I should damn well think it does. Why, supposing I don't like it?"

Joel had to unclench his teeth to speak. "If you don't like it, you don't buy it, Mr. Hattersley."

"Bullshit," Hattersley retorted. He wasn't smiling any more. "Don't be a horse's ass. I want to look at that stone. Right now. You hear me?"

"Yes, I hear you."

"Well, come on, then."

Lennox thought about driving his fist into the other man's face. Kicking him on the ground. Saw the blood spurting from the fleshy nose, an overripe tomato under his heel . . .

Lilah was still smiling easily, either too vapid to feel the tension, or rather enjoying it. Her eyes were travelling around his naked torso unconcernedly, lingering on the scars.

Lennox forced the violent images to fade. He couldn't lose control, not over something as trivial as this.

Show him the stone, get him out of here.

"It's in the shed," he said heavily, turning to lead the way.

Having won his point, Hattersley was all smiles again. He

patted the girl's rump as they walked around the back of the house. "Designed this house himself," Lennox heard him tell Lilah. "Built it with his own hands too. Some job, hey?"

"You built this place yourself?" she asked him, stopping. He nodded. She gazed at the low, elegant lines of the house. "All the carpentry, everything?"

"Uh-huh," he grunted, quickening his stride so they had to hurry after him.

In the cool of the shed, he drew the canvas off the carving and stood back. Hattersley and Lilah moved in and studied it eagerly. There was a silence. "Well," Hattersley said. "Well."

"I don't think you need worry about your five thousand dollars, Keith," the girl observed at last.

"Don't think I do," Hattersley agreed. The man's face was greedy. "It's superb."

"Yes," she nodded, "it's superb."

"It's going in the wall, next to the main fireplace." Hattersley began sketching in the air with his fat hands. "There's a narrow window right beside it, to give some side light, pick it out. In winter, when the fire's lit, you'll be able to sit there, watch the firelight play over it. It'll be sensational. Sensational."

The blond wasn't listening. She had turned from the carving to gaze at Lennox. She had a way of looking at him that was unselfconscious, yet somehow disturbing. Her eyes drifted from the hawk-like, moustached face to the forearms folded across his chest, veined and muscled. She studied the width of his shoulders, the taut, scarred waist. She looked at his crotch. At the long, lean legs in the faded denims. Then she smiled directly at him. She had a slow, pretty smile. It showed pink gums and a lot of white teeth.

Lennox didn't smile back. He wondered how anyone kept such white skin in an Arizona summer. She must live indoors.

"Look at all this stuff." Hattersley gestured at the wealth of carving lying around the shed. "This boy has talent, real talent. Guess I must be one of your best customers, right, Joel?"

"You've bought a lot of my work," Lennox acknowledged in a quiet voice.

"Damn right, and it ain't cheap, neither." Hattersley chuckled. He took Lilah's arm and led her on a tour of the workshop, greedy eyes darting among the stones. "Look at that nude. And that horse's head. Great work. Is that for sale?"

"No, it's not."

"Beats me why you don't open yourself a gallery downtown, boy. You'd clean up. Long as you kept shop with a shirt on."

"Maybe he'd do better with his shirt off," the blond murmured.

"That thing there, that kind of animal, what's that, mythological? Some Navaho thing?"

Lennox nodded.

"Is that for sale?"

"No."

"Damn. I like that thing. Pay you top dollar."

Again, he tried to unclench his teeth. "It isn't for sale."

The blond squeezed Hattersley's arm. "Maybe Mr. Lennox doesn't want us wandering around his studio, Keith. You've seen your carving. Let's not trespass."

"Are we trespassing?" Hattersley asked Lennox. "Yeah, look at his face. He wants us out. When he gets that mean look, he could almost scare you, couldn't he?"

"Yes, he could," Lilah said, watching Lennox. "He has a ruthless face. I wonder whether he has a ruthless character?"

"Ruthless?" the other chuckled. "You ask Uncle Ho whether that boy's ruthless."

"Did you get those wounds in Vietnam?" Lilah asked him.

"You're looking at an authentic hero," Hattersley said. "Killed, how many, more'n twenty of them, right?"

"So those are battle wounds." She reached out and laid her finger gently on the star-shaped scar just under his ribs. The flesh flinched, like a nervous horse's. "That must've hurt."

"Came back with a chest full of medals," Hattersley said. "America ought to have gave him a hero's welcome. Instead, the kids spat on him. Didn't they, Joel, boy?"

Lennox felt the blood pounding in his temples. His vision was blurred, stained with red. They had to go, *now*, before he exploded. He replaced the tarpaulin, trying to keep his hands steady, then silently held the door open for them to leave.

As she passed him, the blond brushed against him. He knew it was deliberate. He felt a soft breast yield against his arm. Again, his flesh jerked involuntarily.

He locked the shed and walked with them to the Cadillac.

"I guess a drink's out of the question?" Hattersley said, making a joke of it.

"Sometime when I'm not working," Lennox replied. His voice was tight in his throat.

The blond was looking around at the rocky hills, the cacti, the low adobe house. "You live in a beautiful place, Mr. Lennox," she said. "You have a beautiful home. And you have a wonderful talent."

He looked back at her without speaking. Her features were out of focus.

"Come on, honey," Hattersley called. He got into the Cadillac and started the engine.

Lilah stayed put. Her blue eyes were on his. "I'd like to come back sometime," she told Lennox in her babyish voice, "when you're in a better mood. Can I do that?"

He looked away, not trusting himself to speak.

"I think you're very special." She looked at his body, seeing the muscles that were rigid and strained. He saw her pupils darken, then contract again. "Keith's not special," she said softly. "He just wants to be. He likes you a lot. Don't be angry with him." She offered him her hand. He didn't take it. Apparently unoffended, she walked over and got in the car.

Hattersley backed up in a cloud of dust and roared away from the house, honking his horn. Lennox caught a glimpse of the girl's face looking back at him through the rear window.

He went back into the house once the dust had drifted high into the cloudless sky. He looked around the sparsely-furnished room. He was trembling. The rage was in him. It swelled his muscles, churned in his gut.

He felt something rise up his trachea, choking him. The heat did that to you. Not the dry heat of Arizona, but the moist, fetid heat of Asia. It suffocated you, like rotten ooze smothering your mouth.

Something buzzed past his ear suddenly, a fly, maybe just a distant noise. He flinched wildly away from it.

Joel clenched his teeth, hearing the breath hiss through his nose. His skin was bathed in sweat. It dripped down his chest, slid across his ribs.

It was time to feed the girl.

He tried to get himself under control.

•   •   •

She was sleeping so soundly that she did not even stir as he opened
the door of the cell. He put the tray down and stared at her. She
lay on her back, her head on one side, her face to the wall. Asleep,
she looked like a child.

He turned his head on one side to study her better. She had
evidently washed herself. She smelled a great deal better. She wore
only her pants and T-shirt. Her bare legs were thin and white.
There seemed to be no flesh on her. Her arms were outstretched,
the chain linking them to the headboard.

Which one of us, he wondered wryly, is the greater prisoner?

His gaze dropped to her naked thighs. Then he frowned in
puzzlement and bent forward.

Eden stirred and opened her eyes dreamily. He reached out,
his fingers biting into her thigh.

"What the hell is that?" he demanded.

The girl rolled away from him swiftly. She lunged at the sheet
and dragged it over her body. He jerked at it roughly. It was cheap
cotton and it tore apart with a long rip. She shrank back against
the wall and swung her knees up to her chest, clamping them there
so he couldn't see. He reached for her. For a moment they wrestled
fiercely. But she had no strength to match his. He easily pulled
her hands out from around her thighs.

"What the hell is it?" he repeated.

He held her down, his finger tracing the scars on her ankles,
behind her knees, across her thighs. Then he knew.

"Needle marks," he whispered. "Those are track marks, aren't
they?"

She didn't answer. As soon as he released her, she grabbed
the sheet and dragged it up over herself.

He straightened, feeling numb. "It wasn't a disease after all,"
he said. "It was drugs."

"No," she choked.

"Yes. You've been going through cold turkey. That's what's
been making you sick."

She shook her head. But the big green eyes were staring with
guilt and fear.

"Why the fuck didn't you tell me?" He heard himself screaming at her. "You bitch!" He lashed at her face, open-handed, and

saw the blow drive her head to one side. A line of blood appeared between her lips. "I thought you were dying!"

"I *am* dying!"

"Bullshit," he shouted. "Nobody dies of cold turkey."

"What do you know about it?" she spat at him, her eyes blurred with tears. "I need a doctor! I need *help*!"

He reached out and grasped her thighs. She shrank into a ball again. He leaned down and peered at the marks on her legs.

He touched the raised weals with his finger. "How long have you been hooked?" he demanded. "Five years?"

"A year," she said through gritted teeth. She was trying to cover herself with her thin arms.

"Liar." She flinched, as though expecting another blow. "How the hell could you do this to yourself in only a year? Stick a dozen needles into yourself at once? You're a junkie!"

"Leave me alone," she quavered. She clamped her hands protectively between her thighs, shrinking from him. "Get away from me!"

He understood the gesture. "You think I want to rape you? You think I would touch you with a ten foot pole?" he demanded incredulously. His voice was shaking. "You're disgusting. Look at you. Like a shrivelled up little frog."

Then the girl seemed to explode. She raised herself on her arms, screaming curses at him, hurling expletives at him with a rage that sobered him.

"Who the hell are you to sneer at me?" she screamed. "You're the one who's sick! You're sick in your head! You wouldn't be doing this if you weren't sick!"

"Shut your mouth!"

"Fuck off!" She was like some small, feral animal with blazing eyes and bared teeth. "You're insane," she screamed. "You're sick, can't you see that? You're crazy!"

He grasped at her. She clawed at his face frantically, her nails tearing at the eyes behind the black holes. Her fingers scrabbled at the material. She felt it rip.

And then she had pulled the hood right off, and was staring into his face.

She saw the hawk visage; saw the dark moustache and the bony cheeks. The dark, curly hair. The black eyes that glittered into her own.

The day in Laurel Canyon came flooding back to her. The man who had pulled her from her horse.

She drew back, appalled. "Oh, Christ," she whispered. "You!"

His face convulsed with fury. He grasped her hair. The wrenching shock swung her around, facing the wall. She clung to the steel frame of the bed. He slammed her down on her face, pinning her to the bed. He was breathing harshly. She could smell him, male and acrid. She knew suddenly that death was inches away.

"I swear to God it was an accident," she said desperately. "Whoever you are, I won't tell!"

He held her like that, it seemed, for an age. Then he abruptly released her.

"I won't tell," she said, not looking around. Her eyes were tight shut. "They'll never know I saw your face, I swear they won't! I'll keep it a secret!"

She heard the door crash shut.

11.

⟶ Sacred Heart

march 1938

Barcelona

The children are harder to bear than anything else.

Mercedes has not wept for months. She is no longer squeamish.

But now, after sixteen air raids in two days, it is the children who make her cry.

Sometimes they have wounds she cannot bear to look at, and scream like rabbits while they are treated, unbearably. Sometimes they are stoical beyond belief, huge eyes staring at the doctors in silence while their flesh is spoiled by steel and thread.

Often they are brought into Sagrado Corazón Hospital naked and unmarked. But they are quite dead. Killed by the blast, as the doctors tell her, their small organs pulped inside their bodies. So small, so innocent, so limp, they emerge from the fallen masonry with open eyes and open mouths, limbs dangling like the limbs of rag dolls.

There is a terrible wrongness about those bodies. There is a terrible wrongness about the women who scream like animals over them, on their knees, hands clasped in futile prayer.

She is sobbing steadily as she leaves the ward, but no one tries to comfort her. They know how she feels about the children. Others are crying too.

The systematic pounding of the city with high explosives has reduced everyone and everything to exhaustion. She is so tired. There are too many people to deal with.

Women with babies and children queue for bread in the streets. Meat is unobtainable, even horse. People do not shrink from eating dogs or cats. Along the Ramblas, men sit selling the tarry tobacco they have extracted from discarded butts.

How has the republic held out so long? Franco is better-armed this year than ever. Better organized and better-financed, he finds victory just eluding his grasp. But not for long.

By the end of this month, the nationalists will sweep through Aragón towards the sea, finally cutting the republic in half. Soon, only the two great cities, Madrid and Barcelona, will remain, crammed with refugees and starved of food. And then they too, will fall.

Though six months of hard fighting remain, the end is clearly in sight. Everyone knows it. In the meantime, Mussolini's bombers drone over Barcelona.

The distant thudding began, an irregular heartbeat that could be felt through the floor of the basement.

Mercedes met the eyes of the soldier opposite her. They were a deep, clear green, and they were staring at her with a directness that disturbed her.

She looked away. Forty people had crowded into the basement. Many were strangers who had come in off the street. The others were her fellow-tenants, many in their dressing-gowns at this hour of the morning. Faces were drawn. No one spoke.

She could feel those green eyes still on her. Despite herself, her gaze was drawn back to the man. He was very handsome. Dark brows, rocky cheekbones and a thrusting chin gave him a bold, animal beauty. He wore a thick moustache, clipped above a wide mouth that was now smiling at her, showing white teeth. She saw the Stars and Stripes pinned to his black leather jacket. An American volunteer. Another film star here to posture at war against a Spanish backdrop.

She looked away without answering his smile.

The thudding seemed to be drawing closer. "Don't worry,"

the superintendent said loudly, "we're quite safe in here. Snug as bugs, aren't we?"

"They've been coming every three hours for two days," an old woman quavered. "Maybe this is the last time."

"Why should it be?" an old man asked dryly. "They'll keep coming back until some air cover arrives."

"Or until they run out of bombs, which is more likely," someone else commented.

There was a particularly loud explosion. A woman screamed. Dust drifted down from the beams.

Mercedes looked up. She could hear a sound up in the foyer. She strained her ears to catch it again.

There it was. A thin voice calling something. The voice of a child.

"There's a child in the foyer," she exclaimed.

Everyone looked up. "I don't hear anyone," the superintendent said.

"There's a child up there," she repeated.

"You're hearing things."

"There is!" Mercedes had been squatting by the boiler, her back to the wall. Now she rose to her feet. She pushed her way through the crowded cellar towards the door.

The American soldier opposite spoke to her in accented Spanish. "Where the hell are you going?"

"I'm going to bring her down."

"You can't go upstairs." He grasped her arm in strong fingers. "The bombers are nearly overhead."

She pulled her arm free and ran up the winding flight of stairs. But the hallway of the apartment block was empty and dark. There was no sign of the child. Maybe she *had* been hearing things.

The explosions were much louder now. Mercedes felt the floor vibrate. A giant was striding across the city on leaden feet. She thought of the bloodstained bundles in the hospital. She went outside.

The street was deserted. Cars had been abandoned, some with doors left open. Along the sidewalk, a row of linden trees were coming into leaf. It was cold and windy.

Then, a hundred yards up the street, she saw the little figure, skipping. Skipping, as though the holocaust were not sweeping in on silent wings.

Who could have forgotten her out here? Where were her parents? Hiding. Dead, perhaps.

Mercedes cursed violently and started running after the child. The child hopped in a clumsy way, first on one leg, then on the other, the rope swinging over her pigtailed head. She was singing.

"Little girl!" Mercedes shouted as she ran. "Come! Come here!"

The child heard her at last. She stopped and turned. Her eyes widened at the sight of Mercedes coming towards her.

"Here!" Mercedes called. "Come!"

There was an explosion, so close that the shock wave thumped Mercedes and the ground jumped underfoot. Smoke was rising over the rooftops. Suddenly the child started running in the opposite direction.

"God damn!"

Mercedes gave chase. Her longer legs gave her the advantage, but the child seemed to flutter along on the wind. She rounded a corner and was gone.

The giant was drawing closer.

Mercedes came to the corner and swung around it, her heart pounding.

Suddenly, over the rooftops, she saw a group of black crosses floating against the sky.

Another group followed behind it, surreal.

She searched the street frantically. There, thank God. The little girl was only a few feet away, crouching beside a tree. Mercedes darted forward. The child's face stared up, white and vacant. Mercedes suddenly saw the slant eyes and moon face of mongolism. The child was retarded. That was why no one cared. She snatched the little body up and went back round the corner.

The child was unbelievably heavy. She clung to Mercedes's neck, her legs dangling around Mercedes's hips. Mercedes desperately wanted to stop for breath, but dared not.

A sense of doom was filling her. Her lungs burned. She fought onward.

There was a sudden glare of ochre light. Heat seared her. She felt that she was in slow motion as a vast sound crushed her chest, swept her off her feet.

She lay on the pavement, her back numb, surprised to find that she was not dead. Everything was fragmented. Things were raining down on her. She tried to cover her face with her arms. Her ears roared and sang, but in her mind was silence.

Through a fog of swirling black smoke, she saw the child. She staggered towards her. She was alive and screaming, her knees and hands bloody.

Half the street seemed to be blocked with debris. Mercedes gathered the child in her arms. She began plodding ahead, her refuge impossibly far away. Her back ached and her head had been cut.

She was thinking of a long-ago day in the forge, of a coin that seared her palm, of pain that filled her mind with red light. The child was so heavy. She had to fight against the dreamy unreality that she knew came from shock.

Then she saw someone running towards her, shouting furiously. It was the American volunteer. She couldn't make out what he was saying, but she was glad to see him.

He took the child out of her arms and dragged her down the street towards the tall building. She stumbled and tottered, her strength and breath almost gone. His fingers dug into her arm painfully. The breath sobbed agonizingly in her throat.

They made the shelter of the foyer. Mercedes was faint and sick and wanted to vomit. She felt the American's fingers wind around her hair and pull tight.

"You maniac," he shouted at her as he dragged her down the stairs. "You mad bitch. You crazy *puta*."

She tried to fend him off. He cursed her unremittingly in a hoarse voice until he ran out of breath and they tumbled down the last stairs to the basement.

People screamed as they burst in, covered with dust and blood. Someone took the child, whose eyes were glazed with shock, but who had nothing worse than grazes on her hands and knees.

"They're right overhead," the American gasped. "An apartment building just down the road took a direct hit."

"Which one?"

"A tall one, on the corner of the square."

"Thank God, no one is in there, now. It was evacuated last night."

The ground was rumbling and shaking under the pounding of the high explosives. The American and Mercedes collapsed beside the boiler. The American put his arm around her shoulders. She pushed him violently away.

She had never been closer to death than up there. But she could not stop thinking about the coin and the day she learned that her father was not her father.

She touched the cut on her head. It was sticky with blood and starting to swell. Her hair was gritty with dust. Her brain throbbed.

The child started screaming again. She wanted her mother. The giant was stamping around outside. Each time he brought his foot down, a building was crushed, a street disembowelled. If he stamped too close, their own building would collapse and their cellar would become a mass tomb. A woman took the child in her arms and comforted her, but she continued to cry.

After the raid, the crowd milled aimlessly in the street, marvelling at the chaos of rubble and exclaiming at the sharp smell of explosives in the air. There was an almost jolly air of mutual congratulation, which Mercedes knew well. They had survived. Nobody was dead.

Hundreds of windows had been broken, despite the shutters. The street glittered with broken glass. Near the bombed building, a tram lay pathetically on its side.

Mercedes's head pounded. She felt bruised and feeble. As she turned to go back into the building, there was a touch on her shoulder. The American soldier had come up to her.

"I'm sorry I called you names," he said, in his accented Spanish. He kissed her on the cheek, his moustache prickly against her skin.

In the light, his eyes were greener than ever, startling against his brown skin and black hair. She wiped her cheek roughly. "You pulled half my hair out," she said, glaring at him.

"I'm sorry about that too," he said. "I apologize from the bottom of my heart." He reached out. "You've got a cut on your head. Let me take a look."

She avoided his hands. "I'm all right," she snapped

"It looks nasty," he said in concern. "You might have a concussion."

"I can deal with it."

"You should wash it."

"I am going to."

The American laughed quietly. He had the white teeth of a tiger. Her eyes brightened with anger. "What are you laughing at?"

"The thought of myself, running around looking for you, with the whole Italian air force dropping bombs on us."

Despite herself, her frown eased. "Well. Thank you for coming for me," she said grudgingly.

"Are you sure you're all right?" he asked.

She nodded and without further answer, left him standing in the street.

Her apartment was on the fifth floor. No one used the beautiful panelled elevator after bombardments. It was a long climb.

The apartment was not large, but had once possessed considerable grace. Like the other wealthy families in this block, the tenants had left for France at the beginning of the war. The Central Committee had requisitioned the whole building. Mercedes was meant to share the apartment with two other nurses, but the apartment's population was a floating one, and for the time being she had the whole place to herself, with its marble bathroom, its echoing, parquet-floored *salón* and its cut-glass chandeliers.

There was almost no furniture in the place apart from the huge four-poster bed, which must have been too heavy to carry. There were some ornate iron chairs from the balcony, and in niches, various white marble busts of blank-eyed women.

The rest was white space. Mercedes loved it. The superintendent ensured that there was abundant hot water, a precious commodity in wartime Barcelona, and the view across the park was beautiful.

She examined the cut in the mirror and decided that it wouldn't need a suture. She washed it carefully and took two aspirins for the headache. Her back was going to be bruised where she had fallen. The American had been right, she decided. She had been crazy to run out into the street in the middle of an air raid. By now she'd learned about the folly of heroism. Her judgement must have been warped by tiredness and the memory of those dead children.

She'd have to walk to Sagrado Corazón this morning. There would be no public transport. And there was nothing for breakfast. She felt light-headed. She washed herself and went downstairs.

The American was standing in the street outside, towering over the group of men he was talking to. To her annoyance, he walked across to intercept her.

"Hello again," he greeted her. She merely nodded. He moved into her path, stopping her. "My name is Sean O'Keefe. Sometimes people call me Juan. It's the same thing." He was holding out his hand. She took it reluctantly. It was big and rough. "I'm in the International Brigades," he told her. "I've just gotten back from Aragón. I've been trying to find some friends I used to know, but they've gone. Nobody can tell me where they are. I don't know where I'll get a place to sleep tonight."

"Go to the railway station. They'll give you a blanket on the floor."

"That's a terrible idea. You live in that apartment block, am I right?"

"Yes."

"Maybe your family would have a room they could rent me for a week or two?"

"No."

"Really? Why not just ask them—"

"I live alone," she said shortly.

"No family?"

"Not here."

He looked surprised. "All alone in Barcelona, in these times? That's rough. You ought to have someone to take care of you."

"I have to go," she told him. "Goodbye."

He started walking at her side, looming over her. "Where are you going, *guapa?*"

"I'm not your *guapa*," she said coldly.

"What's your name, then?"

"Mercedes Eduard," she admitted reluctantly.

"So where are you going, Mercedes Eduard?"

"To Sagrado Corazón."

"You're a nurse?"

"Yes."

"Good for you." He took her arm familiarly. The gesture was common enough these days, even between strangers, but with him it had a possessive quality that made her bristle. She pulled her arm free from the insistent grip. "If you're trying to pick me up, you're wasting your time."

When he smiled, two sets of lines curved into the handsome face, one coming down from the corners of the green eyes, another set curving up from the deeply cut mouth.

"You think I came all the way from West Virginia to pick up skinny little Spanish girls like you?"

"I'm not Spanish. I am Catalán." As an afterthought, she added, "And I'm not skinny."

"Yes you are."

They looked at one another. He was tall and strongly made. His bare brown throat was sinewy and his shoulders pulled the leather jacket tight. The hand that held the sling of his rifle was veined and muscular.

Beside him, she was definitely slight. Two years of war had pared every ounce of superfluous flesh from her. Her face had lost the round softness of eighteen. But she was strikingly beautiful. She had a dark and sombre loveliness that was making this American volunteer devour her with his eyes.

She was not too unworldly to interpret his stare accurately.

"This is a stupid conversation," she said. "I have to get back to the hospital."

"The Lenin barracks is in that direction. I may as well go there. I'll walk with you."

She quickened her step, but he kept at her side.

They turned right at the corner and walked towards the old centre. There was little motor traffic. A fire engine clanged by, on its way from one fire to the next.

Whoever had loved this vivacious city in the summer of 1936 would have wept to see it now, silent and bowed. Barcelona was in rags, gaunt with weariness and hunger.

The bombing had been monstrously destructive. She was choked with grief.

"They're using a new type of bomb," he observed casually. "They must have delayed action fuses. They seem to go through the roof, and down through a dozen floors before they detonate. Take the whole building out. Very effective."

"Yes," she agreed bitterly, "very."

"What you did, saving that child—that was one of the craziest things I've seen, Mercedes."

"You were crazy to come for me," she replied shortly.

"There's something about cowering in a cellar, like a rat, that gets on your nerves. I was cursing you. Calling you every kind of name. When that big one went off, I couldn't stand it any more. I just shot out. It looked like the end of the world. I thought the next one would fall right on me, for sure. By the time I found you I wasn't in a very good mood."

"You called me a whore and a crazy bitch."

"The kid was wrong in the head, after all that. A loony."

"What difference does that make?"

"Makes you a little crazier than me, I guess. However, the child is still alive. You did the right thing. You were very brave."

He studied her profile. She said nothing.

"When you ran out of that basement," he went on, "I felt sick. There was something about you I couldn't get out of my mind. You had a desperate look. As though you'd stopped caring about yourself. I didn't want you to die."

They had reached a big intersection. She pointed down the street. "The barracks is down that road and to the left. Goodbye."

"Mercedes—"

But she was already running away from him, towards Sagrado Corazón. She felt his eyes on her back, but this time he didn't try to follow her.

Sagrado Corazón was a small hospital which had been run by nuns until the nuns had been driven away. It was now officially called the V.I. Lenin Infirmary, but the old name stuck. It took the overflow from the huge General Hospital down the street, and had specialist pediatric and maxillofacial units. Both kinds of nursing were technically and emotionally demanding.

By early evening it was clear that the intense bombardment had stopped for the time being. The faces around her were empty with exhaustion. At least the hospital had not been hit. Some people said that was because of the huge red cross they had painted on the roof, but Mercedes knew it wasn't. It was random chance.

She found herself thinking of the American volunteer with the green eyes. Why had he come? Why had any of them come to shed their blood on Spanish soil?

Ten thousand French. Five thousand Germans. Thousands more English, Americans, Poles, Italians. Swiss, Czechs, Hungarians.

Not sent by their governments, as Hitler and Mussolini had
sent whole armies, but volunteers.

Casualties among them had been dreadfully high. They threw
themselves into battle with the fervour of crusaders. The English,
in particular, had proved themselves lions. Three quarters of them
had already been killed or wounded.

She alone seemed to be unable to appreciate their heroism.

Too many of her dreams had been extinguished with José-
María, Federica, and the rest of them. She had seen too much torn
flesh, too many children's faces twisted in pain.

Others seemed to have a faith that endured. She no longer
had.

She knew that the war was lost. The republic's allies were
abandoning her. Aid had stopped coming. In Gerona, Francesc
was converting lorries and tractors into armoured fighting vehicles.
Ploughshares were being beaten into swords. Betrayed and corrupt, the cause had been abandoned.

She was not part of the movement any more. She could not
share their convictions. She had few friends these days, male or
female. Two years after Matilde, she was still a virgin. Since José-
María, no man had ever come near her. She had wanted to be
alone. And she remained alone.

Had the American found a place for the night? She had been
harsh with him. He'd come to her rescue, after all. She felt guilt
at the way she'd brushed him off.

Her shift ended and she set off home. She was ravenously
hungry and bone-tired.

The evening was cold and windy. She was wearing a jacket
and a knee-length cotton dress, and the icy air whipped her bare
legs. Because of the air raids, there were no streetlights, no lighted
windows. Even the automobiles crept along with no more than a
glimmer of yellow from blinkered headlamps. Barcelona was a city
of darkness.

San Lluc

Francesc arrived home late. Conchita had been waiting for him,
and when she heard his key in the lock, she came downstairs to

meet him. They held one another without speaking in the empty forge.

She could feel his fatigue in the heavy way he leaned against her. He was working himself to death. His face, always grim, had grown gaunter. The bones of his brows and cheeks seemed more prominent. His hair and beard were now all grey. Even the deep blue of his eyes seemed to have faded, like an old shirt that had been washed out too many times.

"You'll feel better after this," she said, putting the food in front of him.

"Have you heard from Mercé?" he asked.

"A letter came this week," she nodded. "And she sent some pictures."

"What does she say?"

"Read it after you've eaten." She reached out and brushed back the hair that hung over his brow. "You look awful, Francesc," she said. "You're killing yourself."

"I'm not dead yet," he grunted.

"Is the work going well?"

"It's impossible to find good men these days. Only clumsy boys and weak old men."

She noticed that there were new cuts on his hands, some of them deep and unhealed. But she said nothing. Though he was supposed to supervise the work of others, she knew that he could not bear to see poor workmanship. He still wrestled with iron and flame, despite his disability, and his fifty-two years.

Alone here, she had nothing but her job at the cork factory, which since the war began had been collectivised, and was run by a workers' committee. She thought of little but Francesc and Mercedes. The war had compelled them each to live their own solitary lives. It was as if their existence as a family had been suspended by the war, as though they had put off their lives to a distant day that all three now knew might never come.

After he had eaten, he read Mercedes's letter. He studied the photographs she had enclosed. One showed her standing with a group of other nurses, wearing white smocks and caps with red crosses. The dark beauty of her face squeezed his heart. He missed her acutely, missed her wild, wayward spirit. He could only guess how much Conchita suffered.

"Mercedes will come back," he said gently. "She is a survivor."

"Even if she survives, she'll never come back to us, Francesc. We've lost her. We lost her a long time ago, when she was still a child."

"She'll fall in love. She'll make a new life with a good man. That's a woman's fate. We would have lost her in any case."

Conchita's face was pensive. "When she got back from the front last year," she said at last, "I thought she might have had someone there. Someone who died. She had that look about her. She never said anything. I just guessed. Did you feel that?"

"I don't have your intuition," he said tiredly. "She just looked exhausted to me."

"Do you think she's still a virgin?" Conchita asked him.

The question made him shrug. "Who knows? She'll be twenty soon. She's grown into a beautiful woman. She'll fall in love," he repeated. "Her youth is her shield. She has enough strength to face what's coming. When it's all over, she'll still have the rest of her life ahead of her. Time to rebuild in."

"But so many horrible things have been done. On both sides. There's so much hate . . ."

"There has always been hate in Spain. It's what we do best."

"That's a terrible thing to say, Francesc." She rose and started clearing the table. "Spain was a good country until this war started! The evil came with politics and giving weapons to barefoot rabble like those animals who killed Matilde."

"It also came with army officers in polished leather boots," he said dryly. "And men who like to ride in Hispano-Suiza limousines."

Sighing, she finished tidying. She made coffee for them both, putting a dash of brandy in his.

He was waiting for her in the bed when she came through, looking more relaxed after his bath. The harsh lines around his mouth and eyes, which made him look so old, had eased slightly. He even had a smile for her.

"Got the energy to make love?"

"I was wondering the same thing about you."

"Get into bed with me and see," he suggested.

She drew the curtains and started to undress. He watched her over his coffee, his eyes warm.

Where time was paring the flesh away from Francesc's body, it was adding curves to hers. Conchita was thirty-eight this year. She was already becoming matronly. Her bosom had filled and rounded. She was growing plump in places that had always been slender before—her hands, her cheeks, her arms.

She felt regret at the disappearance of her girlish figure, but not a great deal. Francesc had never really shed his Victorian preference for full-figured women, and she knew instinctively that he preferred her this way.

He reached for her as she got in beside him and drew her close. She snuggled into him with a little whimper. "It's so good to have you back. I only live for your return. I'm nothing without you. I love you, love you."

He said nothing, just crushed her with his arms. He had never been good at tender words, but he expressed his feelings in other ways. He kissed her gently. She could feel his hunger. She reached down and wrapped her fingers around him. "Have you missed me too?" she whispered, squeezing him.

He groaned, his mouth seeking hers. They kissed with a kind of desperation, cramming the week's loneliness and worry into this wonderful moment. Her full breasts fascinated him, excited him as they had not done when she'd been slenderer.

"My little partridge," he said huskily. "My plump little bird." He cupped the mound of her sex in his hand, feeling her already moist and eager. He caressed the silky-wet folds of her, making her writhe with frantic desire until she could stand it no longer. She clambered over him and sank down onto him, guiding his manhood into her with little gasps of pleasure.

"Oh, that's so good," she murmured, settling down on his loins and resting her hands on his chest. Her eyes were misty. "So good. God, I miss you."

He laced his big hands around her waist and began to rock her gently backwards and forward. She felt him inside her, deep in her body. "So—good," she whispered. "So good . . ."

She stopped talking, her lips parted. Francesc rocked her, watching her eyes close, her cheeks flushing as the pleasure built up in her. He could not find the words to tell her, but these moments were as precious as life itself to him. When all the horror was ended, he vowed, he would make it up to her. They would have time together, an ocean of time in one another's company, with nothing to come between them.

Their lovemaking was the unhurried, skilful affair of people who know each other well. She arched back with a sharp moan that was like a sob. His fingers bit into her hips as he too, came. With vivid intensity he felt the heat and sweetness of their union. The moment endured brightly, then began to fade. She drooped forward against him like a cropped lily, her arms spreading around his neck.

"Francesc, my love, my love..."

He held her, inhaling the clean womanly scent of her hair, marvelling in her presence. Now, as so often at these times, he was aware of wonder at the way she had changed his life. What would he have been now, had Marcel Barrantes not come into the forge that cold autumn evening? She had been a gift from the gods, a golden crown placed on his undeserving head by some kindly deity that forgave sins. He felt himself begin to slacken inside her until he slid out, limp. She smiled at him, as she always did.

Afterward they lay at peace in the dark until sleep came.

Barcelona

At the entrance to her apartment block, Mercedes stopped short. The American was waiting for her.

"You again!"

He smiled. "Me again."

"What are you doing here?" she demanded angrily.

"How would you like a fresh omelet, Mercedes? With some good country ham?" He leaned closer. His deep voice became a husky whisper. "Or maybe a sausage or two? A bottle of good *rioja*? Peaches and cream to follow?"

She stared at him, feeling a physical pain twist her empty maw. "What are you talking about?"

"I'll provide the ingredients if you'll do the cooking."

"You're a liar," she said brusquely. "Where would you get such things in Barcelona?"

For answer, he unslung his knapsack and opened it. The contents clinked. She peered inside suspiciously.

She saw bottles, a loaf of bread, half a ham, several tins and other things wrapped in cloth. He closed the bag again.

"Where did you get all that?" she demanded in astonishment.

"From a good fairy. Is it a deal?"

"You're a black marketeer," she accused him sharply.

He smiled at her and shook his head.

"If you're not a black marketeer, then you're a looter. And the police will shoot you."

"I doubt it. But we're wasting time here and I'm hungry. Let's go and start cooking." He started climbing the stairs. "What floor is it?"

"Stop!"

He paused and turned to her. "Well?" he asked.

"Wait. Let me think." She was pondering fiercely.

"Perhaps we'll have the cheese to follow," he said, watching her. "Or maybe we'll melt some over the omelet."

Her mouth was full of saliva. She had to swallow. She thought of the bag of dried chickpeas that was all she had to eat upstairs. *A real omelet.* She wrestled with herself. The thought of hot food was almost unbearable.

"You can't spend the night in my apartment."

"I still don't have anywhere to sleep, Mercedes."

"You'll find somewhere. You're evidently resourceful enough, Señor West Virginia. I'll cook the food. You leave afterwards." She swallowed saliva again. "Otherwise, nothing."

Their eyes met in the dull light. He was so much bigger than she was. But her face wore an expression that brooked no argument. He sighed. "All right. I'll go afterwards. What floor is it?"

"Fifth," she said, hiding her triumph.

He turned and began climbing again. Her weary legs followed his broad back, and the omelet.

She unlocked the door and let him in. He stepped into the apartment and propped his rifle in one corner. Then he looked around with a long whistle. "This is some place, Mercedes." He wandered around the bare *salón*, admiring the white marble busts. "My God. Is this how the other half lives?" He peered into the other rooms. "A bit bare, though. Where's all the furniture?"

"The owners took it with them."

"You've got this whole place to yourself?"

"For the time being."

"You could accommodate six of me in this mausoleum," he accused.

"I could. But I am not going to." She led him to the kitchen and watched as he emptied the knapsack onto the table. In addition to what she had seen, there were various dried sausages, a dozen eggs wrapped in a newspaper, a bottle of olive oil, bottles of armagnac and red wine, tins of corned beef, sardines, peaches, asparagus. Mercedes was dazed at the sight of so much food. "Where did you get all this, for God's sake?"

The American sniffed a sausage luxuriously. "A friend."

"What kind of friend?"

"Tell you the truth, I hardly know the guy. He works in the U.S. consulate."

"And I suppose you have plenty of American dollars to buy black market goods?"

"Sure. I'm a rich man." He unfolded a clasp-knife and sawed off a round of salami. He held it out to her with his tiger's grin.

She felt giddy. The pain in her belly intensified. She gulped. "It's obscene," she said. "All this food, and people out there starving."

"Yes. Terrible. Want a piece of salami?"

She shook her head. "I'm not going to eat like that, not after all this time." She rolled up her sleeves and started breaking eggs for the omelet.

He lounged against the wall, chewing the salami and watching her. "I hope you're a good cook," he said.

"I'm good enough," she replied. She was almost regretting having given in to his proposal. After two years of constant hunger, this bounty seemed gross. She tried to quell a sense of shame as she prepared the food.

She felt his stare on her. No doubt he was anticipating that she would melt a little once she had drunk and eaten. Well, he was in for a disappointment. And if a full belly gave him any clever ideas after dinner, she thought grimly, she had the means to discourage him. She was not afraid.

He picked up a bottle of wine and started opening it. "Got any glasses?"

"In the cupboard."

He poured two glasses of *rioja* and offered one to her.

Mercedes wiped her hands on her apron and took it. He met her eyes. "To the republic," he said with ironic gaiety, clinking his glass hard against hers. "May it run its next little war better."

The wine was smooth and rich on her tongue. She closed her eyes as she swallowed, feeling the dark glow slide into her belly. When she opened her eyes again, he was still watching her.

"Where are your family, Mercedes?"

"Up north. In Gerona."

"Are they in this war?"

"My father is."

"What does he do?"

"Before the war he was a blacksmith. He's in charge of making armoured cars out of tractors and automobiles."

"Yeah. I've seen those things. Ingenious, but they don't stand up too well to German Panzers."

"We're doing what we can," she replied shortly.

"Sure you are. Got any brothers or sisters?"

"No." She could feel the wine in her veins. She took another gulp and shuddered slightly as it went down. "I've forgotten your name."

"Sean O'Keefe."

"And what brought you to this badly-run little war, all the way from West Virginia?"

The handsome face creased into its beautiful smile. "Youth and impetuosity."

"What battalion are you with?"

"The Líster Battalion."

He said it with pride. It was a crack battalion, led by one of the most successful and charismatic of the Communist generals. She raised a cool eyebrow. "I'm impressed. This is going to be ready in a minute. Can you put some things on the table?"

They ate facing one another, too hungry to talk much. The hot food filled her with a glow she had almost forgotten. The omelet was wonderfully good. It had a taste that was gloriously new, as though hunger had cleansed her palate. They finished off with tinned peaches and condensed milk.

"By God," he sighed, "that feels better. I haven't had a square meal since I got here."

He poured Armagnac into their glasses and they sat watching one another with a kind of replete wariness.

"You haven't answered me. Why did you come to Spain?"

"Same reason as the others. To fight for my convictions."

"Are you a Communist?" she asked him.

"Red hot. Maybe I'm not too precise on the theory. But you don't forget the kind of upbringing I had. It gets kind of ground into your pores."

"I thought everyone in America lived like a king."

He smiled slightly. "You heard about the Great Depression, I imagine? During the Depression I was earning two dollars and fifty cents for a ten-hour day. Cutting coal out of the hills. That's maybe twenty *pesetas*."

"Our coal miners get less money than that."

"We never saw any money." He took out a wallet and extracted a thin disk, which he put in front of her. She picked it up. It was a cheap tin token, stamped M.C.M.C.—25¢.

"Is this money?"

"Company money," he said. "The initials stand for 'Mingo County Mining Corporation.' I got one of them for an hour's work. The only place you could spend it is at the company store. Prices there ran about double what was fair. If you took it to an outside store, you paid a surcharge. So it was only worth maybe fifteen cents." He took the token back and replaced it in his wallet, as if it were a religious medal.

She frowned. "That happens in America?"

He lit a cigar and puffed at it until it was glowing. Through narrowed eyes, he considered the coal. "America isn't all milk and honey. I've been beaten, shot with buckshot, tear-gassed till I went into convulsions. I know what the class-struggle is all about. When I heard what was happening in Spain, I saw I could fight back, legitimately, with a rifle in my hand. I had to come. I had no choice."

She studied the silvery scars on his tanned face. His hands, too, were hardened, the knuckles scarred. He had an animal quality of aggression. A killing look.

She was afraid of him suddenly. She got to her feet and began to clear up. Given what she now knew about him, his tale of a friend at the consulate sounded thin. She wondered exactly how and where he had come by the food.

"It's getting late," she said curtly.

"You're turning me out?"

"I need my sleep."

He puffed smoke lazily. "And here I was thinking my sob story had touched your heart."

"It did. But now you must go."

He leaned back, smiling at her with those deep eyes. He was really very handsome. And like some very handsome men, he had an air of laughing confidence, a tantalizing sureness of himself.

"And what if I've decided to stay the night, after all?"

"I don't think you will."

He toyed with the glass, still smiling at her. "How would you set about evicting me, Mercedes?"

Mercedes didn't answer. She put the plates in the sink and began to wash them.

He rose and came up behind her. She felt his arm slide around her waist. Her heart lurched and she tried to pull free. But he was too strong. His body was iron-hard with muscle. It cost him little effort to draw her against him. He was smiling into her eyes. "I'm not going to hurt you," he murmured. "You're a lovely woman, Mercedes. You shouldn't be alone..."

"Let me go!" She turned her face away frantically. His lips touched her temple gently. With his free hand he was caressing her hair. The delicacy of his touch was belied by the steely strength in the arm that was wrapped around her waist, immobilizing her. One hard thigh pinned her against the sink. She was panting, her heart racing with fear and anger. She couldn't get her hand to her pocket.

His mouth closed on hers. His lips were hot. His breath smelled of brandy and cigars. He kissed her lightly at first, then with increasing passion. She felt his tongue begin to probe her lips and her head spun.

With a fierce effort, she broke free and fought away from his restraining arm. She dug into her pocket and dragged out the little pistol.

She pointed it at him with both hands, gasping for air. She saw his eyes widen slightly. He grew very still.

"Is that thing loaded, Mercedes?"

"Yes, it is," she panted. She pulled back the hammer. "And the safety is off." The gun was a woman's weapon, as neat and deadly as a little black snake. Though it trembled in her hands, she kept it aimed at his heart.

"Well, I'll be damned," he said softly. There was a glint in his eyes that was almost like amusement, though she had never seen a man laugh in the face of a loaded gun before.

"Get out of here!" she ordered.

He shook his head regretfully. "No. I guess you're going to have to shoot me."

"What?" she gasped.

"Here I am and here I stay." He picked up his cigar and blew on the coal. "I'm not moving."

"Get out of here!"

He shook his dark head. "No, I believe I'll face the bullet."

"I'm not joking," she snapped, her voice rising. "I'll use this. I mean it."

"I've been shot at before," he commented mildly. "Just make it quick."

"Go!"

"No."

Her fingers tightened around the knurled grip. Her heart was still racing. For a moment she considered firing a shot past him. But there was something massive about his presence, something that forbade histrionics. She met his eyes. In their green depths lay both mockery and challenge. She couldn't pull the trigger, not even to try and scare him. Unbelievably, he was outfacing her, despite the pistol in her hand.

Then he seemed to surge at her, one hand clamping around her gun-wrist. He spun her around. His arm clamped around her throat, robbing her of breath. She gagged helplessly, her windpipe crushed under the hard muscle. The blood roared in her ears.

He wrenched the pistol away and released her.

"Don't you ever point a weapon at me again," she heard him say, through her rasping breaths. "Don't you do it, Mercedes. I ought to paddle your backside for pulling a trick like that." He grasped her chin hard and tilted her face up to his. "You use pretty extreme measures to defend your virtue," he said grimly. "I don't find that kind of thing very funny."

She pulled away from him and went to the sink to get a drink of water. There was bile in her throat. Sean O'Keefe watched her as she drank painfully.

He took the ammunition clip out of the gun and ejected the

round from the breech. Then he tossed the hardware onto the table and walked over to her.

She shrank back from him. "Don't touch me!"

"What the hell is wrong with you? Are you so damned afraid of male advances that you have to keep a pistol in your pocket?"

With easy strength, he picked her up in his arms. Her shoes fell to the floor. As if in a dream, she felt him carry her to the bedroom. She was drowning. She thought, with dazed matter-of-factness, I should have shot him. He's going to rape me. There was nothing she could do to resist. She was utterly defenceless. Her will seemed to have died in her.

He laid her down on the huge four-poster bed and began to undress in front of her, stripping off his belt and shirt. "Would you really have shot me?" he asked.

She didn't answer. It was as though all emotion had drained out of her, leaving her empty. He undressed with perfect naturalness, as though he had undressed before strangers a thousand times before. He was beautifully made, his body hard with muscle. There was majesty in his nakedness.

He came to her and took her in his arms. The smell of his skin enveloped her. For all his formidable strength, he knew how to be gentle. His mouth sought hers without roughness. She felt his fingers unfastening her blouse.

"Would you really have shot me?" he murmured. "What a way to go." He kissed the corners of her mouth, her cheeks, nuzzling into the hollow of her jaw, next to her ear. Mercedes felt his hand reach inside her blouse to touch her breasts. She looked into the American's eyes and felt something stir inside her.

He was perfect. She did not know him, nor he her. He came from far away, from a remoteness to which, if the war did not claim him, he would return. Her virginity was a burden which she suddenly knew she had to shed, before it began to grow heavier and start bearing her down.

He kissed her mouth. Her lips parted tremblingly, her face tilting to meet him. She closed her eyes and drew him down onto her.

"Take me," she whispered. "Yes, yes, take me!"

He mounted her, forcing her thighs apart. He slid into place. She looked up into his face, her eyes wide and intent. As if for the first time, Mercedes realized how beautiful he was. Pure, like some potent male animal. She felt an almost painful response in her heart to his beauty, as though a sharp blade had pierced it, leaving her wounded. She wondered when the wound would ever heal. Then he slid one hand under her waist and lifted her hips so that he could penetrate her.

She felt her maidenhead give way and cried out at the fierce pain. He bore deep into her, piercing the darkness of her inward being. She arched like a bow, but could not escape the pain. Slowly it dulled to a flame. She felt wetness. She opened her eyes, which now brimmed with tears, and saw awareness start to dawn on his face.

"Mercedes?" He lifted himself up on his elbows and looked down. Then he withdrew from her and sat up. He switched on the little lamp at the bedside. In its light, they looked at one another.

"Oh, shit," Sean said quietly. "You're a virgin!"

"I *was*," she corrected him.

"I thought—when you said—" He was obviously disconcerted.

She felt almost sorry for him. "It's done now."

"But if I'd known I wouldn't have gone at it like a bull at a gate!"

"What other way is there?"

"You're bleeding."

She stood up. Her legs were shaky, the way they'd been under fire at the front. She went to the kitchen and rinsed herself. She went back into the bedroom with a bowl of warm water.

"I thought you were going to come back with the gun and shoot me," he said ruefully.

"Too late for that." She sat beside him and washed the blood off him with her fingers. Curious, she studied the implement that had undone her. It was still rigid. The tip was enclosed by a hood of skin, which could be pulled back to expose the swollen crown. "That's very clever," she said, gently retracting the skin with her fingers.

"It's my own invention," he said solemnly. His body was magnificent. Satin-skinned, yet so strong. Everything was beautiful, the muscular chest, the dark nipples, even the rampant sex she held in her hands.

He reached between her thighs and touched her. She winced slightly. But he was infinitely gentle. His fingers touched her skillfully, and in the end, he eased the pain. His touch became erotic, stirring her need. "That's nice," she whispered. He knew where the secret stamen lay among the petals. He knew how to touch, how to awaken. Her belly quivered with little currents of electricity. "Come to me again," she whispered.

"Maybe we should let you rest awhile first."

"No. Come to me."

He mounted her again and entered her. The pain was sweet. He began to thrust into her, with force, and yet without brutality. It had a power she never imagined sex could possess. The old four-poster was creaking, as if in anguish. His force filled her. It gave her meaning.

Desire awakened, that urgent coursing she had almost forgotten. It was as though he was erasing Matilde, as though Matilde had left some infinitesimal trace on her skin, some kind of scented dust that was now at last blowing away, and leaving her forever. Her nipples puckered and hardened into points. Confusion faded into sureness of purpose.

His face was concentrated, his eyes burning into hers. She moved with him. Waves of emotion grew, intensified. She had not known there was so much need in her. So much hunger, so much empty ache that needed to be assuaged.

A searing rush of heat flooded her loins and her mind, cramping her whole body into an arc on the bed.

She cried out to him, wordlessly. She was blind with tears. She clung to him, like something battered by the sea, as he broke on her, calling her name. He seemed to forget how strong he was for a long moment, crushing her in his arms until she could no longer breathe.

Then he shuddered into relaxation.

"You are wonderful," he whispered. "Wonderful. Wonderful."

Seville

It is a sumptuous dinner, sumptuously attended.

The duchess's servants have provided a magnificent banquet

tonight. Really, you would hardly know there was a war on at all.

Many of the guests, of course, are in uniform. The women are outnumbered by the men. But there are so many unattached men floating around Seville these days that it is hard to make up a well-balanced party.

The dark man sitting beside the hostess, with his chin in his hand and his heavy lids drooping, is Gerard Massaguer, the big wheel in SAFNI. He is listening, apparently intently, to a thin German diplomat.

His Italian wife, Marisa de Bono, sits a few places down from him, sandwiched between two elderly generals, both of whom are attempting to monopolize her attention before the ladies retire. Marisa is very slim, with bobbed golden hair and clear violet eyes. In her ears and at her throat are splendid sapphires. They send out splinters of azure light which rival the sparkle of her eyes.

The Berlin diplomat speaks excellent Spanish.

"It gives the Führer great personal satisfaction," he is telling Gerard, "to assist General Franco in this magnificent triumph. The Führer takes an especial pride in the fact that so many young German volunteers have recognized their duty and have come to Spain to fight."

The young infantry lieutenant-colonel who sits beside him has been getting steadily drunker as the evening wears on. "Volunteers?" he repeats. "That's an odd word."

The diplomat ignores him. "It is wonderful to see a country in the terrible grip of Bolshevism achieve liberty, despite the criminal interference of Great Britain, France, and other decadent, pro-bolshevist nations."

"No doubt," the lieutenant-colonel says, "it also gives the Führer a great personal satisfaction to be able to try out so many of his new weapons on Spanish soil."

The diplomat fixes his monocle in one eye and peers at the lieutenant-colonel, who has dark shadows under his eyes and who bears five gold wound-stripes on his uniform. "The Führer is most eager that General Franco does not lack for efficient modern equipment," he says reprovingly.

"And most eager to test this equipment by slaughtering Spanish civilians."

"Are Bolsheviks and Jews to be given the name of Spaniards?" the German diplomat asks pleasantly.

"At Guernica," the lieutenant-colonel replies bitingly, "there were only Spanish nuns, priests, mothers and children. The attack was carried out on a market day. Fighters machine-gunned the townspeople as they fled in panic. Bombers finished the job off with incendiaries."

The Berlin diplomat smiles thinly. "You are as lurid, sir, as a Jew journalist of the gutter press."

The officer flushes hotly. "I am an officer of the Spanish army."

The diplomat turns his back on the infantry officer. "Without men like you, Señor Massaguer, this war would be a far greater struggle. How are your efforts proceeding, sir?"

"Reasonably well," Gerard replies lazily. "We're conscious of our debt of gratitude to your Führer. And to the German people. We do our best to repay it."

The lieutenant-colonel stares at Gerard with bloodshot eyes. "The currency Señor Massaguer uses is somewhat devalued, however. Spanish blood is not worth much these days."

Gerard glances at the man in irritation. "You are determined to insult someone tonight."

"I didn't know that a bloodsucker like you could be insulted," the soldier replies.

"You're being very boorish," the duchess tells him austerely. "Perhaps you're over-tired."

"Tired, yes," the soldier says loudly, his voice beginning to slur somewhat. "Tired of seeing this war run by profiteers and parasites."

People around them have stopped talking. An embarrassed hush is starting to fall over the table. "If you're not feeling well," Gerard says harshly, "perhaps you should retire before you make a fool of yourself."

The lieutenant-colonel puts down his napkin and rises to his feet. One of his legs squeaks mechanically. Heads turn in curiosity. "I leave the field to the hyenas and the vultures," he says in a drunken voice that everyone hears. He jerks himself out of the room.

In the vacuum, someone says, "Shell-shocked."

"Hysterical," says an archbishop helpfully.

The duchess, their so-charming hostess, saves the day by brightly suggesting that it is time the ladies retired to let the gentlemen enjoy their cigars and brandy. The company rises to its feet, the women troop out, chattering brightly, and the men settle down to Havana tobacco and French cognac.

It is two o'clock in the morning by the time Gerard and Marisa get home.

Marisa tip-toes into her son's bedroom, to make sure the child is sleeping.

He is curled up on his side, sucking his thumb in his sleep. She kisses his cheek softly. He frowns.

In the bedroom, Gerard already has his shirt off. As usual, he has left the heavy gold cufflinks in the sleeves for Marisa to pick out. She goes to the dressing table and unclips the sapphires from her ears and throat. She puts them in her brimming jewel case. She looks at the sparkling heaps of her jewelry.

"Gerard," she asks him, "are we profiteers?"

He pulls off his trousers. "The word is meaningless. That man needs a good, hard kick in the balls. If he's not careful, someone will see that he gets one."

"But are we?" she presses.

"Of course not," he says irritably and goes into the bathroom.

She unfastens the shimmering gown and hangs it in the cupboard. She sits down at the mirror. She examines her face. It is unlined. It still holds that look of innocence. Her body too, is still fine, slender and taut.

When Gerard comes out of the bathroom, she smiles at him in the mirror. "Did that officer spoil the party for you?" she asks him.

"It was the hostess he insulted, not me."

She puts the brush down and turns to him. "We're so rich, Gerard. Richer than we ever dreamed we'd be. And that's all because of the war, isn't it?"

"So what?"

"That man called us profiteers in front of everyone. It's such an ugly word."

He walks over to her and dips one blunt finger into her jewel case. It comes up dripping a string of pigeon's blood rubies. "Do you really care?" he asks softly.

She smiles slightly and caresses the stones. "No," she says. "I don't really care."

He kisses her, then gets into bed and picks up a book.

She undresses. Slim and naked, she too goes to the bathroom. A little while later she comes to bed and snuggles up to her husband. She closes her eyes, thinking back to the party. All those women, making up to Gerard . . .

She is quite aware of Gerard's adulteries. She is not unduly troubled by them. She is an Italian, after all, and was brought up to anticipate unfaithfulness in her husband. Her father was just the same.

And Gerard is very generous in his gifts to her. Her jewelry is already the talk of Seville. They live in a magnificent house, with a dozen servants. Their furniture is exquisite. They have marvelous paintings, porcelain, carpets. They know everyone who matters. And everyone who matters adores them. They are on the crest of the wave, and the wave has a long, long way to go.

No, she decides. She does not really care if they are profiteers. She does not care what they are, so long as the wave does not tumble and fall onto the shore.

Barcelona

There had never been anything like it in her life. There would never be anything like it again.

Love took Mercedes by storm. It breached her citadel, overturned her tower, made her its absolute hostage. Its power over her was like no other emotion she had ever known, out of all proportion to the time it had taken to blossom, or the cruel scarcity of their days together.

He had only a fortnight's leave. They spent every hour they could in the huge bed. Sometimes, despite her overwhelming happiness, strange moments of grief came over her when she thought of Matilde or José-María. Looking back on those relationships, she could see their fragility, their delicacy.

Sean was so strong, so vivid. He flooded all her senses. His touch was different. He was so sure of himself. He moved into her with a bone-melting purpose. José-María's body had been frail and slender. Matilde's had been soft. There were no soft places on Sean's body. He was hard and powerful, in control of himself. He touched the same places Matilde had touched long ago, tracing the same paths to her pleasure. Yet this was as different as the sun from moonlight.

Matilde and José-María are lying dead in the ground, she thought. And I am alive. She felt a twist of strange emotions in her heart, sorrow and exultation in one. Matilde had foreseen this. *This will mean nothing to you in the end.*

She let the memory of Matilde and José-María fade, deliberately, and drank Sean in, talking, listening, making love.

He'd had the same sort of life as Francesc's, and had the same kind of unquestioning commitment to his cause. Unaccountably, however, he reminded her more of Gerard Massaguer. There was little physical resemblance, apart from the dark hair and skin. But Gerard was a killer too, where Francesc was not. Both men had that ruthless sense of purpose. The association was disturbing and she shuddered it away.

At first, he refused to believe that she had been at the front.

"What on earth possessed you to go? For your father?"

"For myself. I thought it was the right thing to do."

"Where were you?"

"At a place called Granados."

He raised an eyebrow. "In Aragón? The Fascists retook it this year. Granados is a heap of rubble now. You'd hardly know there was ever a town there at all." He took her hands. They were lean and pretty, like the rest of her. The nails were short and unvarnished. These days, only whores and rich men's mistresses wore nail polish or lipstick. "How long were you there, my darling?"

"From January to April 1937," she replied quietly.

"Were you involved in any fighting?"

She shrugged for an answer.

He studied her face. "Don't you want to talk about it?"

"No."

He grunted. "Shit. That means you had a bad time. I'm sorry, Mercedes."

"I had no worse a time than anyone else."

"You'll tell me about it when you're ready."

"It seems so futile. All those deaths. For nothing." She raised her dark eyes to his. "And it gets worse the longer it lasts. There's so much treachery. There's no real idealism any more, Sean. It's all greed, ambition, cruelty."

"Is that how it seems to you?"

"I don't care about the revolution any more," she said. "Two years ago, when I went to the front, I was someone else, someone with ideals and hopes. I'm not that person any more."

"I'll never change," he said, touching her face. "I've been a trade unionist all my life. I'll be a Communist until the day I die. It's the only idea that makes any sense to me. When this is over, I'll go back to the States and fight for working conditions there. I'm going to do my share for the common man." He saw the expression on her face. "You think I'm a hopeless idealist, don't you? You don't know what it's like, Mercedes. The company owns people. It owns your soul. Miners work ten hours, six days a week. When you get sick, they stop paying you. If you get hurt bad, they fire you. When profits go down, they lay you off. It was the inhumanity that my father couldn't stand any more."

"Was he like you?"

"Not as big. But he looked like me. They called him Red Mike O'Keefe. They also called him Black Mike O'Keefe, on account of his hair. It was the same colour as mine. But mostly it was Red Mike."

"And your mother?" she asked.

"As Irish as Paddy's pig. She's very special. She doesn't talk much, but she's strong. She gets what she wants. I'd never have got out of Mingo County but for Ma."

"What did she say when you wanted to come and fight in Spain?" Mercedes asked.

"She cried."

Mercedes remembered her own mother's cheeks, wet with tears at the station. "Do you write to her?"

"I'm not a great correspondent," he said. "I guess she knows the way I feel about her."

She slid her palms around the powerful tendons of his throat, down his broad chest, over the hard points of his nipples. The hair on his chest was harsh, crackling under her fingers as though it were electric.

"How do you feel about me?"

"I adore you." He opened her gown. Her body was as smooth as marble. She was slim and pale-skinned. Her breasts were small. He bent to kiss the soft hollow of her collarbone, the shallow valley between her breasts, the aching tips of her nipples. "I adore you," he repeated. "I've never known anyone like you, Mercedes."

She saw that his manhood had risen from his loins in a rigid, veined column. She bent and took him in her mouth.

His fingers bit into her arms for a moment. She kept still, feeling him throb in her mouth. He was salty, hot and full against her tongue. She bit into the firm flesh, at first gently, then with increasing pressure. He groaned her name, his thighs parting. She slid onto her knees between his thighs, her arms going about his taut waist. His muscular body arched backwards in ecstasy. She felt his fingers knot in her hair.

His arousal excited her with a long, slow flare in the blood, like petrol igniting. Her sense of power over him was thrilling. She had him enclosed, at her mercy. He was hers. He had been so sure that he was going to be the master of the situation, so sure that he was the teacher, she the pupil. But she had made love too, though not with a man, and she knew something about the techniques of pleasure.

Then he pulled himself out of her mouth and collapsed beside her. He was gasping for air, his face dark with passion.

"My God," he said. "Where did you learn to do that?"

"Some of the children used to do it on the playground, when I was at school. Don't the girls do it in West Virginia?"

"Not the nice girls."

"I never told you I was a nice girl," she said quietly. "You should have stopped me if I was offending you."

"We Americans are very straitlaced compared to you Europeans," he said gently, taking her in his arms. "And I didn't say it wasn't wonderful. Just...nobody ever did that to me before."

"Then I've taught you something," she smiled. Her dark eyes were bright. She drew him onto her and guided him between her thighs. "There," she whispered, as she claimed him. "Sean, I love you. I can't bear the thought of your going."

"I'll always come back to you. Always."

•   •   •

And then there were only two days left in paradise.

She was overwhelmed by such grief that he knew he had to get her out of Barcelona.

With his genius for obtaining the unlikely, he borrowed a motorcycle from somewhere, and they rode up to Tossa del Mar, a little fishing village along the coast. Away from Barcelona, the air was crisp and the terrible sense of doom faded.

The village was pristine, lovingly whitewashed. Reflected sunlight filled the streets with luminosity. Here and there, geraniums blossomed from a window box, or a brightly-painted doorway relieved the starkness of the whitewash. A little castle towered over the rooftops, frowning out at the Mediterranean.

As they walked down the stone steps to the sea, they passed three young girls coming the other way. Each carried a large clay water jar balanced on the top of her head. At the sight of Sean's tall figure they fell silent. Three pairs of bright eyes surveyed him quickly as they passed.

He stopped and stared after them. The heavy water jars on their heads gave each girl a gliding, archaic grace. The swaying hips and swinging arms moved economically as they climbed the steep stairway without apparent effort.

"What are you staring at?" Mercedes asked him jealously.

He shook his head. "I just wonder if they have any idea what a pretty sight they make with those jars balanced on their heads."

"Of course they do," she said dryly, taking his hand. "That's why they don't carry them under their arms. Come on. I want to show you better things than girls' backsides."

She led Sean down to the little beach. Two dozen small fishing boats lay higgledy-piggledy on the tight semicircle of sand, framed by the steep cliffs with their hedges of agave and prickly pear. The water was like glass. The few boats in the shallows seemed to float on air. Farther out, the turquoise turned to ultramarine, then to a dazzling sheet of gold that stretched to the horizon.

He was enchanted. "In the States, this would be a huge resort. They'd build hotels and nightclubs and bring in trainloads of tourists."

She smiled. "That'll never happen here." They clambered over the rocks and kicked off their shoes in the sand. A few old men were working on their boats or untangling nets, and gulls drifted lazily overhead, but apart from that they had the whole cove to themselves.

They lay on the hot sand side by side, fingers entwined. The ripple of the waves lulled them.

"This is heaven," he said quietly. "I could stay here forever with you."

He was due to go back to the front on Monday. She looked at him through eyes that were blurred.

Sean saw her tears. "Don't think about it," he said.

"Just come back to me," she choked.

"I'll always come back to you."

He held her close. Their lips touched, warm and intimate. He laid one hand on her cheek and looked into her eyes. "The war will be over soon, Mercedes. When it ends, I want you to come to the States with me."

"Go to America with you?" she repeated in astonishment.

"Yes." His eyes were serious. "By now you must know how I feel about you."

"But we've only known each other ten days!"

"What does that matter?" he asked. "You will never feel this with anyone else, Mercé. Never in your life."

They walked back up to the village and ate in a *fonda* near the little white church. The dim restaurant was filled with fishermen, their laughter and their smoke. The only thing on the menu was mussels, fresh from the sea. They ate a mountain of them, gorging themselves. Sean was captivated by the atmosphere of the place. Mercedes ate in silence.

She thought of skyscrapers, streets full of huge automobiles, a world of ships and bridges and factories, in which people were dwarfed by what they had created. A world utterly different from the little villages of Catalonia. It was an idea that terrified her.

But Sean was right. He had already become her new life.

And in the end, perhaps that was all that mattered.

They got back to Barcelona in the evening to find that there was a power failure.

"Lérida's going to fall any day now," Sean commented. "Then the Fascists will have a clear run north, along the river Segre, to Tremp. Tremp is the hydroelectric plant that supplies Barcelona with electricity. In a few days, all the lights in Barcelona are going to go out. Permanently."

"Don't talk about the war. Let's make tonight last forever."

They lit a thick, ivory-coloured candle that had been plundered from some church, still scrolled with gilt. By its pale light they went to bed and made love.

Their lovemaking had become more sensual lately, less hurried. The feel of his hot skin against hers was ecstasy. She pressed against him, her mouth seeking his as their limbs twined. His tongue was like a flame entering her mouth. She could feel him hard and thrusting against her belly. She reached down and took him in her hand.

"I love you, Sean," she said huskily. "I love you more than you'll ever know."

The candle's flame was reflected in his eyes, making them glow like emeralds. He drew the sheets away from her and studied her body in the candle's gentle light. Her skin shone like ivory. He caressed the fine curves that ran from her ribs down her flanks, along her thighs. "There's so much difference between one body and another. Some are ugly, some beautiful. Yours is the most beautiful I've ever seen. And I know so little about it. I've only ever touched it in the dark."

He parted her thighs. She allowed him to, feeling no shame or embarrassment. His fingers trailed across her loins, touching the secret skin there. "I've never seen this before," he said.

She lay on her back, looking up at him. "Didn't your other women let you look at them?"

"Not like this."

"Were they ashamed to let you see?"

"I guess so. Like I said, we're not very sophisticated in West Virginia."

She tilted her head on one side. "So? Is it interesting, Señor West Virginia?"

"It's very pretty." He touched her, tracing the shape of her sex with his fingertips. "Like a flower. Very discreet."

"Discreet?"

"Well, a man's arrangement is kind of obvious, isn't it?"

She smiled. "Yours certainly is."

"But this is so neat. Secretive, nestling away here underneath you. You just have to close your legs and it's gone." His touch was erotic, making her stir. "Be patient with me," he said softly. "I'm just an ignorant Mick."

He bent and kissed her between her legs. Her lips there clung to his. Mercedes felt sweetness leap. Her hands moved down to cradle his head. His tongue found the growing bud and pleasure was suddenly wildly intense.

"Sean . . ." she whispered.

He did not answer. He was lost in her. The perfume of her body was intoxicating. She tasted of musk, ambergris. He explored her with his tongue, licking, caressing.

Pleasure took her, contracting the muscles in her lean stomach, forcing the breath in and out of her lungs with increasing speed. He was learning, teaching himself by her responses. She swayed her hips against him, wanting more. Even in this he was harsher, more demanding than Matilde would ever have been. He used his tongue and teeth as though he wanted to devour her.

She could sense how much it was exciting him too. She knew that he was taking pleasure from this, could tell that by the way he moved, held her.

He came to her and thrust into her, his weight pinning her to the bed. She was so wet that he slid deep into her body without resistance. Their lovemaking was almost painfully sweet and intense. Her climax was a golden spear that stabbed into her, making her cry out on a long, shuddering note. She felt him convulse, felt him spurting hot and thick into her. He kissed her in between gasps. Her own musk was on his lips.

She felt him relax slowly. The intensity of the sex seemed to have dazed him. She could feel his muscles twitch as they eased into quietude. He slackened, slid gradually out of her. She whispered his name over and over again, stroking him. "You're my soul," she told him. "My life."

Three nights later, when he'd gone back to the front, she stood at her window and stared out over the park and the darkened city beyond. Here and there, the tiny glimmer of other candles showed against the night. A dimly lit tram crawled along like a glow worm.

She wondered if he would come back to her.

She put out the light and went to bed.

12.

Long Ago, Far Away

Tucson

He was still reeling as he made his way upstairs.

His hands shook violently as he poured himself some whisky and gulped it down. He had lost control. He had let her pull the hood off. She had seen his face.

She had seen his face.

He was cornered. Now the only way to be truly safe was to kill her. He clenched his teeth against the bile that rose in his throat.

He poured a second shot and went into the main room. It was flooded with light and glowed brightly. He tried to draw solace from the familiar textures and colours all around him.

He had furnished the house as soon as it had been built, three years ago, and had changed little since then. With the exception of the ponderous walnut chest, which had been carved in Aragón in the early sixteenth century, none of the furniture had been made more than a hundred miles from Tucson. The rough workmanship, mellowed by time, was unpretentious and soothing. Many of the things were Indian. The brilliant geometric patterns of the rugs contrasted with the more muted devices of the basketware, and the irregular curves of the pottery.

There were only two of his own creations in the room, a marble bust of a woman with serene, smooth features, and a rougher slab of sandstone carved with lizards and snakes, which he had set into the wall above the fireplace.

He walked to the sandstone carving and laid his hand on it. The sweat on his palms stained the honey-coloured stone.

It had been his fault that she'd seen his face. He'd been unbelievably careless. It was his fault she had to die.

He had always known the girl might have to die. It was something he had always had to face.

He had killed before, many times, in many ways. He had fired bullets into human flesh. Had burned, hacked, ruptured the human engine. Had seen its vital cords unravel, its fluids gush. It would not be difficult to kill that fragile girl.

He need not even use a gun or a knife. Something in the food, something that would put her to sleep without her even knowing it.

A gentle death was a reward. He knew that. You could ask little more from life. Except revenge.

He could bury her out there in the desert. In the clean dry soil. In a sacred place. All places were sacred, there.

He could—

Nausea rose in him. No. He couldn't. He could never kill that girl. Something forbade it, something deeper than thought. It would be easier to kill himself than to kill her. Much easier.

So what are you going to do?

Eden sat hugging herself.

His face was burned into her mind's eye. The same face she'd seen, three years ago, in Laurel Canyon. Tough, aquiline, with hard cheeks and jaws. A face that should have been strikingly handsome, except that the strong features had been defaced by bitterness. By a frightening tension. A sensation of imminent violence. And she would never forget those eyes. Black. Impenetrable.

How could he ever let her go now? She could swear not to describe his appearance to the police. But he would have no reason to believe her.

They could make an Identikit. Issue thousands to every cop in America. Put up posters. Go on television. Search for him.

Of course, it would be like searching for a needle in a haystack. She didn't even know what state she was in. And the face was not that unusual. He could dye his hair, shave the moustache, go far away. Disappear with his money.

But he might not be prepared to accept that risk.

Who was he? Why had he chosen her?

Vacantly, Eden wondered whether she was doomed.

He emerged from the haze slowly and drained the glass. He looked at his watch. He was short of supplies. He had to go into town, do some shopping.

He tidied up, then locked the house carefully. He had fitted wrought-iron guards to all the windows and expensive locks everywhere. He did not want burglars getting into the house, finding what he had built in the cellar.

Looking back, he had done so little planning. It had all been so very easy. Going to California. Taking the girl. Bringing her here. He'd hardly thought about it. It had been a picnic. It was important to keep calm, now that victory was in the palm of his hand. No more losses of control.

He walked out into the blazing sun and got into the van.

Driving along the saguaro-lined dirt road, he thought about the other thing, the addiction.

There had been something dimly familiar about the "illness." That shivering. The sweating through icy skin. The pains in her back. He had not been able to put his finger on it. But he ought to have known.

The girl was a junkie.

He thought of Eden's thin body. The haunted face that should have been pretty. Those turkey trots along her veins. The white, almost translucent skin. Heroin did that. It gave you that dead fish's belly look. He'd seen it in Saigon. There had been no shortage of heroin there.

Those scars . . . the girl had been a heavy user.

Pity came to him suddenly. *Poor kid.* She was so young, so very young.

He tried to force the emotion out. She didn't deserve compassion. While he'd been losing his soul in Vietnam, she'd been wallowing in the lotus swamp. She'd been born with every advantage. Born on top of the shit pile. It was almost funny. She'd turned out even more screwed-up than he was.

She was asleep and did not wake when he next went into the cell. Her face was exhausted. The dark hair clung to her forehead and cheeks. The vulnerability of the bare throat and jawline was almost painful. There was a bruise on her face where he must have hit her during the struggle.

He watched her for a long while.

Eden. Chained to the bed.

Chained as he had once been.

He waited for the surge of triumph. It didn't come. It had been there at first, that swelling sense of achievement. But now he felt something else. A painful tug of pity. An emotion that choked him.

A silken thread that ran from somewhere deep inside him to somewhere deep inside that girl.

He looked at the track marks on her legs. He'd seen worse. Eden had avoided the infections that humbler addicts got. But the scars were livid in the pale flesh. Little pinpricks to let in dragon seed. And the monster took root within.

He bent over her and slid the key into the handcuffs and unlocked them. The skin beneath them was scarred and abused. It would heal. He drew the chain through the headboard carefully, trying not to rouse her. But one of the cuffs clanked against metal. Eden stirred. Then her green eyes opened and stared into his.

He was not wearing the hood. She backed up into the corner, away from him. Her face seemed to crumple. "Are you going to kill me?" she asked.

"The cuffs are coming off for a while, that's all."

It took her a moment to register the chain in his hands. She looked down stupidly at her own wrists. "Are you taking me out of here?"

"No." Pity for her squeezed him inside, but he forced hardness into his voice. "First piece of shit you give me and they go right back on," he said. "I'll chain you hand and foot. Understand?"

Eden touched her bare wrists dazedly. "You're not wearing the hood. That means you're going to kill me, doesn't it?"

"No. It doesn't."

She stared into the face of her kidnapper. He could see fear in her eyes. They were an emerald green. They had once been bright and insolent. Now they were set in deep sockets, overshadowed by a tangle of black hair. Her cheekbones stood out starkly.

She suddenly covered her eyes with her hands. "I don't want to look at you! It wasn't my fault the hood came off. Put it back on. Put it back! I hardly saw your face. I didn't even get a look at you. I wouldn't know you again if I met you in the street—"

"Calm down, Eden."

"You're going to kill me."

"I'm not."

"You're lying. You wouldn't have come in without the hood if you were planning to let me live!"

There was a silence. "How do you feel?" he asked.

"I've been better," she replied, without uncovering her eyes.

"You should have told me about the heroin."

"You should have told me you were going to kidnap me."

He turned to go. "Don't waste the water washing," he said over his shoulder. "You're dehydrated. That's why you look so wasted. Keep drinking. I've brought you extra."

He slammed the steel door shut.

She took her hands away from her eyes and touched her wrists. Why had he freed her? Out of a sense of pity, because he knew she'd have to die?

Without the weight of the chains, her arms felt feather-light. She lifted her arms high above her head, revelling in a sudden sense of freedom. Her shoulder still ached where he had hurt her, but she felt a breath of euphoria touch her. She could leave the bed for the first time and move around her tiny domain. She swung her legs off the bed.

Her first attempt to rise was unsuccessful. Disuse and general weakness had robbed her legs of strength. They gave at the knee and she collapsed back onto the bed.

Gritting her teeth, Eden forced herself to try again. The muscles in her thighs shuddered and clenched. She cried out and leaned against the wall for support and this time did not fall back. Pain stabbed from her heels right up into her spine.

With infinitesimal movements, she started to shuffle. The cell was so tiny that there was just room to edge around the bed. But despite that and despite her geriatric legs, triumph flamed in her. She crept around to the other side of the toilet, terra incognita. Now too, she could reach up and touch the aluminum grilles in the cement wall. A cool breath of air touched her outstretched fingers.

She lifted her hands towards the ceiling. Stretched out her arms. Edged back to the door and leaned against the cool steel. Happiness made her laugh aloud. To be able to move an extra few feet, to be able to touch the far wall, was as keen a pleasure as any she had known.

Freedom. How relative freedom was!

She reached high, swaying her waist, feeling things pull tight in her thin frame.

She moved around for a few minutes until her legs protested intolerably, then sank back onto the bed and massaged the quivering muscles. Later, she would try again. She rolled over and examined the tray. A piece of fried chicken and some tired-looking potato chips. The food nauseated her, but now she had her legs to think of. They needed the protein even if her stomach didn't.

She reached down and lifted the plate onto the bed.

Costa Brava

The businessman from Madrid stared expressionlessly at Mercedes's motor yacht, his hands in his pockets. His mouth was pursed as though he were whistling, but no sound came out.

"I bought her three years ago," Mercedes said. "I paid over a million dollars for her."

The businessman did not react, continuing to whistle silently.

"You've seen the way she's fitted out. She was built at de Vries in Holland. Every detail is immaculate. She will cruise at eighteen knots. She will sleep four couples in the utmost luxury. The decks are Burmese teak. She has the latest satellite navigating equipment —"

"She's three years old," the man interrupted shortly.

"She's a classic!"

"I can't go any higher." He glanced at his watch. "And I have very little time. Excuse me. I need to make a telephone call." He turned his back on Mercedes and walked back to the boatyard office.

Mercedes turned furiously to Paco, the boatyard owner. "The bastard!"

"It's a ridiculous offer," Paco said.

"Two hundred thousand dollars? It's an insult," she replied savagely.

Paco shrugged. "So don't waste any more time with him."

Mercedes's mouth was a hard line. "I can't afford to let him go. You haven't exactly come up with a line of prospective buyers."

"You haven't exactly given me much time," he retorted. "If you want a good price for a boat of this quality, it's essential to be patient."

"I cannot be patient," she said brusquely. "I have no choice."

Paco frowned. "You're not seriously thinking of accepting this offer?" She was silent and his expression changed. "Two hundred thousand? Señora Eduard, I find it hard to believe you need the money that badly. This boat is worth at least three quarters of a million dollars. If you give me just three months more, I'll be able to find—"

"I don't *have* three months," she said, the strain in her voice almost breaking. "I don't have three *weeks*, Paco!"

The man from Madrid was coming back. The summer sunlight glanced off the dozens of snowy white hulls, making the boatyard a dazzling place. He put on dark glasses and addressed Mercedes brusquely.

"I have to get out to one of my factories. Well?"

Mercedes gritted her teeth. "If you raise your offer to a quarter of a million, I will accept it here and now," she said.

The factory owner from Madrid was a handsome, blunt-featured man. "You'll accept two hundred thousand, Señora Eduard," he said coolly. "You have no choice."

"What do you mean?"

"You're in trouble. You're selling everything you own. You have some kind of demon on your tail. That isn't a secret any more."

Her face had gone white and strained. "I have no idea what you're talking about."

He smiled slightly. "Don't you?" He took a cheque book from his inside pocket and uncapped a gold pen. "I'm going to write a cheque for two hundred thousand dollars. That's drawn on a New York account. You want it?"

Paco stared at Mercedes Eduard in astonishment. She stood absolutely still, her face mask-like. Then she inclined her head slowly. She did not speak.

The man from Madrid wrote the cheque, tore it out and passed it over to Mercedes. "Anything else you want to sell, come to me." He was smiling broadly. He did not even glance over his shoulder at the motor yacht he had just bought. "A pleasure doing business with you," he said as he took his leave. "I hope you can outrun your demon, Señora Eduard."

When the telephone rang, Joaquin de Córdoba picked it up, but did not speak even when he heard Mercedes lift her own receiver.

"Hello?" she said

"There's someone else on the line," said the harsh voice that de Córdoba instantly recognized. His heartbeat accelerated violently. "Who else is listening?"

"A family friend."

"A family friend, huh?"

"An advisor. Joaquin de Córdoba. You spoke to him once before."

"Is he a cop?"

"He's just a friend. An old family friend."

"Well, this is Paul. I'm another old family friend. From way back."

Mercedes took a breath. "How is my daughter?"

"She's bad. Cold turkey's pretty rough. You know?" He let the frozen silence stretch out, then laughed. "Did you think I wouldn't find out? The girl's a junkie. She's covered in track marks. With a habit that heavy, withdrawal's bound to be agonizing. Isn't it?"

"Please." Mercedes's tone was quiet. "Tell me. Is Eden sick?"

"She's worse than sick. She's pretty near dead."

De Córdoba caught his breath. "What do you mean?" Mercedes demanded urgently.

"I mean she won't last forever."

"What's wrong with her?"

"Get the money. Fast. Or you're going to get her back with her eyes closed. Permanently."

"*What's wrong with her?*"

"Pretty much everything."

"You must get her a doctor. Please! Get her help!"

"I can't call a doctor. You know that. I'd have to let her die down there before I call a doctor." He laughed again. "Don't you think it's ironic? Your daughter turning out a drug addict?"

"Please! If Eden is ill—"

"You could almost call it divine retribution."

"Listen to me!"

"No. You listen to *me*. And you listen too, Mr. Eavesdropper. You may learn something about your friend there. Are you listening, old friend?"

"I'm listening," de Córdoba said quietly.

"Did you know that her husband was Los Angeles's favorite drug runner? Did you know that?"

De Córdoba was silent.

"Yeah." The voice was slightly breathless. "He was. What do you think of that, old boy?"

"I don't know what you want me to say," de Córdoba said hesitantly.

"I'll bet you don't. Her husband ran cocaine in from Colombia for years. Carried it in his freight planes. That's where the money came from to buy the yachts and the houses and the limousines. As money goes, it's the dirtiest money around. That's why it's so ironic about Eden. Her precious little *baby*." He spat the words out with a venom that made de Córdoba wince. "All those years, you never cared about what happened to other people. Now it's come home to you. Hasn't it, Mercedes?"

She spoke with an effort, as though her voice were rusty. "I had nothing to do with my husband's—with his business dealings. I never involved myself."

"You lying bitch."

"It's the truth."

"You knew where it came from! You were spending his money, and you're trying to tell me you didn't notice it was dripping blood?"

"I'm guilty of that," she said in the same rusty voice. "Yes."

"Is that why you've taken Eden?" de Córdoba asked. "To punish Mercedes Eduard for what she did?"

The voice was silent. Then it spat out, "Just get the money."

The line clicked dead.

Mercedes came into de Córdoba's room after ten minutes. She was pale, but she met his eyes directly. "It's the truth," she repeated. "I was never involved in Dominic's business. It took me years to find out what he really did. And by then we had Eden." She shrugged painfully. "What could I do? I waited until I thought Eden was old enough. Then I left him."

"Please—" he began, embarrassed.

"As for the money I have, I swear to you that Dominic gave me nothing when I left him. I invested in the stock market over the years. I made a lot of money. Part luck, part skill. Whatever that man believes, none of the money I have came from drugs. I swear it."

"You don't have to justify yourself to me," he said gently.

"I know I don't have to." She was still holding his eyes. "But I want to. I want you to believe me. Do you?"

"Yes," he said without hesitation. "I do."

Tucson

He put the tray down at her bedside and looked at her.

"How're you doing?" She did not answer. "I brought you an extra blanket," he said. "Here." He folded it gently around her trembling shoulders. "This'll keep you warm."

She looked up at him with eyes that screamed wordlessly. Today the sickness had come back without warning. Today had been like the worst of those very first days. She'd been bad at breakfast. Had vomited immediately afterwards. As the sunless, shadowless day had inched forward, she'd gotten worse. Now she was racked with pain and fear, her skin whorled by gooseflesh. Each hair was erect, each root a focus of pain.

"I can't take it any more," she said through chattering teeth.

"Yes, you can," he said. He had shaved today. He wore jeans and a thin T-shirt. His muscular arms were tanned. She could smell the sunlight on his skin. Up there in the real world, it must be hot. But down here it was icy cold, colder than arctic.

"I wish I could die," she whispered, huddling into the blanket. "I wish my heart would just stop beating."

"Come on, now. It isn't that bad."

"How the fuck would you know?" she spat at him.

"You'll get over it. You need to eat." He sat down beside her. Eden shrank instinctively from him. He lifted the plate onto her lap. "Come on."

She stared down at the fried eggs and bacon. "Jesus." She closed her eyes and twisted her face away from the nauseating smell. "Take it away."

"You need it."

"I'm not eating that crap any more."

"What's wrong with it?"

"All that fried shit. It's so unhealthy."

"Suddenly you're a health freak," he said wearily. He held out the plastic fork. "Come on, Eden. Eat something."

"Fuck *you*." She snatched up the plate and flung it across the cell. It smashed on the cement wall, spattering egg. "*Get out of here!*"

His face hardened. "You can do without, then. And you can clean that up yourself." He rose.

She turned her anguished face up to him. "Why won't you give me any more *pills*?"

"You're going to have to learn to do without pills and injections," he said, preparing to leave.

"Wait!"

"What?"

"How long have I been down here?" Her voice was pleading. "I tried to work it out, but I couldn't. I've been so sick. I can't remember."

"Don't think about it."

"Don't *think* about it?" Her eyes met his. "Have you got a dog? You wouldn't treat your dog like this, would you? I'm going insane! Is that what you want?"

"No."

"No window, no books, not even a lousy magazine!" She was crying now. "You don't know what it's like to be chained in a cellar like a dog!"

"Yes, I do," he said quietly.

"Can I have a radio? Please?"

"No."

Her expression grew desperate. "A book, then."

"No."

"A newspaper, a magazine, anything—"

"No," he said. "You don't have the right to demand anything."

"You can't leave me like this," she said, her voice rising. "You *can't*! I'm strung out. I haven't got one damned thing to distract me. Please—" Her voice trembled. She plucked at the blanket in agitation. "Please, for God's sake! You can't leave me in here as if I was some kind of animal!"

"What will you eat if you won't eat eggs and bacon?"

"I don't want *anything*. I can't keep anything down, can't you see that?" She covered her face in her hands briefly. "Oh, goddamn. Anything fresh. Some fruit. That's all."

"I'll bring you something in a little while." He put his hand on the doorknob.

"Bring me something to read," she begged. "A jigsaw puzzle, anything."

"I'll see," he said.

He locked the door and went upstairs. He breathed in the clean air and rested his eyes on the clean surroundings. It was foul down there.

He hadn't really thought of her as a person, not at the planning stage. He'd thought of her the way a farmer thinks of an animal. As a creature to be catered for. But without feelings.

Not that he'd wanted her to suffer. He'd made the cell secure, but not cruelly so. She would have been relatively comfortable except for the cold turkey, which he could never have foreseen. He hadn't done *that* to her. She'd done it to herself.

But Eden was not an animal. She was a person.

That had come almost as a surprise.

Her sickness, her rages, her passions, had almost shocked him at first. He hadn't anticipated that she would be so . . . *alive*. No. Despite all his planning, he hadn't anticipated that. It was as though one of his carvings had awakened under his fingers, writhing with fierce life.

He was worried about her. How long would it take for the symptoms to go?

He'd seen guys go through cold turkey, or try to. They shook, they sweated, they thought they couldn't go through with it. But mostly they got over it in a few days. Then they usually went back again. Not all of them, but most did. The dragon's jaws did not relinquish its prey so easily.

But this was taking a lot longer than a few days. Maybe because she'd been such a heavy user. Or because she was so slight.

As far as he knew, there wasn't any easy way through it. The main thing was to keep her eating and drinking. She was right. He had been giving her a bad diet. Not enough fresh produce. He'd have to re-think her menu.

Fruit. She'd said fruit.

In the kitchen, he started chopping fruit to make her a fruit salad. He sliced the soft flesh carefully, trying to make it look attractive. He'd cheat a little, put in some sugar to give her some energy. Maybe she'd eat a salad later, some tomatoes and lettuce—

Half-way through, he stopped short, the steel blade upraised. What the hell am I running here? he thought. A five-star hotel?

For a while, he stared down at the sliced peaches and bananas. He debated throwing them into the trash. He hadn't done all this in order to provide a health camp for Eden van Buren.

Then he sighed, shook his head and went on chopping.

When he came in two hours later, she had cleared the mess up. The pieces of the broken plate were piled on the tray. She looked no better. She was still shivering like a whipped dog. He could see her ribs, stark under the T-shirt, the knobs of her spine. She turned those haunted green eyes on him.

"Feeling any better?" he asked. She shook her head. He sat beside her again. "I made some fruit salad. Peaches, apples, bananas, pineapple. Try it."

She took the spoon and dipped it listlessly into the fruit salad. She ate a little. For a while he thought she would stop, but she kept spooning tiny morsels of the stuff up. He felt an absurd sense of victory.

"Good," he said.

"Did you bring anything to read?"

"This." He gave her the book. She took it eagerly.

"*Survive the Savage Sea*? What is this?"

"It's about some people who survived a shipwreck." He watched her face as she leafed through the book, the spoon still in her fingers. It was gaunt and fragile. Her eyes were hungry, as though she needed the book more than the food. Even her shivering had slowed. Her cheeks were haggard, her eyes hollow. Her hair was a knotted tangle. But she had fine facial bones, and the shape of her mouth was a perfect leaf, symmetrical, soft.

She smelled sour. Her clothes were rank. So was the bed. He calculated the length of time she'd been imprisoned here without a bath. No wonder. She probably couldn't tell she stank any more.

He rose to leave again. She looked up quickly. "Wait. Have you spoken to my mother again?"

He kept his face expressionless. "Don't ask. Don't ask me anything about that side of it. Not ever."

"But—"

"Nothing."

He let himself out and locked the door.

Santa Barbara

Five years ago, Dominic van Buren had set aside enough pure, uncut cocaine to last him the rest of his life.

Or so he thought.

Staring now at the sealed packages that remained in his safe, he realized with a spasm of horror that he was soon going to run out. In five years he'd used more coke than he'd planned to in a lifetime.

He felt rage and anxiety churn in his gut. He slammed his fist against the heavy steel door. Fuck. *Fuck*.

He'd given too much away. Given too much to little blond girls who hadn't even known how to appreciate it. Pretty soon he would end up having to go out and buy some more. At today's gigantic prices!

He slammed the door shut, grinding his teeth. Him. *Him*, having to go out and score, like some kid off the street. The worms of anxiety were wriggling out of his stomach, slithering up his gullet. Not enough. Not enough coke in the safe, not enough money in the bank to buy any more.

God damn those little girls. He felt like going out and finding them all, squeezing their little slim throats.

He sat down at his desk and cut the white powder into lines.

His fingers trembled as he inserted the rolled-up bill into his nose. He inhaled deeply, feeling the drug ram into his sinuses. The icy fingers spread up into his brain, soothing him, easing his ill-temper.

He snorted all the coke, then leaned back in his chair with a sigh. He closed his eyes. The worms all slithered back into his stomach. They wriggled a while, then burrowed back into their homes, quiescent, still. Still.

There, now, he thought. What was all that fuss about? There was plenty of coke left in the safe. Plenty of money in the bank to buy more if it ever looked like running out. Why, he was a millionaire.

Even his murderous rage against the little blond girls had faded. The coke had bought him some marvellous sex over the years. And he'd used most of it himself, really. He was using more and more these days. He was snorting four or five times a day.

Be frank, he thought, unrolling the $100 bill. Eight or ten times a day. He dabbed up the remains of the powder and rubbed it absently into his gums. Or was it more?

He sat there, staring ahead. He felt okay, now. What he didn't like, lately, was the feeling he got between toots. That frantic feeling. The rages. The worry he didn't have enough coke or enough money to last. It was irrational. Disturbing.

Was it as much as twenty times a day? Thirty?

Looking back over the past weeks, he seemed to see himself shuffling in and out of his study every half hour or so, swinging open the safe, reaching for the neat little packages.

Damn. Was he experiencing those panics thirty times a day? More?

He had a sudden vision of his mother, sitting on the lawn in front of the psychiatric hospital. A strand of saliva glistening on her chin. Her eyes, empty, burned out.

Jesus. Was he going to end up like that, after all?

Despite the friendly presence of the coke in his brain, he felt anxiety churn in him anew. The worms started moving in their burrows. Wriggling. Squirming.

They said coke wasn't harmless any more. They said—

Was he becoming hooked on the damned stuff? Of course not. He'd been using it all his life.

All his life.

Imprisoned in a yellow deck chair on a green lawn, white-coated attendants drifting to and fro in the background. With that dead sound in his own head.

Walking down endless corridors, past countless rooms, in each room a bed, on each bed a woman lying staring at the ceiling with lifeless eyes and lolling hands.

Fear was terrible, sudden. *No.* He couldn't end up like that, the way Mother had ended up. He'd die first.

Maybe he should cut some more lines, take another toot.

But he had to be careful. It was running out. And with the price it was today, he couldn't afford to have to start buying it.

He thought of all the people he'd shared coke with. All those greedy-eyed little blond girls. Damn them. Goddamn them. Just how much *was* left? The worms were all out now. They were starting up his gullet again. They'd be in his throat soon.

He jumped to his feet and hurried back to the safe.

Tucson

She devoured *Survive the Savage Sea* in one great gulp. She sat huddled in the bed, trembling and icy cold, turning the pages feverishly. As soon as she had finished the book, she sagged back in exhaustion. Her mind was as unaccustomed to exercise as her body.

Sometime later she awoke with a start as the lock rattled. He came in, carrying the tray. She handed the book back to him.

"Was I supposed to draw some moral from this?"

He raised one eyebrow. "Finished already? You must have sat up all night reading."

"There aren't any nights down here," she said bitterly. "No dawns, no sunsets. No hours or minutes."

"You look better this morning." He reached out and took her pulse. Surprised by the action, she looked down. The bones of her wrist were as frail as a bird's in his strong fingers. Her skin was a sickly white against his. He had powerful, capable hands; they were roughened by work, but not clumsy or crude. "Am I gonna live?" she muttered.

"You're okay." He let her wrist go and put the tray in front of her. There were several pieces of fruit, cheese, some whole wheat rolls, a plastic mug of milky coffee. "This healthy enough for you?"

"At least none of it's fried." She started drinking the coffee. He did not leave, but stood watching her. She glanced at his face from under the tangle of black hair that covered her eyes. "What are you looking at?" she asked sullenly.

"Cold turkey's as much a state of mind as a sickness."

"Oh, really?"

"It can't kill you."

"Well, thank you so much," she said acidly. "If you're wrong, I'll be sure and let you know."

"It's staying on heroin that kills you. Not coming off it. You're over the worst now. You'll start feeling better soon."

"If I don't lose my mind first."

"How long have you been on the needle?"

"I told you." Her voice was low. "A year."

"That's a lie. Of course, you had the money to buy all you wanted. Plenty of money. The super-rich can afford the super-drug. Isn't that right?" His eyes were dark and intense. "You're going to be grateful to me, Eden."

"Why?"

"I've done something for you which nobody else could have done."

She stared at him.

"I'm making you sweat the poison out of your system. You're sick. But not as sick as you were. You're being purged. You're going to be a free woman for the first time in your life. Cleansed."

She shook her head slowly. "Jesus. I don't believe it."

His dark brows came down. "I've given you a new chance. How many people would give their everything for a new chance, a chance to start again? Think about it."

"And then you're going to kill me."

"I'm not going to kill you."

"Oh, bullshit." She slammed the mug down. "Don't treat me like a child. You're letting me see your face. Do you think I'll ever forget you? If you let me go, the first thing the cops will do is have me make an Identikit—"

"If your mother doesn't call the cops, you'll live."

She studied his face. She'd long since decided that he was at least half-way crazy. But there was a strange confidence about him sometimes, a massive calm. He carried himself like a man who had done a lot of things. Or a man who had been through a lot of things. "You're pretty sure of yourself."

A network of lines appeared around his eyes and mouth. He was either in his thirties, with a young body, or in his twenties, with an older face. "It's all gone without a hitch so far," he said.

"It hasn't been exactly difficult," she pointed out ironically. "You didn't have to fight your way through bodyguards to get to me."

"Oh, it took me a long time to get to you," he said in the same quiet way.

She broke a roll open and put some cheese and a slice of pear inside. "Yeah. You've had me in your sights for a while, haven't you? That time you ambushed me in Laurel Canyon—what were you going to do to me then?"

His expression changed subtly. "I just wanted to see you, face to face."

"Why?" She bit into the roll.

"To see what you were like."

"But why? Why me? What had I ever done to you?"

"You might just work it out one day."

"Now what the hell is that supposed to mean? Huh? You said something, then. You said, 'it's too late for apologies.' What did you mean by that?"

"Nothing."

"Is it something I'm supposed to have done? Why did you choose me?"

He turned to go without answering.

"Were you in Vietnam?" she asked suddenly.

He turned slowly back to her. His face had gone flinty and frightening. Suddenly the food was dry as dust in her mouth. She choked it down. "Just a guess," she said in a smaller voice. "Pedro saw you that day. He said you moved like a trained soldier." The eyes were terrifying now. "Listen," she said urgently, "it doesn't matter. I won't say anything. It's just, like, if you were in Vietnam, I feel sorry for you."

"You feel sorry for *me*?" he creaked.

"I was against the war. I went to rallies. I nearly hit Nixon with an egg, once. But I'm not one of the ones who threw shit at GIs. I know you had no choice. I know you went through hell out there. I feel for what you went through. Really, I do..."

Her voice trailed off. He kept staring at her with that disturbing intensity. She remembered his frightening strength, his capacity for violence. "I don't want your sympathy," he said at last. "Shove it up your ass."

She didn't answer. He walked out.

He was raging inwardly.

She felt sorry for him.

She felt sorry for *him*.

God *damn*. Little junkie bitch peering up at him through that filthy, matted hair and telling him she felt *sorry* for him. Like he was some kind of cripple. Some kind of mad person.

Maybe that was it. Maybe she thought he was crazy.

Crazy?

The thought enraged him further. "I'm not crazy," he said aloud through gritted teeth. He had done this for a purpose. For a *reason*. His actions were not those of a deranged person. Nor of a disturbed one. He'd planned every step. He'd thought about it for years. *Years*. All he wanted was justice.

She'd asked, "Why did you choose me?" Choose! As though *he'd* had any choice! As though he'd ever had a chance to choose, from the day of his birth! Did she think of him as some kind of psycho? Some jumble-brain who'd picked her out at random? Picked her name out of the phone book with a pin?

He stood, filled with his rage. It choked him, held him in its grip like a huge fist. He could feel his hair standing on end, his nipples tight, his stomach clenched. Yet he loved its power. Loved the sense of purpose it gave him. He was both its victim and its worshipper. He could kill her, now, right now.

He ought to go down there and—

He ought to go down there and—what? Tell her? Explain why he was doing it? Tell her the whole sad story?

And then kill her?

He started taking deep, shuddering breaths. The oxygen flooded into his brain, cooling him, gradually easing the tension. The anger left him slowly. It ebbed out of his muscles. He shook his arms to help them relax.

The world steadied around him. The room came into focus. The wood. The stone. The clay tiles on the floor.

Her smell was in his nostrils, rank. An animal smell. A zoo

smell. In the jungle he'd looked after himself better than she did down there. Jesus, she stank. It seemed to cling to his clothes. It hung on him like guilt.

He couldn't stand it any longer. He had to get her clean somehow. Get the cell cleaned too.

He stood for a while, thinking. Then he picked up the keys to the van. He had to do some more shopping.

He pushed his trolley around K Mart, relishing the cool breath of the air conditioning on his skin. It was 107 degrees outside.

What size would she be, Small or Medium? Small. Anyway, it wasn't critical. She wasn't going anywhere in the things.

He got a lightweight track suit, pink. Five T-shirts, plain white. A packet of seven plain cotton panties. Then, on thought, an extra packet. He hesitated over the brassieres. Thinking of those tiny breasts, he figured she wouldn't be too bothered about a bra. He got a couple of cotton camisoles with scraps of pink lace on them.

Moving along, he picked up socks, a pair of pink slippers, and a pink comb. And a pink plastic hair band. To keep the hair from falling over her face.

In the cosmetics section he got a bottle of shampoo with a picture of herbs on the label. Three bars of soap, pink. Some baby powder. A bottle of cologne. A toothbrush, pink. A tube of Colgate.

He looked down at the contents of his trolley. The checkout girl would think he was shopping for a wife who couldn't get out.

He added a pair of sheets, two pillow cases and a laundry bag. Then he headed to the checkout.

Eden had been bad again today. Her stomach felt as though it had been stabbed. The twitching was back. And every time she closed her eyes, jagged lights flashed in her brain. She wasn't suicidal, the way she'd been at first. But she was bad.

Her mind would not let her be. All it would think about was heroin. Junk. Scag. Smack. The feeling of it in her veins. The healing glow. The lift, away from this earthbound rockscape where she lay wrecked and broken.

She did not know that her body was struggling to regain its chemical balance. Rusty Fagan, with his reading of the drug literature, could have told her that during the time she'd been injecting heroin, her brain had stopped producing the endorphins that naturally suppress pain. When the heroin had been abruptly taken away too, there was no barrier between her brain and the general pain of being alive. It would be some time before the levels readjusted themselves.

Rusty could also have explained that her natural metabolic rate had accelerated many times in order to compensate for the heroin's deadening effect on her body's vital functions. Now, as Rusty might have put it, her system was like a boat's propeller lifted out of the water, screaming in overdrive.

But Rusty was dead, and all Eden knew was that she felt frantic, yet exhausted; raw, yet unreal; in pain, with no way out.

It still mattered more to her than the fact of being kidnapped. Being cut off from heroin was the far greater torment. Having been cut off from the world was no great punishment, not when the world had long since ceased to matter to her. Now and then, just occasionally, the thought came to her, Jesus, I've been kidnapped. The rest of the time, her only thought was of heroin.

Even here, in this tiny grey cell, her brain would not stop working out ways to get heroin. It was not impossible, even here. There was a way. Through him. If he could be persuaded to go out and get her some, she could be high again. And away from this misery. Back into heaven.

He need not even get her a needle. She could snort it. Or smoke it. The way she'd started. After such a long period of withdrawal, smoking it would be a rocket.

Caressing the flame under the foil. Watching the powder melt, bubble, become volatile.

Drawing that rich, greasy smoke deep into her lungs. Feeling the first ecstatic lift. The slow rush. The golden glow. And then it was all gone, all the pain, all the tension. You held it down as long as you could, your lungs becoming vast, cloudy chambers. As you sagged back, the tinfoil slipped from your fingers. Like the best sex, better, like nothing else in the universe...

Her head was spinning wildly. Just thinking about it had set her pulses racing.

How? How would she persuade him to go and score for her? Again, there was a way. She would offer him something. The same thing she'd given Rusty. What all men wanted.

She got up jerkily.

Since he'd unchained her, she'd hardly spent ten minutes at a time on the bed. She would jerk to her feet and move around her cell. Around the bed, around the toilet, around the bed, around the toilet, creeping through the little spaces until her joints ached and she was exhausted. Then she would sprawl back onto the bed and lie there. And her limbs would jerk, and her back would ache, and her bladder would hurt until she couldn't stand it any longer, and would jump up and squeeze around the bed, around the toilet, around the bed, around the toilet . . .

She was sitting on the toilet, relieving her bladder for the eighteenth time in three hours, when she heard the bolt clatter.

"Wait!" she called. "Wait!"

The door swung open. She was still hauling up her jeans when he came in.

"Jesus," she snarled, "I told you to wait!"

"What for?"

"Don't I have any damned privacy around here?"

"This is for you." He was carrying a bundle in his arms. He dropped it on the bed. Her eyes widened as she saw what it was.

"Clean sheets!"

"Yes. We're going to get you and this place cleaned up. You stink."

"Is that surprising?" she snapped.

"I've got you some clean clothes too. But first you're going to take a shower."

"A *shower?*"

He held out the blindfold. "Put this on."

Costa Brava

Mercedes sat holding the telephone, waiting for Gerard to be put on the line. She stared with unseeing eyes at the note pad in front of her, covered with her intricate calculations. Eight million dollars. A million of that was Gerard's. Seven paltry million. Was that all it came to, the sum total of her life?

She had not lied to de Córdoba. Her money, almost all of it, had come from the stock market. You didn't need to have been an expert to have made money in the strong bull market of the mid-sixties. She had bought IBM in the 1950's and Xerox in the 1960's. The stock had kept on rising for a decade. And she'd kept buying. Without telling Dominic. By the end of the 1960's she had been a very rich woman, at which point she had got out of the stock market, and had put her money into certificates of deposit and Treasury bills.

She'd once estimated her personal worth at something around thirty-five million dollars, not counting the house. A fortune. But when it came to selling those assets, it had all slipped through her fingers. She hadn't raised a quarter of that.

It was all gone: the cars, the boat, the investments, her art collection, her jewels.

There was only the house left.

The agents had valued the house at around eight million dollars. The contents, they said, were worth around another million. They'd assured her they could find a buyer within a year. She'd told them she would settle at a much lower figure for an immediate sale. They'd pricked up their ears, said they would do what they could. She was waiting impatiently for them to contact her.

If she sold for five, that would leave her two million dollars when it was all over. Not exactly wiped out. But very different.

She had already destroyed her fortune. She had boiled thirty-five million dollars' worth of possessions down to seven million in cash. She could never buy back what she had lost. And when she paid the ransom, she would have nothing at all.

She did not want to think about a future without her house, without all her possessions. She would cope. All she could think of was Eden, Eden back and safe, and in her arms . . .

Gerard's voice came on the line. "Mercedes?"

"Gerard!"

"Any news?"

"The kidnapper called again."

"What did he say?"

"Nothing. Just threats and insults."

"Any compromise over the money?"

"None. He wants his ten million."

"You'll get it back." Gerard Massaguer's voice was like gravel pouring into a bucket. "When this is over," he said grimly, "I intend to use every ounce of power I have to track this man down. I'll have him gutted like herring. He'll wish he'd never been born."

"All I want is my daughter back." Despite herself, she was crying. She fought the tears back. "I'm sorry, Gerard. I didn't mean to cry. How are you?"

"Tired. I've just come back from Seville. I went to see Marisa."

"How is she?"

"The same. Nothing has changed. Nothing ever will. Do you know how long she's been in there? Thirty-two years."

"I'm sorry, Gerard."

"Thirty-two years. She's sixty-nine, Mercedes. She's spent nearly half her life in that place."

"I'm sorry," she said again, helplessly.

He grunted. "She would have been better off dead. Like the rest of them."

"Don't say that."

"Why not? She's a skeleton. She's lost nearly every human feature. Except the capacity to suffer. I told them to let her die."

"Gerard!"

He laughed harshly. "Yes. They were shocked too. I asked them whether they considered what she had as a life worth living. They said she doesn't want to die. She just wants to suffer. I would administer the poison myself if she wasn't—" He paused. "If she wasn't all I have left. How close are you to raising the money?"

"Another week. Maybe more."

"And then you'll be broken."

"Then I'll have Eden back. That's all that matters."

"Is it worth it, Mercé?"

"What do you mean?" she asked sharply.

"I mean, is Eden worth your financial destruction?"

"She's my child!"

"And will she thank you for destroying yourself?"

"That is not the point!"

"Will she be any different? Will your sacrifice make her love you any more? Or turn her into a good daughter? You talk about having her back. You never had her, Mercedes. She rejected you."

"She's only a confused child—"

"You're giving up everything, Mercedes."

"I know that."

"To save a child who is already corrupt—"

"No!"

"—doomed—"

"*No!*"

"—and beyond all salvation. You're spending ten million dollars to ransom the life of a heroin addict. A piece of human flotsam who will go back on the needle as soon as she is set free."

"I'll change her. I'll start over with her. I'll save her, somehow . . ."

"Save yourself. That's more important."

"If it was me who'd been kidnapped—wouldn't you sacrifice everything you had to save me?"

"The comparison does not hold," he said roughly. "You are worth a hundred of Eden. The Pharaohs had a god who weighed souls, Mercedes. Weigh Eden's soul. Ask yourself what it is worth."

"To me, she's more important than life itself. I can't weigh her. There aren't any scales to weigh her. *She's my child.*"

"What if she ends up like Marisa? What if she ends up spending the rest of her life in a place like that? Will it have been worth it, then?"

"Gerard, you're asking me terrible things!" Her voice broke. "Don't you understand? I have no choice!"

"It seems to me," he said heavily, "that you *want* to be destroyed."

Her breath was coming fast and shallow. "I must do it."

"Do you think she'll be grateful? When it's over, and you have nothing left, the girl will leave you. She'll walk out on you and leave you—"

"You're a selfish bastard," she said, the words jerking out of her unbidden. "You always were a selfish bastard. You always will be. You understand *nothing*."

"Mercé, don't be a fool—"

"Keep your million." Mercedes's hand shook as she replaced the telephone, cutting him off.

Tucson

The blindfold brought it back with frightening sharpness. The night he had taken her. How long ago? Days? Weeks? Months?

His fingers bit into her arm as he guided her out of the cell. She was suddenly terrified. She tried to put her hand out, to ward off obstacles.

"Keep your hands by your side," he commanded. "You won't hit anything."

She stumbled. Across a concrete floor.

"Steps," he said.

She climbed. Wooden stairs. As they went up, it got a lot warmer.

She felt sunlight touch her skin. In a house. A dry, clean smell. Wood and polish. The floor under her bare feet felt like the clay tiles at Santa Barbara. The air was warm. Actually hot. A dry, baked heat. It almost took her breath away. A desert heat. Maybe she was in Mexico, somewhere like that.

He steered her left, right, left again.

A door opened. He pushed her forward. A cooler place. A soap smell. A glassy sound to the echoes. A bathroom. The door closed behind them. The bolt clicked.

"Okay," he said. She felt his fingers unfasten the blindfold. The white light hurt her eyes. She blinked around her.

They were standing in a bathroom. It was simply furnished, with white tiles and white ceramic fittings. A basin, a bath, a tiled shower cubicle. Clay tiles on the floor. There was no mirror. There was a window, with pebble glass, but although it was tilted open, all she could see was a sliver of blue sky. After her grey cell, the colours were super-saturated.

He looked down at her from his superior height. "Take your clothes off, Eden. You're going to take a shower."

"Not with you here," she retorted.

The craggy face didn't change. "I can chain you in there and just leave the shower running on you for an hour. Or we can do it the easy way."

She pulled the hair away from her eyes. "Please. Let me wash on my own."

"No. I'm not leaving you alone in here."

She looked around. "There isn't even a shower curtain!"

"Here's some soap. And some shampoo. Wash your hair." He gave her the things, then pointed to a wicker laundry basket in one corner. "Put your dirty clothes in there."

She stood for a moment, irresolute. What if he raped her? Well, he could do that anyway. Then the thought of clean, warm water suddenly broke through. A shower. Soap. Shampoo. The sweet smell of the soap was intoxicating.

She couldn't wait any longer. She yanked off her clothes and naked, stepped into the cubicle.

The impact of the water was painful on her hypersensitized skin. She stood under the jet, eyes closed and let it stream over her face, her breasts, her outstretched arms. It drummed on her like rain on a tin roof, sluicing down and streaming off her fingertips. She spluttered happily. Suddenly she didn't care about his watching her any more.

She shampooed first, lathering her matted hair into a thick foam. It rinsed away grey. God, she must have been dirty. She lathered twice more until the hair squeaked between her fingers and her scalp felt tender.

Then she started soaping her body. The soap slid across her skin with a sense of release. She glanced at him. He was leaning against the basin, watching her with those deep-set, dark eyes. She turned her back on him and soaped her loins and her thighs. The lather was bliss.

How wonderful. How wonderful to feel the water course over her skin, washing away the prickle and the itch.

She washed every inch of herself. The lather! The froth! The dizzy sweet smell! She took the nail brush and scrubbed her dirty fingernails clean. She crouched and scrubbed her toes. When there was nothing left to wash, she just stood under the water with no thought of ending the experience. Finally, he reached in and turned the taps off.

"That's enough. Dry yourself, now." He handed her a big towel. Eden buried herself in its folds. Clean. How marvelous to be clean!

"Enjoy the peep-show?" she asked him, wet hair clinging to her face.

"You're nothing much to look at," he said dryly.

"Why did you watch, then?"

"Brush your teeth." He passed her a pink toothbrush, already loaded with toothpaste. She stooped over the basin and brushed. The toothpaste burned her unaccustomed mouth fiercely. When she spat out, the froth was stained pink.

"Come on," he said, taking her arm. "We're going back down."

"Oh, shit!" Suddenly, the intensity of her freedom was too sweet to give up. The luminous white bathroom. The sliver of blue sky out there. The first breath of outside air on her skin. "Oh, no, please! Not right now!"

"Come on, Eden." He swung her around and looped the blindfold over her eyes again. The darkness pressed into her eyes. She started crying weakly. "You bastard. You cruel bastard..."

"Move." He jerked the towel away from her and pushed her to the door.

"My clothes!"

"They need to be washed. Or burned."

He hustled her, naked but for the blindfold, out of the bathroom. She was hardly dry yet. She sniffed feebly as they went back along the same route. Through the patch of sunlight. Down the wooden stairs. Into the cool. It must be a cellar of some kind. She recognized the clatter of the bolt on the door. A cell built into a cellar.

He jerked her to a stop. "Just stand there. Don't move. Don't touch the blindfold."

She stood without moving. Water from her soaked hair trickled down her back. She felt weird, standing there in her bare skin, the black scarf around her eyes. Vulnerable. She clasped her hands in front of her private parts. She could hear him moving around, arranging things. Now what the hell?

Then he took her arm again and pushed her forward. She heard the door shut behind them. He unfastened the blindfold.

She was back in the cell. She looked down at the bed. It had been stripped and made up with the clean sheets and a clean pillow case. The blanket was new too. Laid out neatly on the blanket was a pile of clothes. Clean new T-shirts, pairs of pink cotton panties, camisoles, socks, a pink track suit.

Next to them was a pink comb, a pink hair band, a bottle of cheap cologne, and a plastic bottle of talc.

She was speechless. At last she said, "You like pink."

"What's wrong with pink?"

"You must think I'm a doll. Is that why you kidnapped me? To have a dolly of your own to dress?"

"Don't you like this stuff?" he asked, frowning.

"Oh, it's great. For a thirteen year-old." But she was already hustling into the clean clothes. They felt wonderful on her skin, crisp and sanitary. "Oh, my God," she whispered. "That feels so good..."

She pulled on the track suit and sat on the bed. She took the comb and ran it through her wet hair. When she'd combed it all back sleekly, she took the hair band and slid it on. She looked up at him with a mixture of defiance and shyness. "Better?"

He was actually smiling. He had straight white teeth. For a moment he was young, handsome. "A hundred times better," he said. Their eyes met for a moment. Then his smile went out. "From now on, you'll get a bath every three days. You'll wear the track suit. You'll change the other clothes every day. Put the dirty ones in the laundry bag. Understand?"

"Yes."

He gestured at the perfume, the talc, and the plastic things. "I'll leave that stuff in here. Do anything silly with any of it, and I'll take it all away. Everything. I'll leave you in here naked as a jay. Understand?"

"Yes." She picked up one of the camisoles. "It's really hot up there," she said, looking at it. "Where are we? Mexico?"

He didn't answer for a moment. "How did you guess that?"

"Is that where I am?" she said in satisfaction. "Somewhere in the middle of the desert, right? I know that desert smell. Dry and clean."

"Clever girl," he said without inflection, and turned to go.

"Hey," she said. He turned. "Thanks."

Alone in the cell, she looked around. She was clean. Her world was clean. She stroked the clothes. She picked up the talc and the cologne and stared at them. God, the luxury. The riches.

He would have avoided the first night of the exhibition if he could have done so. He hated such occasions. But Kolb, the gallery owner, had been so pressing that to refuse would have been conspicuous. So he had graced them with his presence, but on sufferance.

He stood awkwardly holding the beer, staring over the girl's shoulder at the crowd. She had fenced him into a corner, using her notebook and pencil the way a lion tamer uses his chair and whip. She was bizarrely dressed, pretty, clever. She was the arts reporter for a big paper, and her eyes were bright with purpose.

"Your work is very highly focussed," she said. "I'd say it reflects a very intense preoccupation with natural forms. Would you agree with that?"

"Well . . . I guess."

"There's an absence of *synthetic* content. You don't make many compromises. Some people say that's because of your life-style." She looked at him, with his worn leather jacket, denims and boots. "You have a reputation for reclusiveness, Mr. Lennox. Don't you like people?"

"I don't have any problem with people," he mumbled. He was tongue-tied in front of her aggressive interviewing style. "I just need . . . privacy."

"You're a very private man, aren't you?" She scribbled in her notebook. "Would you call yourself lonely?"

"I'm never aware of . . ."

"Yet you don't associate with other artists. For example, Sandra Wilmot, the other artist in this exhibition, is quite a gregarious person. You don't feel you're missing out on the fellowship, what one might call the *sodality* of other artists?"

"I'm not quite sure what you . . ."

She smiled brilliantly. "The interchange of ideas. The stimulation of other viewpoints."

"I have my own ideas."

"That much is obvious." She wrote again. He wondered what she could find to write about his terse replies. She looked up. "Mr. Lennox, this is some of your best work to date. The sculptures are bigger and more complex than ever before. As an artist, you've made great strides in the past two years."

"Uh-huh."

"Your prices, if I may say so, reflect that. Some of these pieces here tonight have pretty heavy price tags. And I notice two have sold already."

He shrugged. Over her shoulder he watched the glittery people wandering around the gallery, staring at his sculptures, and at Sandra Wilmot's paintings. He could see Sandra Wilmot herself, a blimp in a muu-muu, surrounded by admirers. He did not feel anything for her work either way. It seemed ephemeral to him.

So did the glittery people and their smiling faces and never-still mouths. They were like wraiths, drifting hungrily in search of something real to fasten onto. In fact, the only substantive things in the long, carefully lit gallery were his own sandstone carvings, massive, solid and silent.

"You never associate with other artists?"

"No."

"But where does the stimulus come from?"

"I don't know."

"You've banished yourself up in there in the hills, hardly seeing a soul from day to day. You're known to discourage visitors. That isn't the way most artists like to live."

"I'm not most artists."

"I guess that's an answer. You've never had any formal training. Is that true?"

"Yes."

"Is it also true that you started off carving gravestones in Prescott?"

"I worked for a memorial mason for a while . . . before Vietnam."

"Ah, yes. The war. Would you say that Vietnam helped shape your—"

"I don't want to talk about Vietnam."

"Well, I just want to get at the roots of your creative impulse."

"I don't want them got at."

"You don't enjoy being interviewed, do you?" the reporter said with a sharp little smile. "That's okay. But it does mean I'm very much left to my own devices. You can't complain if you don't like what I write about you."

"I won't read it anyway." He was simply stating a fact, and hadn't meant to be rude; but he saw the anger in her eyes. He glanced at his watch. He'd been here two hours. He could leave now, get back to the house. It was way past Eden's mealtime. "Excuse me," he said abruptly and slid past her pad and pencil.

He side-stepped some people who'd once bought some of his work, avoided Kolb's eye and made his way towards the exit.

"Hi, there."

A small blond woman stood in his way. He looked down into the wide-eyed smile. Familiar. Her name came to him. Lilah. Keith Hattersley's girl. He grunted something and kept moving.

"Joel, wait!" Her hand caught the sleeve of his leather jacket, but he pretended not to notice and pulled free.

His van was waiting in the lot outside the gallery. He got in and drove off with a squeal of tyres. He hated crowds. He hated questions, faces thrusting into his, eyes probing his...

He hustled through the six o'clock traffic. The evening sky was tinted green, with a few streaks of yellow in the west. The lights of the city had started to twinkle.

Driving up towards Golden Gate, Joel forced himself to ease his boot off the accelerator. No need to rush. She would be all right. But the anxiety was always there at the back of his mind. He hated leaving the house. What if something were to happen to him? What if he got in an accident, didn't get back for two or three days? She would be trapped down there. Without him, she would die.

The thought disturbed him. He had to force himself to ease off the accelerator again.

He was glad he'd let her clean up. It had been wrong to keep the girl in that filthy mess. Unnecessary.

He thought of her naked body under the shower. She was so thin and angular. Almost like a child, but for the small breasts and the triangle of black pubic hair. Almost sexless. Yet there had been something intriguing about her shape. Her body had a grace of its own. Not the conventions of feminine curve and swell, but the spare beauty of a leafless tree, of a thing that had been pared down to its bare anatomy.

He'd wanted to see her naked. He admitted that to himself. He'd thought it was simple curiosity, an abstract thing. But it hadn't turned out so abstract. She was a woman, not a girl. Her femininity was stronger than he'd anticipated. It had affected him. It was as though a barb had caught in his mind.

He had an image of the water running down her flat, pale belly, dripping through those shadowy curls, sliding down her lean thighs. Of the sharp, dark nipples, tightened under the downpour. Her arms outstretched, like a priestess. Unexpectedly, he felt the swelling of desire.

He cursed under his breath. *No*. He didn't want her affecting him in *that* particular way.

Christ, no.

He shook his head angrily, as though to shake away the image of those rigid brown nipples. It was too long since he'd had a woman. Much too long.

It was dark by the time he got back to the house. He went to the kitchen, and heated the meal he had prepared earlier, tortillas topped with beef, tomatoes and small but fiery wild chiltepins from the desert. He sliced cheese on top of the tacos, and put them under the flame to grill.

It occurred to him, almost for the first time, to wonder what he was going to do with the money.

Ten million dollars.

It was a gigantic fortune. A mountain of money. His primary purpose had been to take it away from Mercedes. To inflict a shattering blow to the world she'd built up. To make her whole life seem meaningless.

But afterwards, the money would be his. His by right. He had earned it. He had paid for that money. It *was* his.

What was he going to do with ten million dollars? He could burn it. Send her a photograph of it burning.

He could spend it. Leave Arizona. Go buy himself an island in the South Pacific. An apartment in Rome. A chalet in Switzerland. Anything. It seemed unreal. But foreign parts did not call him. He did not want to leave Arizona, or the house he had built. It was too much a part of him. He loved it too much. Loved the desert and the mountains and the stillness and the peace. He'd never felt any desire to leave this vast, open land where he had suffered and become a man.

He watched the cheese melt and bubble, and tried to think what he could do with the money that would be worthwhile. All he could come up with was that he would never again have to sell a sculpture. He would never again have to sell a piece of himself to those greedy-eyed wraiths. Or accept a commission from the likes of Keith Hattersley.

She was sitting on the bed as he came into the cell. She looked up. He stopped short, staring at her.

She was transformed. The hair that framed her face now gleamed like a raven's wing. She had slipped on the hair band to keep it neat. She was clean and pale as ivory. Sitting there, neat and tidy in her pink track suit, she was a different being from the half-wild creature he'd grown accustomed to. A slim, pink flamingo in a cage.

Beautiful.

"What's the matter?" she asked, frowning at his expression.

"Nothing." He shut the door and gave her the tray.

She looked at the food without relish. "Tacos."

"Don't you like tacos?"

"I don't like spicy food."

"This isn't a goddamned hotel," he snapped. "Eat or go hungry."

"Okay, okay." She sat back with the tray in her lap and crunched into a tortilla. "It isn't bad," she said. "But then, I'm famished. You're kind of late, aren't you?"

He didn't answer. He wanted to tell her about the vapid people at the gallery, about the ridiculous questions the reporter had asked him. But of course he couldn't. He watched her eat, aware of her smell. She had used the talc and she was fragrant. There was something new in the cell, something disturbing. She was unbelievably changed. She was more feminine. Dangerously so. She was all glossy and clean and sweet-smelling and he felt that she had gathered strength from the change.

The green eyes met his. "Did you cook this?"

"Who else would cook it?"

"So it's just you. Doing all this. You don't have any . . . partners."

"Sure I have partners," he said, angry with himself for his carelessness. "There are lots of us. I'm the only one you'll ever see."

"Where are the others? Here in Mexico?"

"I told you never to ask me anything about that side of it."

"That side of it? What other side is there?"

"Just forget it. Just concentrate on getting through this. It's all that concerns you."

She shrugged sullenly and kept eating. He wanted to leave, but something stopped him. He sat down on the end of the bed. She raised one eyebrow. "Staying for dinner?"

"I may as well take the tray back when you're through."

"Suit yourself." She finished a taco. "I could use the company. Will you bring me some more books?"

"I'll see."

"When am I gonna get out of here? I mean, you must have *some* idea."

"I told you. Forget it."

"Oh, sure. As a matter of fact, I have so much to do in here that the thought of getting out barely crosses my mind." She was just picking at the food now, though the plate was half-full. He couldn't get over how changed she was. She still looked sick, but she had shed that desperation. She was more poised. Much more poised. Like the Eden he'd imagined. A little rich girl, sassy and polished.

"How are you feeling?" he asked.

"I feel like shit," she said with unexpected venom. "I need a fix."

"Don't be ridiculous. You're over it now."

"Because you say so?"

"Because it's been more than two months."

The green eyes widened in the pale oval face. "Have I been here two months?"

"More or less."

"God. It feels like I've been here forever."

"A month is plenty to get over cold turkey."

She pushed the tray aside. "Cold turkey's nothing," she said. "Addiction's not about cold turkey." She pressed her finger to her temple. "Addiction's up here."

"Haven't you ever tried to come off heroin before?"

"Why should I?" She gave him a mocking look. "Heroin's wonderful. What do you think people take it for? It's beautiful. It's been the happiest time of my life. Don't you believe me?"

"You must have had a damned poor opinion of your life up till then," he said, disgusted.

"Oh, I did. I have a damned poor opinion of most things."

"Including yourself."

"I'm rotten." She said it with a funny little smile. "I don't have much self-esteem. But heroin changes all that."

"It makes you feel better?"

"You learn to love yourself. You learn to love what's inside your head. You just float. Nothing can hurt you any more." Her eyes grew dreamy. "No depression. No pain. Like being in heaven."

"You've got to stop thinking about it," he said brusquely.

"What else should I think about? I dream about heroin every hour of the day."

"You're a fool. You're just a spoiled little bitch."

"Gee. No one ever said that to me before."

"You think your little sojourn in heaven will last forever? Don't you know how heroin will degrade you in the end, drag you down to the sewer, where all the other junkies end up?"

"It's like being in love with a man," she said. "You know he can be mean, but he excites you so much. You can't stop loving him. You don't *want* to stop. He's a pimp. He beats on you, but you learn to love that too. When he's with you, he lifts you up so high. And when he goes, you're just waiting for him to come by again." She sat up. She looked feverish now, her eyes brilliant, her lips scarlet. "I bet you know where you could get some."

"I don't buy a lot of heroin," he said dryly.

"But you know where to score. This is Mexico, right? Oh, I bet you know who the local dealers are. I bet if you wanted, you could go out and score for me. You could, couldn't you?"

"You're crazy," he said. But he was fascinated by the eerie beauty that had come over her.

"You wouldn't have to get a needle. Just some tinfoil and a lighter—"

"No!"

"I'd pay you. I'd pay you well." She licked her lips. "It'd be worth your while."

"That's enough!" he said harshly. "If you think I'm going to supply you with heroin in here—"

"You don't know how good I could make you feel." She smiled, wide and false. A whore's smile. A vampire's smile. "I'm good in bed," she said huskily. "Very good. And I'm clean now. Don't you think I'm pretty?"

"I think you're sick."

"I'll do anything you want me to." He couldn't believe what she was saying. What she was doing. She edged over to him, holding his eyes. He smelled the sweet innocence of the talc. She reached out and took the lapel of his jacket in her fingers. "I'll blow your mind. I'll fuck you, suck you—"

"Shut up," he said savagely.

"I'll be your doll. You can dress me up. You can do anything you want to me. Anything. You can come all over my face—"

He knocked her arm away and grasped at her mouth, crushing the foul words. His fingers bit into her cheeks, distorting her face.

Her huge green eyes stared at him. He heard her whimper against his palm. Her skull felt like a bird's, fragile, brittle.

"Eden," he said shakily, "don't ever say that again. Not ever. You understand me?" She whimpered again. "Say that again and I'll hurt you. Bad."

He released her. She shrank back. The marks of his fingers were livid on her cheeks. Her saliva was on his palm. He wiped it on his denims. He could hear his own heart pounding.

He was terrified by how aroused he was. He was terrified by how much he wanted her.

"Forget about heroin," he said, fighting to keep his voice normal. "Get it out of your mind."

She touched her mouth with trembling fingers. They came away bloodstained. "You always have to hurt," she said with bitterness. "Couldn't you just have said, 'no thanks'?"

His mouth was bone-dry. He swallowed hard. "You don't—"

"I don't what?"

"You don't understand."

Looking exhausted now, Eden leaned back against the cement wall. "Of course I don't understand. I don't understand anything. Why did you choose me? What do you want with me?"

He sat silent, breathing unsteadily. They looked at one another across the gulf of their mutual incomprehension.

"What's your name?" she asked simply.

"You know I can't tell you that."

"I have to have a name for you."

"Joel." It just came out.

"Joel?" She tasted it. "Joel. Is that your real name?"

"It's real enough."

"You're going to have to kill me when this is through," she said. "I know too much. I know your face. I know where we are. I even know your first name, now. You could never let me go. Could you?"

"If the police don't get involved, I'll let you go."

"And if they do?" When he didn't answer, Eden smiled crookedly. "So why the big fuss about getting me some junk? My last days might as well be happy ones."

"You're not going to die."

"We're all going to die, Joel." She touched her hurt mouth

again. "I went on a detox program once," she said, almost casually. "My mother and father forced me to. While I was in there, they had my lover killed. They thought he was evil, because he used to go out and score for me. Big, evil pusher. They thought if they removed him, I wouldn't do any more drugs. So they had him *eliminated*. I guess my mother arranged it. She has more guts than my father when it comes to that sort of thing. It looked like suicide. A bullet through the head. But it was murder."

He stared at her. "You're making this up."

"Why would I make it up?"

"Because you live in a fantasy world."

"You don't know much about my mother. My mother has contacts you wouldn't believe. When you get your money, better go where she can't find you. She has sharp claws."

"Did this man turn you on to heroin?"

"No. I learned to smoke heroin in twelfth grade. It was the first time I got really out of it, you know, really stoned. God, it was so good..." She lay back, her lids drooping. "You can't imagine how good it was. It was like coming home." She was, if possible, even paler than before. Her face had a greenish tinge, like someone about to be very seasick. "But Rusty, he turned me onto using the needle."

"Then I would have killed the bastard too."

"My hero." She touched her throat and choked a little.

"What's the matter?"

"I think I'm gonna be sick pretty soon. I never liked Mexican food. And my stomach's kind of screwed-up." She winced again. "You never tried drugs?"

"I smoked hash once or twice."

"In Nam?" She didn't wait for an answer. "That's where a lot of guys learned about drugs. I found out about drugs at school. A little group of us, we used—we used—"

"Hold on." He moved to her quickly as she started to retch, and pulled her over to the toilet. She clutched at him frantically, her stomach heaving. He put his arm around her shoulders and held her head over the bowl.

It all came up in a rush. He felt her thin body convulse in his arms. She was so frail that the sickness seemed to shake her the way a dog shakes a rat. He kept a tight hold of her through the dry spasms that followed. Then he flushed the toilet and wiped her clammy face with the towel.

"Oh, God." She gulped. "I feel . . . terrible . . ."

"Easy now," he said gently. "No more tacos, I swear."

"Very . . . alluring . . . huh?"

"Just relax."

"I bet you can hardly . . . resist me."

She sagged over to him, resting her head wearily on his shoulder. He put his arms around her. She lay against him with her eyes closed. He looked down at her. There were hectic spots on her cheeks now. Her eyelashes were very long. She looked pathetically vulnerable.

He was ashamed of the rampancy between his thighs. He tried to ignore it. "Feeling better?"

"This feels good," she mumbled against his chest. "Please don't go. Just hold me."

He tightened his arms around her. After a while, he stroked her hair lightly, uncertainly. It was silky and soft. He didn't mind the faint, curdled smell of her sickness. Mingled with the talc, it reminded him of babies. Of tender things.

"You don't have to go yet, do you?" she asked without opening her eyes.

"Not for a while," he said huskily.

"I get so lonely down here."

"I know."

"That damned light never goes out. Not ever. Can't you rig it so I can turn it off?"

"It's too late to put in a switch now."

"Then couldn't you turn it off from outside? Just at night? God, this feels so good . . ."

She was silent for a long while, just nestling in his arms. Her body seemed to be melting against his. Such strange feelings went through him. Such strange thoughts. For a while, he was somewhere else. In some sweet and lovely place that he'd dreamed of since before he had words. A place he'd only seen in dreams. Somewhere far off and long ago . . .

"We could make love anyway," she said at last, dreamily. "That would be almost as good as heroin."

He bit his lip, hard. He wanted to get up and leave, but his erection was thrusting so violently out of his loins that she would see it. And know. "I don't want to make love to you."

"Yes, you do. I wouldn't mind. You're very handsome."

"God damn," he said quietly, "are sex and drugs all you think about?"

"And rock and roll." She said nothing more for ten minutes. He thought she was asleep until she stirred in his arms and he released her at once. She moved away from him, pushing the black hair away from her temples. Her face was softer, bruised-looking. Her eyes were unfocussed. She smiled at him. "You were sweet to me. Thanks."

He took a deep breath. "Why not get some sleep now?"

"I might, at that."

He trusted himself to stand up at last. His legs felt weak. He picked up the tray and prepared to leave. She was already curled up on the bed, watching him with green slits of eyes.

"I've got an idea," she said.

"What?"

"If you let me speak to Mama, I could tell her not to go to the police. For my sake."

He considered. "Maybe."

He was quite drained as he locked the cell door. He stopped and looked at the board where the house's fuses were located. There was a single trip that would turn the lights in the cell out. He went over to it and switched it off.

It would be dark in there for the first time in two months.

He picked up the tray and went upstairs.

When he next came down to her, she would not look up at him.

"What's the matter?" he asked.

"I'm ashamed," she muttered, hanging her head. "About what I did. The things I said."

"It was kind of crude."

"I guess you think I'm the worst kind of slut."

"No," he said gently, "I don't think that, Eden."

She looked up at last and he saw that her pale cheeks wore a dark red blush. "I'm sorry, Joel."

He found himself smiling at her. He liked hearing her call him Joel. It touched him, warmed him inside. "The woman that blushes is not quite a slut," he said.

"Is that a quotation?"

"Sort of."

"I just felt so terrible..."

"I know." He gave her the book he was carrying. "I bought you this."

She laughed shortly when she saw the cover. "*Kick Heroin?*"

"What's so funny?"

"The title. It's like one of those do-it-yourself books that make it sound so easy. *Learn Chinese. Build a Yacht. Kick Heroin.*"

"Read it. It'll help."

She tossed the book wearily aside. "I've been given books like that before." But he knew she would read it, later. He turned to the door again. "Aren't you staying?" she asked quickly.

"I can't."

"Why not?" she demanded, almost fretfully.

"I have things to do."

"I don't." She was frowning. "You could stay and talk to me for a minute. I swear I won't try and seduce you."

He smiled again. "I'll stay and talk to you when I bring your dinner tonight."

She brightened. "Promise?"

"I promise," he said gently.

He had finished Hattersley's commission, so he called the builder to arrange for him to come pick it up. In the afternoon, he began a new sculpture.

He had chosen white Carrara marble, a material he didn't often use, partly because he felt it was cold and alien to this landscape, and partly because it was so expensive. The block was a big one and had cost him a great deal of money. But this time he had a feel for the material, smooth and white and pure.

He had been making dozens of sketches, using thick crayons. He had selected three main drawings to work from. With them in his hand, he prowled around the marble block, marking it, at first lightly, then more boldly. Despite the drawings, the ideas in his mind were still not fully formed. They would develop as he worked. That was increasingly the way, these days. If he'd been properly trained, he supposed, had gone to art school, he'd have been more sure. He would have started with sharper ideas and gone a more direct route. But as it was, he had to feel his way, like a blind man.

What he wanted this time was not an artifact, not a finished thing. He wanted something dynamic. A sense of the figure *emerging* from the stone. The idea wasn't original. He'd seen photographs of Michelangelo's last works and they all had that sense. Male figures agonized in the struggle to wrench themselves out of the rock that imprisoned them. That was something like what he wanted, but in his mind the image was not so . . .

He could not find words to express himself. The ideas floated in his head, tantalizingly, but without definite form.

He began work with the biggest chisel and the heavy club hammer. The first cut was clean and accurate. The white stone sheared smoothly. He worked quickly, taking out big, wide flakes. The crystalline pieces fell away in obedience to his wishes. He paused to re-mark the stone when his lines had gone, kept on cutting, stopped to re-mark once more.

It was bakingly hot in the shed. There had been no rain since May. But today there was a haze in the sky. A muggy feeling in the air. Maybe a storm was coming.

The stone lost its manufactured, blocky shape. It began to look like something natural, weathered. Pleased, he pulled off his shirt and kept working. His body moved more and more smoothly as he went on. It had become automatic, an instinctive thing. The ringing note of the chisel pierced him sweetly. Through half-closed eyes, he watched the white stone slowly changing, wearing away, taking an inner shape. Just like Mr. Schultz's wax, when he'd been a child. Transforming itself in its hands as though it were a thing alive and he no more than a watcher. The best game there was. Watching it happen, as though it were nothing to do with him. Not to do with his mind, at least. Coming out of somewhere deep inside, the way web came out of a spider.

Sweat streamed down his chest and back, an indication of how heavy the air was today. He didn't usually sweat so much. Maybe he'd dig a swimming pool one of these summers. He'd never wanted one before. Now he thought it might be nice. Not one of those synthetic blue lozenges. A stone pool that looked as though it had just happened. Somewhere to float at twilight and watch the stars come out. He swung the heavy hammer, feeling the thud right through his bones, watching the flakes drop, the inner shape start to emerge.

"Anybody home?"

He recognized the little-girl voice before he turned. She was standing behind him, silhouetted against the light. She wore a checked shirt and Levis and handsome, hand-tooled boots. The blond hair was fluffed out around her face.

The pleasure of his creativity drained away. He lowered the hammer slowly, feeling a dull anger, a dull alarm.

"What are you doing here?" he rasped.

"I told you I might drop by." Lilah walked to him, swaying her hips. "I told you I thought you were special. I like special people."

He'd been so absorbed with his work that he hadn't heard the car pull up. He clenched his teeth. "I didn't invite you."

"I know. Keith isn't with me." She examined the marble block. "Hey. That looks interesting. Is that a commission?"

"No."

"It's for you? For the house?"

"Yes."

She was studying his body the way she had done the time before, openly, with pleasure. "You're magnificent, Joel. But you know that, don't you?" She smiled up at him. Her name, picked out in gold letters, nestled against the white skin of her cleavage. "Are you angry with me for coming?"

"You shouldn't be here."

"I just wanted to see you. You ran away from me the other night. At the Kolb Gallery. You can't stand crowds, can you? You hate all those fakes and phonies." She held out a newspaper. "I brought you this. There's an article about you. That woman who was interviewing you at the gallery." He didn't take the paper, so she opened it and showed him the place. There was a big photograph of one of his works. Lilah smiled. "It's an interesting article. She doesn't like you much. I'd guess you got under her skin." She read aloud, " 'Joel Lennox the artist is a fascinating, sensitive personality with an outstanding talent. Joel Lennox the man is brusque, ill-mannered, plain ornery. Trying to get a spoken sentence from him is like trying to squeeze blood out of one of his sandstone carvings.' " She laughed softly. "You must have been very rude to her."

"I'm afraid I'm working right now," he said, speaking with an effort. "I'm going to have to ask you to leave."

"Sure. Right away." But her eyes mocked him from under long lashes. "Have you finished Keith's carving?"

"Yes."

"Mind if I take a look?"

"I'd rather you just left."

"This is it right here, isn't it?" She lifted the tarpaulin and looked down at the stone. "Oh," she sighed. "That's so beautiful. You have such a wonderful talent—"

He jerked the tarpaulin out of her hand and faced her, the anger naked in his aquiline face. "You're not listening to me. I didn't ask you to come here. I want you to go now."

" 'Brusque, ill-mannered, plain ornery,' " she said gently. "But you fascinated her. You fascinate me, Joel."

"I'm not running a fan club."

"Don't you ever get lonely?"

"No. I don't like visitors."

"Only the ones you invite, huh?"

"I never invite anyone."

"Never?"

"Never."

She nodded her blond head at the house. "Then who's the gal you've got in there right now?"

He felt as though she'd rammed a knife into his heart. "I don't have anyone in there," he stammered, dry-mouthed.

"Pink cotton panties, small? Camisoles with a bit of frill?" She put her head on one side. "They're on the clothes line right now. Don't tell me you wear that stuff when nobody's looking?"

His mind whirled. He opened his mouth, but no words came out. He'd hung her things out on the line. He'd been unbelievably stupid.

Lilah gave him her slow smile. "She doesn't have a lot of money to spend on her underwear. You should buy her something lacy. Something sexier."

He still had the club hammer in his fist. His fingers tightened around the wooden shaft.

"Is she the model for Keith's carving? Is she a Navaho? Is that why you're ashamed of her? Maybe she's hiding in the house.

Embarrassed to come out." Lilah sauntered away from him. He stood rooted to the spot, grasping the hammer. She paused in front of the new carving and picked up one of the drawings. "Is this her too?" She studied the slim, crouching figure in the sketch, then glanced at the marble block. "She's pretty. Kind of skinny, though. Her titties wouldn't fill two teacups." She turned to him. "I've always been . . . fuller-figured. Since I was a girl. Would you like to sculpt me, Joel? In the nude?" She leaned on a workbench, cocking one hip. "I'd like to pose for you. I've been photographed." She giggled. "The photographs were kind of artistic."

"I don't need a model," he said hoarsely.

She reached across herself, hugging herself so her breasts pushed up at the vee of her shirt, smooth and white. "You're adorable," she said softly. "You're the most attractive man for a hundred miles around, Joel. You must be used to girls chasing you by now. Am I being too obvious?"

"I don't need a model," he said again.

"Are you worried about Keith? You needn't be. I live my own life."

He swallowed dryly. "And I don't have any girl in the house. Somebody left those things here. A—a friend."

"Nice of you to wash them for her." Her eyes dropped to the silvery scar under his ribs. The sweat had dried in streaks of marble dust on his tanned skin. She sighed quietly. "Okay. I'll go. Will you do me one favour first?"

"What?"

"I'd love to be shown around your house."

"*No.*"

She looked at him for a long while. "Keith was right. You *are* frightening. There's something about you. Like an earthquake waiting to happen." She moistened her lips with the tip of a pink tongue. "It's scary. And very exciting."

He walked stiffly at her side as she went back to the car. She had come in a little yellow Ferrari Dino. The drive along the dirt road had covered the car with ochre dust. "I bought it myself," she said, turning to him as she opened the door. "I have my own money. I'm not Keith's kept woman."

"Bully for you," he said tightly.

She leaned forward, her voice soft. "One day, I'm going to

show you things your little squaw hasn't dreamed of yet, Joel. I'm going to make your earthquake happen." She smiled, slipped on sunglasses and got into the car.

The dust of her leaving hung in the air long after the growl of the engine had died away in the desert stillness.

Costa Brava

The man said he loved the house. The woman said, "It's far too big." But Mercedes could sense their excitement. They touched everything, feeling the quality of the curtains, stroking the marble, turning on the taps. She tried not to hate them. She could have asked Maya to show them around, but she'd known she had to face up to this herself. Maya was sitting with Joaquin in the garden, waiting.

They walked around the indoor pool, where Maya's rain forest grew lush and abundant. The man dipped his hand in the water and murmured approval.

"This structure was architect-designed and custom-made," the estate agent said, pointing up at the glittering glass dome. "It ensures year-round swimming."

"Nice."

"It's a wonderful house, don't you think? A unique home."

"But so big," the woman sighed. She wore a leopard-skin jacket despite the heat and a tight leather skirt. She had a huge diamond ring that glittered. She was in her thirties, the man in his late forties. A bond dealer from Barcelona, the estate agent had told Mercedes, and his second wife. The woman's eyes never stopped moving, taking it all in. "You're leaving the plants, of course."

"Yes," Mercedes said quietly. "The plants stay."

"What about the pool furniture?"

"We can come to an arrangement about that. About all the furniture, if you like."

The man looked up sharply. "You'd be interested in selling it?"

"For the right price, I would consider it."

"The furnishings are extremely valuable," the agent put in smoothly. "As you've seen, they're of extremely high quality."

The man smoothed his glistening hair back, considering Mercedes with shrewd eyes. "You just want to walk out of here, is that it? Take nothing with you but the cheque?"

"That might suit me." She turned before he could ask any further questions and led the way out.

"I think you'll agree," the agent intoned, "that the taste throughout is exceptional—" She heard him droning on in the hushed tones that estate agents and funeral parlour directors use.

They came into the entertaining area. The couple from Barcelona looked around silently. Mercedes could see the woman's red-nailed fingers biting into her arms. She'd sell her soul to have this house, she thought. They'll buy it if they have the money. But do they have the money? Instinct told her they were a long way short.

"The fireplace is English," Mercedes said. "Eighteenth century. A lot of the panelling also came from England. It was in the library of a stately home. I had a local cabinet maker make up the rest to match."

"The glass doors open onto a patio," the agent said, moving forward. "The columns are solid marble—"

The telephone began to ring. Excusing herself, Mercedes turned and picked it up.

"Hello?"

"Mama!"

"*Eden.*" The tone of her voice made the others turn sharply. She sat down, her legs weak. "Oh, Eden, is that you?"

"It's me, Mama."

"Where are you?"

"Here. The same place."

"How are you, darling? Are you all right? He told me you were sick."

"I've been sick. I'm getting better now."

"Has he hurt you?"

"No. Not yet. Oh, Mama. I'm so sorry about this." Mercedes could hear Eden start to cry and felt her own throat choke. "Mama, I miss you so much."

"Darling." It was all she could say. "Oh, darling..."

The estate agent was trying to steer the couple from Barcelona out onto the patio, but they were hanging around the door, just within earshot, fascinated. Mercedes was hardly aware of them.

"He won't let me talk for long," she heard Eden say. "Mama, have you got the money?"

"I'm trying to get it. I'm trying. Tell him, Eden. Tell him I'm trying. But it's so hard—"

"When will you have it?"

"It'll be a little while, yet. I'm doing everything I can, but it'll be a little while, yet. It's so much."

"Oh, Mama."

"Soon, darling. I swear it on my life. I'll get you out of there soon, baby."

"Have you called the police?"

"No. They don't know anything."

"Mama, don't call the police. For my sake. Please."

"I haven't."

"He'll kill me if you do."

"I haven't. *I haven't.*"

"Are you sure?"

"Trust me!"

"Mama, I can't speak any more. I have to go now. Mama, I love you—"

Eden's voice was suddenly cut off. "Eden!" she said distraughtly. "*Eden!*" She thought she heard a man's breathing for a moment. Then the line clicked dead. She covered her face with her hands, rocking with pain in the chair.

The estate agent finally managed to push the clients outside. "As you can see," he began, somewhat breathlessly, "the gardens have been beautifully landscaped. No expense has been spared—"

An hour later, the couple from Barcelona dropped the estate agent off at his office and drove to a country restaurant in their B.M.W. The woman was quivering with her revelation.

"Did you hear that?" she burst out as soon as they were on their way. "They've got her daughter!"

"Who've got her daughter?" he asked.

"*I* don't know who. Kidnappers. That's why she's selling out!"

"Oh, come on, Pilar..."

"I *heard* her, Jaume!" Her eyes gleamed with exhilaration. She dug her nails into his shoulder. "She asked if they'd hurt her.

And the girl asked if she had the money yet. And she said she'd have it soon. Jaume, you know what this means? She's desperate! She'll take anything!"

He took his eyes off the road to glance at her uncertainly. "Are you sure about this?"

"I've never been so sure of anything in my life." She was panting slightly with excitement. "Jaume, this is a golden opportunity."

"Well, I don't know—"

"We could have that magnificent house, and everything in it, for a song!"

"That woman's no fool—"

"They've got her like this!" She reached down and clutched his privates in her hand, squeezing hard. He gasped.

"Not so tight, *querida*!"

"It doesn't matter how clever she is. They've got her like this, Jaume." She squeezed hard enough to make him whimper, then relaxed her grip a little. "If we let this go by, we're the biggest fools in Spain."

He sleeked his hair back, a habitual gesture. Now he too was starting to feel excitement. "What should we do? She wants five million dollars."

"Offer her one."

"A million dollars? For that house?"

"For the house and everything in it." She was rubbing him now, feeling him swelling under her fingers. "For every stick of furniture, every blade of grass, every stone."

"She'll never take it."

"She'll take it. If she doesn't, the kidnappers will start cutting her daughter's fingers off." She kissed his cheek. "Even if we have to go as high as a million and a half, even two, it'll be the deal of a lifetime. The deal of a lifetime!"

He stared at her for a minute. The car started to wander and he swerved it straight again. "My God, Pilar. If you're right—"

"I *am* right."

"We'll have to act fast."

"This afternoon," she said succinctly. "Are you hungry?"

"Not any more."

"Good," she said huskily. "Pull over, Jaume."

She was still crying as he led her from the telephone back down into the cellar. He locked the door and untied the blindfold. She wiped her eyes and looked up at him blearily. "She sounded so— so grief-stricken. I never heard her sound like that before. She's always been so strong. So remote."

"Do you think she was telling the truth?"

"Yes."

"But then, you would say that, wouldn't you?"

"I think she was telling the truth." She sighed shakily. "I've never heard her sound like that. Not ever. I never knew she cared that deeply. I never had the feeling I was part of her life."

He stared at her. "Was she . . ." He hesitated. "Was she a good mother?"

"She's *concerned*." Eden grimaced. "She always did what she thought was best for me. She never consulted me, not ever. She just *did* it. Like, when they found out about the heroin, she had me put in the Hebron Clinic. No questions, no alternatives. She just did it. Like having Rusty killed. You know any other mothers would do a thing like that? She's the strongest person I'll ever know. Stronger than good or bad. She's just Mercedes. But she would never let me down, not in anything practical."

His face twisted. "She wouldn't, huh?"

"After I skipped out of the clinic, my father never gave me another penny. Said he wouldn't pay for my junk. But Mama never cut my allowance off. Despite everything, she would never let me sink. Even though she knew what I was doing with the money."

"I guess she knew what you would do if you didn't have the money," he said dryly.

She wiped tears off her cheeks. "Want to hear something funny? The first few days after you grabbed me, put me in here, the thought went through my head that she might have arranged it all. Organized it, as a way to get me off heroin. She's capable of something like that. But she'd have more finesse."

He sat down on the bed beside her. He hadn't meant it as an approach, but before he could stop her, she had pressed herself against him, resting her head on his chest.

"Hold me," she commanded.

The muscles of his body had tensed in reaction. With an effort, he put his arms awkwardly around her.

The slim body nestled into his embrace. "Not like that," she complained. "You're so stiff. Hold me like you did before."

His breathing was unsteady. He drew her into him, trying to relax. She was like a child. Like a sick little sister, needing comfort. But he could feel the soft swell of her breasts against his ribs.

She sighed contentedly, closing her eyes. "You're so strong," she murmured. "But you'd never really hurt me. Would you?"

There was no answer he could give. Words stuck in his throat. He lowered his face so that his mouth touched the glossy black hair. It felt like silk against his lips. He inhaled the clean shampoo smell, and felt a wave of dizziness rise up inside him, spreading through his brain. There was a pain in his chest, a throbbing in his heart.

"You smell good," Eden said dreamily. "You smell of man. Rock me, Joel."

He swayed her gently in his arms, as though she were a child. He felt her slacken utterly against him. He could feel the articulations of her body moving as he rocked her, as though she were a beautifully-constructed doll. His mind was filled with wonder. How could she relax so completely in his arms? He was her kidnapper. Her enemy.

She had no sense of self-preservation. None whatsoever. She was an innocent, nestling in the jaws of the dragon.

Why had no one looked after her?

He felt it again. The silken thread that passed from deep inside him to deep inside her. Stronger now, tugging at his guts painfully, hurting him. Did she feel it too? Did she feel its insistent tugging?

He kept rocking her until he heard her breathing become deep and slow. Her head lolled back like a cropped lily.

He looked down into her sleeping face. The long lashes were still wet with tears. Her lips were parted. She was so lovely. The oval face was angelic.

He stared at her, lost. Eden. Eden sleeping in his arms.

What had he done to her?

What right had he to do this to her?

He felt a sob rise in his throat and choked it back. He pressed her face to his, cheek to cheek, feeling the wet of her tears against his skin. She murmured something. She was as light in his arms as a cloud.

He laid her down on the bed and wrapped her in the blanket. She didn't wake. Exhaustion had sealed her lids.

He smoothed the black hair away from her face with his roughened hand. Her skin was so pale that he could see the faint blue veins branching along her throat, at her temples. Precious, he thought. Beyond value. He sat staring at her and it was a long while before he could tear himself away.

The book, *Kick Heroin*, fascinated her. It also disturbed her. It was like looking at herself in a distorting mirror.

She'd approached the book with cynicism. She'd thought it would moralize. It didn't. It had been written by an ex-addict and it was shorn of all self-righteousness. It was brutally candid.

She'd turned straight to the section about withdrawal and had read it with wry self-recognition. All the symptoms were painfully familiar. There were several suggestions about how to cope with withdrawal. None of them included being locked in a ten-by-six concrete cell.

Among other things, she read that her prolonged stomach troubles were a common aftermath of withdrawal. She also read that disorientation and depression could continue for several weeks after the initial symptoms were over. She read about the various cures that were available. None were appropriate. Anyway, it was too late for cures. She had already been through the fire.

She hadn't wanted to read the rest of it, but she'd been drawn to. The experience was proving painful. Through the plain, hard text, she'd begun to see a shadow of herself, of her own nature.

One sentence in the book had leaped out of the page at her: *Junkies don't want to look at themselves.*

The truth of it jolted her. She'd never wanted to think about herself. She'd never wanted to *be* herself. From the very start, she'd taken drugs to get away from being herself. But why? What was so hideous in her own nature that had to be escaped all the time? Terminal boredom? Or something worse?

Even now, her mind flinched automatically from introspection. Like a child at the edge of a black well. Terrified of what lay in the strange depths.

That was why she'd inevitably gravitated to heroin. Toward Lethe. The river of forgetfulness. She'd wanted oblivion and heroin was the only drug to have ever given her that. The lotus flower, closing around her. Sealing her in its perfumed embrace.

That had been the hardest part of her imprisonment. Nothing had been so terrible as being forced to look at herself. To live with herself. To be with Eden, day and night, listening to her sob, smelling her filth, watching her self-abasement.

That was why she dreamed of junk all the time. For something that would take Eden away again.

She was imprisoned, not in the cell, but within the even narrower confines of her own cranium. She touched her temples. Within those thin ivory walls.

Where did she go to when she was high? She'd never considered the question before, not from the viewpoint of being stone cold straight. It was hard to visualize the place she got to. It was a place long ago, far away. A place before.

A place where everything after was shut out.

She laid the book aside and closed her eyes. She wished Joel was here to hold her. She saw his face in her mind. What did he do when he left her? His hands were roughened, often cut. Maybe he worked in a quarry, on a construction site.

She had spent hours trying to imagine his life outside the cell. Did he go to some *cantina* and sit, alone and silent, drinking beer? Did he just sit waiting for his ten million dollars?

She thought about Joel constantly. He'd become the focus of her life. Hardly surprising.

She had started to miss him when he was gone.

She wondered whether he missed her.

When he next came in, he brought her a little vase of brilliant red wildflowers. She was delighted.

"Poppies!"

"Desert poppies. They won't last long."

"They're lovely." She touched the flowers to her lips. "So velvety. So red."

"I thought they'd brighten the place up."

"Where am I going to put them?" She folded down the toilet seat and put them on top. "There."

They smiled at each other. He picked up the book. "Have you read it?"

"Most of it."

"And?"

She shrugged. She didn't want to acknowledge how much the book had disturbed her. "He's sincere, anyhow. But my life wasn't like that. Degraded, desperate. I always had enough money to avoid that."

"What about your boyfriend, the dealer?"

"Rusty?" She smiled. "Rusty didn't like me associating with other junkies. He always came between me and that world."

"Because he didn't want you to see where you would end up."

She looked up at the tall, broad figure. "Rusty just wanted to protect me. He cared for me."

"The way a farmer cares for a sow he's fattening for market."

Her smile faded. "You sound just like my mother. Rusty never let me touch bottom. I was never one of those pathetic junkies who hang out in parks and outside all-night drugstores, with nowhere to go and nothing to do but stare at the neon. Rusty took care of me."

"What did you do when he died?"

"Oh, I hung around Spooky. He was a friend. A dealer. We used to shoot up together."

"Was he an addict too?"

She nodded slowly. "Yeah. They all are. I did see some pretty vile things at Spooky's. I remember once seeing Spooky give himself a bad hit. All the veins in his arms were screwed-up. He shot up, but the blood just seeped out of the vein. It made like a lumpy blister under his skin. He kept saying, *oh, shit*. He managed to suck it back into the syringe, and squirted into a spoon. Then he started separating the clots so he could re-inject it. I had to turn away." She sat back. "Another time I remember going with him to take a junkie to the hospital. She'd OD'd. She was delirious. She went into a coma in the hospital. I remember their faces. The way they looked at us. Like we were dog-shit on their shoe. She died the next morning and we all just split. We just left her body there for someone to pick up."

She saw lines of repugnance form around the dark eyes and

hard cheekbones. "And you still didn't realize where you were headed?"

She was silent for a while, thinking. "Once," she said slowly, "I remember groping in the garbage for a needle. Fishing it out and jamming it in. I was worried. Not that it might be infected, but that it might be blocked. Then I kind of sat back and looked at myself. I wondered..."

"What?"

"Just wondered what I was turning into."

"And?"

"It was too late. I'd already become what I was turning into."

He sat down beside her and stared into her face with his intense black gaze. "It's *not* too late, Eden. You're not a junkie any more."

"I'll always be a junkie."

"*No.* You've already kicked heroin. Didn't you read that book? It's over."

"It'll never be over."

"You weren't born to be a junkie," he said harshly. "I've seen plenty of addicts, Eden. In Vietnam and other places. They were all cripples before they ever took a shot. If it wasn't drugs it'd be booze, or Jesus. You're not like that."

"How do you know what I'm like?" she asked tiredly. "It's something inborn. Some taint. My father takes drugs, you know."

"That's because he's a cocaine merchant," he said impatiently. "It isn't hereditary."

"He's not a cocaine merchant. He just uses it."

She saw him stare at her. "Your father was one of the biggest coke dealers in LA," he said.

"That's bullshit."

"He flew cocaine in from Colombia for fifteen years, Eden. You think your father became a millionaire freighting bananas and Papayas?"

She felt a cold chill close around her heart. "Jesus."

"Didn't you know?" he demanded. "Didn't you guess?"

"No! How do *you* know?"

"It wasn't hard to find out. Your father supplied the best coke in town. He was famous for it."

"Jesus," she said again, feeling nausea choke her. Something was shrivelling inside her. "My mother never had anything to do with that. I know she didn't."

"Do you?" he asked ironically.

"Yes!" She felt herself shrink, become grey and silent.

He searched her face. When he spoke, his voice was oddly rough. "Maybe she didn't. I thought you'd know by now," he said. "I shouldn't have told you."

She was silent for a full minute. "I've never looked it in the face before," she said in a low voice. "But somewhere inside, I knew, all along."

"It has nothing to do with you," he said shortly. "You weren't to blame. And you didn't start taking drugs because of any *taint*." He studied her face and saw she wasn't listening. He rose. "I'll come by for the tray later."

He locked the door as he went out.

Eden sat, shrunken and empty, staring at the wall.

She dreamed she'd been bound in chains. She dreamed she was immobilized, crushed by the weight of the fetters.

Mama and Daddy were there. But they wouldn't help her. They didn't even seem to know she was there.

They were arguing. Having one of their fights. She could see Mama's face white and strained, and she knew it was a bad fight. Daddy started shouting. He shouted horrible things. One after another. About Mama.

She wanted to cover her ears, but her arms were paralyzed by the chains.

Then Daddy looked at her at last. He had a frightening expression on his face, as though he was very drunk. He started shouting at her. He got to his feet and she caught a glimpse of the thing sticking out of his groin, thick and erect.

But it wasn't that that made her scream. It was the things he was saying. His mouth was moving and the words that came out were terrible. They were destroying her, destroying everything around her. It was all a jumble, a roar. The walls were coming down. And the ceiling was falling. And she couldn't get away. And Daddy kept talking. She knew what he was saying and she couldn't bear the pain. She screamed louder and louder to drown him out. She knew if she could drown out his words, the walls would stop falling, and their house would be safe from destruction. She screamed so loud that it tore her chest, deafened her.

She was awake, abruptly, drenched in sweat. She was clinging to Joel. He had come into the cell again. She could feel the hard muscles of his body through his shirt.

"Did I scream?" she gasped.

"No. You didn't make a sound. You were thrashing around."

"I was having a nightmare. About my father." She pressed her face against his chest, hard. She was feeling unbearably shaky. "Jesus. I can never scream when I have that dream. If I could scream, it would go away..."

"It was only a nightmare," he said.

"It keeps coming back. All my life. I hate it."

She drew back. Her heart was still pounding against her ribs like a hammer. He looked concernedly into her face. "It's shaken you up. You're sweating. And shaking. Take it easy."

She drew an unsteady breath. "It's okay. I'm glad you're here." She hauled off her soaked T-shirt. She threw it into the corner and lay back, folding her arms above her head to let her skin dry.

Then she saw his face. "What's wrong?"

"Put a clean shirt on."

"When I'm not so clammy. Am I offending you?" She looked down at her own small breasts, with their peaked nipples. "You've seen me before."

He looked angry. "You're too..."

"Too what?"

"Too open," he said harshly. "Didn't anyone ever teach you to be defensive? Protect yourself?"

She raked the hair away from her temples. "I guess not."

"You go through life like a stupid child that never got stung by a bee or burned by a flame. You think everything's safe, everything's open to you."

"Just because I took my shirt off?"

"Because of everything you do! You ask for trouble!"

"I didn't think seeing my tits would drive you to rape me," she said wryly. "They're not exactly seductive."

"For all you know—" He bit off the words.

She met his eyes. "If you'd wanted to rape me, you'd have done it the other night, when I invited you to. I couldn't stop you." But she folded her arms over her breasts, covering them, all the same. "Sorry."

"You need a keeper."

She smiled. "You're my keeper." She reached for a clean T-shirt and hauled it on over her head. "There," she said, shaking her hair free, "is that better?"

He nodded. For the first time she noticed the black blindfold in his hand. "What's that for?"

She saw the Adam's apple convulse in his throat as he swallowed. He seemed to hesitate. "How would you like some exercise?"

She stared at him. "What kind of exercise?"

"A walk."

She couldn't believe it. "Outside? On the *outside*?"

He nodded. "But I have to know I can trust you."

"You can," she said urgently. "I'll do anything you say, Joel. Anything."

"I'll have to cuff you and put the blindfold on. Don't touch until I tell you."

"I won't."

"I'm going to put you in the back of the van and drive you to a place where you can walk. Understand?"

She nodded, not trusting herself to speak. He held out the blindfold. "Come on."

The journey was uncomfortable, even painful. Being jolted in the back of the van brought back sharp memories of the night he'd taken her, the last time she had seen the outside world. It was stiflingly hot and dust crept into her nose and mouth.

But none of that mattered. The prospect of being outside, out in the blessed sun, made her weak.

At last, the jolting stopped. The roar of the engine cut out.

He unbolted the back of the van and she felt his hands take her arms, helping her out. She felt a hot wind buffet her, like the breath of a huge bonfire.

He unlocked the handcuffs. "Don't touch the blindfold," he warned. "We're going to walk a little way."

He took her hand. She clung to its strength with both of hers. "Joel, I'm frightened—"

"There's nothing to be frightened of. Just walk with me."

She stumbled at his side, clinging to him. The ground underfoot was uneven. Heat swallowed her. The wind was all about her, beating against her, whistling and moaning through vegetation. Dust kept lashing across her face, making her cough. Once she tripped over something and almost fell, but he caught her and kept her upright.

At last he let her stop.

"Okay," he said, letting go her hand. She felt his fingers unfastening the blindfold. It fell away. Her eyes were tightly shut, but the sun burned scarlet through her lids. She covered her eyes with her hands to shut out the pain.

"It'll take you a little while to get used to the sun," he said, close by.

She eased her hands away. She opened her eyes.

13.

~Sean

may 1938

Barcelona

She felt him stroking her hair. It was a dream at first. Then she heard his voice.

"I love you," he whispered.

She felt something seize her heart, crushing it. "Sean!"

Sean was kneeling beside her bed, as though praying. He put his arms around her and drew her close to him. She clung to him, choked with tears. "Oh, Sean. Oh, thank God you're back."

He kissed her mouth, her eyes, her sobbing throat. His cheeks were harsh with stubble and he smelled of acrid sweat.

"Come into bed," she said with a throb in her voice.

He stripped and came to her. His throat was tight. She kissed his mouth with burning passion, pulling him onto her with all her strength. Later, they would make love slowly, with eroticism. Right now, sex was a desperate need that could not be toyed with.

He mounted her roughly. Mercedes lifted her knees high up around his waist, reaching down to guide him into her. He groaned as she touched his rearing flesh. She looked into his eyes and drank in the blind look on his face as he sank into her.

"Oh, God," he whispered. She could feel him filling her, pressing against her womb.

He made love to her with a kind of savagery, thrusting into her flesh with long, violent strokes. Physically, there was more pain than pleasure. But neither was seeking pleasure. Their lean bodies were in the grip of something more urgent, the escape from loneliness and death. They came at the same moment, shuddering violently and clawing at one another, calling out each other's names.

Afterward, he cradled her in his arms while she cried. Then he sank down heavily beside her and seemed to melt with exhaustion into sleep.

She got a day off work and on his insistence, they went up to San Lluc to see her parents.

It was mid-May and the countryside was coming into its glory. Mercedes's eyes were glutted with colours, the silvery glint of olives, the cloudy green of pines, the rippling yellow of wheat fields.

They arrived in the village at around noon.

Sean steered the rumbling motorcycle into the square, and paused to stare up at the façade of the *ajuntament*, fluttering with flags. Opposite it, the village church stood with smashed windows and open door, as though gaping dully at the change that had overtaken it. No mass had been celebrated there since the summer of 1936, and it was now used only for storing the village cooperative's farm machinery.

High over the town stood the hulk of the convent.

She pointed the way to the forge. He guided the machine down the narrow earthen streets, the noise of the engine bouncing off the stone walls on either side. Dogs and children scattered in their path.

In front of the forge, Sean stopped and propped the motorcycle up on its stand. He switched off the engine and the silence rushed into their ringing ears.

Sean gazed at the ancient, honey-coloured stone houses. The arched doorway of the forge was shut and padlocked. In front of it stood a colourful row of potted geraniums and ferns that Conchita had put there. The mass of bougainvillaea opposite was coming into purple bloom. The street was empty but for a few chickens scratching busily in the earth.

"This is where you grew up?" he asked her.

She nodded. "That's the forge over there. I was born in that house."

"It's like a doll's house."

"Is it?"

"Enchanting. I've never seen anything like it."

She laughed and went to him. He took her in his arms and kissed her.

She had missed him so terribly, with such desolation in her heart. As she clung to him, in front of the house in which she had been born, she felt her love for him pierce her heart like a sword.

Conchita opened the front door. She stood watching them without speaking until at last they noticed her. Mercedes ran to her mother. On the doorstep the two women embraced tightly, silently. Sean followed.

"*Mamá*," Mercedes said breathlessly, "this is Sean."

Conchita reached out and took his hand. "Hello, Sean," she said. "I'm glad to meet you."

Sean stared down at her, as though entranced by the intelligent grey eyes that met his. Conchita's face was oval, like her daughter's, with the same flawless porcelain complexion and an ineffable sweetness of expression. The dark hair was touched with grey at the temples. She was studying him with a gentle, intense gaze.

He stepped forward and kissed her on both cheeks, lightly.

"I'm glad to meet you too," he said.

She smiled at last, fleetingly. "Come inside. Your father will be back in time for lunch," she told Mercedes. "At least, I hope he will. He's so busy these days. I know he'll make a special effort." She led the way upstairs.

Looking at them, she knew with certainty that they were lovers, that Mercedes had found her man. She thought, He is so handsome. And my God, how much she loves him. Look at her face.

Mercedes took Sean's hand and led him around the house from room to room. Sean stared at the white-plastered walls and terra-cotta floors, the low, vaulted ceilings, the little spotless rooms with their plain furnishings. It seemed biblical in its simplicity. So clean, so neat, glowing with polish.

She took him to her bedroom and he saw the little bed, feeling his love for her twist in his heart.

He was helplessly in love with this strange, intense girl. Sexually, emotionally and in every other way, she held him in the palm of her hand. He was captivated by her. Though he had been the conqueror at first, it was he who was now the vanquished. No matter how many women he had possessed in his wanderings, and he had possessed many, he had come to think of Mercedes as the first, the only one. Every minute he was with her he felt the spell deepening, twining ever more tightly around his heart.

The last thing he had been looking for in Spain had been a passionate love-affair. He had thought he was coming here to fight a war, but increasingly it seemed to him that the reason he had really come to Spain had been to find Mercedes. To find love.

He had been drawn here, by some fate that had reeled him to this girl, this love, this moment beside her in the bedroom of her girlhood.

Francesc returned from Gerona at two o'clock, limping heavily on two sticks. Sean saw a middle-aged man with a grey beard and piercing blue eyes, magnificent from the waist up, shattered below. He recognized at once his iron character, his purpose.

They shook hands, each assessing the other's strength.

They sat down to a meal of roast lamb, the sort of meal both had only dreamed of for months.

After lunch, Mercedes and Sean went out for a walk in the sunshine. Conchita watched them through the little kitchen window. She turned to Francesc, who was still sitting at the table.

"You like him?"

Francesc stretched his weary shoulders. "He's a fine young man. Has a belly full of fire. Not afraid to speak his mind either."

She smiled faintly. "You were very like that, at his age."

"And what am I now?"

"Oh, much the same. Just quieter. Not so cocky." She went to him and slipped her arms around his husky shoulders. "They *are* lovers."

"Yes, I think that's obvious."

"She adores him."

Francesc stroked her arm with his big hands. "Yes. She does."

"There's no chance that he'll stay here when the war is over. He'll have to go back to America. And he'll take her with him." She stared at him, her eyes blurring.

The road wound towards the next village, through oak woods and spreading farm land. She hadn't made a deliberate choice to follow it, yet it was the same path she and Matilde had taken two summers ago, gathering figs and blackberries, a week before her death.

They walked down the road, arms wrapped around each other's waist. He was enraptured.

"This is such pretty country. So gentle. So sweet and soft. I can't remember when I last looked around at the countryside and didn't have to wonder whether there was a Fascist behind the next bush, or a dive-bomber in the clouds."

Across the plain, cypresses seemed to float on the haze. Soon the pastures would start to take on the golden tints of summer. Among the green blades now, millions of poppies bloomed in scarlet whorls and streaks, sometimes running into broad lakes of blood.

"God, it's so lovely. Look at those poppies! When this damned war is over, Mercé, we're going to live in the woods somewhere. Buy ourselves a farm and live close to nature for the rest of our lives." He took her in his arms and kissed her. "You don't know how lucky you are to have been born and raised among such beauty."

Farther along the road, they came into the farmyard where she and Matilde had drunk from the well. A ragged dog rushed out to bark at them. But no one came to the door this time. Whoever was in the house stayed indoors. Sean hauled the bucket up from the well and drank from it.

"Drink some, it's wonderful," he said, gasping at the coldness of the water.

She shook her head. Before they reached the clump of oaks where Matilde had crowned her with cornflowers and gentians, she made Sean stop.

"I'm tired," she said. "Let's rest."

She settled down at the roadside. He sat beside her and looked at her in concern, touching her hair. "What is it? What are you thinking about?"

She turned to him. "Sean . . . have you ever had to do something terrible? Shooting a woman, killing someone who was helpless?"

He was silent for a while. "No," he said at last. "But I've stood by while things like that were done. I guess that makes me just as guilty as the ones who pulled the trigger. Guilty forever."

Her eyes were haunted. "At Granados . . . I shot a man. A prisoner. He was wounded and someone was trying to kick him to death. I took my revolver and shot him in the head."

"Oh, Jesus," he said softly. "You never told me before."

"I just pulled the trigger and he was dead. I never stop dreaming about it." She held him close. "I'm guilty forever. Like you."

"I thought I knew you. But I don't." He looked at her with a strange expression. "I don't know you at all. I don't think I ever will."

"I don't think I'll ever know myself," she said wryly. "Before the war, I used to think I knew what I was. I was so young then. My God. It's like a void. A gulf into which so much of me has fallen. And vanished without any trace. I don't know who I am any more, Sean."

"Oh, Mercedes . . ."

"Except through you." She held his hands. "I have a meaning through you, Sean. It's as though all the broken pieces of my life come together through you. While you were at the front, I knew what I'd be without you. Something sterile. Leafless. Something without wings. Don't leave me again, Sean. Don't take my soul away."

He couldn't look into her eyes any more. He drew her into his arms and held her tight.

august 1938

Seville

Gerard Massaguer accepted the glass of champagne from the steward, and looked out the window at the blue Mediterranean far below. The Dornier flying boat was luxuriously appointed, and very fast. They had taken off from Rome at dawn, had refuelled in Palma de Majorca three hours later, and would be in Seville in time for a late lunch. Supplied to Franco courtesy of the Luftwaffe, it was the ideal machine for rapid Mediterranean crossings.

He and Liesl Bauer were the only passengers today, with the steward and a crew of three.

He sipped the champagne reflectively. It was a Spanish *cava*, better than Italian *spumante*, but inferior to a good French marque. However, it was quite acceptable at fifteen thousand feet.

He glanced at Liesl, his young secretary, peacefully asleep beside him, uninterested in champagne or the sea below. She was a Berliner, a gifted linguist. She had been recommended to him by Johannes Bernhardt, the Nazi businessman who had set up HISMA.

She lay with her pale golden hair tumbled over one shoulder of her severely cut black suit. Her mouth looked bruised, and her lids were heavy. He had probably rather worn her out last night. She seemed continually astonished by the inventiveness of her employer's sexual imagination, but was pleasingly eager to learn. He smiled. It gave him some satisfaction to feel, at the brink of forty, that he could still wear out a twenty-two-year-old girl.

The trip had been a success from all points of view. The interview with Mussolini had gone well.

He rang the steward for another glass of champagne. He was growing hungry.

"Have you anything to eat?" he asked the man.

"There is cold roast quail, Señor Massaguer. Or caviar. Or cold consommé."

"Bring the quail. And plenty of toast."

"Very good, señor."

He stretched out his legs and pulled the beautiful camel-hair overcoat over his shoulders. It had been a personal gift from Ciano, Mussolini's son-in-law, perfect for air travel. It was chilly at this altitude. There was no turbulence, though. The Dornier flew straight and steady in the fine summer weather

The war was almost over. Which was rather a pity, in one sense. The longer the war went on, the richer he would get.

But he was already a very rich man indeed. And once the war ended, another game would start, the game of exercising the power they had fought for. His position in Franco's post-war government was assured. Given time, he would make his way into the cabinet. A portfolio, ideally, combining the exercise of power with scope for financial benefits.

The Ministry of Finance, maybe. Perhaps the Exterior. He was still young, and he had a long, glittering ladder to ascend. He felt a warm pleasure, almost sexual, fill his loins. He glanced at the sleeping girl, and wondered what it might be like to make love aboard an aeroplane.

The food arrived. He tore at the quails with his teeth. He was growing weary of Seville and its African airs. He was sick of the throb of flamenco guitars and the flamboyant rustle and stamp of *sevillanas*. He longed for the cool winters and green summers of Catalonia. He longed to see Mercedes.

Beside him, Liesl awoke. She blinked at him and smiled. He tore off a piece of quail, put it on toast and popped it into her mouth.

"Time you woke up," he said. "You've been asleep since Palma."

She swallowed. "I was worn out."

"You've been working too hard," he said solemnly.

"I must look a mess." He watched her applying lipstick and powder. The smells of the cosmetics always aroused him. In the bright light through the aircraft's windows, her skin was as fine as Dresden porcelain. She was a lovely creature, a real find. Every detail of her body was perfect. He knew. He had missed none of it.

He rang for the steward to clear away the tray. When it was gone, he picked up the cashmere travelling rug and laid it across both their laps.

"Thanks." She smiled. "I was a little cold."

"I'll warm you up." Under cover of the rug, he slid his hand between her knees, and caressed the silk-stockinged expanse of warm thigh.

"*Ach, du!*" She looked around hastily. "Someone will see!"

"Nobody's interested," he purred.

"Gerard, no!"

"Hush." His fingers found the suspenders, and traced them down to the satin pants. He eased the filmy material aside and slid his fingers into the hot, moist crease of her sex.

"*Liebchen,*" she murmured weakly. His caress was hard, ruthless. Her flesh moistened. She moaned, her lids drooping. After a while, she gave up looking to see if anyone was watching, and slid a little farther down in her seat, parting her thighs to allow him better access. Her mouth opened and her cheeks started to flush.

He watched her face with hooded eyes, seeing the sheen appear on her forehead, despite the crisp air. With his free hand, Gerard unbuttoned his own trousers and took himself out. Then he guided her hand onto him. Her fingers wrapped eagerly around his tumescent flesh.

The Dornier made a slight adjustment in its course as the Spanish mainland came into sight and flew on steadily for Seville.

Marisa was waiting for him at the airport with their own car and their private chauffeur. Her face was as white as paper. As soon as he saw her, he knew that something was terribly wrong.

She ran across the tarmac to meet him. He hurried ahead of Liesl and took his wife's elbows in his hands.

"What is it?" he demanded brusquely.

"It's Alfonso," she blurted out in Italian. "He's terribly sick. He collapsed yesterday. Oh, Gerard, Gerard—"

His grip on her arms tightened furiously. "How, sick?"

"The doctors say it's a brain fever." Her violet eyes were swimming with tears. "They're putting needles into his spine, they say they have to draw off fluid or he'll die—"

"Where is he?" Gerard asked tightly.

"In the hospital. Alonzo Guzmán is looking after him personally. Come, Gerard, come quickly."

He swung around to Liesl. "You'll have to use the official car, Fraulëin Bauer," he told her. "Present my apologies to the minister. I'll write my report in person, as soon as I'm able. Explain the position. And get the baggage home."

"Yes, Señor Massaguer," she nodded obediently.

Gerard hurried to the waiting limousine with Marisa. As it accelerated away, he listened in silence as she spilled out the story.

The boy had become ill after Gerard had left for Rome. He had been shivering, complaining of headache. She had put him to bed. The doctor had told her not to worry. But the illness had grown disastrously worse. Alfonso had begun screaming with pain, sometimes vomiting violently. He seemed unable to bear light or noise. Then he had collapsed. In terror, she had rushed him into hospital, where she had first heard the dreadful words "brain fever."

The doctors had done lumbar punctures. But the child could not be roused.

"He still hasn't regained consciousness. I came straight from the hospital to pick you up," she told him, blotting her eyes with a handkerchief. Her beauty had been crushed. She was trembling uncontrollably. "He sees nothing, hears nothing. He's going to die!"

"He's not going to die," Gerard said grimly. He stroked her short blond hair roughly, trying to comfort her. But there was lead in his chest.

The child was in an isolation ward on the second floor. The doctor in attendance led them silently in and lifted the sheet for them to see.

Alfonso was lying on his side, dark lashes closed over his swollen eyes. He did not stir. His thin ribs hardly seemed to stir with life.

Gerard knew then that the child was going to die. He grasped at the iron rails of the bed for support. "Is it meningitis?" he asked mechanically.

"It's meningococcal septicaemia," the doctor said quietly. "A grave form of the disease. The cerebrospinal fluid we drew off confirms the diagnosis."

"Is he going to survive?"

The doctor laid the sheet back over the child and gestured for them to accompany him out of the room. Marisa was crying helplessly. Gerard had to hold her up. The doctor took them to an office, where Alonzo Guzmán, the eminent pediatrician, joined them.

Guzmán sat them down, looking grave. "This is a very serious illness," he told them without preamble. "It is very rapid and there is only a small chance of survival."

"But there *is* a chance!" Marisa exclaimed, staring feverishly from one doctor to the other.

"There is hope," Guzmán answered her obliquely.

"Then save him, save him, for God's sake, save him!"

Guzmán was pulling at his beard. "There is always hope. But in this case, as my colleague will confirm, our hope has to be tempered by the aetiology of the disease."

"What are you talking about?" Gerard rasped.

"This is an inflammation of the lining of the brain," the other doctor said. "There is massive fluid production. This has resulted in severe pressure, which is usually fatal. If it is not fatal, there is consequent . . . damage."

"What kind of damage?"

"Mental defect. Possibly with blindness."

Marisa uttered a harsh, animal wail, then slid silently onto her knees, her mouth fixed open. The younger doctor came forward and bent down to her in concern.

Gerard sat immobile. He wanted to reach out to his wife, but his body felt heavy. There was a deep roaring sound which he at first thought was machinery, but which he realized must be inside him somewhere, caused by the rushing of blood in some vessel.

He rubbed his face and caught the musky smell of Liesl on his fingers.

The younger doctor had managed to raise Marisa to her feet. He looked at Massaguer and Guzmán anxiously. "I'll take Señora Massaguer out, and give her something to alleviate the shock."

Gerard nodded without speaking. The doctor led Marisa out of the office. Gerard sat in silence for a long while. Guzmán toyed with his pencil, waiting for him to speak. At last Gerard looked up, his lids drooping heavily over his eyes.

"The hydrocephalus—can it be relieved?"

"Yes. What we cannot do is fight the infection adequately. We have no suitable drugs." He cleared his throat. "In our opinion, a great deal of damage has already occurred to the brain. Had the boy come in twenty-four hours earlier, we might have been able to do much more. The disease is extraordinarily rapid in its effect." He paused, looking at Gerard's exquisite suit and diamond tie pin. "This is no reflection on your wife, of course. She was not to know. I wouldn't mention it to her."

Gerard felt a spasm of hatred for the smooth, unemotional manner of the pediatrician. He gritted his teeth. "The brain damage you talked about. Mental defect. Blindness. Has that already happened to my son?"

The professor nodded without hesitation. "Almost certainly."

His fingers tightened around the arms of the chair. "There's no possibility of a mistake?"

"We are all agreed. Casares, the brain specialist from Córdoba, saw the child last night. He checked for reflexes. There were none. Every indication is that there has been considerable damage."

"Enough to make the boy a cabbage?"

"If you wish to put it like that."

"He'll never come back to me the way he was?"

"No."

Gerard closed his eyes briefly. When he opened them again, the room seemed bright, unreal. "Then I do not wish the boy's life saved," he heard himself say. Guzmán was silent. "No matter what his mother says," Gerard went on in a monotone. "Tell her what you have to. Lie to her. But don't let him live. You understand?"

"You're formally asking me to suspend treatment?" the professor said carefully.

"Whatever it takes."

"Whatever it takes, Señor Massaguer?"

"Exactly."

The pediatrician stroked his beard. "I'm afraid I'm not quite clear. Are you asking me to—"

Anger convulsed the heavy face across the desk from him. "You know damned well what I'm asking you, Guzmán." Gerard's voice was a frightening rasp. He slammed his hand down on the desk with a crash. "You know who I am. Don't play the virgin with me, or I'll have them cut your balls off and ram them down your throat."

Guzmán paled. Gerard rose to his feet and walked to the door. There he turned and pointed a thick forefinger at the doctor. "Don't let him suffer. You hear me?"

Guzmán nodded silently. Gerard went to find Marisa. He walked past the door of Alfonso's room without looking in, or pausing in his stride.

He had a strange memory. There had been a huge olive tree growing outside the *masía* when he'd been a boy. The tree had not been pruned for a century or more, and the thick, gnarled branches had spread sideways, keeping light from the front of the house. One day his father had ordered the gardener to cut off the heaviest of the branches.

He had watched as the white flesh was sawn through until the heavy branch had crashed to the ground, with a jar that had made him leap with fright.

He felt now like that tree, as though a living part of him was being cut through, and had dropped to earth. There was no pain yet. That would come later. For now he felt only the terrible loss of the amputation.

Marisa had wanted to stay at the hospital, but once the morphine had taken effect, he had brought her home. She was lying in her bedroom now, neither asleep nor awake, tears sliding silently down her cheeks. A maid sat by her.

He was in his study, mechanically preparing his report on the Italian mission. The words crawled from his pen like ants, covering the paper with industrious, empty activity. He wrote and wrote, but had no idea of the meaning.

Guzmán telephoned personally two hours later.

"The boy passed away peacefully a few moments ago," the pediatrician said heavily. "He felt no pain. May I present my condolences to you and Señora Massaguer."

"Thank you," Gerard said tonelessly. "I will come in to make the arrangements tonight." He replaced the receiver.

He looked around him, at the leather-bound volumes on the shelves, at the framed photographs of Franco, Mussolini and Hitler on the walls, the precious Chinese vases. The antiques. The open window. The palms rustling in the slight breeze. The empty sky beyond.

He felt his whole being focus on Mercedes with a sudden terrible pain.

Now, he thought, I have only one child.

Barcelona

The train was late. She stood among the milling crowds in the railway station, apparently the only person who was not going somewhere or coming back from somewhere. Humanity swarmed around her like a river around a stone. Midsummer heat made the air thick and breathless.

The railway system was enormously overburdened in this blistering summer of 1938. Those who foresaw the end, and had the means, were starting to pack their belongings and head for France. The exodus from Catalonia had already begun.

As she looked around her, Mercedes saw many families who were evidently emigrating—men, women and children ploughing towards the platforms, followed by porters heaving trolleys piled with luggage.

An announcement began and she strained to hear the echoing words above the roar all around her. She caught something about the Tarragona train, but whether it was an arrival, or yet more delay, she could not tell. People began streaming down to the left.

"What did they say?" she demanded from a soldier next to her.

"The train from the front. It's coming in on Platform Four."

"Platform Four?" She hurried towards the barrier, fighting her way through the crush of bodies headed in the same direction. Her path was blocked on all sides. She was going to miss him if she couldn't force her way through!

The train was already coming into the station with a deafening din. Clouds of black smoke and white steam billowed up to the high glass vaults. Arms and heads protruded from every carriage window and the engine was bedecked with flags.

Using her elbows and shoulders, she moved as fast as she could manage, dodging people, suitcases and piles of baggage. The yellow irises she held were crushed against her chest, petals scattering. But she reached Platform Four just as the train came to a halt with a long scream of brakes.

Men were piling out of the carriages among clouds of steam. Almost all were soldiers, wearing motley summer uniform of khaki pants and open-necked shirts of various colours. Many were wounded and hobbled on crutches. Over the booming loudspeakers she heard the squeal of women greeting their menfolk. Families mobbed, swarmed. Embraces and tears surrounded her. Mercedes climbed onto a bench, and peered frantically over the bobbing heads. Where was he? How would she ever spot him in this melee?

Then she saw him. He was on the steps of a carriage, hanging onto the open door, scanning the crowd with deep green eyes. He was so beautiful! Her heart was squeezed tight inside her. She waved her bouquet madly, the yellow petals by now bruised and flapping. He caught sight of her at last and she saw his face crease up in a joyful grin.

They fought towards each other and met half-way. She sobbed with sheer joy as he swept her up into his arms and crushed her to his chest.

"Sean, oh, Sean! Oh, God, I've missed you, *amor!*"

He held her without speaking for a while, then covered her face with kisses. He was leaner than he had been seven weeks ago, but as always, he looked magnificent. She dug her fingers into the hard muscles of his shoulders, as if to convince herself he was real.

He drew back a little and studied her. "You're ravishing," he said huskily. "I can't believe my eyes. And your hair is beautiful!"

She swung her dark locks, smiling up at him with misty eyes. She had been letting her hair grow ever since they'd become lovers, because he'd said he liked it long. Now it was shoulder-length, heavy black coils that glinted in the light. Her oval face was glowing with happiness. "These are for you." She proffered the tattered bunch of yellow irises. "They got crushed while I was waiting for you. Oh, my love, thank God you're back! How long have you got?"

"Two days."

Her happiness was almost shattered. "Only *two days!*"

"Yes. I only got away because I told Líster you were pregnant. I have to get back to the front in forty-eight hours." He kissed her mouth, hard. "Let's get out of here. I'll fetch my gear." He was back in a few seconds with his duffel bag and his rifle over his shoulder. He reached for her hand and forged an easy path through the throng.

In the sunlight outside, Sean hugged her again, his strength almost crushing the breath out of her lungs. He looked rangy. His skin was baked to the colour of new bronze by the sun. "You've lost weight," she told him, trying to fight down her acute disappointment at the briefness of his visit.

"Sweated it off. I must smell like a goat; I'm sorry. Haven't had a chance to bathe." The station was on Paseo Colón, right on the harbour. He took a deep lungful of the salty air. "Jesus. It's good to smell the sea again. You know the worst thing about war? It stinks."

"I know," she smiled. "And you are pretty gamey. I'll run you a bath first thing when we get home."

"You mean afterwards?"

"I mean *before.*"

He grinned and studied her trim figure hungrily. She was wearing a new yellow dress, to match the irises, with a little white collar. "You look wonderful. Do you have to be at the hospital today?"

"No, I've got the day off. And tomorrow too."

"Angel!" he said happily and hailed a taxi.

Driving up Paseo Colón towards Montjuich, he held her in his arms, his eyes full of love. They had not been together since June. She wondered how she had survived without him and how she would survive again, when he had gone.

"Have you been studying?" he asked her in English.

"Every day," she answered him in the same language.

"Every day," he mimicked her soft accent, smiling. She had been learning English, at his suggestion. She had discovered that she had a natural aptitude for languages and could already read the English newspapers without a dictionary.

She ran him a bath at the apartment and while he wallowed in it, put his filthy clothes in the little laundry to soak. In the pockets were a few coins and some pathetic home-made cigarettes. She made him a cup of coffee, not the ersatz stuff concocted out of burned acorns, but real Brazilian coffee, bought at a prohibitive price on the black market and saved for his return.

She brought it into the bathroom and watched his face as he incredulously sniffed, then tasted the brew.

"What did you do, sell your soul?"

"Something much more tangible," she smiled. "Something soft, warm and furry."

"I'll tan your hide," he growled menacingly.

"You have a dirty mind. I sold one of my rabbits."

"Your what?"

"My mother brought me some from San Lluc last month. I've started raising them on the balcony. They're no trouble to keep. You can always get bits of old cabbage and grass to feed them. They're worth a fortune nowadays. As a matter of fact, it's rabbit stew for lunch."

"You'd kill a fluffy, adorable bunny and eat it?"

She nodded. "From its floppy little ears to its little cotton tail, Buster."

"What a rapacious capitalist you are," he said, amused.

He closed his eyes with pleasure as he drank the coffee.

She looked at his naked body in the bath. As always, she felt a long burn of joy in her possession of him. His frame was majestic, but thinner than she had ever seen him. His ribs showed under the brown skin. His belly was as flat and hard as a board. His face wore lines of tiredness and there were shadows under his eyes. His lips looked dry and cracked.

"Has it been bad?" she asked him quietly.

He drained the cup and passed it to her. "Oh, it's been so-so."

But she could tell from his face, his body, that it had been bad. "They say it's been a great victory. They say we could win the war, now."

"Yeah, we heard that rumour too. It's been a great something, that's for sure. You wouldn't have any decent cigarettes?"

"I've got some cigars for you. But not before you've eaten. Do you want to tell me about it?"

"There's not much to tell," he said with a touch of bitterness. "We took them by surprise at first. Crossed the Ebro in boats and on pontoon bridges. You heard about that?"

"It was in all the papers," she nodded.

"They didn't expect that. If we'd had the proper equipment, we'd have smashed right through to Madrid. But we had no air support, no proper artillery. There was nothing we could do once they started shelling us. We ran out of steam at Gandesa. We just lay there in the sun while they threw everything they had at us. Shelled us night and day. Sometimes they strafed us." He propped himself up on one elbow. Every muscle was suddenly taut, stretched. "We were supposed to dig in. But you couldn't even scrape yourself a hollow, because it was solid rock. No shelter, not even a tree to hide behind. No water anywhere. We kept attacking these little rocky hills and they kept driving us back. And the sun... Amazing how quickly the dead start to stink in that heat. You can't bury them. They swell up in a few hours. Their uniforms split open. They smell like..." He lay back in the water and looked up at her with haunted eyes. "A lot of my friends died like that, Mercé," he said. "A lot of nice American kids. They made it this far. Now they're left to rot out there on the *sierra*. I lay next to a boy named Harvey Mandelbaum for six hours while he bloated up and busted his shirt open, and the flies made a meal of him. I thought I was going to die too. I can hardly believe I'm seeing you. I can hardly believe you're real."

"I'm real," she said gently. Her eyes were wet with compassion. She reached out and kissed him tenderly. "I'm here, *amor*."

He sighed. "Thank God I can talk to you. You know what

I'm talking about. Any other woman, I wouldn't be able to say these things. But you understand . . ."

And he has to go back in two days, she thought. "Don't take any chances, Sean," she implored him. "Not now. It can't last much longer."

"No, it can't. This is the end, Mercé. This is going to be the last offensive. There isn't another one left to make. From now on, it's all downhill. We've only embarrassed Franco, but Franco doesn't take embarrassments lightly. He'll throw the works at us now. Pass me the razor, darling."

She held the mirror for him while he lathered his cheeks and shaved himself. She'd always thought his shaving in the bath a disreputable habit, but his father had done it, and his grandfather before him. She watched the hard muscles ripple under the slick wet skin and felt her hunger for him twist in her belly.

Clean-shaven, he was dazzlingly handsome. He grinned at her, brilliant white teeth flashing. "Better?"

"Wonderful." She kissed him. "Do you want to eat?"

"No, I do not want to eat."

She rose. "I'll wait for you in the bedroom."

She was feeling shy enough to draw the blinds, so that the light in the bedroom was cool and dim. She took off her shoes and the yellow dress and lay down, wearing only her slip. She could feel herself trembling. It had been so long . . .

They had seen so little of one another since that weekend in San Lluc. A weekend in June, spent at Perpignan, in France. And now these cruelly short two August days. That was all.

Sean came into the bedroom, towelling his hair. He was naked. "I've been looking at your bunnies. They're really cute."

"You went on the balcony like that?"

"Sure. Show all the other girls what they're missing. Why is it so dark in here?" He walked over to the window and reached for the blind.

"Don't," she pleaded.

"But I want to look at you."

"Just come to me now. Look at me later." She held out her arms.

He left the blinds down. In the soft light, his skin was like old gold. He took her in his arms, and buried his face in the soft flesh of her throat. She held him tight, stroking his neck. "Thank God you're back," she said softly. "Every day you're away is an eternity. I worry about you so much . . ."

"Mercé," he said in English, "I love you."

Their lovemaking was the savage rite it always was, the first time he got back, a headlong thunderstorm, like desert rain.

She left him sleeping like the dead, sprawled out on her bed, and got up to bathe and make lunch.

After they had eaten she gave him one of the cigars she had bought him.

"I got these in especially for you."

He examined it reverently. "Same place as you got the coffee?"

"More or less."

"Well, thank you kindly, bunnies." He lit up. They were squatting cross-legged on the bed together, wearing the white and blue hospital dressing-gowns she had borrowed from Sagrado Corazón. The afternoon sunlight streamed in through the opened window, with the distant noise of the city. He inhaled luxuriously, then blew out a long plume of smoke. "My God, real tobacco. We've been smoking dried potato leaves out there. There ain't no cigarettes to be had."

"Is that what it was? I wondered."

"Sometimes we get *kif* off the dead Moroccans," he told her. "Gives you a terrible headache, but it takes your worries away for a few hours."

"Would you take cigarettes off the dead?"

"Honey, some people yank the gold teeth out of their mouths."

"That's horrible!"

"Yeah. The gold's not worth very much either. It's a rough war. Christ knows I'm sick of it." He drew on the cigar again, then put it down reluctantly. "I'm not used to cigars any more. It's making my head spin." He took her hands in his, and looked into her eyes. "Mercedes, I came back to marry you."

She felt her heart turning over inside her. "Marry?"

His fingers gripped hers. "I know it's gone out of style lately. There are no churches left open any more. But if you want a Catholic ceremony, we can probably find a priest somewhere who'll do it. Personally, I'll settle for a civil wedding. Not very glamorous, but we'd each get a proper certificate. It would be legal enough to get you into the States with no problems when we go back."

Her head was spinning. "Sean, I don't know—"

"It's the only way," he said urgently. "Listen to me. The International Brigades are going to be disbanded any day now. They'll be sending us home before the winter."

"How do you know?" she asked, staring at him with dark eyes, her oval face suddenly pale.

"Neville goddamned Chamberlain and his Non-Intervention Committee. That man is so keen on peace, he'll lie down and let the Nazis piss in his face if they shout loud enough. Part of the deal is that all foreign volunteers will be withdrawn from Spain."

"When?" she asked in dread.

"Before the winter. The International Brigades are finished, anyway. All the best men are already dead. They were killed long ago. The thing only has propaganda value. And that's no value at all any more."

"Oh, Sean!" Her heart was racing in her breast. "You want to get married *now*? In the next two days?"

"There won't be time later," he said. "They'll ship us out in a hurry. If we marry now, you'll be able to come with me then. Or if I have to go back without seeing you, you can follow me. And if I'm killed before then—"

"Don't say that," she pleaded.

"If I'm killed," he repeated, "that piece of paper might just get you into the States without me. If we get things ready this afternoon, we could be married tomorrow. Maybe a night in a good hotel. And at least it would be done." He saw her face and was angry at her lack of enthusiasm. "What's wrong?" he demanded. "Jesus, Mercé, don't you love me enough to say you'll marry me?"

"Of course I love you. You're everything to me. But leaving Spain. Leaving everything behind me—"

"Leaving *what*?" He grasped her arms, his fingers biting into her flesh to command attention. "It's going to be a bloodbath, Mercedes. You know that! It's all over, can't you understand? The Fascists have won and when they take over, the first thing they'll do is destroy anyone who could ever challenge them again. They'll slaughter thousands of people, anyone who ever lifted a finger against them. And that includes *you*. There isn't going to *be* anything to stay behind for! It's finished, finished!"

She felt sick. "And you're asking me to run away from it all and leave my parents to face all that without me!"

"If they have the sense, they'll get out before the end. They can go anywhere in the world. Mexico, Canada, the States. Even to Russia. Stalin's promising to take republican refugees from Spain."

"*Russia?*"

"Anywhere away from the Fascists. But that's their business," he said urgently. "*Their* lives. You have to think of yourself, my love. You're young. You'll adapt to a new country. You already speak English well. America may not be perfect, but it's still the land of opportunity. There's hope in America. There's none here, not for the next ten or twenty years. The whole of Europe is going to go up in flames! We have to get out. What else can we do? Listen, didn't you always know you would marry me? This is a bit sudden, but you've known in your heart that someday you would be my wife and come to the States with me. Haven't you? *Haven't you?*"

She went to the window for air. She looked out over the sunlit hill of Montjuich, with its castle on top, and the distant buildings of the city. Peace and quiet reigned. The summer sky above was limpid, a deep blue that faded to violet along the horizon. She inhaled the warm air deep into her lungs. It smelled of traffic, trees, the city.

He was right. She could do nothing to save her parents and they could do nothing to save her.

Sean had given her a meaning. He had given her happiness; not a passing mood, but a state of being that endured, that soaked every fibre of her existence. But love also meant being a hostage to fate. Love meant knowing you could be broken into pieces again, at any time. It was a privilege which carried heavy burdens.

Going to America might be a question, in the end, of whether she could survive without him.

She turned around and looked at him, sitting on the bed. His beauty squeezed her heart. The deep green eyes met hers with that brave light she loved so much. She unfastened her gown, revealing her slender, naked body and went to him.

. . .

She cried all through the wedding.

They stood in a bureaucrat's dingy office with three other couples and repeated the soulless words some anarchist had travestied from the Catholic rite. Most of all, she hated the homily which the union official gave them immediately afterwards, while she looked down at the cheap ring Sean had bought that morning and had put on her finger.

"All right. There are three certificates. You get one each, we keep one in our files. When you want to get divorced, you both come in with your certificates and tell us why. Then we burn all three copies and you're free. But this is a serious step, so don't come back if you just fancy a fling in the hay with someone else, because you'll get a swift kick in the backside if you do. Now take care of each other."

They emerged from the office, clutching their certificates. His uniform was still damp from yesterday's wash. She had refused to get married in her nurse's uniform, as was the fashion. She was wearing a cream skirt and blouse and was carrying a bouquet of white flowers. She had on a little white beret to which she had pinned a scrap of veil. They looked like what they were, beautiful, poor and young.

In the hallway, the other couples posed for photographers. A group of soldiers struck up a ribald song. Some confetti was thrown. Elated, Sean hurried her out into the street and lifted her high into the air and swung her around.

"Mrs. Sean O'Keefe, I love you," he shouted in English. "We're on honeymoon, you realize that?"

His face was radiant. Not a soul they knew was there to see them married, no fellow-soldiers of Sean's, none of her friends from Sagrado Corazón. She had not even sent her parents a telegram. He'd suggested she go down to San Lluc next week and tell them in person. She looked down at him, clinging to his muscular arms, and suddenly realized how alone they were and how very much they depended on one another.

"Put me down, you fool," she said, laughing through her tears.

"The world is ours! Ours!" he sang, grinning up at her.

An old woman who was passing by stopped and smiled at them. "Have you just got married, children?"

"Yes!" Sean said, letting Mercedes down at last and hugging

her. "We've just got married, mother, and now we're on honeymoon."

She looked at them with wrinkled eyes. "You are such a beautiful couple. So healthy and handsome. May God bless you and make you very happy. Are you on leave, soldier?"

"Yes," he nodded.

"When do you go back?"

"Tomorrow," he replied, his smile fading.

The old woman dug into her bag and pulled out something. She pressed it into Sean's hand. It was a cheap wooden rosary. "To protect you," she said confidentially.

They went to lunch at the Palace Hotel, where they had pooled their resources to book a suite for the night. It was a beautiful old nineteenth-century hotel, as white and ornate as a wedding cake, with yellow canvas awnings. It looked out over the Plaza de Cataluña, an island of grace in the drab desert of war.

There was silver cutlery on the white linen and flowers on the table. The waiters treated them like a visiting king and queen, serving the meagre dishes and the cheap wine with so much ceremony that it seemed like a feast.

But they did not notice the food. They stared at one another with eyes that saw nothing but their own love.

In the afternoon they made love on the enormous bed. Her body arched against him with a depth of passion she had not reached before, her soul bathed in flames.

"Mrs. O'Keefe," he said. "God knows it doesn't suit you, but it suits me fine."

Later, he took her to the Metropole to see Charlie Chaplin in *Modern Times*. He had already seen the film. She had not. He told her it was the funniest thing in the world. The smell of the cinema reminded her piercingly of her grandfather, dead in his grave these eight years. The Tivoli in Palafrugell had been closed last time she'd been to see it. It had looked sad and tawdry. She thought of the way her grandfather had died, alone and ill and fighting for every breath.

She stared at the glimmering screen, listening to the audience roar. Their own lives, she thought, were like flickering dreams, thrown across the dark for a while, then gone. The tiny figure of the clown, enmeshed in the huge cogs of a world gone mad, at first made her laugh until she cried and then just made her cry.

Sean took her out before the end. They walked along the Ramblas towards the Paseo Marítimo, arms wrapped around one another. Mercedes rested her head against his shoulder, her eyes half-closed so that everything was a bright blur around her. She felt herself in a daze, her heart aching with a mixture of happiness and pain which she could not define.

She knew she would never forget this day. She knew that until she was old and wandering, she would look back on this day with a lump in her throat and with the memory of his strong body in her arms. She knew what they possessed now they would never possess again.

They stopped beside the statue of Columbus towering atop his immensely high column, pointing with his bronze finger towards the New World. Sean looked out across the sea. "This is where the road to America began," he said. "Four and a half centuries ago. *'In fourteen hundred and ninety-two, Columbus sailed the ocean blue.'*"

"I should go home and feed my rabbits," she said, looking towards Montjuich.

"Not on your honeymoon," he remonstrated.

"They'll be hungry."

"So am I. For you."

She smiled up at him. They turned around and walked back to the Palace Hotel.

The room was beautiful, its ceiling stuccoed, its furnishings relicts from a grander and statelier age. They undressed and sprawled on the bed.

Sean gazed at her, at the smooth lines of her naked back and shoulders, at the dark sweep of her hair. The triangle of dark hair nestled between her thighs, as perfect as if it had been painted on by a miniaturist. Her breasts were round and high. He watched them stir as she moved, the nipples erect. "Are you really my wife?" he asked wonderingly.

"According to those dirty bits of paper I am," she smiled.

"You don't sound too convinced."

"Yes, I am. And if you want to roll in the hay with anyone else, that man will kick you up the backside. That's my guarantee."

"I don't want to roll in the hay with anyone but you, darling." He caressed the curve of her hip, tracing the perfect line from her thigh to her slender waist. Her buttocks were taut and smooth as marble. Every detail of her was perfect, immaculate. He took her foot in his hand and studied it intently as if it had been the finest work of art. The toes were slender and long, the nails pearly. Down the instep a pale blue vein wriggled elegantly.

"Have I got nice feet?" she asked.

"You've got nice everything."

"So have you. This is especially nice." She lay with her head on his belly and caressed his manhood. He responded eagerly, surging up under her fingers.

"If you touch me there," he murmured, "you'll have to marry me."

"I already have. This monument is now my property." She studied him intently. "I think I might put a little statue of Columbus on the top, just here."

"Would that be comfortable?"

"It would be very impressive." She drew her fingers along him. "With a little gilding and an inscription."

"What inscription?" he smiled.

She spoke in English. "*In nineteen hundred and thirty-eight, I deflowered Mercedes Eduard.*"

"That doesn't even rhyme," he complained. "And *deflowered*? Where did you get a word like that?"

"I looked it up in my dictionary. The Spanish word is *desflorar*. It means the same thing. To pluck the flower. You plucked mine, didn't you?"

"It's pronounced 'plucked,' not 'plook-ed.'"

She copied his pronunciation. "What a silly language. *Pluct.*"

"It rhymes with 'fucked.' Though I agree, *plook-ed* sounds more painful."

"It hurt like hell at the time," she told him.

"Not any more?"

"Not any more. Tell me about West Virginia."

"I already told you. What you're doing down there is very nice..."

"I don't mean about strikes and marches and police. I mean tell me what it's *like*. How people live. What sort of friends we'll have. Where we'll live. What we'll do."

"Well, it's beautiful. Mountains and forests and rivers. The people are ...they're ..."

"Go on."

Her fingers were still exploring him. He sighed voluptuously. "Mercé, either stop doing that, or stop expecting me to talk to you."

"Why? You said it was nice."

"You're distracting me."

She took him between her lips, closing her eyes and sank slowly down.

"Oh, God," he whispered. He filled her mouth, swollen and hot. She could taste the salt of his desire. She reached down to cup his balls, her heart laden with the pleasure of her tenderness for him, her power over him. Gently she bit into the resilient flesh, tormenting him.

Sean covered his face with his hands, arching to her. She possessed him utterly in that moment, held his soul on her tongue. He was hers, more intensely than any civil or religious rite could have made him. Away from the bright circle of this moment, all was uncertainty, all was darkness and doubt. In their lovemaking lay the only conviction she knew.

She concentrated on giving him delight, on taking her pleasure through his. She could feel him swell on her tongue, could hear his breathing become ragged, until he grabbed at her arms and tried to draw her away.

"Mercedes," he gasped, "stop. Now!"

She drew him onto her. He entered her, shuddering, his face dark and clenched. "Oh, Jesus, Jesus . . ."

He cried out, a hoarse groan, as he came in a gush, his essence gouting into her body. Her own orgasm was immediate and fierce, making her grit her teeth, her nostrils flaring, her eyes fluttering closed. But she was quite silent. Her being had concentrated into the animal intensity of possessing him, of drawing him into her, entirely, forever. She did not stop moving against him, would not let him stop either, no matter how raw he felt, until pleasure flared anew for them both and they settled into the driving cadence of their lovemaking.

She smiled up at him slightly, her eyes smoky. She lifted her knees, opening herself further to him, urging him deeper.

The future, the past, all dark. All meaningless. This moment, all or nothing. This moment, if need be, for always.

She reached down and grasped the hard, slippery shaft of his cock, feeling him thrust in and out of her flesh. Her fingers closed around him, hard, stopping him from entering her. Then she opened her fingers just enough for him to force his way through, into her loins.

She kept her hand there, compelling him to make love to her like that, thrusting through her clenched fingers before he could reach the softer flesh of her sex.

She opened her eyes and saw by his face that she had taken him into a world which was new to him. His pupils were drugged, so huge that his eyes seemed black. The muscles of his shoulders were tensed and veined, the skin glistening with sweat. He was on top, but it was she who commanded, who could shut him out and let him in. She could lead him beyond conventionalities, beyond the boundaries of what he knew and expected. He was looking down at her with an expression that was almost bewilderment. Beneath the physical pleasure that contorted his face lay a kind of awe.

She tightened her fingers, making it cruelly hard for him, feeling him drive through her hand and into her. Assessing his power, challenging him. Until the cords stood out on his neck and she knew he was going to come again.

Then she released him and grasped his shoulders as he went into her all the way and the eruption of heat and joy began. At last she spoke, a wordless cry that rasped in her throat and vibrated in the stillness of the room.

Too weak to do anything more than hold hands, they lay together and watched the afternoon dim into evening. The first stars came out. The sky turned violet, purple, ultramarine. She though of what he had to go back to in the morning and wept.

When it grew too dark to see, they turned on the lights. The marble-tiled bathroom contained a bath that was on a scale with the rest of the furnishings. It was an immense thing on claw feet, deep enough to be filled to chest level. There was scalding water too. They filled it and sat in it together, soaping each other's bodies.

"I'll go up to San Lluc next week," she said, "and tell Mama and Papa."

"Will they be angry with you?"

"I don't know. I don't care. I care more about your going

back to the front. I'm so afraid for you. Are you afraid?" she asked him simply.

"Sometimes."

"Keep being afraid," she said to him. "That'll stop you from doing anything stupid."

"I'm beyond stupidity. You know something? I remember when the war was like a Sunday outing. Literally. I remember people driving down from Barcelona on the weekends, with their womenfolk, and picnic baskets and flasks of brandy. Come to take a few potshots at the enemy, as if they were grouse or pheasants. Monday morning they would go back to the office."

"You thought it was a picnic too, didn't you?" she said. She squeezed a spongeful of water down the dark hair on his chest. "You came out from West Virginia with your tail wagging, dying to shoot a few capitalists, just for the fun of it."

He smiled wryly. "Maybe I did, at that. And it *was* kind of fun, at first. There was camaraderie. We felt as if we were achieving something. That's all changed now. Now it's just a sickening mess." He touched her breasts, pale and firm, the nipples erect. "You're so beautiful. I love you so much. You're the only woman in the world."

"I wish you didn't have to go back. I wish you could pull out, now."

"The war's going to be over in a few months. Why are we sitting in the tub, talking about killing?"

"Because we got married in the middle of a war."

"Come on. Let's get out and go get some food."

"I don't know if I'm hungry." She was watching him with dark eyes. "Do you think it's possible," she said softly, "that we could make love again?"

"Hell, I don't know."

She reached for him under the water. His cock was soft and slack, but as she stroked him, she felt him harden and swell. He reached for her breasts, cupping them in his big hands. He leaned forward and kissed her mouth. Her tongue reached out to lick his, tracing the shape of his lips. "Oh, God," he whispered, his eyes closing. "Mercedes, you astound me."

"A honeymoon as brief as this should be memorable. I love that word. Honey-moon."

"Nights of sweetness."

"One night of sweetness."

"I never knew sex could be like this . . ."

"Sex is for the pleasure of lovers."

"Yes."

"I thought you were the big seducer," she whispered, squeezing him.

"But I never met a woman like you."

"Am I shameful?"

"Shame*less*."

"Just because I like to make love with my wonderful new husband? I think that's normal. We Catalán women have been liberated from our shackles. Didn't you know that?"

"I'm finding out." He rubbed his thumbs across her nipples, making her shiver with pleasure.

"Ahhh . . . I need you so much, *amor*. I want you to kiss me. Now. Will you?"

He nodded without speaking. She slid out of the water and sat on the edge of the bath, wet and naked. She slipped one thigh over his shoulder and drew him to her. She cupped his face in her hands and smiled down at him with dark eyes. "I want you to remember this, Sean. Forever. I want you to remember how much I love you and want you."

"I'll remember. Always."

She drew his mouth to her loins and shuddered as he kissed her there. She rubbed her foot slowly up his muscled back. She needed him to taste her. Not to forget. A profound, sad tenderness uncurled in her. She wanted to nourish him, cherish him. She wanted to protect him, always.

She wanted him not to die.

The next day at three he boarded the train back to Tarragona and the front. By a supreme effort, she held her tears back until the locomotive began to move. Her husband leaned out of the carriage window, waving and shouting to her until his voice was drowned in the clamour of the engine and his face was lost in the clouds of steam.

She stood, weeping, in a throng of weeping women, watching the train recede along ribbons of steel, leaving a vacuum that was like the grave of all their hopes, all their loves.

october 1938

Seville

The artist worked with the plodding care of the untalented academician, gazing at Gerard Massaguer long and lugubriously in between brush-strokes.

They were in the internal courtyard of the house in Seville. Gerard sat cross-legged in the high-backed chair, hands folded in his lap. The artist, Camillo Álvarez, sat opposite him. Neither man spoke.

In Gerard's opinion, Álvarez was a third-rate hack. Whenever he caught sight of the canvas, he winced. The man was portraying him as a ponderous dummy with goggling eyes. Exactly the way he portrayed Franco.

Marisa wanted it done, and since Alfonso's death, he did not, could not, deny her anything. She had not recovered. Since today was a Friday, she would be at the cemetery even now, putting fresh flowers on the grave. Tonight she would cry for hours. She would go to mass five, six, seven times over the weekend.

The remembrance of the boy's death had come over him like a shadow, deepening the clefts which had recently appeared at the corners of his mouth and nose.

The painter cleared his throat.

"Eh?" Gerard queried.

"The expression, Señor Massaguer."

"What?"

"The expression. You are tending—forgive me—to frown."

Gerard forced his face to relax. "Is that better?"

"The eyes. Not so heavy. Perhaps you could raise your glance a little."

Gerard complied. He had expected to be tormented with boredom, but the two-hour sittings each morning had freed his mind to wander. He had even come to welcome the enforced immobility which allowed him to plumb the well of his own thoughts. He stared at the fountain with unseeing eyes, thinking of the one subject which had come to dominate him this autumn, Mercedes Eduard. His daughter. He had begun to think the words these days, belatedly, but with a powerful stirring in his heart. *My daughter.*

His child.

Since Alfonso, he had been haunted by the thought that Mercedes, too, might be dead. She was not. She was alive. He had the proof in his pocket.

It was a report from the nationalist spy network in Catalonia. He had commissioned it through a colonel of Intelligence several weeks ago, paying for the service with a crate of Scotch whisky. It had arrived yesterday.

He had instructed them to start at San Lluc, not knowing that Mercedes had not been at San Lluc since the autumn of 1936. The spies had picked up the trail quickly, however. Catalonia was riddled with informers and agents and they had been very thorough. There was a wealth of information in the neatly typewritten pages. And several revelations had been less than agreeable.

He thought of the day they had talked at Las Yucas, years ago. He remembered the earnest, childish declaration that she would fight for the republic against the army. He had warned her, then. He had warned her clearly. But she had meant it. Oh, yes. She was his flesh, all right. What she had said she would do, she would do. Just like him.

She had become a *miliciana* in 1936. A militiawoman who had faced armed combat in Aragón, side by side with the rabble of the *barrios*, with bus conductresses and hard-faced factory sluts.

She had taken arms against the *generalísimo*. Even now, Franco was preparing laws which would give him immense powers to punish those who had resisted the National Movement. There were records, papers, files which would be captured and which would condemn. There would be vast purges. Some said he intended to imprison or execute every human being who had lifted a hand against him.

Mercedes was facing the camps or the firing squads for that crime alone. And there was worse, far worse.

She was said to have shot a wounded prisoner at Granados. In the head, at point-blank range. In front of witnesses. One Juan Ramón Ramírez, a turncoat now in the nationalist zone, claimed to have seen the event.

A story like that would be enough to hang her. Quite dispassionately, Gerard knew that Franco's court-martial would require a legion of Red atrocities in the aftermath of the war. They would be needed to displace the weight of atrocities on the nationalist side. Rumours like that, whether true or not, would be fiercely targeted. Witnesses could always be found when they were needed. Retribution would be terrible.

And he himself, unwittingly, had drawn the attention of nationalist intelligence to the girl.

Álvarez cleared his throat again. "My apologies, Señor Massaguer."

"What?" Gerard snapped.

"The expression—"

He forced the tension out of his face once again.

They did not know who the girl was, of course. Or so he trusted. That was one thing, at least. And she had been less conspicuous since 1937. She now worked in Sagrado Corazón hospital, tastefully renamed the V.I. Lenin Infirmary. She was a nurse, out of the combat zone, though still aiding the republic.

But there was a final shock. She had just married.

"Married," of course, according to some improvised republican gibberish, which would count for nothing after the war. What frightened him was that she had chosen a foreigner, an American volunteer named Sean Michael O'Keefe.

The figure of O'Keefe tormented Gerard's imagination. The information was skimpy. He was twenty-eight, a miner from West Virginia. No address had been found. Described by the report as a dedicated Bolshevist and a good soldier, O'Keefe had been promoted to the rank of captain in the International Brigades.

The International Brigades were already being withdrawn from the fighting. Next month, they were due to be sent home.

Which meant that Mercedes, his only remaining child, his flesh, his hereafter, might leave Spain soon and go with her American husband.

The thought filled him with dread. If she were to leave before he saw her, to float upon the winds of the world and perhaps be lost to him forever! And yet, if she stayed in Spain, she was doomed.

Álvarez plucked a large silver watch from his waistcoat and consulted it. "With your permission, Señor Massaguer, the sitting is over."

"Very well."

Gerard rose and studied the canvas. The portrait was almost finished. It was an incredibly ugly work. He knew that he had aged suddenly since the death of his son, his features growing heavier and more melancholy, his once-thick hair starting to thin and grey. But surely he did not have that turgid flesh, that stony stare? That stuffed horror was not him?

He made some neutral comment and left the painter to pack up.

He went to his study and sat at his desk. What was he going to do about Mercedes? How was he going to shield her? The important thing, of course, was to be in Catalonia with the vanguard of the invasion and to get to her quickly. Build whatever protection he could around her life. He had influence and more important, he had money. There was much he could do.

Especially if he cleared the ground first.

He unfolded the report and studied it. There was information about Francesc and Conchita Eduard too. The blacksmith, as Gerard had expected, had been aiding the republican war effort from the start. He was director of an armaments factory in Gerona and would certainly be shot after capture. To a man with his past record, no mercy would be shown.

The woman, Conchita, still lived in San Lluc. She was the only one in whose favour something could be said, some story of a nun from the convent whom she had sheltered for a while. However, the nun had apparently been murdered sometime later, and even that might turn out to be another nail in the family coffin.

He felt nothing for Francesc or Conchita. The woman had never meant anything to him. He could hardly remember her face any more. Whatever happened to her now was irrelevant.

The blacksmith had always been an enemy, from the day they'd met on the plain of Pals. He remembered the hate that had smouldered in the cobalt blue eyes. Gerard felt an answering hatred flicker in his own heart. *He* was the girl's father, not that slouching cripple, that muddle-headed anarchist. Eduard's filthy paws had soiled the girl. It was the blacksmith's fault that Mercedes now faced death. His poisonous teachings had dragged her through the mire.

I should have disposed of you years ago, he thought. He should have eliminated Eduard and Conchita and put Mercedes in a convent school. He had waited too long.

But then, there had been Marisa and the boy to think of. It hadn't seemed so important, then.

Should he tell Marisa about the girl? Not now, of course. Perhaps not ever. No one need know anything. He felt no shame about the girl's politics. They would change. She was very young, only twenty-one. In any case, it was the flesh and blood that mattered, not the politics. If she was like him, she would already have understood the emptiness of dogmas and faiths.

As for the birth, a pedigree was just a piece of paper. New ones could be written.

He sat at his desk thinking for a while, then reached for the telephone.

Barcelona

A gramophone was playing dance music in the hospital.

The melody drifted faintly from the medical faculty, despite the shuttered windows and locked doors. They were having a party inside. Now and then came the muffled sound of cheering and laughter.

It was no secret that several hundred right-wing sympathizers were living in the medical faculty building. For the most part, they were friends and relations of the medical staff, wealthy bourgeois who had been in hiding since the beginning of the war. Now they were beginning to emerge from their hiding-places. They had begun to congregate at Sagrado Corazón some weeks earlier. Eagerly, they were awaiting the collapse of the republic and the arrival of Franco.

The hospital, always a focus of right-wing feeling, had changed markedly since the summer.

The atmosphere among many of the staff had become one of veiled excitement. The statue of Christ, which had been removed from the foyer in 1936 and tossed into a cellar, had reappeared in its niche as if by a miracle. Its plaster face scrutinized all arrivals again, a chipped plaster finger laid triumphantly on the Sacred Heart. There were half-whispered conversations which started with the gleeful words, "After it's all over," or "When the army gets here."

The gramophone began to play a popular Fascist song. Through it came singing and louder cheers.

"¡Viva España!"

"¡Viva España!"

"¡Viva España!"

It was the nationalist war cry. Mercedes, who heard it on her ward, and who knew that many of the medical staff were at that party, felt a wave of disgust pass through her.

Could they really anticipate the arrival of the Fascists with joy? Had they forgotten how Mussolini's bombers had bombarded this defenceless city? Had they forgotten the slaughtered children?

They would be eating and drinking in there. Yes, because the new tenants had astounding supplies of food. Such people, richer and cleverer than the common rabble, had their hoards. The smell of their cooking—two meals a day—had tormented the wounded for weeks.

For months, the only food available to ordinary people in Barcelona had been rice. Mercedes had not eaten properly since Sean had left. She was already suffering from what she knew were the signs of malnutrition—bleeding gums, a peevish feebleness, an inability to concentrate on anything. Her heart pounded frighteningly at any exertion. Her last period had not come. She suffered from dizzy spells.

Yet it had not occurred to her to accept, when one of the doctors had invited her to the faculty building for a meal. She could not have eaten with them to save her life. It astounded her that any doctor could feed himself, knowing that his patients lay starving in their beds.

She turned away from the window and looked around the ward. It was heavily overcrowded, the beds jammed up side by side. The faces of the men were grey and defeated. They lay in silence, listening to the distant music as though it were the sound of Franco's armies, already marching down the Avenida Diagonal. The normal chatter of the ward had died away.

These wounded men had been, in Mercedes's eyes, brave beyond belief. They had submitted to horrors. They had endured mutilation and disfigurement, treatments that were sometimes more agonizing than their wounds. None had been adequately fed, despite their injuries. And so few ever complained. They had faced their torment with cheerfulness. Now they lay silent, cowed by the music of a distant gramophone.

What would happen to them when the city fell? Some said they would be dragged from their beds and murdered by the Moors. They were already beginning to discharge themselves, melting away in the night, with unhealed wounds and limbs still in casts.

She pushed her trolley out and down the corridor to the next ward. Ward 37 was the Facial Surgery ward. To work here was a privilege, for it called for the utmost reserves of tact, self-control and nursing skills.

Since it was on the ground floor, sandbags had been piled up against the windows here. The artificial light was dim and cast an unnerving light on an already unnerving scene. There were only six men on this ward, but their injuries were appalling. They had lost eyes, jaws, faces. Four breathed through tubes inserted into their tracheas. One had been extensively burned and his face was a mask made of red sealing-wax by a child. The surgeons had been patiently trying to manufacture ears, lips, nostrils from gobbets of flesh cut from other parts of his body.

Mercedes kept her expression cheerful as she came in. All made some sort of noise in greeting. Those who had eyes followed her as she made her way to the last bed, where the most recent injury lay. His face was entirely swathed in bandages. Two tubes protruded from the dressing. One went into the trachea to give him air, the other into a nostril, so that he could be fed. He had been brought in three days earlier from Gandesa, his face shattered by a mortar bomb. It had taken the surgeons five hours to pick the splinters and smashed bones from his face. Now it was time to remove the dressing and assess the repair work.

She drew the curtains around the bed and looked down at him for a moment. He was a big man. His muscular shoulders were naked above the sheets. The hair that showed above the bandages was black.

She touched his shoulder gently.

"I'm going to remove the bandages," she told him. "Then a doctor will come and take a look at you. Do you understand?"

He nodded slightly. Mercedes turned the lamp on him. She unfastened the pins and then, with a forceps, began to unwind the outer bandages.

"I'll try not to hurt you," she said as she worked. "Just lift your hand if I do."

But he flinched and whimpered wordlessly as she worked.

Beneath the bandages, the man's face was a mass of stained gauze packs.

Suddenly, her hands began to tremble violently. Nausea made her almost vomit, her shrunken stomach twisting inside her.

It was something that happened occasionally and only on this ward. It was the thought of Sean. If he should come back to her like this. If one day she should unwrap the bandages on an unknown patient and find Sean's destroyed face beneath . . .

Her head was spinning. She had to lay down the forceps for a moment and close her eyes. Then she felt a hot rush of shame at her own weakness in the face of this man's silent suffering. She was a nurse, not an actress in some sentimental film. She picked up the forceps again and forced herself to keep working. As she worked, she kept talking to him in a quiet, reassuring voice.

She lifted the gauze pads with infinite care, one by one. Beneath them, the eyes were completely swollen shut, tracked with the black scribble of stitching. The fleshy part of the nose had gone, leaving two crusted holes in a stub of bone. The lower jaw had also been blown off, and when she picked the packs out of the mouth, the man's tongue lolled out of his torn throat, swollen and distorted with stitches. Most of his teeth had been lost. It was a face from a nightmare of pain and degradation.

"It all looks fine," she said calmly. "Very clean. No infection. Dr Pla will be pleased. Your eyelids are very swollen, but you'll be able to see again soon, when the swelling goes down. I'm just going to clean some of the stitches."

She began working with little pads soaked in saline, bathing the skin, taking immense care over the eyes and nostrils.

"You were wounded at Gandesa, weren't you?" she went on. "My husband's at Gandesa. He's with the International Brigades. He's an American. Maybe you met him? His name's Sean O'Keefe. He's a big man, like you. A captain. I haven't heard from him in weeks. We haven't been married very long. I'm sorry, did that hurt? I've nearly finished."

There had not been even a photograph among this man's possessions to show what he had once looked like. His name was

Sebastiá Fuster, and he came from Olot, a small town up in the mountains. He was twenty-six. Eventually, someone would come to see him here. Whoever it was, mother, sweetheart, sister, would have to look at that face and pray. Even with months of skin grafts and reconstructive surgery, Sebastiá Fuster was never going to smile, eat or talk normally again.

"I write to my husband every day," she said. "I never hear anything from him. The mail doesn't get here from the front any more. I don't even know if he gets my letters."

As she was finishing, he reached out and laid a large hand on her arm to catch her attention. A grunt came from his chest. Then he made a gesture of writing on his other palm.

"There's a pad and pencil next to your bed," she said, giving them to him. "They're always there."

Blindly, he began to write on the pad. Mercedes struggled to decipher the scrawl.

SAW JUAN O'KEEFE TWO WEEKS AGO, GANDESA. WAS WELL.

Her heart jumped. "Thank you," she said, touching his shoulder. "Thank you. That means a lot to me."

He wrote again. The ruined tongue stirred in the shattered jaw as the pencil scratched. YOUR HUSBAND—GOOD MAN. VERY BRAVE.

"Yes," she said, "he's very brave. You're all very brave."

SOME MAIL COMES. KEEP WRITING.

"I will," she said.

He fumbled a fresh sheet over. I.B. GOING HOME, he scrawled. ALL OVER FOR EVERYBODY. BEST THING.

"I understand," she said, looking compassionately at the travesty of a face. "Don't tire yourself any more. We'll talk later, when you feel stronger. The doctor will want to see you."

The pencil hesitated over the paper, then wrote one more line. ALL STUPID WASTE.

She touched him again. "I'll go and call Dr. Pla now. I'll be back later to put on another dressing."

She put the pad and pencil back on top of his locker and rose. After a moment's hesitation, she drew the curtains back. This ward was not a place for coyness or privacy.

Those who could see craned their necks to look at the newcomer's injuries. As she pushed her trolley out of the ward, she heard the man with the red sealing-wax face murmur, "Poor bastard."

She summoned the doctor and then went to sterilize her instruments while she waited. She had another recurrence of her trembling and had to lean against the wall.

Oh, Sean, she prayed, *come back to me.*
Come back to me alive and well.

Sierra de Montsant, Aragón,

Sean O'Keefe sniffed the icy mountain air. "We're not far from the coast now. I can practically smell the sea." He fell into step beside his sergeant, a wizened cockney named Bill French. "We could make Tarragona by tonight."

"Yes, if it was just you an' me. But it ain't." The Londoner nodded at the men. The breath clouded at his mouth. "They're exhausted. It's got to be thirty miles to Tarragona."

"I guess. We'll have to push them," Sean said.

"We can't push 'em much 'arder, or they'll start to drop."

"That means another night in the open. And another day on the road. I don't know which is worse."

Sean left the sergeant and clambered wearily to the crest of the ridge. It was a rocky and bleak landscape, the vegetation monotonous scrub. The road ahead was dotted with trudging figures. The sky was leaden, but the cloud-cover was way too high to provide any sort of cover from enemy aircraft. Although they were well behind their own lines by now, they had heard the Stukas whining and growling all morning and had heard the thud of their bombs. Five miles away, black smoke smudged the horizon where a tank or a truck was burning.

Sean looked back at his own men. They were strung out like the beads of a broken necklace, but he knew they were safer that way. Bunched up in an orderly column of four, they were too tempting a target for the fighters. So far, probably because they had no vehicles, not even a motorcycle, they had mercifully been ignored.

More and more of the men were shedding their weapons now.

"We're well behind the rest," he called to French. "Keep them moving, Frenchy. The sooner we get away from those fucking Stukas, the better."

The sergeant obediently dropped back to chivvy the men. Sean could hear his sharp voice echoing among the rocks like a terrier yapping.

He sat on a rock and fumbled in his greatcoat for a cigarette. The frost bit into his chest with the first lungful of tarry smoke, making him cough painfully.

It was growing piercingly cold as winter approached. The men who trudged across the mountainside were muffled in greatcoats and blankets. They had come along this same road four months earlier. Then it had merely been precipitous. Now it was pitted with bomb craters and blocked with burned-out trucks. They had to go around these obstacles, stumbling over rocks and the ubiquitous wild oak whose jagged leaves tore at their hands and clothing.

There were so many wounded that almost every pair of whole men had a comrade slung between them, with limbs or head bandaged. Those who could not even hobble had either been left behind, or had been given the dubious privilege of riding in trucks which were such easy prey for the Stukas.

"Move it, *muchachos*," he growled at the first handful who caught up with him. "Pick your goddamned feet up. You're not strolling around the brothels yet."

He sat growling the same thing to the rest of them as they passed by. Most were Americans or British. A few gave him grim smiles, the rest hardly looked up. He counted them off in his head. They were all still together, such as they were. All were grey with dust, their uniforms filthy and ragged, their faces pinched.

From here on, however, the land sloped towards the sea. Thirty miles to Tarragona. From Tarragona there would be motor transport up to Barcelona. And in Barcelona, the International Brigades were to be demobilized. Disbanded, retired, withdrawn. They were going home. In days he would be with Mercedes again. He felt his heart leap.

They had not seen each other since August and he ached for her with a kind of desperation. Unthinkingly, he touched the little bundle of her letters which he kept in his breast pocket, letters so worn they did not even rustle any longer.

His love for her choked him sometimes. During the summer's

heat it had made him tremble. In this winter of defeat, it boiled in his chilled blood. He carried her with him wherever he went. There had not been an hour of the past three months when he had not thought of her. Even at Gandesa, when the Fascist artillery had shelled their positions until tons of splintered rock had filled the air, and the columns of dust had towered to the heavens, and it had seemed as though the whole world was exploding.

When the last stragglers had passed him by, he rose to his feet, and made his way through them back towards the head of the column and rejoined the sergeant.

"We've 'ad our arses well and truly kicked, 'aven't we?" the sergeant said dryly, nodding at the ragged column. "Most of us dead, and the rest bein' sent back to where we came from."

"The whole world's going to be at war against Fascism soon," Sean said slowly. "We've struck the first blow. That's what counts. Isn't it?"

"I dunno," French shrugged. "I dunno what counts, Cap."

He gave Sean a shrewd glance from faded blue eyes. Not an affectionate man, he'd grown fond of the big, oddly innocent American. Over the time they'd been together, he'd seen maturity come over Sean O'Keefe. He'd seen the war carve away the last vestiges of soft youth from his face and body, and had seen grey begin to fleck the thick black hair and moustache. He thought of it as the iron coming out.

In French's experience, war turned you into either a man or a rabbit. There were a lot of rabbits. Sean had become a man. And that made him exceptional. Yet there was a naive aura around him, an innocence that was vulnerable. He would learn, French thought. He would learn by and by.

They did not hear the Stukas until the first was almost upon them.

There were two, one a few hundred yards behind the other. Sean spun around and saw the crooked wings streaking low over the ridge towards them. He saw the cheerily twinkling lights that were actually machine-guns firing. He saw his men begin streaming off the road, abandoning the wounded where they fell, hurling themselves into the thorny scrub like panicking animals. Then he and French both hit the earth together.

The fighter screamed over them, its passing like a vast blow. They heard it climbing upwards, its engine yodelling savagely. The second Stuka swept over the ridge and began its strafing run. The fluttering of the machine-guns was like giant wings. The bullets ripped up the road like a plough.

Sean kept his face pressed into the dry earth, horribly aware of how exposed they were. He was cursing himself violently for not having kept a better look-out. Grovelling here in the road, they were sitting ducks. He heard French moaning, "Oh, fuck. Oh, fuck. Oh, fuckin' 'ell."

The second plane exploded past them, raking at the lines of floundering men. Its wings tilted from side to side as it hunted. Sean scrambled to his feet when it had gone, tried to drag French up.

"We've got to get off the road!"

"Get down," French was shrieking at him.

"We can't lie in the fucking road," Sean gasped back. "Come on!"

But French had fought himself free and was sprawling on the ground again, still yelling at Sean to get down. The fighters were both banking against the leaden sky. Sean cursed him, turned, and began sprinting towards an outcrop of rock twenty yards away, where there was shelter. French's shrill voice pursued him, until it was drowned out by the approaching Stuka behind.

He did not look back, just flung his pack off and ran like a hare before the hounds. The banshee wail swelled, engulfing him.

He felt a great wind buffet his body. He was swept off his feet, tumbled like chaff, scoured along the rocks. He heard his own voice screaming, pleading. Until at last he came to rest, his limbs outflung.

He tried to rise and knew that it was not the wind that had buffeted him.

Unthinkable pain overwhelmed him, but there was no air in his lungs to scream and no strength in his arms to beat at the claws that were rending him.

He lay looking up at the grey sky, unable to move or breathe. Broken, he thought. Not working.

He saw Bill French's face appear overhead, staring down at him in horror.

"Sean! Oh, Jesus Christ, Sean!"

The little sergeant was trying to lift his head up. The fighter's guns had punched huge holes in Sean's body and it lolled like a broken doll's. Dimly, he saw that French was becoming daubed with scarlet. To his vague surprise, the sergeant was crying.

He tried to smile at Frenchy, but did not know whether he had succeeded.

He wanted to tell French that it had not been wasted. He did not feel that he had squandered his life. Looking back, the years in Spain seemed to him constructive years, a time of decision and achievement. He was aware, at this outermost extreme, that it had all been logical. All a pattern, with a purpose and a meaning. It had led somewhere. It would lead on, through this, to other goals, other scopes.

He tried to tell French that with his eyes, but French only sobbed.

Things were breaking up inside him, the machinery of life disengaging and falling apart. His head lolled sleepily. His throat had flooded, warm and salt. His last thoughts were sweet ones, of Mercedes. He felt a moment of joy that she would live, even though he would die. He felt the full sweetness of life and saw her face looking at him, the dark eyes radiant. How strange and lovely she was.

The terrible pain faded. The earth opened kind jaws and swallowed him.

14.

Saguaro

Tucson

She opened her eyes.

She had been a creature of the dark so long that the light stabbed into her brain like a dagger.

The first thing to come into focus was the sky. It towered over her, filled from horizon to horizon with a vast, roiling mass of clouds. Their tops were brilliantly silvered, but their bottoms were black, and only a few rags of blue were visible. The coming storm loomed, dizzying her with its height and power. She groped instinctively for Joel's hand. His fingers twined through hers.

Slowly, she lowered her gaze to the landscape around her.

At first it made almost no sense to her. She had last set eyes on the soft contours of southern California. This world was so alien, so strange, that he might as well have dropped her on the surface of another planet. The soil was orange. The plants that grew all around her had extraordinary shapes: towering, ribbed bodies with twisted arms; sprays of thorny wire that ended in a handful of leaves; confused masses of thorns and spikes and bristles; and all of it swaying in the big wind that buffeted their faces.

She clung to Joel's hand, gaping. And slowly, her brain began to make some sense of it all, resolving it into a desert landscape of cactus, prickly pear, mesquite and tamarisk. In the distance, a range of dim violet mountains crawled along the horizon, over-shadowed by the storm that was heading their way.

Dust kicked itself up into swirls and devils, or cartwheeled between the cacti, bowling tumbleweed along the way a child bowls a hoop. It rushed through the scant foliage of the trees and whistled shrilly through the thorns of the cacti.

She turned to him at last. He'd been watching her. She had to raise her voice over the wind. "It's so beautiful!"

He smiled. "There's a storm coming. I wanted you to see it."

"It's wonderful!" She gazed around. There was no sign of humanity as far as the eye could see, not a house nor a telegraph pole. Just the vastness of the desert and the sky. She started walking forward, tugging him along beside her. "What are they called?" she demanded, staring up at the huge barrel bodies.

"Saguaro."

"Oh, yeah. Of course." They were the dominant life form on this alien planet, fleshy kings of the arid land. They stood like giants, their ribbed and spiny bodies sometimes sprouting arms that beckoned or warded off, sometimes towering to forty feet without a branch. In places, they were grouped thickly enough to form a forest. In others they were lone monoliths. The wind was so strong now that even they were swaying ponderously, heavy arms waving.

"And those?"

"Ocotillo."

"And those?"

"Cholla."

Once, this world would have seemed sparse and barren to her. Now, after weeks of deprivation, it overwhelmed her with its richness. There was too much to take in, too much to see.

She exclaimed with delight at the ripe purple fruit on a prickly pear and reached out to touch. He caught her hand quickly.

"They're covered with thorns you can't even see. Take you a week to pick them all out of your fingers."

"Are they good to eat?"

"Not bad."

The beauty of it all was flooding her senses, astonishing her with its variety.

He let her wander where she wanted, clinging to his hand, answering her questions as they formed. She thought she was in

Mexico. In fact, they were still on his own land, a couple of miles from the house. But she would never know the difference; the immense Sonoran desert that stretched from Arizona into Mexico, and down the peninsula of Baja California, all looked the same to the inexperienced eye. It would take a native to tell one part from another.

The baking heat of the day was fading as darkness fell. Already, the cool air smelled of rain. Thunder was growling in the distance.

"Saguaros can live for hundreds of years," he told her. "A big one like that will weigh three, four tons."

"What are those red things on the top? Flowers?"

"No, the flowers are white. Those are the fruit. The Indians eat them. They're sweet."

She picked up a piece of wood, part of the skeleton of some plant. It was a lacework tube light as a feather and she marvelled at its witchery. "Do Indians live here?"

"Not in this valley. Farther along, past that range of mountains."

"I can see why you let me out." She turned full circle. "There's nowhere to run to, is there?"

"Nowhere."

She looked up at him. "Is this place your home?"

"You could say that. It's the place I love best."

Eden still held the bit of dead wood in her hands. The wind whipped the black hair around her face and she shook it free. "Why are you doing this?" she asked him.

He almost didn't catch the words over the wind. "Doing what?"

"This kidnapping."

"For the money."

"No," she said. "You don't care about the money, Joel. You're not a money person."

"How do you know?"

"I've been around money people all my life. They're not like you. A money person would never come and live in a place like this." She moved closer to him, green eyes intent. "And you're not a criminal. You've never done anything like this before. If *I* had to kidnap *you*, I think I'd do a better job." She saw his mouth move in a slight smile. "You're scary, but not because you're bad.

You're scary because you've been hurt. And it's never got better."
She was almost touching him now. She held the wooden lacework
tube in her hands like a wand. "That's why you're doing this.
Because of the hurt. Did my mother hurt you, Joel? Is that why
you're hurting her now?"

He seemed rooted to the spot, unable to speak or move. His
eyes were fixed on hers. The sky was becoming lurid, and the
ochre light was reflected in her eyes, making them glow. Her hair
was streaming around her pale, oval face, whipping and unfolding
in the wind.

"What did she do to you?" she asked.

Still he couldn't speak.

"What did she do?" she asked again.

Lightning glared around them, and a sudden crash of thunder
rolled overhead, making them both jump. The spell was broken.
Or perhaps it merely changed.

He reached for her hand and started pulling her along. "Come.
I want to show you something."

"What?"

"Come!"

"It's going to storm!" But she ran with him, slithering down
the sandy slope, swerving past the thorns that grabbed at her. The
desert looked trackless to her, but he seemed to know his way.
He led her through a clump of mesquite trees, their feathery
branches whipping in the wind.

"Look."

He was pointing to a tall saguaro that loomed up in front of
them. She saw at once that it was different from all the others.
Instead of growing in a pillar, like the rest, it had begun to flatten
half-way up its length and had spread into a broad fan. Two arms
were upraised around the fan. The fan was a face. A woodpecker
had made a hole that was the mouth. Wrinkles in the green flesh
made eyes and cheeks. Two strange ears grew on either side of the
head.

Even in this bizarre landscape, it was a bizarre creature.

"It's a man," she exclaimed.

"It's a spirit."

She stared at it. "Why did it grow like that?"

He didn't answer. She took his hand and they stood looking

at the weird plant together. The first drops of rain began to fall. The sky overhead was almost black.

She showed him the water drops in her palm. "It's going to rain like hell in about thirty seconds. What'll we do?"

"We'll get wet."

"What about the lightning?"

"What about it?"

She laughed suddenly, throwing her head back. "You're right. Oh, God, it's good to be out." She lifted her face to the lowering sky and opened her mouth for the rain to fall in.

Thunder rolled overhead again. As if on that signal, the rain came on a gust of cold wind. It beat down on them in big drops that pattered among the foliage and thudded into the sand. Eden felt her T-shirt begin to cling to her skin. She was in a kind of ecstasy. The wildness of the elements was intoxicating, sweeping her spirit up in a wave more powerful than any drugs could provide. The rain tasted sweet on her tongue. It was warm. She felt Joel's strong fingers entwined around hers.

Then the heavens opened.

Rain gushed down in torrents. The distant mountains had vanished. They could barely see fifty yards. The world had become a white mist in which a few lone saguaro loomed. In seconds they were utterly drenched.

She put both arms around his waist and hung on tight. His arms came around her. She could feel his body jerking, but whether he was laughing or crying, she could not tell.

The rain was elemental, a primeval force older than time. It obliterated other realities, dominating the crouched world. It lashed them, blown by the wind; it beat on them, poured down their bodies, turned them from clothed humans into huddled beasts. It quite dwarfed them. All around, lightning ignited whitely, and a huge crash rolled across the valley, seeming to pass overhead.

Eventually, he led her, stumbling, to the thicket of mesquite trees. He pulled her down and they collapsed onto the earth under the partial shelter. She huddled into his arms and he drew her in between his thighs. She pressed her face to his wet, muscled throat, inhaling the smell of his skin. Water streamed down onto them through the branches.

He began to rock her, the way he had done in the cell. He rocked her gently and slowly, his big body sheltering her.

The thunder came in gigantic peals. The variety of its voices was astounding. Sometimes it was like boulders rolling, at other times like vast iron bells. Then there would come a staccato drumming, the steel hoofs of a stallion dancing on the roof of the world; then the crash of cities falling.

"How long will it last?" she called against his throat.

"A half hour. Maybe an hour," she heard him say.

"I wish it would last forever." She rubbed her face against his skin, feeling it slippery and smooth. In his arms she felt no fear, no pain. She touched his throat with her tongue. There was salt mixed with the rain. She could taste the musk of his skin. She opened her mouth wide and bit into his throat gently. He shuddered, his arms tightening around her.

She lifted her mouth to his, seeking. Their lips brushed, but he turned his face aside. She knew better than to press him again. He would take her when he wanted to. And maybe then she would unlock some of the secrets that lay in him.

They clung together through the downpour. Time seemed to be immobilized, as though the very world had stopped turning to watch the spectacle. She felt as though they had entered some place around which other forces moved, the eye of the hurricane, the pivot of the machine. A vacuum in the order of things. She felt her mind touch the stillness. There was peace in the midst of the storm; silence in the heart of chaos.

Silence. Peace.

Then the cogs stirred and the machine began to tick again.

She realized that the thunder was more distant. It was still raining, but not so fiercely now. And the sky was lighter.

It had rained for perhaps three-quarters of an hour. It was hard to tell. Maybe she had even slept. She felt so strange, as though something had happened that had changed her. As though she'd passed through some rite of passage. Maybe I'm going to be different now, she thought.

Joel stirred. His mouth had been pressed into her wet hair and now he looked up slowly. "It's passing on."

Eden sat up stiffly and pushed her hair off her face. She looked at him. He was beautiful, she thought suddenly. When the pain left his face, he was absolutely beautiful. Who had flawed him? She reached out and touched his cheek.

"Joel," she said. "Joel. Is that really your name?"

His mouth moved in a strange smile. "'That which the palmerworm hath left hath the locust eaten; and that which the locust hath left hath the cankerworm eaten; and that which the cankerworm hath left hath the caterpillar eaten.'"

Eden stared at him. "What's that?"

"It's the beginning of the Book of Joel."

"In the Bible?" He nodded. "What else does it say?"

"'And I will restore to you the years that the locust hath eaten, the cankerworm, and the caterpillar, and the palmerworm, my great army which I sent among you.'"

"You know it all by heart?"

"I was made to learn it all by heart."

"By whom?"

"By a man who called himself a priest." He was still smiling at her, but she saw the shadows in his eyes.

"Say some more. Please."

"'And it shall come to pass afterwards, that I will pour out my spirit upon all flesh; and your sons and your daughters shall prophesy, your old men shall dream dreams, your young men shall see visions.'"

"It's beautiful. What does it mean?"

His eyes left hers, looked upwards. "The rain's nearly stopped. Come."

He rose and pulled her to her feet. Only a few drops were now falling. The light was still weird, but not so lurid. The sky overhead was an upside-down sea of silvery mist. The dark mass of the storm was moving north, growling as it departed.

Eden inhaled. "Oh . . . that smell."

"Creosote bush."

"Which one is it?"

He showed her the common, unassuming shrub. A few battered yellow blossoms still clung to the twigs. She crushed the leaves in her palms, and inhaled the marvelous fragrance. Elusive, pungent, it was the very essence of the desert.

"It's medicinal," he said. "Heals wounds. Cleans out the stomach."

"Does it?" She picked a spray to take with her.

She was soaked; her T-shirt clung transparently to her small breasts, her tracksuit bottom bagged with the weight of the water it had absorbed.

"I'm going to wring myself out." She kicked off her shoes. She pulled off her shirt and pants, and twisted them into ropes to get the water out. He stood staring at the west, where a golden streak of sun was fighting through the mist. "That was the most beautiful thing that ever happened to me," she said.

Joel turned to her. Naked but for the cotton panties he had bought for her, she smiled at him. "Truly."

He walked slowly to her. "Didn't you ever regret becoming an addict?" he asked quietly.

Eden felt a lump form suddenly in her throat. "Oh, shit. What did you bring that up for?"

"You must have known what you were doing to yourself."

"Of course I *regretted* it," she said, her mouth quivering. "And no, I didn't know what I was doing. I thought I could handle it. I didn't think I'd end up a junkie. Nobody does."

"But everybody knows."

"Maybe *you* know. I didn't." She felt like crying. "Did you have to remind me about that? Huh? That's the first hour in the past year that I forgot I was a junkie."

"You're not a junkie," he said. "You're cured. I cured you."

"It ain't that easy, pardner," she said, mimicking his Western accent. "Junkies don't get cured."

"Look," he commanded, pointing to her naked thighs. The track marks were fading in the milk-white flesh, the scars healed. "They're cured."

She inspected herself. "I'll soon make new ones."

"You're *not* a junkie, Eden!"

"Show me a needle and I'll show you a junkie."

"Jesus," he said, his voice harshening, "you make me so mad sometimes . . ."

"I have that effect on all my friends," she said dryly.

"Get dressed," he commanded.

"Don't be such a puritan."

"Come on."

"The saguaro don't mind. The sky doesn't mind. Only you mind." She swung suddenly and flung her clothes high into the air. They fluttered absurdly, fell hooked among thorns. "There," she said in satisfaction.

"Very adult," he said.

"Does my body upset you?" She spread her feet and held her arms wide, and thrust her navel forward, her small breasts up. "Does it? This ugly little thing?"

He did not want to look at her, play her games, but her body dragged his eyes irresistibly to it. She was a pale starfish against the vastness of thorn and sand. The pink triangle of her panties mocked him.

"You're not ugly," he said, his tongue clumsy in his mouth.

"Skinny, ugly, irresponsible little junkie," she said.

"You're not."

"I am."

"Eden . . ."

"What am I, then?" she demanded, walking towards him.

"You're beautiful." The words seemed to jerk out of him, without his volition. "Precious."

"Precious?" She shook her head and laughed softly. "Been a long time since anybody called me that. My Mama used to call me precious, once upon a time, long ago." She cocked her hands on her hips. "Ten million bucks *is* pretty precious though, huh?"

"That's not what I mean."

Her green eyes glittered. "What *do* you mean, Joel?"

He turned away from her abruptly, not trusting himself to speak. His heart was thudding unsteadily, as though it had forgotten its rhythm. He went and retrieved her clothes from the bushes they had landed in. He brought them over to her.

"Your wardrobe's not that large," he said, thrusting them at her. "Put them on."

He was almost surprised when she obeyed. He caught a last glimpse of her breasts as she shrugged the shirt on. They were perfect, high and firm, the tips erect.

She knew. She enjoyed using her power on him. Right now it was a game. Soon, he knew, it would be no game. He had taken few lovers in his life, though many women had pursued him; but he knew what she was doing to him. And what he was doing to her.

He clamped his teeth hard and rubbed his wet face with his hands.

. . .

When the last mutterings of the storm faded, a profound stillness
fell over the desert. A big black raven drifted among the saguaro,
the first living thing she'd seen since the storm began. They walked
together, not talking or touching. The evening was luminous. The
wind had died down and all around was the heavenly smell of the
creosote bush.

Water glistened on the plants. Droplets congregated among
the thorns of the saguaro, rimming each plant with a nimbus of
golden light.

In the west, a high window had appeared among the clouds
and streams of light were falling on the distant hills.

"So beautiful," she said.

"There'll be a rainbow pretty soon."

"Joel, look!" She stopped dead, grabbing his arm. A rabbit
scuttled across their path, long ears flattened back.

"It's only a rabbit."

"Yeah, I know." She stared after it wistfully. "I wish I'd
caught him. I'd take him back with me."

"He wouldn't like your cell."

"No," she said quietly. "I guess my cell's no place for a
rabbit."

They met each other's eyes for a moment.

The window in the sky was widening and light was pouring
down through it in glory. The mountains were misty purple and
gold. He stopped to gaze at them. Eden looked at him.

He was so tall and straight. His body was magnificent. She'd
once thought his face, lean and aquiline, was cruel. In this context,
it wasn't. It was simply harsh as the desert was harsh.

It was his eyes which had seemed so disturbing. They stared
sombrely out from under his brows, seeming to threaten. But now
she had seen the pain in their depths. They were the eyes of a
young prophet. Listening to him quote from the Old Testament,
she had heard echoes that haunted her. In this desert setting, she
thought, he was almost an Old Testament figure. Maybe John the
Baptist had looked a little like him.

"Say some more from the Book of Joel," she said quietly.

He quoted without hesitation, his voice gentle as he stared at
the mountains. "'And it shall come to pass in that day, that the
mountains shall drop down new wine, and the hills shall flow with

milk, and all the rivers of Judah shall flow with waters, and a fountain shall come forth of the house of the Lord, and shall water the valley.'"

"Who made you learn all that stuff?" Eden asked.

"I told you."

"Was he your father?"

Joel's mouth was suddenly grim. She saw lines tighten around his eyes. "He called himself my father."

"And he wasn't?"

"No."

"Did he raise you?"

"I grew up in his house."

"And are you religious?"

"No." He turned unexpectedly and started walking again. She had to hurry to follow him.

"Hold my hand," she pleaded. He took her fingers in his. "Your hands are so big," she said. "Strong and rough. What do you work with, stone?"

She felt him flinch. He swung around. "We've been out long enough. We should be getting back."

The window had stretched to cover half the sky now and the evening was bright and golden. The light was in their faces as they turned back.

Suddenly he stopped. "There. Look!"

Eden lifted her head and saw the rainbow.

It arched upwards out of the valley, soaring high into the luminous air. Its summit was invisible, but the other end reappeared far off, descending into a golden mist.

And as she watched, it strengthened, the colours intensifying until they glowed with outlandish brilliance, and a second rainbow appeared in tandem with the first, but more faintly, its less distinct brother. The colours shimmered, changing subtly as the light and the mist changed. Starkly outlined against it, the gaunt arms of an ocotillo reached upwards, and a towering saguaro stood indomitable.

Eden felt the awe of the spectacle fall over her. In that vast hush, after the raging of the storm, the rainbows wore an unearthly smile. She felt the promise of healing, of happiness, tug at her heart. Rainbow promises, always just out of reach, yet leading on, beckoning, always smiling.

Her eyes filled with tears and she had to swallow. "Oh, god-damn," she said, and her voice shook. "Look at that."

He put his arm around her and drew her in. "It means every-thing's going to be all right," he said gently.

"Is that another of your biblical aphorisms?" she asked, wip-ing her eyes.

"'I do set my bow in the cloud, and it shall be for a token of a covenant between me and the earth.' But it's always meant that, from before the Bible. The Indians believe it too."

The rainbows glowed and faded. The violet band, the most delicate colour, was sometimes hardly visible. Then, as the light changed, both rainbows were suddenly gone.

The evening sky yellowed. The mountains turned blue, then indigo. He led her through the dripping desert, holding her hand. He realized that he had lost the blindfold somewhere in the rain-storm. But in any case, he could not face chaining her and blind-folding her now. It didn't matter so much if she saw the van. He had taken the plates off as a precaution. And it would be dark by the time they got to the house. So he just led her to where it was parked, off the dirt road.

"This is more civilized," she said, clambering in through the door. She curled up in the seat beside him. "It's hell in the back."

"It's secure," he said and heard the defensiveness in his own voice.

He started the engine and wheeled the van around. As they drove through the gathering dusk, she said, "Thank you," very simply.

"I wanted you to see that."

"I know. That's why I'm thanking you."

"Tell me something," he said, looking ahead. "Do you really still think about it?"

"About junk? Yes."

"How often?"

"All the time."

"Do you know how long it's been since you last had a shot? It's eight weeks. How can you still want to think about it?"

Eden sighed. "I don't *want* to think about it. It's just there, like being hungry, or thirsty. Think is the wrong word. It would be like having a leg cut off. You wouldn't always be thinking about that. But your body would always know it wasn't there."

"Is that how you feel? That you're not whole without heroin?"

"I've never been whole," she said in a low voice.

He didn't know what to reply. They drove in silence for a while, until Eden spoke again.

"Back there, during the storm—when you held me in your arms—that was so beautiful, Joel. I almost felt something happen to me."

"What?"

"I don't know . . . something." She peered out of the window at the blue, blue evening. "I almost believed in that rainbow."

"But you know better, is that right?" he said dryly.

"You puzzle me. You kidnapped me. You chained me in that cell like a dog. You nearly broke my arm, once. Then, in the middle of a thunderstorm, you say I'm beautiful and precious." She looked at his aquiline profile. "You start talking to me like a social worker about kicking junk. It's more than a little crazy, isn't it? Huh? I don't understand what you want from me."

"I don't want you to come out of this and go straight back on heroin," he said shortly.

"Why not?"

"Because you're somebody special," he said angrily. "You've got a mind, you've got character, you've got *fight*. You can't just lie down and die!"

"What the hell," she shrugged. "They're going to drop the bomb on us anyway . . ."

"They're not going to drop the bomb."

"They are. We're all going to be radioactive ash."

"That isn't a reason to inject yourself with that *shit*."

"No, but it stops me from worrying about it."

"Maybe if you did more worrying," he said harshly, "you'd need less dope."

"Ah, but if I took more dope," she smiled, "I'd do less worrying."

"I don't understand," he said in frustration, "how you came to it. How you didn't turn away when you saw it was taking you over."

"Well . . . you don't think about it taking you over. Not at first. It's more like you're chasing it. The first few times you inject, it's wonderful. The best. You're on honeymoon. Every time is closer to heaven. You come down and think, wow. Then you start feeling the twitches. When the high wears off, the world looks worse than ever. You look in the mirror and your face is pulled into a snarl. Then you start feeling really bad." She swallowed. "Sick, frightened. You pick up the needle again and you know that when you come down, you're going to feel like shit. But then you think, well, I'll just shoot up again. And again, after that. You'll stay stoned, and never come down. And that makes it all right. You know there'll always be some more. I didn't even have to go out and score. Rusty was always there with more."

"And making a bundle on the side," Joel said bitterly.

"Maybe." She swallowed again. "So then you know you're hooked. But you're a happy junkie. You love being a slave. You don't want anything else. You don't notice that your life changes from colour to black-and-white. Nothing matters any more except what happens in your head when you're stoned. The rest is all a bad dream. But the junk isn't so strong any more. It wears off so fast you don't take it to feel good any more, you take it to stop from feeling bad. You're shooting up all the time. Every few hours. That's how I got those tracks. I never stopped." Her voice was trembling so much she could hardly keep it level any more. "I never stopped once. Sticking the needle in was a trip in itself. It used to feel like..."

She started to sob, brokenly, helplessly. She put her face in her hands.

Joel stopped the van, and wrapped his arms around her. Grief for herself, for what she had done to herself, came in a paroxysm. He held her as she sobbed aloud.

"Oh, shit," she said, her voice cracked. "It's so horrible. I don't want to go back to it, Joel. I don't ever—want—to go back."

"You're not going back."

"But I'm—so—weak. I'm so *frightened*."

"Eden..." Suddenly he was kissing her face, her brow, her cheeks. He kissed her eyes, feeling the salt wet of her tears on his lips. "You're not going back," he kept whispering. "You're not going back, Eden."

Costa Brava

De Córdoba was waiting for Mercedes at the poolside, staring into the crystal-blue water. She had wanted to go alone to the notary. She had not wanted even Maya to go with her.

She was very pale as she came into the dome, but she held herself upright, and her oval face wore no signs of grief. He rose to his feet. She met his eyes directly. "It's done."

He did not commiserate or show compassion. She did not want that. "When will you have the money?"

"Tomorrow morning. They're paying it in Zurich."

"Good."

"My bankers will call me at the notary's office to confirm the funds are there. Then we'll sign."

"I see."

"They're paying two million for the house and everything in it. I've managed to scrape together enough loans to cover the last million. I have the full amount now."

He nodded.

"It's nearly over," she said.

"Yes. I pray it is."

"It's time to put the notice in the *New York Times*."

"I'll call them now."

"Thank you. I want you to take the money to America, Joaquin. I want you to get Eden back from this man and bring her to me. Will you do that?"

"Yes," he nodded. "I'll bring her back to you."

"Thank you." She sat down beside him. She was wearing an immaculate, formal suit and black gloves. She pulled off the gloves now, and dropped them onto the floor, as though she'd been forced to touch something foul with them. "They've given me two weeks to clear out."

"Where will you go?"

"To a hotel in Barcelona."

"And then?"

"And then . . . I don't know. Back to starting over again, I suppose."

"And Maya?"

"I am going to send Maya away."

"But why?"

"I wanted to give her a beautiful life. I did, for four years. In return, she filled a place in my heart that had always been empty." She grimaced. "It was time to part, in any case. I never wanted to watch her turn into a middle-aged spinster. And then into an old woman's nurse. It's time she broke away and married. Started a family."

"It'll break her heart."

"She's young. She'll recover. So will I." She smiled into his eyes. He felt his heart contract painfully. She was a lovely woman, he thought, one of the few truly lovely women he had known. Her strength awed him. She sat there, stripped of everything she'd owned, and could smile at him. He did not know whether she was raging or crying inside. None of that showed. Only her immense self-possession.

"You're remarkable," he said softly.

"Not so remarkable." She gazed around the crystal dome, the beautiful house that was no longer hers. "You've developed a soft spot for me, haven't you, Joaquin?" she asked, still looking away.

"Yes."

"And I for you. You're very gentle. I admire that in a man."

He swallowed, his heart bursting with what he wanted to say to her, but could not. "You'll need somewhere to live."

"I suppose so."

He did not hesitate again. "You have a place with me."

He saw her eyes fill with tears. Then she looked away quickly. "Thank you, Joaquin," she said huskily. She knew what he was offering.

"I mean it. I have more than a soft spot for you. I love you. Whatever I have is yours. Now isn't the time to talk romance. But I don't want to lose you once this is all over, and Eden is back with you. I want to spend the rest of my life with you, Mercedes. Or at least, near you."

There was a long silence. "That means a great deal to me," she said at last.

"It isn't much of an offer, I know—"

She touched his hand to silence him. "It's a wonderful offer by a wonderful man." She sounded almost gay, but her eyes were brimming. "I have never truly loved a man, not since I was a young woman. But perhaps I could love you. I can make no promises, Joaquin."

"That's good enough for me," he said in a voice that was a great deal less steady than he would have wished.

"Thank you." She leaned forward and kissed him on the lips, the way she had done once before. He felt her lips cling for a moment, pulling out his soul. Then she rose to her feet. "Thank you for everything, Joaquin. Now I must go and see Maya."

Tucson

The house was in darkness as he drove up to it. Eden was still crying in the seat beside him, but weakly now. She was winding down. He knew that the tempest of tears had broken some barrier inside her. Maybe she'd stop resisting the idea that she could live without heroin. If only he could get her to accept the fact that the addiction had been ended.

He parked the van and then sat, irresolute. What was he going to do with her? The thought of locking her back in the cell, after what she'd been through, was hateful to him. He couldn't face it.

And the aching pleasure of her company had twined around his heart. He wanted to be with her.

It would be insane to become careless now.

But he felt that he *was* insane. Not raving mad, just disjointed from the hard, cold reality of his ordinary thoughts. Free, floating. She'd done that to him. So what if she saw the inside of the house? It was just a house.

But she would see the sculptures.

Mercedes had promised no police. But what about afterwards? She would want the money back. She would want revenge. She might go to the police then. They would question Eden. Sieve her memory for every little detail. She would remember the sculptures. His identity might be traced through them. After all, there could not be so many young sculptors living in the southwest, even if you included Mexico.

And once inside the house, there were so many other dangers. The telephone. The television. The radio. His papers. His books. He would have to watch her like a hawk—

She spoke in a tiny voice. "Are you going to put me back down in the cell?"

He shelved his thoughts abruptly. "No," he said in a firm voice. "Come."

He led her into the house and went around, switching on lamps. Eden stood in the centre of the room, staring around her silently. She reached up and touched one of the smooth, antique beams that supported the ceiling.

"You built this house," she said.

"What makes you think that?"

"It's you. Everything here is you." She pointed to the large, handsome sandstone carving that had been set into the wall above the fireplace. "Did you do that? Are you an artist? Did you do all these sculptures?"

"I bought them. I collect them."

"No. They're you," she said. "Only you could have made these things." She picked up a head carved in marble and looked into its smooth and serene face. "Is this a portrait? Who is it?"

"A woman I knew."

"Was she your lover? Did you love her?"

He was fighting to keep control. Things were slipping into chaos, spinning around him. He felt his feet slipping as the world tilted. "Stop asking questions. *Please.*"

"You're a wonderful artist." She put the head down and picked up a clay figure. "If I had just the tiniest fraction of your talent—" She looked around her, at the glowing furniture, the Indian rugs and pottery, the magnificent old Spanish colonial chest that stood next to the fireplace. "This is the most beautiful house I've ever seen."

He couldn't help laughing.

"I mean it," she said earnestly.

"I thought the same when I saw your house in Santa Barbara."

Her eyes widened. "You were there? When?" His face closed and he turned away without answering. But light suddenly dawned on her. "You were the burglar!" she exclaimed. "You broke into the house, didn't you? While I was still at Mount Pleasant? It was you! You smashed all my glass horses. And my dollhouse."

He went to get towels for them both and held hers out to her.

"Tell me the truth," she pleaded. "That was you, wasn't it?"

"Yes," he said with an effort. "It was me."

"Why? Why did you break all my pretty things?"

"I was angry."

"And then," she said, thinking hard, "you must have come to Mount Pleasant to see me. That was just afterwards. I remember now. That's where you got the photographs! You had photographs of me jumping, and I wondered where they'd come from. You took them from the house!"

"Dry your hair. It's wet."

She stared at him a moment longer, eyes wide and wondering. Then she plunged her head into the towel and began rubbing her hair briskly.

He went into the kitchen and put the coffee pot on. Then he rested his forehead against a wooden dresser, feeling sick. He squeezed his eyes shut and saw jagged lights dancing. What was he going to do? Couldn't lock her up. Couldn't let her go. And she was breaking down his defences all the time. He was naked to her. She had only to ask, and he answered. It tore out of him without his volition. She would lay him bare. She would know. She would find out everything.

He jerked as he felt her hand rest on his back. She'd come up behind him on bare feet. "What's the matter?" she asked.

He turned to face her. Her hair was tousled, a dark, cloudy halo around her face. Her eyes were concerned. "What is it, Joel?"

"Don't ask me anything more," he whispered.

"But I have to know," she said. "Why did you do it? What were you looking for?"

"The years that the locust hath eaten," he blurted out. "The years."

"The years? What years?"

He pulled away from her and her green eyes. He went into the other room and pulled off his wet shirt. She followed him. "Joel? What years?"

"Jesus Christ," he snarled, whirling on her, "shut up, Eden!"

She flinched, but didn't draw back. She reached out and laid her hand on the big scar under his ribs. His flesh was warm. "Did you get this in Vietnam?"

"Yes!"

"Poor soldier," she said compassionately. "Know what we are? The Doll and the Steadfast Tin Soldier. From the fairy tale. You know."

"I never heard any fairy tales," he said. "You've got to get washed. Dry clothes. You're soaked."

"So are you." She smiled. "Let's get in the tub together."

"No."

"Come on! I promise not to try and rape you. We'll be like brother and sister."

He grasped her arm with enough force to make her gasp with pain and hustled her to the bathroom. He thrust her in. "Wash yourself. I'll get you some dry clothes."

When he came back, she had undressed and was sitting in the bathtub, her knees brought up to her breasts. She was soaping her thighs thoughtfully. "They were in love," she said. "She was a paper doll and he was a tin soldier. Someone threw him out the window and he ended up in the sea. Or something. But he was steadfast and he came back to her in the end. Then somebody threw him in the fire and he started to melt. So the paper doll flew into the fire too, and they were both burned. It's Hans Christian Andersen. I had the book when I was a kid."

Joel looked down at the slim, pale body. He felt the silken cord stretching tight, pulling between them.

"You had so many toys," he said in an unsteady voice. "So much love. Nursery rhymes. Fairy tales. Everything you ever wanted."

"Didn't you?"

"No. I had nothing."

"Didn't they love you, the people who brought you up?"

"I think they hated me. I know they hated me. They hated everything."

"What happened to your real parents?" she asked.

"They died."

"I'm sorry," she said gently. She lay back. The curly triangle of her pubic hair drifted in the water. He tried not to stare at it. Her face was tired. Emotion had drained her. He saw that there were shadows under her eyes, that their greenness had dimmed. Paradoxically, he thought she'd never been more exquisite.

She looked down at her own body, and covered the dark triangle with one palm.

"I've never had an orgasm," she said inconsequentially.

He'd stopped being bewildered by her butterfly changes of theme. He waited for her to go on.

She smiled faintly. "Whenever I say that, it makes the man I'm with want to try and give me one. To prove he's a better lover than all the other guys, show what a marvellous dick he's got. It never works. I'm non-orgasmic. I get my kicks through chemicals." She looked up. "That's what I always imagine it must be like. Like the rush you get when you first shoot up. Is it like that?"

"I've never tried heroin."

"But you've taken drugs. Is it like drugs?"

"No, it's not like drugs."

"What is it like, then?"

He rubbed his face tiredly. "You ask the goddamnedest questions."

"Is it good?" she insisted, watching him.

"Yes, it's good."

"Beautiful?"

"Sometimes."

"So you didn't miss out on everything in life. I got the doll houses, you got orgasms. Which of us has done better?"

"Don't you—" He hesitated. "Don't you feel anything?"

"Oh, sure. It's nice. It doesn't gross me out or anything."

"Have you been with a lot of men?"

She smiled. "You're blushing. Why are you shy with me? I'm not shy with you. I feel I've known you all my life. I could tell you anything. I *want* to tell you. Yes, I've been with lots of guys."

"How many?"

"Maybe a dozen. It isn't always easy to remember. I was often stoned when it happened. In fact, the first time a man ever made love to me, I was so out of it on acid I didn't even realize. That was at Woodstock." She brooded for a moment. "Come to think of it, I've been stoned pretty well every time I've ever made love."

"Maybe that explains," he said dryly, "why you never had an orgasm."

"I never thought of it like that." She took her hand away from her loins. "Well?" she said, fluttering her eyelashes. "Aren't you gonna try and make it number lucky thirteen?"

He couldn't help the laughter that bubbled out of him. She was delighted.

"You're so beautiful when you smile," she said. "You almost never do. I'm going to make you laugh."

"Are you?"

"I feel like we've already been lovers. Do you feel that?"

"No," he said. "I don't feel that."

She tilted her head on one side. "Aren't you falling in love with me?" she whispered. "A little?"

It was hard to breathe. He opened the door. "I'll make us something to eat," he said. "Then you're going back to your cell."

They ate in the kitchen, at the broad oak table that was scarred and chipped by a century's use. She adored everything in the house: the design, the furnishings, the atmosphere. She was awed by his sculptures. She took a naive delight in it all, like a new bride arriving in some frontier home.

"I love it here," she said. She'd only picked at her food. Now she played with the candle that she'd insisted he light. "If you kept me here forever," she said dreamily, "I'd never go back to junk."

"I'm your kidnapper, not your keeper."

Eden cupped her face in her hands. The candle flame glowed in her eyes as she looked at him. "You could call the whole thing off, you know. Tell my mother to keep her ten million. What do you want it for, anyway?"

"Then none of it will have meant a thing," he said roughly.

"Yes it will." She smiled. "You'll have me. I'm worth more than ten million dollars."

Joel didn't answer her smile. "No. I want her to pay."

"What for?" she demanded, sitting up. "Just what did she ever do to you? You said something about the years. She stole time from you? You went to jail because of her?"

He rose to his feet abruptly. "I'll wash up."

"I'll do it. Please. Let me." She gathered the plates, and started to wash them in the sink. He sat watching her. "I suppose," she went on, "if you told me what she did to you, and I told Mama, she'd know who you were."

"She'll never know who I am. She doesn't know what she did to me."

"She doesn't *know*?"

"If she walked into this room right now, she wouldn't be able to identify me."

"You're not crazy, are you?" she said suddenly, turning. "I mean, really crazy. Irrational. Doing this because you hear voices or something."

"I'm not crazy," he said grimly. "I've got a reason."

"But you won't tell me?"

"Not now."

Eden sighed, and turned back to the dishes.

He stared at the slim figure, barefoot and tousle-haired. Eden. Eden here in his kitchen. Washing the plates. He felt that it was a dream. That if he closed his eyes for a minute, she would be gone.

But he did not close his eyes. He was transfixed by her overwhelming importance in his life. He had no words to explain what she was to him. He only knew that he had staked everything on her.

His sanity.

His soul.

The evening was no more than pleasantly cool, but she insisted he light a fire. He made it out of twigs and thin branches, so it would blaze prettily for an hour or two, then fade.

Eden curled up beside him on the sofa, nestling against him. There was nothing sexual in her desire to be held. He knew that now. The occasional ventures into sluttishness were disturbing, but not real; roles she had learned from men who'd used her. She simply loved to be held in his arms, with the innocence of a child. She had been with men, but in anything but a purely physical sense, she was virginal. She was unawakened.

She rested her head on his shoulder, staring into the flames. "I'm exhausted."

He was silent.

"I really was against the war, you know," she said. "It drove me mad. I used to watch television and have to go and be sick. I went to everything: protests, meetings, marches. Maybe I was just a screaming kid. But looking back, it was the most worthwhile thing I ever did in my life. All the rest . . . all the rest was just waste."

"You haven't lived very long," he said quietly. "You're only twenty."

"It'll be my birthday, soon," she said, remembering.

"In three weeks' time."

"Twenty-one," she mused. "Will you give me a party?"

"You'll probably be gone by then."

She didn't reply to that. She laid her hand gently on his side, where the scar was. "What was it like for you? Vietnam?"

He spoke with an effort. "I don't ever talk about it."

"Not even to me?"

"Why should you be different?"

"You said I was precious." Her fingers pressed lightly. "How did you get this?"

"In an ambush."

"Was it bad?"

"They sent me home."

"Tell me about it. Please."

"What's there to tell? You saw it all on TV."

"Was it really like that? Burning villages? Massacres?"

"Yes," he said shortly.

"Joel . . . maybe it would do you good to talk about it."

"Wouldn't do you any good to hear about it."

"What did they do to you?"

"They violated me."

"Well, I'm not going to force you to talk about it." She took her hand away from the scar. She laughed unexpectedly and rolled onto him, resting her elbows on his broad chest. She smiled into his face. "Hey. This is kind of weird, isn't it? I mean, things have come along. A while ago I was scared to death of you. Now look at us."

"I never meant this to happen," he said, mesmerised by her smile. "It's crazy."

"So what? It's happened. I'm not a prisoner any more. I'm a house guest."

"Except you can't leave."

"Who says I want to leave?" She leaned forward and touched his cheek with her mouth. "I might get to like being kidnapped," she said, her breath warm against his skin. Her weight on him was feather-light. "My desert hideaway. It's like . . . I'm safe. You're responsible for me, now. I belong to you."

"You don't belong to me, Eden," he said huskily.

"I could," she whispered. She searched his eyes, then kissed him again, on the other cheek. Her mouth was so gentle, so soft. Her hair fell forward, caressing his face. "You'd keep me out of harm's way. Wouldn't you, Joel?"

"Eden..."

She kissed his temples, his brow. She kissed his fluttering lids, her lips like velvet. "You're magnificent," she breathed. "You're like the sunrise. You came into my life for a purpose. To save me."

"*No.*"

"You did. You did."

"I can't even save myself," he said painfully.

"I'll save you. You save me and I'll save you." She cupped his face in her hands and kissed him on the lips. He was overpowered by the sweetness of it. He felt her smile. "Your moustache tickles. I might have you shave it off."

He lay as if in a trance, his mind numbed, yet almost agonizingly aware of every nerve-ending. He felt her tongue touch his lips, pressing delicately, exploring his mouth. Her kiss was an intoxicating, flickering thing. It was gentler than any caress he'd ever known, but he felt the power in it take his soul in both hands, as easily as she cupped his face. The silence of the house flooded around them, the vastness of the desert.

She drew back a little and looked down at him with dreamy, intent eyes. "I'm putting a spell on you," she said. "You can't escape."

"You're so beautiful," he whispered. "Every day you become more beautiful."

"Maybe I am healing, after all." She pulled up her shirt and took his hand, guiding it to her breast. He cupped the soft swell, feeling the nipple nuzzle into his palm. Her long lashes drooped. "That feels good," she murmured. "Doesn't it feel good to you?"

He found himself kissing her now, kissing her with passion. He didn't want to do this, but there was a fire in his mind and he was running before it, being swept along on its hot wings.

Her mouth was soft, moist. Her tongue met his, eager and warm. She pressed to him. He felt her trembling eagerness.

His hands moved hungrily, stroking her lean ribs, caressing her breasts, her erect nipples. Her body was a miracle. Her delicacy was miraculous, her softness, her grace. Every line, every curve of her was exquisite.

She wound her arms around his neck, eyes half-closed, murmuring. He was spellbound, intoxicated. He had drunk Lethe water and sweet forgetfulness was enclosing him. Everything had faded out of him except his need for her. Passion had never done this to him before, consumed him so completely.

They slid slowly to the floor, sprawling on the rug in front of the fire that whispered. Her skin was like flower petals and smelled as sweet. She cradled his head against her breasts. Her nipples were taut centres of need. He took them in his mouth, bewitched. She shuddered and whispered his name.

After a while she pushed him onto his back, and pulled his shirt up over his head, and tossed it aside. She looked down at his body, the firelight dancing in her eyes.

"Beautiful," she whispered. "You're so beautiful." She ran her palms across his chest to where his throat joined the curving wings of his collarbones. "If I was a sculptor, I'd sculpt you. In some golden stone, the colour of your skin."

He couldn't speak. The enormity of what he was doing dawned on him. He felt a burning flush of shame, of self-disgust.

She smiled her secret smile into his eyes. "You never thought this would happen, when you first took me. Did you?" Her fingers traced the dark, crisp hair that began at his throat and grew all down his belly to his loins. "But I feel I've been waiting for you all my life, Joel."

"Not like this. We can't do this."

"We can't?" She slipped beside him with heart-melting grace, and rested her head on his arm, her eyes still holding his. "What's the matter?"

He gathered her into his embrace, suffocating on the emotion in him. "We *can't*," he choked.

"Why not?"

"We *can't*."

"Have you got scruples? You want me, don't you?"

His breathing was wildly irregular. "I want you. I've never wanted anything the way I want you."

"Well, then." She drew him to her breast almost maternally, and guided her nipple to his lips. "I'm wet," she said gently. "I can feel it. That's so rare."

"Eden, please . . ." She saw that his face was agonized. "I can't. I can't."

She smiled painfully. "Why not? It's nothing physical. I know that. I can feel you against me."

He pulled away. *"No."*

She sighed and rolled onto her back. She stretched her arms back over her head, the firelight playing on her pale skin. Joel fought for control, his lungs seeming unable to take in oxygen. Blackness was hovering at the edge of his vision. For a while he thought he might faint.

When he'd mastered his panic a little, he turned to her and saw that tears were streaming down her cheeks.

"Eden..." he said helplessly.

"Don't apologize," she said. "It's logical. It fits in with everything else in my life."

"I didn't want—"

"I've been screwed by a dozen guys I didn't want. And the first man I really want won't have me."

"Eden—"

"The first time I really feel something wonderful, it turns out to be a mirage."

"You don't understand. There are things that—there are factors you can't possibly imagine."

"You could try me," she said, staring up at the ceiling with blurred eyes.

"I will tell you, one day. I swear it." He wiped the tears tenderly off her cheeks. "I'll tell you. But I can't tell you yet."

She closed her eyes. "I want to sleep."

He gathered her in his arms. "I'll put you to bed."

"Not down there. Please. I want to sleep with you."

"That's impossible," he mourned.

"Don't you trust me?"

"I don't trust myself."

He carried her down the stairs limp in his arms, and laid her on the narrow iron bed. She looked up at him, childlike. "Are you ever going to let me out again?"

"Yes."

"When?"

"Tomorrow."

"Promise?"

"I promise."

Before he went upstairs, he turned off the lights in her cell.

•   •   •

She didn't wake when he brought her breakfast in. She was sleeping like the dead, her black hair tumbled. He left the tray there and went upstairs.

He went to the shed and worked on the marble sculpture with a burst of mindless energy. The figure was taking shape, emerging from the stone. She crouched, slender limbs straining against the walls that imprisoned her. He struck with fast, accurate blows, unthinking. He should have worn goggles for the work and chips of marble got into his eyes and mouth, making him curse. But he did not stop until sheer exhaustion made him sag back, panting. At last he tore himself away from his work, washed, and went to make lunch for Eden.

When he came into the cell, she looked up at him angrily.

"Where've you *been*?"

"Working."

"I missed you. I woke up and found you'd been and gone." She got up and put her arms around his waist, lifting her mouth to be kissed. He kissed her clumsily, not knowing how to deal with her affection. She pressed to him like a cat. "Don't do that again."

"You were sleeping so soundly. I didn't want to wake you. How are you feeling?"

"Great—now."

"Good." He pushed her gently away. "Eat."

She sat down, examined the tray of food, then looked up. "Can I come out?"

He shook his head. "No."

Her expression tore at his heart-strings. "Please, Joel."

He'd meant to tell her he wasn't going to let her out again, but he couldn't say the words. "Later," he told her. "When it gets dark. It's still daylight. Somebody might see you."

"You mean it?" she said, brightening. He nodded. "We could eat together again," she said. "I could cook for us. I'm not a bad cook. Please?"

"You can cook, if that's what you want," he said helplessly.

She smiled. "That's what I want."

She started eating with more appetite than he'd ever seen her have before. Her diet was still mainly fruit, with some cheese and bread. She wolfed it down, chattering about yesterday, about the storm in the desert, about his sculptures, about what it had felt like to be outside again.

He watched her, marvelling at the change in her. Health and energy seemed to be pouring into her, even as he watched. The gaunt look was vanishing. She had put on weight. Her skin seemed to bloom. Like the transformation that came over the desert maybe a dozen times every century, when the rains fell at just the right time, and the barren earth was suddenly covered in dazzling acres of poppies, dandelions, goldfield and owlclover; and what had been wilderness became a garden, and what had been dead teemed with life.

She was so beautiful. She made his throat ache. She was like a butterfly that he had caged, and he ached to open the door and set her free.

But how could he? How could he ever set her free?

Costa Brava

De Córdoba carried the suitcases down the marble stairs to the Jaguar. There was no one to help him. Mercedes had let all the servants go on the weekend. Apart from the concierge on the gate, the whole estate was deserted and silent, awaiting the departure of the old, the arrival of the new.

His injured back protested as he loaded the luggage into the trunk.

Then he stood in the cool morning sunshine, staring up at the magnificent mansion that had been Mercedes Eduard's. The rows of white columns, the high crystal dome, seemed to glow in the autumn light. The trees set around the house were beginning to take on their autumn colours, golds and russets creeping in among the fading green. It had never looked, he thought, more lovely. It was an enchanted place. A Xanadu.

He thought of the girl he'd never met, the daughter for whom Mercedes had sacrificed everything. Would she ever know? Would Eden ever understand what her mother had done for her?

There was no sign of the two women. They were saying their farewells somewhere inside the house. Maya would not be coming with them to Barcelona. Mercedes had forbidden it.

He could only imagine how her battered heart must feel. She was coping with not only the terrible worry over Eden, and the loss of all she possessed, but also the destruction of a loving friendship which he knew had been real and lasting. She was bleeding in a dozen places. But her strength, as always, awed him.

And she had won, as they'd all known she would win.

He would be staying with Mercedes in the Palace Hotel in Barcelona, until Eden was returned. Maya was returning to Seville, to her mother. A car was coming within the hour to take her to the airport. It was unlikely, de Córdoba thought, that she would ever see Mercedes again. Once Mercedes had made up her mind, there could be no going back. Maya would know that.

He heard the crunching of tyres on gravel and turned. A taxi was pulling up beside the Jaguar. The driver got out.

"Fare to the airport. Señorita Duran?"

"She'll be out in a minute," de Córdoba said.

The driver stood with his hands in his pockets, staring up at the house. "What a place, huh? Some people know how to live."

"Yes," de Córdoba nodded. "Some people know how to live."

The other man walked up and down, whistling to himself, kicking idly at the gravel.

At last the door opened and Maya Duran came out. She was wearing a plain Chanel suit with gold buttons, the sort of outfit that suited her to perfection. But her face was another woman's. She was paper-white, holding herself in with a huge effort. She looked exhausted with crying. De Córdoba hurried to her and took her arm, leading her down the stairs. He could feel her whole body trembling.

"Thank you," she whispered. She touched his hand with her own. It was ice-cold. The taxi-driver held the door open. She turned to de Córdoba, but seemed unable to speak. He had seen faces like hers before, on the dying, on the condemned.

"I'll do everything in my power," he said gently.

"Thank you," she whispered again. She seemed incapable of movement, so he kissed her cheek, and guided her into the car, and closed the door. The driver flipped de Córdoba a salute and got in the front.

De Córdoba stood back. As the taxi wheeled around, and

headed back towards the gate, he saw that Maya's face was in her hands. He watched the taxi drive down the avenue of cypresses.

Mercedes emerged a quarter of an hour later. Like Maya, she was beautifully dressed. She was composed, but there were heavy bruises of weariness under her eyes and she moved with a frailty he'd not seen in her before. She locked the door and came to the car.

"All ready?" he asked. She nodded. She did not look back as they drove down the avenue. They stopped at the gate house to leave the keys with the concierge and then moved out into the road.

He drove without speaking, waiting for her to break the silence. She did not do so until they were on the Barcelona highway.

"Next week is Eden's twenty-first birthday," she said at last.

"Perhaps that's a good omen."

"What is he waiting for?"

"I don't know," de Córdoba replied.

"Is this usual?"

"No."

She turned to face him. "The advertisement has been in the *New York Times* every day for two weeks. He must have seen it. He must know I have the money ready for him. Why doesn't he reply?"

"Perhaps it's a last game with you. A last twist of the knife."

"Maybe he'll just kill her now. Now that I'm ruined."

"No," he said decisively. "He wants the money. And you're not ruined yet. Ten million dollars in cash makes you a very wealthy woman, Mercedes."

"Compared to what I had—"

"But he doesn't know that. He may be waiting to make sure there'll be no double-cross."

"He can't ever know that. Just as I can't ever know he'll give Eden back to me." The woods on either side of the highway were gloriously tinted, their ochres and reds shimmering in the sun. "It's autumn already," she went on, looking out of the window. "Eden has been in his hands for over two months."

"But she is alive."

"She was alive when she called me, weeks ago. She may not be alive any more."

"You said she sounded healthy."

"She sounded terrible. But it was her voice."

"We've done everything he asked. We have not contacted the police. We have the money in full. We're cooperating. He has no reason to hurt Eden, now or later."

"There was a case in Italy," she said, speaking with difficulty. "They kept the money and the victim was never returned."

"Yes," he nodded. "That has happened. But it's extremely rare. If kidnappers killed their victims more often, families would be less inclined to pay the ransoms. It would be counter-productive. You've seen my files. You know that in the vast majority of cases, the victims come back safe and sound. I think it will go well, even if he plays cat-and-mouse for a while."

"I'm not without claws of my own," Mercedes said grimly.

"We have to keep calm," he said gently. "This is the most demanding part of all. But the end is in sight."

"Perhaps there'll be a message at the hotel," she said.

It took two hours to get to Barcelona. Before noon, they were checking into the Palace Hotel, overlooking the Plaza de Cataluña. It was a graceful old building, painted a pristine white, with yellow canvas awnings on all the balconies.

There were no messages at Reception.

De Córdoba's room adjoined Mercedes's suite. It was elegant and very comfortable. The ceiling was stuccoed, the furnishings old-fashioned and grand. He glanced at the telephone. From this morning on, the entries in the *New York Times* classifieds would carry a notice of the new number.

He slid open the glass door and stepped out onto the balcony.

He looked down at the orderly chaos of the huge intersection below.

Tomorrow would be the sixteenth day since they had started advertising in the *New York Times*. WANTED, CASTLE IN SPAIN. ANY PRICE PAID. I HAVE THE MONEY. PLEASE GET IN TOUCH.

Still there was no reply. It was a worrying development. He could not imagine what could be holding things up.

He thought of Maya Duran's shattered beauty. Those who loved Mercedes Eduard, he reflected wryly, seldom recovered from the experience intact. *Everyone I've ever cared for*, he'd once heard her say, *has been destroyed.*

Tucson

Joel stared at the newspaper spread out on the table. The message was there again, as it had been every morning for the past two weeks. It had changed slightly this time. There was a new telephone number, and an added line: WE ARE READY TO DEAL — PLEASE CONTACT US IMMEDIATELY. He could sense the desperation behind that sentence.

He raised his head slowly and looked out at the porch. Eden was sitting in the old bentwood rocking chair, a book on her lap. She was not reading. She seemed to be staring across the desert, or perhaps she was asleep. Her long black hair fluttered slightly in the afternoon breeze. She was wearing a denim skirt and a sleeveless white shirt, clothes he had bought her in Tucson. As always, his heart lifted at her sheer grace, at the pure line of her throat and arms. He could never hope to sculpt lines as vivid as that, as pure as that.

He thought, as he had done each day for two weeks, What am I going to do? And as he had done each day, he folded the newspaper without answering the question.

He rose and walked out to her. She looked up, her eyes warming. Since he'd started letting her roam around free during the day, her skin had picked up a golden tan. It set off the green eyes stunningly. It was the final polish on the process of healing that had transformed her from a sick child to a healthy and beautiful young woman, one week from her twenty-first birthday. She was wearing a Navaho necklace of silver and turquoise beads that he'd given her. He sat beside her.

"You okay?" she asked.

"Yes. You?"

"Wonderful," she smiled. "It's getting cooler, isn't it?"

"The winter's coming."

She stretched languidly. "Will it be as beautiful as the summer?"

"More beautiful," he promised.

"I feel like every fibre of me has relaxed."

"You look well," he said. "You're transformed."

She lifted the denim skirt, a habitual gesture, and studied her slim brown thighs. "They're healed," she said. "See?"

Joel nodded. The track marks that had once been so livid were no more than silver flecks. The skin was like satin. She cocked one knee to trace the old scars with her fingertips. His eyes ventured between the smooth swell of her thighs; then he averted his gaze quickly.

"I have strong thighs, don't I?" she said absently. "That's through riding. I wonder how Monaco is? Poor boy. I suppose he hasn't been ridden for months. I've forgotten what it's like to sit in the saddle." She studied the marks on her ankles. "They'll never disappear completely. Will they?"

"They might."

She shook her head. "Uh-uh. You can't ever leave it behind completely. It'll always be there. Waiting."

"Are you still thinking about it?"

Eden smoothed her skirt flat over her legs. "Yes, I think about it. Not every five minutes, like at first. Maybe every hour."

"Every *hour*?"

"You don't know what good progress that is. I don't think I'll ever stop thinking about junk completely. Don't think I want to. It's like, while I remember it, and how shitty it all was, I'll be guarded. Do you know what I mean? If you can't trust yourself, you're careful. It's when you forget, think you're safe, that it comes back and hits you in the face."

"You'll have to learn to trust yourself some day," Joel said.

"Yeah," she said. "It's so easy here. I just don't have to worry about it. You're standing between me and the big, bad dragon." She held out her hand and he took it. Her fingers were slim and cool in his. She smiled at him, her eyes clear and happy. "Hey. Aren't you going to work this morning?"

"Yes. I was just reading the paper."

"Come on, then."

They walked to the shed, hand in hand. She curled up in her place, an old wicker chair, and opened her book. She lowered her head, but he felt her eyes on him as he picked up the chisels. No matter how deeply involved he was in his work, he could not ever forget her presence.

At first he'd started letting her out at night, like an owl. Then for part of the day. Finally, he'd stopped locking her up at all.

The cell had lain empty for ten days now. She no longer went there unless he had to leave the house. Then he would shut her in there, in case someone came. But he could not bring himself to turn the lock. That would have torn some precious, delicate fabric between them.

The rest of the time she was free to go anywhere in the house or its immediate environs. She slept in the spare room upstairs. She was steadily filling it with strange or pretty things she found in the desert, stones, weird pieces of wood, plants, bits of pottery, anything that caught her eye.

They called it, "house arrest."

At first he'd wondered whether the new freedom would make her grow more restless, whether she would start to chafe at her confinement. But she showed no signs of it. Only of a deepening peace.

Of course, letting her out was an outrageous risk. But she was as concerned not to be seen as he was. On the single occasion that someone had come to the ranch, she'd hidden herself voluntarily, with the instinctive wariness of a desert animal.

It's insane, he thought. Who is the prisoner, and who the jailer?

Her presence lit up his life. He loved her so much.

She spent most mornings like this, curled on her chair with a book on her lap. She was content to just be, sunning herself, soaking up the peace. Her eyes seldom left him. She followed his every movement.

He worked at his usual brisk pace, shedding the tensions and doubts. The marble sculpture was approaching completion. As with all his best works, it had actually begun to look larger than the original block he'd begun with.

After two hours, his skin was dripping with sweat. He went out and plunged his head under the tap, letting the water run. Then he came back into the shed and studied the work. Eden came to stand beside him.

The dynamism of the sculpture was remarkable. The sensation of suffering, of achievement, was almost tangible. He felt a pang of satisfaction at the contrast between the smooth, feminine body and the jagged rock that enclosed her. Not all the limbs were free. Parts of the figure were still buried in the rock, still in the throes of birth. He stood staring, drinking in the pleasure of the thing.

"It's wonderful," she said. She'd long known that she was the subject. She reached out now and stroked the tense line of the torso. "I wish I had a fraction of the strength you've given me."

She lifted his big hand to her mouth and kissed the knuckles softly. "You're a great artist. It's a beautiful thing. What are you going to do with it?"

"It's yours," he said, surprised that she would ask.

She said nothing for a while. Then she said, "I knew you'd say that." She knew that too-obvious signs of emotion disturbed him, but she reached up and pulled his head down to her. "I adore you," she whispered. "Thank you, Joel." She pressed her mouth to his, her lips moist and soft.

For a moment he crushed her in his arms, his passion fierce and immediate.

Of all the situations he had ever been in, this was the strangest. The strangest time of his strange life.

Then he pushed her away, as he always did. "Let's eat," he said in a flat voice.

She made lunch, humming, while he washed. She was no cook and could prepare only the simplest of meals; but he never complained and seemed actually to enjoy her food.

She took an intense delight in mundane domestic duties like cooking. That he had allowed her to take them over, she felt, was a major privilege. Letting her become the woman of the house. Once, the idea of being the woman of a house would have made her lip curl. Now it filled her with quiet joy. Watching him eat her food. Keeping his house clean. Washing their clothes and pinning them out in the desert sun. Ephemeral tasks that left nothing behind, and yet were as important as the march of centuries.

After the storms that had shipwrecked her, this haven was supremely precious. She did not want to think of any life outside this house, this desert garden. She had deliberately shut off all such thoughts. She felt as though for the past weeks she had been soaked in peace. Drenched in it, so that it had nourished her, the way the increasingly frequent rains were nourishing the saguaro, filling their gaunt summer shapes with sap. Soon, white flowers would open their scented petals at dusk. And then the sweet scarlet fruit would ripen.

She felt his eyes on her and smiled. "I know you're watching me," she said.

"You're putting on weight."

"Am I getting too fat?"

"You're exquisite."

She turned quickly, shot through with the pleasure of the compliment. But she saw by his face that he regretted the words, so she didn't comment. "I feel so well. I've never been so healthy in my life. Not even before I started mainlining. It's as if I—" She broke off, her eyes drawn to the billowing dust outside. "Joel," she said urgently, "someone's coming."

He turned swiftly, his face tense. But the yellow sports car had already pulled to a halt outside and a woman was getting out.

The woman walked up onto the porch, and through the open door into the house. She wore a cowgirl outfit, tight denims tucked into ornate boots, half-open blouse, scarf and a Stetson. She stopped short as she saw Eden and took off her sunglasses to stare. Eden stood frozen, the knife still in her hand. Then the intruder turned to Joel with a smile. "Hi there, Joel honey. How's every little thing?"

Eden glanced swiftly at Joel. He was pale and his whole body was rigid. He did not move as the blonde woman walked up to him and kissed his cheek.

"Am I butting in?" she said brightly, unfazed by the taut silence.

"We're just about to have lunch," Joel said quietly.

"Well, don't mind me." She pulled off her hat and shook her platinum-blond hair free, then came over to see what Eden was making. "Don't look so frightened, honey. I'm not going to eat your lunch. Or you." She was smiling prettily, but there was something about her that chilled Eden's heart and made her stomach sink. Eden saw that she wore a name chain, Lilah. The gold letters sparkled against the pale cleavage of her breasts. Despite the cowgirl outfit, she had the whitest skin Eden had ever seen. "What's your name, honey?"

"Eden," she said with dry lips.

"Well, if that ain't a real purty name," Lilah said, exaggerating her Arizona drawl. "Guess you can see my own name right there at my throat, can't you?"

"Yes."

She walked around Eden slowly. Her cool blue eyes were taking in every inch of Eden, from her bare feet to the turquoise beads around her neck. "So this is your little squaw?" she asked Joel. "You have better taste than I suspected. She's a sweet thing."

"Lilah," Joel said quietly, "I told you twice before I didn't want you to come here. You just don't listen, do you?"

"But like I told *you*, you fascinate me. I just can't stay away." She smiled sweetly. "And I'm not so easily snubbed." She turned back to Eden. "Where you from, honey? Back east?"

"California."

"Ah. Might have guessed. Only thing missing is the flower in your hair. San Francisco?"

"Los Angeles."

"Uh-huh." She dipped a finger in the salad dressing Eden had made and put it into her lipsticked mouth. "How old are you, honey?"

"Twenty," Eden said.

Lilah tilted one eyebrow and sauntered away. Joel and Eden stood in silence, unmoving. Lilah stared around her, pivoting full circle until she was facing them again. "You have a beautiful house, Joel," she said, swinging her hat. "I knew it would be. You're quite domesticated. Everything in its place, and a place for everything. Unusual in a man. Or is that your little flower child here?"

Joel spoke tautly. "Go away, Lilah."

She looked from him to Eden, still smiling. "Something's not right here. Is it?"

"Everything's fine."

"No, it isn't. I have a nose for these things. Something stinks here. And I think it's you, honey." She met Eden's eyes. "You're hiding from something. What is it? Are you under age? Is your Daddy looking for you?"

Joel moved forward, his jaw clenched. "I'm not going to ask you again."

"You always had a reputation as a loner, Joel. But since she came, you've turned into a hermit. You don't show your face anywhere any more. And you hate anyone coming up here. You're terrified someone will see her. Who is she?"

"She's just a friend," he said through clenched teeth.

"Why are you hiding her? What's wrong with her? Are you on the run, honey? You got police trouble? Drugs trouble?"

Joel saw the colour drain from Eden's cheeks. "Get out of here, Lilah," he rasped.

"A man like you," she said softly. "And a little tramp like her? Doesn't figure, Joel boy. You could do better. A lot better."

He walked to Lilah stiff-legged and grasped her arm. She cried out at the pain and tried to struggle. But his strength was much greater than Lilah's.

He dragged her relentlessly to the door. On the porch, he thrust her towards the steps.

He hadn't meant to push so hard, but anger had been flaring in him. She fell, clattering down the wooden steps and sprawling in the dust. Instantly, bitterly, he regretted the action.

He did not move to help her up. She rose slowly, dusting herself. Her eyes were icy as she looked up at him. "This is gonna cost you, Joel boy. You can bet your boots on that." She didn't look back as she walked to the Ferrari.

Barcelona

The telephone began to ring.

Mercedes got to it first and picked it up. "Yes? Yes, put him through. Quickly!" She looked up at de Córdoba. "It's from America," she said. He watched her, a slim, elegant figure in an imposing hotel suite, clutching the telephone to her ear.

But as soon as the connection was through, he knew it was not the kidnapper. Her face seemed to sag, emotion draining from it. The conversation was a long one, but she answered mainly in monosyllables. At last she said goodbye and replaced the receiver.

"Who was it?" he asked.

"Dominic's lawyer. He's suffered a collapse. He's been admitted to a clinic."

"I'm sorry. A heart attack?"

"No." She spoke wearily. "A mental collapse. He attacked a young girl in his home. A child prostitute. He's in a psychiatric hospital in Los Angeles. He had to go there to avoid prosecution."

De Córdoba was taken aback. "Has this sort of thing ever happened to him before?"

"Dominic is a cocaine addict. He always liked his own merchandise too much. He's been turning into a psychotic for years. I always knew it would happen. His mother died in a place like that," she said. "His worst fear was always that he'd end up the same way."

"God help him."

"Funny, isn't it, how our destinies pursue us?" She turned to him, looking older and wearier than he'd ever seen her. "Joaquin," she said quietly, "why doesn't he contact us? Why doesn't he call?"

"I don't know," he said hopelessly. "I don't know."

Tucson

He came into her room early, barely an hour after the sun had risen. She lay fast asleep in a splash of sunlight, her long lashes fanned out across her cheeks. He stood watching her. His heart contracted at her loveliness. She lay like a child, her cheek pillowed in one hand, the other arm stretched out fearlessly.

No defences, he thought. No defences at all.

He sat beside her and stroked her hair with tender fingers until she stirred and the green eyes opened mistily and looked into his.

"Happy birthday," he said.

She smiled slowly. "Oh, yeah. Big day, huh?"

"Big day."

"I'm twenty-one. All grown up." She reached up and linked her arms around his neck. She drew him down. "Sorry," she murmured. "Must have dragon breath."

She smelled so good, of young womanhood. Her mouth was soft. He closed his eyes helplessly as they kissed, feeling himself utterly lost. Her lips parted and he felt the warm moistness of her tongue. He tried to resist, but his will failed him. His fingers tightened in her hair as the kiss deepened and he explored the inner sweetness of her mouth. She arched her throat to taste his tongue on her palate. Her hands slid under his shirt, caressing his skin, setting him on fire.

As always, it was he who drew back. "I've got a present for you," he said unsteadily.

"I want you," she said softly, "for my present."

He turned away, forcing gaiety into his voice. "Come on, get up. Don't keep her waiting."

"Her?" That aroused her curiosity. "What is it?"

"She's outside. Come and take a look."

She swung herself out of bed and pulled on jeans and a shirt. "Do I need shoes?"

"You'll need boots." He held them out to her.

Her eyes widened. "Oh, Joel. You *haven't*."

His craggy face gave nothing away. "Haven't what?"

She started pulling the boots on frantically. "Oh, I can't wait."

She ran out ahead of him. He followed more slowly, hearing her squeal of joy as she clattered onto the porch.

When he came out, she had her arms around the horse's neck, her face pressed to the gleaming coat. "Oh, Joel," she said tearfully. "Oh, Joel."

He was drunk on her pleasure. "You like her?"

"Oh, Joel," she said a third time. "She's a pure-bred Arabian. She must have cost a fortune."

"Well, I knew you'd turn your nose up at anything but the best horseflesh."

She turned to him, wet-cheeked. "I love you."

He flushed. "They called her Roxanne at the stud. But you can call her what you want."

She came to him and cupped his face in her hands. She kissed him so hard he thought she had cut his lip against his teeth. He unhitched the reins from the post and held them for her. "Get on."

She swung herself up into the saddle and slid her toes into the stirrups. She was aglow. "Oh, my God, that feels good. What a beautiful saddle!"

"It's Mexican."

She looked down at him. "This is how we first met," she said. "Remember?"

"I remember," he said.

She wheeled the mare away from him and cantered across the yard. He leaned against the porch, watching her, marvelling at the horse's fluid, dancing movement. Underneath the silky white coat, the aristocratic muscles were sharply defined, the slenderness of the long legs belied by their strength. The feathery tail was held high and proud.

And she rode beautifully. He was astounded by her grace. It was as though she had suddenly taken on a new kind of existence. Her black hair streamed behind her, her slim body fused to the mare's, light as thistledown, yet utterly in control of the surging power, the drumming hooves.

She wheeled again and broke into a gallop, rising out of the saddle. He watched her fly past, his heart leaping into his mouth for her. The silken cord that stretched between them had suddenly become alive, vibrating cruelly in his guts.

Jesus, if she were to fall—

He had a dreadful vision of her delicate bones fracturing, the satin skin torn. The vision became physical pains in his loins. Terror took him. His fingers clenched around the wooden rails of the porch. He could not bear to watch any more and turned his head aside, shutting his eyes.

His head was full of thunder, of roaring wind and swirling dust. *And I looked, and behold, a whirlwind came out of the north, a great cloud, and a fire infolding itself and a brightness was about it, and out of the midst thereof as the colour of amber, out of the midst of the fire.*

An eternity passed before he heard her voice. "You weren't even watching!"

He turned slowly. She was alive. She was panting and radiant, wiping her forehead. Sweat had begun to stain the mare's white coat.

"You weren't watching!"

"I was watching." He forced a smile to his trembling lips. "Be careful. Please."

"Watch!"

She wheeled around and the animal seemed to spring off the desert earth into the air. He half-expected her to sprout wings and soar into the cobalt sky. Dust swirled around her as she galloped away again. The stabbing in his loins was crippling him, making him want to curl up and moan.

He cursed himself wildly for buying the animal. What had he done? Fool, fool, and fool again. He had given her the means to destroy herself!

He heard her calling, above the thunder, her voice high and clear as a kestrel's.

Was this love? This terrible tie that could break your bones inside you and strip the skin from your flesh?

She had stopped wanting to gallop, and was putting the mare more quietly through her paces in front of the house, when the Pima County Sheriff's Department car came rolling slowly down the road.

Joel felt a hand like death clutch at his heart. For a moment he thought wildly of the M–16 locked in the closet. But he could not move. He seemed nailed to the wooden posts.

Eden had seen the police car too. He saw her head turn. He sent her a mental scream, *go, run, get away from here!* But she did not receive his message. She halted the mare to watch, her hair clinging to the sweat on her face.

Two officers got out of the car and walked over to Joel. One was middle-aged, florid, with a jowl that bulged over his uniform collar. He carried a black plastic clipboard. The other, young and dark, kept his hand on the butt of his revolver. Both wore reflective sunglasses. Joel saw himself reflected in the four distorting mirrors.

"Hi, there." It was the older man who spoke. He was smiling widely. "You Joel Eldred Lennox?"

Joel nodded, his tongue cleaving to the roof of his mouth.

"Hi, Joel. Officers Hanrahan and Daly from the Sheriff's Department." The jowly man nodded at the low adobe house. "Nice place you got here. Beautiful view too. I guess you're right on the Saguaro National Monument. Good place for solitude. They tell me you're one of our town's leading artists."

Joel found his voice at last. "How can I help you?"

"We're pursuing some enquiries."

"What sort of enquiries?"

"Missing-person files. Just routine." The florid officer turned to look at Eden, still sitting motionless on the white Arabian, dust drifting around her. "And who would that be, Joel?"

He knew who had sent them. Not Mercedes. Lilah! He moistened his mouth. "She's a friend."

"Uh-huh. She staying with you?"

"Yes."

"How long has she been here?"

"A couple of months."

"Does she have a name?"

He was silent.

The officer was still smiling. "No name? You just call her *say-look*?"

The younger man spoke up. "We're gonna have to ask her a few questions, Mr. Lennox. Mind calling her over here?"

"She's done nothing wrong." He didn't recognize his own voice. "She's been recovering from a serious illness."

"Sure. We ain't gonna upset her, Joel. But we'll still have to talk to her."

The younger man waved to Eden and called, "Miss? Would you come over here, please?"

Eden responded unhesitatingly, walking the mare over to the two officers. Joel pushed himself off the railings, his muscles taut. The two officers moved back unobtrusively. Their expressions were unchanged, but both had their hands on the butts of their guns now.

His mind was whirling with possibilities. They were experienced policemen, but they would be unprepared for his savagery. He could go for the fat one first. Get his weapon. Try and beat the younger man to the draw. Lock them both in the cell. Get in the van and drive out of here—

"Good morning." Eden was smiling tranquilly down at them from horseback. "Anything wrong?"

"Not a thing, miss." The fat man seemed to never stop smiling. "Like I told Joel here, we're just pursuing some routine enquiries. My name's Hanrahan. He's Daly."

"Has somebody made a complaint?"

"Not at all. Might I be so bold as to ask your name?"

"Sure. I'm Eden."

"Eden who?"

"Just Eden."

Hanrahan wrote on the clipboard. "That's a beautiful animal you're sitting on."

"Joel gave her to me today. It's my twenty-first birthday."

"Well, happy birthday, Eden. Not a bad present, huh?"

"Never had one like it."

"You're from out of state, I'd guess?"

"I'm from Los Angeles." She was utterly relaxed, her voice level and pleasant.

Joel felt sick. The younger officer never took his eyes off him, still resting his palm on his gun.

"You got an address in LA?"

"Not exactly."

"Not exactly? How's that?"

"I've moved around a lot."

Hanrahan was flipping through the pages on his clipboard. "Would you have any ID, Eden?"

"Not a thing," she said, smiling. "You've got a list of missing persons there, haven't you?"

Hanrahan nodded. "That's right, Eden."

"I'm not on it, officer. I'm not a runaway."

"Never said you were."

"Nobody wants me."

"Now *that*," the florid policeman chuckled, "is what I'd call a questionable statement. Look, Eden. If it's not too much trouble, we'd like to take you down to the sheriff's office. Just to help us eliminate a few lines of enquiry—"

"You're arresting me?" she said, frowning.

"Of course not. We're just asking you to help us."

"I don't want to go."

"It would help if you were a little more open with us. Like giving us your full name and address."

"We could come back with a warrant," the younger officer said, "and take you down in handcuffs."

Joel moved forward again, taut as a bow. "Hold it right there," the younger officer said harshly, half-drawing his revolver. "You move like that again, mister, and I'm likely to misconstrue it."

"Take it easy, Daly," the fat man said mildly.

"He's just trying to protect me," Eden said.

"From what?"

Her poise was absolute. "You want to know who I am and what I'm doing here, right?"

"That's right," Hanrahan said easily.

"Okay," she said, with a little sigh. "I'll tell you. I'm a heroin addict."

Hanrahan's face changed subtly. "Is that right?" he drawled.

"Yes. Or at least, I was, up until this summer. That's when I met Joel. We fell in love. He's been helping me come off heroin. That's why he brought me here. For the peace. The solitude. It's the perfect place, don't you think?"

"You been through cold turkey?"

She nodded. "Joel helped me right through it. He gave me the support I needed. I could never have done it without him. I've been clean for two months."

"I don't see any needle marks on your arms, Eden."

She slid off her horse and unbuckled her belt. "I hope I'm

not going to offend you two gentlemen. I never used my arms. The marks show too much." She lowered her denims. "That's where I injected myself. There and in my ankles."

The two officers were staring in fascination at the tanned thighs, and the briefs stretched tight over the mound of her sex. Both had apparently forgotten Joel's existence.

He could move now, club them both to the earth with ease, rout them—

But he didn't need to. She was routing them without lifting a finger. He could tell by the way their faces had changed.

"Well, well," Hanrahan said softly. "Never seen anything like that before."

"I had a heavy habit. I was in a bad way. Joel saved my life. He saved my soul." She zipped up her jeans and tucked her shirt back in. "He's still very protective towards me. He thinks I'm ashamed of people knowing the truth. But I'm not."

"That's a very sensible attitude. You've been very frank and I appreciate that. Perhaps you wouldn't mind telling us your real name and address, now?"

"Sure. My real name's Antigone Pringle-Williams."

"Antigone?"

"That's why I prefer Eden. My address is Lexington Road, off Sunset Boulevard, Beverly Hills."

Hanrahan wrote. "Sounds like a real nice address."

"It's not like here, Mr. Hanrahan."

"We're gonna have to check this information, uh, Eden. You understand that?"

"Sure. My parents know I'm an addict. They've practically given up on me, to tell you the truth. But you won't find anyone at home right now. They're both in Europe, on location. My father's an actor, you see."

"We'll find some way of checking." Hanrahan took off his dark glasses. His piggy eyes were relaxed. "Want to know how I know you're telling me the truth?" he asked.

"The horse," Eden said.

"That's right," he nodded. "I been around horses all my life. I watched her all the time you were sitting on her. A pure-bred Arabian like that, if she'd sensed any tension in you, her ears would've been flickering like sparrows on a line."

"I'm telling the truth."

Both men had their hands off their revolvers now. Even Daly had slackened and was smiling.

Eden went to Joel and linked her arm through his. She could feel his rigid muscles against her. She looked at the two officers candidly. "I'm sorry you've both had a false alarm."

"Nothing's wasted, Eden. And you're bringing a little glamour into our humdrum lives. We may come back to check one or two things later. You don't mind?"

Joel felt Eden nudge his ribs. "No problem," he said in a husky voice. She nudged him harder. He forced more words out. "Sorry I wasn't more cooperative back there. It's kind of a touchy subject."

"It's always best to be open with the police, Joel. We ain't the monsters we're cracked up to be. You take care, now."

They walked to their car and drove slowly back the way they had come.

They stood together on the porch, watching the sunset. There was not so much as a rag of cloud in the vast sky that shaded from yellow up to green, then to the high blue emptiness of space. The desert was silent. The forests of saguaro and ocotillo became black silhouettes, stark against the evening sky. Stars began to sparkle, cold as diamonds on blue velvet. They could hear the horse munching peacefully among the oats they'd given her.

"It's corny, isn't it?" she said. "Some of the most beautiful things are corny. Sunsets, rainbows, true love." She leaned against the railing and stretched up her arms. He saw her outline against the sky, slim and feminine. Her hair was very long now. It fluttered in the evening breeze, long and soft. "I love this place. I hate California. I've always hated California. Everybody wants to go there, but it's like a mirage. You know? Promises that don't come true. A mind-fuck. It isn't really America. This is America. This is the heart of America."

He was rigid with tension, hardly listening to her talk. Eden touched his arm. "Joel. Don't think about them any more. They're gone."

"They'll be back."

"I fooled them."

"Not for long."

"They probably won't even check. And if they do, they'll

think I'm who I said I was. They'll realize that woman was just being malicious."

"They'll be back," he said through gritted teeth. "It's all over, Eden. We've got maybe a week. Maybe less. We're going to have to get out of here."

"I'll go with you anywhere," she said simply.

"Your mother's ready to pay the ransom. I'm going to collect it. And then I'm giving you back to her."

"You're not serious!"

"I'm deadly serious." He saw her profile against the sky, clean and youthful. "I may have given you more freedom lately. But I'm still your kidnapper."

"You're not," she said urgently. "You're my friend!"

"Don't kid yourself," he retorted harshly. "I'm your enemy."

She was silent for a long while. "I haven't thought about junk lately," she said at last. "Not for whole hours at a time."

"Good."

"I've thought about you."

He forced himself to speak normally. "You won't ever need drugs again. You're free."

"No, I'm not free. I couldn't make it without you."

"Don't say that," he said sharply.

"But it's the truth," she said simply.

"What kind of fantasies are you spinning now?" He turned on her. "We're not in some Hollywood movie. We're not going to live happily ever after!"

"We can work this out."

"We can't. Eden, you're going to make your own life from now on. Without drugs. Without any help. And I'm going to disappear. We'll never see each other again."

"You know that's not true," she replied calmly.

"It's exactly what's going to happen."

She touched his cheek. "I love you."

He knocked her hand away. "Jesus! You don't even *know* me."

"I know enough about you."

An explosion of anger made him punch the timbers, making them shake. "You think I can kidnap you for ten weeks, take ten million dollars away from your mother and just declare a *truce*?" His fingers bit into her arm. "You're a child, Eden. You think like a child, talk like a child. She'll scream for the police the moment you're free. Those cops will be back up here with the whole Pima County force."

"I'll stop her."

"Nobody can stop her. Maybe she'll stage a fake suicide for me, the way she did for your friend, Rusty. A bullet through the brain."

"Don't say that," she blurted out, her voice breaking.

"It's over, Eden. *Over.* I'm going to have to go on the run. I'll never be able to come within a hundred miles of you again."

She clung to him. "We'll work it out. I'm not leaving you, Joel. You talk about sending me back to her. But that's just a phrase. I never lived with Mama, not since I was fourteen. I love her, but I have nothing in common with her."

"Eden—"

"If you let me speak to her, I'll work it all out. We'll tell her to keep the ten million—"

"*No!* She's got to pay!"

"You've had your revenge, Joel. Whatever you've got against her, she's paid. I heard it in her voice. You've hurt her. Terribly. It's enough, now."

He thrust her away and sat down heavily in a chair. He put his temples in his hands. His head was spinning.

She touched his shoulder gently. "They'll only know what I tell them, Joel. And I'm not going to tell them anything."

"Oh, Eden," he groaned. "You're so innocent."

She sat beside him. "I need you," she said simply. "You saved me. Now you're responsible for me."

He shook his head dumbly.

"If I go back now, I'll be mainlining in a week. I don't have a hope in hell." She laid her silky head on his shoulder. "I don't ask anything from you. Just to be around you. We'll both go on the run. We'll both disappear. South America. Canada, maybe. We'll find another house like this one. Somewhere in the country . . ."

She talked on, her voice dreamy. Her fantasies were pastel-coloured, innocent. She spun them out like cotton candy.

Joel did not listen. He sat in terrible solitude, cold as death. He'd pursued revenge blindly, like a god. In the name of revenge, he was going to lose everything. His home. His identity. His tranquillity. And ultimately, Eden, the only human creature he had ever truly loved.

It had been a catalogue of senseless errors, from first to last. He should never have become involved with her emotionally. From the first step, from the moment he'd seen the track marks, it had all gone terribly, fatally wrong.

And now it was collapsing, whirling out of control. He was no longer at the centre of things. He was sliding to the edge, spinning off into the void.

He was being swept to destruction.

He got up and pulled Eden to her feet. "Come on."

"Where to?"

"You're going back to the cell."

"For how long?"

"Until it's time to give you back."

"Joel, no!"

"Move."

She started struggling as he pushed her indoors. She had gained strength over the past weeks; she wasn't a bundle of bones any more. Inside the house, she succeeded in pulling free of him.

"You *can't*," she said breathlessly.

"It's not safe any more. I should never have let you out."

She retreated as he advanced on her. "I'm not going back down there."

"You are."

"No!"

He lunged at her. But fast as he was, she evaded him and swung a heavy walnut chair between them. "It would be a betrayal, Joel. Of us. Of everything."

"Don't make me hurt you," he said grimly, his black eyes seeming to smoke.

"You can't do this to me. Not after what's happened between us."

"It was never meant to happen." He grasped the chair and flung it aside. One of the legs splintered against the wall.

Eden gasped, shrinking back from him. "Joel, don't."

"It's over. It's all over." His face had closed. It was a mask to terrify. He was no longer the gentle, protective man who'd nursed her so tenderly. He had turned back into the dark warrior who'd first broken into the ranch, moving towards her with dreadful intentness.

"What's happened to you?" she said. Tears welled in her eyes, blinding her, spilling down her cheeks. "Joel, stop! I can't stand this!"

He took her wrist without answering and pulled her to the stairs that led down to the cellar.

She struggled against him, but despair was draining all the strength from her muscles. She grabbed the rail, like a child, digging her heels in.

"I don't want to hurt you," he said and she heard the anguish in his voice.

"Then don't," she pleaded. "Don't do this to us."

He kept his face turned away. "I have to."

"There's another way! There is!"

"There's no other way." He jerked her arm and she came slithering forward.

"I love you," she wept. "I can't bear it. I can't bear it."

He had to drag her down, step by step, fighting all the way. By the time they reached the cellar, he was breathless. Her hair had become tangled and her face was white as death.

Joel looked down at her. In a lightning glare he saw her as she had once been, sick and unclean. It hit him like a blow, making him stagger.

"Don't," she was whimpering, "don't, don't, don't, don't."

He had to push himself on, as though against a huge force. He had waded through swamps like this in Vietnam, his brain firing frantic messages to his failing limbs, the dead weight of his own existence dragging him down. She felt so heavy, so agonizingly hard to move.

At the door of the cell his strength almost failed him. They were both sobbing for air. He made a gigantic effort and dragged her into the little grey room.

"If you do this to me," she said wildly, "I'll never forgive you. I'll kill myself!"

"It's only for a while," he said desperately.

"You're destroying me. Don't, *don't.*"

"Calm down."

"You can't send me away," she screamed. "I'm gonna shoot

up as soon as I get out. I'm gonna shoot myself so full of junk I'll never come down!"

"You won't."

Her eyes were wild green slits. "It'll be your fault. I'm gonna OD myself, Joel. I'm gonna screw every man in sight for enough money and then I'm gonna shoot it all up my arm in one blast. It'll be your fault!"

His fragile self-control snapped. *"It's your fucking life,"* he screamed back. *"Do what you want."*

Desperation exploded in her. She raked at his face with her nails, making him reel back. He managed to grasp her wrists before she could do any damage. She kicked and wrenched. Her strength appalled him. She was like an animal fighting for its life, twisting and clawing against a superior force. They grappled in a desperate silence, hardly knowing what they were fighting against or for. He slammed her against the wall of the cell and she felt as though her ribs had cracked. She managed to get a hand free and clawed his cheek, feeling her nails dig into the skin over the hard bone.

"Eden," he cried hoarsely, "Eden, stop!"

It ended suddenly. She gave a broken cry and went limp. They collapsed onto the bed together, gasping. She reached for him again, not to hurt this time, but to cling to him.

"Please," she whispered, pressing her mouth to his, "please don't send me away from you again. I love you, Joel. I love you so much. Please, please."

There was a fierce pain in his chest, as though his heart were physically breaking. The blood was pounding in his head like hammer blows. Eden's lips were parted against his, her breath hot and moist.

"Please," she said again, her voice changed.

He gathered her in his arms. Their kiss was sudden and wild, impelled with the force of a river bank bursting. He rolled onto her, crushing her slim body onto the iron bedstead. He muttered her name huskily, combing the dishevelled hair away from her face, his mouth hot on her eyelids, her cheeks, her open mouth. His mouth was almost brutal in its need, savaging her answering lips, his hands sliding across her breasts, her flanks, the curve of her hips.

She was weeping with emotion, wrestling with his clothes until her hands found their way under them and slid across the warm, muscular flesh of his back. A different kind of fire raged now, more urgent than before, more consuming. She felt Joel's thigh slide between hers, his hips thrusting to her in a primal movement which her own body answered intuitively.

She dragged his shirt off, frantic to feel his skin against hers. She was whimpering constantly, her eyes blind. He buried his face in her throat in a kind of despair. She shuddered as she felt his teeth take her, so close to the hot current of arterial blood, biting at the delicate tendons of her shoulders.

"Bite me," she whispered, "oh Joel, oh Joel..." Her own body felt so fragile and slight against his strength, his passion almost crushing her, on the borderline of hurt. He jerked her T-shirt up to expose her breasts. She knotted her fingers in his thick hair as he kissed the valley of her breastbone. His breath was hot and hungry. He cupped her small breasts in his hands, devouring the suddenly-swollen peaks, his teeth and tongue tormenting her.

She arched up to him, nestling her breasts in his face, feeling the roughness of his beard against the soft skin. She did not know how to give herself to him, how to express the longing that was greater than she was. She wanted to envelop him, love him, heal him...

He slid down and plunged his face against the naked satin skin of her belly.

"Tell me you love me," she implored him. "Tell me, tell me—"

"I adore you," he gasped. "I worship you."

Eden moaned as his fingers ripped at the copper buttons of her jeans, pulling them over the swell of her hips. Frantic to be naked, she rolled away from him for a moment. She kicked her jeans off, tore off the rest of her clothes, then came to him, naked but for the turquoise beads at her throat.

His arms took her in a lover's embrace. Their mouths locked. The touch of Joel's hand between her thighs was an almost shocking pleasure that made her bend like a bow against him, the breath searing her lungs. She did not know the sensations she felt, yet she recognized them as if by instinct. Untouched joys, new, all new. His fingers slid between the petals of her sex, seeming to caress her very soul. She felt herself wet, slippery with need, so wet that she was barely substantial, as though her flesh had melted at his touch.

It had never been like this. It took her identity away, consuming her. It was more than pleasure. It was a rich flood that rose through her whole body, a river rising through parched earth.

Her own sex was a new world. Among the pleasure lay a greater pleasure, an even more urgent centre of need. He found it with expert gentleness, the swollen bud responding to his fingertips with a spasm of life. Sensation peaked unbearably in her, her trembling body arching in the grip of the rising flood.

Eden felt a sense of wonderful awakening, of discovery. So. So this. This was what it was all about, after all.

Suddenly, she had remembered. Remembered how it had always been, that desperate searching without finding, that endless straining for a pleasure that was never there.

And now here it was. What she had never found, but always craved. What she had always known he could give her.

It was coming, like an express train thundering to the crossing. She reached for him, her fingers fumbling with his belt. She knew she was going to come, this time, at last. She wanted him inside her when it happened, wanted him to feel it, be with her, be in her.

She was talking to him, pleading with him, without knowing what words passed her lips, or whether he even understood. Her fingers found him at last, erect and hard, a thick column of power that filled her hands. He felt wonderful. His body tightened against her, his head thrown back at the fierce pleasure of her possession.

"Come to me," she begged, "come to me now."

"Eden," he said softly, "Eden . . ."

"*Now*," she gasped. "Please—I'm going—I'm going to come."

"Yes," he whispered, his mouth against her cheek, "yes, yes, yes."

But he would not come to her. She was already tumbling over the edge of the waterfall, helpless in the current. Why would he not come to her? She wanted to reason with him, plead with him, but her words had become inarticulate groans. It was too late, she thought with a wild corner of her mind, too late—

It felt the way she'd always known it would feel, somewhere at the centre of her brain. Not like heroin, not like anything else. It had a beginning and an end, but the in-between was the heart of a mystery. From her loins up into her viscera, up into her breasts, down into her thighs, through her brain.

"Come in me," she heard herself saying. "Joel, come in me."

She felt him shake his head. She opened her blurred eyes and saw the naked agony in his face. Pity for him tore at her heart while her own climax was still rippling, alive.

"My darling. Why? What's wrong?"

"It's—a—sin."

Instinct made her know she could not argue with him. She slid down to him and took him in her mouth. He was salt and hot, filling her mouth. She heard his voice, broken and yet ecstatic. She thought of the times she had done this before, not out of love, but as an empty act of obeisance. Then it had been a punishment. Now it was beautiful, sacred.

She did not want to tease him, did not want to give him a chance to refuse her this. She held his shaft tight in her hand and sucked hard on the swollen plum in her mouth.

He cried out again and she exulted to hear that it was her name he cried.

She felt it begin, the way it had begun with her, a deep inner convulsion. She felt him swell suddenly, felt the seed surge under her fingers, rushing upwards. Then he was coming in her mouth, gouting, salt and thick against her palate. She stayed with him as he tried to escape, every muscle shuddering. She gulped at the flood of his seed, swallowing him, wanting him in her to compensate for the act of union that should have been.

Joel's movements became slower, weaker. She realized that he was crying like a child. She let him slide from her lips at last, spent, and cradled his head in her arms.

"I love you," she said gently, again and again. "I love you so much."

He wept against her breasts, his shoulders shaking in inconsolable grief.

It took him a long while to stop. She held him in dreamy tranquillity, filled with the wonder of what had happened to her, feeling changed, new and strange to herself.

"Was that a sin?" she asked him, when he'd finally stopped.

"Not as great a sin as the other," he said. His voice was infinitely weary. "But a sin."

She stroked his sweat-matted hair. "Why? It was so wonderful."

"It was what I was always afraid of." He sat up, naked and magnificent. But his face seemed to have splintered with grief. His eyes were empty as he looked at her. "If I'd told you before, it could never have happened."

"Told me what?" she asked.

"She's my mother too."

Eden closed her eyes, shutting him out. She heard her own voice ask, "Who's your mother too?" even though the knowledge was already there and the anguish already beginning to put out its thorns.

"Mercedes Eduard is my mother." Her skin was like ice, her brain numb. "I'm your brother, Eden."

15.

~Confession

Mercedes awoke in the grand four-poster bed. Everything was white silk, trimmed with lace—the pillowcases, the sheets, the canopy overhead, even the night dress she wore. She lay among the tumbled white froth, letting her nightmares seep away.

When she had stopped trembling, she sat up and poured coffee from the silver pot that had been placed beside her bed. The Limoges cup was wafer-thin against her lips, so fragile she could have bitten it through with her teeth. There were croissants and marmalade, too, but she ignored the food. Two maids flitted around her bedroom.

"What sort of day is it?" she asked.

"Cold and rainy, Señorita."

Her bath had already been filled with hot, lime-flower-scented water. The bathtub itself was carved out of pink marble and stood on lion's claws, like the royal sarcophagus of some ancient civilization. She lowered herself into the steaming water and lay with her eyes closed.

One of the maids brought in a pile of hot, fluffy white towels. "It's Easter Sunday," she reminded Mercedes. "You're going to the big reception tonight, at the palace."

"I hadn't forgotten."

"Will you wear the white gown?"

"Yes."

"And you'll be able to wear the sable," the girl said, her voice excited. "And the diamonds." She took the sponge and lathered Mercedes's back and shoulders. "It's going to be lovely."

"I'm going out this morning," Mercedes said. "I have an appointment."

"You'll need an overcoat and boots, Señorita. And gloves."

"Put them out."

"Yes, Señorita. The new coat, perhaps. The one the Señor brought from abroad. I'll tell the chauffeur to get the car ready."

"No. I won't be taking the car."

"The weather's too wet for walking," the girl warned.

"I'll take the subway train."

"But, Señorita! It's Easter Sunday. The trains will be packed. And in this weather — "

"I'll take the subway."

"Of course, Señorita." The maid's eyes flickered slyly. *She thinks I'm going to see a lover*, Mercedes thought. "Shall I do your underarms?"

Mercedes lay back and raised her arms over her head. The maid lathered her armpits and shaved them gently with a silver safety-razor.

"Your visitors have started arriving, Señorita," the other girl said. "There are three of them in the hall already. Imagine, coming at this hour. Some people have no consideration."

"I'll see them before I go out."

After her bath, Mercedes sat at her dressing-table and looked at her own reflection in the mirror. The woman who looked back was beautiful and calm.

The black hair was longer than it had been during the civil war. It now reached to her shoulders, framing her face and throat. She had put on weight since the winter of 1939; her collarbones no longer stuck out like the wings of a seagull and her breasts were once again rounded. She opened her gown to look at her body. She would never in her life be plump. The marks of hunger had been erased from her flesh, but not from her mind. She would never have the rich curves that her mother's body had achieved after childbirth. She was like some new breed of womankind, taut and slim, devoid of those lush, vulnerable convexities, stripped of superfluous flesh.

In one month's time she would be twenty-five years old. Her face bore no lines. The smooth cheeks and full mouth were those of a young woman. But her eyes held something much older. A darkness. A blackness.

They were waiting in the entrance hall, three women. They were always women. They always had the same eyes, desperate and beaten. All three were shabby-looking, their hair lank with rain. Their threadbare clothes contrasted painfully with Mercedes's Italian wool suit and crepe-de-chine blouse. She did not ask them into the salon, though a fire was burning there. The silk and mahogany trappings of that grand room would have been inappropriate.

She heard them, one after another, whispering in the hallway, like a priestess taking confession.

A brother who needed his political records "purified," all references to his socialist sympathies expunged, so he could get off the freezing sidewalks where he played his violin for pennies in a mug, and get back his job in the orchestra.

A son who had been in jail six months, without charge or trial and who was dying of tuberculosis.

A daughter who had been arrested for prostitution.

"Everyone is a whore or a thief these days," the mother said sadly, but without bitterness. "How else can people live, Señorita?"

"I'll do what I can," Mercedes promised.

"If the police would just leave her in peace. She might meet a decent person. Somebody who would take care of her."

"I'll try." She wrote the details in her little notebook and saw the women out, allowing them to kiss her hand and shower her with benedictions.

"God bless you, Señorita. God bless you."

The uniformed concierge hurried to open the door for her as she crossed the lobby.

"A nasty day, Señorita. Mind the puddles." He tipped his hat to her.

She walked out under the portico and into the Plaza Mayor, pulling the collar of her leather overcoat up around her cheeks. The beautiful seventeenth-century façades looked down serenely on the bronze equestrian statue that stood at the centre.

This had been the smartest and most beautiful square of the city for over three hundred years. But once out of the Plaza Mayor, the scene changed. Four years after the end of the civil war, Madrid, like Barcelona, continued to bear the marks of bombing—ruined buildings, vacant plots, streets still closed to traffic.

Grinding poverty was evident in the clothes people wore, in the way they moved. The gaunt face of hunger was everywhere. Even at this first hour of the morning, people were queuing in the streets for food. Every butcher's shop, every baker's, every grocer's had spawned a huddled line of women with baskets. Empty-cheeked men prowled in search of some trick that would supply them a cup of coffee and a roll.

People avoided her as she walked, not even raising their eyes to hers. Her bearing and her clothes marked her off as one of the victors. A woman of power.

The furtiveness of people sent a pain through Mercedes's heart. They slunk away from any show of strength. Nowadays a man in a trench coat who might be a secret policeman, even a well-dressed woman like herself, cut a wide swathe on the pavements of Madrid.

She sat in the compartment, surrounded by the dank smells of winter, poverty and trains. She was aware of the covert glances the other passengers gave her. The men stared at her face, the women at the cut of her gloves and coat.

A shabby young girl was looking with undisguised longing at Mercedes's soft leather boots. I was once as you are now, she thought. She gazed out the window at the darkness rushing by.

Reflected in the glass of the window, Mercedes's own image stared back at her.

Her self-control suddenly faltered. She felt a wild fluttering at her heart, a pain filling her chest. She felt she couldn't breathe any more, that she was choking.

For something to do, she took out the crumpled piece of paper and stared at it blindly. The writing was a blur, but she knew it by heart already. The address was the answer to two years of searching.

No, she thought. I will not give in to this. Mustering her resolution, she fought the emotion slowly back into its lair.

The street was a mean one, in a grey district of factories and workers' houses. The house was above a tobacconist's, in whose window was his entire stock, a few trays of hand-rolled cigarettes. She rang the bell and felt, rather than saw, eyes appraise her from behind the faded net curtain.

The woman who opened the door was in her early forties. She was small and shabby, with shingled brown hair.

"Teodora Puig? I am Mercedes Eduard," she said hesitantly. "I've come—"

"Yes, I know who you are," the woman said brusquely. She stood back and jerked her head. "You'd better come in."

Mercedes entered the house. "I was told you had information about my mother."

Teodora Puig's eyes gleamed in the dark passage. "I didn't bring you here out of charity. I have information to sell. Not to give."

"I have money. I was told you were with her during her last months. Is that true?"

"Come." The woman led her into a small parlour which was crowded with furniture and ornaments that had once been genteel, but were now dusty and frayed. Over the mantel was a large oleograph of Christ, one finger laid on the Sacred Heart. "I can't offer you real coffee," Teodora Puig said. "We don't have any. We make ours out of burned acorns. But then." She surveyed Mercedes's clothes spitefully. "We haven't *adapted* as well as some people."

"How much do you want?"

"A thousand pesetas."

Mercedes had far more than that in her handbag. She nodded. "Very well. I'll give you the money. After you tell me what you know."

"The money first."

"No," Mercedes said quietly.

The woman laughed sharply. "So you can double-cross me?"

"I've given you my word, Señora."

"Your word?" Teodora Puig spat. "The word of a traitress and a whore?"

Mercedes felt the colour rush to her face. Anger clenched her stomach. "I want to know what happened to my mother. Where she went. How she died. Do you really know something? Or are you playing a game with me?"

"Oh, I know everything," Teodora Puig replied.

"When did you meet my mother? At Argelès?"

"No, long before that. On the road to the French border, at the end of the civil war. In January 1939. Do you know what it was like on that road?"

"I can imagine," Mercedes said quietly.

"In your beautiful leather coat and boots? I doubt it." Teodora Puig took out a cigarette and lit it. The smoke she exhaled smelled tarry and acrid. Mercedes sat, waiting. The woman had fallen silent, staring into a corner distractedly.

"We had to walk by night," she said at last, "because the planes would strafe us by day. So by day we slept under hedges and in barns and by night we walked. Mothers carried their babies. Men lugged suitcases. Those who couldn't walk were pushed in handcarts.

"There were thousands of us on that road. The wounded, the blind, the elderly. It was like an army of scarecrows. They were together, your mother and father. How your father made that journey, with his legs, I'll never know. It must have half-killed him. Your mother was carrying another woman's baby in her arms. She'd started out carrying a suitcase, but after the first day, she dropped it to take the child." She exhaled smoke. "That's what she was like, your mother."

"Yes," Mercedes said, almost inaudibly. "That was what she was like."

"Your parents were frantic with worry about you. They kept hoping they would meet you on the road. They asked everyone if they'd seen you. The weather was cruel. Freezing cold. None of us had coats, or even blankets. Looking back, if we'd slept out in the open at night, instead of walking, half of us would have frozen to death on the way. As it was, everyone was coughing by the time we got to the border and the children had fevers. We were soaked to the bone.

"There were so many people at the border. Like the gates of heaven on the Day of Judgement. The French would only take the women and children. They wouldn't let the men through. Your mother wanted to stay with your father, but he made her go on ahead. She cried like a child. Everyone was crying. I never saw people cry like that, not even during the worst years of the war."

Mercedes felt the hot tears swelling under her own lids. She kept them back with an iron effort of will. The other woman finished her cigarette and carefully pinched out the coal. Made from the butts of butts, it would serve to make other cigarettes yet.

The rain had started coming down again. It beat against the window of the little room, streaking the grime that had gathered there.

Teodora Puig went on, "The gendarmes searched us all as though we were criminals. There was an old woman who had something clutched in her fist. They couldn't get her to give it up. It took two men to prise her fingers open in the end. A handful of earth. That was all she had brought with her from Catalonia. They made her throw it away.

"We waited at the border for three more nights, sleeping in barns and garages hoping the men would be let through. They weren't. Then the French police rounded us all up and put us on lorries like cattle and took us away." She laughed shortly. "I say like cattle, but it was worse than that. We'd lost everything. We were just inconvenient things, to be disposed of. You can't imagine the feeling, to be a *refugee*, to be *nothing*."

"Where did they take you to?"

"A long way north. We ended up in a little village called Loué, not far from Le Mans. They deloused us and disinfected our clothes and put us in the local barracks.

"None of us knew what was happening to our families in Spain. Your mother was distraught. She had no idea where either you or your father were. She didn't know whether you were in Spain or out, alive or dead. She knew that if either of you had been captured, the Fascists would have shot you. Her only hope was that you were both in hiding somewhere.

"She was in touch with all the refugee organizations, but they had no news. She would ask anyone who had come from Spain if they had seen you, or had a message. I don't think an hour passed that your mother didn't think of you or your father. She always expected that you and he would turn up in Loué one day, alive and well.

"Then an official letter came for your mother. It said that your father was dead. Shot by firing squad. His body had been unclaimed and had been disposed of by the state. Later, we heard that he had been buried in San Lluc, in a common grave with thirty others. You know about all that, of course?"

"Yes," Mercedes said quietly. "I know about all that."

"Conchita took the news badly. She didn't scream and wail. She was above that sort of thing. But she stopped eating and she got very sick. We thought she was going to die. We nursed her for weeks. We saved her life. But she didn't really want to live. She was so afraid you might be dead too." Teodora Puig cocked her head at Mercedes. "There had been no news of you in twelve months. Not a letter, nothing. You weren't dead, of course. You were lying low. Thriving. But she didn't know that. She'd been so strong up till then. But even when she could get out of bed again, she was so weak. All the life seemed to have been crushed out of her.

"The World War had started and we'd hardly noticed. But suddenly our quiet little world was turned upside down. In May 1940, the Germans invaded France. In three weeks they were in Paris.

"The gendarmes hustled us onto a train going south, down to Perpignan. We thought they were sending us back to Catalonia and that we were all doomed. In Perpignan, they put us in a stable yard. We slept on filthy straw, in the open. The children started getting sick. A lot got pneumonia. The babies got a diarrhea that couldn't be stopped. Your mother, weak as she was, helped nurse the children. They started to die. You could see the life pouring out of their little bodies, their eyes going dim. I don't know how many died in the end. A lot. And your mother started coughing.

"They sent us to the concentration camp at Argelès-sur-Mer. It was so crowded. There were ten thousand of us crammed in there. You've heard about Argelès?"

"Yes. I've heard about it."

"There were no beds in the barracks. We had to sleep on the naked earth. Men on one side of the camp, women on the other. There was no heating. We had only one blanket each and the winter was coming. You can't imagine the cold. Or the hunger. By then, food was short and the French had started to hate us. They said we were taking the bread out of their mouths.

"That was a hard, hard winter. A lot of us got sick. Your mother couldn't stop coughing. Then she began to cough blood. I knew she was going down, from the minute we arrived at that camp. She'd given up hope of seeing you again. She'd said good-bye to you in her mind. She had nothing more to live for. You see? In the second week of January, she collapsed. So we took her to the infirmary."

Teodora stopped talking as though the story had ended and lit another cigarette. She was huddled in her chair like a weary bird after a long journey.

Mercedes spoke quietly. "Is that when she died?"

"Yes," Teodora Puig said at last. "She had pneumonia. She was so very thin. No more than skin and bones. We hadn't eaten properly in months. It was clear she couldn't survive.

"A priest came from Argelès to hear her confession. Then she died. In my arms, as a matter of fact. We had become friends, you see. She never saw her child or her country again." Teodora exhaled smoke at the ceiling. The red-rimmed eyes were vacant now. "She died on January the 12th 1941, in the morning. We buried her in the camp cemetery. And that was the end of her."

Mercedes felt the tears scald her eyes. She had reconciled herself to Conchita's death a long time ago. It was over two years since she'd received the news. She had had time in which to grieve. But the bare account of her mother's exile and suffering had torn something open inside her. A sense of utter desolation gripped her there, in the shabby little parlour. Despite all her resolve, she put her face in her hands and sobbed.

Teodora Puig did not watch her, but sat smoking in silence. After a while, she said, "There. So now you know what you wanted to know. Your mother left a few things in a box. There's a letter for you in it. She wrote it in the last few months. I'll go and fetch it."

She rose and returned a short while later with a battered tin box. She tucked it firmly under her arm and held out a claw. "The money first," she said brusquely.

Mercedes fumbled in her bag and gave the woman the money. She was desperate to get out of this oppressive little room. She took the box and hurried blindly from the house.

She knew what she had wanted to know.

She'd spent two years searching for the details of her mother's death. Now she had them. Conchita had gone into the darkness, far away and alone. A stranger had held her as she died.

The thought haunted Mercedes.

She had never really known her mother as an adult. She had

been barely adult when she'd left home after Matilde was killed, burning to throw herself into the war.

That glorious war. She remembered herself as she was then, lying in her bed, dreaming about a crusade of knights and banners, hardly seeing the terror in her mother's eyes, hardly hearing Matilde weep beside her. She remembered the way she had yearned to be a part of it all. Not knowing. Not guessing how bitterly she would come to hate that war. With what finality it would shatter everything she knew and loved. Not dreaming how it would leave her.

The letter Conchita had written her was brief. The lines blurred as she read them, again and again.

> Argelès-sur-Mer
> 15 November 1940
>
> My dear daughter,
>
> I have thought of you so many times, always with the hope I would see you once more and hold you in my arms. Now I know that we will not meet again.
>
> I long to go to God and am not afraid to die. It has not all been wasted. Throughout it all, Mercedes, you were my chief happiness. One day, perhaps, another child will be yours. I have nothing else to leave you but this hope, which is also my blessing.
>
> Pray for me, as I shall for you, and all of us, that we will some day meet again in heaven.
>
> Mama

Mercedes sat by the window, watching the rain which beat down on the Plaza Mayor outside. Figures crawled across the stone plain, made small by the vastness of the architecture. She tried to form a prayer for Conchita, but no words would come, only a desolate sense of longing.

The war had taken them all, all.

Matilde. José-María. Francesc. Conchita. Sean.

She remembered how calm she had been the day she'd heard

that Sean had been killed. She had heard the news with flat disbelief, at first. It was not true. It *could* not be true. There had been some mistake. Someone with a similar name. Or perhaps he was only wounded and they had got the facts wrong.

She could not accept that Sean's bright light had been put out. That she would never feel those strong arms around her again, or see the deep green eyes flash in laughter.

Sean had been too vivid to die. Too full of life. They could not have killed him. He had been too strong, too clever for death.

Besides, there were all their plans. Their future together. Their life. America. Their children. All that could not have been taken away. It was impossible.

When, after a few days, his things had been sent back to her, acceptance came that it was true, that there had not been a mistake. She'd had one wild outburst of grief, crying that had torn her open.

And then it had passed and she'd been left almost unable to mourn, as if in the midst of the general catastrophe, her own catastrophe had been diminished. In reality, the news had been a shattering blow. It had left her without hope, without a sense of future.

It had destroyed something in her forever.

During the few more weeks that she had continued at Sagrado Corazón, grief had been hollowing her away from within. So that when the end came, she had collapsed, with barely a sound, like a house of cards touched by the breath of a child.

She had stood numbly on her ward, watching as sick men climbed out of their beds to flee on their crutches. They had urged her to run too. Even the doctors had told her to go.

She could have run with the others. Francesc and Conchita had begged her to come, to meet them in France. She had said she would meet them in Perthús.

But she could not flee the doom that was coming.

The Fascists had bombed the port and city day after day. Rows upon rows of corpses had piled up on the streets, men, women, children. All the hospitals had been overflowing. In Sagrado Corazón, patients had huddled in the corridors, on the staircases, in the gardens outside. She could not leave. Even when Franco had been at the very gates of the city, and everyone who could walk had begun streaming north, Mercedes had stayed at her post, a wingless drone clinging blindly to the hive while the others swarmed madly around her.

And then the hive had been empty and silent. Barcelona had been a vacant city awaiting the nationalists.

On 26 January, a day of brilliant sun, they had arrived. They had marched up the Diagonal. Barcelona was theirs. A mass of thanksgiving had been celebrated in the cathedral, the first open mass in Barcelona for more than three years.

Sagrado Corazón had been flooded with other uniforms, other voices. There had been no mercy for the remaining wounded. Those who'd been unable to flee were dragged from their beds to prison. Even the faceless man from Olot had been taken. Later, she had heard that he had died of an infection, which had saved the firing squad's bullets.

Nationalist wounded were put in the vacated beds instead. Mercedes had found herself nursing the enemy, but with no sense of irony or injustice. Only a dull apathy. Those had been days of triumphal processions, of marches and echoing loudspeakers, of celebration and revenge.

Then the arrest.

They had come to the hospital with the warrant, and had driven her away in a car to the women's prison at Las Cortes. She'd been thrust into a cell crowded with women and children, where she'd curled up in a corner and closed her eyes, as though her spirit had died within her.

The rest of it, the interrogation, the charge, the trial, the sentence of death, had all passed as though in a dream. Looking back, she had experienced it all without emotion. Certainly not fear. Perhaps only a sense of degradation and later, not even that.

They had moved her to another part of the prison, where women sentenced to death were held awaiting the firing squad. Strangely, she had been the only one in that strange and dreadful cell to have ever fired a shot in war, or taken an enemy life. The others had committed crimes of the tongue or the pen—or, denounced by anonymous "witnesses," had simply been present when crimes had been committed by others. Some were even younger than she was, white-faced virgins destined to wear a shroud before a bridal veil. Others were stout matrons, despairing for their families and children.

For all these women, the Prosecutor had asked the same sentence, death. In all cases, the Defence—supplied, of course, by the nationalists—had asked for thirty years' prison. In all cases, the judge had decided on death.

But there was always the possibility that the death sentence would later be commuted. None of them knew which it was to be.

They lived awaiting the clattering of the bolt that would announce their fate. Most had been waiting this way for weeks and months.

Mercedes had been plunged in the utmost indifference. Daily, she had heard the firing squads in the courtyard. She had seen the others pray and weep and vomit. It had not touched her. She had been insulated by her apathy.

In March she'd been given the stark news of Francesc's execution.

By then it had seemed to her that it was living that was unnatural, not dying. In the midst of so much darkness, one more light going out was part of a logical process. All she'd been able to think had been, I'll be with you soon.

But later, she'd found tears. A woman from San Lluc had been brought into the cell for one night. She had witnessed Francesc's death. She had whispered the story to Mercedes in the darkness, gripping her hand tight.

They had arrested Francesc a few miles from the French border. He had been unarmed, but the anarchist union card he carried had been enough. He had been taken back to San Lluc in a lorry. There, accusers had been waiting.

The firing squad had been busy in San Lluc. On that day, thirty had already been shot, against the wall of the church. The wall, and the cobblestones below, bore a dark, spreading stain.

Francesc had been brought back in time to stand with the last batch, against the church wall. It was already evening. There had been a discussion as to whether the light was good enough for the soldiers to aim, or whether the executions should be resumed in the morning.

It had been decided to get them over with before supper.

A priest had administered last rites to those who wanted them. Francesc had not. He had let his sticks drop to the ground, the woman said, and had drawn himself upright without them. He had faced the rifles without flinching, though others had sobbed and cowered, and held out their arms, as though to ward off the bullets with their hands.

In the failing light of evening, the order had been given to take aim and fire. Francesc had fallen with the others and the soldiers had gone off to eat. The bodies had lain there until dawn, when the burial party had come to shovel them into a mass grave in the village cemetery.

In the space of a few days, San Lluc had become a town of ghosts. The *guardia* had forced those who remained to clear the church of all the lumber and machinery that had been stored in it. On their hands and knees, the women had been made to scrub the flagged floors, the cobwebby walls, the desecrated altar—but not the clotted stain on the wall outside.

It had still been there when the bishop had come from La Bisbal to re-sanctify the church, and for all anyone knew, it was there yet.

Hearing the story, Mercedes's exhausted body had produced tears. They'd seeped from her like sap from a wounded tree. She'd lain in her corner, grieving for her step-father, for all of them. She'd looked around the cell at the human wreckage gathered there. Was this what had become of their glorious revolution? Was this where the bright river of blood had led?

The next day, the woman from San Lluc had been taken away and Mercedes had never seen her again.

In April, the pace of executions had stepped up.

She had watched the women taken out, one by one; some screaming and struggling, some calm as saints, some in a dead faint. She had heard the crash of the firing squads in the courtyard.

By then she had not eaten in weeks. She had not even known how ill she was, or what was happening to her body. Malnutrition had shrunk her, so that she weighed less than when she'd been fifteen years old. Grief had hollowed her face and dulled her eyes. Her hair had started to fall out. She had lost three teeth.

When Gerard Massaguer had walked into the cell, with the order for her release, he had not even recognized her.

The long line of limousines edged slowly past the entrance of the Palacio de Oriente. It was a cold night and steam eddied around the cars' exhaust pipes.

Floodlit, blurred by rain, the façade of the former royal palace rose like a white cliff face of neoclassical pillars and columns into the darkness. She and Gerard sat in silence, listening to the rain drum on the roof of the Hispano-Suiza and watching the wind-screen wipers sweep to and fro. Mercedes shivered despite the warmth of the car and drew the fur more closely about her shoulders.

At last it was their turn. Gerard helped her out of the limousine and walked her into the lobby. She had to squint against the dazzle. The magnificent marble staircase seemed to rise upwards into a blazing sun.

It was only as they ascended that she realized an enormous spotlight had been set on a tripod on the first landing. It was an olive-green, military thing, incongruous among the marble balustrades and velvet drapes. The Moorish guard who stood rigidly to attention beside it was sweating visibly in the heat it shed, his turban limp. The purpose of the lamp became clear as they turned the corner. Its merciless glare lit the staircase for the group of newsreel cameramen who were filming the arrivals.

"Franco doesn't want the world to miss a moment of this," Gerard murmured into her ear.

He smiled benevolently at the cameras. But as she passed under the searing beam, Mercedes felt a moment of absolute nakedness and wanted to turn and run back down the stairs into the dark. As if sensing her panic, Gerard's fingers tightened around her arm.

At the top of the stairs, in the kinder light of crystal chandeliers, they joined the throng of guests preparing to meet Franco and his wife. Almost all the women had arrived in furs. One or two wore tiaras. Of the men, about a quarter were in evening dress, like Gerard. The rest wore uniforms of some kind. The purple capes and skull-caps of bishops glowed brightly among military dress uniforms and the rococo gold braid of diplomatic livery.

From the salon beyond, an orchestra could be heard playing Schubert. Footmen moved discreetly among the assembly, gathering overcoats and hats.

Pietri, the strikingly handsome French ambassador, stood nearby, talking to his no less handsome Argentine counterpart. Both held their plumed tricorn hats under one arm. Beside them, the Bulgarian ambassador fiddled with his own plain top hat a bit wistfully.

Carlton Hayes, the American ambassador, had arrived after them and was ascending the staircase with his wife. Both Americans winced a little under the spotlight — and not altogether, Mercedes thought, because of the dazzle. But they put a brave face on it and smiled for the cameras.

Heberlein, the German diplomat, turned his back studiously on the Americans as they reached the top. The wide lapels of his greatcoat set off his cadaverous face. His expression implied a bad smell nearby.

The Japanese ambassador, Yakichiro Suma, also turned his back conspicuously on the Hayeses. He stood with his hand on the pommel of his gold sword, beaming at all around him. His shaven football of a head sat oddly on his intricately embroidered tunic. He wore the bristly little Hitler moustache that so many Japanese favored these days.

Somewhere in the gathering would also be the British and Italian ambassadors. Madrid was one of the few places in war-torn Europe where both Axis and Allied diplomats were stationed; and Franco was one of the few leaders who could summon them all to the same reception. Of the warring nations, only the Russians did not have an ambassador here.

"Good evening, Mrs. Hayes," Gerard said pleasantly, bowing over the American woman's hand. "Good evening, Mr. Ambassador. Good to see you both. Happy Easter."

"The same to you, Señor Massaguer." Hayes unwound the white silk scarf from his neck and shook hands with Gerard. He turned to Mercedes, his eyes warming. "Hello, Mercedes. It's a nasty night out there. You, at least, look like spring."

"Thank you, Mr. Ambassador," she said dully. She was wearing a simple white gown and elbow-length white gloves. The diamond necklace at her throat sparkled coldly. More than one onlooker had found her almost painfully lovely.

At the far end of the room, the *caudillo* appeared with his wife. He wore the highest military uniform in the land, that of captain-general of the navy.

Beside him, aquiline and increasingly regal as she entered her forties, Doña Carmen was splendid in one of her customary black gowns.

"If Franco gets any fatter," Gerard muttered, "he won't fit his uniforms. The man's becoming a caricature of himself." He took two flutes of champagne from a passing tray and put one in her hand. "You're like a sleepwalker," he remonstrated. "What's wrong with you?"

She closed her eyes briefly. "Nothing."

"Nothing? I know you better than that. You're trembling. You haven't eaten all day, I suppose." He signalled to one of the Moorish attendants. The man brought over a tray of hors d'oeuvres. Gerard gathered a heap of smoked salmon and caviar biscuits onto a plate and made Mercedes take them. "Eat," he commanded.

"I can't."

"*Eat*. You'll be fainting, next."

She forced herself to chew the delicacies. They tasted of the tears she could not shed, salt and bitter. But she felt the food go some way towards lessening the dizziness.

Gerard watched her, his arms folded. He would be forty-four this year. His brows and moustache were still coal-black, though his temples were now silvered. He was an outstandingly handsome man. Middle age was blunting his features, making them harder, more intensely masculine. She had never seen the square face hold pity, or tenderness. She had seen it flinty with anger, sensual with desire, but never moved by any soft emotion. Like her own face, it was a mask. A mask of power.

"Smile," he commanded. "Doña Carmen is coming to talk to us."

Franco's wife had a regal bearing that the dictator himself completely lacked. She swept up and reached out to take Mercedes's hand in both of hers. "Tell me, Mercedes, how is your dear aunt?"

Mercedes made an effort. "Much the same, Doña Carmen."

"No change?" The large eyes turned to Gerard. "The eminent German doctor—?"

"Her humble Spanish priest is of more comfort than the eminent German doctor," he replied. "No, Professor Schulenberg was unable to help."

"So very tragic." The bodice of Doña Carmen's gown was sprinkled with seed pearls. She seldom wore showy jewellry, seldom varied her costume, nor the way she wore her hair, swept off her face in burnished chestnut waves. "It is a horrible thing for a mother to lose an only child. But you, Don Gerard, have lost both child and wife. How do you bear your loss?"

"I have a small gift of faith," Gerard said gently, folding his hands.

"Ah!" Her face lit up. "Faith. That not so *small* gift. You answer like a bishop, Gerard. I think you must have more than a little of the priest in you."

"I felt the call," Gerard said smoothly. "If my dear elder brother hadn't lost his life in the Moroccan war, I'd almost certainly have joined the church. But destiny forced me to take Felip's place. Abandoning the priesthood was one of the great regrets of my life." He smiled gently. "Still, I've been able to serve my country in some small way. That makes up for it."

"You would have made a wonderful monsignor, Don Gerard."

Gerard inclined his head piously. Mercedes glanced at him. His ability to slip the mask of hypocrisy on and off never stopped dumbfounding her.

It was eighteen months since Marisa Massaguer had been committed to an insane asylum in Seville. Her derangement, a form of uncontrolled grief, had proved untreatable. She no longer recognized anyone except the image of her dead child, Alfonso, an image which caused her excruciating pain.

Mercedes knew that the collapse of Marisa's mind, like the loss of Alfonso, had caused Gerard real anguish, in some dark inner recess of his soul. And yet he did not scruple to use her condition for his own ends—to milk sympathy from Doña Carmen, for example, or to perpetuate the fiction that Mercedes was Marisa's niece.

She imagined Doña Carmen's appalled expression if she knew what her real relationship to Gerard Massaguer was. How they would all gape at her if they knew who she really was, what she had really been!

Doña Carmen shook her head sadly. "Poor, poor Marisa. But you must not let your aunt's tragedy frighten you away from marriage and motherhood, Mercedes. Indeed, no!" Doña Carmen looked earnestly into Mercedes's face. "They are the consummate, sacred goals of Spanish womanhood."

"Yes, Doña Carmen."

"We must find you a suitable husband one of these days. How old are you? Almost twenty-five, isn't it? High time you left off being a spinster." With a gleam of teeth, she had moved on to another guest.

"You're a fucking hypocrite, Gerard," Mercedes said quietly.

He shrugged. "Hypocrite, coward, traitor, whore. What do those words mean? Just sounds, Mercedes."

"What kind of priest would *you* have made?" she spat at him.

"As good a one as any of these arse-lickers in purple." He tilted one eyebrow at her. "And what do you think Doña Carmen would say if she knew she'd been holding hands with a real live anarchist *miliciana?*"

"At least she believes in the rubbish she talks."

"Come. I want a word with Hayes."

They moved towards the American ambassador, and joined his circle, which included Sir Samuel Hoare, the British ambassador and his wife. Gerard turned casually to Hayes.

"The tide of the war seems to be turning in the Allies' favour, Mr. Ambassador."

Hayes nodded. "Yes, thank God. For the first time since 1939, there's a little light at the end of the tunnel."

"Perhaps the prospect of a negotiated peace is no longer an impossibility."

"A *negotiated* peace?" the American repeated. He shook his head. "We're not about to negotiate with Hitler and Mussolini, Minister. The time for that is over. The war can have only one end—an unconditional surrender by Italy and Germany."

"An Italian surrender may not be far away," Gerard said. "But a German surrender? You and I have both met Herr Hitler. How long will it take? Another five years of war? Another ten?"

"However long it takes," Hayes said sleepily, "that is what we're going to get."

"Even if it means destroying Germany? With the real danger in the east?"

Hayes's eyelids drooped even farther. "The real danger?"

"Oh, come, Mr. Ambassador. Soviet Russia is the real threat to the west. If Germany is destroyed, we'll lose our only real bulwark against bolshevism."

"The Russians are bearing the brunt of this war right now," Hayes said dryly. "On our behalf."

Gerard took out his gold cigarette case. "Cigarette?"

Hayes studied the case. It was solid gold, the lid embossed with a swastika in a wreath of laurel leaves. "The Third Reich is adding to its gold reserves by pulling fillings out of the teeth of Jews who pass through the death camps," Hayes remarked impassively. "Why don't you throw the wretched thing away?"

"If you win the war, I'll have it melted down and re-cast as an American eagle," Gerard smiled. "Or a British bull dog."

"By then it'll be too late for that." Hayes's pouchy eyes were sad. "Spain is going to find herself out in the cold when the war is over, I'm afraid. She's unlikely to be invited to join the new United Nations."

"Why not?"

"There's the question of human rights, for one thing. The United Nations is going to be a league of democracies. Not of totalitarian states."

Gerard's black eyes fixed on Hayes. "Then you'd better keep Soviet Russia out."

"Minister, the Russians have already paid their entrance fee," Hayes said gently. "In blood. Franco's hoping that just being anti-Communist is going to be enough to get him back into the fold, once the war is over. But he's wrong. Believe me, he's wrong."

Gerard drew on his cigarette. He and Hayes had always enjoyed a confidential trust, if not an intimacy. Hayes was well aware of Gerard's influence. And Gerard trusted the experienced diplomat in his turn. "Is that the way Roosevelt feels?" he asked.

"Yes. I rather fear I may be the last American ambassador in Spain for a long time."

"Even with the Russians so powerful?"

"Even with that."

"Franco's preparing reforms, you know."

"Yes, we've heard rumours. But I doubt they'll be enough. Something more than a facelift is needed."

Mercedes, who had been silent up until now, spoke quietly in English. "Franco was put in power by Hitler and Mussolini," she said to Hayes. "He modelled his regime on theirs. It was forced on the Spanish people by violence. It is maintained by violence. It has no legitimacy whatsoever."

"Yes," Hayes said, glancing at her in surprise. "We know that."

Gerard's grasp of English was not good, but he had understood the tone of Mercedes's words. "My niece has some romantic left-wing sympathies," he said.

"Her sympathies do her credit." Hayes smiled slightly at Mercedes and patted her arm.

"Spain's isolation won't last long," Gerard said. "By the 1950's, it will be over. America can't afford not to be friends with Spain, even if Franco stays in power." He exhaled a plume of smoke upwards and ground the cigarette out in an ashtray. "Which he will. Let's have some more champagne."

It was late by the time they got home. The servants had kept the fire burning brightly in the grate. Gerard poured himself a brandy and went to warm himself in front of the flames. Mercedes pulled off her white gloves and threw herself down wearily on a chaise-longue. She kicked off her shoes.

"Thank God that's over," she sighed.

"Tired?"

"Exhausted." She let her head loll. Her eyes drifted around the room.

All the paintings in the salon were family portraits. Over the mantelpiece hung a sombre oil painting of Gerard himself, done in Seville, during the civil war, by Camillo Álvarez. The artist had painted a stormy sky behind the dark figure, and though it was not a flattering work, it had caught Gerard's brooding power.

Above the sideboard was a portrait of Marisa, painted in Rome. She was holding a parasol, laughing over her shoulder at the viewer. It was a shimmering, glamourous work in a palette of silvers and whites. Whenever she saw it, Mercedes was reminded of the gay creature she had first seen as a girl, peering out from behind a tree in the schoolyard in San Lluc — and of the tragic ruin she had met in the asylum in Seville last year.

Opposite hung a photograph of Alfonso, their dead child, her half-brother. The child's face was solemn, the black frame matching the grave eyes. She met those eyes now, with a painful contraction of the heart. They were so like Gerard's. So like her own.

Gerard was watching her, swirling the brandy in his glass. "What upset you today?"

"If you must know, I heard how my mother died."

His handsome face grew still. "How?"

"I found a woman who was with her in the refugee camp. In Argelès-sur-Mer."

"How did you find her?" he asked.

"Through the women who come to me for help. I always ask them if they know anyone who was at Argelès. I had to know how my mother died, Gerard. It was haunting me. I have such nightmares about her..."

"And now you know."

She looked up at him. "She died of pneumonia and malnutrition."

"I see." He picked up his glass and drank reflectively. "I'm sorry."

"Is that all you can say?" Her eyes were swimming with tears. "You're *sorry*?"

"You accused me of being a hypocrite earlier tonight," he pointed out. "What more do you want me to say?"

"Your glorious Fascists drove her and my father from their home," Mercedes said. Tears spilled down her cheeks. "She died in a stranger's arms."

"There was nothing you could have done." He held out the brandy-glass. "Drink this. It'll do you good."

She took the glass in both hands and choked on the fiery liquor. "The war has taken everything from me, Gerard. Everything I ever loved."

"Nobody wins in a war," he said impassively.

"You've won," she said bitterly. "You and that pack of gangsters at the palace."

"Nobody can stop history. And don't throw your grief in my face, Mercedes." The black eyes were formidable. "The war took my wife and child from me. Whatever you've been through, you cannot imagine the pain of losing a child. I really am sorry," he said more quietly, looking down into her face. "But she's better off dead. The way things are, now."

"I want to go to her grave."

"Out of the question," he said flatly. "Let the dead bury their dead."

"I'm going."

"You're not." He held the glass to her lips again. "Finish it."

She poured the rest of it down her throat. "You don't give a damn about her, do you?" she said bitterly.

"I will be dead myself, soon enough. So will you. All of us are born to die. I get sick of the pretence that we're all going to live forever. Besides, your mother meant very little to me, Mercedes."

"Enough for you to fuck her!"

"How many women have I fucked since Conchita Barrantes? Five hundred? Six hundred? We didn't have a romantic relationship, Mercedes. It was a rough-and-tumble thing. There's always a struggle with virgins."

For a while the words didn't sink in. Then she looked up, shocked. "You mean—you *raped* her?"

"Well, of course."

"You never told me that before!"

He shrugged. "Does it matter?"

Her throat constricted. "You *bastard!*"

"I was eighteen. She was a year or so younger. I assure you, neither of us took it very seriously."

"I hate you so much sometimes," she said in a low, trembling voice. "I could kill you."

"Remind me not to turn my back on you tonight, in case I get a dagger between my ribs," he said dryly. "Did you think your mother and I had a tender affair?"

"I thought at least there'd been . . . attraction."

"She loathed me."

"I know she did, afterwards. But before—"

"There was nothing, before. We met in a field. I tumbled her on her back. We went our ways. You were the consequence."

"Do you rape all your women?" Mercedes asked in a brittle voice. "Is that what you like best?"

"Don't be gauche." He wiped her tears away with his thumbs, then bent to kiss her.

"Don't touch me." He tried to take her hands, but she fought away from him. "Don't touch me!"

His fingers bit into her arms, pulling her around to face him. He stared into her face. "You're beautiful," he whispered.

"I hate you," she said fiercely.

He laughed, showing his even, white teeth. "Nonsense. You've been in love with me since you were fifteen years old."

"How can you call it love?" She rose and walked to the fire, crushing her hands together. "I know what love is. I loved Sean. This is something else, something horrible..."

He lay back on the chaise-longue, watching her with that dark amusement in his eyes. "Don't be so melodramatic, my dear."

Her face was a white mask with dark red lips and burning eyes. She stood under his portrait, her eyes strikingly like those in the painting. "Why? Why did you have to do it to me?"

"You talk as though you had no part in it."

"I *didn't*," she said passionately. "I had no choice. No hope."

He stifled a yawn and glanced at the gold watch on his wrist. "Let's not forget that I saved your life," he said languidly. "I rescued you from the firing squad. You were a skeleton. I nursed you back to health with my own hands."

"You seduced me, Gerard. Before I was even in my right mind again, you raped me. Just like you raped my mother. I couldn't fight you. Do you think I *wanted* it?" Fraught with pain, she clenched her fist and struck the stone mantelpiece. "Do you think I wanted to become my father's mistress?"

"I think of us as a man and a woman. Not as father and daughter."

"But you *are* my father."

"In what sense? Because I took a village girl a quarter century ago? I didn't bring you up. The blacksmith did. He was your father in any real sense and he's dead."

"I've always thought of you as my father," she said in a low voice. "Ever since I knew."

Gerard rose and walked over to the walnut case that held the costly Blaupunkt radiogram. The voice of Radio Berlin drifted in slowly. The announcer was presenting, in honeyed tones, "a luminous moment in German culture," the Beethoven violin concerto, about to be performed by the Berlin Philharmonic. The orchestra was being led by the brilliant thirty-five-year-old conductor, Herbert von Karajan.

The sublime opening movement spread its wings. As the violins began to soar, Gerard came to her. He laid his hands lightly on her arms. "It was the Jews and the Christians who made sex something obscene. They poisoned us with their taboos. All rubbish. Lightning doesn't strike the house when we make love. Devils don't dance on the roof tiles. There's nothing in logic or nature to forbid it. My dear one, what about you and that nun? Wasn't that just a little eccentric?"

"That was innocent. This isn't!" She faced him. "What if the servants found out I was your daughter?"

"They won't. Unless we're very foolish."

"It's bad enough saying I'm Marisa's niece," she went on wretchedly. "If they ever knew the truth . . . all those people at the palace tonight—what would they say if they knew? They'd be appalled. Horrified."

"They'd probably burn us at the stake, given the current moral climate," he agreed urbanely. "But they don't know. Nobody does. Nobody ever can, now. Everybody who ever knew is gone."

"I felt like telling them all tonight," she said, her face taut. "I felt like screaming it at them. That I was your daughter. And your lover."

"You would only have destroyed us both," he shrugged. "And what good would that have done?"

"It might have saved our souls."

"We don't have souls." He smiled into her eyes. "We're divine, Mercé. You're my goddess. I'm your god."

"You're insane."

"Am I? Come." He led her to the window and drew the heavy velvet drape aside. Outside, rain drifted relentlessly down on the Plaza Mayor. Nobody was stirring in the square. The bronze king on his bronze horse stared with blind eyes at the lights of Madrid which glimmered in the darkness beyond. "Look where we are," Gerard said gently. "At the pinnacle of this city. There's nobody in Madrid greater than us. Nobody in Spain. We're unassailable. We hold it all in our hands at last. It's all ours, my love. All of it. Beyond, the whole world is burning. There's nowhere else. We're gods, Mercedes. Can't you see that?"

He drew her close. Exhaustion made her sag into his arms. He was so sure of himself, so authoritative. His strength was immense, not just a strength of the body, but of the spirit as well, mastering her, crushing her will. He was so utterly sure of what he did, so utterly indifferent to what she felt or thought. She was the focus of a burning, obsessive passion; and yet she was helpless, almost irrelevant. Her only power was a passive one, the capacity to awake his desire.

His breath came more quickly. He led her to the chaise-longue and pushed her down onto it. She felt his fingers unfastening her gown. Then she heard him undress himself.

She became limp, her eyes closing, her neck sagging back, like a woman in a trance. The prelude was always like this: the help-lessness, the inevitability. She felt the firelight on her naked skin, felt him part her thighs.

Then his weight crushed her and she cried out as she felt him penetrate her, thrusting deep into her body. She pressed her face into his chest, biting her lips to silence any more cries.

But her body betrayed her. It became an animal thing, apart from her mind. It ignored the scream in her mind. It allowed itself to be seduced by what she knew to be evil. It was, indeed, no longer hers. Nothing was hers any longer. She was his, as com-pletely as a slave.

"Mercedes," he whispered roughly, his face flushed with pas-sion. "My goddess. My goddess . . ."

She did not speak. Her body arched against him. The scream went on. He thrust into her with devouring strokes, consuming her. The brilliant flower budded and opened within her, displaying its scarlet throat, its leopard-spotted petals. The petals expanded, caressing the erogenous areas of her body with knowing skill.

She whimpered in anguish, not at what he was doing, but at her body's betrayal. She felt as though her mind were tearing apart, as though her very life were being crushed.

He's my father, she thought, again and again. I am his daugh-ter. There can't be pleasure in this evil. I won't accept it. But he thrust pleasure on her, whether she accepted it or not.

With Sean, she had always been the teacher, he the pupil. She had led and he had followed. With Gerard, she had no will at all. With absolute control, he urged her towards the almost unbearable summit, sustaining it until she thought she could bear no more.

"No," she moaned, "no, no, no, no!"

She felt his mouth at her throat, felt the heat of his breath. She was whirling in the maelstrom, sucked deeper and deeper into the whirlpool. Between her thighs, her body was wet and hot. He plunged into her like a stallion, ramming against her womb.

Suddenly, her mind was no longer there. There were no more words, only submission and submersion. There was no longer anything to lose. With inarticulate gratitude, she felt her own resistance disappear. Release was imminent and she greeted it with a final eagerness, as the tortured greet death.

The end came with ferocious energy. She could not silence her own long cry of passion, ending on a whimper of defeat. She felt him surge within her, heard his triumphant groan.

Then her strings were cut and she sagged brokenly away from him, her eyes burning with tears. The intensity of it had left her dazed.

She felt the familiar hollowness. It had happened again. Her soul had been sucked out. It floated somewhere else, away from her, estranged from her.

This was the way it always was, afterwards. The river had been crossed another time. She was lost again, wandering on a distant bank, among strange sights and sounds.

Gerard looked down at her without speaking. She covered her face with her hands, feeling the hot tears flow. Then she sat up. She was trembling uncontrollably, her limbs jerking. She reached for her gown and pressed it to her naked breasts.

The Beethoven concerto flowed into the room. The fire crackled quietly. Everything was as before.

She was still numb. She watched Gerard with unseeing eyes as he walked across the room. The firelight gleamed on his skin. His body did not have the majesty of Sean's, but it was hard and sinewy. She watched the shadows mould his torso as he poured brandy into the glass. His face was relaxed, calm.

He sat beside her. "You hold so much back from me, Mercedes."

"I have nothing to give you, Gerard," she said dully.

He put his arm around her and made her drink. "You'll understand yourself better. In time. In time, you will accept how wonderful this is."

Her teeth chattered against the rim of the glass as she drank. "I wish I were dead."

"You need a break. We'll go somewhere warm, away from this wretched weather. Somewhere away from the war. The Canary Islands, perhaps. Or North Africa. I'll arrange it."

His voice flowed over her. She did not listen to the words any longer. She heard only the contentment in his voice, the pleasure in having conquered her once again. He held her and kissed her. She did not respond, just sat in apathy, her eyes fixed on the beckoning arms of the flames.

Later, the numbness wore off.

She sat on her bed, hugging herself, rocking slowly to and fro in grief.

There was no pain greater than this. No suffering worse.

Not in the worst times of the war, not when Sean had died, not in the death cell in Barcelona, had such a weight of unhappiness crushed her. There had always been some escape open to her. Now she had none. She was imprisoned in this beautiful apartment, in the heart of the enemy camp, with only evil for company. But it was worse than that. She had become her own prison. She had become her own death cell.

She hated herself with an intensity that was unbearable. It suffocated her. She was vile. How vile she was! A creature not fit to breathe. *A traitress and a whore.* She had betrayed everything that was good in her life—Sean, Francesc, her mother—all the people she had loved. All the beliefs she had once lived by. She had embraced evil with eager arms. She was estranged from herself.

She stared into the roaring void that had to be crossed again. In the night silence of the house, voices raged at her, screaming their disgust and loathing.

Through this, through this howling wilderness of self-abomination and terror, she had to make her way back to normality. No; not normality. To the fragile, unreal balance she had come to think of as normality. To the glassy poise she had to cling to in order not to go mad, or kill herself.

Until the next time and she was destroyed all over again.

How had this happened to her? Without her volition and yet with her compliance. As she'd emerged from the darkness after her imprisonment, and had first stirred her crushed wings during that icy spring of 1939, her first feeling had been a wave of love and gratitude for her rescuer.

She'd been re-born adoring the man who'd saved her from death, who'd given her refuge, who sat day after day by her bedside, talking to her gently, spooning food into her mouth as though she was a child.

She'd clung to him. She had wept when he left the room. The servants had to console her, like a feverish child, when he went to work in the Ministry.

When he returned and took her in his arms and kissed her on the lips, she had felt her heart lift with joy. She'd purred under his caresses like a cat.

And even when he had slid into the bed alongside her, she had suspected nothing. She'd been incapable of suspicion. He was her saviour, her father, come for her at last, the way she'd always dreamed he would.

But as the weeks went by, and her physical health returned, it had all begun to change. Her mind, not yet formed after having been broken, had grappled in perplexity with the things he did. The caresses that touched her breasts, her loins. The sound of his breathing, becoming harsh and greedy in her ear. Kisses that devoured her. The pressure of his desire against her.

She did not remember the first time her father had made love to her. But she knew there had been pleasure. There had always been pleasure. He knew how to awaken it in her, knew how to use it to silence her crying.

Her sickbed had become a bed of passion, imperceptibly, insidiously.

She had emerged into the light as her father's concubine. The object of his physical love. By the time she was well enough to leave her bed and walk, she was already enslaved. By then, she was already on the rack, torn apart by two diametrically opposed forces—her love for him as a man, and her love for him as a father.

There had never been a choice. There had never been a moment when she could look the situation in the face and grapple with it. It had all happened too imperceptibly.

Suddenly, she could not bear the thought of crossing that wilderness again. It was too appalling. And the knowledge that she would have to do it again and again and again mocked her. How could it ever end, except in madness or death?

Mercedes slipped through the doorway of the cathedral. Evening was falling. The lamps had not yet been lit and the great echoing space was dark. The icy wind from outside swept through the deserted pews. An old woman was lighting a candle, her lips moving silently. Mercedes saw the little yellow light reflected in each dull eye.

What am I doing here? she asked herself. *What have I come for?* She pulled the black lace mantilla closer around her face. Usually, she knelt in the darkness and tried to pray. But this time she hurried to the confessional.

There was an astringent smell of incense in the carved wooden cubicle. She knelt and put her face to the grille. She could just make out the silhouette of the priest on the other side. He was resting his cheek on one fist. She wondered whether he was awake. Then she heard him stir.

"I am listening." He spoke with the voice of an old man.

"I'm not a believer, Father," she said unsteadily.

"Not a believer in what, my child?"

"Not a believer in God."

He hesitated. "Then why are you here?"

"Because I believe in sin."

"Are you in sin, my child?"

"Yes." Her voice broke. "I am in terrible sin, Father."

"Terrible sin?" he repeated with a sharper note.

"I'm entangled in it. I have no way out."

"A sin of impurity?"

"Yes, Father, a sin of impurity."

"With others?"

"With one other."

His voice gentled again. "There is no sin so terrible that God will not forgive it. And there are worse sins than sins of impurity. With whom are you committing this sin?"

"With my own father." Her stomach was tight with pain as she said the words.

The priest did not respond, perhaps because he was too shocked.

She hurried on, the words spilling out. "He says there's nothing wrong in what we do. He says there's no heaven and no hell, no God, no Devil." She wiped the tears from her face. "I don't know what I'm doing here. I've been coming here for weeks. I haven't believed in your God since I was a child. I just have to tell someone. I have nobody else to talk to. If I can't, I'll go mad.

I think I am mad, sometimes." She was trembling. She had come here to spill her pain, to get relief. But confession was ripping her open, not healing her. "I live in a nightmare. I'm so terrified that people will find out the truth. We're always on the brink of destruction."

Suddenly she saw the dim outline of the priest's face, turned to the grille, as though he were trying to make her out in the darkness.

Terror took her.

Her confession unfinished, absolution beyond her reach, she ran blindly from the cubicle. Four or five women, mostly elderly, were waiting to give their confession. They turned to look at her as she ran.

Outside the cathedral, the sky was stained scarlet, as though blood were streaming from heaven.

The next morning, she awoke in a panic, unable to remember her name, or where she was. She terrified the maids by clinging to them in desperation, demanding, "Who am I? Who am I?"

The confusion passed; but she was aware of a profound disturbance, like cloudy particles swirling in her mind. The thought that the amnesia might return frightened her to death. Gerard took her to the psychiatrist again, who prescribed pills, and told her not to touch alcohol. She agreed apathetically to all his suggestions. For a week after that she woke saying, I am Mercedes Eduard, I am Mercedes Eduard, in her mind.

One evening she went back to the cathedral, and kneeled in the confessional. But the old priest was not there. A younger man was in his place. She confessed to routine sins of pride and envy, and was given a rosary to say. She did the penance with the same dull studiousness that she took the psychiatrist's pills. She did not go back.

A month later she became ill.

She went to the doctor several times, but the upset did not respond to treatment. The doctor did some tests.

A week later he called her into his consulting rooms, and made her sit in the comfortable armchair. His expression was odd, half-knowing, half-disdainful.

"You are not suffering from food poisoning, Señorita," he

told her briskly. "You have quite another condition altogether. I'm afraid you must prepare yourself for a shock. You are pregnant."

She locked herself in the bedroom.

Then she hurried to the dressing table and pulled open the drawer. In her clumsiness, it fell to the ground. The contents spilled across the carpet. She fell to her knees and groped among the bottles until she found the morphine tablets. She fumbled the bottle open and shook the little grey pills into her palm.

Were there enough of them to kill her? She went to the bathroom, and there, among the pink marble fittings, crammed the pills into her mouth four and five at a time. They were bitter and chalky on her tongue. Nausea rose in her. She choked as she gulped them down.

She stumbled out of the bathroom and sat on the bed again. She took the bottle of cognac from her bedside table. She filled the water tumbler with the spirit and started drinking.

After she had drunk three glassfuls, she was afraid she would vomit and stopped. She prayed that she had taken enough to kill her.

She curled up on her side, and felt a sudden flood of relief— as though she had chosen life, rather than death. She felt an achievement of some obscure kind. A solution.

No more. It had all ended. The despair, the agony, was all over. She lay without thoughts, peaceful for the first time in months.

16.

~Payment in Full

The call came, as so often before, late at night. They had been sitting across a small table, playing whist in near-silence, listening to the distant hum of traffic in the square below.

Their eyes met. "You get it," she said quietly.

He picked up the telephone. "Joaquin de Córdoba."

"This is Paul."

He recognized the abrupt tones at once. The relief cracked in his voice. "We've been waiting for your call for nearly three weeks."

"I'm ready to trade. I want the money by noon on Wednesday."

"Where?"

"Mexico."

"*Mexico?*" He stared at his watch blankly. "That gives me less than three days to assemble the cash and fly from Spain to Mexico. It's impossible."

"You should have assembled the cash already," he snarled. "Why the fuck did you send up the signal if you haven't got it yet?"

"We've got it. It's just a question of assembling it—"

"Assemble it, then!"

"I'll try my best," de Córdoba said. There was a kind of desperation in the kidnapper's voice that made his heart sink. Had something gone dreadfully wrong? He tried to keep his own tone calm. "There is no problem with the money. It will only take time."

"There *is* no time," the voice said savagely.

"Why not?"

The voice verged on hysteria. *"Don't argue with me!"*

"Where in Mexico?"

"Hermosillo. You know where that is?"

"Yes."

"Go to the Hotel San Sebastian in Hermosillo. I'll contact you again when you get there. What's your name again?"

"Joaquin de Córdoba."

"Wednesday, de Córdoba. *Wednesday.*"

"You haven't told me what denominations."

"What?"

"What denomination banknotes. Twenties, hundreds, five hundreds—"

"Nothing smaller than fifties. No thousands. No consecutive numbers. And all used. You understand?"

"Perfectly."

"The money has to be in a bag I can carry."

"Ten million dollars," de Córdoba said gently, "even in five-hundred-dollar bills, will fill a large suitcase and weigh a great deal."

"Just do it."

"If I'm not there by Wednesday, I beg you to be patient. This is not so easy to organize as you think—"

"Just do it."

"Please—may I speak to Eden? Just a word, just to hear her voice—"

"That's not possible."

"Why not?"

"Because I say it's not."

"We need proof that Eden is still alive. Mercedes Eduard is extremely concerned. It's been several weeks since she last heard her daughter's voice—"

"Eden's alive." The bitter venom that he knew so well slid into the harsh voice. "And tell that abnormal bitch if she were a better mother, none of this would ever have happened."

The line went dead.

De Córdoba replaced the receiver. Mercedes was sitting white and tense. Her cards had fallen to the floor and lay scattered around her feet.

"He wants the money by Wednesday in Hermosillo, Mexico."

"That can't be done."

"We're going to have to try."

"How did he sound?"

"He was screaming. He sounded very tense."

"Why?"

"I don't know. He refused to let me speak to Eden."

"Then how do we know she's still alive?"

"We're just going to have to take his word for it."

"What else did he say?"

"Just the usual abuse."

"What else did he *say*, Joaquin?"

He hesitated. "He called you an abnormal bitch. He said to tell you if you'd been a better mother, none of this would have happened."

She looked away without speaking.

De Córdoba reached for the telephone. "I'll call the airport."

Tucson

She was no better when he next went down to the cell. She was still shivering, sitting hunched on the bed with her head in her hands. It was so like her illness during the first days of her imprisonment that he was appalled. Her light had gone out.

He sat down beside her, helpless in his pain. "Eden, I'm sorry."

She would not raise her head to look at him.

"Eden. Please . . ."

She looked up at him slowly. The green eyes were dulled. She was very pale. "You did this out of self-pity," she said. "Because I was a spoiled child and you weren't."

"I did it for *justice*," he said tightly. "And you cannot imagine what my childhood was like, Eden."

"How can you blame her for that?"

"She was my mother!"

"But you came at the wrong time."

"At the wrong time, yes," he said bitterly. "I was an incumbrance on her life. An obstacle to her ambitions. So she *sold* me. Like a dog. She sold me to those monsters to torment."

"And so you had to torment her in revenge. Her and me."

Joel grasped Eden's arm. Her skin was clammy. "How can you ever understand? You were never beaten. You were never starved, chained, terrified out of your mind with horrors. No one ever gave you a minute's pain. There was never an hour that you wished you were anyone different or anywhere else. I used to wish I was dead, Eden. At eight years old, *I wished I was dead*. They chained me in the cellar like a beast."

"So you did the same to me."

"I didn't want you to suffer—"

"Bullshit. You wanted me to suffer, exactly as you suffered. That's how spiteful and senseless it all was."

"I was half-mad, Eden," he said, almost pleadingly.

"And now you're sane?" she asked bitterly.

"No. I'm screwed-up. Maybe I'll never be sane. But this was my way of righting the balance."

"There isn't any balance, Joel. Just a lot of other screwed-up people. Let me go." She tried to pry his fingers loose from her arm, but her muscles had no strength. A long shudder took her and she started rocking to and fro. "Oh, God. God. Let me go."

"Eden!" He put his arms around her, frantic to console, to explain. "Eden, I was her legitimate child. Not some bastard. Not some *mistake*. She married before she left Spain. An American volunteer, Sean O'Keefe. I've seen his photograph. But he died before I was born. And rather than bring me up alone, she sold me to Eldred Lennox. 'And they have cast lots for my people; and they have given a boy for an harlot and sold a girl for wine, that they might drink.'"

"You don't know," she said. "How can you know anything about what it was like for her, then?"

"I know what she did to me! She shed me like a parcel and

married your father. Became rich on the fruits of evil. Lavished on you the things that should have been mine!"

"You can't punish her for what she did all those years ago!"

"Those years are *me*. I am the years, the years the locust hath eaten. She must pay. It's between me and her. Nothing to do with you. 'Behold, I will raise them out of the place whither ye have sold them and will return your recompense upon your own head.'"

"It makes me sick to hear you quote that stuff. It's evil!"

"It's the Good Book," he said with a terrible smile. "I was raised by it. I was made to memorize it, chapter and verse, with the chains and the darkness to encourage me. It has a fine, vengeful spirit, Eden. Nothing goes unpunished. *Nothing*."

"Revenge doesn't solve anything. We're all chained together."

"Yes. We're all chained together. Revenge is an ax. It cuts chains free."

She was crying now, exhaustedly. "Maybe she thought they would take better care of you than she could. He was a clergyman. A man of God—"

"He was a devil," Joel said savagely. "She sold me to the devil. For two thousand dollars. I saw the papers, Eden. The woman who brought me up showed them to me, on her deathbed. My mother took two thousand dollars and I was given to people who destroyed me—"

"How could she guess those people were monsters?"

"Everyone knew! They'd been rejected by every adoption agency in California!"

"Everybody suffers," she wept. "Look at me, Joel. I had the childhood you missed. And look at yourself. You're strong. You have a wonderful gift. You're in control of your own life. And I'm worthless, doomed, defiled. Which of us had the better deal?"

"You're *not* worthless," he said fiercely. "You're the only one of us all who stands a chance. You're going to take it, Eden. You're going to soar."

"I loved you so much," she said brokenly.

He took her face in his hands. Her skin burned like fire against his palms. He saw that her lips were dry and cracked. "You're the flower of my life. I'll always love you, Eden. You're my sister. You're more. You were chained to me all my life. What I'm doing now is cutting the chains. Setting us all free."

Her trembling was more feverish than ever. "What are you going to do with the money?"

"I'm going to burn it."

"It's crazy, crazy, crazy. You're destroying everything you've made of your life, for the sake of hurting a mother you've never known!"

"For the sake of justice."

"I could tell you so much about her." She clutched at his wrists. "Things you don't know. How gentle she can be. How wonderful she can be. How everyone who knows her loves her."

His face closed. "I don't want to hear that."

"But it's true! She isn't what you think she is, heartless, cold. She's human. She's like you—"

"*No.*"

"Face her, Joel. Meet her."

"I don't need to meet her."

"You do! You need her!"

"All I need," he said tautly, "is to know that she has been punished."

"You've gone through this whole thing imagining she's something she's not. Joel, please listen to me. Please, please. Let me speak to her. Let me explain—"

"You can explain when it's all over."

"*It'll be too late.*" He was almost afraid of her sudden passion. It seemed to be burning in her, cracking her surface, drying her skin before his eyes, consuming her beauty. "Listen to me, Joel, listen! I'm so afraid of what will happen. So afraid. I feel so sick, Joel. So sick. Don't go through with it. Don't, don't—"

She could not speak any more. She was hunched over as if in unbearable pain.

"I have to go through with it," he said in a dead voice. "We're going down to Mexico tomorrow. Get some rest."

He rose and went out of the cell, locking the door behind him.

Houston, Texas

Joaquin de Córdoba stared out of the window of the airliner. Thirty thousand feet below, Texas lay stretched out, a tawny vastness beneath cloudless skies. The man beside him had slumped in sleep, and his head nudged de Córdoba's shoulder from time to time.

He felt exhaustion tug at him, somewhere below the level of his consciousness. He had not slept in two days. Of the last thirty-six hours, he had spent twenty-three in airliners. Barcelona to Madrid on Monday afternoon. Madrid to New York overnight. In New York he had collected the first installment of the money, six million dollars. It had been waiting for him at First National, and as requested, they had provided an unobtrusive escort back to the airport.

From New York he had flown, again overnight, to Miami, where he had picked up the remaining four million dollars at a different bank. Again, he had been escorted back to the airport.

The money was unbelievably heavy. The larger component, packed in an aluminium Globetrotter suitcase, had been made up of small-denomination bills. It was almost beyond his power to lift. It was in the hold now. He had personally stood and watched it being loaded.

The smaller component, packed in a leather Vuitton valise, was lighter. Sixteen bundles of five hundred used $500 bills. Four million dollars, packed neatly under the few changes of clothes he had brought with him. It was tucked under his feet now, nestling up against his calves.

The light money. His eyelids drooped. The downward tug of exhaustion was strong, treacherous, pulling his mind into the dreamy reverie that would lead to sleep. The heavy money and the light money. The big money was light. The little money was heavy.

He jerked suddenly into wakefulness, felt his skeletal muscles quivering with the nearness of sleep. He sat up, shrugging the sleeping passenger off his shoulder. He dug the heels of his palms into his reddened eyes. He could feel tiny blood vessels bursting under the pressure. He took a deep breath and turned blearily back to the view. He could not sleep. He dared not sleep, not until Monterrey.

The diplomatic accreditation arranged for him by Gerard Massaguer had carried him effortlessly through Customs and Immigration so far. He expected the same when he disembarked in Mexico tomorrow.

He checked his watch. Another two hours to Houston. Then a five-hour wait for the onward flight to Monterrey. And from Monterrey, the last leg, to Hermosillo. He prayed that the kidnapper would be patient.

Tucson

The Dodge Ram was ready. He had packed it with all the water and food they would need, the sleeping bags, the tent, the spare clothes. He had serviced the car himself, replacing all the hoses, packing spares. He'd bought it nearly new a week ago, and apart from the worn tyres, which he'd replaced, it was in good condition. They'd be comfortable in its strength, even over the rough terrain they would need to cover.

He knew where they were going to cross. East of Nogales, at a place he'd used before. A twenty-five-mile midnight run across the desert and they'd be in Mexico. The chances of being stopped were slim. Nobody checked for illegal entrants *into* Mexico.

He'd considered packing the M–16. He badly wanted to, but it was not an easy weapon to hide in a compact recreational vehicle. He had no hand gun either. So he had to be content with the heavy, razor-sharp Commando knife, which he stored in the glove compartment.

Now that the end was so near, he had recovered his sense of purpose. For those few wonderful weeks, he and Eden had floated free. A remission. A gift. Now they were on course again, moving towards their destiny.

It was four o'clock in the afternoon. They would set off after dark.

He lay down and tried to get some rest. His thoughts returned anxiously to Eden. She seemed to be getting worse. She hadn't eaten in two days. Had barely drunk a glass of water. She was already weak and exhausted. He prayed that she'd managed to eat the food he'd left last time, the fresh vegetables, the temptingly ripe fruit she loved.

He should never have told her. It seemed to have crushed her. To have taken away her spirit.

She would recover, he told himself. She would be all right.

• • •

He went down at dusk, to see if she had eaten. She had not. The food was untouched.

She was sleeping, though it did not look like sleep. She was never still. Her body twitched and jerked. She was moaning feverishly. He touched her forehead and was frightened by the heat of her skin. Now and then her eyes half-opened, milky green slits that rolled blindly.

Her skin had changed further. It was dryer than ever. It seemed to have darkened.

He sat watching her, feeling a cold blade enter his heart. She had been like this during the worst of her withdrawal phase. Could it have returned? Could the shock have triggered off another bout of withdrawal symptoms? He did not know.

He left her to sleep another couple of hours.

He came for her at nine. She was awake by then, but her face terrified him.

"I'm sick," she whispered. "Hold me, Joel."

He took her trembling body in his arms and held her close. No, he thought. You can't do this to her. You have no right!

"What is it?" he asked her. "Is it the cold turkey again?"

"I don't know. It feels different."

"What does it feel like?"

"Feels so—hot. So sick, Joel."

With infinite gentleness, he fed her two aspirin and made her swallow them.

"Drink some more," he pleaded. "Just a little."

Most of the water spilled down her chin. She choked at last and shook her head. *"Can't."*

"You'll feel better soon. It's just Valley fever. It'll go."

He held her, cradling her head against his chest, stroking her hair.

After twenty minutes, the trembling began to slow. He touched her forehead. She seemed less hot.

"How do you feel?" he asked.

"Better."

"Okay. We have to go."

She looked up drowsily. "Where are we going?"

"I told you. To Mexico."

He helped her to her feet. But when she tried to walk, her legs folded. He caught her just in time.

She smiled wanly. "You're gonna have to carry me."

He lifted her in his arms. She felt so light he was sickened.

He carried her upstairs and out to the Ram. He put her in the front seat with a pillow under her head and wrapped two blankets tightly around her. He pulled the seat belt across her.

"How's that?"

She didn't open her eyes. "Okay."

"Try and get some sleep."

He got into the driver's seat and fired up the engine. He drove down the road between the tall saguaro and did not look back at the house he was leaving behind.

There was another vehicle following the same route, about two miles up ahead, a battered truck with no plates, heading for a drug pickup maybe, or to collect illegal immigrants waiting for their guide at the border. But certainly not police. Earlier, they had slowed enough to let him come up behind them, get a good look at him. He let them do it, so they knew he wasn't any trouble to them and he knew they weren't any trouble to him. After that, he kept his distance.

The clouds of dust they were leaving were a convenient marker for him to follow through the night. The desert vegetation was weird in the headlights, armies of ghosts with twisted limbs and clutching hands. The route was a lot rougher than he remembered it. The Dodge had been jolting and leaping like a buck rabbit. He had hit a big saguaro earlier on and thought he'd wrecked the radiator. But the green flesh had been too soft to do much damage to the Ram.

Eden was back in her restless sleep. From time to time she moaned and muttered, never any words he could understand. When he hit a big pothole she would cry out or whimper. He tried to drive with one hand as much as he could, using the other to steady her. She was being jolted cruelly. At times he thought her neck would snap as her head lurched from side to side. But she did not wake.

He touched her forehead. It was burning hot again. But no

longer sweaty. The sweat seemed to have dried up in her and her skin was parched.

He smashed his hand against the steering wheel in frustration. *Goddamn.*

He pulled to a stop and got the water bottle. Supporting her head tenderly in his arm, he tried to get her to drink. The water spilled from her slack lips. None went down.

He bathed her face and throat with his wet palm. "Not much longer," he promised her urgently. "Another couple of hours."

She muttered something unintelligible.

He kissed her mouth. It felt dry and cracked. "I love you," he whispered.

He checked the compass and set off again. Maybe she would sweat the fever out tonight. Maybe come the dawn it would break and she would be through it.

Maybe.

Los Angeles

After their morning rounds, the doctors decided to let Dominic van Buren out of his room to enjoy the autumn sunlight. The complications were troubling, but the intermediate medication had taken good effect and the violent episode had been dealt with. An orderly was called who helped van Buren to rise and pull a dressing gown over his pajamas. He wiped van Buren's mouth with a tissue and brushed his hair. He asked van Buren if he needed to go to the bathroom. Van Buren didn't answer, so the orderly took him to the urinal anyway, took his penis out and held it while he urinated. Then he guided him down the corridor to the garden.

At the door of each room, van Buren paused to stare in at the patients who lay listlessly on their beds, or sat with their heads in their hands, or sang, or laughed or wept. The orderly was forbearing at first. Then he grew impatient and propelled the old man along with more vigour.

Still van Buren's head swivelled slowly at each doorway they passed, peering in with eyes that seemed to search for a familiar face.

The sun was shining. The garden was green and pleasant. The

orderly steered van Buren to a comfortable-looking yellow deck chair in the middle of the green lawn and pushed him gently into it.

"Soak up a little sun," the orderly, who was black, advised cheerfully. "Winter's gonna be coming soon."

He crossed the lawn to join a group of other orderlies sharing a cigarette. Van Buren's eyes followed the white coats as they drifted to and fro.

Monterrey, Mexico

The morning hit de Córdoba in a dizzy wave. He had forgotten this dry Central American heat, the vastness of Central American skies. He sleepwalked through Immigration, surrounded by the familiar soft-toned Spanish of Mexico. The aluminium suitcase, marked and sealed as a diplomatic bag, was whisked through Customs uninspected.

A handsome young man from the Spanish consulate was waiting for him at the gates.

"Colonel de Córdoba? I'm Oliverio Marqués. Welcome to Mexico. The consul has ordered me to extend any help you need. I've booked your onward flight to Hermosillo," he said, holding out the ticket. "It doesn't leave for some hours. I'm sure you'd care for a wash and a meal. Perhaps a rest?"

De Córdoba rubbed his face wearily. He was longing for sleep. He felt like death. "Is there somewhere we can go?"

"There's a clean hotel not far from the airport. My wife is expecting you. My car is just outside."

"Very well. Thank you. Be careful with those," he begged, as Marqués helped de Córdoba load the suitcases onto a trolley. "If those go astray, we're both dead men."

Oliverio Marqués smiled. Then he saw de Córdoba's expression and his smile faded.

Sonora, Mexico

He was awake before dawn, listening to the first chirp of birds. Eden was huddled in his arms, motionless. He had zipped them both into the one sleeping bag last night, and they had slept like lovers, their limbs entwined, their bodies pressed together. The bunks in the back of the Ram were comfortable. She had passed, he thought, a restful four hours. She had moaned a little for a while, but then had settled into a deep sleep. He would let her sleep until she awoke. She needed the rest desperately.

He lay cradling her head against him, watching the sky through the back window. It turned slowly from blue to rose-pink. He prayed that the fever had broken.

In the vast peace of the dawn, he reflected that today might be the last day they ever spent together. He would never again hold her in his arms, his half-sister, his half-lover. But he did not feel grief. Not yet.

He had loved her as a sister and as a woman. And yet he felt no confusion. No sense of impropriety. Not any more. They had given one another the gift of sex, once and for always. Whenever, after this strange day, he thought of her, it would be with joy.

Now, without anger, without pain, he saw what he had not seen before, that what he held in his arms outweighed everything else he had done—this treasure, this unforeseeable discovery. Loving Eden mattered infinitely more than justice. She had healed him more than revenge could do.

She was the first woman whom he had ever loved. The first human being he had ever unquestioningly adored. And she had taught him to see himself—to discover a part of himself that he would never have known if he had not reached out to touch her.

They had touched one another. They had made one another whole. Perhaps that had been the real motive, all along, the real impulse of destiny. To bring the two of them together. To teach each about the other. About themselves. About how they had both been used. *And they have given a boy for an harlot and sold a girl for wine.*

He had freed her from her enslavement. He had no doubt that she could free him from his. His love for her was the most over-whelmingly important thing he had ever discovered. Perhaps he was free already. Perhaps she had already performed the miracle, and freed him from the rage, the bitterness, the flaring resentment that had poisoned his life.

Was it too late to stop what he had set in motion?

She stirred in his arms and muttered his name. Then she began to whimper.

"Eden?" It was light enough to see, now. He reached out and unzipped the sleeping bag. She rolled onto her back. He lifted himself up onto one elbow and looked into her face.

His castle of bright dreams was annihilated in one terrible crash. She's dying, he thought numbly.

Her lips had cracked like a dry lake bed. Her face was gaunt, her cheeks sunken. The colour of her skin was terrifying, a clayey ochre yellow that bore no resemblance to human flesh.

"Eden," he said desperately, shaking her, "Eden, wake up!"

He kissed her parched lips. White froth had dried at the corner of her mouth. Her skin seemed to sear his.

He got the water bottle, and began to bathe her face, trickling the water over her lips. He was praying, for the first time since Vietnam. Take me, instead. I have always been your scapegoat. You cannot take this innocent child! She has not transgressed!

She woke slowly. When she opened her eyes, he saw that the whites too were stained with yellow.

"Where are we?" she whispered.

"In Mexico. In the desert." He was sick with anxiety for her. "How do you feel?"

"Weak. Shitty."

"Worse than last night?"

"Maybe a little better." Her eyes closed again.

"I'll make us some breakfast. Try and go back to sleep again."

He left her in the sleeping bag and got out of the Ram. In the first rays of the risen sun, the mountains all around were peach-coloured, folded with soft purple shadows. The scrub was autumn-dry, autumn-pale. Desert woodpeckers were busy among a stand of saguaro nearby. The horizontal rays of the sun deepened the cacti's ribs, emphasizing their stark beauty.

He set up the gas stove and put the coffee pot over it to brew. He made another fire out of dried wood and propped the skillet over it on stones. The sizzling of the eggs and bacon, the smells of cooking, gave him a little solace among the immense solitude. For the first time in years, the desert seemed desolation to him. A wilderness that dwarfed and threatened. There was no place for humans here.

He tried to recover his sense of purpose. To pitch his will

against the wilderness, fly the banner of his independence over the empty places. He felt terribly alone.

He took her a plate of food, but she could not eat.

"Please try," he implored her. "It'll make you feel better, I swear it."

To please him, she sat up and tried to chew some bacon. But it was too much of an effort. And the salt taste of the food made her gorge rise. She began to retch violently.

He held her tight, feeling her frail body convulsing. He could not bear it. She was going back into the darkness.

She drifted back into sleep. As he zipped her into the bag, he had a dreadful vision of the bags he had seen zipped up in Vietnam.

After that, he couldn't eat either.

He drank some coffee, packed up the Ram, and started the engine. According to his reading of the map, the road to Cucurpe lay due west. He checked the compass as he drove. The desert was rocky here, but flat. By keeping a careful look out, he managed to avoid jolting Eden too much. Every few minutes, he turned to look at her in the back. She lay like the dead, her black hair tumbled over her face. He prayed for her as he drove.

He hit the road to Cucurpe after two hours. There was no traffic on it at this hour. He doubted whether there was ever much traffic on it. It was a wretched road, pot-holed and disintegrating at the edges. But it was little-used and he did not want to take the main route to Hermosillo.

Cucurpe was as wretched as the road that led to it, a shanty town of dusty obscurity. But it had a gas station. While the sleepy attendant filled the Ram's tank, he went to the doorless telephone booth and called the San Sebastian Hotel in Hermosillo.

Señor de Córdoba had not yet checked in. But there was a reservation in his name for tomorrow night.

Tomorrow night?

He felt a wave of panic as he hung up. By tomorrow night, Eden might be dying. She might be dying now. He had to get her to a doctor. But he dared not. They were going to have to spend another night in the Ram, maybe another two. Unless he took the risk of a hotel.

Rage blinded him. What were they doing? Why was it taking so long? Why hadn't they assembled the money sooner?

He forced himself to stay calm. He could not lose his self-control. Eden's life hung from his fingers now.

He got in the Ram, swung it around in a cloud of dust and set off back up the twelve-mile road to Magdalena.

In Magdalena, at mid-morning, he found a *farmacia*. He struggled with his rusty Spanish.

"We're on holiday. Americans. My wife—she's sick. Fever. Weak. Won't eat. Throws up everything I feed her."

"You should bring her in here." The pharmacist, a young woman, looked at Joel's unshaven, taut face with unease. "Better still, go to a doctor."

"She's sleeping right now. I don't want to wake her. Haven't you got something?"

She spread her hands. She had large, liquid black eyes and the smooth features of Papago ancestors. "It could be anything. I don't know what to suggest. Does she have any other symptoms?"

"She's burning up with fever. And her skin—" He touched his face. "Yellow. Her eyes too."

"Her eyes and skin are yellow?"

"Yes."

"Then she has jaundice," the girl said positively. "It could be serious liver disease. But it's probably caused by hepatitis."

"Hepatitis!" Light flooded his mind. He cursed his own slowness savagely. Of course. *Of course.* She had been incubating serum hepatitis, one of the heroin addict's commonest diseases.

"There are two types," the pharmacist was saying. "Type A and Type B. Type A is usually contracted through—"

"She has type B," he said bleakly. "I should have known. She's a diabetic. Injects herself with insulin."

"Ah." She nodded emphatically. "Then she probably does have hepatitis B. An inadequately sterilized needle is almost always the cause—"

"How dangerous is it?" he cut in urgently.

"Well, it's a serious illness. Especially if she's a diabetic and she's not eating. You must take her to a doctor or a hospital right away. They'll do tests to confirm if she has got it—"

"We come from Phoenix, Arizona," he said. "I think I'm going to have to take her back to the States."

"That would be best."

"Can't you give me anything for her in the meantime, for the journey, until I get her to an American hospital?"

"There isn't any specific treatment for infective hepatitis," she said.

"No treatment?"

"Just rest."

"Nothing else?"

"Rest is the most important treatment, until the patient's fever settles and her appetite comes back. She shouldn't be moved around. She should definitely go back home and get to bed as soon as possible." She saw his anguished expression. "Most people," she said gently, "are only jaundiced about a week. Then they make a complete recovery. It just takes time. Bed-rest and time."

"I see." He felt a little reassured by that. "Can't I give her anything for the fever?"

"It would be better to let a doctor prescribe any drugs. You don't want to damage her liver any further."

"No, I don't want that. She won't get any worse?"

"There can be complications. They're rare, though." Her eyes moved to the queue of customers starting to form behind Joel. "Take her to a doctor."

"Okay," Joel nodded. "Thank you." He left the pharmacy and did some shopping in a food store. Then he walked back to the Ram, thinking hard. If the only treatment was rest, then perhaps she would be all right until the payoff. If she didn't get any worse. But there was no way he could keep her in the Ram for another forty-eight hours. They were going to have to book into a hotel. Something humble but clean. Somewhere she could just lie in bed and sleep, out of the heat, while they waited for de Córdoba.

He'd parked the Ram in the shade of a peeling garden wall, away from prying eyes. He got into the back and looked at Eden. She was lying half-awake, muttering to herself. Her skin was yellower than ever. Again, he cursed himself for his tardy recognition of the symptoms.

He woke her. She seemed a little stronger.

"Joel? Where are we?"

"Magdalena. I've brought you some fruit juice. Try and drink."

He raised her and touched the mug to her lips. She gulped

once or twice and swallowed with difficulty. "It's so hot," she moaned. "I'm burning up, Joel."

"I'm going to take you somewhere cool right away. I think I know what's wrong with you now."

"What?"

"You've got hepatitis."

"Oh, shit," she said wearily. "You sure?"

"I think so."

"Are you gonna take care of me?"

"I love you, Eden," he said seriously. "More than my life."

She put her arms around his neck and smiled up at him. "I love you too," she said. "Don't worry about me. Hepatitis ain't nothing. Junkies get it all the time. You get it off the needles. My sins are catching up with me. That's all."

"You've never sinned in your life."

She tried to laugh. "That's what you think. Now somebody wants me to pay." She put her mouth up to his and kissed him. Her lips felt like paper. "Where are we going now?"

"I'm going to find us a hotel where we can rest up."

"With a bath," she said. "I'm dying for a bath."

"Sure," he promised, stroking her hair. "With a bath and everything."

Barcelona

Mercedes Eduard too, found prayer an unfamiliar ritual. She sat with her hands clasped and her head bowed, just as she'd done as a child, long ago. The words of those far-off prayers came in drips, mingling with the things she wanted to scream.

Heavenly Father . . . for we have sinned in thought, word and deed . . . but especially in our deeds . . . she's so young, dear God . . . her sins are so pale and small . . . look on mine instead, scarlet and black, like evil orchids . . . worthier game for your sword . . . I beg you to take me instead and spare her . . . take me instead . . . I love her so much . . . so much.

She took several long, shuddering breaths. It will be all right, she told herself. Eden will be back with me soon. Soon. And then, no more mistakes. No more pain. We will understand each other from now on.

But she felt a terrible foreboding.

Weariness weighed on her like a mountain.

Eden had already suffered for so long. If the kidnapper had meant to make Mercedes grieve, he was too late.

While he'd been planning, someone else had been devising a punishment far more apt, far more ironic for Mercedes Eduard. She had rejected her son. Her daughter had rejected her.

Yet she loved Eden so much. From the day she'd first held Eden in her arms, Eden had mattered more than life itself. She loved Eden the same way she'd loved Sean, from the depths of her being, without reservations, without reason or understanding.

She felt the blood pounding in her ears. Fate had allotted her a punishment that was beautifully cruel.

After a while, she rose to her feet and went to the window. She looked out at the city, and remembered it as it was once, battered by air raids, under a pall of black smoke. Destiny had driven her into that air raid shelter with Sean. Into what other strange refuges would destiny drive her in time?

Sonora

She slept, motionless, for almost four hours. He sat on a chair beside the bed, never taking his eyes off her. His heart was filled with prayers for her, with love for her. In the heat of the afternoon, stillness came over the little town. Its sordid streets emptied. The children vanished, the shops closed, the traffic melted away. Somewhere a radio played, sentimental Mexican ballads, but distant enough to be pleasing, rather than otherwise.

The hotel was primitive, but the cleanest he could find. The room was simply-furnished and quiet. Its window looked out onto a patio where a cactus garden grew wild.

At sundown, life began again outside in the street. The room was filled with ruby light. It gave Eden's skin a spurious glow of health, and he drank in the deception.

The sound of voices and motorcycles disturbed her. She began to whimper again, moving restlessly under the sheet. He took her hand. She was still terribly hot. He had to get her to drink, even if he forced her, or she would burn up before his eyes.

She awoke suddenly, in a state of confusion that bewildered him.

"Rusty?" she cried out, her fingers tightening around his. "Rusty, where are we? What are we doing here?"

"I'm not Rusty," he said gently. "I'm Joel." He went to the basin and came back with a wet sponge to mop her face.

She shrank away from him. "Who are you?"

"Joel," he said. "I'm Joel. Your brother."

She let him sponge her face, but her eyes were wild. Her face was all tremors and twitches. "I need a fix," she said. "It's time for my fix."

"You've forgotten," he said. "You don't need a fix any more."

"I do!" She was frantic. He had to restrain her from climbing out of bed naked. "Where's my gear? Where's my junk?"

"Baby, don't," he begged, close to tears. "You went through cold turkey. You're healed. You're cured. Don't you remember?"

"I'm sick," she whimpered, clinging to his hands.

"You've got hepatitis. Remember?"

"I need my fix. Oh, God, I feel so bad! I need my fix, Rusty. Don't make me wait. *Please!*"

She struggled with him feebly. He was shattered with grief. He could not find any more words. At last she subsided, crying weakly. He took her pulse. It was fluttering and weak.

Get her to a hospital. Now.

She seemed to slide out of the delusion. "Joel? What have I been saying?"

"Nothing," he said, weak with relief that she had returned. "Silly things."

"I thought you were Rusty. I thought . . . I must have been dreaming."

He kissed her brow. "How do you feel?"

"Exhausted." She lay back, her yellowed face pinched. "I hurt all over."

"One more night," he promised. "And one more day. De Córdoba is arriving in Hermosillo tomorrow night. It'll be over. Soon."

"It'll never be over," she said. She took his hand and lifted it to her lips. "Whatever happens tomorrow, you'll come to me again."

"You know I can't—"

"You will," she said. Her eyes burned into his. "You *will*. I'll be waiting for you."

"Yes," he said, to pacify her. "I'll come."

"I'll be waiting for you, Joel. Until you come."

He swallowed hard. "You haven't eaten or drunk in nearly four days. You're going to have to drink something now. Even if I have to pour it down your gullet. Understand?"

She smiled feebly. "I love it when you're masterful."

"Okay." He filled the glass with a mixture of water and peach nectar and brought it to her. "Get it down in one go," he said.

She took it in both hands. "Chug-a-lug."

She drank slowly, as though it hurt her to swallow. Her eyes closed. He saw her slender throat gulp. He noticed that bruises were appearing on her arms where he'd held her as she struggled. He cursed his clumsiness. He'd have to be more careful from now on. She was so frail.

She seemed a little better after she'd drunk. She rested with her eyes closed. "You're right," she said dreamily. "That has improved things a little."

"Good."

After a while, she opened her eyes. "I have to go to the bathroom. That's what your water's done for me."

He helped her to rise and walked her to the bathroom door. There she stopped and laid a hand on his chest. "I can manage from here on. A girl has to have some privacy."

He watched her grope her way into the bathroom, supporting herself on the fixtures. He shut the door and waited.

She took a long time, ten minutes or more. He was just about to go in and see if she was all right, when she shuffled out of the door. She had a lopsided smile on her face. "Well, whaddaya know. I got my period."

He stared at her.

"You don't think that's much of an achievement, do you?" She leaned against the door. "While I was on the needle, I stopped getting my periods. I never had a period in a whole year. Sick, huh? Now here they are back. I'm a woman again, Joel."

He took her in his arms. "Congratulations."

"Yeah. It feels good." She sniffed a little against his neck. "Never thought I'd be so pleased to get my period."

"Do you want me to go out and get you something?"

"No. It ain't much of a show. I tucked some paper in my pants. That'll hold the flood. Take me back to bed, Joel. Hold me in your arms. Please."

He lay with her, cradling her in his arms. "You came out of the darkness," she said softly. "But I was waiting for you all my life, Joel. I was never complete until you."

"Nor I until you," he whispered.

"You made me kick heroin. You made me come. You made me a woman again."

"Don't talk. You don't have to."

"I'll never be able to explain how I feel about you. Want to hear something funny? When I was a kid, I used to dream I had a big brother. I guess a lot of only children have those sorts of dreams. I used to weave whole fantasies around you. My big brother. My protector. My friend." She touched his lips with her fingertips. "When I grew up a little, I stopped dreaming about a brother. I used to dream about my ideal man. He'd be strong and wise and handsome. He'd be special. Different. And now here you are. But I never knew it would be the same person, brother and lover and friend and teacher, all in one..."

"As you've been to me," he whispered. "Sister and lover and friend and teacher. All in one..."

She drifted back into sleep, her limbs twitching against him. It was getting cold. He pulled the blankets up over them and drew her close.

At four o'clock in the morning, she woke, choking. She seemed unable to walk. He carried her to the bathroom, trying not to panic. He held her head over the basin, rubbing her back. The choking eased slowly.

"Sorry," she mumbled at last. "False alarm."

Then she vomited a pint of blood.

Before dawn, she had vomited three times more, always the same dark, clotted blood. He saw that her gums were bleeding too. And her nose. He was numbed. The universe was crashing down around him. He knew that if she died, he would die too. And burn in hell for eternity.

She was confused again, apathetic. She did not seem to know where she was. For a while she thought she was in the Hebron

Clinic and called him Rusty several times. Later she called him Daddy. She begged for her fix, panting and trembling.

The trembling grew more intense. Her hands flapped from time to time, as though she were swimming, or trying to fly.

He saw the stains on the sheet, and realized that what she'd thought was her period had been vaginal bleeding.

There was no answer from the night porter. He went out, as the sky began to lighten, to try and find a doctor. The sun was up by the time he managed to locate one, an old man who spoke some English, and who wheezed and cursed as he pulled clothes over his pajamas.

By the time he got the man to the hotel room, Eden was in a stupor, her hands flapping constantly, her breath coming fast and shallow.

"She's jaundiced," the doctor said, blinking at the girl who lay on the bed.

"I told you," Joel snarled at him. "She's got hepatitis!"

"Don't shout at me, young man. I ain't deaf." The doctor felt her pulse, peering blearily at his watch. "Nor senile." He pulled her eyelids back with his thumbs. Then he prodded, apparently aimlessly, at her sides and stomach. "In fact, there ain't nothing wrong with me. Unlike your friend, here."

"What's wrong with her?" Joel demanded.

"Hepatitis," the old man said irritably, "like you said."

Joel grasped him by the throat and swung him around. "What's wrong with her?" he screamed in the old man's face.

The doctor scrabbled at Joel's hands. "Her liver is collapsing."

"Is she going to die?"

The old man was afraid of Joel's expression. "Not at all," he said. "Not at all. We got to get her to a hospital. Let me go, young man."

"Where's the nearest hospital?"

"Hermosillo. Thirty miles away. I'll call an ambulance."

"I'll take her myself."

He wrapped Eden in the blankets, then lifted her in his arms and carried her out. The doctor followed. By now a group of people were standing in the lobby, attracted by the drama. They watched Joel impassively as he carried the unconscious girl down the stairs and out to the Ram. He put her in the back, packing cushions around her. "Don't die," he told her seriously. "You're going to be all right."

"Señor—" The receptionist was standing nervously by. "Forgive me—the room has not been paid for."

"There's my fee too," the doctor said cautiously.

Joel pulled a handful of money from his pocket and threw it at the two men. They flinched back from the fluttering bills.

He got in the Ram and spun the wheels all down the street.

Hermosillo, Mexico

De Córdoba had been sitting, staring at the suitcases. He'd just called Mercedes to tell her he was in place, but he had not had time to wash and have a drink, yet.

When the telephone rang, he picked it up, feeling very old.

"Joaquin de Córdoba."

"This is Paul. Is the money ready?"

"Yes."

"You got a car?"

"I hired one at the airport."

"What is it?"

"A yellow Buick with a vinyl top."

"Put the money in the car."

"Now?"

"Now, yes, now." There was a dead note in the kidnapper's voice that disturbed de Córdoba. "Take the road to Nogales. When you get through a village called Carbo, keep a lookout for an abandoned cantina on the right. It's surrounded by saguaro. You can still see the name, La Moreneta, painted on the front."

"Wait!" De Córdoba's heart was pounding. "Let me write this down."

"You don't need to write anything down. You make sure there are no other cars on the road. You leave the money inside the cantina. Just put it on the floor."

It seemed too crude, too simple. "But—anyone might find it there!"

"Not anyone. I'll be watching. And I have a rifle with telescopic sights. So don't try looking for me. You understand me?"

"I understand you. The money is in two bags. An aluminium suitcase and a leather valise. There's four mill—"

"Leave them there. Get back in your car. Drive back to Hermosillo. Go to your room. Wait there. When I have the money, I'll call you in your room and tell you where to find Eden."

"Wait—how is Eden? Can I speak to her? Hello? Hello?"

The line clicked dead in his ear.

Los Angeles

The orderly stopped the trolley and pushed the door of van Buren's room open. He peered inside. "Mr. van Buren? Medication time."

Then he saw van Buren's leg, white and thin, protruding from behind the bathroom door.

He ran in. The dressing gown cord had been looped around the taps of the basin. There were no suitable fixtures in the ceiling for such a purpose. The man had tied the cord around his throat and had just sunk down onto his buttocks, pulling it tight around his windpipe and carotid artery.

The face was congested and blue. The orderly dragged the inert body to its feet and clawed the impromptu noose from the bruised throat. He checked for heartbeat and breathing. There were none. He ran out into the corridor and screamed for a doctor.

Then he went back to the immobile patient to begin resuscitation.

Barcelona

It was four o'clock in the morning when the call came through. Mercedes had not slept and she picked up the telephone at once.

"Mercedes? It's Joaquin."

Her heart seemed to have stopped beating. "Have you found her?"

"Yes. I've paid the ransom in full and I'm with Eden now. Mercedes, I have very bad news for you."

She closed her eyes instinctively. "She's dead."

"No. She's in a local hospital. In intensive care. She's very sick, Mercedes. She has a very serious form of hepatitis. Fulminant hepatic necrosis. She must have got it from an infected needle, before the kidnap. She is in a coma."

Every sentence was like a hammer-blow, battering her to her knees. "Is she going to die?" she asked quietly.

"It's possible," he said. "The doctors want you to come to her. As soon as you can."

"I'm coming," she said. "If she wakes, tell her I'm coming."

17.

~The Anvil

Hermosillo

"I begged him..."

It was not even a whisper. It was a rustle. Mercedes had to strain to make out the words.

"I begged him, Mama... not to go through with it..."

"Don't talk, my darling. Don't talk."

"...didn't want it to end like this..."

Mercedes had been warned not to touch or kiss Eden, in case she contracted the disease. But now she pulled the surgical mask away from her face and touched Eden's papery lips with her own. Eden's breath was sickly-sweet. The disease had done that.

"Mama, I missed you so much."

"I missed you." She looked helplessly at the machines that surrounded Eden, at the plastic tubes that went into her arms and nose. The technology was frightening, not reassuring. It seemed suddenly terrible to Mercedes that Eden should have to die with all this around her. She had seen death in many forms, but never so systematic, so unemotional. The monitors, the gauges and meters that hovered with Eden's hovering life, would measure her departure down to the last discharging neuron, the last flutter of her heart. They would tell the precise instant when life became death and Eden was no more.

No mystery. No dignity. No pity.

She felt a flare of rage. A desire to smash it all, to release Eden from the needles that pierced her flesh, the liquids they pumped into her and sucked out of her . . .

The nurse who sat in the corner stood up quickly, as if sensing Mercedes's rage, and came to check all the monitors.

Mercedes stroked Eden's hair. She saw the lips move again.

"Mama . . ."

"I'm here."

"Stay with me . . ."

The gaunt face on the pillow seemed carved out of gold, a funeral mask. The eyes were neither open nor closed. Mercedes did not know whether Eden could see her, whether she was even truly aware that her mother was by. Perhaps she was talking to a figure she saw in dreams.

The nurse's eyes were disturbed over the green mask. "I'm going to call the doctor," she said. She hurried out.

Mercedes stood watching her daughter. So many things she had planned to say to Eden, when she was with her again. Yet she was dumb now, too drained even to pray.

The doctors came in, gloved and masked and bustling. A nurse took Mercedes's arm gently.

"Mrs. van Buren? You'll have to leave for a while."

She walked out. De Córdoba was sprawled in a chair in the waiting room, his head sunk on his breast. She let him sleep. She had nothing to say in any case and no appetite for consolation.

As she walked past the desk, a secretary waved to her. "Mrs. van Buren? There's a call for you. Use the yellow booth over there."

She let herself into the booth and lifted the receiver.

"Yes?"

"How is she?" asked the harsh voice.

Mercedes's fingers tightened around the telephone. "What do you want?"

"Is she alive?"

"She's dying," she spat into the instrument.

She heard something like a gasp, or a sob, bitten off. Then the voice returned. "I want to see you."

"What for?"

"I have to see you. You have to see me."

A few minutes later, she emerged from the booth to find de Córdoba waiting for her. He looked ghastly.

"Mercedes," he said, his voice faltering, "they want you to go to her."

Mercedes walked from the hospital at noon the next day, with de Córdoba at her side. She was dressed in a plain, dark, Paris suit. She wore dark glasses and a hat and most of her face was hidden. Externally, at least, she showed no emotion.

De Córdoba, by contrast, was drained. His patrician face was lined and baggy and disordered strands of silver hair hung across his brow.

In the lobby, he took Mercedes's arm gently and pulled her around to face him. "It's insane to go alone. Let me come with you, Mercedes."

"No." She spoke with an effort. "He would see you. He would stay hidden."

"I could keep my distance."

She shook her head.

"He may be planning to harm you, Mercedes! He may be luring you into a trap!"

She gestured at the hospital building. "After what he has done to me already, what further harm can he inflict?"

"He could take your life."

"I could take his."

"You're a woman, alone! He told me he had a rifle with telescopic sights. He may well be deranged, Mercedes." He snapped his fingers. "He could kill you like that."

"Then let him."

"You cannot mean that."

"I mean everything I say. I am going alone, Joaquin. Don't make me argue with you. I have very little strength."

He released her and let his arm drop. His face folded into hopelessness. "I'm sorry."

"I want to see his face, Joaquin. That is all."

"Be careful," he begged. "I'll wait for you here."

"Go to Eden. I'd like someone to be with her."

"I'm sorry, Mercedes. Sorry it turned out this way."

She touched his cheek. "Thank you, Joaquin. For every-thing."

He nodded, unable to speak.

She drove into the desert, in the direction she'd been told to go. It was a landscape that seemed unreal to her, a vast anvil on which the sun beat, upon which all the elements beat without mercy. It seemed to her the most lifeless place she had ever seen. A place to die. Was that why he had brought Eden here? As a scapegoat, into the wilderness, to bear all sins?

The jagged mountains that ringed the plain were carved with purple shadows. As she approached them, the sandy plain gave way to rockier outcrops, where a different vegetation grew—a scrubby plant with grey leaves and sporadic yellow rags of blossom. Now and then, among the scrub, she saw the occasional green spire of a tall cactus.

The stands of cactus grew denser. She stared at them as she drove. They were ribbed, columnar. Some sprouted limbs that seemed frozen in an unearthly dance. Others were solitary, mon-olithic. They began to fascinate her. They were a strange com-munity, these majestic plants. They had life, an indomitable, blind life that thrust from the arid earth and survived, even here. While they stood, this was not wilderness.

The sky overhead was a deep blue, flecked with a few high, pearly clouds which cast faint shadows on the earth below. The car was air conditioned, but she did not want its artificial, icy breath on her skin. The autumn warmth was not excessive. She drove slowly, with the windows open. At first she'd thought this landscape had no smell but the smell of dust and the road. But gradually she became aware of something else. An almost imper-ceptible, aromatic tang, fainter than a memory, yet persistent. Perhaps it was the cacti that gave it off, or perhaps the unassuming grey shrub with the yellow flowers.

She passed through a village, a cluster of straggling adobe houses buried under their own poverty. Yet something about the place reminded her of San Lluc. Not the prosperous San Lluc of today, thriving more with each new crop of tourists, but the San Lluc of yesterday, of her childhood. There was the same poor innocence, the same unawakened peace. The past was still here. Not yet obliterated.

The package had arrived in July. It was now October. In the intervening three months, she felt that she had relived her entire life. Had acted it all out in memory, in pain. We do not know when we are happy, she thought. Then it is gone. Then we grow old and we die.

She reached the foothills of the mountains by early afternoon and saw the sign she had been told to look out for. She found the little dirt road and turned the car down it. The huge cacti were on all sides now. She saw that the green ridges of the stems were lined with golden thorns, and that birds flitted constantly among the branching arms, finding food and shelter.

When the road petered out, she parked the car as she had been instructed and got out. She found the track, a rocky footpath that ascended among the ochre rocks. She started to climb. It was hard going. Sean is buried in a place like this, she thought. She had been to the grave that Bill French had made for him, high in the Aragonese mountains. She had seen the cairn of stones they had erected where he lay.

She reached the top. She was out of breath. She wondered how much farther she had to go. Then she caught the smell of burning and knew she had arrived.

He stood by the pile of smouldering ash, a taller man than she had expected, more impressive. He was unkempt. He had obviously been sleeping in the open for several days. His hair was wild and the lower half of his face was dark with stubble. But there was something regal about him. The face, aquiline and harshly-carved, was strikingly handsome. The eyes, black and glittering, were extraordinary, the eyes of a young prophet in the wilderness.

He was imposingly built. Under the dishevelled clothes she could see he had the same sort of body as Sean's, hard and active. The same sort of man, dark-haired, strong of muscle, devoid of fear.

He moved slightly as she approached, as if he wanted to salute her in some way and had forced himself to be still.

She faced him across the pile of ashes, elegant in her Paris suit, surreal in this wild setting.

"Well," she said quietly. "Here I am."

"How is she?" he blurted out in the curt voice she knew so well.

Mercedes took off her sunglasses and her hat. "You did not need to bring me all the way out here to ask me that. If you call the hospital, they will tell you."

He seemed fascinated by her face. She saw the hunger in his eyes as he drank her in, the wildness. "You know who I am?" he demanded.

"Yes," she nodded. "I know who you are. Better than you know yourself."

"Did Eden tell you? Did you guess?"

"I suppose I guessed." She shrugged. "In the end."

"You thought I would never reappear in your life." He bared his teeth like an animal. "You must have forgotten all about me. All these years."

"No," she said. "I never forgot you."

She saw his face jerk. He was evidently holding himself in with a great effort. Forces within him were trying to tear him open. She could sense the strain, like the electric omens of an earthquake. He kicked at the ashes with his boot. "You know what this is?"

She didn't look down. "My worldly wealth."

"Yes," he nodded. "Your worldly wealth, Mercedes. I've burned it. All of it."

She smiled faintly. "Do you think that matters to me?"

"Nothing matters more to you," he retorted.

"You're wrong. Nothing matters less."

"Liar!" He took a step forward, his fists clenching. "What kind of human being are you? You weren't fit to have children!"

"Perhaps not," she agreed quietly.

"You let her turn into a drug addict. You corrupted her. I saved her." He struck himself on the chest, his eyes blazing. "*Me.* Your first-born. The son you sold like an unwanted dog."

She didn't flinch. "Tell me—what did they name you?"

"They named me Joel. 'The vine is dried up, and the fig tree languisheth; the pomegranate tree, the palm tree also, and the apple tree, even all the trees of the field, are withered: because joy is withered away from the sons of men.' They called me Joel," he spat at her, "because they were *holy people*."

Her eyes were abstracted. "I only saw them once. I can remember their faces. And I remember your face as I gave you into their arms. You had just begun to learn to smile."

"It must have broken your heart," he said bitterly.

Her eyes focussed on him again. "You broke my heart, Joel, long before you were born."

"Do you know what they did to me?"

"I can see what they did to you," she said.

He kicked violently at the ashes. The silvery dust exploded around him, drifting in the pure desert air. "You sold me for two thousand dollars."

"I never took a penny," she said gently. "Your adoptive parents gave a thousand dollars to the doctor, and a thousand to the lawyer who made the arrangements. There were, in any case, fees to be paid. Nothing was given to me. I could not take you to a regular adoption agency. They asked too many questions, even in those days."

"But you knew what those people were!"

"A priest and his wife. People of God. They were desperate for a child. I thought they would give you the love I could not."

"They'd been rejected by every adoption agency in California!"

"Because of their age."

"Because they were deranged, cruel, twisted people! Religious maniacs!" Spittle formed whitely on his lips. "Monsters! People who only wanted another human creature to torment!"

"If that is so, I did not know it." She studied his quivering face. "Do you think I deliberately gave you to people who would make you unhappy? Do you really think that? My poor son. I wanted you to escape the dark, not go into it."

The gentle tone of her voice made his eyes flood with tears. He was trembling violently. "Why didn't you keep me?" he stammered. "Why? Why did you have to give me away?"

"I've told you," Mercedes said. "Because I wanted to save you from your legacy. But you have sought it out."

"It belonged to me! You owe it to me!"

"Then take it," she said wearily. "Take what is yours, Joel."

"How did my father die?"

"Your father is still alive."

His mouth jerked. "I've seen my birth certificate. My *real* birth certificate. It says Sean O'Keefe died a few months before I was born."

"Sean was not your father. Sean died in the last months of the civil war, years before you were born."

"But the certificate—"

"The certificate was forged."

"You're lying!"

"It was falsified to give you a background that people would not shrink from. To hide the truth. Otherwise, not even those people you called monsters would have taken you."

"What truth? Goddamn you! *Tell me!*"

For a moment, their faces had a strange similarity. The same piercing black eyes, the same intense beauty. A watcher would have had no doubt that they were mother and son.

"You were conceived incestuously." Her voice was low and calm, but not compassionate. "The man who is your father is also my father."

He shook his head, as if he'd been struck. "I don't understand."

"I mated with my own father," she said. "I became pregnant with you. It is you who are the monster, Joel."

She saw that he was numb. Full understanding would not come for a while. She studied him, almost dispassionately, assessing his strength. Would he survive? He had possessed the strength to come this far. To put himself through the furnace. To lay his heart on the anvil. Perhaps he could endure this last blow too.

"That is why I gave you away," she said gently. "To try and spare you. To spare myself. To give us both a chance to escape. But you did not want to escape."

Joel was struggling to hold himself upright, his hand pressed to his side, as though something there was tearing him. "I would rather have had—this knowledge," he said laboriously, "—than go through—what I went through."

"I did not know that. The future is veiled, Joel. We all walk in the dark. We act for the best, as far as we can see. I am sorry for your pain. Truly I am. I did not will it." She looked into his eyes for a long while. "You have grown into beauty. Your father, too, is a handsome man." She turned. "There isn't any more to say. Goodbye, Joel."

"Wait!" He took a pace forward, his hand stretched out, fingers trembling.

"What is it?"

"Eden. Tell me how she is. *Please.*"

"How strange. I remember asking you that once, with the same desperation."

"I never wanted her to suffer. I only wanted—"

"Eden is dead."

She saw it hit him, saw him stagger like an ox in the killing shed.

"*No.*"

"She died this morning. A few hours ago. Before dawn. I left her in her coffin to come here. If it's any consolation, the doctors say it was not your fault. She was doomed. She would have died in any case."

He opened his mouth in a terrible scream. "No!"

"And you did save her, in a sense. You redeemed her from the slavery of her addiction." Her eyes were huge in her pale face, filled with immense grief. "That was a good deed, Joel. A candle in a dark, dark world."

He fell to his knees among the ashes, his face seeming to disintegrate, cracking open to spill his grief. "Mother," he whispered. "Mother!"

Mercedes turned and walked back down the rocky path to her car.

february 1974

Los Angeles

Eden parked her car in front of the ranch. She got out and walked to the stable door, where Monaco's brown face peered out.

She stood stroking the horse for a long while, her eyes far away. Then she went into the house.

"Mama?" she called. "Mama, I'm home."

Mercedes came out of the kitchen, drying her hands. "You're late," she said reprovingly. "I was starting to worry." She kissed Eden's cheek. Eden had still not lost that frail look. Her beauty was unbearably fragile, a thing of crystal that could be shattered at a blow. She had just begun to go out on her own. It would be weeks more before she regained her full health and Mercedes hated her being away for more than an hour. "Where were you?"

"I was at the clinic, with Daddy."

"How is he?"

"Much better. He's started talking again. In fact, we talked all afternoon."

Mercedes smiled faintly. "About what?"

"About us. About the three of us. About how we became the way we all are."

Mercedes's smile faded as she took in Eden's expression. The colour left her cheeks.

Eden turned and walked to the window. "At first," she went on, "I thought he was wandering in his mind. Deluded. But then it came to me. My nightmare."

"What nightmare?" Mercedes asked, dry-mouthed

"I've been having it for years. I dream I'm bound in chains. I can't move. You and Daddy are in the room. But you won't help me. You don't even seem to know I'm there. You're arguing. Having one of those awful fights you used to have. You remember?"

Her mother's face was like stone. "I remember the fights."

"I always see your face looking white and strained, and I know it's bad. I want to cover my ears, But I can't lift my arms. Then Daddy sees me. He has a horrible look on his face. He starts shouting at me. Sometimes he's naked and I can see his cock. But that's from another time. From when I saw him with Françoise."

"It's only a dream, darling," Mercedes said.

"That's what I always thought." Her green eyes held her mother's, clear and cool, wise beyond their years. "It doesn't end there. The things Daddy says to me are terrible. They destroy me. They destroy everything around me. I know what he's saying, yet I can't hear it. It's all a jumble, a roar. The walls are coming down. And the ceiling is falling. And I can't get away. And Daddy keeps talking. I can't bear the things he's saying. So I start screaming, louder and louder, to drown him out. I know if I can drown out his words, the walls will stop falling and our house will be safe." She took a deep breath, unclenching her hands. Her nails had bitten into her palms, leaving red half-moons in the soft flesh. "I always wake up at that point. The funny thing is, I never do scream. Not aloud. I used to think that if I could only scream aloud, the dream would go away and never come back.''

"My poor darling," Mercedes whispered.

"But it isn't a dream. Is it, Mama?"

"No," Mercedes said with an effort. "It's not a dream."

"It's a memory. It came to me today, when Daddy told me who I really was. I was there. In the house, in Santa Barbara. It must have been a little while after we came back from that trip to Europe. I heard you fighting. I came into your bedroom and I heard what Daddy was saying about me."

"Eden—"

"That I was not your child."

"Oh, Eden," Mercedes said in anguish.

"That I was adopted."

Mercedes put her face in her hands.

"That's why, whenever he was really angry with me, he used to say the same thing to me. *You little fuck.* It was years before I began to understand what that meant. It wasn't until today that I really knew. A little fuck is someone conceived in a moment of casual sex. A bastard. A by-blow. Born on the wrong side of the blanket. The sort of unwanted child who ends up with an adoption agency.''

Mercedes lifted her face, stained with tears. "You were never unwanted." She took Eden in her arms and held her tight. "We wanted you so much, my darling. You were the answer to our prayers.''

"Why did you tell Daddy you were sterile?"

"Because of something that happened to me. Something terrible.''

"But you'd already been married. You'd already had a child. Didn't you tell him any of that?"

"No. Your father knew none of those things." She wiped the tears from her cheeks. Her features seemed blurred, as though the tears had dissolved the clear lines of her face. "I couldn't face having another child, Eden. I couldn't. I believed myself to be tainted. Polluted. Not fit for motherhood.''

"But why? Because of Joel?"

"Because of the circumstances of Joel's birth."

"Because you gave him away?"

"Partly."

"What else?"

They faced each other, both of their faces strained and tense.
"I can't tell you," Mercedes said.

"Why did you give him away?"

"I can't tell you!"

"Always secrets, Mama." For a moment, Eden's face fell into
the bitter, sullen lines of her adolescence. "Always mysteries,
places I mustn't go." Then the bitterness faded and her new, calm
beauty reasserted itself. "All right. I won't pry. But you must tell
me everything else. I have a right to know."

Mercedes took a shuddering breath. "God. I need a drink."

"So do I."

"You can't. The doctors said — "

"I'm damned well going to. And screw the doctors. Go into
the garden, Mama. I'll bring you a drink there."

She took the bottle of wine out to her mother in the shade of
the big oak tree. She sat and poured two glasses. They toasted one
another silently and drank.

"Did you love Sean O'Keefe more than Daddy?" Eden asked
after a while.

Mercedes's mouth turned down at the corners. "It was a different thing. I loved Sean very much, yes. In a way, time was kind
to us. We had only the first joys. Our love never had time to turn
into boredom, disillusionment, bitterness. It was still fresh and
beautiful when Sean died. And that's how it'll always be."

"And Joel is his son?"

Mercedes looked away. She was silent for a long while. Then
she leaned back in the chair, bruises under her dark eyes. "Yes,"
she nodded. "But Sean died before the child could be born. I was
a widow and pregnant. And I was desperate to get out of Spain.
I went to the American ambassador in Madrid, a man named Carlton Hayes. He had been a good friend to me. He helped me get
to America. Later, he helped me get American citizenship. I came
to Los Angeles, because Ambassador Hayes had a contact here, a
job where I could use the only gift I had—the fact that I spoke
both Spanish and English. I had the baby. I had no choice about
putting him up for adoption." She spread her hands. "Besides the
other factors, I was working eighteen hours a day as a bilingual
secretary in an export-import firm dealing with South American

fruit. I couldn't have cared for a baby and survived. So I gave him away. Eden, if you think that didn't tear my heart out, then you're wrong."

"Poor Mama. Poor Joel . . ."

"I should never have married again. I was scarred with guilt inside. But I was so lonely. Your father came along and . . ." She shrugged. "After we got married, I did everything I could to avoid another pregnancy. It wasn't as easy then as it is now. But I couldn't stand the thought of having another child, so I did what I could. Without telling Dominic. He was so eager for children. It broke my heart. I nearly told him. Perhaps I should have told him. But you get past a certain point and . . ."

"Oh, Mama."

"Dominic wanted to adopt. At first the idea was repugnant to me. Then I saw the beautiful logic of it. I had given a child away. I should take another woman's child as my own. I could have motherhood without passing on my taint. I could atone. Oh, Eden, the day we got you was the happiest day of my life. For the first time, my life had a meaning. A purpose. It never had one before. It's never had one since."

"Your life does have a meaning, Mama. You're the most purposeful person I'll ever know."

Mercedes reached out and took her hand. "We didn't name you Eden. Your birth-mother had already called you that. It was a beautiful name. A place before sin and pain. A garden of innocence. It was what we wanted your life to be."

"Why didn't you ever tell me? Why did you hide it?"

"It wasn't our decision alone. The agency actually advised us to keep it a secret. They said it could harm you to know the truth."

Eden winced. "Was the truth so ugly?"

"No. Your mother was a single girl from a good family. That's all. But it was fairly common advice in those days. Nowadays, things are different. Attitudes have changed. In those days they talked about a 'legal re-birth.' It was all a big secret. The real records of your birth were sealed by court order. They issued a new birth certificate, with a false name, a new date and place of birth. You became our child, in law, in fact, in every detail. And we wanted that, Eden. The next five years were the happiest years of my life. Of Dominic's too, I think."

Mercedes drained the glass. Eden refilled it, watching her mother's face. "Something went wrong, though."

"I found out the truth about him. About the drugs, the cocaine. That he wasn't just bringing enough for his own use. That he was bringing in massive consignments and making a fortune out of it. Yes. Something went wrong, all right. I don't think I ever spent a peaceful night after I found out. I couldn't stop thinking what would happen if he got caught. What would happen to you, I mean. I made up my mind I would leave him as soon as you were old enough. Then he began to change, around the time you were five or six. He had started to rot. That's the only way I can describe it. He changed. His pleasure started to matter more and more to him. He had lots of affairs. Not just Françoise. Lots of others. Younger and younger girls, children sometimes. You were the only link that kept us together. Then, when we got back from Europe, I had a disaster." Her face went taut. "I'd fallen pregnant during that tour. I think it must have happened in Venice. A terrible mistake. I was forty-two years old, then. The abortion wasn't easy to hide. Dominic found out. He found out that I'd deceived him all our married lives. I couldn't tell him why I'd done it. But it wouldn't have helped, in any case. He had turned against me. And against you. Against us both. He called it a shattering loss of faith. Perhaps it was. I have no right to judge him." Her fingers tightened around Eden's momentarily. "That nightmare of yours—I remember that night so well. Dominic was so drunk. He hardly knew what he was saying. He was shouting at me, breaking things. You woke up and came into our room in your pajamas. He turned on you. He said such terrible things, my darling. That you weren't his. That you were a parasite I'd foisted on him. You just stood there, frozen. He said you had no right to be here, that he hated the sight of you, that you were the child of a whore, that he was going to put you out on the street where you belonged—"

Eden covered her ears with her hands, shutting out the terrible words that had haunted her unconscious for so long. Even after all these years, the pain and the nausea were overpowering. It was a long while before she dropped her hands again and looked up with pain-dulled eyes at her mother. "Oh, Mama . . ."

"You screamed yourself into a fit. I thought you had been scarred forever. Yet the next morning you woke up laughing and sunny, as though nothing had happened. We thought you must have forgotten it. Blotted it out in the night. But a few months after that, you began to change. You started becoming so wild. Rebellious. By the time you got your periods, you were uncontrollable. We'd lost you."

"It's been there all my life," Eden said in a shaky voice. "It's always been there, Mama, festering inside me. It made me hate myself. I took drugs to get away from what I was. To stop the pain of knowing my whole existence was a lie, that I was just a little fuck."

Mercedes reached for Eden and the two women wept in each other's arms.

Later, they sat facing each other. Eden's eyes were misty emeralds.

"I'll never take drugs again, Mama. Maybe I'd have been tempted if it hadn't been for the hepatitis. But it nearly killed me —and I'm never going back again."

"I know."

"I've never had a sense of self-worth until now. It didn't matter what I did, I always knew I was worthless. Joel changed that, Mama."

Mercedes stroked her daughter's hair gently. "You've made yourself a new life, Eden. Free of the past. Free of drugs. You know who you are. What you are. You've grown into an exceptional young woman. I'm so proud of you."

"I'm so proud of you," Eden said unsteadily. "Now that I know everything."

Mercedes shook her head with a faint smile. "No. You don't know everything, Eden. My life is not one to be proud of." She lifted her fingers and touched Eden's mouth to silence the protest that had begun. "I don't want your pride in me. All I can pray for is your forgiveness."

"What for?"

"For what I am. For what I've done. You don't know me yet, my child. Perhaps you'll never know me fully. Perhaps that's best. But as the years go by, there are things you're going to find out about me. Things that may appall you."

"I can't believe that."

"Believe it. It's in me. In my blood. A taint."

"Come on!" Eden twisted restlessly. "All that medieval Spanish gloom and doom."

"No, Eden." Mercedes's face was sombre. In the past nine months, she had aged perceptibly. Her beauty was passing into a new phase, from the bloom of maturity to the austerity of age. "I thank God that you don't have my blood in your veins."

"That's a horrible thing to say!"

"No. I had a child and he was cursed."

"Joel is *not* cursed! Just hurt and confused."

Her eyes were hooded. "Whatever evil I've committed, remember that evil was also committed against me. I pray that you'll try and understand. That you'll never come to hate me."

There was a swelling in Eden's throat. "Mama, how could I ever hate you? You've loved me so much. You gave up everything you had for me. And I was not even your child."

"Oh, you are my child," Mercedes said gently. "I learned that while Joel had you. You are my beloved child. The only thing that matters to me, in the end." She looked around. "And here I am. A guest in your house."

"How can you call yourself a guest? This house is yours!"

"No, it's yours." She glanced at Eden's clean, youthful profile. "And you're getting stronger day by day. I won't be able to pretend I'm nursing you any more. Soon, I'm going to leave you."

"You don't ever have to leave the ranch!"

"What we have right now is more precious to me than I can say. I want to keep that the way it is."

Eden caressed her mother's arm. "Where will you go, then?"

"Back to Spain."

"That's so far from me!"

"Yes. Out of harm's way. I'm going to stay with a friend. A dear friend."

"So many things about you I don't know . . ."

Mercedes smiled. "Many things," she agreed.

They sat in silence, watching the evening fall over the garden. The shadows lengthened. A little gust of wind stirred the branches of the tree over their heads.

"If you want," Mercedes said, "I'll help you get a court order to unseal your birth records."

Eden lifted her head. "What for?"

"So you can trace your real mother."

"I don't want that," Eden smiled. "You've just said it. You

are my real mother. There's something infinitely more important that I have to do."

"What?"

"I have to find Joel."

Mercedes's face was suddenly anguished. "Leave him be, my darling. You and he have done with each other. It's over. Forever."

"No, Mama. It's not over."

"He can only bring you terrible pain."

"I'll never love another man," Eden said quietly. "Not the way I love Joel. When Daddy told me this afternoon that I wasn't . . ." She shook her head. "Now there isn't any sin in loving him the way I do."

"It's grotesque!"

"Maybe. But we're not blood-related. That's all that matters to me. He has to know that. He said he would come to me. He hasn't. So I have to go to him and tell him who I am. That he's not my brother. That if he wants to marry me—"

"No!" Mercedes gasped in agony.

"That if he wants to marry me," she said clearly, "he can. He's not in Arizona any more. I don't know if he's even in America. Maybe he stayed in Mexico. I've been trying for so long to find him. I can't understand why he doesn't contact me. As soon as I'm strong enough . . ."

Mercedes interrupted in a strained voice. "He thinks you are dead."

Eden's head whipped around. "What?"

"That is why he hasn't contacted you, I told him you had died. I told the hospital to say the same if he called."

"Mama! How could you!"

"It was best."

"Best?" She was pale with shock. "How could you have done such a cruel thing?"

"I wanted him away from you. You are on the brink of a new life. And he is a doomed creature, Eden. He would drag you down into a hell you cannot even imagine."

"He's not doomed!" Eden said sharply. "You're wrong. I can save him. Just as he saved me. I owe it to him. He loves me so much!" She fought for self-control and bit back the fierce words that rose to her lips. "That was a terrible thing to do to him," she said quietly.

"It was a terrible thing he did to me," she said with grim emphasis. "He nearly killed you. And he took more from me than money. But I didn't tell him you were dead to punish him. Only to protect you."

Eden shook her head slowly. "Your claws are too sharp, Mama."

"I had to have sharp claws! You have none!" She took a deep breath, then went on more quietly, "You're not like me, Eden. We were made in different forges. You are gentle. I am not. You have never had any defences. I've always had to use my claws to keep harm from you."

"I love him."

"I prayed that would pass."

"It hasn't passed. It never will."

Mercedes fought with herself almost visibly, her mouth trembling with emotion. Then she rose and walked into the house without a word.

After a while, Eden followed her.

Her mother was sitting by the window in the dark house, staring out.

"I cannot stop you from going to find him," she said in a flat voice. "But I warn you, he may have been destroyed. I told him something, the day we met in the desert, that might have shattered him. If he has survived it, and he wants to tell you what it is, he will. I can not. It belongs to him. And him alone."

"Secrets and mysteries," Eden said quietly. "Darkness and hidden things. Do they ever end?"

"No," Mercedes answered.

The house was in darkness. Eden walked around slowly, putting on the lights, one after another, until the house blazed and the darkness had been driven back. Then she turned to her mother.

"You're right. I'll never have claws like yours. I am different. I believe I can save Joel. Perhaps he'll drag me down to hell. I don't believe he will, though I'd go into hell smiling to bring him back, if I had to. I just don't have a choice, Mama. He's my destiny."

"Then you must go to him."

Eden kissed her mother's cheek. They smiled at one another, one smile sad and secret, the other innocent, luminous.

·   ·   ·

Mercedes sat motionless where Eden had left her, thinking of that tall, forbidding figure in the desert. How his eyes had burned, the way her own had once burned, with that same dark passion, that anger, that power.

Her son. Her nemesis. He'd stood facing her as though he did not know whether to kill her or fall at her feet. In the end, he'd fallen at her feet.

Perhaps she should have knelt with him. Taken him in her arms. Begged for his forgiveness. Shown him some of the grief, some of the tears that she had shed for him almost thirty years.

But she had been unable to do that. Partly because protecting Eden had been of overwhelming importance to her just then. But partly because her nature forbade it. She had been forged differently. The hammer had shaped her when she was red-hot, with cruel blows, and she had taken a shape she could never, now that the iron was cold and hard, alter.

So she had turned her back on him and walked away.

What could she have done for him, in any case?

Strangely, she felt no anger against Joel. Not any more. It had faded away. He had destroyed her little empire. He had taught her a pain that even she, expert in pain, had not known. He had taken her beautiful home from her, her possessions, her wealth, and had burned them all to ashes in the desert. Yet it could have been worse. Wisdom said that. It could have been far, far worse. He had saved Eden. That had washed all the bitterness away.

She'd started with nothing. She'd ended with nothing. Wealth was only a dream. The world itself was only a dream, a flickering image thrown across the dark.

Her son had reminded her of something she'd forgotten. How immaterial riches were. And how overwhelmingly important life was, that dancing light in the darkness.

What lay beyond the darkness? Anything? Nothing? The answer was no longer as remote as it had once been.

She looked back over her own life, and wondered whether it all balanced out in the end, the good with the evil, the joy with the pain. When the time came for her soul to be weighed, would it be found wanting? Weighed down by its sins?

Mercedes sighed and felt her muscles relax, her strung nerves slacken. The tension flooded out of her. She would interfere no longer in Eden's wishes. No persuasion had ever changed her own decisions. She knew that she could not alter Eden's. Let her put herself on the anvil.

Perhaps Eden would do what she could not do. Kneel with him in the ashes. Take him in her arms and heal him with her tears. Perhaps in doing that, she would not be destroyed. Perhaps they'd even find the enduring happiness that had eluded their mother all her life.

Did she regret anything? The killings? The lies? The betrayals? All, in their way, had been necessary. Inevitable. Just as Eden's fate was inevitable. Regret was irrelevant.

She was, in the end, human. She had known many of humanity's passions, dark and bright. She did not regret that. Above all, she did not regret the love. She had poured out so much of it in her life. And so much of it had been poured into her. Strange love, cruel love, sweet love; love like a rainbow, and love like thunderbolts. None wasted. None mourned over.

And what of her own future, that ebbing tide? So much of it would be linked to her two children and their fate. She closed her eyes and saw them standing before her, the dark and the bright angel, the natural and the acquired, the boy and the girl. She would pray for their happiness, their salvation, as she had been taught to pray, long ago. But she would not stay here, near them. Her presence in their lives could not help. Not now. Perhaps not ever.

Joaquin was waiting for her in Spain. Her faithful knight errant. She did not know if she could give him the love he deserved, but she would try. It was not too late to try.

Francisco Franco, at eighty-two years old, was dying. A handsome and able young king had been groomed to supervise the transition to democracy, and to sit once again upon the throne of the Bourbons. That would be something to see. Perhaps she and Joaquin would live to see the kind of Spain she had dreamed of as a girl, and had taken up arms to defend in that searing summer of 1936.

Yes. There was always something to see.

She rose to her feet, a beautiful, dark woman. She smiled to herself. The hammer strikes. The iron is shaped. The work proceeds. Life moves on.

~Epilogue

february 1974

Arizona

Clouds towered over the desert like the walls of the city of heaven.

They seemed not to move. But their swelling ramparts were soaring into the upper atmosphere. Soon their tops would spread into the anvils from which the thunder would be struck and the storm would sweep down over the desert.

Winter had changed the landscape little since Eden had last set eyes on it. The heat had gone. As the thunderclouds overshadowed the earth, the air cooled further. But nothing else seemed to have altered. The colours were the same. The saguaro still reigned over their kingdom.

As she drove up into the hills from Tucson, leaving human traces behind her, she felt their power increase. Sentinels? Magi? Did the outflung arms beckon or ward off?

He was not dead. He was here in the wilderness, poor scapegoat, poor outcast, alone and suffering. But not dead. She was sure of that. She felt his presence as surely as she felt her own. And she had never in her life felt her own presence so surely.

It seemed to her, in these strange days, that she had just been born. That everything before had been a cloudy dream. That her life lay before her, ready to be formed anew.

She knew she would find him. She had no doubt about that. She would find him and heal him.

She drove onward, lost in her thoughts. She thought about Mercedes and Dominic. About the shadowy mother who had borne her and whom she had never known.

She thought about what she herself had been; about what she was now; about what she might be in time.

The possibilities. The possibilities. They shuddered in her, the way wind shudders in the unfurling sails of a yacht about to leave the shelter of her anchorage. She felt the richness and terror of her own many futures, that multifarious Sinbad treasure that only youth possesses.

She remembered, like a dream, the past nine months of her life. The despair of lotus land. The night Joel had come out of the darkness for her. The little grey cell and her agony there. The vastness of the desert above, the cleansing, healing desert. The vaster force of love and how it had transformed her.

And finally, her thoughts returned, as they always did, to Joel. To what he had suffered. To what Mercedes had done to him. To the destiny that tied her to him forever.

As she turned off the main road onto the trail that led to the ranch, confidence abruptly drained out of her.

What if he was dead? What if her instincts had been no more than wishful thinking and Joel was gone from here?

Worse, what if grief had shattered his mind?

She choked. It was hard to breathe. She wound the window down as she drove, to let oxygen into the car. There was a smell on the clean desert air that flooded her mind with sharp, almost visionary memories.

On such a day as this, he had taken her out of her prison, into the wilderness. The sky had opened and the heavens had poured deliverance down onto them. They had clung together through the storm. They had kissed in the heart of chaos.

And after they had come through, she had thought, with a sense of wonder, maybe I'm going to be different now.

And she remembered what the smell was. The elusive, pungent sweetness of the creosote bush. Soon, when the rain thrashed the leaves, the fragrance would fill the world, healing, cleansing.

The ranch came into view at the end of the trail, its unassuming shape blending into the landscape. Memories were almost overwhelming her. There it was. The house in which she had begun as a prisoner and had ended by finding her freedom.

Where she had discovered love.

Where sickness had ended.

Where her final purgatory had begun, that final illness that had almost killed her and had put the final seal on her renunciation of heroin.

She was talking aloud now, praying, but did not know it.

The first thing she saw as she reached the ranch was the horse, the white Arabian he had given her.

She stood motionless in the corral, watching her arrival. The growing breeze stirred the silky mane. Eden sat motionless, staring back at the mare, gripping the steering wheel so hard that her knuckles blanched.

Then, reassured, the horse lowered her head to the alfalfa at her feet and began to eat.

Joel was alive. He was here.

She got out of the car. Her legs could almost not carry her. She walked forward, dizzy with emotion.

And then he came around the house.

He had been working. He still held the hammer in one hand, the chisel in the other. He was bare-chested and she could see the weight he had lost, the hollows beneath his ribs.

He stopped, transfixed by the sight of her. His eyes were huge and black. They stared at her from beneath the wild tangle of hair. He had grown a beard. Beneath it, his face, always aquiline and austerely carved, was gaunt.

She fought against the pressure that crushed her chest and tried to speak.

"I didn't die."

She saw something like terror flicker in his eyes as she spoke. She knew he was afraid his mind was giving way.

"I didn't die," she repeated, more urgently. "I'm real. She lied to you. She lied to us all. I'm not her daughter. Oh, Joel! I have so much to tell you. So much to give you. We're going to spend our lives together. We're going to heal each other. I'm going to give you—" She ran out of words. He stood immobile, as though rooted to the soil. She could not move to him either. They seemed frozen. Did he hear her? She reached out her shaking hands.

"I'm going to restore to you the years that the locust has eaten," she said.

The tools dropped from his hands and she saw the tears stream suddenly down his cheeks.

And then she was in his arms, clinging to him. His strength crushed her. She felt his sobs, tasted the salt of his tears.

And in their union she knew there would be no more partings. No more pain.

Silence in the midst of the storm, peace in the heart of chaos.

About the Author

Marius Gabriel was born in South Africa in 1954. He became a full-time writer while a postgraduate at Newcastle-on Tyne University in northern England. With numerous paperback romances to his credit, *The Original Sin* is his first venture onto a larger canvas. Mr. Gabriel has also been a musician and an artist. He lives in Spain with his wife Linda and is currently at work on a new novel.